THE
Rails to
LOVE
ROMANCE COLLECTION

9 Historical Love Stories Set Along the Transcontinental Railroad

THE
Rails to
LOVE
ROMANCE COLLECTION

Amanda Cabot, Kim Vogel Sawyer,
Diana Lesire Brandmeyer,
Lisa Carter, Ramona K. Cecil,
Lynn A. Coleman, Susanne Dietze,
Connie Stevens, Liz Tolsma

BARBOUR BOOKS
An Imprint of Barbour Publishing, Inc.

Print ISBN 978-1-63409-864-9

eBook Editions:
Adobe Digital Edition (.epub) 978-1- 68322-032-9
Kindle and MobiPocket Edition (.prc) 978-1- 68322-033-6

Published by Barbour Books, an imprint of Barbour Publishing, Inc., P.O. Box 719, Uhrichsville, Ohio 44683, www.barbourbooks.com

Our mission is to publish and distribute inspirational products offering exceptional value and biblical encouragement to the masses.

 Member of the
Evangelical Christian
Publishers Association

Printed in Canada.

Contents

Outlaw on the Pueblo Excursion

by Diana Lesire Brandmeyer

Dedication

For Pastor Randy Bolt and his wife, Jean

Chapter One

The string quartet Mary Owen's father had hired for her small birthday dinner played in the background. The receiving line thinned to a few more single men waiting for an introduction.

She'd been pleasant to each of them, asking a question to judge their excitement for adventure. None would go west, even to visit, and one thought riding the trolley thrilling. She planned on repeating the responses to her father in the morning. Proving that she had indeed attempted to find someone interesting enough to consider marrying.

"William Crossen."

Her father shook the man's hand.

"My father is a friend of Mr. Wagner."

"Yes, he told me you might be attending. Let me introduce you to my daughter, Miss Owen."

"Charmed, Mr.—"

"Wy— William Crossen, Miss Owen."

"Thank you, I've met so many for the first time tonight. Tell me, what do you think about traveling to Africa?"

"I haven't considered it. Are you planning a trip?"

His eyebrows scrunched. He didn't care for her question. She almost sighed but held back. One more handsome gentleman, but not one who would gallop beside her up a mountain or blaze trails through a forest. "Not at the moment, but asking questions helps me remember to whom I've spoken."

Attending and trying, as her father requested, to find someone she might marry was the only way he'd allow her to go with Aunt Cora on a small adventure. Even now, she had yet to see the tickets. She would get them at breakfast, if Father felt she held up her end of this event.

And she had. The gloves riding her arms up to her elbows begged to be unbuttoned, slid off, and tucked away. The dress, a breathtaking wonder Father ordered from Paris for her, held her tight at the waist. Did Queen Victoria feel like this? Bound to responsibility with cloth and silk?

Would her mother, if she had lived, understand how much Mary wanted to be like Aunt Cora? Or would Mother have trained Mary to be like her, a lady at all times, content in the life she lived?

Aunt Cora, her father's sister, bounced in and out of Mary's life with her exciting travel tales and trunks full of exotic trinkets and clothing. Her spinster life intrigued Mary.

"All you need is one, Mo." Father whispered in her ear, startling her. "Marry, and you'll be taken care of forever."

"You promised not to call me that." Mo, the nickname he used when trying to get her to follow his chosen path, his clear intention tonight. He'd combined the initials of her first and last names to get it when she fussed about not having a middle name like her friends. The problem arose when she wanted to go a different direction from his. And she did.

"I sense you are not present in your mind tonight. Why is it so difficult for you to think of being married? I'm to blame for not giving you another mother."

"Father, you say that, and yet you aren't married. Perhaps marriage isn't as wonderful as you wish me to believe."

"What you don't remember is the joy I shared with your mother. That is what I wish for you, dearest. I haven't found another who could outshine her. It wouldn't be fair to marry someone I couldn't love as much as my dear wife."

"Maybe that is my problem as well. You've made your marriage to Mother sound so perfect that I want the same. I want to love someone who loves adventure and doesn't intend for me to wed, live, and die in the same home. He isn't in this room. I wonder if he exists."

"You promised me after this trip, this adventure, you will accept someone." He gave her arm a gentle squeeze. "You will understand so much more when you have children, the need to protect them."

She met his eyes, surprised to see a bit of moisture in the corners. "I said I would try. Please, can we enjoy my birthday together? I dislike being at odds with you. Especially as you will be leaving for New York in a few days and I will be off on my grand adventure."

"You need to take care of Aunt Cora as well. That's why I'm letting you go. I'm afraid she'll skip meals and something will happen to her. Well, that's not a cheerful thought, nor is this evening turning out the way I'd hoped. We should have held this at home, with your friends."

"I see them often enough. Besides, it feels as if you've already paraded every marriageable male in St. Louis and Topeka in front of me."

"And none of them, not even one, interested you a little, Mo?" Her father led her to the dining room.

"None, Father. They were all content to stay where they were, no desire to see the world. And shallow. It's all about how they will work in the family business. If I become a missionary nun, at least I'll go places and work with God."

"You could work with a husband, help him in his career by making sure his home is run in a timely and efficient manner."

"Father, you can't be saying that as if you mean it. If you felt a wife's role crucial to a man's career, you would have remarried despite your declaration of how much you loved my mother."

"Maybe tonight will be different."

Topeka was worlds away from her life in St. Louis. In a few days, she would be on a train with Aunt Cora. Sent away again, but this time by her own choice.

◆ ◆ ◆

Wyatt recognized the glassy look in Miss Owen's eyes. Had she met too many people? Or perhaps, like him, she wanted to be elsewhere? At least being a male, he had more choices than to be paraded in front of wealthy men seeking a wife.

Potted plants hugged the corners along with a few women who seemed to wear a cloak of invisibility that kept most suitors from seeing them. Was it intentional? Could there be women who didn't want to marry? The question Miss Owen asked him about Africa intrigued him, as it was far from the usual conversations he'd had in receiving lines.

Maybe he'd find a story here if he stuck it out through the evening.

◆ ◆ ◆

Mary's heels felt the bite of the too-tight tapestry shoes. They matched the green in her dress, and she'd been so sure they would loosen as the night went on. Her mistake now had her sitting alone next to a potted tree. Her shoulders relaxed as she took in the occupants of the room, the unmarried women huddled together, chirping like birds, probably hoping one of the eligibles would single them out. Hiding by the tree worked to her advantage.

"—leaving Sunday on the Pueblo Excursion train." A male voice with a touch of excitement continued. "Should be quite the adventure."

She caught the words and held them close. Did Father have anything to do with this?

Chapter Two

As Mary approached the dining room the next morning, Aunt Cora's voice drifted down the hall. When she heard her name, she paused to listen.

"If you don't let Mary go, you'll drive her to the jungles in Africa."

"Why would you think that, Cora?"

"Have you not paid any attention to your daughter these past two years? She reads those missionary magazines over and over."

"It's a passing fancy. Saving the world is nothing more than a fantasy. Once she marries and has children of her own—"

Mary wanted to rush in and explain that it wasn't a childhood dream, but she held back.

"What if she doesn't?"

"Last night she might have met someone. I saw her chatting with a few men who would make decent husbands."

"By your standards. What if she wants to marry for love? Have you even asked her?"

"Nonsense. We've discussed her need to marry. Love hasn't come into the conversation. She doesn't have to live the way you do, Cora."

"Brother, that's incorrect and you know it. You know why I chose this life. You might as well put her on a ship to Africa tomorrow if you aren't going to let her go with me on this excursion."

"Cora—"

"No, I don't want to hear your excuses. When a telegram arrives saying she has been eaten by cannibals or lost her leg because of a snake bite, remember you could have prevented it."

Cannibals! Mary covered her mouth.

◆　◆　◆

Squaring her shoulders and preparing for battle, Mary entered the dining room. Aunt Cora sat across from Father.

"We didn't wait for you, dear. We thought you might sleep in this morning after last night's event."

"The pancakes and sausage are quite good, Mo." Her father pushed back in his chair. "I've had a few too many."

Mary filled her plate from the buffet. She had to go on this trip. If she built on what Aunt Cora said about being a missionary, it might sway her father.

At the table, her father stood and pulled out her chair. "Your aunt and I were discussing the trip."

"Yes, Father?" She sat and put her napkin in her lap. "I did what you asked. I met every male in Topeka last night."

"Did you find any that you'd care to see again?" He picked up his coffee cup and drank.

"There were so many, and they all seemed the same. Boring. Not one took me seriously when I asked about going west or liking adventure."

"That's good. It means they were stable, good providers. They won't be wandering off, leaving their family to fend for themselves." He set the cup on the saucer. The coffee sloshed, breaching the rim.

"You've taught me how to shoot, Father. I think I can take care of myself. If I don't marry, I won't have to protect a family." She sliced though the pancake and then stabbed it with her fork. He wasn't going to let her go with Aunt Cora.

"Brother, this is nothing more than a quick trip to Colorado. Let her go so she can see what adventure is about." Aunt Cora placed her hands in her lap. "Mary, you'll consider your father's request? On this trip, will you think about the men your father presented to you, what they can offer you, and give your father an answer when we return?"

Her pancake swelled in her mouth. She chewed. She could do this, take the trip and decide later. She nodded.

"That's the best I can hope for, then. Mo, you may go, but you must take care of your aunt. Truly, this is the real reason I can give for acquiescing to your request. Your aunt must eat often or, as you know, she passes out."

"Really, Brother, I am quite capable of feeding myself."

"But if something was to go wrong—"

"I promise to take care of her, Father."

His shoulders sagged. "Then I will allow this trip." He reached into his suit pocket and withdrew the train tickets. He set them on the table. "I'm not fond of this idea, but if you promise to consider marriage when you return, you have my blessing."

Mary's heels bounced against the carpet. Should she run to her father and hug him? She stilled her feet. She wasn't a little girl anymore. He needed to see that. "Thank you, Father. I will do as you ask." Then, before he could change his mind, she reached over, grabbed the tickets, and placed them in her lap.

"It's going to be a grand adventure, Aunt Cora."

◆ ◆ ◆

Wyatt Crossen leaned against the edge of the pocket door of his father's office after dinner. He crossed his arms waiting for his father to criticize his choices.

When his mother excused herself for the evening and his father suggested they go into the library for a discussion, he knew his father would issue another demand concerning his life.

His father sat in the largest chair by the fireplace. "Come, sit."

With heavy feet, he made his way to the smaller chair, his mother's. Did it make her feel as unequal as it did him?

"It's time you find a wife."

And there it was, the biggest demand of all.

"I'm not ready. I can't support a family on my wages."

"You could, if you worked for me." His father tapped the armrest.

"We've been through this argument. I want to write, not work with numbers in a ledger. It's important to me to make my own way in this world." He regretted his words, knowing they would open a sore that refused to heal.

"Are you saying I didn't?" His father pounded his fingers against the wood.

"No, Father. Without you, the business would have failed, but the difference is you wanted to work in the shipping business. My heart doesn't lie there." And it never would. If only he could make his father understand. "Was there ever a time you wanted to do something else?"

"I did what was expected of me. My heart never strayed."

His father stared past him. Was he lying? "Never?"

"It's bad enough you work for that paper, but to refuse to marry is unacceptable. This family needs an heir. You are the only son. Do you understand it is your duty to provide one?" His father's cheeks flushed, cranberry red next to his white beard.

"Father—" Wyatt leaned forward, gripping the armrests.

"I'm not finished. No one in this family has worked with his hands since your great-great-grandfather bought the shipping company. You are too much like your mother's family, living life through God, letting Him direct all your actions." He punctuated his words with a wave of his hand. "Well, son, that will not get you where you need to be in this life. Just look at them. Preachers and farmers. That's all they will ever be."

Wyatt disagreed. Perhaps his father hadn't worked with his hands, but those before him had. His grandfather told him stories about sailing on the ships, what it was like to be on the ocean in a storm, and in a country where English wasn't spoken. As for letting God direct his actions, that wasn't going to change.

"I sent you to the Wagners' last week. Did you find at least one woman you could imagine being married to?"

"I went because you requested it, but again, Father, I will marry someone I love, a woman God made for me to be my helpmate." Miss Owen had surprised him with her question about Africa, but she was from St. Louis and would return there. Besides, he'd be off in a few days himself. It did seem as if God placed interesting women in his path but then swept them away before he could pursue them.

"Pure foolishness. But realize you and any children you sire will be penniless if you don't marry this year."

"That may be, but I won't dishonor God by making a mockery out of one of His sacraments. I trust He will provide what my family will need."

"What about 'Honor your father?'" Father fisted his fingers and pounded the armrest.

"That's what I did this past Saturday evening by attending the Wagners' function. Along with that, I write under the pen name Wyatt Cross, as you insisted, in addition to a host of other demands these past years." And he'd become used to that name.

"Is it so hard for you to stay in Topeka? For your mother's sake?"

"Not as long as I am free to travel." His father brought out an immature side of him. He knew why marriage and staying in Topeka were important to his parents. Knew it too well. He'd heard so many times growing up how he was a miracle. Their only child. Though his mother called him a blessing from God, his father seemed to think having William was right in life.

"You aren't our prisoner, William. With the money we have, you could travel anywhere you choose." He slumped in his chair. "We're growing old too fast. Someday you'll understand." His father rubbed his balding head.

"I'm sorry. I know you wish the best for me and always have. I'll consider what you are asking and continue to pray for God to soon send the one He has chosen for me."

A muscle ticked in his father's jaw. "God again."

Chapter Three

Mary stood on the platform waiting to board the Pueblo Excursion train. She shivered in the March wind despite the woolen traveling suit she wore. No, it wasn't from the cold. Excitement coursed through her, sending goose bumps down her spine. She was really doing this. Her first adventure, and if she could get Aunt Cora's secret from her, it would not be the last.

"Mary, stop bouncing." Aunt Cora touched Mary's arm. "It's a train ride—"

"Not an elephant ride in India. I know. But to me, it's as exciting. Imagine being cooped up in boarding school for years, Aunt Cora. The only time I had fun was at home when Father let me practice shooting. You were so fortunate that you didn't have to endure the life I've had."

"Yes, your life has been horrible. Attending school must have been similar to incarceration." Aunt Cora scowled.

"But it was. We were told when to eat, when to sleep, and when to pray." Mary knew many girls would've been happy to go to school. But all she'd ever wanted to do was grow up at home and experience all St. Louis had to offer. Her father's ideas about appropriate experiences differed from hers. If he would have let her, she would have volunteered at the orphanage. Instead, he sent her away to boarding school. He might as well have kept her locked up.

"Protecting you," he'd said. From what, she had no idea.

She wanted to travel the world. Her father wanted her to be a wife. They'd been at odds for months. When Aunt Cora had suggested Mary come with her on the excursion to see what else life offered, Father's eyes had narrowed before he'd said no. Then Aunt Cora told him about her illness and how she needed a companion on this trip. He relented.

"It hasn't been a dull life from what you've said in your letters," Aunt Cora said.

"Schoolgirl fun and pranks, and no, I didn't come up with them. Not all of them. It doesn't compare to the excitement you've had, Aunt Cora."

"You have no idea what I have endured, Mary."

Mary chose not to reply, even though she disagreed. Today was a joyful day. Even the rumble of the baggage carts reminded her of low laughter. So many people gathered on the platform and beyond it would be impossible to count all of them. Men, of course, outnumbered the women from what she saw, but there were more than she'd expected.

The crowd came to a halt. Mary overheard a couple close to them talking. She turned slightly to see them, surprised to find them head to head whispering and smiling. They traveled together? And were happy? She couldn't pull a memory of her mother and father ever doing that.

"Get your Pueblo Excursion photo made here." A photographer stood in front of a drooping banner displaying a steam engine in front of a mountain. "Remember this trip forever!"

"Let's do it, Aunt Cora." Mary swayed and clapped her hands. Her purse swung from her wrist, almost hitting her chin. "I'm sure I'll never forget this trip, but it would be nice to have a memory to pull out and look at."

"Goodness gracious. It's a good thing I'm holding our dinner basket, or you'd have it smashed and upside down by now. You must settle down. We can get the picture taken, and by then, it should be time to board."

Mary straightened her back and forced herself not to run to the photographer. She didn't wish to embarrass Aunt Cora, especially if she hoped to travel with her again. She would act the perfect lady she'd been trained to be.

◆　◆　◆

Wyatt Cross jumped from the buggy as it arrived at the station, overnight case in hand. He'd procured a ticket for the excursion by chance. He saw the ad and approached his editor about doing a story. He would be one of many reporters onboard, but he doubted their mission would be the same as his. There were 446 people on this train, but he wasn't interested in why the men took the trip. The women. That's where the stories would be, and, if God was listening, a wife for him.

His bag held tight in his hand, he looked for a porter. It was a two-day trip, but he needed to look good when he arrived in Pueblo, so he'd brought an extra suit. There would be cameras at the other end, and he didn't want to show up in the newspaper his father read looking unpresentable. It would only strain their relationship further.

"May I help you with that, sir?" An employee of the train company appeared in front of him. "Bound for Pueblo?"

"Sure am, George. Take care of this for me?"

"May I see your passage ticket, sir?"

Wyatt pulled the colorful ticket from his coat pocket.

George returned the ticket along with a numbered metal check. "Only one stop along the way. Your bag will be waiting at the hotel for you when you arrive."

"Thank you." Wyatt handed the man a few coins and received a wide grin in return.

"Get your picture taken before you board the train! Remember your—" A shout drew Wyatt's attention away from the attendant. He was about to dismiss the hawker when he noticed a young woman and her companion conversing with the photographer.

The young one, with hair the color of untarnished copper, smiled so hard her cheeks would hurt by the end of the session. He'd seen her before, but where? The older one, maybe her mother or aunt, showed no excitement. Bored, maybe? From her outfit, Wyatt would guess she'd been on many more exciting journeys and this one didn't compare.

So those were two of the eighty-three women on the trip. He'd start his interview with them.

◆　◆　◆

Mary took in the clamor around her. They got their photo taken right away. It was good she'd urged Aunt Cora to act, or they'd be standing in the line that formed.

"Ladies, you won't regret having this beautiful reminder in the years to come." The photographer placed them close together under the banner. "Give me your basket and hand luggage. You don't want that in your photo."

Aunt Cora handed it over. "Mind you be careful of that."

"I will, madam. And miss, what about your umbrella?"

"It's part of my traveling costume."

The photographer nodded, then stepped to the edge of the photo prop and set down the basket. Once he moved behind the camera, he slipped under the dark cloth.

"Thank you for doing this, Aunt Cora."

The photographer poked his head from under the cloth. "Get a little closer to each other, please, and stand very still."

Mary brushed up closer to Aunt Cora until their shoulders touched.

"Hold still just a little longer."

Out of the corner of her eye, Mary glimpsed a flash of green as a child ducked off with their dinner. "Stop, thief!" She fled after him, ignoring the calls of the photographer and her aunt. She had to catch the robber or they wouldn't have a meal on the train. She wove through the crowd, shouting as she went. "Excuse me!"

The crowd parted, but no one stepped forward to help. There wasn't time to purchase another meal, and she had no intention of letting the boy steal it from them. Aunt Cora had to eat or she would faint. Mary promised Father she'd take care of his sister, and if that meant chasing a child, then she would.

There, a green jacket in front of her. She'd caught him. She leapt across the remaining space between them. Her motion knocked the boy to the ground. Mary wobbled but kept her balance.

"That's mine!" She leaned over him, placed her foot on his leg, and yanked the package from him. "Stealing is wrong, and stealing from women is even, even more wrong."

She nudged the boy with her umbrella. "The Bible says thou shall not steal—"

The umbrella handle slid through her hand.

Gasping, she turned her head. Another thief? A man towered over her. His mustache quivered. Was he angry? Her knees trembled. Would he strike her? Was this one of those incidents Aunt Cora told her to be aware of, where one person acted as a decoy and the other stole your money? She stood taller. "He stole—"

"He's probably hungry, miss. I'm sure he'll apologize if you let him off the ground. Won't you, son?"

Her face heated with embarrassment at the compassion and maybe something more in his voice. "I can handle this. I do not need your help."

The boy tugged her skirt. "Missus, I'm sorry. I am hungry. My sister is, too. I promised her I'd find food."

"You sit still and be quiet." She kept her foot on the boy and stared at the man in front of her. Did she know him from somewhere? Then again, Father introduced her to so many men she couldn't be sure. It wouldn't do if word of her behavior made it back home. Gathering her thoughts, she stilled her emotions and directed her attention to the boy. "How old are you?"

"I don't have to tell you."

"Where is your sister?" The boy couldn't be more than eight. The whistle blew its boarding signal. She didn't have time to help this child right now. His clenched lips said he wouldn't give her any information.

She couldn't fix everything, but today, she could help this boy. She opened the basket and withdrew a sandwich, then an apple, and handed them to the boy. "Share this with your sister."

"Thank you. God bless." The boy stood, swayed on his feet, ready to run.

"Go on." He didn't need more encouragement. He scampered away without looking back. It concerned her that he might not have enough to feed both him and his sister. She should have given him more. Father said she shouldn't have such a soft heart for beggars, that they took advantage of her. Still, how did one know if a child was truly in need?

"That was nice of you, though he may not have a sister."

She bristled at the man's warning comment. So much like her father. "But he might. I'll take my umbrella, thank you. I have a train to catch."

Chapter Four

"Mary, I had to pay for that picture, and I'm sure it is ruined." Aunt Cora's heavy eyebrows almost knotted together as they got into the boarding line. "I would have thought better of you. Running after a basket of food as if you hadn't just had breakfast."

"I'm sorry, Aunt Cora. I had to save our dinner. You have to have something to eat." Mary handed her the basket and straightened her suit jacket. "Some of this is a bit mushed with all the jostling."

"Dear girl, this is an adventure. If it is mush, then that is what you eat. If the child had absconded with it, then that would also be part of the story you get to tell after the trip. Adventure isn't about the place you end up. It's the trip you take to get there." Aunt Cora shrugged. "Maybe you aren't ready for this."

"But I am. I was shocked someone would steal our food." Mary wanted to go back and change her actions toward the boy. She could have given him her entire portion and kept Aunt Cora's. That skinny youth in ragged clothes and bony hands might not have eaten in days, though it hadn't slowed him down. Or maybe it was the idea of eating that gave him the burst of energy to run. She did catch him.

She glanced behind her to see if she could spot him. If she remembered his face, when they returned. . . She stopped when her gaze collided with that odious man who took her umbrella. Was he going to Pueblo, too?

Before she turned away, he winked. Her heart kicked against her chest. Should she mention it to Aunt Cora? Or maybe she'd accept her aunt's advice and see where this journey took her. After all, he was taking the excursion trip. Perhaps he liked adventure.

She risked another look. The man held a notebook and scribbled. A reporter. Probably the excursion train would be loaded with them. She dismissed entertaining any more thoughts about him. Father would have a fit if she so much as spoke to the man again. He wouldn't be rich enough to placate her father.

◆　◆　◆

Women of all backgrounds boarded the train in Topeka, Kansas. The first line of an article could be tricky. He'd likely change it after he spoke with some of the women. Wyatt scribbled a few more sentences about leaving the depot and the weather. He glanced up to find the copper-haired beauty who gave food to the boy staring at him. He flashed a wink and a smile. He shouldn't have, but the temptation to tease her was too great.

He'd have to find her on the train and interview her. Must be a good story there. SOCIALITE ON THE EXCURSION. Possible heading for the article? Plucky woman to chase a child. Most of the women he knew would have screamed and pointed for someone else to do the running.

He checked the line behind him. Women were scarce in this monochromatic crowd but easy to pick out with their colorful hats. They traveled in small groups or with a husband. What would it be like to share adventures with a wife? He would concentrate on speaking to the ones without a male companion.

Wyatt closed his notebook and slipped it into his pocket along with the pencil. The line inched forward. Noticing everyone in front of him carried a package or basket onboard, he realized he hadn't stopped to pick up food for himself. His stomach growled. He woke too late for breakfast and skipped lunch. If he wanted dinner, he needed to act fast.

The line stretched behind him. Would he have enough time to purchase something at the station? He decided to risk it. "Pardon me." He moved through the murmuring crowd and ran for the depot. There wouldn't be time for the staff to make a sandwich. If he asked for a hunk of cheese and bread, and the wrapping, he would save time.

Once inside, he rushed to the lunch counter. No one stood behind it. He glanced around for an employee and then saw the sign.

CLOSED.

He forgot it was Sunday.

◆ ◆ ◆

Mary waited until Aunt Cora's dress hem dragged the top step of the passenger car before she followed. Her shoe clunked against the steel. This was real. She relaxed as she passed through the vestibule doors.

The porter took their lunch and hand baggage from Aunt Cora and then led them down the wooden aisle. After he stored the items on the rail above the seats, Aunt Cora tipped him. "Thank you, George."

George nodded and moved a few steps back so they could sit.

"Mary, come by the window so you can see everything." Aunt Cora stepped aside as Mary slid past.

"Thank you. It will be exciting to see what the Kansas and Colorado scenery is like." Mary settled into her seat. "How did you know his name is George?"

"I don't. It's what is done on trains. Call the porter George and tip him well, and you'll always have a friend on the train. It's something I learned from my travels. I believe it has something to do with George Pullman, the owner of the trains."

"Interesting. I'll remember that." Mary peered out the window. The once-overflowing platform emptied as passengers boarded the train. There were a few stragglers. One man came running. She leaned closer to the window. The man who'd taken her umbrella. He should have been onboard by now.

The whistle sounded. Steam released. "All aboard." The conductor sounded off. "Last call."

Would he make it? Her heart jumped. It would be awful to miss this train. Especially if he was to be writing about it.

"What are you gawking at?" Aunt Cora leaned over Mary's shoulder.

Lavender essence, Aunt Cora's favorite scent, freshened the air, but it didn't calm Mary's excitement.

"I'm watching people run to catch the train. Why don't they arrive on time? Do you suppose they had an emergency? Or maybe forgot something?" Mary pressed her face against the window, trying to spot the man boarding.

She'd lost him. Just as well.

"Possibly both. Some like to test the fortitude of others' patience." Aunt Cora settled back into her seat. "I missed a train once in Spain."

Mary whipped around. Aunt Cora had the best stories. "Why?"

"Someday I'll tell you the whole tale. It isn't that exciting. We were at a café, and they had the best paella. We lost the time in laughter." Aunt Cora sighed.

"We? Who were you with?"

"Another time, dear. Another time." Aunt Cora wiped a tear from her eye.

Chapter Five

The train whistle blew. Black smoke plumed into the air. Wyatt ran, regretting the idea to go for food and thankful he'd decided to send his valise to the baggage car. Panting, he grabbed the handrail with both hands as the wheels turned. He swayed on the bottom step as the train picked up speed. That was too close.

Missing this train could have ended his career or at least demoted him from reporter to selling papers on the street. And that would have forced his father's hand. He swallowed back his anger at being ordered around.

"Ticket, sir?" The porter stood at the doorway just far enough back for Wyatt to enter the car. He spotted a purple hat and the copper tendrils of the woman he sought, sitting in the seats that faced each other. The one place he hated. There would be no leg room, but the chance to talk to these two women came before comfort.

"Got it right here, George." He slipped his ticket from his pocket and handed it over with a few coins.

"This car is pretty full. If you'd like to look in one of the others—"

"This one will be fine. I can move later if I'm uncomfortable." He took back his ticket and stuffed it in his pocket. Resisting the urge to whistle, he strode down the aisle, keeping his balance like a sailor at sea, and slid into the seat in front of the most beautiful woman he'd ever seen. How had he missed the green of her eyes when he took the umbrella from her?

Those same eyes looked loaded with ammunition and ready to take him out.

"What are you doing?" Her face reddened.

Did she think he was here to berate her about the child?

"I needed a place to sit, and this seat was open."

Her mouth formed a small *O*, but no words, not even a breath, left her lips. He seized the moment before she might ask him to move. "I'm Wyatt Cross from the *Daily Commonwealth*. I'm hoping to ask you a few questions for a column I'm writing."

"Aunt Cora?"

Good. Now he knew the relationship between them. He stared at the aunt and waited for her reply. Listening, not talking, brought him the best stories.

Aunt Cora patted her niece's hand.

A nice hand, he noticed, smooth and without a blemish, her nails trimmed to exactness.

"Mary, it's your chance to be part of history. Why don't you help this handsome gentleman with his article?"

Mary nodded. "I'm Miss Owen. It's nice to meet you."

So, she wasn't going to tell her aunt about their earlier incident. She didn't appear to remember him from the Wagners' dinner party. The woman who asked him about Africa now sat in front of him. God giving him a chance at the one he thought long gone?

"Thank you for agreeing to talk with me. Where are you from?"

"We're from St. Louis." Her voice was soft against the clacking of the wheels on the track.

"How did you get tickets for the excursion?" He leaned forward to hear her answer.

She pressed against the seat. "I'm not sure." Her eyebrows knit together, and she glanced sideways at her aunt, then back at him. "Father bought them at the depot, or did you, Aunt Cora?"

Aunt Cora coughed. "Yes, we both did in a way. I told your father I was going, and he procured the tickets."

"He must have thought you would be safe with all the dignitaries on this trip." He'd have to do some digging when he returned to Topeka. The man had connections to be able to get tickets for the excursion. But why would he send his daughter and her aunt on a trip that hadn't been tested? "The excursion is the first for the Santa Fe to Pueblo; there could be problems. You must be brave women to take a journey that hasn't yet been experienced by men."

"We both like adventure, or rather my aunt does. This is my first trip. I am going to enjoy it."

"As long as things go well, I assume?" Wyatt scribbled *first-time traveler.* This would be a story to follow up on if all didn't go smooth on this first train journey to Pueblo.

"Even if they don't, Mr. Cross."

◆　◆　◆

Mary held tightly to the edge of the seat. Mr. Cross made her squirm. The space between their legs had to be less than two fingers' width. Her skirt moved as he adjusted his feet.

"It's a bit cramped in these seats. I apologize for mussing your outfit."

Her face warmed, and it wasn't from the woodstove in the corner across from them. She scooted her feet under the seat and smoothed the fabric a bit tauter. "Maybe you could find another place to sit?"

He twisted his body and peered down the aisle, his foot stretched to the side. Once again, he touched her hem.

"Looks pretty full to me. They sold all the tickets, and with only ten coaches there aren't a lot of open seats. I think I'll be here until we stop in a few hours." He sat back in his seat and scribbled in his notebook.

What was he writing now? She leaned forward a tiny bit, pretending to adjust her skirt while hoping for a glance at the paper. Or was he sketching?

He looked up.

She snapped back into place. His Wedgewood-blue eyes and coal-black lashes connected to some feeling she hadn't felt before, not at all unpleasant. Her breathing quickened. Perhaps if she thought of him as a restless child instead of a handsome gentleman, it would be easier to sit across from him until the next stop. He looked as disheveled as a boy.

His coat, while of good quality, had sleeves a bit too long, adding to the childlike vision. One of his light brown waves slipped through his pomade and twirled to the side. She bit back a smile. It wouldn't do for him to think she found him amusing.

"Mary, look." Aunt Cora nudged her shoulder with hers. "Is that snow falling?"

The sky grew dark, and white flakes stuck to the window.

◆　◆　◆

"Snow isn't unusual for Topeka in early March." Weather. He was a reporter and that's the most interesting thing he could say? Wyatt struggled for something more thought worthy to jump the conversation to his desired topic.

"We have snow in March as well, Mr. Cross. Sometimes so much the roads are impassable. Isn't that right, Mary?" Aunt Cora rubbed her forehead. "I do believe I'm getting a headache."

And he'd lost the train right off the track. Now the women were going to discuss aliments. Perhaps he should search for another seat with a woman capable of conversing about more than aches, pains, and hunger.

"Aunt Cora, it's too early for dinner, but maybe all this excitement has left you a bit hungry. Should I get you something from the basket?"

"I'll be fine, dear. Let's just give it some time and see if it disappears. Now, Mr. Cross, how did you get started in the newspaper business?"

Taken aback by her question, Wyatt almost told her he'd begun his profession as a way to irritate his father. "I've always liked to write stories, and this was a way to make my own money."

"So you come from a moneyed family, then?"

Mary's attention turned from her aunt to him. Wyatt's throat closed. Another woman looking for a husband. He'd been mistaken to think she came on this trip for the adventure.

"What makes you think that, Mrs.—" He realized she hadn't introduced herself.

"Miss Owen as well. I've never married." She turned away. "Maybe we should ask George to get the basket."

The younger Miss Owen glared at him. He'd made her angry by upsetting her aunt.

"I can retrieve it for you, Miss Owen." He stood, smashing the younger Miss Owen's dress again. If he kept this up, he'd have to buy her a new one.

"Mr. Cross, if you trample my skirt any more, you're likely to put your boot through it. We can call George to help, and maybe you can find another place to sit." She gave him a candy-sweet smile. "Then my poor unmarried aunt can rest. Your attempt at polite banter has most likely caused her a powerful headache." With that, she punched the buzzer by the window for George.

Eager to be away from the bothersome Miss Owen, Wyatt nodded. Once more, words escaped him.

He ambled down the aisle and paused next to an empty seat beside a young woman who sat next to an older man. Maybe she would be willing to talk. "May I sit here?"

The woman batted her eyes at him. His heart sunk. A woman looking for a husband.

"Of course. I'm Winnie Periwinkle, and this is my uncle Albert."

"Mr. Cross. I'm doing an article for the paper about women on the excursion. Would you mind answering a few questions?"

Miss Periwinkle brushed her shoe along his ankle then rested her foot on top of his. "What would you like to know?"

Trapped. Was this how Miss Owen had felt?

Chapter Six

Wyatt lurched across the platform to the next car. The rushing wind slid under the awning and attempted to steal his hat. He grabbed it before it took flight, holding it tightly to his head as he entered the car. The warmth from the stove hit him, and he relaxed.

He had no intention of finding a wife on this trip, despite his moment of insanity when he noticed the stunning Miss Owen's eyes. No, thank you. He'd take his father's anger. He didn't need the family money or the name. He definitely didn't need Miss Periwinkle either, despite her willingness to answer any question he asked. Her desperate friendliness had him asking a few rapid-fire questions so he could escape her obvious desire for a husband.

He strolled through the swaying car. Happy excursioners filled all the seats. He might as well return to the one he'd left. He resolved to ignore the green-eyed beauty and watch the scenery go by.

He turned to go back. The train had slowed. That wasn't right. He glanced out a window. Snow still fell, but that shouldn't affect the train. What was happening? The reporter's blood raced through his veins. He smelled a story brewing.

He took off toward the engine where he could get answers. Thoughts of his father, marriage, and money dissipated with each step he took.

◆ ◆ ◆

"Aunt Cora, what a dreadful man." Why had they sat so near the stove? Mary traced her cheek close to her hairline, making sure no perspiration made an appearance.

"You'll have to get used to those who are a bit rough around the edges if you want to see the world. If you're serious about missionary work, you'll stand in front of bulls who don't wish you to be in their community."

Mary handed her aunt a cookie. "Will one be enough, do you think?"

"I suppose we'll find out. It is an odd thing that eating keeps me on my feet, or in this case, on the seat." Aunt Cora sniffed the cookie. "I do love the smell of butter and sugar. Many times while in Europe, I longed for a bit of an American cookie."

"Their treats are quite delightful, but I understand. Do you feel it is because it's a memory of home more than the cookie itself?"

"Perhaps."

Mary kicked her hem out in front of her a bit to inspect the damage left by Mr. Cross's boot. A parade of dusty sole marks marched across the bottom. She would have to brush the skirt when they stopped for the night. The realization crushed her hope of an evening of leisure. "Do you encounter many like him on your travels?"

"A few, and sometimes the ones I thought were the worst of scoundrels turned out to be the nicest of gentlemen."

"Tell me about one of them, please?" She patted her aunt's arm. She loved her stories. While at boarding school, she'd retold her roommates the stories over and over. They all dreamed of living like her aunt, though they knew they would not. All of them were destined to marry a man who would improve their families' positions or coffers.

All except her. She intended to live a rich and exciting life, the way her aunt did. She refused to be sent away to a loveless marriage to lose herself because her father deemed a union more important than who she was.

"There was a young man in Spain. Why is the train slowing?" Aunt Cora wrinkled her forehead.

"We aren't to our stop yet." Mary tried to peer around her aunt to judge the reaction of the others.

The murmur from the passengers built. A woman clung to Mr. Cross. She held on to him as if she'd known him for a long time. Mary fisted her hands tightly enough for her fingernails to bite her palms.

◆　◆　◆

Mary sucked in a breath as Wyatt slid back onto the bench across from her. "It appears there is a problem up ahead."

"Why aren't you sitting with your friend?"

"Miss Periwinkle? We are acquainted but not friends. I prefer to be here where I can have the entire seat to myself. As I was saying—"

"What's happening?" Mary couldn't keep her hands still, plucking at her skirt and then her hair. "Are we in danger? There aren't train robbers, are there?" She peered through the window and saw little but snow.

"Seems the snow has caused a problem farther up the line." Wyatt spoke loudly and intentionally.

"How do you know?"

He put his finger to his mouth as if to shush her, then stood to address the car. "I've talked to the engineer. We have to stop at the next town because something happened to the snow plow."

"Do they have a place for us to stay?" Aunt Cora leaned over to Mary. "And so your adventure begins. We shall see how you stand up to changes in plans."

"I'll be fine. It's quite exciting to have things go off the rails. I mean having to stop, not the train itself. I wouldn't care for that." Mary peeked under her eyelashes at Mr. Cross. He stood there, acting important, talking to the gentleman next to them. His voice bounced around the car like a child's ball. "I know this stop. There isn't a place for everyone to stay."

He turned from her and lowered his voice. She couldn't pick up the words. But she knew enough to know she and Aunt Cora needed a plan for the night. Maybe they could sleep in their seats. Not comfortable at all, but what other choice would there be? She intended to find out as soon as Mr. High-and-Mighty sat down.

Chapter Seven

Wicker baskets crackled as their owners opened them. Was that fried chicken he smelled? Wyatt's mouth watered. Missing breakfast and lunch turned out to be a big problem.

"Stuck? The snow plow is buried?" Mary unwrapped a sandwich and handed it to her aunt.

"Eat half. I have plenty." Aunt Cora shoved the sandwich into Miss Owen's hand. "We'll be at the next town by morning, and we can get breakfast."

He could taste the saltiness of the ham piled high between bread. Would the young Miss Owen share with him the way she had the boy? He slid his pencil out from behind his ear and chewed the top while considering how much to tell the women. "We aren't going to make it that far. The engineer said two plows are ditched and one of them is halfway on the track. We're stopping in Larned until they build a temporary track."

"Mr. Cross, where is your dinner?" The older Miss Owen sounded much like his mother. "I hope the railroad has secured rooms for us there."

"I'm not hungry." His stomach roared like thunder.

"But he must be, Aunt Cora. Did you hear—"

"Mary, don't be impolite."

She tore her sandwich in half, leaving herself a mere quarter. "Here. We know you didn't bring a dinner basket with you. What were you thinking? We were told to bring a meal."

He didn't want to take it from her, but last night's dinner was a distant memory. "Yes, I knew. I forgot. I had a late night and slept too long. I missed breakfast and didn't have time to get lunch, either."

She pushed it at him. "Go on, you must eat something."

He reached for the sandwich, brushing her gloveless fingers as he did. A spark of electricity shot between them. He pulled back. Had she felt it, too? "You're cold. Why don't you change places with me, so you can be closer to the stove?" Why did he feel a need to put her comfort before his? Would he have done the same for Miss Periwinkle? He might have, not because he wanted to, but to be polite.

"I'm fine. Thank you." She took a birdlike bite.

"Reconsider, please. It will be cold by the window, and we'll all be sleeping on the train tonight." She was stubborn. He liked that.

"Aunt Cora?"

"Part of the adventure, Mary."

◆ ◆ ◆

He was right. They were stuck sitting on the track for the night. She chose to stay by Aunt Cora. At least they could use each other's shoulders for pillows. Mary leaned against her aunt and tried to doze.

What if they were stuck more than one day? That wouldn't happen, would it? If it did, what would they do for food? Would the railroad send another train? Maybe Mr. Cross knew. How did he find out information before the others? Possibly because he was a reporter? What it must be like to be free to chase a story across the country? What would it be like to be married to a man like Wyatt? Would he allow her to travel with him if she married him?

Her legs tingled and numbed. She moved them but couldn't get it to stop. Much like her father's request. She'd have to answer to her father's wishes soon, but how could she marry someone she didn't know? It wasn't fair that men could choose not to take a wife. Why couldn't her father be like her aunt?

Please, God, help me find the words to explain to him how much I need, want to be different? That I want to be a part of something bigger. Helping orphan children discover who You are would work for me, if it works for You, that is. Always Your will, Father, even if it means I marry someone my earthly father has picked out for me.

Sleep would bring the morning faster, but it continued to evade her. The soft glow from the lamps along the sides of the coach didn't help. She liked a dark room when she slept.

George explained it would be best to keep them lit to protect the ladies. Mary shivered. Safety hadn't been a concern until he said those words.

Mr. Cross closed his eyes and dropped off into sleep. How did he do that? Maybe reporters were given that gift so they could be ready to follow a story at a moment's notice.

Please, God, let the train move tomorrow. She wiggled against the seat. Funny, she didn't notice how hard it was until now.

"Are you awake?" A throaty whisper came from Mr. Cross.

Mary jumped. "I thought you were out for the night."

"Seats are too uncomfortable." He straightened up and rubbed his whiskered chin. "Can I interview you? That would pass the time."

She glanced at the passengers around her. Some played cards and others bowed their heads in slumber. There would be many sore necks in the morning. "We'll disturb Aunt Cora."

"Not if we whisper."

Mary tilted her head to one side and then the other way to ease the kinks that had settled. "What could I possibly have to say that is exciting enough for you to print?"

Wyatt reached into his coat pocket and brought out his pen and paper. "Let's find out. Why are you taking this trip?"

How much should she tell him? Knowing her father might read her words gave her pause. Caution would be best. "My aunt travels all over the world. I admire her and would like to be able to do what she does. Or become a missionary. I've not been away from home before, so my father let me come this time because Aunt Cora can't be alone."

"Why not?" His knees brushed hers.

A finger of fire raced through her. Mary swallowed and pushed back into the seat. He readjusted his position sideways. "My apologies. There isn't much room for legs."

"She forgets to eat and becomes dizzy. I'm here to make sure she has meals on time."

"Is that why you chased the boy?" He scribbled in his notebook.

"Yes. My father asked me to watch over her, and I intend to, even if that means chasing urchins." He had nice hair, though mussed from his attempt to sleep.

His pencil stopped scratching as he looked up. "So, you didn't want to take this trip?"

"I didn't know about this excursion until Aunt Cora told me a few days ago, before we left St. Louis. I'm thankful to be allowed to accompany her." Otherwise, she might be planning her wedding.

"Is it odd you were unaware of this trip? It's difficult to obtain tickets for special excursions as they sell out fast. The paper I work for purchased mine a month ago. They were sold out a week later."

"Are you suggesting my father planned for me to come with Aunt Cora before they argued about it over breakfast?" Anger erased the fire Mr. Cross ignited within her. Why would they conspire against her? She would have said yes without the subterfuge. Did Aunt Cora even need her?

◆ ◆ ◆

Wyatt's instinctive reporter warning bells rang in his head. He'd rattled Miss Owen. Her eyebrows twitched, and her lips turned down. Something was up, but with her lips so tight, he didn't think he'd get much from her right now.

Miss Periwinkle strolled past, leaving a scented trail thick enough to be called a rose garden.

"Excuse me, Miss Owen. Why don't you get some rest? I'll chat with Miss Periwinkle. I have a few more questions I'd like to ask her." Even though it was the last thing he wanted to do.

Her mouth opened and closed. He'd played his cards right and rendered her speechless. Good. When he returned, he might find her willing to speak to him.

Chapter Eight

Mary woke to the bright sun poking at her eyes through the window. The snow on the ground stretched for miles. She yawned and raised her arms, then dropped them down once she remembered where she was.

Aunt Cora still slept. Mary debated waking her and calling for George to get their basket down. They had a few pieces of cake left they could eat for breakfast. After that, Mary was unsure where she would find food. Maybe she shouldn't wait to try. If she did, there may not be anything. She stood and stepped over Aunt Cora's feet. Most of the passengers still dozed. The perfect time to see what was outside the door of the train and search for food.

With George's help, she tugged on her coat. "Could you direct me to the nearest place that might have food?"

"The snow is awful deep, miss. Let the men go searching when they wake."

"I fear there won't be enough. I have to make sure my aunt has provisions."

George steadied her as she stepped on the slick metal steps to disembark from the train car. The cold from the handrail seeped through her gloves. The wind blew hard, picking up the fresh snow and sending it swirling around her. A house stood about four cars away along with a windmill, and a water tower to fill the tank of the train, but she didn't see anything else. Could this be where the stationmaster lived?

She took a step, and snow circled her ankles and slid up her shins. She withheld a shriek. The cold didn't matter. Her goal was to reach that house and see if there was food to be had. Aunt Cora could not go without. Her father had been adamant.

Someone stepped out of the house onto the porch. It looked like Mr. Cross.

Had the scoundrel found a bed to sleep in? He waved at her.

"Wait! I'll bring you what I have."

Mary stopped. It would be a blessing from God if Mr. Cross had what they needed. She heard her father's voice: "...a husband can protect you." Maybe a little watching over from a man wouldn't be so awful.

As Mr. Cross approached, his footsteps crunched in the snow. He handed her a basket. "Keep this by you. It isn't a lot, so you'll have to ration between the two of you. The stationmaster offered what provisions he has. There won't be enough to feed everyone. I know your aunt needs food, so she'll be the first to get breakfast."

"We have cake. You didn't have to bring it for us." Why did she say that? "Sorry. I'm a little grumpy in the morning, especially if I haven't slept well. Thank you for thinking of my aunt."

"Women shouldn't travel without a man. They need someone to look out after them.

Since your father isn't here, I've chosen to do that for you."

He might as well have slapped her face. "If it wasn't for my aunt, I would throw this at you. I can take care of myself. That's the whole point of this trip. I'm proving to my father that I don't need anyone besides God and myself to get through this life. I am capable of finding my own food."

She tried to turn, but the snow snared her foot. She fell face forward into a freezing bank. The basket flew out of her hand. Bread and apples skittered across the snow. She lifted her head to see. The precious food lay on the tracks. If she wanted to get it, she would have to crawl underneath the train, and if she did, the bread wouldn't be edible. She bit back the tears that stung her eyes.

She pushed into a sitting position. Her wool skirts, heavy with snow, made it impossible to stand. She didn't want to ask, but she had to unless she wanted to crawl to the train and have George help her. "Mr. Cross, would you please give me assistance?"

"Here. Take my hand."

She did.

He pulled her up, balancing her against his chest.

Warmth radiated from him. For a moment, she wanted to sink against Wyatt and let him take care of her and Aunt Cora.

"What are you going to do now? You're capable, so you say. What are you going to do for dinner tonight? The engineer said we won't leave until tomorrow morning. After your cake is gone, you're still going to need three more meals."

"All I need is a shotgun, and I'll get some food. I'll get a hunting party together. Tell my aunt I'll be back later." She stomped through the snow toward the stationmaster's house. She knew how to shoot, and she was going to get a gun. There would be dinner, lunch, and breakfast, too. They might get sick of rabbit, but they would have something to eat.

◆　◆　◆

Wyatt bit back a chuckle. Maybe he was right about this woman. She wasn't one to sit back and wait for things to happen or to be given to her. He would pay more attention and dig a little further into what she was like under normal circumstances, and what her desires were for the future. Meanwhile, he let her go on to the stationmaster's home.

While she did that, he'd gather a few men and join her hunting party. She had a good idea. Getting fresh meat for the day would not be a bad plan. Perhaps with the few provisions left, one of the women passengers could make some stew and stretch it further. Good gravy, now he sounded like a woman. What was happening?

One thing he knew for certain, he would avoid Miss Periwinkle the rest of the trip. She had one thing in mind. Marriage. Marriage to anyone.

He could see why she was single. She hadn't stopped talking about herself for one minute last night. She was a great candidate for an interview if one could believe a tenth of what she said. One moment she talked about wanting to climb mountains, and the next she prattled about how she couldn't wait to sit by an evening fire with her knitting. The two things were so far apart from each other, he didn't know what to make of it.

Before he boarded the train, he waited for Miss Owen to make it to the house. He wouldn't mind having to rescue her from the snow one more time. The door closed.

Whether or not she would get a gun was another question. He was surprised she didn't have one on her.

"Can I help you with that, sir?" George hung on to the rail. "It's a bit slippery."

"Here's a basket of food I got from the stationmaster. It isn't much. I'm hoping you can distribute it evenly."

Wyatt handed the basket up to George, who took it and set it down.

"He has a little left, but not much. I fear once the others realize there is nothing on the train to eat, they will hit his door as well, asking for food. I'm gathering a few men from the other car to help hunt."

He grabbed the handrail and climbed the stairs. His foot slipped, but he caught his balance before he fell.

"Careful, sir. Is there something I can do to help?"

"Would you please inform Miss Owen that her niece plans to go hunting with us?"

Imagine that. A society princess out hunting in the snow. Yes, she intrigued him. He wanted to find out more.

◆　◆　◆

The wind had calmed, making it a good time to hunt. Not far from the train, Mary stood outside the circle of men. They made more noise than hens clucking for their dinner. She took a few steps away.

"Where are you going, Miss Owen?" Wyatt caught up to her. "We agreed to stick together."

"You and your posse did. I can do far better on my own."

"It's not that we can't. It's a safety issue. As long as we are—"

Mary spotted movement on the snow. She placed the repeating Winchester on her shoulder, took aim, and fired. "Got it. You were saying? I need to pick up my rabbit, if you don't mind."

"And if you go out there and someone else shoots—"

She aimed and fired again. "Sure is a lot of talking and not much hunting going on. If you and the others are going to provide food, you best be getting to it." She walked away. Miss Periwinkle could have him. Reporters, at least this one, didn't seem to be good at providing during a crisis.

"I'm coming with you. Two of us will look bigger out there and, if God is watching out for us, we won't get shot. Or you could return to the train, and I'll get these picked up and cleaned."

"And then what? You expect me to then cook them?" Which is what she intended to do, but she wanted to know what he thought.

He rubbed his whiskered chin. "Why wouldn't you?"

"Because I bagged them. That's the rule of hunting." He probably didn't think women should have the right to vote either.

"How do you know?"

"My father taught me to hunt when I was small. I would have had more to pick up if I'd had my own gun. This one is a bit too large." She rested the long barrel over her shoulder and stepped away from him. "Are you coming?"

Chapter Nine

In the car, Mary found her aunt conversing with Miss Periwinkle, who held a piece of cake in her lap.

"I've asked Miss Periwinkle to sit with us for the remainder of the trip." Aunt Cora slid over so Mary could sit.

"I hope you don't mind, Miss Owen. Your sweet aunt is such a delight. She even shared her cake with me as I had nothing left from last night." She tittered.

"That was to be for my aunt to eat. I suppose she didn't mention if she is without food she faints?"

"Mary, there is no need—"

"Why no, she didn't mention it." Miss Periwinkle's face drooped a bit, and she looked at the cake in her lap uncertainly.

"She wouldn't. But I will, so enjoy that bit of chocolate cake. Aunt Cora, you may have mine." Mary rubbed her hands together. Her feet felt like blocks of ice from tramping through the snow, but she couldn't very well remove her boots and rub them.

"We'll see. I'm not hungry at the moment. Miss Periwinkle was telling me she hoped to find a match in Pueblo."

"Or this excursion. There are some mighty fine men to pick from, like Mr. Cross. He was sitting with you earlier. What did you think of him?" Miss Periwinkle took a bite of the cake.

"I'm sure he'll return soon. He said he couldn't find another place in the other car."

Miss Periwinkle's face took on a dreamy look. "If Mr. Cross would like to sit here, there is plenty of room beside me. Mama used to say I'm light as a feather and tiny as a hummingbird."

Mary wished she would have stayed out in the cold and dressed those rabbits. Why had she let Wyatt convince her to come inside? Especially since she was mad at him for suggesting it in the first place. It would serve him right if he had to sit by Miss Periwinkle. "I'm sure Mr. Cross would be delighted to sit next to you, Miss Periwinkle. He said you were old friends."

Miss Periwinkle blushed. "He did? Wyatt is the sweetest man. I can't believe someone hasn't snatched him up for a husband since he—"

Wyatt slid into the bench seat. "Miss Periwinkle, you aren't spreading tales, are you?"

Mary noticed he kept inches between them by hugging the edge of the seat.

"Are you warm enough, Miss Owen? I can switch places with you so you'll be closer to the stove. After that spill in the snow and hunting, it wouldn't do to catch a cold."

"Mary. You were hunting?" Aunt Cora drew herself up in an opposing posture. "I promised your father—"

"So Miss Owen is a bit of an outlaw then?" Wyatt wore a huge grin as he reached for his notebook and pencil.

"I am not, sir." *Outlaw indeed.* "I had to find provisions for my aunt. Anyone would have done the same for a family member."

"I wouldn't dream of shooting an animal, Mr. Cross." Miss Periwinkle touched his arm. "Make sure you put that in your article. It's not right for women to behave so wild-like when there are men present to take care of them."

He inched farther away, half-hanging off his seat. "I disagree, Miss Periwinkle. It's good for women to know how to take care of themselves. They can be proper helpmates to their husbands and free them from worry when they must leave them alone."

"Hmpf." Miss Periwinkle crossed her arms and huddled closer to the window.

Wyatt didn't care for Miss Periwinkle. Mary warmed inside despite the outer chill on her skin. "Mr. Cross, I would love to move closer to the heat. Thank you."

◆ ◆ ◆

Outlaw. That's what he'd call her in his article. OUTLAW ON THE PUEBLO EXCURSION made a grand headline. Might even be front page worthy. Mary caught his attention and held it. Women like Miss Periwinkle couldn't begin to garner his attention in her presence.

Here was a woman not afraid to go into a snow-filled pasture and hunt food for her family. Did she have a sense of adventure, too, or just one of survival? One could argue both were needed, or maybe they were interchangeable.

He watched her while she chatted with Miss Periwinkle and her aunt. He shut his eyes, hoping they would think he rested. He'd rely on his memory if they said anything that he could use in his column.

"It's rather dull waiting. Isn't it?" Miss Periwinkle tapped her foot. "If we had a game to play, it would pass the time. Did you bring cards, Miss Owen?"

"She certainly did not." Mary's aunt roused from a rest she'd been taking. "We do not play games of chance in this family. I'm surprised you do, Miss Periwinkle."

"My father allows it. Parlor games are all the rage back home in Boston. There's not much else to do in the winters."

"There is always the Bible to read or stitching that can be done. My niece has been trained in the proper ways of a lady. Didn't you go away to school?"

"My parents sent me to Europe. The rules there are much different. Always an event to attend and a gentleman to take you. Why, we even snuck out of school some evenings to walk along the riverbanks. Nothing like this backward country. That's why I came on this trip. Father is traveling in the train that left behind us. He's a legislator, and he wants to open the West to more people."

She lied, and Wyatt knew it. Earlier she'd mentioned growing up in New York and traveling with her uncle. They were buying a home in Pueblo.

"What does your father do, Miss Owen?"

Mary frowned.

Would she answer? Miss Periwinkle might as well have asked Mary how much her father was worth. Wyatt's fingers itched to get at his pencil, but he remained still.

◆ ◆ ◆

"I'm going to explore the train. Would you like to come along, Aunt Cora?" Mary wanted out of the tight space and away from Miss Periwinkle's questions.

"Walking around isn't good for me." Miss Periwinkle gazed at Mr. Cross. "I tire easily."

More like she didn't want to leave Wyatt's presence. Should she stay? "Aunt Cora?"

"Go along, dear." Her aunt elbowed Wyatt. "Would you be a dear and escort my niece? She's restless. I'll stay with Miss Periwinkle. We wouldn't want her to tire herself too much."

Mary bit back a grin. Her aunt didn't want Wyatt around that woman either. But that meant her aunt did want Wyatt around her. Did she want to see her married as much as her father did? She'd dig into that subject when she came back from her walk. By then, she trusted Aunt Cora would have encouraged Miss Periwinkle to return to her own seat.

Wyatt stood. "It would be my pleasure to escort you, Miss Owen. We can walk to the observation car. Maybe we will see a patch of green or even a buffalo."

"I'd like that. I haven't seen one yet. I hoped to see all sorts of wildlife on this trip." She waited for him to get free. Miss Periwinkle moved her feet into Wyatt's path, as if she could stop him from getting away from her.

"It's a narrow walk all the way there, but I'll be right behind you. It's three cars down." Wyatt rested his hand on her shoulder.

Mary didn't mind the warmth of his hand or the fire that rushed through her. Was Miss Periwinkle green with envy?

Chapter Ten

Mary paced the empty observation car. With all the windows, it should have been pleasant and full of excursionists. Instead, the snow and the sun hiding behind clouds made for a dreary view. "How much longer do you think we will be stranded?" She stood next to the glass, but her breath fogged it, concealing her view.

"The engineer told some of the reporters the new track should be finished by tomorrow. We might be able to pull out in the morning."

Mary turned to Wyatt. "Another day?" Her voice rose in a pitch that hurt her own ears. "You knew this. And yet you closed your eyes. And went to sleep? We don't have enough food for another day."

"Let's not panic everyone. Remember, God said you can't add a day to your life by worrying." Wyatt moved closer to her.

"That's your answer? Don't cause trouble? Don't worry? It's going to be pandemonium once it's discovered. We have to do something. I'm going to gather some men to help find more game. I'm sure I can borrow the rifle from the stationmaster again."

Wyatt grabbed her by the shoulders and pulled her close. "We aren't going to starve, and you aren't going hunting again."

She pushed against his chest. But he didn't let go. "You have no right to tell me what I can do. You aren't my father or my husband. I won't sit here waiting for provisions to be brought. I have my own gun. If I have to, I'll use it."

"You brought a rifle?"

"No, this." She pulled her small pistol from her pocket. "And if you don't let go of me, I'll use it on you."

"Miss Owen. I've been looking for you." George bent over and gasped for air.

Wyatt released her, and she hid her gun in the folds of her skirt. Her heart fluttered. "What's wrong, George?"

"Your aunt fell, and we can't wake her up."

◆ ◆ ◆

Mary rushed through the cars. A man played a violin, and the bow reached into the aisle, poking her in the side as she passed. "Sorry, please excuse." She took no time to look back. *Please, God, I have to get to Aunt Cora. Please let her be awake.* Had she broken the man's bow? No matter. She would find out later and make amends.

She made it to their car and stopped. Men stood in their seats. Miss Periwinkle hovered over Aunt Cora, who lay in the aisle still as death.

Wyatt bumped into her.

She bobbled on her feet.

He steadied her.

Grateful, she took strength from his strong hands on her waist. *Please, God, let her wake up. This isn't the kind of adventure I wanted, Father.* Pulling away from Wyatt's strength, she clung to God's. She knelt at her aunt's side and stroked her cheek. "How long has she been like this?"

Miss Periwinkle, white-faced and breathing shallow, gripped the seat next to her. "Miss Owen, she decided to come with you and Mr. Cross. When she stood, she dropped like a rock. Her head cracked against the edge of the bench."

"Does anyone have any honey or preserves, even sugar?" Mary, frantic for an answer, surveyed the passengers. Blank faces returned her stares. "She needs something to eat."

"We all do." Miss Periwinkle sighed. "If I'd known she was this hungry, I wouldn't have eaten the other piece of cake she offered."

Mary stiffened with fury. She wanted to yank Miss Periwinkle's ankles so she'd fall and hit her own head.

"Think, do you have a sugar cube you slipped in your pocket, a piece of candy?" Wyatt's voice boomed above her. "You there, sir. You had butterscotch this morning. There is no time to lose here."

The man came to life. "Yes, I have a piece."

"I have a bit of preserves."

Passengers sent items to Mary. She'd never had to do this before, but Father explained what needed to be done. The preserves would work fast, but she needed water or tea. "Wyatt, I need to make this thinner."

"George, bring some water, please."

Mary patted her aunt's cheek. "Please, wake up."

Wyatt took the glass from George and handed it to Mary. She spooned it into the preserves and stirred. "Lift her head please, Wyatt."

He knelt and did as she asked.

With great care, Mary dribbled bits of the thinned mixture into her aunt's mouth. "Come on, Aunt Cora. Open your eyes."

◆　◆　◆

Mary's aunt moved, and Wyatt breathed a sigh of relief.

"What's the meaning of this? Why are you all looking at me?" She coughed and then groaned. "My head."

"Be still, Aunt Cora. I'll help you back into your seat. You fainted, and now you have a nasty bump on your head."

Wyatt slid his arms under Miss Owen's. "Sorry, ma'am, but this is the easiest way since you're stuck between the seats."

"No harm, Mr. Cross. It's nice to have such a strong young man to help Mary through this." She staggered on her feet. "I think I'm fine now."

"You are not fine. I need to find you something else to eat before you have another accident. Mr. Cross, do you suppose you can rally the men for another hunting party?"

"Mary, you are not going out there again. I will not have my niece acting like an outlaw. Those men can hunt just as well as you. Besides, I'd like to have you by my side as I feel a bit weak, and Miss Periwinkle isn't much use."

"I'm sorry. If you'd have said you needed the cake—"

"You should have asked." Mary thundered. "What were you thinking? That you are the only person who is hungry?"

Wyatt backed away. This outlaw was a bit more than he could handle. She didn't need a husband. She was ready for adventure. Maybe a little too much.

Chapter Eleven

unt Cora, you seem fine now. I really think I should go help hunt food for us. Father—"

"You will not. Your father doesn't expect you to kill a buffalo to feed me." She twisted in her seat and took hold of Mary's chin. "You have much to learn." She let go and turned away. "I fear I'm not going to have enough time to teach you."

"You only need to tell me how to keep from being married. The rest I can figure out. Besides, as long as you eat, you'll be here a long time." Mary patted her aunt on the hand, and then rose.

Her aunt grabbed her. "It's not what you would expect. What if I told you I wanted to be married?"

"But you always said. . ." She plopped onto the seat.

"That's what I wanted you to believe. I made my choice and had to live with it." She dabbed her eyes. "Growing old alone isn't joyful. You'd do well to remember that."

"I still don't understand. You talk about laughing with friends and missing trains in Spain—"

"I'll tell you about that if you promise not to hunt with the men."

Guilt slid down her spine. She wanted to know more about her aunt's life, but what of her promise to her father?

Miss Periwinkle edged her way into the seat in front of them. "Did you hear? The train behind us will be here soon. I overheard some men discussing it in the observation car. They thought with the snowstorm it wouldn't have left Topeka, but it did. It's the legislature train, and it has a sleeper car. We won't have to search for comfort on these hard seats tonight."

"Why would they let us have the berths, Miss Periwinkle?" Mary tried to follow the logic of someone giving up a place to lay flat. She rubbed her neck and wished she could do the same for her lower back.

"We're women, silly. Of course we will get to use them. The legislative train is full of men. Isn't it grand being a woman?" Miss Periwinkle leaned over and checked her reflection in the window. She patted a stray hair back into place. "I must let Mr. Cross know. I'm sure he hasn't a clue since he's out scavenging for food."

Mary seethed. The woman vexed her with her all-knowing attitude and obvious attraction to Wyatt. But why? If Mary wasn't interested in him, she ought not care if Miss Periwinkle thought him a good catch.

But she did. Mary considered Wyatt's concern for her aunt. Family must be important to him. He was quick to provide for the two of them, also something good to have in a husband. He must care for adventure, since he reported the news from places like this excursion. And there was the matter of how he made her feel when he pulled her close.

But would Wyatt want Miss Periwinkle, the flirt? She had to know he wouldn't be able to afford to outfit her in expensive clothes like she now wore. Mary wouldn't need such things. Her father had plenty of money, so she wouldn't go without, even if she convinced him to follow her desire for adventure by becoming a missionary. God called her to be more than a wife. She knew it in her heart.

"You might want to let the other women in the train know first. They will be ecstatic about this as well. Run along, dear." Aunt Cora moved her legs to the side as Miss Periwinkle exited.

"I imagine they'll have provisions to share, too, Aunt Cora." Mary leaned back in her seat. The weight of her promise to her father slipped off her shoulders, leaving room for excitement to take hold. "Now tell me about the man you didn't marry."

Aunt Cora's eyes shone with the sparkle of tears.

◆　◆　◆

"Mr. Cross. Mr. Cross."

Wyatt turned from the men he'd gathered to hunt small game. Miss Periwinkle stood at the top of the stairs, bundled in a fur coat. It wasn't that cold. What did she want with him? Maybe if he ignored her, she'd go back inside. "I'll go with Johnson if he promises not to shoot me. He does work for a rival paper."

"Mr. Cross!"

The woman's voice triggered a bolt of pain in his head. He waved. Maybe that would quiet her for a moment. "I'd better find out what she wants before she slides off those steps."

"I hear she's looking for a husband." Johnson guffawed.

"I'll make sure to introduce the two of you later."

Johnson snickered. "I think it's too late for me. She's set her hook for you, Cross."

"Well, I'm not getting reeled in." He'd made it clear, or so he thought, that he wasn't interested in her. Miss Periwinkle was meant for someone else. Unlike Mary, who tugged at his heart.

Heavy snow clung to his boots, impeding his progress, but the weight of his reluctance further shortened his stride.

"Mr. Cross, you don't have to go hunting," she yelled from the top step. "Another train is on its way. We've been saved."

He stopped. "Thank you, Miss Periwinkle. I need to inform the men. It was kind of you to let us know."

"You'll be coming back on the train soon, won't you, Mr. Cross?" Her lashes fluttered, lips curved—a pose no doubt meant to draw him in.

"At some point I will. You best go back inside where you'll be warm." *And far away from me.*

◆　◆　◆

"Why must you know?" Aunt Cora's eyes pooled with tears.

Mary wanted to cry with her aunt. She hated upsetting her. "It's only because I admire you so much. I want to be like you and travel, maybe become a missionary. Did you know one woman changed an entire village just by showing them what soap can do? Can you imagine? I want to do something with my life, like Susan Blow. Opening the kindergarten in St. Louis is such a worthy adventure." She stopped and took a breath.

"I didn't want the life I have. It's what was left when a carriage accident took the love of my life."

Mary gasped. "You were planning on getting married?"

"Yes, and it isn't as horrific a thing as you have imagined. Horace and I were going to marry that spring and live in the house my parents gave us. The one I live in now." She caressed her cheek. "We had grand plans. He was a lawyer, and we wanted to have children and take them abroad. We felt it important for children to experience the world."

"But how did you escape marriage to someone else? Every woman must marry or become the old spinster aunt."

Aunt Cora's eyebrow raised. "Providing there are other siblings. You, my dear Mo, will never be an aunt if you don't marry, since you don't have any siblings."

A cloak of loneliness settled on Mary.

"Once Horace was gone, I knew I couldn't love another, and my father didn't insist." Her aunt wiped her eyes. "I thank my father for that. He gave me a precious gift. He sent me on a tour of Europe. I traveled the world. I met so many people and made friends everywhere. Though, I think Father thought I'd return with my grieving finished and willing to marry."

"All those you met, and yet you never found another Horace?" Mary rested against the back of the bench.

"No. There were a few who came close, but they didn't make me as happy as Horace."

"Do you think it's like that for everyone? That you only get one chance at true love?" Worry crept through her. Had she passed up her chance by insisting she didn't want to marry? Is this what her father wanted her to understand, that real love only happens once? Thinking back over their conversations, Father never said she must marry, only that he desired her to.

"Maybe not everyone, but I think it is true for the Owen family. Your father felt the same about your mother. Once he lost her, he couldn't give his heart to another, not even for you, Mo. He wanted you to have a mother, but he refused to marry unless he found love again."

Mary didn't even bristle at the use of her nickname. She had much to consider, like the way Wyatt made her stomach all fluttery and her heart race when he touched her. Had God sent him? If so, what would Father think about her marrying a reporter?

Chapter Twelve

Darkness fell. Wyatt didn't reappear all afternoon, even though Miss Periwinkle told him he didn't have to hunt. The minutes continued to drag by as Miss Periwinkle chattered about all she intended to do once she reached Pueblo.

"The house Uncle purchased has thirteen bedrooms. Can you imagine, Miss Owen?"

Mary shook her head and hoped Miss Periwinkle didn't realize she'd been about to drift off. "That is quite a lot of rooms. What are you going to do with all of them?"

"Uncle hasn't said. He doesn't have any children."

Mary's stomach twisted. Something wasn't quite right. "Miss Periwinkle, why are you with your uncle instead of your parents?"

"They died. Uncle came to the door the day our house was being sold. I didn't have anywhere to go, and he was leaving the city. When he suggested I accompany him to Colorado, I was sure God sent him to rescue me. At least going with him would give me a chance to find someone else to marry." Miss Periwinkle balled her hands in her lap.

A liar. She'd told them earlier she'd been in Europe and her father let her play cards.

"You didn't know him, and you came on this trip?" Aunt Cora perked up. "I'm not sure that was wise, my dear."

"Maybe not, but I didn't have a choice. It was go with him or to the poorhouse." She sat back in the seat, and tears bubbled. "I thought my life would be different. The man I was to marry left as soon as he found out my parents died and left me without an inheritance."

"How awful, Miss Periwinkle." Mary's heart flipped from disgust to hurt. What would it be like to lose both your parents and your home?

Father wished her married, but was it really the worst thing in the world? What if she had to follow a man she didn't know to Colorado? It would be an adventure, but not one with happy excitement. Just horrible dread.

Miss Periwinkle sniffed. "Please, call me Winnie. I will be fine. I do miss my parents. Maybe when this train takes off and I get to Pueblo and see the house, I'll feel better."

Mary pulled a handkerchief from her pocket and handed it to Winnie. "What does your uncle expect you to do? Are you to be a guest? A companion? Or—"

Two men loud with laughter tumbled through the doorway; one of them landed in the lap of a woman. She shrieked.

The still-upright man dragged the other to his feet and saluted the outraged woman with a brown bottle before bringing it to his mouth and tossing back a long swig. "'Scuse me, lady. Didn't mean to land on you. Old Griff here is a bit wobbly on his feet."

Griff punched him in the arm. "You're not so stable yourself." He walked backward and stopped next to Mary. "What do we have here? A whole seat full of pretty women?" He reached over and grabbed Mary by the arm. "I believe red-haired beauties to be my favorite." He yanked her out of the seat.

"Stop it! Unhand me." Mary tried to peel his grip from her arm.

Miss Periwinkle screamed. "Let her go!"

Aunt Cora smacked him with her knitting needle.

Griff laughed. Snot sprayed from his nose. "Can't stop me. I'm taking her." He pulled Mary through the car and out the door. "Get the yellow-haired one for yourself. We'll have us a party, Hank."

Mary fought Griff. She couldn't get away. Why weren't any of the men helping? Where was Wyatt? *Please, God, send him to find me and Winnie!*

◆　◆　◆

Evening crept up fast on the prairie. The clear sky sparkled with stars, and the moon lit the way as Wyatt and the other men traipsed through the snow back to the train.

"Excellent idea you had, Johnson." When Johnathan suggested they explore the Kansas landscape, Wyatt agreed. The open air, though chilly, was much sweeter to him than being trapped on the train. His feet were soaked through. He didn't mind, knowing he'd soon be sitting across from Mary and warming his feet by the heat of the stove. He hoped Winnie Periwinkle had returned to her seat.

"Sorry we kept you away from your admirer. Perhaps by now she's found someone else." Johnson smacked Wyatt on the back. "Don't cry when she informs you there is another."

"She's waiting for you, Johnson. You can find a preacher in Pueblo. Maybe acquire a positon at another paper as well."

"And let you have the run at the best stories in Topeka without competition? No. I don't think so. Looks like the other train made it."

Wyatt nodded. "That should ease the tension around here. Might be some good interviews on that train, too, with all those legislators."

"I hope there is more than one. Too many reporters on board." Johnathan paused in his tracks. "Let's head over there together. I like you, Wyatt. Hate to fight you for a story."

"Excellent idea. I want to check on Miss Owen and her aunt first."

"Don't take long."

"Why don't you come with me? Give you a chance to meet Miss Periwinkle." Wyatt couldn't help the cat's-got-you grin he knew crept across his face, though his chapped lips didn't care for the too-tight stretch. He brushed his gloved finger across them, hoping they hadn't split.

"Might as well, but I imagine she's already found a man or two to talk to on the other train."

"Then you'll not be in any danger of being married by morning." Wyatt turned back to look at another group of men following them who'd stopped at the stationmaster's home to return the borrowed guns. "If we hurry, we can beat the rest of them."

◆　◆　◆

Mary continued to fight Griff. The man had skin of leather. Her nails did no more than leave a red mark. Winnie had been right about there being a place to sleep on a different car. "Why are you doing this?"

"You know why, sweetheart. No need to pretend to be the innocent here." He pushed her into a sleeping berth. She fell backwards. "Paid good money for you. Could have had the other one for free, but I like that red hair. I like fighting women." He reached for her hat.

She kicked him in the chest.

He rubbed the spot where her foot landed and then laughed. "Yes, I do. And I've got me one."

He grabbed the hem of her skirt. "Let's see what color your pretty petticoat is. I bet it's red to match your shiny hair."

Mary screamed and yanked her skirt from his hand. The fabric ripped at the seam.

"Making it easier for me, aren't you, wench?" Griff licked his lips.

Mary sickened. If she'd eaten more, she would throw up on him. Instead, bile stung her throat. "Get away from me or I'll shoot." She went for the gun in her skirt pocket.

Griff pushed her down and landed on top of her, pinning her arm to her side. "Yes, indeed. I do like a woman who fights."

His wet mouth moved against the side of her neck. His beard rasped against her skin.

Mary gagged. *Dear God, please send Wyatt!*

Chapter Thirteen

T he train looked homey to Wyatt with its flickering lights reflecting on the snow. *Homey? Since when had he ever had a thought like that?*

Since Mary. He should have asked her to come with him, but then she would have been the only woman, unless he'd also asked Miss Periwinkle. He shuddered. Better that he hadn't. While Mary would have enjoyed the long walk in the snow, Miss Periwinkle would have complained and made everyone miserable.

He went first up the train stairs; Johnson followed.

George didn't greet them. Odd. The hairs on Wyatt's arms tingled against his skin. High-pitched conversational cadence filled the air. Something was wrong. The car stilled when he entered. Mary's aunt slumped in her seat. Was she ill again? Where was Mary?

"Where's Miss Owen?" Perhaps George went to locate her.

"Some man drug her out of here." A gray-haired woman palmed her chest. "She fought him, but he seemed to expect that. I wouldn't have thought—"

"Mildred, be still." The older man sitting with her grasped her hand. "Someone should have stopped him."

"Where's George? Why didn't he step in?" Wyatt's tapped his foot. He had to find her.

"Haven't seen him in a while. Someone said he was getting food for our car from the other train." The older man coughed. "They pulled those girls out of this car. Went right past us, but I'm too frail. I couldn't stop them with this wretched knee."

"There was more than one? Who else did they take?" Johnson's words were hot on Wyatt's neck.

"That flirtatious Miss Periwinkle." The woman scowled.

Mary's aunt stood. "Thank goodness you're here, Mr. Cross. Did you find her?"

The car swayed under Wyatt as he rushed up the aisle to her. "No. I didn't know she was missing until now."

"What will I tell her father? I shouldn't have brought her with me. He was right." Her face was the color of chalk. "She isn't skilled enough to protect herself on an adventure like this."

"Did you know the men that took them?" Wyatt settled her back onto the seat.

"No. You have to find them. They were evil. Smelled of whiskey. Please hurry."

Where would they have taken Mary? His stomach sunk as he remembered Winnie telling him about the sleeping car. This time of day it would be empty. The perfect place to hide malevolent activity. "Come on, Johnathan. We have evil to stomp."

"Someone make sure she gets something to eat." Wyatt yelled as he pounded back through the car to the door. "You." He pointed at the older man. "You can do that much."

◆ ◆ ◆

Mary struggled underneath Griff. He smelled like old fish and hair tonic. There had to be a way to get away from him. She couldn't get to her gun, and it didn't matter as it wasn't loaded. Wiggling to one side, she freed her hand. She grabbed a hunk of Griff's hair and yanked.

"Ow! What'd you do that for?" He put his face close to hers and gave a reptilian wink. "I think you're asking for more excitement than you're ready for, missy."

A shadow cast by the gas lights wavered against the wall. Did Mary dare hope?

Griff's weight left her body. She scrambled off the bed to the dull beat of punches connecting with solid mass.

Wyatt landed a glancing right cross off of Griff's chin. He forced him down the narrow aisle away from her. "Get out now, Mary."

Her legs wobbled. She hung on to the curtain of the booth while the car spun. There were two Wyatts and two Griffs.

"You've made a mistake messing with this woman." Wyatt guarded his chin with a raised fist.

"But I paid for her." Griff snapped out a head shot, but Wyatt ducked left and blocked his attack.

"Then you were scammed. She isn't for sale." Wyatt threw his weight behind one final gut punch. "No woman should be bought."

Wyatt's fist connected, and Griff rocked back against the wall, chest doubled over his knees.

Wyatt turned and grabbed Mary, holding her close to his chest. "Did he hurt you?"

The car stopped spinning. She breathed in Wyatt's scent. He'd come for her, protected her. She burst into tears.

◆ ◆ ◆

Wyatt held Mary close. What if he hadn't arrived in time?

"Winnie. Wyatt, that other man took her." She broke free of his embrace, steady in her gaze. "We have to find her."

"My friend Johnson is looking for her. I hope he found her as easily as I found you. We split up to check the cars."

"You came in time. He was so. . ." She sniffled.

"Shh. You don't have to talk about it. Unless you want to." If she filled in any details, he might have to shoot the man groaning on the floor.

"No. I want to forget what happened. Thank you for rescuing me."

Wyatt stroked Mary's back. He hated tears, but she had every right to bawl her eyes out. She clung to him, and a protective side he hadn't known he possessed stirred. He vowed to keep her safe the rest of the trip.

Just the trip? He didn't want to admit it, but he loved this outlaw.

Chapter Fourteen

Mary and Wyatt discovered Winnie and Johnson in the next car. Winnie's face held a tinge of green, and her hair resembled a haystack that had been repeatedly stabbed by a pitchfork. Then again, Mary considered she might not look her best either, what with her ripped skirt. She hugged Winnie. "I'm so glad you're okay."

"Had to bang up your man, too, I see, Johnson." Wyatt glared at the man on the floor. "I left the other vermin in the car. We should see someone about getting them locked up."

"Mary, your skirt." Winnie's lips trembled. "And me, a mess. How are we going to go back in our car? Everyone will stare."

"We will march in there and sit by Aunt Cora and let her fuss over us. No one jumped up to save us from these men. Let them see what damage they wrought."

Winnie's eyes widened. "Johnson found me in time. Didn't Wyatt?"

"In time for what?" Had Winnie's attacker hit her on the head?

"To protect your virtue."

Red-pepper heat blossomed across Mary's face. "Shh." She turned to see if Wyatt heard.

"Johnson, help me drag this one next door. I'll keep them in there until you find out where we need to put them. I'm thinking the caboose would be the spot where someone could watch them until we reach Pueblo."

"Why don't we drag them there now, before they get their wits about them and start swinging?"

"Good idea. Ladies, can you make your way back to your car?"

"Yes, we can." Winnie braided her hair. "As soon as we feel presentable."

Wyatt touched Mary on the shoulder. "How about you? I should escort you back to your aunt."

"No, I'd rather see those men contained somewhere as soon as possible." Her heart skipped a beat. He cared about her.

Once the men left, Mary turned to Winnie and tucked a piece of her hair back into her bun. "That's better. About what you asked. Wyatt did reach me in time."

Winnie sighed. "We are fortunate to have been saved."

"Yes, but if you thought what you did, will the others think that, too, because of my skirt?"

Winnie stepped back. "Let me see. Turn for me."

Mary did a slow revolution. White fabric peeked out of the tear. "What am I going to do?"

"I can help." Winnie pulled up the hem of her dress. "See, I pinned my petticoat because it was too long. We can use the pins on your skirt."

"But then yours will drag below your hem."

"I don't care. The older women will think I'm sloppy, nothing more. But the tear in your garment will cause titters for sure and damage your reputation."

"Thank you, Winnie." Mary's heart softened. She was sorry for judging Winnie as selfish and uncaring for eating her aunt's cake.

"It's okay. You would do the same for me."

"Why didn't your uncle help us?" Mary tried to remember. Was he in the car when they were taken?

"He's not my uncle." Winnie hiccupped a sob. "He said he was a friend of my father's. He's awful, Mary. What he wants me to do. . . I can't, I just can't. I won't."

"You won't have to. Aunt Cora and I will find a way to save you."

"Can you find me a husband before we get to Pueblo?"

Wyatt. Would he marry Winnie? He did make a dandy rescuer. But could Mary stand by and watch him wed another? It would be an act of kindness a missionary would do. Maybe she wasn't strong enough to be one after all.

◆ ◆ ◆

Mary explained to her aunt what happened in such a way so no one overheard the conversation. Winnie sat across from them, hugging the window.

"There is no way, Miss Periwinkle, that you are going to sit with that man or go anywhere with him once we reach Pueblo." Cora's voice rose.

"Shh, Aunt!"

Cora lowered her voice. "You will travel with us and then return to St. Louis."

"He has my luggage tag. He said I wouldn't get it back if I tried to run off. I don't have money to replace my clothing."

"Never you mind. If he refuses to give it to me and Mr. Cross, then I'll provide you with a new wardrobe."

Wyatt? Had she decided he would be a good match for Winnie? Mary squirmed in her seat. "Father will help her, I'm sure."

Aunt Cora gave her a knowing look. "I am positive of that, but he won't be in Pueblo when we arrive. Mr. Cross has proved himself useful in certain situations. It won't hurt to ask him for assistance in this manner."

Mary sat back. She couldn't argue with her aunt because she was right. Wyatt was all that her aunt said and more.

"If you'll excuse me, I'm going to the women's lounge." Winnie scooted to the edge of the seat.

"Would you like me to come with you?" Mary wasn't sure her new friend should go anywhere alone.

"I'll be fine."

Winnie left the car, and Mary turned to her aunt. "Do you want her to marry Mr. Cross?"

"Would that bother you?"

"I don't know. No. Yes. Aunt Cora, I'm conflicted. I want to be missionary, but I find myself desiring Wyatt's company."

"Again, tell me, why do you insist on being a missionary?"

"To help."

"You can choose to help from anywhere. Missionaries need support from those of us who aren't living in Africa and India. Even today, offering to help Winnie is a mission act. What kind of things could you do if you married Wyatt and lived in Topeka?"

"He hasn't proposed, Aunt Cora. And then there is Father. He won't approve." She considered what her aunt said. She was right. Missionaries had come to her school to speak and raise money. Maybe she and Wyatt could visit one of the countries so they could speak with authorities and then raise money or even collect soap and send it back. That is, if he asked her to marry him.

◆　　◆　　◆

Wyatt tested the rope that tied Griff's wrist to the bunk in the caboose. Both men sobered and expressed regret, but that wasn't enough for Wyatt to let them go.

"Why did you choose them in the first place?" He stepped back. They wouldn't be going anywhere, especially since he and Johnson decided to take shifts watching them.

"The blonde's uncle said we could have them. He said she would be available in Pueblo, that he wanted to start his business early."

Wyatt clenched his hand into a tight fist, then forced it to relax. He couldn't bring himself to hit a tied-up man no matter how much he wanted to.

"Those are respectable women. You were misinformed."

"Tell them we're sorry. Griff and I were playing cards and drinking with the girl's uncle. When he lost, he offered them to us instead of money."

"That will be the last time he does that." Wyatt settled in with his notebook on a hard bench. "Tell me what you know about him."

Chapter Fifteen

Wyatt's neck hurt. He'd spent too much time guarding the prisoners. The swaying of the train beneath him coaxed and cajoled him to close his eyes. The engineer had received the all clear that morning, and the excursion to Pueblo resumed. There were many cheers of joy rumbling through the coaches.

He and Johnson decided to spend the last night of the trip watching the two men rather than split the time. The caboose had two unoccupied beds that were more comfortable than the seats in the cars, making it a cozy nook for him and Johnson to discuss the state of the world.

"Johnson, with the trains going to more places, there are going to be more towns springing up and newspapers needing reporters. Have you ever thought about moving west?"

"You suggesting something? Trying to oust the competition?"

"No, just thinking aloud. I'd like to try another city or town, but I plan to stay in Topeka." Was Mary still sleeping? He'd popped into her car to check on her and found her resting against the window. She had to be cold. He wanted to pick her up and move her closer to the stove. But he didn't have the right.

"Not me—I want to see the world. All the little towns with their crazy lawlessness will make for great stories. Might even send them to New York for the big papers." Johnson yawned. His voice lowered and slowed as the night wore on.

Wyatt slid off the bottom berth and gazed out the window. The sky sparkled with millions of stars. He wanted to show it to Mary.

He nudged Johnson's foot. "Wake up. I'm taking a little walk."

Johnson snorted. "Checking on your woman again?"

"Yes, I suppose I am."

◆　◆　◆

"Mary, are you awake?"

She jumped. Stopped a scream from escaping her lips when she realized it was Wyatt who touched her. "Is something wrong?" She sat up and rubbed her eyes. The train still moved, Aunt Cora gave a ladylike snore, and Winnie—well, she had a line of drool on her chin. Mary quickly wiped her own just in case.

"Will you come with me to the observation car?" Wyatt whispered.

She blinked, then stood, responding to his request before she processed the thought in her mind.

"I understand if you are afraid, but there are others there. We won't be alone." He held out his hand to help steady her as she stepped over Aunt Cora.

In silence, they made their way to the car. Wyatt spoke the truth. There were several people in the car, all staring out the windows.

Wyatt pulled her to an empty space. "Isn't it beautiful?"

Outside, the moon and stars shimmered on what appeared to be a large lake. The reflections of the dancing stars took her breath. "It's the most amazing sight. Thank you, Wyatt, for waking me. We should have woken Aunt Cora and Winnie, too."

"No. I mean, there's something I wanted to ask you without them being present." He pulled her close to him and whispered in her ear. "I know we haven't known each other long, but I feel in my heart that you are the woman God chose for me."

"Wyatt—"

"Shh." He traced her cheekbone. "I've fallen in love with you and want to marry you, spend the rest of my life with you. I want to take you to Yellowstone for our honeymoon. They've opened a hotel there. I think you'd like to see water fountains that shoot from the earth. So, would you be my wife?"

Her heart beat so hard she felt it would break through her chest. He loved her. Despite what almost happened with Griff and that she could shoot better than he could. He wanted to take her on adventures, not leave her at home. She considered what Aunt Cora had said about being a missionary wherever she lived.

"Mary?"

"I want to marry you, Wyatt. I have dreams of helping those in need. Would you be willing to let me do that?"

"What do you mean?"

"I want to be a missionary, but I don't have to travel. Though I'd like to, even though this trip was a bit more exciting than I expected. I want to raise money to help missionary families."

"I'll join you. We'll go to India, if you like."

He would, too. Warmth spread though her. "Yes, Wyatt, I'll marry you, if my father approves." She lowered her chin and canted her body until her forehead rested against his chest.

He didn't move.

She stayed there, feeling the rise and fall of his breath. "He won't, though, because you're a reporter."

She felt a gentle kiss on the top of her head. Had anyone seen? It didn't matter, because the star show was nothing like the fireworks bursting inside her.

"What if Father says you can't marry me?"

"Don't worry. He will approve, as will mine."

"How do you know?" Mary twisted her fingers together.

"Because my full name is William Wyatt Crossen. My father owns a large shipping company, and I'm his heir."

She stepped back. "I don't understand. You lied to me? And what will our last name be? What am I to call you?"

He scratched his head. "My father insisted I shorten our surname when I became a reporter to distance himself. I've always liked Wyatt better."

"You'll have to figure this out before you speak to my father."

A satisfied smile lit Wyatt's face. "So, you will marry me." He drew her close and kissed her.

Mary's knees knocked, weak as a newborn kitten's. She might have even purred.

◆   ◆   ◆

At the Pueblo station, weary-looking musicians played as the passengers disembarked from the train. There were signs and street vendors everywhere even though the train arrived late.

"Aunt Cora, this is amazing. What it must be like to be greeted like this at the end of every great adventure." Mary twisted from side to side to take in as much of the festivities as possible.

"If you have a family to return to, it is like this without the vendors and massive crowds. But it's even more special to be greeted by someone who loves you. Winnie, you're staying with us at the hotel. Mr. Cross is making sure your luggage is sent to our rooms."

"I don't know how to thank you and Mary for taking me in." Winnie stood taller and her smile appeared softer, not forced as it had been on the first part of their trip.

Mary hooked arms with Winnie. "Think of yourself as my sister."

"No, I think she'll be the cousin you didn't have." Aunt Cora beamed. "I didn't have a chance to have a child. I'm taking Winnie for my own. My brother has his child, and now I have mine."

Winnie turned to Mary. "Is that okay with you?"

"Yes, of course! Sister, cousin—at this point in our lives, either would be perfect. But you must promise to look after my father, too, after I marry Wyatt. If I marry him."

"But you must! He's such a gentleman, and he loves you. Everyone can see that."

"First, he has to decide who he is, and Father has to give his blessing." And that she wasn't so sure about. He didn't care for people who lied or for newspaper men.

Chapter Sixteen

Mary paced the floor of her upstairs bedroom back home in St. Louis. She missed the excitement of traveling with Aunt Cora. Now Winnie went with her. It didn't feel right that she was left behind. Even Wyatt had disappeared after he spoke to her father about marriage. Some things he had to do, he'd said. What would she do if he never returned?

She pulled the curtain aside and saw a carriage pull up. Wyatt stepped out. Her heart thudded. He came. She ran for the stairs, then stopped at the top. She couldn't very well greet him like her father's pet dog. She backed against the wall and waited an eternity for her father to call for her.

"Mo, please come down."

She wasted no time bouncing down the stairs, light as air. "Yes, Father?"

He tweaked her ear. "I know you were up there waiting. Wyatt is here to speak with you." He kissed her cheek. "You have my blessing, if he suits you."

Mary entered the parlor where Wyatt waited. "You came back."

"I said I would. I need to tell you something."

"Continue."

"I've spoken to my father about continuing to write. With my mother's influence, he decided I can write under my own name, if I write for missionary magazines."

Mary's heart quickened. God was going to answer her prayer.

He knelt and grasped her hands. "I love you. Would you be my wife and accompany me on my travels to gather stories for the magazines until such a time as we have a family?"

"Yes, and I will travel wherever you go."

◆　◆　◆

Mary Owen and William Crossen's wedding was the event of the season and the talk of the town. Her father spared no expense, but Mary let him only after he promised to do the same for Winnie when she married.

Mary wore a white satin gown from New York instead of Paris, because she refused to wait for a dress to be made and shipped. Organ notes signaled it was time to stroll down the aisle with her father.

"Mo, I pray for a love as strong and wonderful as what your mother and I had."

"Thank you, Father." Mary wiped a tear away. "I love William, but I will miss you."

"I know." He took her arm and led her to William.

Soon it was her turn to pledge her vow. "I, Mary, take thee, Wyatt-William—"

"My little outlaw, call me Wyatt or William. I will love you forever and always."

"And I you."

◆　◆　◆

The train rumbled against the tracks. Steam billowed white against the blue sky. Aunt Cora and Winnie accompanied Mary and Wyatt to see them off.

"I'll find George and get our luggage settled while you say your good-byes." Wyatt tipped his hat and left.

"Mary, take care and think before you do something adventurous." Aunt Cora hugged her tightly.

"I promise. Winnie, take care of Aunt Cora and Father." She hugged Winnie. "He mentioned having a dinner for you to meet a possible husband. Don't be afraid. He was right. Marriage is wonderful. Aunt Cora, he said the same about finding you a match."

"Hmpf." Cora shook her head. "Winnie, let's host a dinner for my brother."

Wyatt returned. "George has taken care of our belongings. Mrs. Crossen, are you ready to take our first adventure as a married couple?"

"I am. Bye, Aunt Cora and Winnie." The warmth of his hand on hers touched her heart. God had provided.

"Yellowstone, here we come. Bears, waterfalls, and geysers are the perfect way to start our life together." He squeezed her hand. "I love you, Outlaw."

"And I love you."

Christian author **Diana Lesire Brandmeyer** writes historical and contemporary romances about women choosing to challenge their fears to become the strong women God intends. Author of *A Mind of Her Own*, *A Bride's Dilemma in Friendship, Tennessee*, and *We're Not Blended We're Pureed: a Survivor's Guide to Blended Families*. Sign up for her newsletter and get free stuff at www.dianabrandmeyer.com.

The Depot Bride

by Amanda Cabot

Chapter One

Early March, 1886
Cheyenne, Wyoming Territory

She was late. Eugenia Bell frowned as the church bell rang eight times. Breakfast would be ready. Papa and Aunt Louisa would be seated at the table, waiting while she. . . *Just one more.* Eugenia's frown turned into a smile as she focused the camera. Last night's frost had coated the lilac bushes, encasing the slender branches in ice, turning the ordinary brown stems into something gloriously beautiful. *Just one more.*

"Eugenia! Are you out there?" Though Aunt Louisa would never shout, her voice carried clearly through the still morning air, a hint of annoyance coloring her normally sweet tone.

"Yes, ma'am." Eugenia rose and headed inside, knowing she could delay no longer. "I'll be ready in a minute." Quickly she doffed her coat, washed her hands, and followed her aunt into the breakfast room.

Though Papa had already seated himself, he rose to hold out Aunt Louisa's chair and waited until Norton, the butler who'd been with them since the house was built, placed plates of food in front of them before he bowed his head.

When Papa had given thanks for the meal, he took a sip of coffee and turned to Eugenia. "What was it this time?"

"Lilac bushes." Eugenia couldn't help smiling as she thought of the scene that had greeted her this morning. "Oh, Papa, they were the most beautiful thing I've ever seen. The way the sunshine was sparkling on the ice made it more brilliant than a crystal goblet. I've never seen anything so wonderful."

Though Aunt Louisa gave a small sniff to indicate her annoyance, the corners of Papa's mouth curved up in what appeared to be amusement. "It seems to me you said the same thing last week, only that time it was the sun setting behind the seamstress's shop."

Eugenia continued spreading marmalade on a piece of toast. "Madame Charlotte is not simply a seamstress, Papa. She designs the finest gowns in the city."

"And I have the bills to prove it." Papa directed his attention to Aunt Louisa, who had already eaten one of the two soft-boiled eggs that, along with a single piece of toast, constituted her normal breakfast. Marmalade, Aunt Louisa had once declared, was not good for the digestion. Neither Eugenia nor Papa agreed.

Papa slathered an extra-thick coating of marmalade on his toast as he smiled at Aunt Louisa. "The next time you and Eugenia are there, you should determine whether Madame Charlotte is able to make a suitable wedding dress."

"Wedding?" The bite of bacon that had tasted so delicious a moment ago threatened to lodge in Eugenia's throat. She knew Papa wanted her to marry—he'd told her countless times that her mother had been his wife for more than four years by the time she was

Eugenia's age—but this was the first time he'd spoken as if her wedding were imminent.

Papa nodded. "Chauncey and I spoke after last night's meeting. I gave him permission to court you."

"Chauncey Keaton?" The words came out as little more than a squeak.

Papa nodded again. "He's the only Chauncey I know. He's a fine man and one I'll be proud to call my son-in-law." Papa continued stirring sugar into his coffee as if this were an ordinary conversation. "Chauncey will make sure you're well cared for."

Eugenia did not doubt that, but she wanted more. She wanted love. Though Mama had been gone for more than ten years now, Eugenia could not forget their conversations. *"Love is the most wonderful thing in the world,"* Mama had said as she'd told Eugenia about the day she'd met Papa and how she'd known he was the man she wanted to marry from the first time she set eyes on him. *"He made my heart beat faster,"* she had said, *"and when he touched my hand, I thought I would swoon."*

Though Chauncey had never set Eugenia's heart to pounding and she had never come close to swooning over his presence, she could not argue with Papa. Chauncey was a fine man. Like Papa, he'd made his fortune in cattle. Men respected him for his business knowledge. Women considered Eugenia fortunate to have caught his interest. But that wasn't enough.

"I'm not ready to marry," she said firmly.

Papa looked up from his scrambled eggs and nodded. "I know that. That's why I told Chauncey the courtship will last at least six months. I want you to have the chance to see that he's the right man for you. You know I want you to be happy."

"Yes." Although Papa was rarely home, when he was, he was kind to Eugenia, asking about her days, bringing her small gifts, even noticing when she wore a new dress.

"I bought you that camera, didn't I?" When Eugenia nodded, he continued. "I'll admit that I didn't like the idea at first, but you proved me wrong. You're a fine photographer."

Though Eugenia wished Papa hadn't chosen the same adjective he'd used to describe Chauncey to also describe her skill with a camera, she was pleased by his praise. "Thank you, Papa. I enjoy taking pictures."

"I know that. Your photographs were what gave me the idea for a new project." He took a bite of the eggs, chewing them carefully before he spoke. "Everyone in Cheyenne is excited that we're getting a new depot."

"Finally." Aunt Louisa wrinkled her nose. "The old one is a disgrace. Why, the men won't even wait there. They use the hotel lobby instead."

"All of that will change with the new building. It will be the finest depot on the UP line and the finest building in Cheyenne." Papa's eyes glowed with enthusiasm, reminding Eugenia that, as a major stockholder in the Union Pacific Railroad, he had a vested interest in it. "I want to ensure no one forgets this event, so I've decided we need a book to commemorate it. I want to document every step with your photographs."

For a second, Eugenia could not speak. Not even in her dreams had she imagined anything like this. "Oh, Papa, that would be wonderful!" She hadn't thought he understood how important photography was to her, how much happiness it brought her, but it seemed he did.

"I need a special writer to tell the story," Papa said. "I've had my eye on a man from Denver. If everything works out the way I hope, he'll be in Cheyenne next week." Papa inclined his head as he addressed Eugenia. "Since you two will be working together, I've offered him a room here. I will expect you to make him feel welcome."

"Of course." As she pictured a man of her father's age, Eugenia tried not to frown. No matter how boring the writer might be, working with him would be a small price to pay for the joy of seeing her photographs in a book. And maybe, just maybe, she would find a way to convince Papa that Chauncey was not the man for her.

◆ ◆ ◆

Mason Farling was bored. Straightening his shoulders, he tried not to yawn. When Mr. Hudson had hired him as a reporter for Denver's premier newspaper, he'd thought he would be writing articles of substance, covering important news. Instead, he'd found himself assigned to nothing more than church socials and parades. Today was the worst. He'd been here for two hours listening to women debate the merit of a bake sale over a rummage sale. Mason feared the seasons would change before they made a decision. Either that or they'd insist he drink another glass of the sickeningly sweet punch that had made his teeth ache.

Desperate, he spoke for the first time since the debate had begun. "Ladies, I know I'm here only to report your decision, but if I might make a suggestion, I wondered if you'd considered combining both ideas? It seems to me that people might become hungry as they shopped and would visit the baked goods tables. And those who came for a cake or pie might be enticed by the other items." When no one spoke, perhaps because they were shocked to hear his voice, Mason added, "I think offering both food and general merchandise would increase attendance."

The response was immediate. Everyone began talking at once, and though it took what seemed like an interminable amount of time, the result was that they agreed with him and adjourned the meeting.

Taking a deep breath as he emerged from the overly warm building, Mason shook his head as he wondered how much more of this he could tolerate. The problem was the alternative was worse. No matter how much he hated feeling as if he were wasting his time with meetings like today's, he did not want to return to the farm and listen to his stepmother crow that she'd been right and that Mason would never be a writer.

As he approached the newspaper office, Mason said a silent prayer. *Lord, You know what is in my heart. Guide me along Your path.*

"There's a letter for you, Mr. Farling."

Mason stopped, startled by the mail clerk's greeting. This was the first time he'd received a letter at the office. The few times his family wrote, they sent the mail to his boardinghouse. Curious, he opened the envelope as soon as he reached his desk. As he scanned the contents and the author's signature, Mason's astonishment grew. *Is this Your answer, Lord?*

He read the letter again, making certain he had not missed anything. "I was impressed with your article about the ladies' quilting society," the author had written. "You turned an ordinary event into something that appealed to many readers."

Mason remembered that meeting and how he had struggled to present the ladies' quilts for the homeless project in such a way that others in the community would contribute fabric and thread. Not once had he considered that anyone outside of Denver would read the article, much less form an opinion about him based on it.

"I have a new project," the letter continued. "I want to produce a book to commemorate the construction of the UP depot here in Cheyenne. I have already engaged a photographer and hope you'll consider being the writer to tell the story that accompanies those photos. It would involve living in Cheyenne for the next eighteen months. I am willing to offer you a salary of. . ."

Mason swallowed loudly. He hadn't imagined it. This man was offering him more than twice what he would earn in Denver during that time. "In addition, I will provide room and board at my home." Mason had no doubt that the accommodations would be far more luxurious than his boardinghouse. Erastus Bell, the man who'd sent this incredible letter, was one of Cheyenne's millionaire cattle barons. He was offering Mason an opportunity that came only once in a lifetime.

And that wasn't all. "I appreciate that accepting my offer means leaving your current position with no guarantee that it will be available once my project is completed. I've taken the liberty of speaking to Cyrus Taggert." Mason recognized the name of the owner of one of Cheyenne's newspapers. "He has agreed to offer you a position if you choose to remain in Cheyenne once the depot is built."

Mason closed his eyes and gave thanks. Erastus Bell's letter was truly the answer to prayer. The only thing that could possibly go wrong would be that the photographer was as difficult to work with as the crusty old man who'd accompanied Mason on some of his assignments. But, Lord willing, that would not be the case.

Chapter Two

"Yrou look particularly lovely this evening," Chauncey Keaton said as he handed his coat to the butler and turned toward Eugenia.

Though Norton normally escorted guests into the parlor, when she'd heard the knock on the door Eugenia had decided to meet Chauncey in the hallway. She couldn't help wondering whether the compliment was sincere. Her gown was one he'd seen before; her hairstyle was the same as always. If she looked different tonight, it must be because of her excitement. The depot project was all she'd thought about today.

"Thank you," she said with what she hoped looked like a genuine smile. Though she hadn't worn anything special today, Chauncey had obviously taken extra pains with his appearance. His hair was freshly cut, and his shirt appeared new. The contrast of his dark hair and eyes against the sparkling white shirt was dramatic, leaving no doubt why many of the young women in Cheyenne were attracted to him.

As Norton returned to the servants' portion of the house, Chauncey pulled a small package from his pocket and handed it to Eugenia. "I hope you'll enjoy this."

New clothes, a haircut, a gift. There was no doubt about it. Chauncey was a man who'd come courting. Eugenia kept the smile firmly fixed on her face. "Thank you," she said for the second time as she undid the wrappings, revealing a beautifully shaped bottle of perfume. If there was one thing Eugenia loved, it was fragrance, so she opened the bottle and sniffed.

Achoo! Achoo! No matter how she tried, she could not control her sneezes. She recapped the bottle and set it on the console table.

"Is something wrong?" Chauncey asked. "The clerk at the emporium told me this was the finest perfume they carry."

Eugenia nodded. The cut glass bottle alone made the perfume a luxury. "I'm certain it is. The problem is there's jasmine in it. I'm sorry, Chauncey. You had no way of knowing I'm allergic to jasmine."

The man's crestfallen expression tugged at her heartstrings. Though she did not love him, Eugenia didn't want him to be hurt. "It's the thought that matters," she told him, "and yours was a good one. Thank you." It seemed as if all she did today was say thank you.

"Papa will be home soon. In the meantime, let's join Aunt Louisa in the parlor."

After Chauncey greeted her aunt, he took the seat next to Eugenia. "How did you spend your day?" he asked.

This was a neutral subject, better than the fact that she was allergic to his gift. Eugenia gave Chauncey the warmest smile she could muster. "I took some photographs this morning." She rose and retrieved the print she'd brought out to show to Papa. "This is my favorite."

Chauncey studied the photograph for a moment, furrows forming between his eyes. "What is it?"

"A lilac bush. I thought the way the ice coated it was beautiful."

Chauncey appeared to be perplexed. "All I see are a few branches. Where's the rest of the bush?"

Eugenia closed her eyes for a second, reminding herself of her resolve to honor her father by being polite to Chauncey. Perhaps it was too much to expect him to appreciate her photograph. "I have others with the whole bush," she told him, "but they weren't as dramatic as this one." And they hadn't touched her heart the way this one had.

Though Chauncey nodded, Eugenia could tell that he was merely humoring her. Fortunately, Aunt Louisa joined the conversation. "Did Erastus tell you about his new project?" When Chauncey shook his head, she continued. "He's going to produce a commemorative book about the depot. Eugenia will be the photographer."

It happened so quickly that Eugenia wondered if she'd been mistaken in thinking that Chauncey was displeased, but it seemed as if his lips curled in what looked almost like a sneer before he flattened them. "It's good that you have a hobby," he said, his patronizing tone making her cringe. "That will keep you occupied until we're married. Afterward, you'll be too busy to bother with things like that. Taking pictures is hardly a suitable activity for my wife."

But she wasn't his wife yet.

◆　◆　◆

It wasn't difficult to understand why the city fathers wanted a new depot, Mason realized as he stepped off the train. This one was shabby and ordinary in the extreme, nothing more than a rectangular box of a building. A city that was reputed to have more millionaires per capita than any other in the United States deserved something with more. . . He paused, trying to find the correct word, finally settling on *substance*.

A man wearing a dark coat and one of the flat-brimmed hats that Mason associated with drivers approached him. "Are you Mr. Farling?" the man asked.

"Indeed, I am."

"Mr. Bell asked me to take you to his home." He reached for the two bags that contained Mason's belongings. "Let me get those."

To Mason's surprise, the man led him to a simple wagon rather than a fancy carriage. Though Erastus Bell was a wealthy man, it appeared he was also a practical one. The wagon was probably used on his ranch, perhaps hauling feed to the cattle that were the source of his fortune.

His house, Mason discovered as the wagon pulled to a stop on Ferguson Street a few minutes later, was not simple and, in all likelihood, not practical. The imposing two-story building with the wide porch spanning the front and two sides was much larger than a widower, his spinster sister, and his daughter needed, and the intricately carved railing and columns on the porch combined with the tall leaded glass windows told Mason no expense had been spared.

When he knocked on the front door, Mason was greeted by a butler whose livery matched the driver's.

"Right this way, sir. Miss Bell and her aunt are in the parlor." To Mason's surprise, though the driver had sounded as American as he, the butler's accent was British, confirming Mason's belief that appearances were important to Erastus Bell.

As the man who'd introduced himself as Norton slid open the pocket door, Mason took a deep breath. A second later that breath whooshed out, and his heart began to pound. He formed a vague impression of dark furniture arranged on a Persian rug with lighting provided by a crystal chandelier and wall sconces. Those were expected. What was not was the presence of the most beautiful woman Mason had ever seen. Standing perhaps half a foot shorter than his own six feet, she possessed perfect bone structure, curves in all the right places, vibrant auburn hair, and green eyes—eyes that had widened with surprise.

"Mr. Mason Farling to see you, ladies," the butler announced in a predictably solemn tone.

The woman who'd stolen his breath rose and extended her hand. "Welcome to Cheyenne, Mr. Farling." Her voice was even, making Mason wonder if he'd imagined the surprise in her expression. "I'm Eugenia Bell, and this is my aunt, Miss Louisa Bell."

"It's a pleasure to meet you both." Somehow he managed to make the expected reply as he took the seat she'd indicated. Mason couldn't understand it. Never before had he been tongue-tied, but from the moment he'd set foot inside the Bells' parlor, he'd found himself struggling to form a coherent sentence. All he could do was stare at the beautiful woman whose home he would be sharing for the next year and a half.

Declining her offer of tea or coffee for fear that he'd be unable to swallow even a sip, Mason looked around. There had to be something he could say. When his glance fell on a photograph resting on the end table, he found himself almost as entranced by it as by the lovely woman who sat only a few feet away from him. The photograph was unlike any he'd ever seen, a picture of some kind of bush, its branches encased in ice. Instead of including the entire bush, the photographer had focused on only a few branches, showcasing the beauty God instilled in every detail of His creation.

"That's a very unusual photograph," he said, pleased beyond all measure that he'd managed to construct a simple sentence.

Though Mason saw nothing amusing in his comment, the older woman chuckled.

"Do you like it?" Eugenia Bell asked.

Her aunt made a little tsking sound. "Now, Eugenia, you know it's rude to ask a question like that."

Mason shook his head, regretting that something he'd said had subjected Miss Bell to even mild censure. "I don't mind answering. I'm intrigued by the picture. In fact, I wish I could meet the photographer. I'd like to ask him why he chose those particular branches and how he captured the sun sparkling on the ice so perfectly."

This time there was no doubt about it. The aunt was laughing, although she was obviously trying to hide it. She pinched her lips together, then nodded briskly. "You've already met the photographer, Mr. Farling. It's my niece."

Mason blinked in astonishment. "You?"

Chapter Three

Under other circumstances, Eugenia might have laughed at Mason Farling's shock. His reaction to Aunt Louisa's statement made it clear he was like most men and did not believe a woman could be a photographer. Papa had felt that way initially, and Chauncey still did.

Eugenia knew she shouldn't have been surprised, and yet she was. For a moment when Mason had looked at the picture, she had thought he admired it. More than that, she had thought he understood why that scene had touched her so deeply. That had led her to believe they would work well together, but then he'd stared at her as if she were a creature from another planet.

"What's the matter, Mr. Farling? Do you think that just because we wear skirts women are incapable of handling a camera?" Eugenia kept her tone mild in deference to Aunt Louisa and the fact that Eugenia would have to spend a great deal of time with this man. She needed to be civil, even if his attitude infuriated her.

For the second time in less than a minute, he appeared surprised. "That's not at all what I thought, Miss Bell. I will admit I was shocked that you were the person who'd taken that extraordinary photograph, but it was not your gender that surprised me. It was your age."

His blue eyes were serious as he continued. "I've had the opportunity to work with several photographers and have seen many others' pictures, but never before have I met anyone your age with such skill. Normally it takes years—even decades—to develop such talent."

While Eugenia blushed at the unexpected compliments that warmed her heart more than she'd thought possible, Aunt Louisa clapped softly. "Well said, young man. If you feel that way, you'll probably be pleased to learn that my niece is the photographer Erastus chose for the depot book."

"That's the best news I've heard in days." Mason's lips curved into a smile as he fixed his gaze on Eugenia. "Your father made me an exceptionally generous offer to write the stories, but I never dreamt that my words would be paired with such beautiful pictures. This will be a book no one will forget." His smile widened, and he took a step toward Eugenia. "I look forward to being your partner."

When Mason extended his hand for the traditional shake that men who were partners would exchange, Eugenia placed her hand in his. The handshake was not what she had expected. Not at all. But then again, Mason Farling was not what she had expected. Instead of the boring, middle-aged man she had thought Papa had hired, Mason was one of the most handsome men she'd ever met, with hair as golden as the prairie grass in autumn, eyes as blue as the summer sky, features as finely formed as the sculptures she had seen in the museums she and Aunt Louisa had visited in New York and Philadelphia while Papa had been occupied with business.

But physical beauty was not the only thing that made Mason memorable. His touch was one Eugenia knew she would never forget. When their fingers and palms met, tingles raced along her arm, and her heart began to pound as if she had run up three flights of stairs. Never before had she felt like this, but never before had she met a man like Mason Farling.

◆　◆　◆

Mason looked around as he entered the dining room. It was what he would have expected from a house this size. The table was large enough to seat two dozen, the china so delicate he was afraid his meat knife might break it, the water goblets fashioned of wafer-thin crystal. This was a far cry from the farmhouse where he had grown up or the boarding-house where he'd eaten most of his meals for the four years he'd been in Denver.

Erastus Bell led the way toward the table and took his place at its head. Though Mason had thought either Eugenia or her aunt would have been positioned at the other end of the table, they were standing behind the chairs closest to Erastus.

"I've put you next to my sister," Erastus told Mason. "Chauncey, you have your usual place at Eugenia's side." The moment he'd arrived and introduced himself to Mason, Mr. Bell had insisted that everyone be on a first-name basis.

After he'd seated Eugenia's aunt, Mason pulled out his own chair. One good thing about this arrangement was that he would be able to watch Eugenia. Although, the truth was he wanted to do more than watch her. He wanted to touch her again, to see whether his memory of the way his heart had raced when he'd felt her palm against his was accurate. He hadn't expected that any more than he'd expected her to be so young, so beautiful, so appealing. And he certainly hadn't expected that she would be the photographer whose pictures would accompany his stories. That was the proverbial icing on the cake of an already intriguing assignment.

Mason glanced at the man seated across from him. He couldn't say that he was impressed with Chauncey Keaton, though he'd felt an instant affinity with Erastus. Eugenia's father was a large-boned man whose leathery skin, the product of years spent outdoors, seemed at odds with his finely cut suit. And yet Mason realized that Erastus's appearance was probably typical of many cattle barons. While some merely invested their money, others were active participants in everything from branding to roundups. Chauncey Keaton, on the other hand, had the pale skin and perfectly shaped fingernails of a man with little acquaintance with manual labor, even though he also raised cattle.

"I'm sorry I wasn't here to greet you when you arrived," Erastus said to Mason after he'd blessed their food. "Unfortunately, I got tied up with several major UP supporters."

Mason shook his head. "It wasn't a problem. Your daughter and Miss Bell—sorry, Miss Louisa—" Despite Erastus's decree, Mason could not address a woman her age without some sort of title. "The two ladies made me feel welcome. I also had an opportunity to see some of Eugenia's photographs. You must be very proud of her."

As he dipped his spoon into the thick soup the butler had placed before him, Erastus nodded. "I am, indeed. I believe that together you and she will create a book that will impress everyone involved with the Union Pacific."

"You always have good ideas, Erastus."

Though Mason could not imagine why, Eugenia appeared surprised by Chauncey's compliment.

Erastus nodded at Chauncey. "It's kind of you to say so, my boy." He directed his attention back to Mason. "I know I told you I wanted you to document the depot's construction, but today's meeting made me think we should expand the scope and feature the railroad's primary supporters here in Cheyenne as well. What do you think?"

"I like the idea. It sends the message that the depot is more than a building. It's part of the community. You might want to incorporate that concept into the title."

Eugenia laid down her soupspoon as she asked, "Do you have a title in mind, Papa?"

He replied without hesitation. "*The Magic City Depot.*"

"That's a great title." Chauncey's words were infused with enthusiasm, making Mason wonder if he ever disagreed with Eugenia's father.

"What do you think of that title, Mason?" Eugenia asked.

Mason was glad he'd taken a bite of bread, because it gave him a chance to collect his thoughts. He didn't want to offend his patron, but he also would not lie. "This is my first experience with a book," he reminded Erastus. "I'm not sure how or when authors choose their titles. I suspect it might be similar to creating a headline for an article."

When Erastus nodded, as if he were truly interested in Mason's opinion, Mason continued. "I usually wait until I've finished writing the article to compose the headline. Even though I know all the facts before I start writing, sometimes my slant changes."

Eugenia gave him what appeared to be a grateful look. "That makes sense, doesn't it, Papa, especially since we don't yet know everything that will be included in the story?"

Her father chuckled. "All right, my dear. I can see you didn't like my idea."

"I never said that, did I, Mason?" Eugenia accompanied her question with a wink.

As solemnly as he could, Mason said, "I don't believe you did."

Erastus's chuckle turned into a full-fledged laugh. "It looks to me like I made the right choice. I can tell you two are going to work well together."

The conversation became casual for the rest of the meal, with Chauncey telling an amusing story about how he had met the Bells' neighbor and fellow cattle baron Barrett Landry at the emporium and how Barrett had found choosing the perfect gift for a lady just as difficult as Chauncey had. When he'd concluded the story, the way Chauncey looked at Eugenia left no doubt that she was the recipient of the gift. The man was staking his claim and wanted Mason to know it.

After dinner, as Erastus led the way to the smoking room, saying Eugenia and his sister would join them in the parlor in half an hour, Chauncey slowed his pace and turned toward Mason.

"I don't know how much Erastus has told you about Eugenia."

Though he suspected he knew where this conversation was headed, Mason decided to play along. "He said nothing other than that she's his daughter. It was Miss Louisa who told me Eugenia would be the photographer on the project."

"She's a lovely woman."

That was an understatement. Eugenia was more than lovely. She was spectacularly beautiful. Mason nodded and said only, "Yes, she is."

Chauncey straightened his shoulders as if to increase his height. "I don't want you to get any wrong ideas about her. Erastus has agreed that she will be my bride."

Mason parsed the other man's words, noticing that he hadn't said Eugenia had agreed. From her father's view, the match made sense. Erastus would have the comfort of knowing that his ranch would eventually be transferred to another cattleman. That was logical, but it felt wrong to Mason. Marriage wasn't a business merger. It involved—or it should—love and attraction. The problem was he hadn't seen any sparks between Eugenia and Chauncey. When Chauncey looked at her, his expression was that of a man admiring an expensive possession. As for Eugenia—Mason could be mistaken, but it had seemed as if she avoided looking at Chauncey.

That was not what Mason would have expected from a betrothed couple, and yet what did he know? It was not as if he had any experience with love, not as if he had anything to offer Eugenia.

Mason forced his lips into a tight smile. "It seems congratulations are in order. Congratulations, Chauncey." Now, if only he meant it.

Chapter Four

"Using two different colors of sandstone will make the depot unique," Eugenia said as she wrapped her cloak tighter around her shoulders. It was earlier in the morning than she was usually outdoors, and though the calendar claimed that spring was less than a week away, winter's chill still reigned in Cheyenne. Forgoing breakfast, she and Mason had achieved their goal of reaching the site of the new depot before any of the workers arrived to begin the excavation.

"The UP was wise to include red as well as buff sandstone for their building," Mason said, gesturing toward the piles of stone that had been delivered over the past few weeks. "The depot will be very different from the capitol." Located nine blocks north on Hill Street, the territory's capitol building would be an impressive edifice featuring both a different style and color from the depot.

Eugenia shivered, wishing she'd taken Aunt Louisa's advice to wear her warmest boots. "Papa won't admit it to his railroad friends, but he doesn't really like the Richardsonian Romanesque style the UP chose. He would have preferred more angles and fewer rounded arches. I think he's wrong, though. The arches appeal to me."

After slipping her gloves into her reticule, Eugenia focused the camera and took a photograph of the stacks of sandstone waiting to be transformed into what Papa claimed would be the finest building in the territory.

"I agree. It'll be impressive when it's completed, almost as impressive as your camera." Mason watched as she rotated the plate holder at the back of the camera. "I've never seen one where the back moved."

Eugenia couldn't help smiling at the expensive piece of equipment. "It's called a Flammang's Revolving Back Patent Camera," she told him. "Papa bought it for me once he realized I was serious about photography. I think he liked the impressive name. What I liked was that being able to rotate the plate holder instead of the whole camera makes it much easier to photograph both portraits and landscapes."

"So this isn't your first camera?"

Eugenia shook her head. "I knew Papa wouldn't approve of my taking pictures, but I was intrigued when I saw a Walker Pocket advertised in a magazine, so I sent away for it. It was far simpler than this one—no mahogany or brass on it." And the seventeen dollar price tag that included the processing equipment as well as the camera itself was a far cry from the hundreds of dollars Papa had spent on the Flammang.

"Your father just wanted you to have the best."

"Yes." Giving Eugenia the best had always been Papa's goal, and according to him, where husbands were concerned, Chauncey was the best. She clenched her teeth and refused to think about Chauncey.

"Here come the workers." Eugenia watched as close to a dozen men arrived and picked up shovels, ready to begin work. There was no fanfare, no special ceremony, simply a small crew of men digging into the ground. While she focused the camera and took several pictures, Mason wandered around the site, striking up conversations with two of the men, somehow managing to not disturb their work while he spoke.

He looked up and caught Eugenia's eye, beckoning her to come to him. "Would you take a photo of Mr. Hobbs?" he asked. "He's a day laborer who's joined the railroad section hands to work here."

Eugenia was struck by two things: the fact that Mason introduced the man as "Mr. Hobbs" rather than simply "Hobbs," as her father would have, and that he wanted a photograph of him. Smiling at the man who was perhaps ten years her senior, she adjusted the camera and took his picture. Half an hour later, when she'd taken a photo of a second man and several of the ever-growing hole in the ground that would one day contain the foundation, she and Mason left the site.

"You took a lot of notes," she said as they made their way back to Ferguson Street.

"Each man had a different story to tell. Take Mr. Hobbs, for example. He has six children and hasn't been able to get steady work because of the weather, so to him this job is a godsend. Mr. Tarkington is a UP employee. He's used to hard work but says this will be harder than anything he's done. He expects higher wages than he's normally paid."

Eugenia knew she shouldn't be surprised at all the information Mason had managed to extract from the workers. Not only was he a skilled interviewer, but his friendly manner disarmed people. "Did the railroad agree?"

Mason shrugged. "That's the problem. It seems no one actually talked about payment. They just hired the men." He paused for a moment then added, "I'm glad you were here to photograph them. I want to include at least one of their stories."

"The workers?" Eugenia didn't try to hide her surprise.

"Why not? They may not be wealthy like the stockholders your father wants me to interview, but without them, there would be no depot."

"You're right." Eugenia revised her opinion of Mason. He wasn't simply a talented writer; he was also a compassionate man.

◆　◆　◆

"A strike!" Chauncey's face was as red as an apple's skin. "How dare those men go on strike? If this continues, the depot will never be finished."

Mason made a show of cutting a piece of his pot roast as he debated whether to say anything. Work had started on March 15, but only three days later all eleven men had gone on strike over pay, obviously irritating Chauncey. Deciding to cut the man's tirade short, Mason said as calmly as he could, "It seems to me the problem could have been avoided if the railroad had discussed wages at the time of hiring."

Erastus laid down his fork and glared at Mason. "Everyone knows that section hands are paid a dollar fifty a day."

"But this isn't the same work section hands normally perform," Eugenia said, her voice as even as Mason's had been. "They might be justified in believing they should be paid more." Though surprised, Mason couldn't help but be pleased that Eugenia agreed with him.

Chauncey made no effort to hide his outrage. "Two dollars a day? That's ridiculous."

The only thing that was ridiculous was Chauncey's attitude. He was acting as if the money came from his pockets. "It's not ridiculous if you have six children to feed and clothe," Mason said, his voice rising despite his best intentions.

Eugenia turned toward her father. "What do you think will happen, Papa?"

"The UP won't back down. They're already looking for a contractor to manage everything. Probably John Coots out of Kansas City. He's in charge of the headquarters building in Omaha. Coots brings his own crew so he doesn't have to hire many locals." Erastus continued buttering a piece of bread as calmly as if men's livelihoods weren't at stake. "You can be sure he won't hire any of the strikers."

Eugenia paled. "How will those men and their families live?"

"They should have thought of that before they struck." Chauncey's voice rang with satisfaction, as if the thought of families starving were of no account.

Taking a deep breath and reminding himself that nothing would be gained by saying anything more tonight, Mason made a mental note to pay a visit to Ned Hobbs. There must be something he could do to help.

◆ ◆ ◆

Eugenia stared at her reflection in the mirror as she secured her hat. It had been more than two weeks since the workers had gone on strike. As Chauncey had predicted, work had stopped, leaving her and Mason nothing to document. Instead they'd wandered through the city together, ostensibly to give Mason a better idea of the town where the depot would reside. In reality, Eugenia suspected he was looking for ways to help Mr. Hobbs and the others. She doubted that Papa, such a staunch supporter of the UP that he would tolerate no negative comments about it, would approve, so she told him nothing of her suppositions. But she couldn't help being pleased when Mason mentioned that Mr. Hobbs was now delivering lumber.

Drawing on her gloves, Eugenia headed downstairs. It was time for Chauncey to arrive.

"You're looking particularly lovely today," he said as he entered the house.

Eugenia forced a smile. It was mean spirited of her to notice that he said the same thing every time he saw her. Chauncey couldn't help it that he wasn't a man of words like Mason.

"Thank you, Chauncey. I'm looking forward to our afternoon together." While it wasn't exactly true, feigning enthusiasm was the least she could do. After all, she had promised herself that she would give him a fair chance to prove he could be the right husband for her. "I always enjoy tea at the Mitchell-Hathaway bakery." That was no lie.

As he held her coat for her, Chauncey said, "I brought my carriage, but I wondered if you'd prefer to walk. The sun is warm for early April."

"That would be pleasant." Eugenia tucked her hand into the crook of his elbow, and they set off. As Chauncey had said, it was a lovely early spring day. While it was too soon for Eugenia's lilac buds to open, the weather was warm and sunny.

"I'm glad you agreed. This will give us extra time together before I leave."

"You're leaving?" Eugenia felt ashamed of the way her heart soared at the prospect. "Where are you going?"

Chauncey preened like one of the sage grouse Eugenia had seen on the prairie. "Your father has been approached by several meat packers in the East and asked me to negotiate the contracts."

"That will be good experience for you."

"I'm looking forward to it, but I'll miss you. I'll be gone close to a month." Chauncey frowned. "That's one of the reasons I wanted this time with you."

A month! Knowing it was wrong to feel so relieved that she would not see Chauncey for so long, Eugenia made an extra effort to be polite. She and Chauncey spoke of ordinary things until they reached the bakery. When they entered, Eugenia sniffed appreciatively and smiled as the proprietor approached her. "Oh, Esther, something smells delicious."

Eugenia looked around the front room of the bakery. As was typical for this time of day, Esther's husband, Jeremy, stood in the far corner, a brush and palette in his hands as he painted a portrait.

"The dried apple pie is just out of the oven. I also have gingerbread and a nutmeg oat cake." Esther showed Eugenia and Chauncey to a table. "Which would you prefer?"

"You may have whatever you want, my dear." Chauncey reached across the table and patted Eugenia's hand. "Have all three if you like."

"I couldn't eat that much, but they all sound and smell wonderful."

Esther tipped her head to one side, considering. "Why don't I cut small pieces of each?"

"Perfect." When the proprietor left to prepare their plates, Eugenia smiled at Chauncey. "Esther's kindness is one of the reasons I enjoy coming here. She makes every visit feel special."

"She's a good baker—I'll grant you that—and a fine-looking woman for someone her age. What I don't understand is why she married a cripple." Chauncey pointed toward Jeremy. "Surely she could find someone better."

Eugenia couldn't hide her shock. It was true that Jeremy walked with a limp, the result of having lost a foot during the war, but that was no reason to condemn him. "Jeremy's a fine man and a talented artist," she said, her voice rising with anger. "Papa agreed that he would commission one of Jeremy's Christmas star portraits for my first Christmas as a bride."

The special Christmas ornament that had brought Esther and Jeremy together had become famous in Cheyenne, with a number of women wanting to adopt Esther's family tradition of having the bride and groom's portrait encased in a star-shaped frame. From the day Esther had shown Eugenia her star, Eugenia had dreamt of her own.

"We'll find someone else to paint ours," Chauncey told her. "I don't want to pose for a cripple. It would make me uncomfortable."

What made Eugenia uncomfortable was realizing that Jeremy had overheard the conversation. She bit her lip to keep from criticizing Chauncey, but try though she might, when she imagined her Christmas star ornament, she could not picture Chauncey's face next to hers.

Chapter Five

W e're finally making progress."

Eugenia laughed at Mason's obvious enthusiasm. "If you can call taking a building apart progress." The existing depot building housed an express office on the east side, a ticket office and women's waiting room on the west. Today the western half was being moved a few hundred yards and placed on the opposite end of the neighboring hotel to make room for the new depot. "It's not very exciting to photograph."

"Are you still thinking about what people will say a hundred years from now?" The twinkle in his eye told Eugenia that Mason found her preoccupation with the future amusing.

"You know I am."

When she'd been sorting through the contents of two old trunks in the attic, Eugenia had found a household management book that must have belonged to one of her ancestors. In addition to a few recipes, it included hints on how to make candles dripless, reminders to bring in pails of water when a freeze was expected, and suggestions on how to sweeten the smell of the privy. What would the author think if she could have seen Eugenia's home with its electric lights and indoor plumbing? And if that much had changed since the eighteenth century, what wonders would the twentieth bring?

"I hope someone finds our book in 1986 and sees what life was like here."

"I'd like that, too, but I don't imagine your father would be pleased to hear you call it *our* book."

Eugenia chuckled and shrugged her shoulders. "Then I won't tell him." Just as she hadn't told him how laughter had become an important part of her life since Chauncey had left Cheyenne or how her heart raced each time she was with Mason. She most definitely had not told Papa that she'd begun to dream of a future where Mason was more than simply the man writing stories to accompany her photos.

The smile Mason gave her made Eugenia wonder if he'd read her thoughts. Surely he hadn't! But when he spoke, his question was innocuous. "Are you taking your camera to the party tonight?"

Last Sunday had been Easter, and to celebrate the end of Lent's solemnity, Papa and the other cattle barons had decided to host a party at the Cheyenne Club tonight. Eugenia was expected to attend such events, and since Papa wanted Mason to learn more about his colleagues, he'd received an invitation.

"I wanted to, but Papa says that would not be seemly. His friends don't all approve of my involvement in the book, so tonight I'm supposed to be nothing more than Erastus Bell's daughter."

"And the most beautiful woman at the dance."

As a blush stained her face, Eugenia ducked her head. Never before had Mason said anything like that. Oh, he'd been friendly, and she'd seen admiration in his eyes when he'd looked at her photographs, but this was the first time he'd paid her a personal compliment. It felt good, so very good, to realize that unlike Chauncey's flattery, Mason's words were sincere. Eugenia's skin tingled with pleasure, and warmth spread through her veins at the thought that Mason regarded her as a woman, not simply his partner.

The pleasure she'd felt over Mason's compliment lingered all day, and she took special pains with her toilette as she prepared for the party. Even Aunt Louisa, who considered events like tonight's dinner and dance a waste of money, told her she looked exceptionally pretty. Now, as she descended the stairs, Eugenia saw Papa and Mason standing at the foot, looking up at her.

"I told you Eugenia would be the belle of the ball," Papa said, his face wreathed in a proud smile. "Mark my words, Mason. You'll have to fight the other young bucks to get a dance with her."

Eugenia caught her breath at the prospect of being held in Mason's arms. She hadn't been certain Papa would approve. In the past he'd insisted Eugenia dance only with men he considered potential suitors. Perhaps he was being more lenient now that he'd given Chauncey permission to court her. Whatever the reason, Eugenia would not squander the opportunity.

She extended the heavy cardboard booklet that Aunt Louisa had pinned to her gown. "My dance card is empty, Mr. Farling."

If Mason was amused by her formality, he gave no sign but withdrew a pencil from his breast pocket. "May I have the pleasure of the first waltz, Miss Bell?"

It was indeed a pleasure, Eugenia reflected an hour later. She had waltzed dozens, perhaps hundreds, of times before, but never had it felt like this. The touch of Mason's hand on hers, the warmth of his palm on her waist, the sparkle in his eyes as he gazed at her all combined to make it a dance she knew she would never forget.

Though it was their first time waltzing together, she and Mason moved like longtime partners, their steps perfectly matched. With no need to concentrate on the patterns of the dance, Eugenia was free to revel in the pleasure of being in Mason's arms. If only the dance could last forever.

◆　◆　◆

"Is something wrong, my friend?" Jeremy Snyder motioned Mason toward the table in the farthest corner of the bakery, the spot where they'd spent many an hour talking about everything from Jeremy's paintings to Mason's articles. Though Mason had never been here with Eugenia, when she'd said it was one of her favorite places, he'd decided to explore the Mitchell-Hathaway Bakery. As Eugenia had promised, Esther's baked goods were exceptional, but what brought Mason back was his growing friendship with her husband. Jeremy had become the older brother Mason had always wanted.

Right now that older brother substitute saw too much.

"I didn't know it was that obvious," Mason said as he accepted the mug of coffee Esther placed in front of him.

"Maybe not to others, but part of being an artist is assessing people's moods. You look troubled."

That was one way of describing it. "I'm afraid I've done something foolish."

"You never struck me as a foolish man." Jeremy shook his head slowly.

If only that were true. "What else would you call having inappropriate feelings for a woman?"

For a moment, Mason thought Jeremy was so shocked that he could not respond, but it appeared he was merely collecting his thoughts. "Do you love this woman?"

That was the question. "I'm not sure. I think of her all the time, and I'd do anything in my power to make her happy."

Jeremy nodded slowly. "That sounds like love to me. So, what's the problem?"

"Her father would never approve. He hired me to do a job, not court his daughter."

"So, we're speaking of Miss Bell."

Mason nodded, his heart skipping a beat at the thought of the woman who'd captured his imagination the first time he'd seen her. "She's the most wonderful woman I've ever met, but I have nothing to offer her. Besides, Chauncey Keaton claims they're practically betrothed. How can I compete with a man like that? He's rich and well connected."

"And you're an honest, hardworking man who loves her. Don't sell yourself short, Mason, and don't give up hope. If Miss Bell is the right woman for you, God will show you the way to win her."

Mason must have looked skeptical, for Jeremy continued. "Believe me, Mason. I know what I'm talking about. I was in your shoes once and look at me now—married to the perfect woman, thanks to God's goodness. It can happen to you, too."

"I hope so."

Chapter Six

Tthis calls for a celebration." Mason gestured toward the depot site, where a tall wooden plank fence surrounded the excavation that had finally resumed. It was early May, and as Papa had predicted, the contractor the UP had chosen had not hired any of the men who'd participated in the strike in March but instead had brought his own crew. Eugenia had taken a number of pictures of the work, while Mason had scribbled in his ever-present notebook. Now that they were finished, he wore a grin as he said, "Can I interest you in one of Esther Snyder's pastries?"

"Oh, yes." Eugenia saw no reason to hide her enthusiasm. "Others may disagree, but I'm convinced she bakes the best cakes and cookies in Cheyenne."

Of course, even if Esther's creations tasted like sawdust, Eugenia would have accepted Mason's invitation simply to have a reason to spend more time with him. Memories of the waltz they'd shared were never far from her thoughts, and though he hadn't referred to it, Eugenia knew she wasn't imagining the new warmth she'd seen in Mason's eyes. The night they'd danced together had been a turning point, changing what had been a friendly partnership into something more, something Eugenia was almost afraid to name.

She placed her hand on the crook of his arm and enjoyed their leisurely stroll north on Central Avenue. When they reached the bakery, she was surprised to discover that for once it was devoid of customers, although Jeremy stood behind his easel in the far corner.

As the doorbell tinkled, Esther Snyder emerged from the back room, her face wreathed in a smile. "Look, Jeremy. Two of our favorite people are here."

Eugenia blinked in surprise at the realization that Mason had been here often enough to have gained "favorite people" status. "I was going to introduce Mason to you," she told Esther, "but obviously there's no need."

"Indeed not. Mason is one of our best customers, although I suspect the real attraction is not my baked goods but my husband."

As Jeremy wiped his hands on a rag and approached them, Mason gestured toward a table for four. "Would you two join us for some cake and conversation?" Though he hadn't said anything, he'd obviously noticed that Esther was with child and might want to sit down.

Jeremy nodded. "If you're sure we won't be interrupting." His eyes lit on the camera Eugenia was carrying. "I'd like to learn more about that apparatus of yours. The last one I saw was a daguerreotype."

When they were all seated with an assortment of cakes on a platter in the center of the table and cups of steaming coffee and tea before them, Eugenia addressed Jeremy. "Photography has changed a great deal since daguerreotypes. We no longer use silver-plated copper plates. Now it's Mr. Eastman's American film." When Jeremy nodded, encouraging her to continue, she explained. "That's paper coated with two types of gelatin. It's lighter than the metal plates, and we can make exposures in far less time than before."

Mason lifted the camera from the floor where Eugenia had placed it. "Show him how the back rotates."

When Eugenia had finished the demonstration, pointing out how simple it was to switch between portraits and landscapes, Jeremy was silent for a moment. "I guess I'd better worry," he said. "These newfangled inventions will put me out of business. People won't want to wait the days it takes for me to paint their portrait when you can give them one in hours."

"Speed isn't everything," Eugenia said, sensing the depth of Jeremy's concern. Painting portraits and landscapes was his livelihood. It couldn't be easy, fearing he might lose the ability to provide for his family, especially once the baby arrived.

Mason swallowed a bite of cake then laid his fork on his plate. "The way I see it, you're both artists. Eugenia captures a person's image at one moment in time. Her photographs are very realistic and show exactly what that person looked like and what he was doing then. When Jeremy paints a portrait, he seeks to depict the depths of his subject's personality. Neither one is better than the other. There's a need for both."

What a sensitive man! Eugenia's heart soared at the way Mason had defused a potentially painful situation, and she couldn't help contrasting that with the cruel comments Chauncey had made when he'd brought her here. Eugenia loved her father. She wanted to honor him, but surely there was a way to convince him that Chauncey was not the right man for her.

◆　◆　◆

"Eugenia!" Papa looked up from the ledger he'd been consulting. "I thought you and Louisa were at the dressmaker's this morning. You know I want you to have a new gown for our party. Nothing but the finest will do for my daughter."

But the finest was not Chauncey Keaton. Eugenia swallowed, trying to tamp down her nervousness. Though Papa rarely denied her anything, this was different. "Aunt Louisa is having her fitting now. I'll join her in a few minutes, but first I wanted to talk to you."

Papa looked concerned. "Is there a problem with the party? I thought everything was settled."

"There's no problem with the party." Eugenia knew how important the gala was to her father. He'd invited everyone in Cheyenne who supported the UP, and the fact that several railroad officials were coming from Omaha would make it the largest event prior to the cornerstone ceremony. "The invitations have gone out, and the food is all ordered," she said, reassuring him.

"Good, good." The furrows between Papa's eyes disappeared for an instant then reappeared. "What's wrong? Do you need a new camera?"

"No, Papa. The camera is fine. I wanted to talk to you about Chauncey."

Her father's eyes narrowed. "What about Chauncey? He's a good man."

Remembering the way Chauncey had treated Jeremy, Eugenia could not agree with her father. "There's no easy way to say this. I don't want to marry him."

"Nonsense!" Papa sputtered. "He'll be a good husband. He's a good cattleman, and I know he'll take good care of both you and the ranch."

The fact that Papa had repeated the word *good* so many times told Eugenia how upset he was, for it wasn't like him to repeat himself. Though she didn't want to distress her father, she couldn't pretend.

"I don't love him." There. She'd said it.

"What do you know of love?"

"I know what Mama told me. I know how she felt about you, and I don't have those feelings for Chauncey."

Papa shook his head, his expression reminding her of the way he'd looked when she'd been a small child and had somehow disappointed him. "Feelings grow. You need to trust me, Eugenia. I only want the best for you, and that's Chauncey."

But it wasn't. It couldn't be.

◆　◆　◆

The next two weeks were a whirlwind of activity, getting everything ready for the party, and throughout that time Eugenia refused to think about Chauncey. He was still back East and would be there for at least another week. In the meantime, she savored every minute she spent with Mason. Though preparations for tonight's party kept her busy, she and Mason visited the depot site each day, looking for anything new to document.

The plank fence encircling the construction site was now covered with posters for local businesses and traveling shows. When she and Mason had visited the bakery for some of Esther's gingerbread, Eugenia had joked with both her and Jeremy, suggesting they advertise there. They'd demurred, saying they had no need to attract new customers, especially since Esther was providing the desserts for tonight's gala.

Eugenia moved from the kitchen to the dining room to the parlor, mentally checking items off her list. Everything was ready. All that remained was Eugenia herself. She climbed the stairs and entered her room. The seafoam-green silk gown Madame Charlotte had designed for her was the most beautiful one Eugenia had ever worn. Intricately draped and trimmed with Venetian lace, it was a true masterpiece. As Eugenia slid it over her head and admired the effect in her cheval mirror, she smiled, wondering how Mason would react when he saw it.

His reaction was everything she'd hoped for and more. As Eugenia descended the staircase, Mason stared at her for a long moment then chuckled.

"This is the first time I've been speechless in. . ." He paused, considering. "The truth is, I can't ever remember being at a loss for words. You literally took my breath away."

Though Papa and Aunt Louisa were standing at Mason's side, Eugenia had eyes only for him. "That's the nicest compliment anyone has ever paid me. Thank you, Mason. May I say you look particularly dashing tonight?"

"You've seen these clothes before."

"Maybe so, but your smile is brighter than normal." And, oh, how that smile made her heart race.

"If so, it's your fault."

Papa cleared his throat, bringing Eugenia back to reality. "Are you ready? The first of our guests are arriving."

Dutifully, Eugenia stood in the receiving line between Papa and Aunt Louisa, then moved into the parlor to circulate among the guests while they waited for dinner to be served. Everyone seemed to enjoy the hors d'oeuvre, and when they sat down for dinner, she heard nothing but praise. By any measure, the party was a success. The only thing that could have made it better would have been if Eugenia could have spent the evening with Mason.

As it was, she'd spoken to him only in passing, but she'd been aware of him no matter where she went or what she did. She saw the way he brought a flush to the older women's cheeks and knew he was being as charming to them as he was to everyone. There was no flattery in Mason, just honest compliments.

As the hours passed, Eugenia smiled so much that her face hurt. Still, she could not regret a single minute, for the evening was everything Papa had wished for.

"Great job, Eugenia," Papa said when the last of the guests had departed, leaving Eugenia alone with her father, her aunt, and Mason. "I could not have asked for anything better."

"Thank you." Eugenia led the way into the small sitting room, noticing that her father appeared tired. "Would you like some warm milk?" When she'd been a child, it had been Papa who'd encouraged her to drink it before bedtime, saying it would help her sleep. It was only later that she'd learned that he'd never outgrown his fondness for the children's beverage.

"That sounds good." He turned to his sister. "What about you, Louisa?"

Aunt Louisa nodded. "With a dash of nutmeg, if you please."

"I'll get it." Eugenia rose. Though she could have summoned a servant, they'd all worked so hard that she didn't want to disturb any of them.

"Let me help." Mason stood at Eugenia's side and slid the pocket door open so she could precede him.

When they reached the kitchen, Eugenia pulled a pan from the cupboard and filled it with milk.

"I want to echo your father," Mason said as he leaned against the doorjamb. "You were the perfect hostess. Thanks to you, everyone had a wonderful time."

"What about you? Did you enjoy the evening?" Though this had been part of his job, Eugenia hoped Mason had found some pleasure tonight.

"I did. Only one thing would have made it better."

Though she'd been about to light the stove, Eugenia turned to look at Mason. There had been an unexpected note in his voice, one that made her wonder what his one thing was. For her, it would have been to have spent more time with him.

"What's that one thing?" she asked.

"I wish we could have danced."

Eugenia inhaled swiftly as memories of the minutes they'd spent in each other's arms rushed back, overwhelming her with their sweetness. It would be wonderful, so very wonderful, if they could repeat that. She looked at the open space in the middle of the kitchen. "There's no music, but if one of us hums, we could dance right here." Without waiting for his response, she began to hum a waltz.

Mason smiled. "You really are perfect." He opened his arms and drew her into them. Within seconds, they were dancing in the kitchen, their feet moving as smoothly as if they were in a ballroom with an orchestra providing music.

Afterward, Eugenia could not have said how long they danced. All she knew was that as they twirled and dipped, Mason's gaze never left hers. And then he stopped, his eyes darkening with emotion as ever so slowly he lowered his lips to hers.

Chapter Seven

It was the most wonderful thing she'd ever experienced. Eugenia spun in a tight circle, her arms outstretched. Now that she was in the privacy of her room, she could savor the memories she'd made this evening when she'd been in Mason's arms. His lips had been soft and firm, sweet and spicy all at the same time.

She smiled as she lowered her arms and walked slowly around the room, trying to regain her bearings. Though she'd dreamt about kisses, she had never realized one would be like that. The pressure of Mason's lips on hers had sent waves of delight through her body, and when he'd wrapped his arms around her, she had wished the moment would never end. But it had.

When they were both breathless, Mason had released her and pointed toward the stove. Somehow Eugenia had warmed the milk. Somehow she had carried on a conversation with Papa and Aunt Louisa. Somehow she had managed to control the silly grin that threatened to pop out every time she thought of Mason and that kiss. But now that she was alone, she no longer had to pretend. Mason's kiss had been the most wonderful moment of her life.

◆　◆　◆

It was the stupidest thing he'd ever done. Mason paced the floor of the spacious bedchamber Erastus Bell had given him. It was dumb, dumb, dumb, and yet he couldn't regret it. The moments he'd held Eugenia in his arms had been more wonderful than he'd dreamt possible. When she was close to him, he'd felt as if they were two parts of a whole, that she was the half of him that had been missing. And her kiss. . . Was there anything on earth so sweet?

Mason frowned as he continued to pace, striding from the window to the door and back again. Though he was a man who made his living with words, he could not find any that did justice to the way he'd felt when he'd kissed Eugenia. That kiss had been indelibly etched on his memory. It had been incredible, unforgettable, and oh so wrong.

Eugenia's father trusted him. He'd hired Mason to do a job, not fall in love with his daughter. Erastus had made no secret of the fact that he wanted Eugenia to marry Chauncey Keaton, and while Chauncey would not have been Mason's choice for her, he must respect his employer's wishes.

He couldn't undo what he'd already done, but he could—and he would—ensure it wasn't repeated. The Bible warned about avoiding temptation, and Mason would. He'd continue to work with Eugenia, because that was part of the agreement he'd made with Erastus, but he could not continue to live here where he'd be tempted to take her into his arms again. And again. And again.

Mason paused and stared out the window, racking his brain for an elusive memory. What was the name of that boardinghouse Jeremy had mentioned?

◆ ◆ ◆

Eugenia hummed as she descended the stairs, a smile wreathing her face at the memory of where last night's humming had led. That had been wonderful, so very wonderful, but. . . The smile faded slightly at the prospect of the next half hour. Though she was eager to see Mason again, it might be awkward, especially with Papa and Aunt Louisa watching them. They'd have to be careful not to catch each other's eye, just the way they had last night when everyone drank cups of hot milk. But once they left for the depot, she and Mason could talk about those unforgettable moments.

As she entered the breakfast room, Eugenia's eyes widened at the sight of only three place settings.

"Has Papa already left?" she asked Norton. The butler was arranging chafing dishes and platters on the buffet.

He shook his head. "No, Miss Eugenia. Mr. Farling said he wouldn't be here for breakfast."

"Oh, I see." But she did not. Though Mason had missed several breakfasts, this was the first time he'd done so without her.

Neither Papa nor Aunt Louisa seemed concerned by Mason's absence. Aunt Louisa chattered about how well the party went, while Papa beamed with pride. It was only Eugenia who had difficulty forcing herself to eat, when all the while she wondered where Mason had gone.

At last the meal ended. As the three of them left the breakfast room, the front door opened, and Mason entered the house.

"Could I have a few minutes of your time, Erastus?" he asked. There were circles under his eyes, as if he'd slept little, and his face was paler than normal. Either of those would have been cause for concern, but what worried Eugenia the most was the studious way Mason refused to look at her.

Papa nodded. "Of course."

As he followed her father to his office, Mason's glance landed on Eugenia then skittered away, as if he'd touched a hot stove. Something was wrong. Terribly wrong. But what?

Feigning interest in a book, Eugenia stationed herself in the library where she could watch the entrance to Papa's office. Sooner or later, Mason would leave, and when he did, she would be waiting.

The door opened, and Eugenia rose, meeting Mason in the middle of the hallway. "Is something wrong?" she asked. It wasn't the most graceful of introductions, but she was too worried to couch her words carefully.

He shook his head. "Not anymore." Once again, Mason failed to meet her gaze. He studied the toes of his shoes as if they contained the answers to the mysteries of the universe. "I explained to your father that I'm moving to Mrs. Tyson's boardinghouse."

Eugenia felt the blood drain from her face, and she reached out, placing her hand against the wall to steady her suddenly wobbly legs. "You're leaving?" The words came out as little more than a croak.

"Not Cheyenne," he said, his voice as cool as if they were casual acquaintances, not partners, not a man and a woman who'd shared the most wonderful kiss in the history of the world. "I'm certainly not abandoning the project," he added. "As I told your father, living at the boardinghouse will give me the opportunity to spend more time with the men who are actually building the depot. You know I think their perspective will be an important part of the book."

"But why?" It made no sense. Mason already spent a fair amount of time talking to the men as they worked. Surely that was enough.

He shrugged his shoulders as if his coat had suddenly become uncomfortable. For a second, Eugenia thought he might refuse to answer, but then Mason raised his head and met her gaze, his eyes so filled with pain that she wanted to cry.

"You know why," he said.

There was only one reason she could imagine, and that wrenched her heart more than she'd thought possible. Despite everything that had happened, Mason did not love her.

Chapter Eight

I missed you." Though Chauncey smiled as he entered the parlor and took the seat she'd indicated, Eugenia felt a shiver snake its way down her spine. Perhaps she was being fanciful, but the expression in his eyes reminded her of a man she'd seen in an art museum back east. The man had been staring at a Rembrandt painting, and she'd heard him mutter, "I'd do anything to own that."

She forced herself to smile as Chauncey continued speaking. "New York, Philadelphia, and Boston are great cities, but they seemed empty without you. I missed you," he said again.

Eugenia wouldn't lie and say that she'd missed him, but she knew she needed to say something. After all, this was the man Papa wanted her to marry. "I'm glad your trip was a success. Papa told me how pleased he is with all you accomplished." While he'd been gone, Chauncey had sent lengthy weekly letters detailing the progress of his negotiations.

"It's an honor to help him. I feel like we're already partners, even though it won't be official until you and I marry."

Partners. This was the first Eugenia had heard of that. "Papa didn't mention making you a partner."

"There's no reason he should have. It's between us men."

Eugenia tried her best not to bristle. Mason would never have said anything like that. Mason respected women. He was kind. He was fair. He was as close to perfect as Eugenia could imagine. If only he loved her. But he did not.

Mason came to the house each morning after breakfast and escorted her to the depot. Once they checked the progress and she documented the day in at least one photograph, he escorted her back home, all the while being unfailingly polite. If she'd only just met him, Eugenia knew she'd be content with the way he treated her, but they weren't new acquaintances, and she could not forget the kiss they'd shared. The wonderful, unforgettable kiss that Mason obviously regretted.

There was nothing to be gained by pining over him. Whatever had been between them was gone. Eugenia fixed a smile on her face as she turned to Chauncey. "Will you stay for supper? I'm sure Papa will want to hear all about your trip."

Chauncey nodded. "I'd never turn down the opportunity to be with you and your father."

Rising, Eugenia said, "I'll let Cook know there'll be four for supper."

"Four?" Chauncey's eyebrows rose, and Eugenia thought she saw a hint of satisfaction in his expression. "Does that mean that journalist left town?"

"No, but he doesn't live here anymore."

This time there was no doubt about it. Chauncey was pleased. "Good. Very good."

But it wasn't.

◆　◆　◆

"It's been more difficult than I thought possible," Mason told the man who walked slowly at his side. When he'd entered the bakery, Jeremy had taken one look at him and suggested they go for a walk. It was only when they were outside and would not be overheard that Jeremy had asked him what was wrong.

"I do everything I can to act as if we're simply colleagues, but what I want is to sweep her into my arms and beg her to marry me."

"Why don't you do that?" Jeremy asked. "You told me once you believed Eugenia returned your feelings."

It was true that in the weeks since he'd moved out of the Bell mansion Mason had caught Eugenia regarding him with something that looked like longing. The emotion was easy to recognize, for he saw it each morning when he gazed at his reflection while shaving.

"I have nothing to offer her, at least not compared to Chauncey Keaton. He can give her the life she deserves. And, even if he couldn't, he's the man her father wants her to marry. I'm just the man hired to write a commemorative book."

Jeremy paused at the street corner to let a carriage pass them. "Will Chauncey make her happy?"

It was a question Mason had asked himself countless times. "I hope so. When I see them together, she's always smiling." Admittedly, it wasn't the way she'd smiled at Mason while they'd danced, but it was a smile.

Jeremy did not appear impressed. "I imagine you're smiling then, too."

"Of course. That's what one does at events like those."

"But you're not smiling on the inside."

"That's true."

"Maybe Eugenia is doing the same thing you are and is putting on a brave front." Jeremy was silent for a moment, perhaps wanting Mason to consider what he'd said. "Don't you think you owe it to yourself and Eugenia to find out how she really feels?" His lips thinned. "I wasn't sure Esther loved me, but I also knew I couldn't spend the rest of my life without telling her of my love."

And look where that had brought him. Esther and Jeremy were one of the happiest couples Mason had ever seen. "How did you get to be so wise?" he asked his friend.

"Me, wise?" Jeremy laughed. "If I have any wisdom, it's come with age and many hours of prayer. So, are you going to talk to Eugenia?"

"I want to, but first I need to ask for her father's permission. I don't know whether he'll agree. To be honest, Jeremy, I doubt he will, but you're right. I have to try, and the timing has to be right." Mason paused, reflecting on how important timing was. "Erastus is preoccupied with the cornerstone ceremony right now. Whenever I see him, it's the only thing he talks about. My best chance of getting him to agree is to wait until the cornerstone is laid."

Though Jeremy had started to nod, he stopped and raised his eyebrows again. "That's a month from now. Are you sure you want to wait?"

"No, I don't want to wait. Not a single minute. But I need to."

◆　◆　◆

It was an excuse, Eugenia admitted to herself as she left the house and headed south on Ferguson. Chances were that Mason didn't need the page that had somehow slipped out of his notebook this morning, but returning it would give her an opportunity to see him again. That was why she was walking more quickly than usual, rather than strolling and admiring the stores she passed.

Her pace did not slow when she reached Madame Charlotte's dress shop. Though Aunt Louisa had urged her to look at the modiste's designs for wedding gowns, Eugenia had not. No matter how often Papa sang Chauncey's praises, no matter how many gifts Chauncey brought her and how many compliments he lavished on her, Eugenia knew she wasn't ready to marry him.

If she agreed, both Papa and Chauncey would be happy, but every time Eugenia thought of marrying Chauncey, she shivered. She couldn't explain why she shrank from the very idea, why it filled her with foreboding. It was foolish, for surely there was no reason to fear Chauncey.

When she reached the corner of Fifteenth Street and turned west, Eugenia's mood lightened. The boardinghouse where Mason lived was only a few yards away. Soon she'd see him, and even if it was only for a moment or two, those moments would brighten her afternoon.

What did not brighten her day was the neighborhood. Why had Mason moved here? Though the boardinghouse was only six blocks from her home, the area was so different that it could have been in another city. This was a less prosperous part of Cheyenne, the buildings poorly cared for, an area that lacked trees and plants but had saloons and a brothel on the next block. Papa called the neighborhood seedy. Eugenia called it sad.

Though the street was almost deserted, her eyes widened when she saw a well-dressed man talking to a woman whose clothing was little more than rags. The man had his back to her, but as Eugenia watched, he slapped the woman, the blow so fierce that she slumped to the ground. An instant later, he began to kick her.

"Stop that!" Eugenia cried, rushing toward the woman. She knew she couldn't overpower the man, but somehow she had to stop him from inflicting more harm. Oh, how could he do something so heinous? What kind of a man would kick a poor woman?

"Stop that!" she shouted again. This time the man turned, and Eugenia's shock turned to horror. "Chauncey?" Surely it couldn't be, but it was. Though his face was distorted by fury and a scowl, this was indeed Chauncey.

The man Eugenia's father wanted her to marry took a step toward her. "What are you doing here?" He tried to modulate it, but she heard the anger in his voice. The question was, was he angry that she was near Mason's boardinghouse or that she'd seen him mistreating the woman?

"Why I'm here doesn't matter. The question is, why were you attacking that poor woman?" Eugenia looked around, but the battered woman was nowhere to be seen. She must have taken advantage of Chauncey's distraction and slipped into the alley.

Chauncey came closer, his expression once more serene. It was almost as if he'd slipped on a mask to cover his fury. "I don't know what you think you saw, but I was merely protecting myself. That woman tried to rob me."

Lies. All lies. Eugenia had seen him approach the woman, not the other way around. "You're lying, Chauncey. I don't know what you two said to each other, but there's no way you can justify hurting her."

As he took another step toward Eugenia, Chauncey's expression changed, and this time she saw concern reflecting from his eyes. Concern but no remorse. Was this the reason she'd felt a frisson of fear every time she thought of marrying him? Perhaps she'd been led here to prevent her from making a huge mistake.

"I know what I saw," she said firmly, "and what I saw tells me you're not a man I want to marry." No matter what Papa said, she would not agree to marry someone who treated the poor and unfortunate with such cruelty.

Though she sensed that he was trying to hide it, Eugenia saw alarm in Chauncey's expression. "Don't be hasty, Eugenia," he said, his voice huskier than normal. "Won't you give me a second chance?"

She shook her head as the memory of his kicking the poor woman filled her with horror. "I can't forget what I saw."

Chauncey came so close that she could smell the Macassar oil he used on his hair. "Can you forgive me?" Before Eugenia could respond, he continued. "Jesus told us to forgive seventy times seven."

That was true, but it wasn't that simple. "I'm not the one you should be asking for forgiveness. It's the woman you hurt."

Nodding as if he agreed, Chauncey said, "I'll find her. I'll make everything right with her. I'll give her money for clothes, and I'll get her a room in a boardinghouse so she has a place to eat and sleep. Please, Eugenia, give me a second chance. Don't disappoint your father."

Eugenia was silent for a moment, considering what the announcement that she would never marry Chauncey would mean to Papa. Though he tried to make light of it, she knew how concerned her father was that something might go wrong during the cornerstone ceremony. He spent hours each day trying to be certain every detail was covered. How could she add to his worries? And then there was Chauncey himself. Though Eugenia didn't expect to change her mind about marrying him, everyone deserved the opportunity to change.

She took a deep breath, exhaling slowly as she formulated her response. "All right, Chauncey. I won't say anything to Papa until after the cornerstone is laid."

Chapter Nine

Today was the day. Eugenia turned to view her gown in the cheval mirror. Though the crowd's attention would be on other things today, she wanted everything to be perfect, including her gown. Today was July 19, the day the depot's cornerstone would be laid, the day she could cease her charade with Chauncey.

She studied the gown, finding no flaw in Madame Charlotte's creation. If only she could say the same about Chauncey. She'd tried to give him a second chance. She'd tried not to think about the poor woman on Fifteenth Street, but what Eugenia had seen that day had made her both cautious and observant.

In the weeks since then, she'd seen the disdain with which Chauncey regarded the construction workers at the depot. She'd noticed the way he picked up the china shepherdess that had been one of Mama's prized possessions as if he were evaluating how much Papa had paid for it. She'd heard the condescension in his voice when he spoke of her photographs. All that had combined to confirm her decision. She could not marry Chauncey. Eugenia knew that as clearly as she knew that today was a beautiful Monday in July, a day when sunshine had replaced the overnight rain.

She would tell Papa of her decision tonight before the celebratory dinner at the Cheyenne Club, and then she would muster every ounce of courage she possessed to ask Mason if he remembered the kiss they'd shared.

◆ ◆ ◆

Today was the day. Mason swirled the brush in his shaving cup then stroked the foam onto his cheeks. Today was the day the Wyoming Lodge of Masons would preside over the ceremony. Eugenia would take photos as they anointed the stone with wine, oil, and corn. They'd all listen to a few speeches. Everyone would applaud. And when it was over, he would find a way to speak to Erastus in private.

Mason picked up his razor and wielded it with his usual precision. It took control not to nick his skin, but that was nothing compared to the self-control he'd had to exert to pretend that Eugenia was nothing more than a friend. The pretense had grown even more difficult when he'd taken Jeremy's advice to study her expression when she was with Chauncey. That had left no doubt: Eugenia was not happy.

Mason could see the shadows behind her smile. What worried him even more was that he also glimpsed something darker, almost as if she feared Chauncey. While that seemed unlikely, Mason could not dismiss his concerns. He wanted to be the man who put the sparkle back in Eugenia's eyes, the man who made her feel safe and cherished.

By nightfall he would know if he had the right to do that, but first they had a ceremony to attend.

◆　◆　◆

"I can feel the excitement." Eugenia smiled as she looked at the crowd that had already started to gather for the placement of the cornerstone. Though she and Mason had arrived a full hour before the ceremony was scheduled to begin, they were far from the first.

"You sound surprised."

"I guess I am. I knew Papa was anxious to reach this stage, but I hadn't realized how many other people in Cheyenne would feel the same way."

Mason surveyed the ever-growing crowd and made a few notes on his pad. "It's an important event, especially for a city that owes its existence to the railroad." He nodded, acknowledging the greeting of one of the workers. "I think the UP was wise to choose today for the ceremony. Laying the cornerstone on the same date that the city was originally surveyed sends a strong message about the railroad being a part of the city."

"And it will be an impressive as well as an important building."

Mason gave her a mischievous grin. "Is that why you're dressed to match it?"

Eugenia's smile matched his as pleasure that he'd cared enough to comment flowed through her. "I'm surprised you noticed."

"I notice everything about you."

As a blush colored her cheeks, Eugenia realized that for the first time in far too long, he sounded like the old Mason, the man he'd been before he moved to the boarding-house. Oh, how she'd missed that man!

"I gave Madame Charlotte a chip of the red sandstone and asked her to try to match it," she explained. Cheyenne's premier dressmaker had surpassed Eugenia's expectations.

"It appears that she succeeded. You look very fetching in your new gown, Miss Bell."

Her smile broadening until she wondered if her cheeks would split, Eugenia nodded. This *was* the old Mason, the one who used to tease her with mock formality.

"Why, thank you, Mr. Farling," she replied, copying his tone. "You look mighty fine today, too."

Mason chuckled, his expression sobering a second later. "I see Barrett Landry. Your father asked me to interview him today. He thinks Barrett may become one of Wyoming's first senators once we achieve statehood."

Eugenia liked the way Mason said *we* as if he were planning to remain in Cheyenne. That would be good. So very good. Though she was tempted to ask if that was indeed his intention, she restrained herself. She would say nothing personal until she'd spoken to Papa. Instead, she nodded at Mason. "You'd better catch Barrett while he's alone."

When Mason headed toward the cattle baron who might or might not become a senator, Eugenia moved into the cordoned-off area. This was where the dignitaries would stand once they'd completed their ceremonial parade into the depot site. This was where the enormous stone would be wheeled into place. But before that happened, Eugenia wanted to take several photographs of the foundation without the cornerstone.

She was so caught up in composing the picture that she didn't hear the footsteps behind her. Before Eugenia knew what was happening, she was on the ground, knocked there by an unseen figure who grabbed her camera.

"Stop!" She scrambled to her feet, her eyes widening as she shouted at the boy who was running away from her. He was moving more slowly than she would have expected, and he kept glancing over his shoulder as if checking on her.

"Stop!" But the boy did not. A quick glance told Eugenia no one was close enough to help her. If she wanted her camera—and she did—she'd have to catch him herself. Thankful that Madame Charlotte had made this gown with a slightly wider than normal skirt, Eugenia raced after the thief, following him behind the old depot building.

With no trains due until after the cornerstone ceremony, the platform was empty. But there, sitting on the step to the depot itself was the boy who'd taken her camera. She guessed him to be no more than ten or twelve years old, with threadbare clothing that made her assume he would try to sell the camera. On another day she might have felt pity for him. Right now all she felt was anger.

"Give it back!" she demanded as she approached him.

The boy simply shook his head. Eugenia took another step toward him, then cried out when a man grabbed her from behind, tugging a burlap bag over her head. In the instant that the world became dark, Eugenia knew the boy had been nothing more than a decoy.

"No!" she shrieked, kicking with all her might. But the man who'd caught her had the advantage of sight, and he dodged her feet.

"Why are you doing this?"

There was no answer. Wrenching her arms behind her, the man quickly tied them, then tossed Eugenia over his shoulder as if she were nothing more than a sack of feed. Seconds later, he dumped her into the back of a wagon. Though Eugenia kicked, it was to no avail. The man grabbed her feet and tied her ankles.

She was at the kidnapper's mercy.

◆　◆　◆

Where was she? While he'd been interviewing Barrett Landry, Mason had seen Eugenia enter the restricted area, but now there was no sign of the woman he loved. Where was she? His eyes searched the crowd, but he saw no beautiful auburn-haired woman dressed in red sandstone–colored silk. Where was she?

A prickle of alarm snaked its way down Mason's spine. She might have gone inside the hotel, but that wasn't like Eugenia. And yet it was even less like her to have simply disappeared.

Practically sprinting, he made his way to the side of the construction site where he'd last seen Eugenia.

"Did any of you notice a woman in a dress the same color as the stone?" He addressed the small group of onlookers who had chosen to watch the ceremony from this part of the site.

A tall, thin man shook his head. "Sorry. I just arrived." The others' responses were similar. Mason was about to give up and look elsewhere when a petite woman with what appeared to be twin boys clinging to her hands nodded.

"I saw a lady like that about five minutes ago," she told Mason. "She was chasing a boy. They went behind the old depot building."

At last, a clue! Mason thanked the woman profusely then raced toward the wooden depot, his heart pounding with fear. There was no sign of Eugenia, no sign of anyone other than a boy who sat on the steps, fiddling with something. As Mason strode toward him, he saw that the object the boy held was Eugenia's camera.

"How did you get that camera?" he demanded. When the boy jumped to his feet and looked as if he planned to flee, Mason grabbed his arm.

"I found it." The boy's sullen reply did nothing to convince Mason. Eugenia would never have abandoned her camera. If she had chased the boy here, it was because he'd taken it.

"I know you stole it," Mason said, his voice filled with anger. The camera didn't matter. All that mattered was Eugenia. "I also know the woman who owned it came after you. Where is she now?"

The boy shook his head. "I don't know."

Mason had no doubt the boy knew more than he was admitting. "You can tell me, or you can tell the sheriff. I don't imagine he'll be too easy on you. Let's start with why you took the camera." The way the boy had been handling it, as if he had no idea what to do with it, told Mason there was more to this than a simple theft.

The boy shook his head again.

"All right. We'll talk to the sheriff." Mason started walking toward the construction site, propelling the boy with him.

"Okay. Okay." The boy planted his feet and stared up at Mason. "A man gave me some money to take it." He pulled a few coins from his pocket and showed them to Mason. Though a mere pittance to Mason, they probably seemed like a fortune to the boy.

"He said I could keep the camera. All he wanted was the lady. He tied her up and put her in a wagon."

Anger and fear warred within Mason. Anger that someone had lured Eugenia here, fear over what the man intended. One thing was certain. There was no time to lose.

"Where did they go?"

The boy pointed toward the west. "Be careful, mister. He's a mean man."

And that mean man had Eugenia.

Chapter Ten

Never before had she felt so helpless, but never before had Eugenia been unable to see, unable to move her arms and legs, unable to do anything to save herself. The lack of sight was the worst, because it distorted everything. Not only did she have no idea of which direction they were heading, but she'd lost track of time. She'd long since given up hope of protecting herself from bumps and bruises. Though initially she had held herself stiffly, she'd soon discovered that accomplished nothing other than making her muscles ache. It was better to remain limp and pray for deliverance. But though her prayers had been constant, the wagon continued to move.

The driver did not seem to be in a rush, and that surprised Eugenia. Did he think no one would realize she was gone? As she considered that possibility, Eugenia frowned. There were so many people at the construction site by the time she'd chased the boy with her camera that it was all too likely she would not be missed for some time. Papa wouldn't be looking for her until the ceremony began, and Mason might think she'd gone to record the parade.

Local politicians and railroad officials had decided to join the Wyoming Lodge of Masons in marching to the site. It would be a short parade compared to the ones the city enjoyed on Independence Day, but it was a parade nonetheless. Since Eugenia had mentioned her interest in it to Mason this morning, he was unlikely to be alarmed if he didn't see her at the site. Though the thought distressed her, Eugenia knew it could be the better part of an hour before anyone was concerned about her absence.

She wouldn't dwell on that, for nothing could be gained by reflecting on things she could not change. Instead her thoughts turned to the wagon's driver. Who was he? Was he working alone, or had someone else hired him to get her out of Cheyenne? Where were they going? If she could remove the sack, she'd have an idea of the direction they were traveling, but all she could see now were pinpoints of light filtering through the weave of the burlap. Those told her it was still daylight but nothing more.

The most important question, yet another one Eugenia could not answer, was why the man had abducted her. It made no sense.

She felt the wagon slow then make a sharp turn to the left. The road was bumpier here, and though she knew it was futile, Eugenia tried to brace herself as the wagon lurched, jolting her up and down and from one side to the other. She would definitely have bruises after this ride. When it emerged, her laugh was devoid of mirth. Bruises were the least of her worries.

The jolting continued for what seemed like hours but was probably only a few minutes before the wagon slowed then stopped completely. Though she was grateful for the respite, Eugenia's apprehension grew as she felt the wagon rock when the driver climbed out. The journey was over. Now she'd have the answers to her questions. The problem was, she wasn't certain she was ready. *Help me, Lord*, she prayed.

Seconds later, the driver lowered the back of the wagon and tugged her out and onto the ground. When Eugenia's legs, cramped from being tied together, began to buckle, her abductor pushed her against the wagon side to steady her then untied the rope that held the sack closed around her neck. With a quick jerk, he pulled the burlap bag away.

Eugenia blinked, trying to accustom her eyes to the bright sunshine. When the momentary confusion caused by the light faded, she stared at the man and gasped.

"Chauncey!" The man who'd abducted her, the man who'd handled her as if she were nothing more than an object, was the man who wanted to marry her.

"Why did you do this?" she demanded, fury overcoming fear. She had seen Chauncey's cruel side, and that had stoked her belief that he was not a man she could marry, but she had never expected him to treat her this way. What could he hope to gain? Even if she had been inclined to accept his proposal, today's events would have changed her mind. And Papa, who'd once sung Chauncey's praises, would be horrified when he learned what the man had done.

Though his lip curled in what appeared to be disdain, Chauncey said nothing. Instead, he gripped Eugenia's upper arm and began to drag her toward the only building in sight, a dilapidated barn. It was impossible to walk with her ankles bound together, and so, though she tried not to, Eugenia stumbled.

"This would be easier if you untied my legs," she said as calmly as she could.

Though Chauncey paused for a second, he shook his head, perhaps remembering how she'd kicked him when he'd first captured her. "I'm not that stupid."

But he was. Surely only a stupid man would risk losing Erastus Bell's esteem. Thanks to his contacts at the railroad and in territorial politics, Papa was a powerful man. No one who'd done what Chauncey had would remain unscathed by Papa's anger.

"I couldn't risk losing you," Chauncey said as he dragged her forward. "I knew you were wavering, and I couldn't let you get away. You're going to be my wife, Eugenia. Make no mistake about that."

"Why? You don't love me." Eugenia wasn't certain Chauncey knew what love meant.

"Love? That's a story for poets and fools. What matters is money and power. Marrying you will bring me both. When your father's ranch is added to mine, I'll be one of the wealthiest men in the territory. Other men will look up to me."

Eugenia shook her head, grateful that at least she could see where she was going. "Surely you can't believe I'd marry you after this. Even if I wanted to, which I do not, Papa would never allow it."

Though he did not break his stride, Eugenia saw Chauncey frown. "Don't be so sure, my dear." The last two words sounded more like an epithet than an endearment and sent a shiver down her spine. "Once you've spent the night here with me, your reputation will be ruined. Your father will have no choice but to agree to our marriage."

Eugenia took a deep breath as she considered her situation. Unless Chauncey untied her, she had no way of escaping. And even if she did somehow manage to get her feet free, where would she go? There was no sight of any other dwelling and she had no idea in which direction Cheyenne lay. For a second, despair threatened to overwhelm Eugenia.

Then she relaxed. It was true there was nothing she could do, but it was also true there was Someone who could save her.

Closing her eyes, Eugenia began to pray.

◆　◆　◆

It wasn't difficult to obtain a horse, Mason reflected as he bent low over the stallion's neck and urged him to even greater speed. The owner of the livery had been more than happy to rent his fastest mount. It wasn't difficult to follow the tracks. Last night's rain had left mud that had not yet fully dried. What was difficult was controlling his anger. How could anyone have abducted Eugenia? No woman deserved to be trussed and stashed in the back of a wagon like a sack of potatoes, least of all Eugenia.

Mason refused to let his mind dwell on the possible reasons for her kidnapping. All that mattered was that he arrived in time to save Eugenia from whatever her abductor had in mind. Mason said a silent prayer for her safety while his eyes scanned the horizon, searching for clues to Eugenia's whereabouts.

There. The wagon had turned off the main road onto a track that, judging from the thickness of the grass, had not been used in months. Was that good or bad? Mason didn't know. All that he knew was that he had to get Eugenia away from here.

The road climbed a small rise. When he reached the top, Mason reined in the horse. Looking down, he could see a small, apparently abandoned building, probably an old barn. Next to it stood a wagon with the horses still harnessed. Though there was no sign of Eugenia or her abductor, this had to be the right place. If they were inside the barn—and Mason saw no alternative—he would have surprise on his side. But that involved stealth.

Sliding to the ground, he dropped the horse's reins, hoping that would be enough to keep him from bolting. Though Mason would have liked to have his mount closer, he couldn't risk the other horses greeting him and alerting the man inside the barn.

Thankful that the grass muffled his footsteps, Mason ran toward the barn, praying with each step that he was not too late and that the horses would not announce his arrival. His second prayer was answered, because the animals seemed more interested in grazing than in a stranger's appearance.

Mason studied the barn as he ran. As far as he could tell, there were no windows, and if this was like most barns, the only door was the one he faced. That was good, because it meant that Eugenia's abductor could not escape. Now the question was whether or not Mason could overpower him. Mason would have the advantage of surprise; the other man would have the advantage of being able to see.

Closing his eyes to a mere slit to help them grow accustomed to what he knew would be the relative darkness of the barn's interior, Mason moved toward the door, opening it as silently as he could. For a second he stood, so surprised by the other man's identity that he felt frozen.

Chauncey Keaton. Even though he saw only his back, there was no doubt who had abducted Eugenia. The very idea shocked Mason. Why on earth had the man who appeared to have every advantage taken Eugenia by force?

Chauncey stood next to Eugenia, his posture menacing. And, though her eyes were fixed on her captor, her expression filled with anger and disgust, Eugenia had no recourse against him. In the split second that it took him to register the details, Mason saw that she was seated on a bale of hay and would have difficulty moving, for her arms were secured behind her back, her ankles tied together. Chauncey would pay for that!

Knowing he would have only one chance, Mason sprang forward, slamming his body into Chauncey's and knocking the other man to the floor. As Eugenia gasped, he landed a blow on Chauncey's jaw. It should have knocked him out, but the man was stronger than Mason had expected. Stronger or perhaps more desperate than he'd thought, for surely only desperation would have led a man like Chauncey to kidnap Eugenia.

The man fought valiantly, his fist connecting with Mason's cheek at the same time that he flung himself upward, flipping Mason off him. A second later, Chauncey wrapped both hands around Mason's throat in a frantic attempt to choke him. Though he could feel his breath shortening and feared that he would be unable to withstand the dangerous pressure, Mason refused to let Chauncey win. Mustering every ounce of strength he possessed, he slammed his fist into Chauncey's stomach. Caught off guard by the force of the blow, Chauncey released his stranglehold on Mason and grunted, then landed another blow.

Neither man was trained to fight, but each was determined to prevail. As he and Chauncey traded blows, Mason found himself tiring. He could only pray that his opponent was equally fatigued. As it was, he had no idea when or how the fight would end. All he knew was that he could not stop, for if he did, that would mean Chauncey's victory and Eugenia's defeat. He could not—he *would* not—let Chauncey win.

Afterward Mason could not say how long he battled Chauncey or how many blows each of them delivered. All he knew was that when he was certain he could not last another minute, Chauncey shifted to the left. It was the opening Mason needed. Gathering his final shreds of strength, he struck a blow to Chauncey's solar plexus. With a loud whoosh, the man who'd abducted Eugenia collapsed, and his eyes rolled backward.

"Thank God."

Mason echoed Eugenia's words as he scrambled to his feet. God had brought him here and had helped him prevail. Though Eugenia looked frightened, Mason could see no sign of major injuries.

"Are you all right?" he asked as he made his way to her.

Though her face was white with strain, those beautiful green eyes shone with relief. "Thanks to you, I am."

As quickly as he could, given his bruised knuckles and bloody fingers, Mason untied first her wrists, then her ankles. Though there was nothing he wanted more than to draw Eugenia into his arms and never let her go, he couldn't take the risk of Chauncey regaining consciousness. Holding out the ropes, Mason managed a small chuckle. "I've got a better use for these."

Before Chauncey could move, Mason turned him over and secured his arms and legs, trussing him even more tightly than he'd done Eugenia.

"I'll send the sheriff out to collect him," Mason said as he helped Eugenia to her feet. The sooner they were away from here, the better. "You can be sure he'll never hurt you again."

Tears filled her eyes. Though Mason hoped they were tears of relief, her next words told him they were not.

"He hurt you," she said, taking one of his hands between both of hers and touching a bloodied knuckle. "Let me help you."

"There'll be time enough for that later." Mason was still shaking inside at the realization of how close he'd come to losing her. He looked around the decrepit barn. This wasn't the way he'd envisioned it, but he wasn't going to let the opportunity slip by.

"We need to talk."

Chapter Eleven

Eugenia stared at the man she loved, the man who'd fought to save her. His clothing was filthy; his knuckles were raw; the trickle of blood at the corner of his mouth and the bruises on his cheek served as further proof that he'd battled Chauncey. He looked like exactly what he was—a wounded warrior—but to Eugenia he was the most handsome, most wonderful man on Earth. Though she was bruised from the ride, thanks to Mason, she was safe.

She moved her feet, trying to remain upright as the blood returned to them, but the smile she lavished on Mason gave no hint of her discomfort. "I don't know how to thank you," she said, her voice fervent with love and gratitude. "I prayed and prayed, and God sent you."

Mason shook his head slightly. As if he sensed how unsteady she was, he reached out and clasped her hands between his. "There's no need to thank me. Don't you know I'd do anything for you?"

His face, his poor battered face, shone with something Eugenia hoped was love as he led her out of the barn into sunshine, and she felt her spirits rise. Though Mason had never said he loved her, surely what he'd done today proved that he cared for her. And maybe, just maybe, he felt more than simple caring. Maybe he loved her, at least a little.

"This isn't the way I planned it," Mason said with a rueful look at their surroundings. Though the prairie was beautiful, the dilapidated barn was not. "I wanted to talk to your father first, but I can't wait." His eyes darkening, Mason tightened his grip on her hands. "I love you, Eugenia. I know I don't have much in the way of material things to offer you, but I love you with all my heart. What happened today only served to reinforce those feelings. When I realized you were gone, my future seemed bleak. I didn't want to think about life without you."

He loved her! He loved her! He'd said it twice. Though she wanted to cry out with happiness, Eugenia's heart was so full she could not speak. The man she loved loved her. Was there anything more wonderful? She nodded, encouraging him to continue.

Mason tipped his head to one side in the gesture she'd always found so endearing. "I'm a man who makes his living with words, but I don't feel very eloquent right now. What I'm trying to say is that I want to spend the rest of my life with you. I know I don't deserve it, but if you love me even a little, I hope you'll marry me and make me the happiest man in the world."

He loved her and he wanted to marry her. The happiness that bubbled through her reminded Eugenia of the night they'd danced in the kitchen, the night they'd shared that unforgettable kiss. And with that memory, the bubble burst. What if today ended like that night? What if Mason raised her hopes only to dash them?

Eugenia pulled her hands from his and took a step backward, needing distance for what she was going to say. "I love you," she said slowly, "but. . ."

His face fell. "But what?"

"I don't understand why you changed after the night we. . ." She hesitated, unwilling to pronounce the word.

As if he understood, Mason nodded. "The night we kissed."

"Yes. I thought it was the most wonderful moment of my life, but the next morning you were gone." And so were her dreams of happily ever after. "Ever since, you've treated me like a casual acquaintance." And that had hurt, oh how it had hurt.

Mason's lips turned down. "I'm sorry I hurt you. That wasn't my intention. I found that kiss just as wonderful as you did. I couldn't forget it—I didn't want to forget it—but I knew you were practically engaged to Chauncey. I also knew your father would never agree to let me court you. So, no matter how wonderful it was, the kiss was wrong. I knew it couldn't be repeated, but if I stayed in the same house with you, I couldn't be certain I would be strong enough to resist."

His words rang true, reassuring Eugenia. Everything he said proved what an honorable man he was. Now it was her turn to reassure him. "I never loved Chauncey. A few weeks ago I told him I wouldn't marry him. I didn't want to add to my father's worries, so I agreed not to say anything to Papa until after the cornerstone was laid."

Mason nodded. "Which is why he had to abduct you today."

"I hadn't thought of that, but it makes sense." She had sensed desperation in Chauncey's words. "No matter what he did, I wouldn't have married him. How could I when I loved you?"

The smile that teased the corner of Mason's lips turned into a full-fledged one. "If you love me, will you marry me?"

Her eyes shining with happiness, Eugenia nodded. "Yes, Mason. A thousand times yes."

"Then let's see what your father says."

◆ ◆ ◆

It was two hours later when Papa stormed into the library. As soon as they'd returned to Cheyenne, Eugenia had cleaned Mason's wounds then retired upstairs to change clothes while he did the same at his boardinghouse. Only when they were both ready had they sent a message to her father and a second one to the sheriff, telling him where he could find Chauncey.

"Where were you?" Papa demanded, focusing his anger on Mason. "You'd better have a good reason for missing the ceremony."

Somehow he hadn't noticed the bruising on Mason's face or the plasters Eugenia had stuck to his knuckles.

"He does," she assured her father. As she explained what had happened, the blood drained from Papa's face. He clenched his fists, and Eugenia guessed he was imagining the punishment he would like to mete out to Chauncey.

"It seems I owe you an apology, Mason," Papa said when he'd gotten his temper under control. "I was too hasty in my judgment. How can I ever thank you for what you've done? You saved my daughter from an unspeakable fate. Name your price. I'll give you anything."

"Anything?" Eugenia asked the question she knew Mason would not.

"That's what I said, isn't it?"

His face solemn, Mason faced her father. "There is something I want, but it's beyond price."

For the first time since he'd entered the room, Papa seemed confused. "What is it?"

"I would like your daughter's hand in marriage. I love Eugenia."

"And I love Mason." Eugenia turned toward her father, hoping he'd understand just how important this was to her. "There's nothing I want more than to be Mason's bride."

Papa's gaze moved from her to Mason and then back again. Taking her hand in his, he extended it to Mason. "You shall be his bride," he said slowly, "but I have one stipulation."

Eugenia turned toward Mason, shaking her head ever so slightly at his unspoken question. She had no idea what her father had in mind.

As if he recognized their confusion, Papa smiled. "Don't worry. It's not difficult. Since it was the depot that brought you together, I want you to include your wedding portrait in the book. After all, Eugenia, you're not just my daughter; you're also the depot bride."

"Indeed she is." The look Mason gave Eugenia was so filled with love that it took her breath away. And then there was no need for words as he drew her into his arms and pressed his lips to hers.

Dear Reader,

Do you ever wonder what inspires an author to write a specific story? In my case, the answer is that I was intrigued by Cheyenne's train depot on my first visit to what is now my adopted hometown. At the time, the depot hadn't been restored and reopened, but there was no hiding the building's beauty. While others might argue that the Wyoming State Capitol is the city's most beautiful building, for me the depot's rounded arches, its clock tower, and the combination of two different colors of sandstone make it my favorite landmark. Now that it's been reopened as a major tourism site, I've attended lectures and parties there, I've eaten in the restaurant, and I've spent hours at the museum devoted to—what else?—train travel. Can you tell that I enjoy the depot?

After hearing all that, you won't be surprised to know that when Kim Vogel Sawyer suggested a novella collection with a railroad theme, it took me less than a second to decide that my story would revolve around the depot. What better part of its history to celebrate than the early stages of construction? And so *The Depot Bride* was born.

I've tried to make my story as accurate as possible by including historical details, such as the initial workers' strike and the anointing of the cornerstone. One thing is pure fiction, though, and that's the commemorative book. If there was one, I have found no record of it. Still, the fictional book provided the perfect way for Eugenia and Mason to meet and spend time together.

I hope you enjoyed their story. And, if you're intrigued by the hints I dropped about Esther and Jeremy's romance, their story is available as an e-book short, *The Christmas Star Bride*. Or, if you prefer a print copy, it's included in *The 12 Brides of Christmas Collection*.

I love hearing from readers, so don't be shy. Let me know what you think of *The Depot Bride*. My web page includes my e-mail address and social media contacts. I look forward to hearing from you.

Blessings,
Amanda

Amanda Cabot is the bestselling author of more than thirty novels and half a dozen novellas, including Jeremy and Esther's story, *The Christmas Star Bride*, and *Waiting for Spring*, which tells Madame Charlotte's story. Although she grew up in the East, a few years ago Amanda and her high school sweetheart husband fulfilled a lifelong dream and are now living in Cheyenne. In addition to writing, Amanda enjoys traveling and sharing parts of her adopted home with readers in her *Wednesday in Wyoming* blog. One of Amanda's greatest pleasures is hearing from readers, and so she invites you to find her online at www.amandacabot.com.

Last Stop, Cordelia

by Lisa Carter

Chapter One

The Sioux warrior dragged her off her horse and onto the back of his painted palomino. And Cordelia Cochrane realized she'd made a mistake. A bad mistake. Possibly a fatal miscalculation. For a newspaper story.

She'd ridden into the middle of an ambush. The ambush set by the Indians as they lay in wait for the search party. And she, like the railroad men, had fallen into their trap.

Cordelia struggled against the Indian's iron grip, her arms trapped against her sides. She cringed at the sound of the firefight between the war party and the railroad men. Pressed against the Indian's chest, she tried not to gag from the pungent aroma of bear grease.

Everyone from her editor to the head of the railroad had warned her. This was no place for a woman. She fought her growing terror. Would she be killed outright? And if not, how much would she suffer first?

God, help me. Please. . .

◆   ◆   ◆

When the Sioux warrior grabbed the lady reporter and hoisted her onto his horse, Neil MacBride sprang out from behind the burned-out buckboard.

"Keep firing!" He thrust his rifle at John Tierney. "I'm going after the woman."

There'd been no word from the Union Pacific surveyors sent ahead of the graders. But with a sinking feeling in his gut, Neil could guess what happened to them.

Breaking cover, shoulders hunched, he ran toward his horse, Mulligan. The lady reporter must've followed the search party to the missing surveyors' advance camp. And only moments before the surprise attack.

Expecting to feel the burning sting of a bullet in his back, he zigzagged. A move he'd learned in battle to avoid certain death at the hands of Johnny Reb sharpshooters. A maneuver he prayed would serve him today in the face of the bloodcurdling cries of warriors.

Despite the popping retorts of the firefight, Mulligan hadn't drifted far. "Good horse." Requisitioned from the army by the Union Pacific, Mulligan was also a veteran of the uncivil war.

Tightlipped, Neil swung into the saddle. He dug his boot heels into the horse and spurred the animal. The horse's hooves pounded the prairie earth. He urged the horse to greater speed.

Ahead, the woman grappled against the copper-toned arms of the Dog Soldier. While the rest of the raiding party battled Neil's men, this Indian galloped for the tree line. He prayed the woman could slow the Sioux long enough for Neil to overtake them.

Clutching the reins, Neil leaned over the corded muscles of the chestnut quarter horse, balancing his weight.

More braves possibly waited in the shelter of the trees. Reinforcements. But Neil couldn't take the chance of using his holstered Colt for fear of hitting the woman.

Had the woman been taken as bait to lure the railroad team into a massacre? Neil clamped his jaw and whipped leather.

Pulling alongside, he grabbed for the blond woman, whose hair tumbled down her shoulders and blew unhindered in the brisk prairie wind. Leaning out of the saddle, he seized the woman around the waist. The Indian snatched at the woman's locks. Crying out, she reached behind her head in an attempt to loosen the pressure on her hair.

A tug of war ensued between Neil and the Indian. Both horses raced ever closer to the looming tree line. Trusting Mulligan, Neil let go of the reins. He lunged as far out of the saddle as he dared.

Neil drew back his fist and punched the Indian. With a grunt, the Indian's grip slackened enough for Neil to pull the woman over the gap between the horses toward him.

She landed with a *whoosh* on her stomach across Mulligan. The Indian pulled a knife. Neil tensed, but hooves sounded behind them. Shots were fired. Bullets whizzed past.

The woman screamed. Neil flinched. But the Indian slumped and then veered his horse toward the trees.

In one smooth motion, Neil turned Mulligan. He pressed his hand against the woman's back to keep her from sliding off.

He motioned at his charging men to give up the chase. The rest of the raiding party dissipated as quickly as they'd appeared, like morning mist over the mountains.

"Rendezvous at the camp," he shouted.

He wanted to put as much distance between them and the Sioux as possible. He dashed across the open prairie. The men followed close behind. The woman trembled beneath his hand.

Reaching the ruined remains of the base camp, Patrick O'Malley pulled his horse up short. "Boss?"

Neil jerked the reins. And getting a good look at the destruction, he grimaced. Mulligan pranced sideways. The woman made a sound in her throat.

Tierney rested both hands on the saddle horn. "You okay, Boss?"

Young Doolittle coughed through the cloud of dust rising from the hooves of the horses. "Is Mulligan okay?"

Trust Doolittle's primary concern to be the horse.

Neil willed his heart to settle. "Thanks a million, lad, for asking. Yes, by the way, I'm fine."

He dismounted. Beneath a tangle of yellow hair, her face lay hidden in horseflesh. Neil started to reach for her but let his hand drop. "Ma'am?" He darted his eyes at O'Malley, at fifty-five the old man of the crew.

They'd fought and survived in the Army of Tennessee because they stuck together.

Because they always had each other's back. And these men trusted him with their lives once more when—at Neil's urging—they signed on to build the transcontinental railroad for the Union Pacific.

O'Malley—the only one ever married among them—shrugged.

Neil cleared his throat and touched the woman's ripped sleeve. She jolted, and Mulligan reared. Young Doolittle, true to form, grabbed for the reins. Neil caught the woman in a flutter of skirts as she crumpled.

A gentle hint of lavender teased his nostrils as he lowered her to the ground. She wobbled. He steadied her.

She was by far the prettiest, sweetest-smelling anything he'd come across since. . . Since ever?

Gaining her balance, the woman in her fancy city skirts whirled. Her eyes were the color of Wyoming bluebells. And the fact that he noticed set his teeth on edge.

He broadened his shoulders. "Are ya daft, woman? Following us out here?" He frowned at the deepening of his brogue.

What in the world had brought the lady reporter out from town and into the wilds? He didn't like to think what a delicate creature like herself would've endured at the hands of—

Her eyes flashed. And not with fear.

◆　◆　◆

Balling her fist, Cordelia socked him in the shoulder. "How dare you, sir!"

She'd show him daft. She'd made a mistake—a mistake with potentially tragic consequences—but a mistake anyone, male or female, could make. And she'd been prepared to express her gratitude until. . .

Until this Irish hooligan insulted her womanhood.

Rubbing his shoulder, the handsome railroad man stepped back a pace. Handsome with sandy blond hair and in his Union army greatcoat. Cordelia might be outraged, but she wasn't blind.

A frown creased the strong brow over his hazel green eyes. "Of all the crazy stunts. . ."

His coat gaped, revealing a revolver strapped to his side and a shirt open at the collar.

A newspaper stringer, Cordelia couldn't help but observe. Her job was to follow the laying of the track and write her eyewitness accounts. She was trained to notice details.

He flung his hand toward the distant ridge. "I just saved yer life, not to mention yer virtue, lady."

She stiffened. "I'll have you know I had everything under control before you came along."

He rolled his eyes. "You looked like you had everything under control about the time the Injun took control of your scalp."

The other men hee-hawed and slapped their thighs. She was sick of being treated like a half-wit. They wouldn't have patronized her male colleagues.

Riding out alone from the end of the rails into Indian country probably wasn't the smartest thing she'd ever done. But she'd be dipped in tar before she'd admit anything of the sort to this blue-belly boor.

"You've cost me the scoop of the century." She panned left to right with her hands, blocking the imaginary headline in the air. "Captivity among the Red Indians."

He bracketed his hands. "Tenderfoot woman buried in lonely prairie grave when she stuck her nose in something not her business."

She drew herself to her full height. "Not my business because I'm a woman?"

"You said it, Miss Cochrane."

He knew her name? Although, as the only female in the bunch of reporters sent to cover the great race between the Union and Central Pacific railroads, maybe not such a surprise.

She tossed her hair over her shoulder. "Your version costs too much to send over the telegraph. You pay for each word."

"A practice"—the man smirked—"*you* might be wise to adopt in everyday conversation."

The youngest one, a boy, snickered. Still mounted, the other two formed a semicircle around Cordelia and her handsome rescuer.

She sniffed. He wasn't that handsome. Not that much.

The handsome one—*stop it, Cordelia*—studied her. She flushed, finding his scrutiny discomfiting.

But he pivoted toward the men. "They did not capture the equipment, did they?"

Something about the way he spoke. . . The brogue came and went.

As for the other men? Irish, every one of them. Veterans by the look of their boots and the dark Union stripe running the length of their army-blue pants. Recruited like so many others to lay rails and join the continent east to west.

The older one shook his head. "Too busy kidnapping the colleen, I 'spect." His accent was thick.

Her blond rescuer—late twenties?—crossed his arms over his chest. "Thank heaven for small mercies." Muscles bunched underneath the man's blue flannel shirt and the army-issue suspenders.

She reddened. Making Cordelia angrier. At herself.

Her self-appointed rescuer gave her a swift, penetrating look. "I reckon we got what we came for anyway."

The bewhiskered man on the middle horse cut his eyes at Cordelia. "Speaking for yerself, Neil?"

So his name was Neil. Her insides did a treacherous flutter.

Neil's mouth flattened. "Hardly, but we'll have to return to town for now." And the look he tossed her way wasn't flattering. "Money a'wasting 'cause someone can't mind her own business."

Her temper flared. "Whose business ought to be in a kitchen?" Maybe he wasn't as handsome as she'd believed.

"Railroad business is not a woman's business."

She lifted her chin. "Horace Greeley sent me here to bring a human perspective to this grand adventure. And I'm not about to miss out on the biggest story since the war."

"Trying to prove yourself?"

She pursed her lips. "Aren't we all?"

His gaze hardened. "Not at the expense of me men's lives you don't, Miss Cochrane."

"I'm afraid you have me at a disadvantage, sir. Your name?"

He scrubbed his hand over the bearded stubble dotting his strong jawline.

"It's Neil," the younger one offered. "Neil MacBride." The boy grinned at her. "I'm Billy Doolittle. The old man here is O'Malley."

O'Malley tipped his cap to her.

"And the one who don't talk much is Tierney."

Tierney, a rough-looking sort, twisted his lips. "As opposed to people who talk a wee bit too much."

Billy Doolittle ignored him. "They served together in the Sixteenth."

She arched a brow. "The Sixteenth. Same as Chief Engineer Grenville Dodge?"

Doolittle nodded. "Where our golden boy came to the attention of General Dodge after Neil saved his—"

"Enough." Neil moved away and took control of his horse again. "Tierney's right. Too much talk. We'd best head to town."

He swung into the saddle. "Put some distance between ourselves and the Sioux before nightfall." He peered at the sun descending behind the ridge. The horses nickered. The men tightened their grip on the reins.

"And what about me, Mr. MacBride?"

He cocked his head. "What about you?"

She planted her hands on her hips. "With my horse gone, do you intend to leave me out here?"

"Don't think the thought hasn't crossed my mind, Miss Cochrane."

Her breath caught.

Neil MacBride gave her a funny, lopsided smile. "But the Indians got far and away enough trouble without adding a crazy lady reporter to their already dire situation."

"You, sir, are no gentleman."

"Sure, and that's a fine way to thank the man who saved you from certain doom." He extended his arm. "What's it going to be? End of rail is a good day's ride from here. Come with us or take your chances."

Her palm itched to slap his hand away, but as dusk deepened, she found herself with no other choice but to play by this aggravating man's set of rules.

She grabbed hold of his hand, and in a flurry of skirts, he swung her onto the saddle behind him.

"Done the hostiles a favor today." He glanced at her over his shoulder. "'Cause I figure you—not smallpox—might singlehandedly bring about their early demise."

She sputtered.

"More than likely, I rescued them from you."

"How dare—"

"Better hang on, lady. 'Tis going to be a bumpy ride." He spurred the horse forward.

Almost unseated, she wrapped both arms around him and held on for dear life. "Y-you are the m—most—"

"You are not the most grateful damsel in distress I've ever come across, either."

"And you are the most patronizing, condescending man, Mr. MacBride, I've ever had the m—misfortune—"

Jolting over the uneven terrain, she cinched her arms tight around his waist. She buried her forehead into the rough wool of his coat and inhaled. Woodsy, sweet, and spicy. Bay rum. And something very male. Very Neil MacBride.

An unexpected combination, which caused her pulse to beat more rapidly. She steeled her resolve. He was a complication she'd best avoid if she aimed to impress Mr. Greeley and secure the plum European assignment he'd promised.

Provided, of course, she survived the Indians and the rough and tumble end-of-rails town. And Neil MacBride.

Chapter Two

Many a ragged colt hath made a noble horse.
IRISH PROVERB

Of course Neil knew who she was.

Every man from the track-laying crew to the machine shop in the end-of-the-rails tent city knew about Cordelia Cochrane. The only female any of them had laid eyes on in months. The only lady, leastways, if you didn't count the soiled doves.

And even if Cordelia Cochrane hadn't been the only woman for miles, he still would've been aware of her. He'd noticed her from the moment she stepped off the supply train.

She was like a sweet breeze across parched prairie soil. With hair like the golden wheat he dreamed of farming one day. Her chignon coiled beneath her straw hat, the black ribbon around its brim fluttered in the ubiquitous Wyoming wind. Her travel clothes were smudged from dust and engine smoke. But her eyes. . . He swallowed at the memory.

Her eyes sparkled with life and intelligence. And he'd found himself hurrying away, his heart pained for something until that moment he'd not realized he lacked.

That evening after the rescue, Neil watched Cordelia across the flickering bonfire. The stars glittered like jewels in the blue velvet of the night sky. And she entertained the men with her stories of her reporting adventures during the war. Young Doolittle hung on her every word. Every now and again, her eyes darted across the flames to Neil as if she sensed his contemplation.

As she spoke, she raised her arms to the nape of her neck, braiding her hair and tucking the strands into the net brushing her shoulders. His pulse skittered, and he clenched the pencil tighter between his fingers.

Soft tendrils of hair curled and framed her oval face. But he missed the shanks of corn silk previously hanging to her waist. His hand twitched, longing to feel those silky strands.

He frowned and bent over his sketch pad. His heart beat at a furious clip. She with her fine, educated eastern ways was as far out of a lowly Irishman's reach as stars in the sky.

Tierney trudged into camp from guard duty. "Your turn, Billy."

Lips poked out, Billy got to his feet. "But Miz Cochrane was getting to the good part."

Tierney snorted. "Get out there, and don't be a lazy dosser. I'd be more afeared for yer scalp if I were you."

O'Malley stretched out on his bedroll. "We best be getting sleep while we can. I'll relieve you in a few hours."

Tierney threw himself onto his saddlebags. "You keep watch, Billy. We'll sleep. Got it, *boyo*?"

Stung, Billy grabbed his rifle. "I ain't ever let you down yet, have I?" He stalked out of the circle of light toward the perimeter of camp where the horses made whuffling noises.

Too restless to sleep, Neil continued to sketch. He kept his eyes down, off the woman. But Cordelia Cochrane drifted around to his side of the fire.

"What're you drawing?"

He slammed the sketchbook closed. "Nothing." He nudged his chin at the pile of blankets he'd loaned her. "It'll be a long ride tomorrow to reach town."

She eased onto the ground beside him. His mouth went dry, and his heart took up a furious cadence.

"You fought in the war?"

He concentrated on the flickering tongues of the fire.

"I begged Greeley to allow me to report from the battlefield." She tilted her head. "Field dispatches. But he refused. Said it wasn't suitable for a female."

"Not a good place for a man, much less a woman."

Her mouth tightened. "Is that how you see women, Mr. MacBride? As 'much less'?"

Neil frowned. "I did not mean it that way. Women are for cherishing, my da always said. And loving."

Her eyes glinted in the orange glow of the flames. "Men don't need that, too?"

The strange, restless yearning he'd first experienced at the railroad depot last week reemerged. A yearning for what, he wasn't sure. For cherishing and loving? To be cherished and loved?

He clamped his lips together.

"Were you drafted into the Union Army?"

"Drafted because I'm Irish?"

She moistened her lip with her tongue. "I didn't mean it that way. I've got nothing against the Irish. In fact—"

"Born in County Clare, but I'm a New Yorker since the age of five."

Her face brightened. "I'm from New York, too."

"Not from the same New York I'm from, I'd be guessing." He curled his lip. "'The well-fed does not understand the lean.'"

"What?"

"An Irish proverb. Ever been to Hell's Kitchen?"

She shook her head.

"I thought not." By the sound of her refined speech, probably from an uptown enclave of wealth. "And for the record, after my parents died I enlisted in the army. I wasn't drafted."

He'd worked hard to eliminate the telltale Gaelic brogue from his speech. Being Irish wasn't exactly a career builder. He'd learned early only brains and hard work would help him to rise above the stigma of being Irish.

"Like the restaurants in the City say, 'No dogs allowed or Irish.'" He was embarrassed at how the Irish crept back into his speech. "For someone like me, the army was my only chance. So I seized it."

"I understand about seizing chances. The *New York Tribune* has enlightened views regarding female reporters." She made a face. "But book reviews and society teas aside, when Mr. Greeley offered me this opportunity, I took it."

She threw him a look as if laying down a gauntlet. "This story is my chance. For more."

Men, apparently, weren't the only ones born with ambition. He found himself intrigued by this woman like none he'd ever met. Although, he supposed his mam had been as ambitious in her own way.

Ambitious enough to scrub rich men's floors to give Neil a rudimentary education. He'd gone to work in the railroad yards with his da after that. But he'd made it a point to further his book learning when and where he could.

"So you're on your own now."

"I'm not alone." He scanned the sleeping men. "I've got me boys." His brow furrowed. What was it about this woman that brought out the Irish in him?

"My dad was a chaplain in the war, his health wrecked. Neither of my parents lasted a year beyond Appomattox." She stared out into the night. "The transcontinental railroad will be the story of the century. I intend to be there when the Central Pacific and Union Pacific meet." Cordelia took a deep breath and released the air slowly between her lips. "This job is all I have, Mr. MacBride."

Despite his efforts to remain distant, he felt for her. She wore her aloneness like the cloak about her shoulders. Not unlike him, he reckoned.

"It's Neil," he grunted.

A smile lifted the corners of her mouth. "Cordelia. So the army gave you an opportunity? For what?"

"The Homestead Act promised one year off the residency requirement for every year served."

She tilted her head. "I never would've guessed you were a farmer. You seem so..."

"So what?"

He'd survived the conflict with his eyes fixed on acquiring his own land in the West one day.

Cordelia gave him a long look. "You seem the ultimate railroad man. Or a soldier. What did Billy mean about you and General Dodge during the war?"

His cheeks reddened. "That story's been done. I was in the right place at the right time. Anyone would've done the same. Not the big deal the general made of it from the field hospital."

When Dodge discovered Neil had practically grown to manhood in a New York rail yard, he'd immediately given him greater responsibility in the Army of Tennessee. Their mission was to repair and rebuild telegraph lines, railroads, and bridges destroyed by the Confederates.

"It was Dodge who brought you into the Union Pacific?"

Recruited by Dodge himself because of the skills Neil had honed in managing men during the war. "I'm a walking boss."

"What does supervising the laying of track have to do with farming?"

"The war reconnected the North and South..." He weighed his words. "This railroad will bring together the East and the West. Unite this country with an unbreakable ribbon of steel. Opening the way for homesteaders like myself."

"Mind if I quote you?" She scrounged in her skirt pocket and held up a black note-pad. "You have a way with words." She scribbled.

The scowl returned to his features. "The so-called blarney tongue? And no, *Miss* Cochrane, you may not quote me. Feel free to claim it as your own. Leave me out of it."

She tapped the pencil against her cheek. "I'm surprised you're able to swing a pickax, *Mr.* MacBride, with that large boulder you've got riding atop your shoulder."

There was a guffaw of laughter from the darkness. Doolittle sauntered into the light, the rifle cradled in his arms. "She's got your number, truly she does, my fine friend."

Neil leaped to his feet. "You're supposed to be on guard duty."

Billy grinned. "Himself got a heap of medals from his time in the war. Gallantry and valor. Neil here is also a whiz with the 'rithmetic, too."

Neil seized the rifle. "If all you can do is stand here acting the maggot, I'll take point myself."

Billy winked at the other men. "Ruffle your feathers, did she now?"

Neil growled as he headed into the darkness. "Grab some shut-eye, and that's an order."

He'd been given oversight of his often rowdy Irish compatriots who provided the unskilled labor that aimed to bridge the continent by rail. An ambitious undertaking.

But Neil was nothing if not ambitious. Again, something he and the lovely Cordelia Cochrane had in common. Lucky for him, his responsibility for the fair-haired maiden of the West ended when he dropped her off in town. Where he'd tip his cap, bid her good day, and wish her fare-thee-well.

A fond farewell? His stomach churned. Something was happening to him that he didn't rightly understand. He needed to get away from her womanly smells and charming ways before it was too late. If it already wasn't.

◆　◆　◆

Cordelia wasn't above admitting to a fondness for riding in the saddle behind her Irish-American rescuer yesterday.

Yet today she'd been handed off—dumped—onto the saddle in front of the amiable O'Malley on the trail toward town. And she was perturbed. At herself. For wishing her arms still around the hard-muscled waist of Neil MacBride.

No way for a seasoned field reporter to behave. Neil MacBride didn't want to be her friend. And despite her best efforts to convince herself his regard—or lack thereof—didn't matter, truth was it did. And his continuing aloofness not only rankled, but stung.

"I'm not sure what I've done to make him dislike me so."

O'Malley chuckled. "Himself doesn't dislike you, and 'tis telling the truth, I am. On the contrary, you've put the fear of God into our lad there."

She shot a look at the broad shoulders of Neil MacBride, riding ahead with Tierney and Doolittle on either side. A nice view of his back—which was exactly what she'd been receiving from the enigmatic man ever since their talk by the fire last night. As if she were a disease he must avoid. And if not avoid, endure.

"Acting like the hounds of hell were nipping at his heels." O'Malley raised his voice. "Wonder why that be?"

"You can shut your gob, Patrick O'Malley." Neil didn't bother to turn around. "Unless you aim to find new employment."

His pronouncement sent the men, including O'Malley, into a gale of laughter. Neil muttered dire warnings under his breath.

Cordelia leaned forward in the saddle. "Good thing then, Mr. MacBride, you'll see the last of me when we reach town."

"Where you'll no doubt be putting another poor sod's life in danger."

She gritted her teeth. "It's my job to report on the progress of the rail, Mr. MacBride. 'Little as a wren needs, it must gather it.'"

He slowed his horse, coming alongside Cordelia. "What did you say?"

"You aren't the only one who can quote Irish proverbs, Mr. MacBride. My grandmother, I'll have you know, was born and bred in County Kerry."

She'd surprised him.

He chewed the inside of his cheek. "It's nothing personal, but neither the railroad or the folks who build it are the type a lady like you needs to associate with."

"I can take care of myself."

He scowled. Transforming that handsome face of his into something less so. Maybe his face didn't do smiling around her. "Stubborn, hardheaded. . ."

She fluttered her lashes. "Or maybe I just remind you of yourself."

Cordelia straightened her shoulders, letting her hands rest on the reins. "I won't get in your way. In fact, I'll never darken your path again."

"I'll believe that when I see it." His mouth flattened. "We've got a schedule to meet."

She raised her shoulders and let them drop. "Why are you so convinced I'll be disruptive to the deadline?"

"Do you not have eyes in yer head, woman, when you gaze into the mirror?"

"What do you mean?"

He glared at her. "I mean any man in his right mind would rather look at you, 'Delia Cochrane, than work."

Heat ballooned from beneath the collar of her shirtwaist. "Oh."

And she fought the urge to shiver at the way Neil MacBride said her name. The prolonged syllables of ''Delia' plucked across her nerve endings like a bow against the strings of a fiddle.

She swallowed. Or, like a caress across her skin.

Chapter Three

If you do not sow in the spring, you will not reap in the autumn.
IRISH PROVERB

Union Pacific Headquarters
Wyoming Territory

I thought you liked me, General."

Grenville Dodge rolled his tongue in his cheek. "I do like you, Neil. Owe my life to you. Gave you a job—"

"And I've worked hard to prove worthy of your trust in me." Neil clutched his battered army headgear between his hands. "There's no rules at the end of rails, sir. Drunks and murderers. Shootings every day. It's too dangerous for a woman."

"You're the only man among this band of ruffians I dare trust with so delicate an assignment."

Neil kneaded the cap. "I'll take a demotion. Blast rock. Dangle from a precipice. Work the line. Anything, sir, but play nursemaid."

The general steepled his hands on the desk. "Miss Cochrane is here at the express wish of a very powerful New York City editor. A man whose newspaper and favor our boss, Thomas Durant, is keen to court."

"But—"

The general snorted. "I'm not asking *you* to court her, MacBride."

Neil clamped his teeth. Of course not. How ridiculous—an Irishman courting an eastern debutante.

Another thing he'd learned early on—though he'd been an American longer than he ever lived in Ireland—once an Irishman, always an Irishman.

One more reason why he couldn't wait to stake his claim out west, where men were judged on the merit of their deeds and character.

"—just supervise her for the duration."

He'd missed a chunk of the general's directive. "How long is the duration?"

"Until we link with the Central Pacific. You can think of her as your last stop. I'll be back and forth between Washington and here. She's your responsibility."

Neil groaned.

The general waved Neil toward the door. "Don't look so forlorn. You might discover you'll enjoy this mission more than you think. I'm not exactly sending you to the firing squad."

"Feels like it."

Dodge laughed. "She'll certainly smell nicer than the company you're used to keeping. Keep her busy, MacBride, but out of trouble."

Easier said than done.

Neil stalked out of the general's office and down the wooden planks of the boardwalk in the makeshift town. This was not a good idea. For a variety of reasons.

Foremost among them—how the loud-mouthed, brash female muddled his brain. He clamped the cap onto his head, adjusted the brim, and narrowed his eyes. He surveyed the end-of-rails headquarters of the UP for signs of mayhem. Which inevitably accompanied the presence of Miss Cordelia Cochrane.

But there was. . .nothing. And it gnawed at Neil like a rat terrier with a barn mouse.

Neil strode past the gambling houses and saloon. He stepped across the rails to the camp on the opposite side of the tracks from the dance halls. He marched past his own tent—larger than the others as befitted his foreman status—and waded deeper into the rows of white canvas tents.

He figured he'd hear her before he saw her. He did. But not the way he envisioned.

With her long, heavy skirts dragging in the mire, Cordelia struggled to pound a stake into the ground. And she was crying. Soft, inhaled gasps of breath as she attempted to erect her own tent.

Tears ran down her cheeks. She swiped at the moisture with her hand, leaving a streak of mud. She raised the mallet over her head. And lost her balance.

She flailed. He lunged forward, but too late. She cried out, and still clutching the mallet, she fell backward into the muck.

"Delia, what're you doing?"

Her head snapped up. "What does it look like I'm doing, Mr. MacBride?" The familiar defiance sparked, but her eyes were puffy and red-rimmed. "I'm trying to establish my living quarters for the duration."

Neil winced. For the duration. But he much preferred the take-no-prisoners Cordelia to the weepy Cordelia. The one with the attitude stood a fighting chance of surviving this assignment. The other would be mincemeat within hours.

"I can see that."

He sensed she wouldn't respond well to coddling. And he, by nature, was not a coddler. He motioned at her grand, failed endeavor. "Aren't the stringers staying at the hotel?"

Cordelia flushed. "I need to be closer to the story." Her mouth wobbled. "Mr. Greeley hasn't yet forwarded my stipend for living expenses."

"So you're down on your luck."

"I'll recover." Cordelia stuck her nose in the air. "I always do."

Mud splattered the front of what had once been a pristine, white blouse. She might be the most bedraggled creature he'd ever seen. He fought to keep the amusement off his face to save whatever dignity she had left.

"You've got no business camping here among the men. 'Tis not proper."

She glared. "You've got no call telling me what is my business."

"How I wish that were indeed true." He crossed his arms over his chest. "But Dodge has put me on Cordelia Cochrane duty while you write your stories."

"I don't need your help."

He cocked his head. "I can see that."

She muttered something under her breath he reckoned might not be complimentary to his gender.

"Not my idea of a good time, either." He offered his hand. "But like it or not, we're stuck with each other until you go yer way and I go mine and our paths blessedly part."

◆   ◆   ◆

A keeper. The Union Pacific had stuck Cordelia with a company spy. Someone to make sure she didn't embarrass the railroad with the truth. Watching her every move. Restricting her access to the real story.

Her gaze flitted to Neil MacBride's square-cut jaw. They'd stuck her with a handsome keeper, though.

She lifted her chin. "And if I refuse?"

He didn't blink. "Then there's a locomotive headed to Cheyenne for supplies within the hour." He leaned forward, hand extended.

She gritted her teeth. Her eyes darted between his hand and the mud. But she grabbed hold. Bracing, he hauled her with a squelching sound free from the muck.

"Right you are." Hands on his hips, he assessed the situation. "Secondly. . .you're not much safer in the midst of my Irish roughnecks than you were from the Indians."

He scanned her mud-plastered locks to what had been one of her nicest yellow-checked skirts. She blushed. He must think her a complete ninny. And it made her mad that she cared what he thought.

"This is not a good location." His eyes cut left and right. "Too close to the sporting women."

He scowled. "And the men, who haven't seen a lady like yerself in a long while—after a few shots of whiskey—might forget the difference."

She mirrored his stance, her hands on her hips. "Pray tell where you think I should set up camp then, Mr. MacBride."

He gave a long, drawn-out sigh. "I think, in light of our enforced proximity over the next few months, we ought to drop the formalities."

She didn't reply but blew a strand of hair out of her face.

He steered her between the tents toward a larger one. The wooden plaque at the top of the tent flap read Walking Boss.

She jerked. "Next to you?"

"Where I can keep an eye on you." And he smiled. A devastating smile, exposing even, white teeth.

Her heart sped up. She willed it to settle. Who knew her heart could be so treacherous, consorting with the enemy?

"I'll pound the pegs and make short work of it. You'll also need a wooden floor or you'll drown in the mud every time we move quarters—every hundred miles. The buildings and tents are taken down, packed on railroad cars, and shipped to the next stop."

He raised her tent roof and also installed an iron stove whose smokestack poked out of a hole in the canvas top. He moved with efficiency, not unlike one of the steam engines. Leashed strength and power.

Watching him work, she wondered if anything ever caused Neil MacBride to lose control. And what it would take for him to do so.

Later that afternoon, she received her stipend in the post from New York. But instead of relocating to the hotel, she decided she liked her new tent accommodation better. Knee-deep in the action. Knee-deep in mud, too. And an arm's length from Neil MacBride.

Sometime over the next day, his cherished army cap went missing. He didn't say anything, but she realized the loss bothered him. As if he'd lost a part of himself, a link with the past. With winter approaching, she vowed to replace the cap with something more indicative of the man he'd become.

The next morning outside the mercantile, she handed him a Stetson.

His forehead creased. "What's this?"

"It's for you. You need a hat. A new American hat for a new American man. Boss of the Plains."

His expression closed. "You have no business buying me a hat." He thrust the Stetson at her.

Refusing to take it, she laced her hands behind her skirt. "You and your stubborn pride. You're not the only one who dislikes being beholden, Neil MacBride. Consider it payment for services rendered."

Neil smoothed his finger over the wide, stiff brim. "What services?" He turned it round in his hands. Examining the hat from every angle.

He liked it. She could tell. Although he'd never admit as much.

"I'd be drowning in the cold mud if not for you. If nothing else, consider it a gift from one friend to another."

His brow arched. "Friends?"

She pretended to study the display in the storefront window to conceal the pricking of tears behind her eyelids. He made the idea of being friends with her sound so ludicrous.

"Wear it, or if you don't fancy the hat, take it back." Her lower lip quivered. "Your choice."

"I like it fine." His voice deepened. "And us being friends. I just hadn't imagined a lady like you would want..."

His hand, strong and warm, touched her shoulder. "Thank you for the gift, 'Delia."

Neil's touch and the lilting sound of his voice set Cordelia's nerve endings tingling.

"It's been a long time since I received a gift. Especially one as nice as this." He shuffled his feet on the boardwalk. "As nice as the gift of your friendship, truly."

She turned. Hat in his hand, he looked at his boots and then at her.

He positioned the brown Stetson atop his head. "A real American. You think?"

With the tip of her finger, she pushed the hat to a jaunty angle. "'Tis a true western man you are now, Neil MacBride."

His lips quirked at her attempt at the Irish. He ducked his head to gain a glimpse in the window. In the reflection, he grinned at himself and at her. "Let the grand adventure begin."

Cordelia's stomach knotted. She had a feeling that for her, it already had.

Chapter Four

Distant hills always look green.
IRISH PROVERB

Days later from atop her horse, Cordelia watched the men lay track with military precision. Construction boss Jack Casement ran the operation like the brigadier general he'd been once upon a war. Scribbling furiously, she tried to capture onto paper the sheer efficiency of the labor.

Teamsters navigated their carts along the fresh-laid rails. On both sides of the wagons men unloaded the steel rails, moving forward as one to place the steel parallel to the embedded ties. Gaugers ensured the rails were a precise distance apart.

Bolters knelt on the track to join the rails. Spike men dropped the spikes onto the grade. Hammer-wielders positioned the spikes onto the cottonwood ties. With three heavy-hitting strokes, the men drove the spikes into the base to secure the rail into the bed of the track.

And then the dance began again: teamsters, gaugers, bolters, spike men. Over and over.

There was a raw beauty in their movements. In their synchronization, a purpose. Poetry in motion. Rhythm in the pinging clang of the hammers.

She'd become used to the roughness of tent living. Hearing the sound of the rain against the canvas as winter drew nearer. And the *ch. . .ch. . .ch* of the locomotive coming and going to the latest stop at the end of the rail. Despite the rigorous, uncivilized conditions, she found herself exhilarated by the West and this grandest of adventures.

Cordelia turned in the saddle. Neil had been quiet while she transcribed her impressions to paper. Hands folded over the saddle horn, he focused on the men—his men—going about their work.

Pride shone in his features. Passion for their noble task burned in his hazel eyes. Like a lover gazing upon his beloved.

With so many men filling graves across the decimated South, she'd long ago reconciled herself to building her career. To never knowing what it would be like to find comfort in hearth and home.

Cordelia was as passionate about her stories as Neil MacBride about his railroad. Yet he reignited within her—not so much a desire for something else—but a desire for something more. Leaving her wondering if both desires were attainable or inherently incompatible.

As for Neil himself? Could any woman ever hope to compete with such an iron mistress? The pit of her stomach tightened.

She studied his face as the sun beat down upon his broad shoulders. The wind ruffled the short blond tips of his hair underneath the Stetson. Seemingly relaxed in the saddle, his perusal of the emerging railroad was focused, intense, and sharp.

And this was a man who desired above all else to farm wheat? But she couldn't say that to him. They didn't know each other that well. Not yet. . .

She cleared her throat. "How much distance do they gain in a day?"

His gaze cut from the grade to hers. Neil flushed as if he'd been caught indulging himself. He took a breath. "Near two miles on an average day."

One corner of his mouth curved upward. "On an outstanding day when General Jack's got a bee in his bonnet, there be more." His hands twitched on the reins.

His attention returned to the work. As if he couldn't somehow bear one mile of track to be laid without him. As if Doolittle, Tierney, and O'Malley were having all the fun.

She could tell he itched to be on the rail bed with the other men. Doing his job. Being a part of the team. And he would've been, except for her.

"I'm sorry."

He half turned in the saddle. "For what?"

"You'd be doing the work you love and with the men you inspire, if not for me."

His eyes widened. "Me, inspire?"

"Yes, you. Your Irish comrades would lay track wherever you told them. They'd follow you anywhere. Like they did in battle."

Neil scrubbed his hand over his beard stubble. "I led some into an early grave. Which is why once this railroad is done, I'll homestead and watch the wheat grow, that I will."

She gave him a cool, measured look. "Sure you will."

He frowned. "What's that supposed to mean?"

Clicking her tongue against her teeth, she steered her horse to higher ground.

He dug his heels into the sides of his horse and followed. "Where're you going?"

"To the meadow to eat lunch."

"Don't go too far. There's guards posted for a reason." He snagged hold of her horse's bridle. "Figured you'd want the entire experience. Food car and all."

The dining car had arrived, and the walking boss who'd assumed Neil's former position called time. Packed into the train car, the men would be served their daily staple of beef, bread, and coffee.

She wrinkled her nose. "So many men in one place at one time."

A smile flickered in his eyes. "Too big a stench in one place at one time."

"I—I didn't mean to imply. . . It's honest sweat. Nothing to be ashamed of."

Neil laughed. "It's better you don't go. Not a good idea to get between a man and his hard-earned grub. No matter how pretty the face."

He thought her pretty? Perhaps he was being sarcastic. Neil MacBride hadn't appeared bowled over by her feminine charms.

In the big grassy meadow, she swung down. "Don't worry about me. I'll stay here in sight of the guards. You go enjoy lunch with your friends."

His face clouded.

She shooed him away. "I'll be fine. You've earned the break from me." She unbuckled the saddlebag.

He dismounted. He grabbed his own saddlebag and slung it over his shoulder. "It's not that. You—" He took the bulging pack from her.

Bees droned. She wished he'd finish what he'd been about to say.

Instead, he plowed deeper into the blowing fronds of grass. "Where do you want it?"

"Right there." She motioned. "But Neil—"

His face lit at his name on her lips. A muscle ticked in his jaw. Heat flamed in her cheeks. She fingered the brooch pinned to the lace collar of her blouse.

Neil hefted the saddlebag in his hand. "What's in here?"

She removed the rolled horsehair blanket she'd stowed behind the saddle. "Mary-Margaret at the tent eatery packed it for me."

"Ah, the Scots-Irish lass. By way of Tennessee." He smacked his lips. "Fifty cents a meal. You're in for good eating."

Cordelia sniffed. "You'd be the one to know." She billowed the blanket over the grass.

Since Neil assumed over watch of her movements, she'd been careful to observe his, too. He didn't frequent the sporting women at the saloon as did so many of the men. Mary-Margaret Gallagher, however, was a different story.

Of course, ever since the young strawberry blond entrepreneur had pitched her eating establishment, lots of men made sure their feet were under one of her tables come suppertime.

Mouth pursed, Cordelia eased onto the blanket and tucked her skirts around her legs. "I'm sure it's no business of mine." She reached for the saddlebag in his arms.

Neil handed the pack over to her, but he didn't let go. "No man among us would turn away a good plate of stew. But it's John Tierney who's sweet on the girl. He never misses a meal."

Cordelia's eyebrows rose. "Tierney doesn't seem the romantic sort." She tugged at the leather.

Neil held on and held her gaze. "John sits there and stares at her the whole time he's shoveling food into his mouth. Strange what calls the heart of different men, eh, 'Delia?"

Her heart hammered in her chest.

"John's more than you might suppose by looking at him. He watched his entire family die, you see, in the Irish famine. He made his way to America alone. Then the war chewed up what was left of his heart."

"He's your friend."

Neil gave her a slight smile. "I guess he's the best one I have. I'm right pleased he's taken an interest in the scrappy Mary-Margaret. She's brought out something in him I feared lost for good."

"So now he only needs to work up enough courage to actually speak to her."

Neil's gaze traveled from her eyes to her mouth and returned to her eyes. "Exactly."

She believed her heart might stop as he leaned forward. Then he seemed to recollect they both still clutched the saddlebag. He let go and shifted away.

"We're moving out tomorrow. It's not too late to head back to Cheyenne."

"Trying to get rid of me?" she whispered.

◆ ◆ ◆

Neil fought the impulse to touch her hand. That or kiss her lips. Getting rid of her didn't seem the coup he'd anticipated. He had to think of her safety, though.

"It's only going to get harder from here. Brutal. The men will get rougher and coarser as the work and the weather worsen. No place for a lady."

She cocked her head. "I appreciate you thinking of my sensibilities, but like you, I've got a job to do. It's not just the Irish who have something to prove to the rest of the world."

Cordelia removed the lunch items one by one from the pack. "Go enjoy your lunch."

Feeling awkward kneeling beside her, his hands gripped his knees. Maybe he was right where he wanted to be. Where he was meant to be. He eased onto the blanket.

Her eyes flew as swift as a bird's wing to his. "What're you doing?"

"Inviting myself to lunch. 'Tis hungry I am. And what you've got looks better than anything else I've seen."

He pressed his lips together. Of all the thickheaded things to say—he wasn't good with words like Cordelia.

She opened her mouth and closed it. For the first time at a loss for words. A smile played along his lips as he helped her unpack the rest of the vittles.

Her eyebrow quirked. "I thought I annoyed you."

"Only when you're being stubborn and unreasonable." The corner of his mouth lifted. "Which, I concede, is most all the time."

She arranged her skirts. "I can't blame you for preferring Mary-Margaret's lunch over the dining car."

"And the lunch companion who goes with it."

By the sweeping tilt of her lashes, he could tell he'd pleased her. Looking at her pleased him. Food for the soul.

He seized a paper-wrapped sandwich. "May I?"

"Suit yourself." She settled onto the blanket with another sandwich. "I haven't cornered the market on stubborn and unreasonable."

Lying on his side, he stretched out, glad to be out of the saddle. "No, I expect you haven't."

"But it's those very qualities that brought us success in our careers." She took a small bite and chewed.

"The railroad isn't my career. Only a means to acquire the start-up money I need for the farm." He tore off a hunk of the ham sandwich with his teeth.

"Mr. Greeley promised me my choice of assignments after this." Her gaze flew skyward, dreamy. "The finest European capitals, the—"

"What do you want with Europe?" Neil gestured at the rolling expanse. "When you can have this?"

She poked his hat with her finger. "Spoken like the truest American I ever met."

His shoulders drooped. "Spoken by a boy from Ireland."

She shook her head. "A man who's fought and worked hard for everything he's got. I know something about that, too."

"Everything I know, I've taught myself."

"I admire that." She smiled at him. A sweet smile. His heart stuttered. A smile meant just for him? Was he being fanciful? But in her eyes, he caught a glimpse of himself as something other—something more—than he ever imagined he could be.

The day had warmed. Not many golden days like this left in the year. He shrugged out of his jacket and rolled the cuffs of his shirtsleeves over his arms to his elbows.

Forevermore when he pondered Wyoming, he'd remember the smell of sagebrush after a rain. And Cordelia, sitting among the green ocean of the prairie.

"Tell me what you saw today." His voice turned gruff. "What will you write in that eastern newspaper of yours?"

Drawing her legs up, she rested her chin on her knees. "A story about what I see?"

Her brown calico skirt brushed against the tops of the prairie grass. Small, yellow curls framed her face into a perfect oval. A meadowlark trilled.

Unable to trust himself to speak, he nodded. And as she described what she labeled a symphony of movement, he drank in the light in her eyes. Her face became animated, passionate about what she loved. Words.

She'd somehow managed in those words to capture the beauty of the prairie, the courage of the men, and the audacity of the entire venture.

A venture to which they both belonged. Joined in a fundamental and totally unexpected way, he, the Irish orphan, with this sophisticated eastern woman. Everything else fell away from him.

The hiss of the steam engine faded. The jocularity of the crew on their lunch respite muted. The wind sighing among the grass went silent.

He was amazed at how well she understood him. How well they understood each other. And he wondered what it would feel like to be the object of her passion.

To be loved by a woman like her. His pulse leaped. Not only a woman like her, but by Cordelia herself.

As she spoke aloud her thoughts, he sketched her likeness. In an effort to capture this moment. Until she ran out of words. Until there no longer existed between them a need for words.

Peace enveloped their prairie island. Her arms clasped around her skirts, Cordelia closed her eyes. And something long incomplete and aching within him righted.

At the clang of the bell on the dining car, her eyes flew open. He laid his pencil down. And the sounds of the outside world intruded once more.

The clang of steel on steel. This hiss of escaping steam. The soothing *ch. . .ch. . .ch* of the locomotive.

"What do you draw, Neil?"

He flipped the sketchpad closed. "Whatever is beautiful. Whatever is true. Whatever is lovely." He rose and offered his hand.

Cordelia's slim fingers caught his hand. Her cool palm lay against his. And yet her touch ignited a quivering sensation within him. Like an iridescent dragonfly flitting against his skin.

She tilted her head. "Philippians. My father was a minister before he became a chaplain in the war."

He found it hard to breathe with Cordelia so distractingly near. "Time to get back to work."

"I'm sorry to be keeping you from yours."

He didn't let go of her hand. "There are compensations I hadn't foreseen."

She stood so close he could've kissed her if he dared. He fought against a sudden lump in his throat. But a poor Irish boy had no business thinking such thoughts about a lady like herself.

"Like lunch?"

He needed to move away. If only to give himself the chance to draw a steady breath. "And your stories." With reluctance, he let go of her hand. "Among other things."

Chapter Five

It takes time to build castles.
IRISH PROVERB

March, 1869
Utah Territory

Neil lost count of how many times he'd relocated Cordelia's tent as the westward trek of the rails moved ever onward.

Something had changed within him since their meadow lunch. He felt as if he grasped at the shadow of his dreams. As the dream of golden waves of wheat—sustaining him through the hardship and terror of war—slipped inexorably from him.

Neil and Cordelia spent a lot of time talking about their past, the present, and their dreams for the future while January snowstorms blanketed Wyoming. A cold wave swept the plains. Gravy and butter froze on the plate.

In February, the worst storm in living memory shut down ninety miles of line. The graders worked in layered overcoats. At times, the UP crew was reduced to making the grade by blasting the frozen ground with black powder.

Later, Neil regretted sharing so much of himself with Cordelia. He'd resolved to keep his thoughts and his words contained and as controlled as his horse, Mulligan. Yet inevitably Cordelia had a way of drawing Neil out of himself.

As the weather slowly cleared, they resumed their forays to the end of the track. The surveyors had completed their job and disbanded.

He chafed with inaction on the days she remained behind the line to interview the end-of-rail residents. As often as not, he suspected she invented reasons to visit the grade so he could be within sight of his men.

The latest obstacle had stopped forward momentum in its tracks. Literally, as the men were confronted with blasting through a mountain. The crew was frustrated.

Cordelia wrote out loud, "The UP's hitherto rapid progress has been more about the open flatness of the plains and less about its much-touted superiority over the CP."

She rested her notepad against the saddle horn.

"You're going to write that?" On horseback, Neil glanced over at what she'd written. "About the UP?"

"It's the truth. Crews are still tunneling through Number Three. Only building the runaround tracks from Echo to Weber Canyon allowed you to get a start on Tunnel Number Four. You've simply rolled the hoop—or the tunnel as it were—down the track to tackle at a later date."

"What about the Thousand Mile Tree?" He jutted his chin in the direction of the ninety-foot giant on the ridge. "One thousand miles of track from Omaha to that tree."

"The Central Pacific has surmounted much harder terrain over the mighty Sierra

Nevada. A triumph of modern engineering."

He scowled. "The point of the race was about which railroad tracks the most miles."

"And here I believed the point was to connect both sides of the continent." She fluttered her lashes at him. "Silly me."

"Truer words, Cordelia Cochrane. . ." He gripped his horse's reins. "O'Malley! Get yourself over here."

O'Malley straightened from working the grade. "Meself?" He pointed to his chest.

"Today would be grand if you can manage it," Neil growled.

Ambling over in no great hurry, O'Malley tipped the peak of his cap to her. "A top of the mornin' to you, Miss Cochrane. How be you?"

"I'm doing well. How about you, Mr. O'Malley?"

"He's fine," Neil answered before O'Malley could. "Doing a decent hard day's labor, which is what I should be doing instead of lollygagging with a know-it-all—"

O'Malley had the nerve to laugh.

Neil jabbed his finger at the man. "You and me are going to do a prisoner exchange, Pat."

Cordelia leaned forward. "Prisoners?"

"A swap. Exchange his freedom for my incarceration for a few hours."

She bristled. "Are you suggesting I've been holding you captive, Mr. MacBride?"

Neil swung his horse toward the direction of the tunnel. "Let's call it time off for good behavior, shall we?"

He gritted his teeth. "I have a burning need to smash rocks." He nudged Mulligan into a trot. He didn't bother to turn around.

◆ ◆ ◆

Cordelia rammed her notepad and pencil inside the saddlebag. "Of all the mule-headed. . ."

O'Malley sighed, not unlike a long-suffering saint before the lions.

"If you've got something to say, Patrick O'Malley, then I suggest you say it."

"You've managed to get under the boss's skin, Miss Cochrane. I've not seen him as rattled under an enemy barrage. What did you do now?"

"I merely observed the Central Pacific appeared to be winning the race in terms of actual accomplishment, notwithstanding the UP's greater mileage."

O'Malley's goatee quivered. "That woulda done it. Our Neil's a mite sensitive about his railroad."

She squared her shoulders. "Heaven help the woman stupid enough to ever try and come between that man and a locomotive."

O'Malley laughed outright. "I reckon that's exactly what you did. And put the poor lad in full retreat."

Without Neil's company, the sunshine lost its glory.

"I'd just as soon head to town, Mr. O'Malley, if it's all the same to you."

She was in her tent when the first rumble shook the ground. The lantern hanging from the pitched roofline swayed. She'd been working at her desk on an article.

O'Malley had not drifted far. He warmed his hands over the fire in the barrel outside her tent. Where he could also keep an eye out for her.

At the second thunderous blast, she rushed outside. "What's happening?"

129

"It reminds me of cannon fire, but—" O'Malley scanned the Wasatch Range where the crew worked the tunnel. "The men were thinking on using that newfangled nitro stuff."

She pressed her fist into her mouth. Why had she goaded Neil? What if he was hurt? "Who else is with Neil?"

"Tierney." O'Malley gulped hard. "Our young lad Doolittle, too."

She caught hold of O'Malley's coat. "What should we do?"

He disengaged from her stranglehold. "I and the rest of the men will be taking the engine as far as we dare to see what we can find. Someone here should help the doc prepare the medical tent for casualties."

"I can do that."

He patted her hand. "And if ye've a mind, girl, I'd pray for yer man and the rest of them."

Tears stung her eyes. "I will."

Despite the rapid beating of her heart as she waited with the railroad doctor for survivors, she realized Neil was far from being her man.

When the engine returned bearing the wounded, she and the doctor were joined in the rail yard by the sporting women.

And Mary-Margaret Gallagher. Who wrung her hands in the folds of her apron at the sight of the men on the flatcar—some bloody, some burned. "John!" she shouted and rushed forward.

The almost unrecognizable man batted away her hands with a fierce scowl. His bushy beard was peppered with small bits of rock. "I couldna get to Neil or the lad. I have to go back. . ."

Cordelia scrutinized the men being helped off the railcar. Where was Neil? *God, please let him be alive.*

Neil and the men were so skilled it was easy to lose sight of the danger. Until today.

Those still mobile crawled off the flatcar. Their clothes tattered and covered in grime, it was difficult to identify them. She followed the doctor's lead and moved from man to man.

She spotted a tall, lean man staggering across the track, his hair coated brown with dirt. "Neil!"

His head snapped up at the sound of her voice. His eyes blazed, the green more pronounced than usual against his blackened face. From a jagged gash in his bicep, blood saturated his ripped shirtsleeve.

In his arms, he carried a slight figure. She picked up her skirts and ran toward him. Billy Doolittle's head lolled.

Neil thrust the boy at her. "Promise me you'll care for him. Stay with him."

She sagged under Billy's weight. "I'll take care of him, I promise. But you—"

"I couldna save his da." Neil tottered. "But I have to—I must save him." His eyes shut.

O'Malley took the boy. In time for Cordelia to grab hold of Neil as he slumped, unconscious.

Hours later, she'd set a camp stool between their two cots. Neither had regained consciousness. Perhaps best with the doctor stitching the wound on Neil's arm. And

Billy. . .? Cordelia felt an unaccustomed protectiveness over the boy.

Not far away, as fierce as a Tennessee wildcat, Mary-Margaret guarded Tierney's bedside. Despite cuts and abrasions, he appeared largely unharmed.

"The nitro worked fine, but a portion of the excavated ceiling collapsed."

"Hush yourself, John Tierney." Mary-Margaret pushed him onto the pillow, and Tierney did as she bid him. Mild as porridge in her hands.

"What did Neil mean about not saving Billy's da, Patrick?"

Billy moaned. The cot creaked as he stirred, yet without waking.

O'Malley exchanged glances with Tierney. "The boy's da fought alongside us."

The older man looked older than his years. "When the General was wounded, Neil managed to get him and the rest of us out of that fix while Doolittle's father held off the gray backs at Pea Ridge."

"And died giving us time to get away." Tierney's eyes burned with unshed tears. "Saving our lives." Mary-Margaret squeezed his hand.

"Billy's da—not me—is the real hero."

Neil tried sitting up and flinched. She eased him down. "Not so fast."

"Billy? Is he alive?"

"The doctor says we have to wait for Billy to awake from the blow to his head he sustained in the tunnel."

She pressed a dipper of water to Neil's mouth.

He drank as if he'd never get enough, but eventually leaned back. "I didn't take you for the nursing kind."

"I told you I'd stay with Billy." She lifted her chin. "I'm a woman of my word."

A tired smile played across his mouth. "You and yer words."

He closed his eyes and drifted away, but into a more peaceful sleep this time. She found herself straightening the sheet, touching his hand, unable to resist brushing the shock of sandy hair fallen across his brow.

What in the world, God, do You want me to do about this Irishman? She sighed. *I'm supposed to go to Paris.*

O'Malley held Neil's battered Stetson in his work-roughened hands. "I found his hat when I pulled him from the rubble. He's not going to be pleased to see it so dirty."

A hat seemed the least of Neil's worries.

O'Malley sighed. "Neil will want this hat when he gets out of that bed."

Bending over Billy's cot, she sponged his face with a cloth.

O'Malley caught her gaze. "When Neil enlisted, he exchanged the derby his da gave him for an army cap. Now, he likes wearing this western hat you gave him. He likes it was you who gave it to him."

She sank onto the stool again. "I'm sensing you're referring to something more than headgear."

"Aye," O'Malley nodded. "This venture has caused us to look at ourselves differently. To look at the world differently."

"You're referring to a man's identity."

O'Malley smiled. "A smart lass, you are. Smart as my friend Neil. Billy's the only one among us actually American-born. He found us after the war ended. He had nowhere else to go."

"And you? Didn't you have somewhere else to go?"

The smile he gave her this time was sad. "Lost my family in the influenza that swept the tenement while I marched through Georgia. I reckon these boys are my job to finish raising. To make sure they're settled, happy, and prosperous. Until then—" He shrugged.

But she knew what he meant. After following the end of the rail, she saw herself differently. Visualized her place in the world differently. Paris differently?

O'Malley shoved Neil's rucksack over to her. "Figure you might find something there of interest, Miss Cochrane. Seeing as how you're such a truth searcher."

Rubbing his callused hand over his bristly goatee, O'Malley shuffled to his feet. "Reckon I'll get me some shut-eye since both my lads are well attended. After I give a good brushing to Neil's hat. Send for me if anything changes."

She rummaged through Neil's pack, and her hand fell upon the sketch pad. Laying it on her lap, she paused. Should she look at Neil's private thoughts? But O'Malley obviously believed she should.

Her breath hitched as she raised the cover to find an intricate rendering of herself. Beneath Neil's talented hand, her face had come to life. He'd somehow managed to capture not only the curve of her jaw and the lift of her cheeks, but that indefinable something in her eyes, too.

In every line and stroke, Neil revealed more than perhaps he intended. Her stomach fluttered. Could a man such as he draw a woman and not have feelings for her?

"You weren't meant to see that."

At Neil's gruff voice, she flipped the sketch pad closed. "I think you made me more than I am. I'm only a reporter."

"I draw what I see. Whatever is beautiful. True and lovely. You're beautiful."

She blushed. "I wish I could draw like you. To be able to show you what I see. You're more than what you give yourself credit for being."

He reached for the sketch pad. "You draw with your words." She handed it to him.

Neil tore the paper with a ripping sound from the pad. He handed her the page. "So you won't forget who you are."

"Will you forget me, Neil?"

As soon as she said the words, she longed to take them back. What on earth had possessed her bold tongue to say such a thing to him?

"No, Cordelia. I will not."

She dropped her eyes and smoothed the page across her apron. "I will always cherish this gift from you. I will always—" She swallowed.

"Cordelia," he whispered. "When the tunnel crashed around us, it was you who flashed through my mind. You with your eyes like prairie bluebells. I want you to know that—"

With a cry, Billy's eyes flew open. "Da? Boss?"

Neil reached across Cordelia for the boy. "It's me, Billy." Flinching from the wound on his arm, Neil sat up and seized Billy's hand. "Easy there, son. It's Neil."

Placing the portrait on the ground, she dropped to her knees beside the cot. "How are you feeling?"

Billy winced. "I'm okay. 'Cept my head hurts."

Neil grunted. Moisture welled in his eyes. "Thanks be to God for that hardheaded Irish skull of yours."

Her mouth pursed. "He's not the only one."

She'd nearly lost him. Lost them both. *Thank You, God, for saving them. Thank You.* No time for weepiness though, when Billy tried to sit up.

Cordelia put a hand on his chest. "Where do you think you're going?"

Billy frowned. "Back to work. I ain't no dosser. Railroad won't build itself, right, Boss?"

Neil exhaled. "You're no dosser, *boyo*. But my advice is to enjoy the lady's tender ministrations while you can."

Billy grimaced, but plopped onto the pillow. "You taking your own advice then?"

Neil leaned back onto his cot. "Why not? I was told once men need cherishing, too."

The unspoken "loving" hung between them.

His gaze flickered. "Unless you wish to be rid of me so soon?"

The way he looked at her then. . . Her pulse accelerated. She didn't wish to be rid of Neil MacBride at all. Not ever.

She rose and took the drawing from underneath the bed where she'd stashed it for safekeeping. "Both of you need to rest."

Neil's hand caught her arm, his fingers curled around her wrist. "You're leaving?" He frowned.

Cordelia bit her lip. "I need to change out of this dress. But I'll return in a few minutes. I promise."

She wanted to weep. She wanted to shout for joy. She wanted to—she didn't know what she wanted to do. Maybe dance.

But she needed a few moments to herself. To marshal her thoughts. To explore these overwhelming feelings inside herself. And preserve Neil's gift to her between the pages of her Bible.

With a tired smile, he let her go. Billy's eyes had closed. But his breathing was steady and easy.

She moved toward the tent opening and angled to find Neil's gaze fixed upon her. With a small flutter of her fingers, she stepped outside and headed toward her tent.

What would Neil have said to her if Billy hadn't awakened when he did?

Could Neil MacBride truly love someone like her? A woman with no practical skills? She feared she'd make a poor farmer's wife.

Yet she, who'd always been so independent, found her happiness and subsequent well-being irrevocably hitched to his. It was both frightening and exhilarating. Because she loved him.

For his grin. For his strength of character. For his adventuresome spirit. For everything that made Neil MacBride the man he was.

Paris? London? Suddenly, neither the Thames nor the Seine held the same appeal they'd possessed a few months ago.

When she looked at him, she saw blue-sky days and prairie. Not an easy life, but a good one. A future rich with love.

To be cherished by such a man. . . Loved. It took Cordelia's breath. Filled her with an indescribable yearning. And hope.

A hope for a life she'd never before allowed herself to dream. But dreams changed. It would prove no hardship to exchange one dream for a better one.

There'd be new skills to learn. New adventures. Although different adventures than what she'd imagined.

And she was pondering how to be a homesteader's wife—how to kill a chicken, how to make candles and soap—when the telegram from Mr. Greeley arrived.

Chapter Six

The only cure for love is marriage.
IRISH PROVERB

Last Stop, Corinne
Utah Territory

Weeks later, Neil nudged the brim of his Stetson. The lovely gift from Cordelia in Wyoming. Good as new, thanks to O'Malley.

Neil reckoned he was a mite ridiculous over the hat. And protective. But the hat reminded him of that perfect time in the meadow with Cordelia.

With the resilience of youth, Billy recovered quickly from his head injury. Neil reassigned Billy to the teamsters to manage the horses. Billy protested being separated from his mates. But being close to the horses soon stilled his grumbling.

They'd arrived at what would probably be the last end-of-rails town. The CP and UP had negotiated an agreement as to where the rails would link. For weeks, the two railroad crews lay track within sight of each other in parallel grades. It'd be a race to the finish.

But to Neil's growing discomfort, he realized his time with Cordelia was also drawing to a close. And over the last few weeks, she'd become distant. Too quiet.

With a troubled look in her eyes, she'd stop midsentence to gaze over the hills. Was Cordelia already separating herself and preparing him for their inevitable good-bye?

Only two weeks old, end-of-rails town Corinne already boasted five hundred frame and tent dwellings. A blacksmith, livery, sawmill, a bank, opera house, and a newspaper office from which the members of the press telegraphed their articles eastward. One last time the gaming houses and soiled doves also followed the rails.

It was merely a matter of waiting for the work train to catch up with the progress of the tracklayers. He and the men could nearly taste the final victory. They'd worked in driving rain and through snowstorms. Enduring high winds and scorching heat. In the burning sun, none complained. They kept at the backbreaking work.

Every day. All day. His tireless Irishmen.

The weather had turned. Turned as lovely as Cordelia herself. The mud was drying fast. The grading camps were thirty miles west of Corinne now.

A continuous line of tents, wagons, mules, and men from there to here. And a farther twenty miles west were the blasting crews jarring the earth with glycerine. Hurling the limestone hundreds of feet into the air. Scattering rock in every direction.

Try as he might, he couldn't imagine Cordelia keeping house in a prairie dugout. Although, the image of the intrepid reporter collecting cow patties for fuel brought a smile to his face.

Other pictures swept his mind. Cordelia and him sharing a life under the big sky of the Nebraska Territory. His child—their child—one day rounding Cordelia's belly.

But the lady reporter weeding a garden patch? His imagination failed as he contemplated her sure and quiet misery. An unhappiness that would destroy them both.

Neil was ready at last to admit it. The truth he could no longer deny. He loved Cordelia Cochrane.

He loved the way she smiled. He loved how her eyes crinkled when she laughed. He loved her intelligence. He even loved—which showed how far gone he was—her independent, fist-in-your-face spirit.

But loving her brought Neil only increasing confusion. About his own place in the world. Who he was and who he'd yet become. He could never hope to offer Cordelia the kind of life and future she deserved.

In a few short weeks, this grand adventure would end. She would return to New York—on the tracks Neil had laid—to pursue her career. And from New York, she'd sail for Europe.

He'd be free finally to stake a claim on a tract of land and build a life. But a life without Cordelia. An empty life. And he wrestled with an equally tough question.

After all these years of chasing the rail, would farming satisfy Neil in the way he'd believed? Was farming how God wanted him to spend his life? Or was that a wrongly placed yearning for a permanence only found in God Himself?

The more he thought about waving rows of golden wheat, the more restless he felt. He stared across the desert flats to the west. He'd come so far—from across the sea.

Across the grassy plains. Tunneling through mountains the likes of which he'd never have foretold. But something drove him to yet see the other side.

Surely he'd already had more adventure than one life could hold. More than his fair share.

He sensed there was more. He wanted more for himself. Further adventures awaited him, he was almost sure of it.

Almost. . . How selfish and greedy to want more when he'd been allowed to be a vital part of the grandest race in history. Suddenly, farming wheat the rest of his livelong days held no appeal.

But what else could a poor man born in Ireland do?

And like so many times over the last few days, Neil found himself on his knees pouring out his heart, his doubts—and beyond words, the longings he didn't rightly know how to express. Into the safekeeping of the One who'd always loved him the most.

Loved him on a ship from Ireland. In the Irish tenement in New York City. On a war-scarred battlefield. In the midst of brutal conditions, implacable enemies, and the herculean task of bridging a continent.

For now, Neil could only finish what he'd begun with the UP and his Irish brothers. And wait in faith for what the Lord would have him do next.

But loving Cordelia while waiting on God's direction was proving for Neil the most challenging task of all.

Chapter Seven

"Done."
END OF RAIL CORRESPONDENT C. COCHRANE

May 10, 1869
Promontory Summit, Utah Territory

Cordelia glanced around at the dry, flat basin surrounded on three sides by the mountains. Hung on a telegraph pole, an American flag flapped in the morning breeze.

In a cloud of steam, a UP construction train unloaded tracklayers and graders. As the train chugged away again, O'Malley grinned at her and Doolittle waved. Even Tierney appeared cheerful. A visceral anticipation hummed among the onlookers and workers.

She scanned the crowd for Neil. His gaze caught hers for a moment before he turned away and said something to O'Malley.

Cordelia fought the sense of disappointment. She reminded herself she had a job to do. As did Neil. Business must come before the celebration.

With a small smile, she tapped her pencil against her chin. The town of Corinne had organized an End of Race dance this evening. And she planned to dazzle Neil MacBride with the one fine dress she'd brought from New York.

Thinking about waltzing across a dance floor with the handsome walking boss set her pulse aflutter again.

"Stick to business, Cordelia," she whispered.

The UP train, carrying Durant, Dodge, and the Casement brothers, arrived. She wove in and out of the gathering of men and women, trying to capture the sense of pride and accomplishment.

What all of them—Irish, freedmen, and the Chinese from the CP—had accomplished together. As Americans. A new breed of Americans, forged by the fires of war, a new beginning for a growing nation—

"Oh, that's good." She scribbled on her notepad before she lost the phrase.

"You and yer words, 'Delia Cochrane."

A warm flush mounted from beneath the lace-fringed collar of her gray-checked gingham. But she kept her gaze on the paper, finishing her thought. Or trying to. Neil's proximity did funny things to her nerve endings.

Her attention was snared by a group of Chinamen with their long black braids who prepared the track for the last railroad tie.

Neil sighed. "Sure and it's the last rail. The last tie."

"Except for the ceremonial spike."

"It's been a grand endeavor, has it not?"

Her eyes cut to him at his wistful tone. "I imagined you'd be more jubilant. Finally, you can lay claim to that homestead."

Neil shuffled his feet, but the CP train with Stanford and other dignitaries rolled into view. The two iron horses—CP's Jupiter and the UP's Number 119—were uncoupled. Both engines were brought to facing positions across the gap in the track. Soldiers lined the grade on both sides. The railroad officials shook hands.

"Ladies and gentleman, may I have your attention, please?" Ever the consummate showman, Durant pontificated on the perils and triumphs the Union Pacific had experienced in reaching this great American milestone.

Not to be outdone, Leland Stanford of the CP spoke of "a riveting example of American ingenuity."

Durant scowled. "A feat of American engineering. . ."

Cordelia rolled her eyes. Neil muffled a laugh with his hand. Dodge and Stanford verbally wrangled over to which railroad belonged the honor of driving the last spike.

Neil leaned close to her ear. "Rivals to the end. Like us?"

"I'd like to think we're more than rivals."

She waited for him to say something more, but his gaze jerked to the ceremony playing out before them. She quelled a rising disquiet. His mind was fixed on finishing the job. And rightly so. Heartfelt declarations would have to wait for the evening.

Cordelia resolved to tell him of her feelings for him. And of the wrenching decision she'd made after hours spent on her knees in prayer. Europe and a future without Neil MacBride had lost its appeal.

She slipped her hand in Neil's. At last, the culminating event of a moment long in the making.

Neil squeezed her fingers. "We need to talk later."

She swallowed. "A telegram came a few weeks ago. Greeley's pleased and surprised by my growing readership. He's offered me my choice of European assignments."

Neil's eyes widened. "Oh. . . I best be congratulating you."

Despite his words, he didn't seem overly pleased. Maybe like her he didn't relish an ocean and a continent between them? But he didn't elaborate.

She bit the inside of her cheek.

Then Stanford brought the silver-headed sledgehammer down toward the golden spike—and missed. Jeers arose. Durant missed, too.

She let loose of Neil's hand to capture the mishap on paper.

Neil scrubbed his hand over his face. "God preserve us from the fancy pants of the world."

"Still believe women don't deserve the vote?"

"You think the fairer gender could do better?"

She gestured toward the grandstand. "There'd be nowhere to go but up."

He laughed.

Finally, the spike was hammered in. Afterward, Cordelia was never quite sure by whom. In their eagerness, the spectators had pressed forward, blocking her view of the actual moment. Nonetheless, she wrote "Done" with a flourish on her notepad.

The engines' whistles shrieked. Telegraph operators sent the message across the vast expanse of the continent. Amidst loud cheering, hats were thrown into the air.

Not Neil's, she noticed with amusement. Not the precious symbol of his Americanism.

The ceremonial spikes were replaced with more functional ones. The locomotives eased forward until they touched.

"Enough with the dandies," called Doolittle. And he led a surge of workmen—CP and UP—onto the steam engines.

As O'Malley climbed aboard, he motioned for Neil. "Come on, *boyo*. This honor belongs to you, too."

She gave Neil a nudge. "Go on. You've earned it."

With a wide grin, he strode toward the engine where he clambered aboard between a freedman and a Chinaman. The engineers of both railroads shook hands.

And it was done. Elation filled Cordelia as she dotted the last *i* and crossed the last *t* on her notepad. A transcontinental journey that had also changed her life.

The last story she'd write for the *Tribune*. Perhaps the last story she'd ever write for publication—if this evening ended as she hoped between her and Neil. And she was at peace about this fork on the track of her life.

She'd fulfilled her mission here, and she trusted God had a bigger purpose for her future. Better than even she with her vaulting imagination could envision.

Perched atop the steam engine with a Chinaman's arm draped around his shoulder, Neil looked younger.

Happier than she'd ever seen him. More at ease with himself, the past and the present. His gaze shifted west. Toward the horizon. Toward the future and bright possibilities.

At that moment, all things seemed possible. And the future beckoned, shiny and new. Like gifts waiting to be unwrapped beneath the branches of an evergreen tree.

◆ ◆ ◆

What now?

Neil scanned the sea of faces thronging both sides of the track. What was next for any of them? United in purpose these last four years, as divided they'd been in the previous four.

He had an uncomfortable inkling he'd just participated in the most significant endeavor of his lifetime. And it was over. As the speeches droned on, the great American army of men began to melt away.

Cordelia pantomimed to him. Lifting her notepad and pointing to what could be the story of the century. He nodded. He'd meet her back in Corinne.

To say their final good-byes? His heart pounded. His discontent grew as the festivities erupted around him.

What was wrong with him? He wasn't sure what to do about his feelings for Cordelia. He knew what he wanted to do, but—

"MacBride!"

He jolted as Grenville Dodge clamped a hand on his shoulder. "Yes, sir?"

"I was hoping to have a quick word."

"Of course, sir. I wanted to thank you for allowing me an opportunity to learn about railroading."

Dodge's face split into a grin. "You've more than earned the chance I gave you. You've a quick mind, mastering everything from surveying to the laying of track. You'll make a fine engineer, Neil."

"I'm not an engineer like you. I don't have your schooling."

"You've been an apt pupil to every task I've set before you over the last four years. You've proven yourself a gifted leader of men." The general's eyes narrowed. "And if you'd allow me one more request, I'd like for you to consider making the railroad your career."

"I don't understand."

"Other railroads need to be built. If we truly aim to connect the country, to link Santa Fe, Kansas, and elsewhere to this shining ribbon of iron."

"You're offering me a permanent job with the UP?"

Dodge shrugged. "Don't think so small. The UP's not the only railway. There's managerial issues here I won't trouble you with. I don't reckon to be long in these parts myself."

Neil crossed his arms over his chest. "Then what are you proposing, sir?"

Dodge's steely gaze met his. "I'm proposing you make your life's work transforming this nation of ours into the industrial giant it can be." He leaned forward. "This will be the age of the railroad. And it is a far-thinking man who hitches himself to this worthy endeavor."

Something pulsed in Neil's veins. And he recognized this excitement as the purpose he'd unconsciously been waiting for over the last few days.

A new adventure. New tracks to lay. New horizons to conquer. A new sense of purpose and direction.

"What about my crew? We've come a long way together from Pea Ridge."

"There's always room for good men. What do you say, MacBride?" Dodge stuck out his hand. "Stick with me. And wherever the rails take us, you'll be an assistant engineer before you can blink." Dodge laughed. "The sky's the limit, Neil. You could have my job one day."

Neil's heart hammered. Chief engineer of a railroad? Was that possible for an immigrant from Ireland?

His breath quickened as he surveyed the majestic Rockies in the distance. The height of which they—he'd—spanned. Perhaps in America, anything was possible.

Is this what You want me to do, Lord?

But he couldn't ask a woman like Cordelia to wander the earth and follow the rails. Nor follow a plow. Neither was the life she deserved.

"What do you say, Neil?"

Dodge waited for his reply, his hand still extended. Neil had no time to pray as he ought, to weigh his decision. *God? What say You? Help me, please.*

A sudden rightness filled his being as birdsong floated across the sagebrush basin. His nerve endings quivered. If he said yes, what then could he say to Cordelia?

But the love of the railroading life and the lure of the track wouldn't leave him alone.

"I'd be most honored, sir, to join this undertaking. Thank you."

Yet as he shook the general's hand, his stomach knotted. He understood what he could never say to Cordelia. And what tonight he must.

Good-bye.

Chapter Eight

*". . .these are the men who won the war to abolish slavery
and built a railroad across a wilderness."*
END-OF-RAILS CORRESPONDENT C. COCHRANE

Gazing at her reflection in the looking glass hanging from the tent pole, Cordelia did a slow turn. She studied the effect of the willow-green silk on her complexion. Her skirts swirled with a satisfying swish.

She touched the elaborate chignon at the nape of her neck. And fingered the lace décolletage of the off-the-shoulder evening dress.

Would Neil like her dress? She'd always relied more on her brains than beauty. But tonight she hoped—oh how she hoped—whatever small amount of beauty the Lord had gifted her with Neil would admire.

She'd never felt about anyone like she felt about Neil MacBride. He was the smartest man she'd ever met. Driven, ambitious, restless. They were a pair, the two of them. How she hoped Neil thought so, too.

From the other side of camp, she heard the discordant strains of a fiddle. Taking a deep breath for courage, she stepped through the flap of her tent. Neil's tent lay dark.

She frowned. Since arriving in Corinne, she'd seen little of him until today as the days wound down toward the completion of the railroad. Toward the finish line of the great adventure that had—for a moment in time—linked all Americans.

Cordelia trembled, and not from the cool air of the spring evening. Had he been avoiding her? Or busy with last-minute details?

After today's ceremony, the work was complete. There could be no more excuses. No more hiding, if that was indeed what he'd been doing these last feverish days.

It was time to acknowledge what existed between them. She bit her lip. Or mourn what did not. Would he dance with her tonight under the stars? Would he speak words of love?

Hiking the hem of her skirt, she picked her way among the army of tents. The men called greetings as she passed—respectful greetings. Otherwise they'd answer to Neil, Tierney, O'Malley, and Doolittle, too.

Crossing the track, she reached the boardwalk and continued to the open-air pavilion the townspeople had erected to celebrate this momentous occasion. An occasion that would signal the death knell of tiny, upstart Corinne, Utah. Like so many other end-of-rail towns, tonight was the beginning of the end.

Would the same hold true for her and Neil?

In the meadow, wooden planks had been placed for dancing. On the perimeter, tables were laden with delicacies from Mary-Margaret's eatery. On a raised dais, musicians plucked desultory tunes.

Yet the gathering had a surreal quality. The merriment forced. As if all these months they'd been pretending. As if tomorrow marked the return to their real lives.

Cordelia shook her head. She hadn't been pretending. She felt more real, more alive, than she ever felt in New York City.

Railroad executives and their bejeweled wives mingled with the others who'd followed the rails to the joining of the track. As couples waltzed, the women's skirts sashayed in a rainbow of color. Lanterns aglow, light flooded the pavilion. Pushing back the darkness as surely as the railroad had pushed away the wilderness.

She scoured the crowd for the one man who set her heart aquiver. But he was nowhere to be found. Disappointment sank like a lead weight in her stomach.

There were also no freedmen or Irish present, either. Except for Mary-Margaret behind one of the food tables. There to serve in what, Cordelia guessed, was her finest pink-sprigged gingham.

And then, Tierney slipped into the circle of light from the darkness beyond. He had eyes only for Mary-Margaret. He whispered something in her ear.

He twined his fingers in hers and pulled her away. The night swallowed them. As if they'd never been.

Cordelia gave a quick, indrawn gasp. Her heart hammered. Gone. Finished. Done.

She clenched her gloved hands at her side. She wasn't ready to be done. She and Neil—they couldn't be finished with each other. Not yet. Where was he?

Cordelia became aware of another pool of light in the distance. She tilted her head at other, fainter strains of music. From another celebration across the tracks.

Gathering her skirts, she followed the sound of the fiddles. And ran—after her dreams—toward the rails turned quicksilver by moonlight.

◆　◆　◆

His back to the glowing bonfire, nevertheless Neil knew the very moment Cordelia entered the circle of light. He pivoted.

She skidded to a stop. She panted as if out of breath. Her eyes darted around the merry band of revelers.

Panicked, stricken, fearful—until her gaze latched on to his. She took a jagged gulp of air to slow her breathing. Fiery, orange flames danced between them.

He told himself to stay away. To leave her be. But he could no more stay away from her than his lungs not draw breath.

She was like oxygen to him. Heady, necessary. He'd starved himself of her for the last few weeks.

Distancing himself. Trying to prepare for when they went their separate ways. Steeling himself against the certainty of pain at her loss.

And despite what he knew he must do, his traitorous feet followed his treacherous heart. He found himself at her elbow.

She gave him that cool, elegant look of hers. Her pulse quivered at the beautiful hollow of her throat. But he made no move to touch her or to speak.

Neil concentrated on committing to memory every beloved feature of her face. The crinkled coil of curls wound onto the back of her hair, burnished to a golden sheen by the fire. The curve of her smooth porcelain cheek. The rosy hue of her mouth. The dress—his breath hitched—like the misty green haze of a soft Irish morning.

He swallowed. "'A handsome woman is easily dressed.'"

A smile licked her lips, but at the sudden intensifying of bow on string, they both turned. The three fiddlers began a fast-paced jig. Boots stomping, they gyrated to the crescendoing beat.

"I didn't see you at the dance."

He trained his eyes on the fiddlers, sawing at the strings. "This is more to my liking. But I would've come looking for you."

It was true. He would have, if she hadn't shown up here when she did.

Her foot tapped to the lively tune. He smiled as her skirts swayed. "There's something in the music that calls to the blood, does it not?"

She gave him a look out of the corner of her eye. "The one-quarter Irish in me, you mean?"

He took her hand in his. "It calls to something in the lifeblood in each of us."

Tierney stepped into the light and began to dance the jig. Neil laughed as Cordelia's jaw dropped. Tierney's brown boots were quick and hard upon the earth.

Arms at his side, faster and faster he danced. The crowd clapped to the pulsing rhythm. The fiddlers accelerated the jig. Tierney kept pace.

Cordelia's eyes were huge. "John Tierney dances like that?"

"A man of many layers. And when he is filled with joy—" Neil took a deep breath. "Like every Irishman, he must dance."

Eyes shining, Tierney extended his hand to Mary-Margaret. Tossing her hair over her shoulder, the girl took his hand, stuck out the heel of her button shoe and stepped out in time with Tierney.

Move for move, jig for jig—matching, at times besting—giving as good as she got. Laughter bubbled from her lips. Her green eyes sparkling, she held her skirt free of her feet. Until gasping for breath, John gave her a gentlemanly bow to the delight of the crowd.

Whereupon the fiddlers—giving themselves no respite—changed with a sliding twang into another fast-paced Irish jig. Other couples joined Tierney and his wild Tennessee rose.

"Come on." Neil pulled her forward. "Your turn."

Both her hands in his, he swung Cordelia around. Her skirts flew, her hair tumbled out of its elaborate bun, and she laughed. Laughed as carefree and lighthearted as he'd ever seen Cordelia Cochrane. He knew because he felt the same.

Round and round. The other dancers and the bonfire blurred. The night faded away till there was only Cordelia and him.

He stopped. Abruptly, irrevocably. Her momentum carried Cordelia a few paces beyond till she, too, stopped. Her brow puckered.

Above the roar of the music, someone shouted, "To Ireland!" Cups were lifted.

He raised his hand for their attention. "And to America." Equally loud cheers.

Cordelia nodded. "America built by all Americans."

He took hold of her arm. "I'd better walk you back. It's going to get only more maudlin from here on out."

Sure as he'd spoken, already the jugs were being passed from hand to hand. "This is not the place for you."

"And you think I belong in the pavilion?"

"Where we belong is something we can only decide for ourselves."

She glared at him. "I don't want to go to the pavilion."

He gave an exasperated sigh. "Sometimes the road is already set, Cordelia. We don't all have a choice."

"This is America. . ."

"Yes." He cocked his head. "So it is. And I've decided to stay with the railroad. Not farm."

"What about us?"

Silence ticked between them.

Her chest rose and fell as she waited for him to answer. But what, in the end, could he say? What could he offer her but a life that would cost her everything she'd dreamed of?

"Neil?" Her tone sharpened. "Answer me."

"There. . ." He cleared his throat and tried again. "There is no us, Cordelia."

She took an inadvertent step backward as if from the force of a physical blow.

He wanted to throw his arms around her, but he kept his hands clamped to his side. Dodge had given him the opportunity of a lifetime. Neil could not—would not—deny Cordelia's chance to make her own dreams come true.

She set off without waiting for him. Oil lamps within set the canvas walls aglow and lighted their path. He had to jog to catch her.

Just outside the closed flap of her tent, she whirled. Stamped her foot. "This is good-bye?"

"I don't think there's much for either of us to say."

Eyebrows rising, she stood on tiptoe, getting into his face. "I think you're just scared. A lily-livered chicken."

She cocked her head. "I don't believe you. I think you do care for me." She lifted her chin. "Love me even."

He clenched his teeth together so tightly his jaw ached. "Don't make me spell it out for you, Cordelia. I don't want to hurt you."

She jabbed her finger into his vest. "I don't hear you denying you love me."

"Why does everything with you have to dissolve into a war of words?"

She cupped her hand around the back of his neck and drew his head to hers till only inches separated their faces. Her sweet breath brushed across his cheek. The scent of lavender wafted across his senses.

His heart thumped in his chest. "What are you doing, woman?"

"Prove you don't love me, Neil."

He gritted his teeth. "Sure, and how would you have me do that? By kissing you?"

"Call it a good-bye kiss, if it makes you feel better. I dare you to show me just how much you don't care. If you can." Her eyes taunted him.

This maddening, unreasonable, hardheaded woman—he seized both her shoulders, crushing the puffy fabric beneath his hands.

She smiled at him then. She'd won, and she knew it. Her mouth moved closer.

"Kiss me, Neil. . . . Kiss me." Her lips parted.

Something curled in his belly. He wouldn't be beguiled by this slip of a woman into changing his mind about what he knew to be best for the both of them. But with her mouth so close, he surrendered his good sense.

He knew he shouldn't. It would prove nothing but prolong the pain. But he couldn't stand this close to her for one last time and not—

Neil kissed her. For all he was worth. And she kissed him back. Her arms reaching around his neck, she knocked off his hat.

With her in his arms, he felt—No. This was never going to work. He thrust Cordelia from him.

She shook from head to toe. "Guess you showed me."

His own hand shook as he bent to retrieve his hat from the ground. "I proved nothing, except I'm a man of my word. I say what I mean, and I mean what I say."

She balled her fist and punched him in the chest. He staggered.

"I reckon"—he swallowed—"I deserve that. I wish you the best in your new life. And I hope Europe is everything you've dreamed, Cordelia."

Her face hardened. "So what will your Irish brothers do after you go build your next railroad?"

"Billy will go with me. O'Malley's got the urge to try California. Tierney. . ." He shot a look over his shoulder past the tents to the ceilidh where the fiddlers had struck up a lament in some minor key.

A dirge. And he thought it fitting. This was the end of everything.

"Tierney's hitching his wagon to Mary-Margaret, who's got a hankering to open an eatery in Cheyenne. I 'spect they'll be married afore the week's out." When Cordelia looked at him that way, Neil's heart lost a beat.

Like she was waiting for him to say something. But nothing he could say would change who they were born to be. Nor the lives they were destined to live, separately.

"Which city will you choose? London or Paris?"

"Does it matter?"

His lips still burned with the remembered feel of hers. "No, I suppose it doesn't. But we'll be doing what the good Lord meant us to be doing."

"Will we, Neil?" She glanced at him over her shoulder. "I wonder."

"'It is a long road that has no turning.'"

Tears stung her eyes. "But don't you see, 'two shorten the road'?"

"Good-bye, Cordelia."

Something sad flickered in her eyes, like the last rays of the sun before dying away to night. Beyond words, she went into the tent. Leaving Neil standing alone and uncertain, assailed by doubt.

With their parting, she'd torn his heart from his chest. Taking it forever with her. Leaving Neil with an aching throb in the empty space she'd left behind.

Chapter Nine

A tune is more lasting than the song of the birds.
And a word more lasting than the wealth of the world.
IRISH PROVERB

The train chugged away from the station. Taking with it, Cordelia. And his heart. Neil's gut tightened. In the end, his passion for rails and her passion for words had driven them apart.

"You're really gonna let the lass go? Just like that?"

He turned toward O'Malley. "It's for the best."

"Best for who?" Billy frowned. "Cordelia luvs you. I know she does. Did you tell her you luv her, Neil?"

Neil clenched his hands. "Doesn't matter."

"Are you daft, man?" Tierney growled. "Love's the only thing that matters, you thick-headed Irish oaf. Not iron track or newspapers."

O'Malley hooked his thumb into his belt loop. "Maybe Neil's not as smart as we gave him credit for being."

"To let a fine woman like her ride out of here. . ." Billy gestured.

O'Malley poked out his lips. "Steel will prove a cold bedfellow, *boyo.*"

Neil resettled his hat on his head. "It's too late." He gulped past the boulder lodged in his throat. "Nothing matters now."

O'Malley squeezed Neil's shoulder. "Why didn't you ask her to stay?"

"I'll be living out of a boxcar. What kind of a life would that be for a woman like Cordelia?"

Tierney spat at the ground. "Did you ever once think to ask Cordelia what she wanted? Did it ever occur to you she might want to be wherever you are. No matter where you are."

Billy nodded. "Our Cordelia's a plucky one. Spirited enough for three women." He gave a low whistle. "Would to God someday a woman looks at me the way she looks at you." The boy scrunched his face. "I don't reckon I'd let her get too far from me."

Neil shook his head. "Marriage, a home. Family. That's not what Cordelia wants. She wants adventure. And I'm only a railroad man."

O'Malley stroked his whiskers. "Speaking as the only one among you with any matrimonial experience, I feel it my duty to inform you, young MacBride, marriage *is* the ultimate adventure." His brown eyes glistened. "A journey not to be missed no matter its length."

Neil's stomach knotted. "You think she'd want me?"

Tierney shoved him toward Mulligan hitched to the railing. "Only one way to find out."

"But she's gone." Neil's shoulders slumped. "I've lost her for good."

"Saints and angels preserve us!" Tierney grunted. "Do I have to do everything myself? Get yerself on that horse and ride after her, MacBride."

"The train? I'll never—I can't—"

"Can't is a coward too lazy to try." Tierney glowered.

O'Malley cocked his head. "That's no Irish proverb I've ever heard."

Tierney's gaze roved toward the Gallagher tent eatery. "Scots-Irish, in fact." A grin split his bearded face. "By way of Tennessee."

"You think there's a chance?" Neil's heart pounded. "The train. . .it'll slow on the approach around the lake."

"Now you're thinking." Tierney clapped Neil on the back, nearly sending him sprawling into the street.

"And if me Mary-Margaret doesn't give you the finest wedding supper Corinne, Utah's ever seen, then I'll be wanting to know the reason why."

Billy jutted his chin. "Bring back our girl."

Clamping his Stetson on his head, Neil untied Mulligan and swung into the saddle. He prayed he wasn't already too late. Clicking his tongue, he and Mulligan dashed the length of Main, churning dust in their wake.

Once outside town, he veered off the road. If he cut across the hills, he stood a chance—a real chance—of stopping her.

Hunched over Mulligan, Neil gritted his teeth. A chance was all he needed. A chance was all the opportunity he'd ever needed.

Neil urged Mulligan into a full-fledged, no-holds-barred gallop. Toward his dream. Toward a life of shimmering beauty like blue skies above prairie grass. Toward a future he never imagined possible for someone like him and someone like her.

Keeping one hand atop his hat and the other clutching the reins, he raced across the windswept terrain. Sides heaving, froth between Mulligan's teeth sprayed Neil. But lifting out of the saddle, he sank his boot heels into the stirrups.

He gave Mulligan his head. Eyes fixed straight ahead, Neil spotted puffs of smoke, coiling like a gray snake, above the black locomotive hurtling toward the incline.

"Help me, Lord, catch the train," he breathed as the wind whistled past. "Help me say the words Cordelia needs to hear so we can be together."

◆　◆　◆

At the collective gasp inside the railcar, Cordelia raised her gaze and caught a blur of motion outside the window. Something chestnut red and fast, drawing parallel to the engine car. Mulligan?

Her mouth fell open, and like the other passengers she leaped to her feet in the swaying passenger car. Her eyes widened. She pressed her nose to the glass.

Waving his hat, Neil shouted at the conductor. Leaning out, the conductor motioned Neil away. But Neil never slackened speed.

A gust of wind sent the Stetson roiling over the open plain like tumbleweed, but Neil and Mulligan kept pace with the locomotive. Pulling ahead in one fluid motion, he spurred Mulligan onto the bed of the track. Directly into the path of the train.

What was the man doing? Had he lost his mind? She pounded the window with her fist.

The conductor blew a warning whistle. Mulligan reared. She put a hand to her throat. Neil almost toppled from the saddle, but he held on.

She envisioned Neil's body crushed beneath flashing hooves and the steel track. "Please, God, no."

Neil regained control of the horse. The conductor braked.

Gravel flew beneath the spinning wheels. She grabbed hold of the seat and braced. The other passengers fell against each other. "What's happening? Who's that man?"

She throttled the bench as if by sheer force of will she could halt the train. The brakes screeched.

The locomotive slowed. Jerking, the fiery iron beast hissed and slid along the rails. Grinding forward, pulled onward by its own momentum. Finally, the train shuddered to a belching stop mere yards from where Neil sat atop his horse.

She'd come to the dance last night prepared to give up London and Paris for him. For a life together. But he'd not given her the chance. He'd not asked her to be a part of his life.

Raw fury gripped Cordelia. She marched down the aisle past railroad executives, past overturned hat boxes, past startled fellow members of the press. She stalked onto the portico between the engine and passenger car.

"Neil MacBride!" She shook her fist in the air. "I've got a few choice words to say to you."

Steering Mulligan off the track, he brought the horse around to her. "I've got a few words I'd like to say to you, too."

Cordelia planted her gloved hands on her hips. "You are the most. . . The most. . ." She felt like spitting railroad ties.

She quivered from the top of her straw bonnet—askew thanks to this crazy man's antics—to her black-booted feet. "Are you daft? Have you lost what little mind I suspect you possess? What in the name of—"

"I love you, Cordelia."

"What?"

"I love you. Perhaps from the first moment you walloped me after I rescued that Indian from you." His Adam's apple bobbed. "Which probably means I'm more damaged from the war than I suspected."

She stared at him. "You love me?"

A muscle ticked in his handsome jaw. Both hands locked on the saddle horn, he grimaced. "This went better in my head."

She grasped the railing. "You love me so much you kissed me good-bye last night and then let me get on this train?"

"I'm slow, but eventually I get there, Cordelia."

She snorted. Most unladylike. But right now, she didn't feel very ladylike. Not after the long, sleepless night she'd endured.

"I made a terrible mistake. I'm so sorry."

"So what changed between the middle of nowhere and last stop, Corinne?"

"Here's the thing, 'Delia. . ."

She steeled herself against the beguiling Irish charm Neil MacBride used with such good effect.

His hazel eyes drifted over the rugged desert landscape. "Dodge knew me better than

I knew myself. There was no last stop, Corinne for me."

Neil's eyes cut to hers and locked. "For me, it's always been last stop, Cordelia. Not the railroad. You. And if you'll have me, I'd be honored to carry your notebooks across London or Paris or wherever the story takes you."

Her heartbeat quickened. "You're asking me to marry you?"

Neil sucked in his cheeks. "Of course, I'd be asking you to marry me. A lady such as yourself, what else would I be doing, pray tell?" His gaze dropped to the ground. "Marriage to me, if that's what you're wanting."

She became aware of a dozen figures crowding the side of the passenger car. Heads leaned out of every window. Listening to every word.

"Do you mind?" She scowled at them. "This is a private conversation."

No one moved. "Give the lad a chance. He seems sincere. He said he was sorry."

She narrowed her eyes at them and then at Neil. "I'd tell you what a sincere something he is, but my mother taught me not to use words like that."

Neil's hair ruffled in the breeze, flopping over his forehead. "So it's no then? As a woman who makes her living with words, is that your last word for me?"

And in his eyes. . .a deep sorrow. Aching uncertainty. Longing. His expression dulled. Hope extinguished.

Neil blew out a measured breath between his lips—lips that had kissed her so wondrously only yesterday. "You're right. Not sure how we'd have ever made this work between two people as different as you and me."

His gaze darted to the passengers hanging out of the windows. "Sorry to have inconvenienced everyone." He turned Mulligan. "I best be finding my hat."

Tears stung her eyes. This wasn't right. This wasn't what she wanted. It was her pride. Her stupid, abominable pride would cause her to lose everything she loved more than life itself.

She clambered down the steps and seized hold of Mulligan's bridle. "Wait. Don't go. Please." His essence tugged at her heart, filled her senses. "I love you, Neil MacBride. I do. Oh, how I do."

"Delia. . ." Neil's chest heaved. "You'll either be the death or the life of me yet. Why didn't you say that to start with?"

"I love you, Neil." She hung on to the bridle, half-afraid she'd lose him yet. "We're far more alike than we're different. We both have itchy feet, that so very American characteristic."

He swung out of the saddle and closed the distance between them. He cradled her against him. He twined his finger around a wisp of her hair.

"Kiss 'er," someone yelled.

She rested her forehead against the broadcloth of his brown vest. "And because I love you and you love me"—her head snapped up—"you love me, right?"

"That is the verra truth. Will you marry me so we can get the story you're hankering after in Paris?"

How right it felt to be in his arms. "The only thing I'm hankering after is a life with you. I'll not be asking you to leave your blessed steam engines, Neil MacBride."

A slow, lazy smile quirked one corner of his mouth. "Have I told you, woman, how I luv it when you speak the Irish to me?" Her insides melted.

"And we will find a way." She tilted her head. "A place where we can be together. Where both our dreams can meet. Like the place where the tracks crisscross each other."

"'The feet will always lead you to where your heart is.'" His arms tightened around her. "The rails will forever lead me home to you, Cordelia."

"Kiss her already, why don't you, man?"

She lifted her face to his. "Yes, please. Why don't you?"

And then at last, he did.

Epilogue

"There is no fireside like your own fireside."
C. Cochrane MacBride

Fort Worth, 1877
Texas and Pacific Railroad

Cordelia laid her pen alongside Mary-Margaret's letter, postmarked Wyoming.

In addition to running her fine eating establishment, Mary-Margaret had her very capable hands full in the raising of her five boys. Born in as many years, like stairsteps. His Irish sons of thunder, John called them. Cordelia smiled. That they were.

She glanced at the watch fob pinned to her shirtwaist. Time to be done with work for the day. Her gaze wandered to the framed sketch pad portrait of herself hanging on the wall. Smiling at the memory, she tucked another letter—from Patrick O'Malley—into its envelope. Her husband would be pleased to hear from his dear friend.

With the completion of the transcontinental, Patrick believed his life and purpose were over. But then he'd met and married a California-bound widow, marooned in her broken-down Conestoga. Happy and prosperous, he was now busy raising cattle and three courting-age stepdaughters on a ranch near Sacramento. Patrick O'Malley had his hands full, too.

As for Billy? Cordelia's eyes watered. The boy—become man—would always have a special place in her heart. Her husband had worked for half a dozen railroads since leaving Corinne, Utah. And Billy Doolittle followed their family from one end-of-rail town to the next.

But in Santa Fe, he left them to follow his own dream. He hired onto the *rancho* of a Spanish family who'd bred horses on the land bordering Mexico since before the United States existed. And there Billy struck gold of a different sort. Not only did he gain the respect of the *don*, but also the hand of the don's pretty daughter.

"Hide, brother. Quick!"

Seven-year-old Annie shoved her brother behind the railcar drapes.

Cordelia's five-year-old son glared. "You're not the boss of me. Stop telling me what to—"

"Hush now, Billy Doolittle MacBride." Annie laid her finger against her lips. "Do you wish to spoil Da's surprise?"

Little Billy scowled. "You're not the boss of me, Annie Margaret MacBride."

Cordelia shuffled the papers on her desk into a stack. "Not so bossy, Annie. More flies with honey, remember?"

Imperious *and* bossy Annie placed her hands on her small hips. "And what of the baby?"

While Cordelia worked on her latest dispatch for the *New York Tribune*, the baby had played on the carpet at her feet. Wherever the rails took them, Cordelia created a home for her precious family. And met her deadlines as she chronicled the ongoing saga of the age of the locomotive for her weekly column.

Omaha, Denver, Topeka. Their current home in Fort Worth, as construction on this particular project neared completion. With every move, her husband rose through the ranks from assistant engineer to superintendent of construction to general agent. There was talk he'd make general manager before long. Cordelia scooped up her baby and set the child upon her lap.

"He's coming!" Sandy-blond Annie dashed for the sofa. "Hurry! Hide!" She threw herself, petticoats and all, over the settee.

Cordelia cut her eyes to the window. With long strides, he headed for the train car they called home. Even after eight years of marriage, pleasurable swirls fluttered in her chest at the sight of him. The same work Stetson on his head. Broad-shouldered and coatless, his shirtsleeves rolled to his elbows.

The children giggled as his boots sounded upon the railcar steps. The door creaked as the hinges swung wide. Removing his hat, he ducked his head as he crossed the threshold inside. His gaze lifted.

Catching sight of Cordelia with the baby, his face lit. His hazel eyes warmed. He gave her that crooked half smile, meant only for her.

With a rush of tenderness, she answered him with a smile just for him. And he crossed the distance separating them. This was her favorite time of day. When Neil returned home every night to her and their children.

Annie popped up from behind the sofa. "Surprise, Da!"

Billy flung himself from behind the curtain. "Happy birthday, Da!" The child clasped his arms around Neil's knees.

Neil winked at Cordelia. "Is it my birthday, you say?"

The Irish in his tongue thickened with her and the children.

Annie launched herself over the sofa and rolled to her feet. "Happy, happy birthday, Da."

Cordelia sighed. "How many times do I have to tell you, Annie? Ladies don't behave like—"

"Apples never fall far from trees." Neil caught the girl around the waist. "And American ladies, so I've been repeatedly told, can do and be anything they wish to do and be."

He grinned at Cordelia. "Especially when the lass reminds me so much of someone else I've luved ever so long."

She sniffed, but her mouth curved into a smile. With Katie on her hip, she came around the desk.

Neil kissed the top of the baby's copper-colored head. "And how's my wee one this fine evening?"

Squirming, Katie reached for her da. Neil took the baby into his arms, and Katie hugged him close.

He twined a strand of Katie's hair around his finger. "Such luvly Irish hair, don't you think, 'Delia?" He quirked an eyebrow.

She wrapped her arms around the baby. "Our Katie is yet another reason why I love all things Irish." With the children hanging on to Neil, together they made one big circle of love.

Annie tugged on Neil's shirt. "There's presents, Da."

Billy smacked his lips. "And cake."

"My, my." Neil's eyes gleamed. "Am I not the most fortunate of men?"

Cordelia cupped his cheek in her palm. "Truer words. . ."

He brushed his lips across her hand. "'Empty and cold is the house without a woman.'"

She fingered his collar. "'It is a lonely washing that has no man's shirt in it.'"

His brow furrowed. "My old friend, Dodge, has asked for my help with a new endeavor on which he's consulting."

She gave his shoulder a playful pat. "And where would the track be taking us this time, Neil MacBride?"

His eyes crinkled. "Have I told you how I like it when you speak the Irish to me, woman?"

Neil nuzzled her nose with his. "The Russians are trying to build their own transcontinental railroad. Think Siberia would be too cold for an American like you?" His face sobered. "But if you've no desire to go, I'll not accept the offer. What say you? We can always return to Omaha."

To build a house on the magnificent wooded lot they'd purchased. But she had a feeling—knowing her husband as she did—like her, he'd always want to be in the thick of the fray.

Hands-on with the work to be done. Wherever the work took him. Because she and Neil shared that most American of characteristics, the urge to wander.

"Of course we'll go. Where's your spirit of adventure?" She fingered his chin. "It's about time you took me to Europe."

"You're sure?"

"It'll give me a chance to interview the czar."

"Heaven help the Russian empire." Neil set Katie onto the carpet. "Take the baby and bring out the gifts, Annie my luv. After dinner, I'll tell you how I once rescued the Sioux Nation from certain extinction."

Cordelia's lips twitched.

Billy tugged at Neil's shirttail. "Don't forget the cake."

"Cake, too." Neil wrapped his big, strong arms around Cordelia. "But first, I must kiss my wife."

Annie took Katie's hand and with Billy ambled toward another room in the rear of the railway car.

"Kiss 'er, Da," called Billy, trailing after his big sister.

Katie toddled after her siblings. "Kiss. . .kiss."

"It doesn't matter where we are, Neil." She tucked her head into the curve of his neck. "Only that we are together. Always."

His breath brushed across the wispy tendrils of hair framing her face. "Always."

Lisa Carter and her family make their home in North Carolina. In addition to writing historical novellas, she is the author of seven romantic suspense novels and a contemporary Coast Guard romantic series. When she isn't writing, Lisa enjoys traveling to romantic locales, teaching writing workshops, and researching her next exotic adventure. She has strong opinions on barbecue and ACC basketball. She loves to hear from readers, and you can connect with Lisa at www.lisacarterauthor.com.

Train to Eden

by Ramona K. Cecil

Dedication

To Mary Jane Smith, a wonderful friend and beautiful lady,
who loved my stories and left us too soon.

Chapter One

July, 1895 Indiana

I should inform the conductor that he has a thief on his train."

At the man's syrupy voice, Anne jerked around in her seat. Her pulse raced, sending her heart vaulting to her throat. *He can't know. There is no way he could know.* Could the bank have dispatched a Pinkerton agent this quickly? Dismissing the thought, she gripped her beaded reticule in her lap and willed her voice to a cool calmness that belied the tumult raging in her chest. "I'm sure I have no notion what you mean, sir."

"Why, you have completely stolen my heart, Miss. . ." He allowed the last word to dangle with expectation and plucked his black bowler hat from his head, sending a strong whiff of lanoline hair oil cascading to her nose.

Anne ignored the man's attempt to obtain her name and injected as icy a tone in her voice as she could manage. The last thing she needed was another inquisitive fellow passenger trying to ferret out her identity. "If I have, I assure you it was entirely unintended." She glanced toward the train car's open door, wishing she had joined her seatmate, Mrs. O'Reilly, who had taken advantage of the fifteen-minute stop at the water station to grab a bite to eat at the depot restaurant.

"Elmer Trowbridge, at your service." He offered her his hand. When Anne declined to take it, he cleared his throat and reached into his gray houndstooth jacket and pulled out a small card, which he handed her. "Salesman extraordinaire of the Dangler Stove and Manufacturing Company of Cleveland, Ohio." He winked and leaned a shoulder against a brass stanchion pole. "I was top salesman last year and am well on my way to repeat this year. So when your mother returns to the train, be sure to give her my card. The telephone number of my company is printed there."

Anne was about to tell him that Mrs. O'Reilly was not her mother when the conductor's voice from outside the train car bellowed, "Aaall Aboooard!"

To Anne's relief, passengers began to file into the car, forcing the ardent stove salesman to sway one way and another to avoid the stream of humanity amid a flurry of voices murmuring "Excuse me, sir. Excuse me, please."

Anne's middle-aged seatmate was less polite. "Would you kindly get out of my road, sir, and allow me to sit?" The rotund Mrs. O'Reilly shoved her way past Mr. Trowbridge and sank into the seat beside Anne with a huff.

"I was just telling your daughter—"

"I have no daughter." The older woman glared at the salesman. "Now be off with ya!" She flourished her ever-present black parasol in a menacing manner, sending Anne's would-be suitor to his seat on the other side of the car, then turned a concerned face to Anne. "Was that feller pesterin' ya, dear? Like I told ya before we stopped, a young lass like yourself, travelin' alone, can't be too careful. Trains are full of thieves, miscreants, and sly-tongued liars."

Warmth suffused Anne's face. What would the good Mrs. O'Reilly think if she knew that some of her descriptions fit her seatmate?

The train began to roll again, and Anne leaned back in her seat and closed her eyes, finally allowing herself to relax. If she pretended to sleep, perhaps she could evade the older woman's prying questions until they reached Union Station at Indianapolis, Mrs. O'Reilly's destination. The farther away from Buffalo Anne could get with the least amount of conversation, the safer she would feel.

Thankfully, Mrs. O'Reilly took up the mundane, rhetorical chatter about her grand-children in Indianapolis that she had engaged in since embarking the train car in Ohio. A faint clicking sound told Anne that her seatmate had resumed her earlier work knitting a pair of mittens for her grandson. Between the gentle rocking of the car, the hypnotic clicking of the wheels along the track, and the softer *click, click* of the knitting needles, Anne soon dozed off.

A sharp jolt yanked her from her nap. Her eyes flew open at the sensation of the train car rocking wildly from side to side. What was happening? A distant rumbling built to a sickening crescendo of scraping and crumpling metal. The car began tumbling, and she grasped the seat in front of her in a desperate attempt to stay upright. There was no longer a distinct floor, ceiling, or sidewalls to the compartment.

Luggage, reticules, shoes…bodies all swirled together as if in a fierce cyclone, pelting Anne with painful, relentless blows. Her screams joined in a panicked chorus with those of her fellow passengers.

God help me! Please help us! Help us all! If she wasn't so terrified, the disjointed prayer screaming from her frantic mind might have surprised her. But the thought seemed to come of its own volition. Would the tumbling never stop? *God, please make it stop!* The answer to her prayer came with a grinding shudder and an angry jerk that shot her forward. Her forehead smacked against something hard. A burst of white light accompanied the searing pain in her head before darkness engulfed her.

◆ ◆ ◆

As if from a long distance away, the clanging of bells and the sound of many shouting voices gradually penetrated her foggy brain. She reached up to wipe wetness from her face, then brought her hand away covered with blood. Screams and moans filled the air around her. Where was she? What had just happened?

Panic gripped her chest like a giant vise. She needed to get out of whatever this place was. She needed to get away.

To her left, she could make out a small rectangle of metal framed by shards of glass. Light. Blessed daylight streamed through the hole. She poked her head through it. Was the opening big enough to crawl through? She had to try. She had to get away from this terrible place. The jagged protrusions clutched at her clothes, ripping her dress, her arms, her legs. Ignoring the pain, she squeezed through the tiny aperture. All that mattered was finding a way out of this dim, confined space filled with hellish confusion. Gritting her teeth, she clutched at the weeds and grass in front of her and finally managed to squeeze her body through the opening.

At last she was in the tall grass. She was free. Despite the trembling of her body, she somehow managed to stand. The grass felt cool to her stocking feet. She had no shoes. What had happened to her shoes? She couldn't remember. Moisture trickled down her head and into her eyes. She touched her head and winced at the pain, then looked at her hand. Red. She was bleeding. An overwhelming desire to leave the confusion and mayhem behind gripped her.

Across the meadow, several yards in front of her, a line of trees beckoned. She headed toward it.

◆　◆　◆

A rumbling that resembled distant thunder halted John Weston's progression down the cows' pens. He glanced out the open doors at the end of the barn but couldn't make out so much as one fluffy white cloud in the faded blue summer sky.

Setting the bag of crushed corn on the barn's straw-strewn dirt floor, he cocked his head and listened. The only sound that met his ears was the bawling of the cows still waiting to be fed.

"Roy had better not be dynamiting stumps again." He picked up the sack of corn and poured a measure into the next stall's trough. Hopefully he wouldn't have to confront his neighbor again about the man's method of stump removal, which scared the cows and cut down on milk production.

John gazed down the line of cows, many with calves, and a sense of satisfaction filled his chest. "Uncle Phil would have approved." The sentiment didn't surprise him, but saying it aloud did. Two years ago he'd thought any meaningful life had ended for him. Working on Uncle Phil and Aunt Clara's dairy farm had felt like a comedown after losing his position as sergeant on the Indianapolis police force.

"John, John!" His young cousin, Matt, raced into the barn, his sixteen-year-old voice cracking with excitement. "Train wreck! There's been a train wreck on the Big Four Line just west of Fortville!"

John plunked the bucket of feed on the barn floor, his reflexive instinct to rush to an emergency perked. "I'd better head over there and see if I can help. You finish feeding the cows."

"Aw, John, I want to go, too." Matt's eyes turned hopeful, like a pup begging for a treat. "Four extra hands are better than two. I won't get in the way, I promise."

"I don't know, Matt. You might see things you'd rather not see—things that could be hard to get out of your head."

Matt's chin lifted in a defiant tilt. "I'm not a baby. Uncle Phil was my age when he went off to fight in the war."

John grinned, unable to think of a reasonable rebuttal to Matt's logic. "All right, if your grandma has no objection, you can come."

"Yippee!" Matt turned and sprinted toward the house, leaving John to hope he wouldn't regret his decision.

A few minutes later, the two jostled along the country road in the buckboard, heading north toward the railroad tracks.

"Hurry up. You're drivin' like we're on our Sunday drive to church." Frustration filled Matt's voice as he leaned forward with his hands on his bouncing knees. "The volunteer fire fellers'll have all the work done before we ever get there, and there'll be nothin' to see."

"I doubt that." John couldn't keep the cynical tone from his voice. "Besides, I thought you wanted to come to help, not because of what you might see."

As they rounded a curve, a movement some yards ahead to their right caught John's eye. At first he thought it might be a small animal preparing to dart into the road in front of them until the disheveled figure of a woman appeared from the tree-lined berm. Her face and tattered gray dress were streaked with blood. She turned and looked directly at their approaching wagon, but her dazed expression suggested that her mind wasn't registering what she saw.

"Whoa!" John pulled the wagon to a stop and handed the reins to Matt. "Stay here." He threw the order over his shoulder as he jumped to the ground. The instincts he'd honed as a policemen kicked in as he strode toward the injured woman—likely a victim of the train wreck.

"Were you in the train accident?" He hurried to close the distance between them.

She didn't answer, but proceeded to stumble down the weeded incline that banked the road. John quickened his pace. The way she swayed with each step, he was amazed that she'd stayed upright this long, and he expected her to fall in a heap at any moment. Now on the road, she stopped and gave him a puzzled look, like she'd never seen a person before. Dried blood matted her reddish-blond hair above her forehead. Her blank stare suggested confusion brought on by shock. She took a teetering step toward him and mouthed something he couldn't hear.

The instant he reached out and grasped her waist she collapsed into his arms. He lifted her up and noticed she was wearing no shoes, only torn and bloodstained white stockings. She looked up at him with huge terror-filled blue eyes that clawed at his heart. Her lips—full, perfectly shaped lips—were trying to form words devoid of sound. Finally, he managed to make out the smallest whisper of "Help me. Help." Then her eyes closed and her head lolled against his chest.

Fear shot through John like an electric shock. He could be witnessing this woman's last moments on earth. *Please, Lord, don't let her die in my arms.* "Don't worry. I'll help you. You're going to be all right." Though he had no idea if she could hear him, saying the words aloud cemented John's resolve to make them come true. "Matt, take the reins!" he hollered as he carried the woman to the back of the buckboard.

"Is she from the train wreck?" Matt's jaw hung slack, his eyes widening.

"I presume so." John laid the woman in the wagon bed, then climbed in beside her.

"Is—is she dead?" Matt's voice turned breathless as he pivoted on the buckboard's seat to peer at the injured woman.

John was glad to see that the sight of gore had lost some of its appeal for his young cousin. "No, she's only fainted. Now get us back to the house as quickly as old Bob can trot, and try to miss the majority of ruts in the road." John pressed his back against the wagon's side and cradled the woman against him, praying she would still be alive when they reached the house.

When they pulled up to the farmhouse, John had Matt run ahead and alert his grandmother to the situation while John carried his precious burden through the kitchen door.

"She was in the train wreck, but she ain't dead, not yet, anyway," Matt blurted as he held the screen door open for John.

"Oh my goodness!" Aunt Clara whirled from the sink, wiping dishwater from her hands. "Put her in the spare bedroom, John." She bustled ahead up the stairs to the guest-troom and hurried to turn down her prize rose-patterned quilt.

"You might want to put away your nice quilt, Aunt Clara." John glanced down at the woman in his arms covered in blood, dirt, and grass stains.

Aunt Clara stood aside, her fists pressed against her ample waist. "I keep this room ready for whoever needs it, and, by the looks of her, she needs it. Now, quit worryin' about the quilt and lay her down on the bed."

John couldn't help grinning. Aunt Clara was in her element: eager to take charge of whatever emergency presented itself. He did as she ordered.

Aunt Clara turned to her wide-eyed grandson. "Matt, heat up a wash pan full of water and bring me a wash rag, some towels, and a bar of soap."

Matt nodded and headed off on the errand. Aunt Clara looked at John. "We'll need to let somebody know she's here. Did she say who she is?"

John shook his head. "She didn't say much—seemed pretty addled."

A soft groan drew their attention back to the woman on the bed. She opened her eyes, and her glance darted around the room, reminding John of a cornered animal. "Where—where am I?" Her weak voice sounded so frightened it broke John's heart. He started toward her, but Aunt Clara got there first.

"Now, now, dear. You are safe." Aunt Clara bent and smoothed the matted strands of hair from the woman's face. "You've been in a terrible accident, but you're safe now."

"Where?" Her blue eyes looked desperate. "Where am I?"

"You're in Eden, Indiana, on our dairy farm." John stepped closer to the bed. "What's your name? We'll let the authorities know you're here, and they will contact your family."

A confused look furrowed her brow. She pushed up to a sitting position and touched the wound on her head, still oozing blood. "I don't know," she whispered, a tone of surprise creeping into her voice. Her widening gaze grew wild as it flitted between John and Aunt Clara, and her voice turned frantic. "I don't know who I am!"

Chapter Two

"I don't know who I am!" The realization struck her like a club to the stomach, knocking the breath from her lungs. The puzzled faces of the man and woman before her offered no help. "Why can't I remember?" A suffocating panic squeezed her chest, and she struggled to get out of bed, but the middle-aged woman in a blue cotton dress and white apron gently pressed her back against the soft pillow.

"Now, now, dear. Don't excite yourself. You've been in a terrible accident." The woman patted her hand. "I'm sure it will all come back to you soon." Though kindly, the woman's unfamiliar round face framed by gray hair secured at the back of her head in a bun, offered scant comfort.

The need to find something familiar—anything familiar—became overwhelming. The man. She had thought him an angel when she first saw him coming toward her on the road. She struggled to remember—anything—and clung with a death grip to every precious memory as if it were a priceless jewel. She remembered being in a dim, frightening place. Seeing a bright portal and crawling through it to the light while razor-sharp protrusions ripped at her clothes and flesh. Running through a meadow toward trees. Seeing a man. A strong man with kind hazel eyes and wearing overalls and a blue chambray shirt. This man. Being lifted up and held against the comforting warmth of his shirt that smelled like a barnyard. How did she know what a barnyard smelled like?

"I know you. You are my angel." She searched his handsome face for a flicker of recognition.

The angel-man stepped closer to the bed, and a wry smile touched his lips. "I assure you I am nowhere close to being an angel." He glanced at the older woman beside him. "My aunt Clara will attest to that."

She grasped his hand, desperate to clutch onto this one scrap of familiarity. "Who am I? Please, tell me."

"All I know is that I found you wandering on the road after the train wreck." Compassion touched his voice and softened his hazel eyes.

"I was in a train wreck?" Remember. Why couldn't she remember? Renewed panic gripped her chest, and she gasped for breath. "My name. I need to know my name!" An indescribable feeling of desolation enveloped her. Frantic for even the smallest measure of comfort, she crossed her arms over her chest and hugged herself. Surrendering to the wave of despair crushing down on her, she began to rock. "My name, I need to know my name." She forced the words through her sobs.

Suddenly the comforting warmth she'd experienced earlier in the arms of the angel-man engulfed her. The same deep, soothing voice she'd heard on the road assuring her that she would be all right whispered soft hushes against her hair.

"I can tell you who you are." He held her and rocked her as if she were a small child. "You are a precious child of God. Your name is Eve." He drew back and gazed into her eyes. His smile warmed her all the way to the center of her heart, and the crippling fear that had bound her like a straightjacket began to loosen and slip away. He gently brushed a strand of hair from her face. "Eve was the name of God's first daughter, and it will do until you can remember another."

Eve. Yes, she liked the sound. Her panic ebbing, Eve blinked away remnants of tears from her eyes. Amazing how having a name to call herself calmed her fear and lent a sense of identity that felt like an anchor amid a raging gale. She settled back against the pillow again and managed a wobbly smile. "I like the name Eve."

His smile widened. "Hello, Eve. I'm John Weston and this is my aunt, Clara Weston."

The sound of footsteps drew their attention toward the open bedroom door. A wide-eyed boy who looked to be in his teens stood at the threshold holding a large, steaming enamel pan, his shoulder draped with towels.

John nodded toward the boy. "This is my cousin Matthew, Aunt Clara's grandson."

Matthew didn't smile or otherwise acknowledge the introduction. He stood frozen in place, staring at her with silver-dollar-sized eyes.

Clara bustled over to the boy and took possession of the items, including a waxy ivory lump he fished from his pocket. "Now you boys clear out while Eve and I have a nice talk and we get her cleaned up."

Minutes later, washed and clad in a voluminous cotton nightgown, Eve settled back against the pillow and, for the first time, enjoyed a measure of ease.

Clara clicked her tongue as she examined Eve's discarded gray frock. She held the garment up to the sunlight streaming through the window. "I'm afraid it is ruined, dear." She shook her head. "Nice material, too—worsted cotton. A shame." She turned to Eve, regret shining in her brown eyes. "I might be able to mend the tears, but I doubt I could get all the blood stains out, and it would never be nice again."

"I don't remember it, so I care nothing about it." Eve managed a weak smile, wishing that the ruined frock was her greatest concern.

"What is this?" Clara bent and squinted at the dress's collar. "Looks like a label of some kind. 'H. R. Kenyon & Co., Buffalo, NY.'" She turned to Eve. "Does that mean anything to you?"

"No." Eve shook her head, and the panic that had abated came rushing back. Fresh tears sprang into her eyes and slipped down her face. Why couldn't she remember. . . something. Anything.

Clara's face crumpled with regret. She dropped the dress to the floor and hurried to Eve's bedside. "Ah, you poor dear." She patted Eve's hand. "I surely didn't mean to upset you more. I just thought—"

A quick rap at the door cut her thought short.

"Aunt Clara. Eve." The angel-man's voice. "Dr. Callahan and Sheriff McCord are here to see Eve, if she's up to it."

Clara's brows raised in a questioning look, and Eve nodded. Though the thought of a doctor poking at her cuts and bruises didn't appeal, the sheriff might have information that could spark a memory.

"Come on in." Clara pulled the quilt up under Eve's chin. Her voice turned stern as John entered the room followed by two older men. "But the minute Eve gets the least bit tuckered, I'm sending you all hikin'." She leveled a sharp look at the trio, and Eve appreciated the woman's motherly protectiveness.

Did Eve have a mother somewhere? The thought pricked at her heart, bringing new tears to her eyes. She blinked them away.

John stepped to the bed, drawing Eve's gaze like metal to a magnet. She couldn't deny his attractiveness, and the quality went far beyond his handsome features.

"Eve." His soft gaze on her face felt like a physical caress. "Do you feel up to having Doc Callahan check out your wounds?"

Eve nodded, prying her gaze from John in order to shift it to the older gentleman wearing a seersucker suit and clutching the handles of a black satchel. Gray. From his shock of coarse hair to his summer suit to his kind eyes, various shades of that color dominated the doctor's looks. Oddly, his monochromatic appearance had a calming effect on Eve, and she relaxed when he pulled a chair up to her bedside.

"Hmm." The doctor's brows pinched as he examined the cut on her head. "I understand you don't remember much about the accident."

Eve winced when he gingerly touched the wound. "Nothing. I have no memory."

"I'm sure it is only temporary, my dear." He patted her hand, but his weak smile and unconvincing tone belied his prognosis. After treating and bandaging her several cuts, he checked for other injuries, including broken bones. Finding none, he pronounced her in otherwise good health and prescribed bed rest and chicken soup.

During the examination, Clara, John, and Sheriff McCord had talked quietly among themselves while casting intermittent glances toward Eve and the doctor.

John stepped toward the bed, his forehead creasing. "What about her memory, Doc? When do you think Eve's memory will return?"

Dr. Callahan shrugged his seersucker-clad shoulders as he stuffed his stethoscope into his satchel and shut the bag with a snap. "Short-term amnesia is not an uncommon phenomenon after such a traumatic event. I expect Eve will remember things in bits and pieces as time goes by."

Sheriff McCord, who stood with his arms crossed over his barrel chest, gave a soft snort. "Amnesia? Convenient, I'd say." The skepticism in his gruff tone and steely glare suggested that he suspected Eve's memory loss was a ruse.

The sheriff stepped to Eve's bedside and trained his gaze on her like a weapon, one bushy salt-and-pepper eyebrow raised. "So. . .Eve." He weighted the pronunciation of the name with a sarcastic emphasis. "Clara says your dress came from Buffalo, New York. Is that where you're from?"

"I don't know." Eve's insides quivered as the sheriff glared down his bulbous nose at her.

"Your accent sounds like New York." He cocked his head, his mustached mouth pursed in an accusatory pucker.

"I—I might be from New York. I told you, I can't remember."

John put a hand on the sheriff's shoulder. "Now Sid, you've got no call to badger her. She's been through enough—"

"Ever heard of the Erie Savings Bank in Buffalo, Missy? Ever been there?" The sheriff leaned in, ignoring John's objections.

Eve pushed down her rising indignation at the lawman's inquisition. Did he have some knowledge that she had a link with that institution? If so, it could help in discovering her identity.

"I don't know. I told you, I can't remember. Please, Sheriff, find out who I am." Eve hated the tears filling her eyes.

"Oh I will, Missy. And I'll find out what you did with that ten thousand dollars you stole, too."

Chapter Three

C lara gasped and covered her mouth with her hands.

Eve felt as if Sheriff McCord had physically punched her in the stomach. "What? What did I do?" She barely managed to whisper the question amid the fear rising up in her chest, threatening to close off her breathing. Had she done something terrible? What kind of person was she? *Who* was she?

John stepped in front of Sheriff McCord as if to make himself a barrier between the lawman and Eve. His stiffened posture turned protective, and Eve experienced a wave of gratitude for her guardian angel-man. "That's enough, Sid." Though an inch or two shorter than the sheriff, John rose to his full height, nearly erasing the difference. "What's this all about? What are you accusing Eve of doing?"

Sheriff McCord shifted to peer over John's shoulder at Eve. His brow lowered and his lips flatted in a grim line. "I got a telegraph from Buffalo that a woman involved in a crime there might be on the train that wrecked." His eyes narrowed to accusatory slits. "The description fits this woman to a T."

"That Big Four line originates in Buffalo. I'm sure there were a lot of people from that town on the train." John's stance and tone remained defensive, calming the new terror rising in Eve's chest. "So what exactly was this person supposed to have done?"

The furrows in the sheriff's brow deepened. "The telegraph bulletin I got from New York refers to the suspect as the Society Bandit. Has a long line of aliases, but her birth name is Annette Bouchard. Raised in high society, she was disowned by her family and turned to a life of crime. With a head for numbers, she gets bookkeeping jobs at banks then embezzles them out of thousands of dollars. Before they realize what she's done, she moves on. The Erie Savings Bank in Buffalo was her last job."

John's hands clenched at his sides, and a warning rippled beneath the surface of the controlled anger in his voice. "You have no proof that Eve is the Bouchard woman."

Sheriff McCord's chin jutted out. "I have no proof she's not, either. And until I do, she's my prime suspect. Besides, Weston, we all know you're not the best judge of character, now don't we?"

Clara hung her head and Dr. Callahan softly cleared his throat, looking as if he wished to be somewhere else.

Though curious about the sheriff's odd comment to John, Eve's concern over what crimes she might have committed swamped all other thoughts.

"I'm afraid I'll have to take you into custody until I can get someone from Buffalo to come and positively identify you, ma'am." A scant hint of apology touched Sheriff McCord's voice as he attempted to step around John toward Eve's bed.

John clapped a hand on the sheriff's shoulder, stopping him. "I'm asking that you not to do that, Sid. Eve is injured." He glanced at Eve. "Look at her. Doc said she needs rest and care. Besides, she's innocent until proven guilty." He raised his strong jaw, his gaze burrowing into the lawman's eyes. "You know it could be a week or more before Buffalo gets anyone down here. Even then, they might not be able to identify her. You heard Mort. Her head injury could be worse than it appears. Are you willing to put an innocent woman's health at risk?"

The sheriff shrugged off John's hand. "What I'm not willing to do is let a suspect slip through my fingers." He looked at Eve. "Get dressed, Missy. If Doc Callahan says you're fit to get out of bed, you're comin' with me." He shot the doctor a pointed look. "Well, Mort, is she fit to leave her bed?"

Eve's insides shriveled with fear as Doctor Callahan's uneasy glance bounced between the sheriff and John, who stood glaring at one another while Clara appeared on the verge of tears. The thought of exchanging the comfort of her bed and the kind ministrations of Clara and John Weston for a hard cot in a jail cell filled Eve with terror.

Dr. Callahan's throat moved with a hard swallow. "Well—"

"Eve isn't going anywhere." John crossed his arms over his chest and widened his booted stance, his gaze never leaving the sheriff's face. "Put her in my protective custody, Sid."

"You can understand why I'd be reluctant to do that, John." The sheriff's scowl deepened.

John glanced down, and his voice turned contrite. "Yeah, I can understand, Sid." He met the sheriff's gaze again, his voice hardening. "But I'm willing to take full responsibility for her and, if you like, I can get Amos Chandler over here to write up the papers all legal and proper."

Sheriff McCord heaved a sigh of surrender. "All right, all right." He waved his hand. "No need to get a lawyer mixed into it yet. I'll telegraph the Buffalo police department and see if I can get someone to come and help figure out who she is."

When the sheriff finally left the room with the doctor in tow, Eve allowed herself to breathe again. Her heart had swelled to watch her champion angel-man battle for her freedom. Still, it didn't dispel the cloud of suspicion hanging over her, and she could only hope it wouldn't bring a storm of trouble down on John and Clara.

◆ ◆ ◆

Three days later, with no further word from the sheriff, Eve began to relax. Surely the lawman would have returned by now if he'd found more evidence pointing to her being the New York criminal. Embezzlement. Could she have committed such a crime? She recoiled at the thought. Still, something akin to guilt scratched at her foggy brain. *No!* "That is not who I am!" The words burst from her lips as if saying them would make it so. Until someone provided evidence to the contrary, she'd refuse to believe herself capable of such an immoral act.

The morning sun shining through the long narrow window on the east wall beckoned, stirring a restlessness within Eve. This room that had first felt like a sanctuary had begun to feel more like a prison.

She swung her legs over the side of the bed, pressed her bare feet against the nubby little braided rug that covered the wood floor, and stood. Glad to take off the voluminous gown, she donned the pink-and-white-striped cotton frock and sturdy shoes Clara had left for her in the wardrobe.

Downstairs, delicious aromas welcomed Eve into the kitchen, where Clara turned from tending a pan of scrambled eggs on the stove to greet her with a wide smile. The older woman's eyes turned watery as they scanned Eve from head to foot, and a pleased expression settled on her round face. "I thought Margaret's clothes would fit you. But are you sure you're well enough to be up?"

"I'm perfectly fine." Eve returned Clara's smile. "The room is lovely, and the bed is comfortable, but three days confined to them are enough. Besides, I'm sure you have plenty to do without waiting on me hand and foot."

"You are no trouble, dear." Lines at the corners of Clara's eyes crinkled with her smile. "To tell you the truth, I've enjoyed having another woman around here again."

"Who is Margaret?" Eve worried that the owner of the clothes she was wearing might not approve of Clara loaning them out. As she considered who this Margaret might be, a thought struck, causing an uncomfortable feeling to twist in her middle. Perhaps John had a wife somewhere.

"Margaret was my daughter—Matthew's mother. We lost her to a ruptured appendix five years ago." Giving a telltale sniff, Clara busied herself with the pan of eggs on the stove.

Gratitude bubbled up in Eve, causing unexpected tears to spring into her eyes. Despite Clara's claim to the contrary, Eve had no doubt that she'd been more trouble than company for the older woman, and now to learn that Clara had given Eve her dead daughter's clothes felt overwhelming. "I can't thank you enough for taking me in." She glanced down at her skirt. "And for everything you've done for me."

"Ah pshaw!" Clara crossed to Eve and gave her a warm hug. "If Margaret was here, she'd have given you the clothes herself. Besides, we've done nothing more than what our Lord and Savior expects from us. 'For I was an hungred, and ye gave me meat: I was thirsty, and ye gave me drink: I was a stranger, and ye took me in. . . .'" She went back to tend her skillet. "'Inasmuch as ye have done it unto one of the least of these my brethren, ye have done it unto me.'" Clara gave an emphatic nod. "I wouldn't want to stand before my Lord on Judgment Day and have to answer when He asks why I turned Him away." Her smile returned. "And I know John feels the same way."

Eve quirked a weak smile. Clara's words had sounded like Bible verses of some kind, but nothing about the quote struck her as familiar. A sick feeling curdled in her belly. A criminal would not be especially religious.

Shaking off the disconcerting thought, she took in the neat little farmhouse kitchen with its stone sink, wood-fired range, and sturdy-looking wood oval table and chairs. Had she ever worked in a kitchen like this one? Again, nothing seemed familiar, and no remembered kitchen skills sprang to mind.

Another prick of dismay. Would a fugitive bank robber have enough money to eat all her meals at restaurants? Eve gave herself a mental shake. She must stop thinking in those terms. Until Sheriff McCord returned with more substantial proof of any wrongdoing by her, she would simply consider herself a guest of the Westons. Besides, Clara and John apparently believed that the charity they showed her bought them some measure of credit from the deity. Still, that didn't negate Eve's responsibility to earn her keep while she was here. "What can I do to help, Clara?"

Clara glanced over at a short wooden cabinet. "You could fetch the slab of bacon from the icebox and slice some down to go with these eggs."

Eve crossed the room to the icebox and opened it. The July day had already turned warm, and the immediate coolness of the open icebox felt delicious. If this was a common experience for her, wouldn't she remember it? The past three days—the only days she remembered—had been filled with such questions. So far, most of her experiences here had felt unfamiliar. She stared into the icebox, knowing she'd found yet another one.

"It's that bundle wrapped in brown paper." Clara moved the frying pan to the back of the stove and walked to the icebox. When she reached in and brought out the wrapped meat, Eve felt useless.

"I'm sorry to be such a dolt."

"Pshaw. You're no such thing, dear." Clara carried the package to a wooden cupboard near the stove and gave Eve an encouraging smile. "It's not easy for anyone to find their way around a strange kitchen. I'm sure I'd be lost in your kitchen, too."

While the two worked together making breakfast, Clara's comment churned in Eve's mind, sparking a barrage of troubling questions. Did she have a kitchen? In what kind of home had she lived? Did she have a husband? Children? Her throat tightened at the thought of loved ones at home grieving her loss. She glanced at her left hand as she reached into the oven with a quilted square of cloth to retrieve a pan of golden-brown biscuits, and the tightness in her throat loosened. No ring adorned her hand. At least she was likely single.

A few minutes later, she felt not only relief, but gladness at that thought when John entered the kitchen. Warmth that had nothing to do with the kitchen stove suffused her face at the sight of her angel-man. His blue chambray shirtsleeves, damp from washing up, were rolled up to his elbows, exposing muscular forearms. *Arms that had held her against his strong, warm chest.*

Eve shoved the thought away. However attracted she might be to John Weston, until she knew who she was, nothing could come of it.

"Well, look who's up." A wide grin marched across John's handsome face as his gaze fastened onto Eve. "It's good to see you on your feet. How are you feeling?"

"Better." Somehow Eve managed to murmur the word even as the sight of her angel-man sucked the air from her lungs. She hadn't seen him since he left with the doctor and sheriff three days ago. Had she always acted this silly and giddy around handsome men? Deep inside, she didn't think so.

"Good. That's good." His eyes remained fixed on hers. They seemed to melt into hers, as if he were trying to peer into her soul. Was he attempting to discern a smudge there, an indelible stain like Hester's scarlet letter? Odd that she could recall Hawthorne's acclaimed novel yet could not remember when or where she had read it.

Even as her brain churned with these thoughts, Eve stood transfixed, unable to move or speak until Clara handed her a plate of biscuits, breaking the spell of John's gaze.

"John, go tell Matthew to hurry and get washed up, or he'll miss breakfast." Clara forked strips of fried bacon onto the platter of scrambled eggs.

John grinned and left the kitchen, leaving Eve feeling bereft.

Her joy returned a few minutes later when he walked through the door again, with Matthew close behind.

When they gathered around the table, Eve's heart quickened as John pulled out a chair for her and his hand grazed her shoulder. His every look, every touch, set her heart dancing. However she might have acted around men before, she must rein in her obviously untamed emotions for her good as well as for John's.

Her unspoken vow had scarcely formed in her mind when John, who'd taken a seat beside her, took her hand in his and obliterated her vow with his touch.

"Shall we pray?" He bowed his head and closed his eyes, as did Clara, who took Eve's other hand and that of young Matthew.

Eve bowed her head. It felt odd. Ignoring the awkwardness of the situation, she let herself become lost in her angel-man's deep, resonant voice without focusing on the words of his prayer: an expression of thanks for the day, the food, and Eve's recovery, including a petition for her full healing.

When John finished his prayer with a strong "Amen," which Clara echoed, he let go of Eve's hand. She experienced the same sense of loss she'd felt earlier when he left the kitchen.

"So what is it like not to know who you are?" Matthew looked across the table at Eve with innocent brown eyes as he fingered a piece of bacon.

Clara emitted a tiny gasp followed by a whispered "Matthew James!"

Eve didn't dare look at John, but judging by the flash of alarm on Matthew's face when he looked at his older cousin, her angel-man's expression was less than approving. For her part, Eve regarded the boy's question as more honest than rude. It deserved an honest answer.

"Odd. I'd say it makes me feel odd." Digging her fork into her scrambled eggs, she smiled. "At first I felt lost and scared, but you, your grandmother, and cousin have made me feel safe."

"So you don't remember if you robbed that bank like Sheriff McCord said?" The inquisitive youngster leaned forward, expectation shining in his eyes.

"That's enough, Matt." The stern tone in John's quiet voice set Matthew back in his chair.

For once, Eve ignored John. "No. I don't think I did. At least, I don't want to think I did."

"I'm sorry, Eve." Regret, dismay, and embarrassment mingled together in John's voice. "Matthew meant no harm." His voice took on a harder edge. "Sometimes his curiosity gets the best of him." He turned his attention to Matthew. "Don't you remember what we talked about this morning in the barn?"

"Baseball?"

Eve stifled a giggle.

"No, Matt. The other thing we talked about."

"Oh." Matthew looked down at his plate. When he looked back up at Eve, his expression had turned contrite. "I'm sorry if I hurt your feelings, Eve." Now his brown eyes looked hopeful. "I didn't hurt your feelings, did I?"

Eve grinned. "Of course you didn't hurt my feelings, Matthew." She shrugged. "Who knows who I am? Perhaps I *am* an embezzler, or a royal princess, or even a lady baseball player if there is such a thing." She paused to pour cream from a little pitcher into her coffee. *How do I know I like cream in my coffee?* The thought wiped the smile from her face for an instant, but she forced it back. "I suppose the good thing about not knowing who you are is that you can be whoever you want to be."

John made an odd throat-clearing sound, and she sensed him tense beside her. Despite his efforts to keep her out of jail, was he beginning to suspect her of being the New York fugitive? The thought pricked her heart. She needed to change the subject.

"So, Matthew, do you have a favorite baseball team?"

Matthew brightened up. "The Chicago Colts, of course."

The conversation turned to baseball until three sharp raps at the kitchen door intruded. When John went to answer it, Sheriff McCord's voice traveled into the room.

"I need to talk to the woman from the train wreck."

Chapter Four

The protective instinct that had spiked in John toward Eve at the breakfast table shot up another notch as he looked into the sheriff's unreadable expression. "Have you discovered something about Eve's identity, Sid?" The sound of chair legs scraping against the floor told him the others had left the table. He sensed Eve's presence behind him.

"No. We even went through every piece of luggage in the baggage car but found nothing we couldn't link to other passengers." Disappointment tinged Sid's tone, but his chin lifted in a determined jut. John had seen the sheriff's stubborn streak enough to know that, like a bulldog with a rabbit in its jaws, the lawman wouldn't let go of this case until he got a resolution. That thought brought both comfort and consternation.

"Come on in, Sid." Aunt Clara's bright voice chimed in from the center of the room. "Would you like some breakfast and coffee?"

Sid dragged his hat from his balding pate and quirked an apologetic smile over John's shoulder. "Thanks, Clara, but my Ethyl fed me." The smile vanished as his gaze slid down to Eve, now at John's side. "I just came from the school where they took some of the injured from the train wreck. A patient there remembers seeing someone that fits your description, ma'am." He glanced at his hands, fingering his gray fedora, and the edges of his gruff voice softened. "I was thinking that if you talked to the gentleman, it might help to bring back your memory."

"Yes. Yes, I would like that." The eager hope in Eve's voice pricked John's heart, and his desire to protect her shot up again.

Without thinking, he put his arm around Eve's narrow shoulders. "Are you sure you're up to this, Eve? Doc told me that some of the injuries are. . .really bad." He gazed into her crystal blue eyes brimming with all the trust and expectation of a child on Christmas morning and fought the urge to pull her against him.

"Yes." Her shoulders straightened beneath his arm, and her chin lifted in a courageous tilt. "If there's a chance that someone from the train knows who I am, I have to try."

"Okay." John took his arm from her shoulder because if he didn't, he'd wrap her in an embrace, and that wouldn't do. He couldn't deny the attraction he felt for Eve. Now, a growing respect equaled that attraction. Whoever this girl was, he wanted to know her better.

◆　◆　◆

A brick building with a bell tower came into view, and Eve's insides twisted. The excitement she'd felt a half hour earlier when she'd agreed to this visit evaporated. She sucked in a ragged, involuntary breath and leaned toward John on the wagon seat beside her.

What if she found family members? The thought of adding to an injured loved one's agony by not recognizing him or her pressed down on her heart like a weight.

"You don't have to do this, you know." John's gentle voice as he reined the horse to a halt in front of the building almost undid Eve's resolve.

The temptation to tell him to turn the wagon around and head back to the farmhouse rose with the lump in her throat. She swallowed it down. Whatever unpleasantness she might face inside this building was worth the chance of learning her identity. "Yes I do, John. I have to know who I am."

John nodded, and a tiny smile lifted the corner of his mouth. A look of wonder and something else Eve was not prepared to name shone in his hazel-green eyes before he jumped down from the wagon.

When he reached up and helped her down, Eve stood for a long moment with his strong hands around her waist. Their gazes locked, and for an instant, she thought he might kiss her. Instead, he put his arm around her back and turned her toward the school. "I'll be with you every step. And any moment you want to head back home, we'll do that."

Not trusting her voice, Eve nodded. She drew in another fortifying breath, gathered her courage along with the folds of her cotton skirt, and headed up the grassy embankment.

Sheriff McCord, who had driven ahead in his buggy, met them at the door. Something akin to compassion flashed across the man's craggy features, and he held out a folded square of white cloth. "It doesn't smell real nice in there. You might want to hold this handkerchief over your nose."

Eve shook her head. "Thank you, but the people in there feel bad enough. I don't want to do anything to make them feel worse."

Two steps into the building, Eve questioned her decision to reject the sheriff's offer. A wave of foul odors smacked her in the face, and she fought the urge to gag. Rows of canvas cots covered the space devoid of desks. Only the bookcases lining the walls interspersed with pictures of George Washington, Abraham Lincoln, and other past presidents evidenced this as a place of learning.

"Breathe through your mouth." John's whispered advice and the comforting strength of his hand on Eve's back gave her the ability to keep her breakfast down and the courage to forge ahead.

Sheriff McCord stepped to Eve's other side. "There's a fellow here who might have talked to you on the train. A drummer of some sort, I think." The lines in the sheriff's forehead furrowed deeper. "Poor feller lost a leg. They took it yesterday, so I'm not real sure if he'll be in much shape to talk. Doc's got him on a heavy dose of laudanum."

Eve stifled a gasp. Was this man a relative? A friend? Whoever he was, he deserved her compassion even if she didn't recognize him. "I'd like to speak with him if he's able."

The sheriff guided them through the maze of injured, many swathed in red-stained white bandages. This must resemble a battlefield hospital. The thought skittered through Eve's mind as she tried to filter out the sound of moans and weeping. At last the sheriff stopped beside a cot where a man lay covered in a faded patchwork quilt, likely a donation from caring locals.

Reluctant to wake the dosing man, Eve studied his pallid features, partially covered by a stubbly auburn beard and mustache. Neither homely nor especially handsome, he looked to be in his midthirties. Nothing about him triggered recognition. The disappointment that realization sparked flickered out when Eve's gaze wandered to the bottom half of the cot. Only on the left side did a long hump beneath the quilt indicate a leg. On the right side, the quilt lay flat against the cot, and Eve experienced a flash of sympathy followed by a wave of gratitude. This could have been her.

"Mr. Trowbridge." The sheriff's voice intruded on Eve's grim musings. "Mr. Trowbridge, you have visitors."

The man's eyelids fluttered and opened to slits, which he trained at first on the sheriff. When his drowsy gaze slid to Eve, his eyes widened, and a smile straightened his mustache to a penciled line above his lips. "Well, hello, Pretty. Glad you came." He winked. "Unless I died and you're welcoming me to the pearly gates." He glanced at John. "But somehow I'm guessing the fellow with you and the sheriff isn't Saint Peter."

"John Weston. A friend."

Eve saw no need to expand on John's brief introduction. Instead, she focused her full attention on the injured man. "I'm so sorry for your injury, Mr. Trowbridge." The words blurted from her lips.

A grin stretched his mouth wider. "If I'd known losing a leg would have won your affection, I might have cut the thing off myself back on the train."

"Then you know me?" Eve studied his features for any scrap of familiarity.

"In what sense?" His grin turned mischievous.

"Be very careful, friend." Though measured, John's low voice carried an unmistakable warning.

Trowbridge's expression sobered. "You don't remember me?"

Eve shook her head, hating the tears filling her eyes. "I don't remember. . .anything."

"I see." Genuine concern flashed across the man's face. "Then I reckon you didn't come out entirely unscathed."

Eve ignored his comment, her heart racing. "My name. Did I tell you my name?"

He shook his head, dashing her hopes. "No, I'm sorry to say our meeting was far too brief." He gave her a sad smile. "Wasn't able to wheedle it out of you." His countenance brightened. "You might have told the lady sitting next to you, though." His brow furrowed in thought. "O'Reilly. I think I heard someone refer to her as Mrs. O'Reilly."

"O'Reilly." Eve's mind churned. Nothing. Then new hope bloomed among a thorn patch of concern. Could this woman be her mother or some other relative? "Did she say if she was related to me in some way?"

Grinning, he gave a wry snort. "She made it emphatically clear that she was not. At least that she was not your mother, correcting me when I made that assumption. I got the sense that you were seatmates by chance, became acquainted on the train."

"I see." Another hope withered, forcing Eve to blink away more tears.

"Hey, there. I'm sure it will all come back to you soon." His voice turned kind, and Eve experienced a flash of shame. She should be consoling him, not the other way around.

"The loss of a leg is far worse than the loss of memory. You are the one who deserves condolences, Mr. Trowbridge, not me."

"Elmer, please." He reached his hand up to her. "Elmer Trowbridge, stove salesman extraordinaire. Nice to make your acquaintance. . . again." His grin widened.

Eve took his hand, marveling at the strength of his grasp considering the trauma he'd experienced. "Until I learn my real name, I'm being called Eve. It's nice to make your acquaintance, too, Elmer."

"Eve. I like it. Apropos, I'd say, since they tell me this place is called Eden." He gave a little chortle. "Just wish my name was Adam."

John cleared his throat. "Thank you, Mr. Trowbridge. We won't tire you any further." He glanced over the cot-strewn room. "Do you happen to know if the Mrs. O'Reilly you spoke of is here?"

Elmer's head rolled against the pillow. "Couldn't tell ya, but I do know the doc has a list of patients' names."

Sheriff McCord turned and headed across the room, Eve assumed, to check the doctor's patient list.

"Thanks." John's tone gentled. "I'm sorry for your misfortune, Mr. Trowbridge, and I'll be keeping you in my prayers. Is there someone, family perhaps, who we could contact for you?"

Elmer shifted his gaze to John. "I appreciate that, Mr. Weston. Never been an especially religious man, but a good word or two on my behalf would be appreciated. As for family. . ." He shrugged. "Grew up an orphan, but the doc has telegraphed my company. They'll be sending someone next week to put me on a train back to Cleveland." He quirked a sardonic grin. "Who knows? This could be the best thing that ever happened to me." He winked at Eve. "It'll be a lot harder for customers to turn down a cripple." For the first time, a hint of sorrow crept into his voice.

"Is there anything I can do for you? Anything you need?" Eve's heart went out to her fellow passenger.

A mischievous glint flickered in Elmer's eyes, but a glance at John doused it. "I could use a glass of water." He rubbed his throat. "Throat's a bit dry."

"Of course." With a parting smile to Elmer, Eve followed John to where the sheriff stood talking with Dr. Callahan.

The doctor's kind eyes regarded Eve as they neared. "I'm so glad to see you up and about. How is that head wound?" He examined the sore spot above her left eyebrow.

"It only hurts when I touch it."

"Hmm." He bounced a smile of approval between her and John. "Looks like Clara is doing a fine job keeping this clean. No sign of infection. Should heal completely in a week or so." His smile faded. "I understand your memory has not returned."

"No. Sheriff McCord thought it might help my memory to talk with folks from my train car."

"But it hasn't." His rhetorical comment held no hint of question. With his arms crossed over the chest of his long white coat, Dr. Callahan tipped his head to one side and looked at her as if studying a laboratory specimen.

"No." The defeated tone in her voice annoyed her. Something inside her hated the thought of needing sympathy, or worse, looking as if seeking it. "So far I've only talked with Mr. Trowbridge, and it seems I never told him my name. He does think I may have told a Mrs. O'Reilly."

Dr. Callahan shared a glance with the sheriff, and his tone turned consoling. "I'm very sorry, Eve, but the only person listed with that surname is a Bridget O'Reilly, and she is among the fatalities."

"Oh." Another disappointment. Unexpected sadness curled in Eve's chest. Even if her acquaintance with Bridget O'Reilly had been a passing one, knowing that Eve had conversed with the woman, perhaps shared a laugh with her, made her inability to remember those exchanges feel like an insult to the dead woman. She couldn't help Bridget O'Reilly, but she could still help Elmer. "Mr. Trowbridge requested a glass of water. Do you know where I might get that for him?"

The doctor cocked his head to the left. "There's a pump and sink in the other room. Nurses should be able to provide you with a glass."

On her way to fetch the water, Eve waded through the cots of suffering humanity, resisting the urge to stop and ask if anyone remembered her. Blank stares from pain-ridden faces suggested that such inquiries would prove fruitless.

A few minutes later, water glass in hand, she headed back to the room where Elmer lay. Opening a door she thought would lead to the room of cots, she found herself outside the school building. She started to head back in when she heard a familiar voice: Sheriff McCord.

"I've made up my mind, John. I can't take a chance on losing this woman. I promised the police chief in Buffalo that she'd be here when his man arrives to verify her identity. Frankly, I'm not sure I can trust you with that, so I'm asking the doc to commit her to the Indiana Hospital for the Insane."

Chapter Five

The sound of breaking glass behind him jerked John's attention from the sheriff's retreating figure.

"Can he do that?" Eve stood on the concrete walkway, her blue eyes wide with fear. At her feet lay what looked to be the shattered remnants of a drinking glass amid a puddle of water.

John's heart, which had stopped beating, convulsed. "I won't let that happen, Eve. I promise." Praying he could keep that promise, he stepped to her. The urge to protect her, to cradle her head against his chest, became overwhelming. He reached out to gather her into his arms, but she knelt and began picking up the larger pieces of the broken glass.

"I've made a mess." The quaver in her voice broke his heart. "I was trying to find my way back to Elmer, but I got lost." A brave smile wobbled on her lips—lips that looked as soft and pink as a rose petal. "It seems I'm always getting lost."

How John wished he could fix her broken memory, but he couldn't. Instead, he did what he could for her. He knelt and cupped her hand holding the shards of glass. "I'll take care of this." He wanted to add "I'll take care of you," but the words caught in his throat. She didn't need more disappointments, and he'd already promised more than he knew he could deliver. "Go get Elmer another glass of water, and I'll meet you inside in a few minutes."

She nodded, relinquishing the shards of glass to his waiting hand. "Thank you, John." The gratitude in her blue eyes, brimming with unshed tears, told him that her thanks encompassed more than his cleaning up this little pile of glass.

Watching Eve disappear into the school building, John's resolve to keep her out of the state hospital solidified. Despite Sid's suspicions, John's gut, or perhaps his heart, told him she was neither criminal nor insane, and he wouldn't leave this place without a promise from Doc Callahan not to commit her to the Indiana Hospital for the Insane.

Later, with that promise secured and his mind easier, John helped Eve onto the wagon for their trip home.

A ways down the road, he turned to her. "Dr. Callahan's not inclined to have you committed to the state hospital." He regretted blurting it out the moment the words left his mouth.

For a long moment, Eve didn't respond. Fearing she might faint, he pulled the wagon to a stop. She expelled a ragged breath. A visible battle to control her emotions played across her pale features, and he marveled at her strength. At length she looked up at him, her blue eyes, which always reminded him of an October sky, clear. She covered his hand holding the reins with hers, sending pleasant tingles up his arm. "Thank you. Thank you, John."

John's heart bucked, and he cleared the emotion from his throat. In another moment he would gather her into his arms, so he flicked the reins against the horse's back, and the wagon began rolling down the road again. "It's Doc Callahan you should thank."

"But you fought for me, and I appreciate that." Her lighter tone turned serious. "Why did Sheriff McCord say he can't trust you?"

John stiffened at the unexpected question, then winced at the painful memory it evoked. He recoiled at the thought of recounting the distasteful event, especially to Eve. But better she learn it from him than from casual gossip she might hear around the community. He blew out a fortifying breath. "Two years ago I worked as a sergeant on the Indianapolis police force. One day some patrolmen brought three members of a pickpocket ring into the station, and I was assigned to guard them while they waited to be processed." He swallowed to moisten his drying throat as the awful memories played through his mind.

"What happened?" Her gentle prompting gave him courage to continue sharing the experience.

"One of the suspects, a woman, complained that her handcuffs were cutting into her wrists." John squeezed his eyes shut, but the events of two years ago refused to go away. Opening them again, he focused on the horse's glossy dark rump. "The police manual's rules of arrest state, 'Officers are enjoined, in making arrests, to act with kindness, to use no more force than is necessary.' So I did as she asked, and loosened them. If only I hadn't. If only. . ." He shook his head, but the motion wouldn't dislodge the memory of what happened next. Another deep breath. He might as well finish it. "While I was taking the statement of one of her cohorts, the woman prisoner maneuvered her hands out of the shackles, ran and grabbed a patrolman's sidearm and shot him to death, then ran from the station."

Eve emitted a tiny gasp. "Oh John, I am so sorry."

John shrugged and unclenched his aching jaws. "They caught the woman and tried and convicted her of murder. The review board exonerated me of misconduct, citing the rule I quoted, but a man died because of my actions. I have to live with that." He forced another swallow past his tightening throat. "I was charged with poor judgment and drummed out of the force. I don't blame Sid for not trusting me." An involuntary snort huffed from his nose. "I can see how your case must seem to him like history repeating itself."

Eve's tone turned defensive. "I'm not going anywhere, and I certainly don't plan to shoot anyone." Her posture stiffened. "I don't know if I had anything to do with robbing that bank in New York, but I'm fairly certain I know nothing of guns, or even how to shoot one."

The wagon stopped, and John realized they were home. He shouldn't have told her. Of course it would sound to her like he was equating her with the woman who'd duped him two years ago. "I wasn't accusing you, Eve."

Before he could make another move, she scrambled down from the wagon and strode to the house.

Watching her poker-straight back disappear through the kitchen door, John's heart sagged with his shoulders, and he blew out a frustrated breath. When would he ever learn to think before he spoke?

But later, while unhitching the horse from the wagon, the memory of Eve's abrupt attitude shift began to scratch at his suspicious cop nerve. The quote from Shakespeare's *Hamlet* sprang to mind: *"The lady doth protest too much, methinks."*

As much as John hated to admit it, he could no more prove Eve's innocence than Sid could prove her guilt. While he no longer wore the badge, he still possessed his police training and instincts. He must resolve to follow the evidence wherever it led and not allow Eve's considerable charms to blind him to clues that might point to her guilt.

◆　◆　◆

Over the next two weeks, despite John's best intentions, Eve daily destroyed his resolve with a look, a laugh, a touch, or a smile like the one she was sending him this very moment.

"How is the cow?" She looked up from helping Clara fill jelly jars with steaming dark liquid and trained those devastating blue eyes on him, turning his mind to mush.

John stepped into the kitchen and forced his mind from the tantalizing lock of red-gold hair curling against Eve's creamy temple and back to his best milk cow that had gone into labor. "She seems to be progressing normally." His heart hammering like a woodpecker's beak against a dead tree, he leaned a shoulder against the wall and managed a tepid smile. *Why did the woman have to be so beautiful?* "We should have a new calf today." Dismay at his own weak will curdled in John's belly. Did he have no defense against her charms? How could he ever assess her with a critical eye?

Aunt Clara wiped her berry-stained hands on a kitchen towel. "Well, I'm praying for a heifer. We could use another milk cow to add to the herd."

That moment the back door burst open, and Matt stumbled in, his eyes wild.

"John, come quick! I think Ginger is dying!"

Chapter Six

S tunned mute, Eve watched John bolt from the kitchen with Matthew in his wake. During her almost three weeks at the farm, she'd learned that Ginger was both a favorite and valuable milk cow. She looked at Clara, whose face scrunched in concern.

"Sure would hate to lose that cow." The older woman shook her head, her hand a bit shaky as she spooned molten wax into jars of blackberry jelly. She lifted her chin and gave a sharp sniff—something Eve had noticed Clara do when worried, as if steeling herself against trouble. She gave Eve a brave smile, but her eyes glistened with unshed tears. "Ginger is one of the last calves I helped Phil birth."

"I'm so sorry, Clara." Eve gave Clara's shoulder a hug. "I hope Ginger makes it, and her calf, too."

Clara turned to Eve and took her hands in hers. "Will you pray with me, Eve?"

The same uncomfortable feeling that always curled in Eve's midsection during the family's prayer time struck again. "I. . ." She felt herself lean back, away from Clara, but the pain in the older woman's eyes compelled her to acquiesce. Offering a warm smile, she squeezed Clara's hands. "Of course I will."

Clara's head bowed, and she closed her eyes. "Dear Lord, I'm sure You've got more pressin' things to attend to, but if You could see fit, I sure would appreciate it if You took a moment to look down on our Ginger and her new calf and bring them through this perilous birth." That sharp sniff again. "It's a little thing, Lord, but that cow, well, she's somewhat special to me, bein' the last calf Phil named and all." Her voice cracked, and Eve squeezed Clara's hands, hoping to offer the other woman some comfort and support.

Another sniff, softer this time, but Clara's hands relaxed in Eve's, and a more peaceful tone came into her voice. "'We know that all things work together for good to them that love God, to them who are the called according to his purpose.' So we ask for Your favor in this, but we accept Your will, knowin' You want only the best for us. We ask this in Jesus' name and for His sake. Amen."

Clara gave Eve's fingers a gentle squeeze and released them, and Eve felt almost sorry for the prayer to end. Though she sensed that praying and perhaps even a belief in God was as foreign to her as life on this Indiana farm, she couldn't deny its calming effect. Was there a benevolent deity who looked down upon her and cared about her? John and Clara thought so. But if that were so, why did God allow tragedies like the train wreck that took lives as well as Elmer's leg and Eve's memory? And what about the possible loss of the Westons' favorite cow?

That question had no sooner formed in Eve's mind than the kitchen door burst open and John, with an arm around Matthew, half stumbled into the kitchen. The boy's face

180

contorted in pain, and he moaned as he gripped his right arm with his left hand.

John helped the pale-faced boy to a chair, while Clara gasped and rushed to them.

"The cow kicked Matt in the arm. It may be broke." As John talked, he unbuttoned the boy's shirt and eased the garment off his right shoulder amid protests of "Ow! Ouch!" from Matthew.

"Oh my goodness." Clara, with concern lines deepening on her face, hovered near her grandson. "Can you move your fingers, Matthew?" She patted his back as if he were a babe.

Grunting and grimacing, the boy clenched and unclenched the fingers of his right hand. "Yeah."

John blew out a long breath. "I doubt it's broke then, but it wouldn't hurt to have Doc Callahan take a look at it." He patted Matthew on his good shoulder, his worried frown melting into a sympathetic grin. "You're gonna have a first-class bruise, though." He nodded at the purplish discoloration deepening on the boy's upper arm.

"I'll heat water and get the Epsom salts." Clara hurried to the sink and pumped water into a teakettle. Setting it on the stove, she glanced over her shoulder at John. "How's the cow?"

"Not good." John rubbed his forehead that had furrowed again in worry. "I don't think the calf's gonna come by itself. It'll have to be pulled." His lips pursed beneath his frown. "I was about to do that with Matt's help when Ginger kicked him. I'll need to get back out there and try to do it myself, or we'll lose the cow and the calf."

"I'm feelin' better. I think I can help." Matt started to get up from the chair, but John shook his head and eased him back down.

"You're done in the barn today, Matt. I can't have you out there doing more damage to that arm. You'll need to stay in here and let your grandma doctor it up."

"I'll help you." The words popped from Eve's mouth before she realized she'd said them. As she watched the proceedings of the past few minutes, a desire to help had gripped her.

The surprise on John's face slipped back into a frown. "I appreciate the offer, Eve, I do. But calving may not be something you'll want to see. I'll have enough to contend with out there without dealing with a female fainting at the sight of blood."

Eve prickled at John's presumption of her weakness, and anger flared in her chest. Stiffening her back, she lifted her chin and shot him a glare. "I have two good arms, and I saw plenty of blood at the school two weeks ago and didn't faint."

"Let her help, John." Clara turned from adding small pieces of wood to the stove's firebox. "Eve's right. She's stronger than you give her credit for." She gave Eve a confident smile before turning a sterner face to John. "You need help, and God has provided it."

John's eyes narrowed in deliberation. At last he exhaled a breath of resignation and bounced a somber look between Clara and Eve. "All right, but she'll need to change into a frock you don't mind ruining." His brow lowered in a grim line as his gaze settled on Eve. "I doubt it'll be worth keeping after today."

Ten minutes later in a patched and stained brown cotton dress that fit her like a sack, Eve followed John to the barn. The sense of victory she'd enjoyed earlier in the kitchen faded with each step, replaced by growing trepidation.

The smell of manure and the sound of bawling cows met them as they entered the dim barn. Eve followed John down a narrow, straw-strewn dirt corridor between stalls of brown and white cows. With each step, she fought the urge to run back to the house. But her determination to prove John wrong in his assumption of her feminine weaknesses trumped her fear, and she steeled herself against what might lie ahead.

At last they entered a stall where a brown cow lay on a bed of straw. The animal's stillness caused Eve's heart to sink. Had the cow died in John's absence? A sudden grunt and movement from the beast relieved Eve while, at the same time, sending her heart vaulting to her throat.

"Shh. There, girl." John patted the cow's brown rump. "We're gonna get this calf out." He turned to Eve, who stood with her back pressed against the stall's weathered boards. "Go to her head and try to keep her calm, but stay away from her legs. That's how Matt got kicked."

For a moment, Eve stood frozen with fear. The thought of approaching the big beast's head, let alone touching it, filled her with terror.

"Eve! Please. Do as I say."

Eve jerked at John's sharp voice, and she found she could move her limbs again. The thought of disappointing both John and herself propelled her to the cow's head.

Tentatively, she touched the cow's jaw. The silkiness of its hair surprised her, sparking an immediate feeling of sympathy for the beast. "There, there." Her courage growing with her empathy, she caressed the streak of white that ran the length of the cow's forehead. "Stay still, Ginger, and let John help your baby to be born."

A warm breath huffed from the cow's nostrils, and her head leaned harder against Eve's hand as if acknowledging Eve's show of compassion. Though happier to pet the suffering animal's head than to deal with the other end, Eve ventured a look at John and saw him take a length of chain from a nearby post.

"I'm going to have to pull the calf out." His jaw clenched, John sent Eve a stern glance from the back end of the cow. "She's not going to like this, so try to hold her as still as possible."

Nodding, Eve stiffened her back and held tight to each side of Ginger's face. Pressing her forehead to the cow's wooly one, she murmured, "Be strong, Ginger, and all will be well. I promise."

At the other end, John pulled on the chain he had evidently attached to some part of the unborn calf, grunting with the effort.

The cow jerked and emitted a loud bawl, but Eve managed to hold tight to her head. She looked back at John and saw what appeared to be a reddish brown blob with legs lying in a pool of blood. Instead of the revulsion she might have expected to feel at such a sight, Eve experienced a sense of amazement and exhilaration. She hugged the cow's head. "Look, Ginger, you have a baby!"

Ginger made no move or sound. Her big eyes closed, and her pink tongue lolled from the side of her mouth.

"Poor thing. You must be exhausted." Eve rubbed the cow's forehead. She had no idea how a cow—or a person for that matter—might react after having given birth, but a marked slackness in the animal's muscles troubled her.

"Eve. Come here, I need you." John's voice, though calm, held an urgency, and Eve hurried to his side.

She stifled a gasp at the sight that met her. John stood in an ankle-deep puddle of blood, shoving wads of rags into the animal's bottom in an effort to stem a gushing, gory flood. A couple steps away lay the lifeless-looking calf, still half-swaddled in the birth membrane.

John wiped the sweat pouring from his grim face with the back of a bloody wrist, leaving a red streak across his forehead. "Take one of those rags and wipe that calf. I don't think Ginger's going to be able to lick the life into her."

Eve obeyed, feeling as if her emotions had gone on a wild roller-coaster ride at Coney Island. *How did she know about Coney Island or what a roller-coaster ride there felt like?* Pushing the thought away, she focused on the hapless calf, rubbing gently so not to injure the infant animal.

Still at work on the cow, John looked over at her effort and scowled. "Hard! You'll have to rub her hard, or we'll lose the heifer." Drenched in sweat and blood, he stepped back from the cow, his shoulders sagging in defeat. "We've already lost the cow to a ruptured uterus."

Eve blinked back tears for the loss of the animal she'd petted and consoled moments earlier. A strong desire to save Ginger's calf gripped her, and she began rubbing the calf's wet hair with all her strength.

John came and knelt beside her. Together, they rubbed and massaged the limp calf for what seemed to Eve an interminable amount of time, though in reality a few minutes. Despair that rivaled what she'd felt when she woke three weeks ago with no memory engulfed her. Tears filled her eyes as resolve filled her chest. Renewed strength flowed into her aching arm muscles, and she rubbed the calf until it shook. "Come on, little cow. Live. Please live."

Chapter Seven

The calf jerked and emitted a tiny bleat. Joy exploded in Eve's chest like a Roman candle going off on the Fourth of July. A happy laugh burst from her lips as unashamed tears streamed down her cheeks. She lifted her face to meet John's widening grin and felt a connection as real and strong as if they'd embraced. For a long moment they sat amid the barn's muck gazing into each other's eyes, their hearts in complete harmony. No words were needed. Within the span of a few short minutes, they'd gone together from the depths of grief and despair at losing Ginger, to the heights of joy at the realization that her calf would live.

John leaned over the now twitching and bleating calf, and for one heart-stopping moment, Eve thought he might kiss her. Instead he stood, breaking the spell, then reached down and helped Eve to her feet. He turned and looked at Ginger's still form, his expression somber. "I'll need to get the milker to extract the colostrum. We'll have to bottle-feed it to the calf if she's to have any chance of thriving." He tossed the last few words over his shoulder as he bounded out of the stall toward the interior of the barn.

Eve shifted her gaze from John's retreating back at the dead cow, her earlier joy wilting into sadness. Sympathy and grief welled up in her chest, accompanied by a surprising twinge of guilt. She'd promised the cow all would be well, and now it lay lifeless.

A soft bleat from the corner of the stall drew her attention to the orphaned calf trembling in its straw nest. A wave of anger rolled over her, washing away all other emotions. Clara had prayed that Ginger be safely delivered of her calf and yet God—if there was a God—had turned a deaf ear to her pleas. The same God had allowed the train wreck that had stolen Eve's memory, taken Elmer Trowbridge's leg, and snuffed out a dozen lives.

John's abrupt return yanked Eve from her bitter muse. Laden with a bucket, short lengths of rubber hose, and a wooden contraption consisting of a seat and foot rests, John walked to Ginger and went to work attaching the hoses to the dead cow's udders.

The calf's pitiful cries filled Eve with compassion, and she hurried to the infant animal's side. "Poor baby." She patted the little heifer's still-damp hair. "I'm sorry about your mama, but don't cry. John and I will take care of you." She looked across the stall at John seated on the wooden contraption he had attached with the hoses to Ginger. As he pumped the treadles with his feet, bluish-white milk splat from the hoses into a bucket fixed at the front of the milking machine. After a few minutes work, he stopped and poured some of the milk into a waiting glass bottle, which he topped with a rubber finger-shaped lid.

John carried the large bottle of milk to where Eve sat with the calf and held it out to her. "Would you like to feed her?"

The offer caught Eve off guard. Her immediate hesitation quickly melted into a desire to comfort the motherless calf, and she nodded. "I'm not sure how well I'll do, but I'd like to try."

◆ ◆ ◆

John wasn't sure what had prompted him to ask Eve if she'd like to feed the calf. Something about the sight of her curled up beside the quivering baby heifer had entirely beguiled him.

He handed her the bottle, then helped her press the rubber nipple to the calf's mouth. With one lick of its pink tongue, the calf tasted the milk and began nursing in earnest.

"Look, she's doing it!" Eve turned a beaming face up to John, and his heart jolted. A riot of red-gold curls framed her rosy cheeks, petal-pink lips, and eyes the color of a clear autumn sky. Her beauty snatched the breath from his lungs as if he'd been punched in the midsection. How easy it would be to fall in love with her. *Easy and stupid.*

It took him a moment to recover sufficient air to reply. "Yes. I think she'll make it." He let go of the bottle, fearing she'd notice his hands shaking. All the while, his gaze remained fixed on the lovely picture she presented. "What should we name her? Ginger Junior, maybe?"

Eve's delicate forehead crinkled in thought. "Her color is closer to cinnamon than ginger." She angled another devastating smile at him. "Yes, I think her name should be Cinnamon."

Holding tight to the bottle being jerked up and down by the hungry calf, Eve glanced at the dead cow, and her smile faded. "What will you do with Ginger?"

"She'll have to be butchered. I have a couple neighbors who I think would be happy to help and share in the meat." In truth, John suspected that none of the meat would stay on the farm, doubting that Aunt Clara could bring herself to cook and eat her favorite cow. "The Lord gives and the Lord takes away."

Eve visibly stiffened, and her somber expression turned almost angry. Easing the bottle from Cinnamon's mouth, she handed it to John. "Seems to me that lately God's been doing a lot more taking away then giving." Despite the July heat, her cold glare and brittle tone chilled John like a blast of winter wind. A tinge of sarcasm crept into her voice. "I'll inform Clara that, as you say, God has both given and taken away. I'll tell her that while the names have changed, the total on her balance sheet remains the same."

Watching Eve's rod-straight back as she strode from the stall, John felt his heart break. How could he convince her of God's love and mercy after the tragedies she'd experienced during the last three weeks—the only time of which she had any memory?

◆ ◆ ◆

As July gave way to August, the answer to that question remained elusive. While Eve seemed happy on the farm, pouring most of her time into caring for Cinnamon, whom John had successfully placed with another cow that had recently lost a twin calf, her disinterest in anything associated with God persisted. Her polite silence during prayers and daily scripture reading couldn't mask her unease with those elements of worship. Though she attended church each Sunday with him, Aunt Clara, and Matthew, her fidgety, distracted demeanor at services suggested that her attendance had more to do with not disappointing Aunt Clara than with worshiping God.

That after more than a month of daily Christian influence Eve's attitude remained one of resignation rather than reverence maddened John. More troubling, the last comment she'd made before stalking from the barn following Cinnamon's birth slinked again from the recesses of his mind to gnaw at his suspicions about Eve's identity. Her use of the term *balance sheet* hadn't struck him as significant at the time, but after turning it over and over in his mind, he couldn't help but deduce that she'd had some experience in bookkeeping: another clue that suggested she might be the fugitive bank embezzler.

Regardless of the warning signs screaming at him of the danger in allowing his affection for Eve to grow, it had done just that. Her every look, every smile set his heart galloping. More than once, he'd had to walk away from her so he wouldn't take her in his arms and kiss her. *"Be ye not unequally yoked together with unbelievers."* The scripture from 2 Corinthians convicted him of his growing feelings for the woman sitting beside him on the wagon seat this second Sunday of August.

"Hyaa!" The frustration building in John's chest shot to his arms, and he slapped the reins down on the horse's rump sharper than he'd intended, causing the horse to jump.

"John, not so hard!" Aunt Clara, sitting with Matthew on the seat behind, leaned forward and put her hand on his shoulder. "We're not in that big of a hurry, dear." She gave his shoulder a pat that irked as much as her gentle chide. "We'll not get to church at all if Bob bucks us out of the wagon."

"Sorry, Aunt Clara." John's mumbled apology was quickly swallowed up by Matthew's eager talk of the coming state fair.

"They're givin' cash prizes for livestock." An audible hesitancy hobbled the excitement in the boy's voice. His next words tiptoed out as if testing the air. "Thought maybe I could enter one of the cows. Everybody says we have the best Jerseys around."

"Oh, I don't know, Matthew." Aunt Clara's voice sagged with regret. "We don't have a big herd. Can't really afford to give up one of our milk cows for a week, especially since we lost Ginger. She was our best milker."

At Matt's disappointed sigh, John hoped to cheer the boy with a compromise. "What about one of the calves, Matt? They give cash prizes for calves, too."

Matt perked up. "Yeah. We could take Cinnamon. What do ya think, Eve?"

John couldn't help smiling at Matt's inquiry. Everyone considered Cinnamon Eve's calf.

"Oh, I'd like that." Eve's bright voice warmed John's heart, which melted when a tinge of worry crept in. "I'd love to enter her in the fair if you don't think she's too young, John." She put her hand on his arm, setting his heart to hammering.

"She'd only have to be there the day of the judging, so as long as either you or Matt stayed with her, I think she should do fine." He gave her a smile which she rewarded with one of her own, turning his racing heart over.

Careful, John. Careful.

Turning his attention back to the road ahead, John clenched his teeth, knowing the feelings exploding in his chest had already rendered the warning blaring in his head futile.

❖ ❖ ❖

"He leadeth me, O blessed thought!
O words with heavenly comfort fraught!
What-e're I do, where-e're I be,

Still 'tis God's hand that leadeth me."

Generally Eve mouthed the words in the hymnals, giving them little or no thought. Today, this one found its way into her consciousness. Did God indeed lead people? She glanced down the pew at the people beside her. John, Clara, and Matthew thought so. Had God led her to this place? If so, to what purpose?

Those questions hung unanswered in Eve's mind as the song's next verse hit home:

> *"Sometimes mid scenes of deepest gloom,*
> *Sometimes where Eden's bowers bloom,*
> *By waters still, o're troubled sea,*
> *Still 'tis His hand that leadeth me."*

The words *deepest gloom* brought visions of the aftermath of the train wreck that had deposited her here: screams of pain and grief, Elmer Trowbridge's amputated limb, Eve's own anguish over her lost past. *Sometimes where Eden's bowers bloom.* Eden. This place had become her home, her sanctuary, and the Westons had become her family.

She looked past Clara and Matthew to John. Her angel-man. A beam of morning sun angled through a stained-glass window to light the back of his head, looking for all the world like a halo.

Eve's heart throbbed. A desire to possess for herself the peace now resting on his handsome countenance gripped her. When Ginger died, John and Clara had accepted the loss as God's will, choosing to focus instead on the blessing of Cinnamon's birth. At the time, their accepting attitude had both frustrated and angered Eve. But now, drinking in the words of the hymn, the notion that a loving, caring God had a larger purpose for all that happened and was leading Eve by the hand through both "scenes of deepest gloom" as well as "where Eden's bowers bloom" felt comforting.

> *"Content, what-ever lot I see,*
> *Since 'tis my God that leadeth me."*

Could Eve do that? Did she have the courage to put every part of her life into the hands of an unseen being?

Like a distant echo, faint words in her own voice formed in her mind: *God, help me!* While more a sense than a memory, the certainty that she'd once uttered that plea settled in her chest. And God *had* helped her. He'd sent her beautiful angel-man to rescue her and bring her into a safe, loving home. And yes, the cow Ginger had died, but her daughter lived, promising future milk production for the farm. Also, John and Clara had donated Ginger's meat to the county poorhouse, helping to feed those who depended on that charity.

Noticing Eve's gaze, John smiled, flooding her with warmth.

Eve's answering smile blooming on her lips faded as she settled back against the pew. They hadn't heard another word from Sheriff McCord since their visit to the school over a month ago. Most days Eve lived in the moment, enjoying life on the farm and helping to care for Cinnamon. But often in the predawn darkness, questions about her unknown past gathered around her like an ominous fog, jerking her awake in a breathless terror. Unsettling images would flash, then vanish—angry faces and the word BANK etched in stone. In those moments when she'd sit up in bed trembling and gasping for breath, her desire—no, her *need* for comfort became tangible. Despite her happy life here in Eden, she couldn't escape the fact that an uncertain future dangled over her head like the sword of Damocles. At any moment, Sheriff McCord, a Pinkerton agent, or some other lawman could appear with a warrant for her arrest and whisk her off to some dingy jail cell.

> *"He leadeth me, He leadeth me,*
> *By His own hand He leadeth me,*
> *His faithful follower I would be,*
> *For by His hand He leadeth me."*

Eve found herself joining in the refrain with full-throated enthusiasm. John and Clara's calm assurance of God's mercy began to make sense, and Eve wanted it. Today, instead of allowing her mind to wander, she listened to the minister's sermon on the Holy Spirit, which he called the "Comforter."

"'And I will pray the Father, and he shall give you another Comforter, that he may abide with you forever. . . . I will not leave you comfortless: I will come to you.'"

As the preacher read the words of Jesus from John 14, tears welled up in Eve's eyes, and a desperate longing screamed from her heart. Peace and comfort. Since waking in that crumpled train car, she'd desired nothing more than a sense of peace and comfort. Whatever lay ahead, she wanted to never again feel lost and alone. Whether her future held the serenity of Eden's bowers or the deepest gloom of a prison's horrors, she wanted the assurance of the salvation and comfort Jesus promised.

"All that is required for you to have the peace of Christ's salvation and the comfort that comes with that is to step forward today and accept it."

At the preacher's words, tears streamed down Eve's face. She rose and squeezed past Clara, Matthew, and finally John to make her way down the center aisle.

◆　◆　◆

Joy and astonishment vied for room in John's chest as he watched Eve walk to the minister and make her declaration of faith. The scene before him blurred, and he had to clear his throat before he could join in singing the benediction hymn.

"God bless you, Eve." The trite but heartfelt comment was all he could manage as he took her hand when a blubbering Aunt Clara finally released her from a smothering hug. Looking into Eve's beautiful face, her huge blue eyes swimming with happy tears, the temptation to declare his love for her then and there tugged hard at John. A thin strand of reason restrained him. As joyous as her decision to join the family of God was, it didn't erase the questions about her past.

The sight of an unsmiling Sid McCord making his way toward them at once alarmed John and validated his sobering thought.

Chapter Eight

*N*ew. Yes, that was the word.

Closing the kitchen door behind her, Eve looked eastward at the first pink streaks of dawn lightening the morning sky. For the past several days, she'd tried to define the feeling that had come over her since her decision to accept Christ. She felt new. Yes, she'd found the peace, the comfort Christ had promised in His Word. No longer did she wake in the night trembling with fear. Even Sheriff McCord's news that, though delayed, a Pinkerton agent had been assigned to her case and could arrive any day hadn't disturbed her serenity. But beyond the sense of calm that had enveloped her, she felt new. Though the facts of her past remained elusive, she'd asked God's forgiveness for any wrongs she had done in her life.

"Therefore if any man be in Christ, he is a new creature: old things are passed away; behold, all things are become new." The words from 2 Corinthians that John had read last night after supper played again through her mind in his deep, resonant voice.

John. The warmth flooding through her at the thought of him and the look he had given her when he read those words had nothing to do with the late-August morning. Her heart throbbed with a deep ache. She *was* new. God had made her new through Christ. Whoever she was before, wherever she'd lived before, now she belonged here in Eden.

She belonged with John. The bold thought at once surprised and saddened her.

Eve blinked back tears misting the rosy hue of the morning sky and quickened her steps toward the barn. The Pinkerton agent Sheriff McCord spoke of could arrive today to rip her from this place. *Away from John.*

"Dear Lord, don't let anyone take me away from here." The final words of her whispered prayer hung for a moment in the heavy morning air as she stepped into the barn. After Cinnamon's birth, she'd begun helping John with the morning milking to let Matthew's bruised arm heal and had continued the habit after the boy's arm was well again. While her claim of wanting to check on Cinnamon was true, she knew it was not the calf but the chance to spend more time with John that enticed her to arise before the sun each morning.

The now-familiar scents of the cows, manure, and straw met her inside the barn's dark interior. Something shot across her path. Startled, she gasped and stopped short, then giggled at her fright when she recognized one of the barn cats. The smells, sights, and sounds of the morning barn with its shifting shadows, mooing cows, and bleating calves had become both commonplace and comforting.

"Did Nubbin scare you?" John's deep voice as he stepped from a stall behind her set her heart pounding.

"You'd think I'd be used to him by now." Eve couldn't stop the nervous giggle that accompanied her light quip and hoped John didn't detect the breathlessness in her voice.

His expression softened with his voice. A dim ray of morning light slipped between the building's weathered wallboards, illuminating his handsome features. "I won't let them, you know."

Eve's heart hammered harder, and her breath caught in her throat as he stepped nearer. Did he have any idea what his nearness did to her? "W–what? You won't let them what?"

He curled warm fingers around her upper arm, sending pleasant tingles from her shoulder to the tips of her fingers. "I won't let them take you away." A grin lifted the corner of his mouth, and he glanced away for a second, looking as boyish as a six-foot-tall man could look. "I didn't mean to hear your prayer, but I don't want you to worry. You must know I'll do everything I can to keep you here."

Eve's heart throbbed, and unexpected tears sprang to her eyes and slipped down her face. "Dear John." She lifted her wet face to him and cupped his bristly jaw in her hand. "I know you'll do what you can, but—"

"Eve." His voice turned husky. He slid his arms around her waist and drew her against him. For one long moment, their gazes held, and she felt as if she were sinking into the depths of his hazel eyes. As if in a dream, she watched his dark lashes sweep down to kiss his cheeks the instant before his lips kissed hers.

For one heart-stopping moment, time stood still. There was no barn, no cows, no world, only Eve and her angel-man floating in a sweet sphere oblivious to any earthly intrusion. Then Eve felt a subtle shift, deep in her being. In that moment, the planets aligned, and she slipped into the niche in the universe carved explicitly for her. All doubt evaporated like the morning fog beneath the rising sun. This is where she belonged: here in the arms of her angel-man.

Too soon he lifted his lips from hers, shattering the spell that had bound them together, while still holding her in the circle of his arms.

Eve slammed back to earth with a jolt. Garish reason crashed over her like an icy ocean wave, demolishing the beautiful dream that had enveloped her. As much as both she and John might want it, they couldn't begin to contemplate a future together until they learned her identity. She pushed away from him and fought fresh tears. "There's no sense in it, John. You don't know who I am. What if I'm the fugitive embezzler the Pinkertons are after?"

A smile strolled across his well-shaped lips, and he gathered her back into his arms. "I may not know the name you were born with, or where and how you lived before you came here, but I know who you are. I know your heart and your soul. You are Eve, and your spirit is as beautiful as your face." His smile quirked into a grin. "I used to be a policeman, remember? I know a thing or two about criminals. If you *were* a criminal, even if you didn't know it, your instinct would have been to run, not to stay here."

Eve's heart crumpled. She loved him even more for trying to convince her, or maybe both of them, of her innocence. For now, it was enough to know that John cared for her and wanted her to stay here in Eden. John trusted in God, and now, so did she. If God meant for her to stay here in Eden with John, God would allow that to happen. But if she had committed acts that would require her to pay restitution and snatch her away rom him, at least she now had the assurance that Christ would walk with her through whatever unpleasantness lay ahead.

Hoping to lighten the mood, she smiled and took his hand. "I couldn't run away if I wanted to. I don't have any money." She turned and began towing him toward Cinnamon's stall. "Come on. I want to say good morning to Cinnamon and brush her coat before I get started milking. I need to keep her looking her best for the fair competition."

◆　◆　◆

ohn stared at the farm's ledger book lying open on the kitchen table, but his mind refused to register the figures on the lined pages. In the two weeks since he and Eve had shared that kiss in the barn, he'd struggled to focus his thoughts on anything other than the woman he loved. Yes, he loved her. That acknowledgement at once thrilled and frustrated him. Since that morning, she'd allowed no other opportunity for such a private moment between them, avoiding any situation where they might be alone together. She'd stopped volunteering to help with the morning milking and now waited to tend to Cinnamon while John and Matthew were busy filling the milk cans and moving them to the springhouse.

Giving up on the ledger, John leaned back in the kitchen chair, expelled a breath of frustration, and shoved his fingers through his hair. Most maddening was knowing that Eve cared for him, too. Despite her increasingly distant attitude toward him, he'd caught her in unguarded moments gazing at him with a look so tender his heart seized. But she'd made it clear: until they learned her identity, she refused to allow their relationship to grow, and despite multiple inquiries, Sid McCord had received no further word on when the Pinkerton agent assigned to Eve's case might arrive.

"John, have you been in my butter-and-egg money?" Across the kitchen, Aunt Clara frowned into the blue speckled crock where she kept the money from her weekly sale of eggs and butter.

"No. Is there some missing?" Pushing the chair back with a screech, John got up and walked to the cabinet beside the sink where his aunt stood peering into the container.

"All of it. Ten whole dollars." A mixture of surprise and dismay played over her wrinkled features.

"Are you sure you didn't spend it on the material you bought to make those new dresses you and Eve plan to wear to the fair tomorrow?" John leaned in to look into the crock.

"No." Aunt Clara's frown deepened as she continued to gaze into the empty vessel, as if by doing so, she could make the missing money appear. "I was careful to keep this back so Eve and I would have a little spending money for the fair."

"Have you asked Matthew, or. . .Eve?" John struggled to make his lips form her name even as his mind raced toward possibilities he didn't want to explore.

"No, I just now found it gone." Aunt Clara replaced the crock on the cabinet shelf. The sadness in her eyes and in the deepening lines around her pursed mouth sparked a quick anger in John.

He patted her shoulder. "Don't worry, Aunt Clara. I'll find out what happened to your money and get it back for you." John headed for the kitchen door, intent on questioning Matthew and Eve, when Aunt Clara's voice stopped him.

"Matthew's off making those milk deliveries to Fortville and Pendleton, so you won't be able to ask him about it until sometime this afternoon, though I can't imagine him doing such a thing."

That Aunt Clara didn't mention Eve fueled John's growing suspicions. Eve's parting words after their kiss two weeks ago echoed in his head. *I couldn't run away if I wanted to. I don't have any money.* Ten dollars would buy a standard coach ticket to New York. "Where's Eve?"

"In the barn tendin' to Cinnamon, I think." Aunt Clara's voice sounded strained as she turned to the sink and began busying herself folding towels and rearranging sundries.

Striding to the barn, John dreaded having to question Eve about the missing money and grappled with how best to word his inquiry. Worse, he dreaded her reaction. Would she get angry, or cry, or look him in the eye and lie? His heart hammering, he walked to Cinnamon's stall, bracing himself for the encounter ahead. When he finally reached the calf's enclosure, his heart sank. Except for the little red heifer, the stall was empty.

Chapter Nine

The sights, sounds, and smells of the Indiana State Fair bombarded Eve's senses. Crowds of milling people covered the fairgrounds like ants on a morsel of discarded food. A cacophony of voices and animal sounds, as well as a mixture of discordant clanging noises and the lilting notes of a distant calliope assailed her ears. The smells of frying foods, popcorn, and livestock somehow mingled together to form a surprisingly pleasant aroma. For the first time since yesterday's strange occurrences, she felt the tension in her body melt away.

When she and Matthew returned from making the milk deliveries to Fortville and Pendleton, Eve had noticed an odd quietness in John's and Clara's demeanors. At first she thought that perhaps the two were miffed that she had accompanied Matthew without letting them know she was going, but when she apologized for doing so, they assured her they didn't mind and even thanked her for helping Matthew. The reason for their strained moods became clearer when, after supper, Clara asked if anyone had borrowed the ten dollars from the crock where she kept her butter-and-egg money. When no one answered, Clara had walked to the kitchen cabinet and taken down the crock. Then, looking into the vessel, her eyes had popped big as silver dollars. Stammering, she'd gazed into the crock as if seeing something astounding. "W–why, it's back." Taking out one of the bills, she'd fingered the money as if to assure herself it was real before replacing it. She'd returned the crock to the shelf and said no more about it.

As John interlocked one arm with Eve and the other with Clara, helping to shepherd them through the throng of fairgoers, Eve wished she could read his thoughts. Did he think she had taken Clara's money, then changed her mind and returned it when no one was around? Did Clara think so as well? The thought saddened her.

John stopped in front of a large white structure marked Fine Arts Building and slipped his arms from hers and Clara's. He glanced at the basket on Clara's free arm. "You ladies go on in and register those jams while Matthew and I get Cinnamon off the railcar and take her to the cattle barn."

Though she'd rather go with John and Matthew to get Cinnamon, Eve knew Clara would appreciate her company. Inside the building, the line to register exhibits, while long, moved rather quickly.

With the registration completed, Clara turned a knowing grin to Eve. "I appreciate your company, Eve, but you're prancin' like a filly that wants to run. I know you're dyin' to see that calf, so if you think you can find your way to the cow barn, you go right ahead."

Concern tempered the excitement bouncing in Eve's chest. "Are you sure, Clara? I hate to leave you here alone."

"Alone?" Clara glanced around the room teeming with women and chuckled. "I don't see a chance of being alone." She patted Eve's hand. "I might even make a few new friends. Now you go on and help get Cinnamon settled in."

Giving Clara a parting hug, Eve headed out of the building and in the direction John and Matthew had taken earlier. A few minutes later, the familiar sound of mooing cows led Eve to the cattle barn.

She scanned the barn's interior filled with row upon row of bawling cows and bleating calves. Her heart sank. How would she ever find John, Matt, and Cinnamon among the crowd? She'd walked several of the straw-strewn aisles when a flash of red caught her eye. Matt had worn a new red bandana around his neck this morning. Quickening her steps, she headed in the direction where she'd seen the color and found Matthew brushing Cinnamon's coat.

He looked up and smiled. "Hey, Eve. Cinnamon seems in great shape." His grin widened. "I think she enjoyed her first train ride."

Eve patted the calf's wooly head and angled a smile at Matt. "John thinks she's worthy of at least a first-place prize if not champion, and I agree." She glanced around the immediate area. "Where is John?"

Matt's expression turned somber, and his gaze dropped to the straw-covered floor. "Eve, I have somethin' I need to tell you." He lifted his gaze back to her, and the sadness in his face sent a shudder through Eve's heart.

Fear clutched at her throat. Had something happened to John?

"It was me that took Grandma's butter-and-egg money," Matt blurted. "I just wanted to get my special girl, Emily, somethin' nice at the midway." The regret in his voice pled for understanding. "I know it was wrong, but John said Cinnamon is good enough to win a money prize. I was goin' to replace Grandma's money with the prize money. Never thought she'd check it before the fair."

A mixture of disappointment and anger tangled in Eve's chest. "Why didn't you just ask your grandma for the money?"

His face puckered deeper with remorse. "I know I should have, but she gave me five dollars two weeks ago and said it had to last till next month." His gaze slid back to the tops of his dusty shoes. "I spent it on a music box and ribbons for Emily's birthday. I knew if I asked for more Grandma would ask me what happened to the money she gave me, and I'd have to tell her." His mouth slanted in a half grin. "Grandma pinches a penny till it hollers. She'd have said I'd spent enough money on Emily and would have refused to give me any more."

Having become familiar with Clara's frugal ways, Eve tended to agree with Matthew's assumption. She also shared Clara's likely sentiment and bit back the scolding perched on the tip of her tongue.

Matthew's voice lowered with his gaze. "So when we got back from milk deliveries and John said Grandma had something to ask us, I got scared and put the money back when Grandma was in the garden pickin' tomatoes. Didn't want them to know what I'd done, and I sure didn't aim for them to think you took it. Can you forgive me?" His brown eyes glistened with sorrow.

Still reeling from the boy's confession, Eve stood mute while fear for John gnawed at her chest. At the dejection on Matthew's face, her heart crumpled, and she hugged him.

He could easily have kept the money and blamed her. That he didn't spoke well of his character and upbringing. "Of course I forgive you, but you know you'll need to tell John and your grandmother." Pushing away, she gripped his shoulders, her greater concern for John swamping any disappointment at Matt's transgression. "Where is John? Is he all right?"

"I was about to tell you." Matt ran a shirtsleeve across his damp cheek. "I already told him, and he headed out to find you. Said he had some apologizin' of his own to do."

A wave of relief rolled through Eve, leaving her weak. "So he went to the Fine Arts Building?"

"Yeah. Then he planned to take in a sulky race at the grandstand." Matt grinned. "Said he hoped you'd go with him."

Eve's heart lifted like the helium-filled balloons she'd seen around the fair, and she gave Matt another quick hug. "Thanks, Matthew. And thank you for telling me. That took courage. I'm proud of you, and I'm sure John and your grandmother are proud of you, too." She glanced down at Cinnamon munching on hay. "Will you stay with Cinnamon while I go find John?"

"Sure." Matthew's beaming face reflected the joy filling Eve's chest as she headed out of the cow barn.

Anticipation at seeing John again and knowing he no longer suspected her of taking Clara's money lightened Eve's steps. As she neared the grandstand, she couldn't stop the mischievous smile stretching her lips. Perhaps she should make him grovel a bit before accepting his invitation to see the sulky race.

A grip on her arm yanked her from her muse and pulled her up short.

"Anne Stanton?" A well-dressed man, still gripping her arm, stepped in front of her. "Are you Anne Stanton of Buffalo, New York?" He pulled back his blue seersucker jacket to reveal a pewter-colored badge pinned to his shirt. "Alfred Douglas, Pinkerton agent." He gave his bowler hat a quick lift as a lazy smile raised the corner of his clipped mustache. "I'm here to take you back to Buffalo."

The fear that sparked at the man's first touch flamed to a conflagration of terror. Blind panic swept away reason. Breaking away from the lawman's grasp, Eve dashed into the crowd milling in front of the grandstand, desperate to find John and to put distance between herself and the Pinkerton agent.

Dear Lord, let John be here! Inside the grandstand arena, the silent prayer screamed from her hammering heart as she scanned the bleachers. The figure of an auburn-haired man in a chambray shirt in the upper levels of the bleachers caught her eye.

"John." Exhaling his name on a puff of breath, she raced up the steps dividing two sections of the raised plank seats then worked her way over to the outside edge where she thought she'd seen John.

"John."

The man turned and Eve's heart sank. It wasn't John.

"Anne Stanton, stop!" The Pinkerton agent's angry voice sounded beneath her.

Desperate to escape, she stepped back, realizing too late she'd run out of bleacher. The sensation of falling, her strangled scream, and the jarring impact of her body hitting the sandy ground all happened in the span of heartbeat. Then blackness.

◆ ◆ ◆

"Eve. Eve, wake up."

The frantic voice sounded like John's, but echoey and faint, as if from a long way away.

"Eve, honey, wake up. Please, Lord, let her be all right. Please, God, don't take her from me."

The crack in John's voice broke her heart. She had to find her way to him and let him know that she loved him, that she wanted to stay with him and never leave him.

"Eve." His voice sounded clearer now, his breath warm against her face.

She needed to see his face. She struggled to open her eyes. Her lids fluttered open, allowing the daylight to stream in and her darling's dear face to come into focus. With the light, a flood of memories poured over her, jolting her fully awake. She sat up in John's arms, where he knelt beside her in the dirt, supporting her back.

"Anne." The word came out in a tone of wonder as the events of the past several months flooded back. "My name is Anne Stanton. I live in Buffalo, New York, with my parents, Ezra and Margaret Stanton, and my little brother, Oliver."

The enormity of the pain she must have caused her family shook Anne to the core, sending an avalanche of regret tumbling over her. Tears blurred her vision and flooded down her face. "Oh John, what have I done? They must think I'm dead!"

Pounded by a mountain of grief and remorse, Anne gave in to the gut-wrenching sobs that overtook her. Cradled in her angel-man's arms, she buried her face against his broad chest, luxuriating in the solace of his murmured endearments and the muffled beating of his heart beneath the soft fabric of his shirt.

"Don't worry, my darling, we will let them know you are here and well." Sadness tinged his voice. "And that you will be heading back to them soon."

Another image appeared before her eyes, rekindling her panic. Edmund. She pushed away from John's embrace. "I can't. I can't go back. I can't marry him. Please, John, don't make me go back."

"Who can't you marry?" The pain in John's eyes slashed at Anne's heart.

"Edmund Bickford, Miss Stanton's intended." The Pinkerton agent stood over them, his arms crossed over his seersucker-clad chest. "Miss Stanton's father is president of Buffalo Bank and Trust. It seems she convinced him to give her two hundred dollars from her trust account to spend on a trousseau, then disappeared."

The man's cool description of her duplicity smacked Anne in the face. John must find her repugnant. Still, the need to explain her actions and perhaps soften his opinion gripped her. She turned to face the man she loved, praying he would understand. "I never wanted to marry Edmund, John. Father chose him for me. Father and Edmund's father are business partners. To them, our proposed marriage is little more than a business deal." She took John's hands in hers, willing him to understand. "I begged my father not to make me marry Edmund, not to force me into a loveless marriage, but he told me to do as he said and that I'd get used to it." Anne hated the tears streaming down her cheeks, blurring John's dear features. "I didn't know what else to do, so I lied to get the money and headed to St. Louis, hoping a distant cousin there would take me in."

A series of indescribable emotions played across John's face, but his silence confirmed Anne's worst fears.

Dropping her gaze to their clasped hands, she managed to croak, "You must hate me."
"No." His tone turned incredulous. "Of course I don't hate you. I love you."

Hearing the words she'd longed to hear her angel-man say sent a fresh cascade of tears down her face.

"Do you think you can stand?"

When she nodded, he stood and helped her up, then immediately went down on one knee. Taking her hand in his, he gazed up into her sodden face. "Anne Stanton, will you do me the honor of becoming my wife?"

Unable to speak through her sobs, Anne nodded, finally managing to squeak out a yes.

John stood, wrapped her in his arms, and sealed their promise with a kiss. Then he turned to the Pinkerton agent, who emitted a soft cough into his balled fist and looked as if he wished to be somewhere else. "Whatever my fiancée owes her father, I'll be happy to repay."

The lawman grinned, his gaze sliding between Anne and John. "Mr. Stanton cares nothing about the money. He simply wants to know the whereabouts of his daughter, and that I can tell him."

John gave the agent his mailing address and that of Sheriff McCord's office, then cocked his head, a bemused look on his face. "So what about the woman bank embezzler from Buffalo?"

Mr. Douglas nodded, a knowing expression blooming on his face. "The Bouchard woman? Apprehended last week in Montreal by the Royal Canadian Mounted Police, extradition pending."

The two men exchanged a handshake, and Agent Douglas congratulated John and Anne on their engagement, wished them well, and with a tip of his bowler hat, headed out of the grandstand.

John drew Anne behind the grandstand and slid his arms around her waist. "Are you sure this is what you want? Sounds like you had a much different life in Buffalo." His gaze broke away from hers. "I wouldn't want you to regret—"

She touched her finger to his lips, silencing him. "Anne Stanton may have belonged in Buffalo, but Eve belongs in Eden."

A grin worked its way across John's lips before he pulled her into his arms and kissed her, as the crowd cheered amid a cloud of dust and the cacophony of racing sulkies and pounding hooves.

Ramona K. Cecil is a wife, mother, grandmother, freelance poet, and award-winning inspirational romance writer. Now empty nesters, she and her husband make their home in Indiana. A member of American Christian Fiction Writers and American Christian Fiction Writers Indiana Chapter, her work has won awards in a number of inspirational writing contests. Over eighty of her inspirational verses have been published on a wide array of items for the Christian gift market. She enjoys a speaking ministry, sharing her journey to publication while encouraging aspiring writers. When not writing, her hobbies include reading, gardening, and visiting places of historical interest.

Love on the Rails

by Lynn A. Coleman

Dedication

This book is dedicated to my granddaughter Leanna and her fiancé as they put their final plans together for their upcoming marriage and life together. May you and Andrew continue to deepen your love, friendship, and relationship with God; each has blessed your grandfather and me all these years and will for years to come.

Chapter One

J effery glanced at the hand-engraved gold pocket watch for the fifth time in less than a minute. He closed his eyes, removed his handkerchief, and sopped up the sweat beading down his forehead and the back of his neck. His bride had been due here thirty minutes ago with the arrival of the Charleston-Savannah Railroad. He'd arranged this marriage because it was what his parents wanted.

Truthfully, he didn't have the time to court and make nice with a woman to determine whether she was worthy to be his wife or not. But on the other hand, he couldn't imagine marrying one of the women of his own social class. None carried a thought in their heads beyond the next social ball. Savannah had its share of social events— enough to keep a couple well entertained throughout the year. But Jeffery always found himself drifting off into business conversations, plotting new ventures during such events. He would dance with a man's wife or daughter all for the purpose of business. No woman had ever succeeded in turning his attention from work. The many who tried soon gave up on him. All of which suited him just fine. . .until the reading of his grandfather's will.

Jeffery caressed the gold watch. . .his grandfather's watch. His heart ached for Grandpa Joe, as the man had preferred to be called by family. He'd been gone for the better part of a year now, and life just didn't seem the same without his grandfather in his life. Grandpa Joe was a self-made man who had taught his son and grandson the value of hard work and industry.

Jeffery flipped open the watch cover and read the message within: *"Whoso findeth a wife findeth a good thing, and obtaineth favour of the Lord. Proverbs 18:22."* *That was Grandpa Joe,* he thought with a sigh, *always praising his wife, even a decade after she'd passed on.* He'd always said he would not be the man he was if it weren't for Grandma Bertha. And that explained his Last Will And Testament, which stipulated that if Jeffery didn't find a wife before his thirtieth birthday. . . Jeffery snapped the watch shut, turned away from the empty rails, and strode back to the station under the shade of the veranda.

A distant whistle blew. Jeffery leaned from the shade into the blistering sun, then back again. With any luck they'd make it to the courthouse in time to be married before the office closed.

He pulled out the letter of response he'd selected following his advertisement posted in a New York City newspaper:

475 W. Broadway
New York City, N.Y.

Dear Mr. Oliver,

 I am responding to your offer in the newspaper. I am a strong woman, in good health, and looking for a husband. I can cook and sew, per your request. I am handy in the garden, and while it is not my favorite activity, I can wash and clean clothing. I have a fair appearance. I would not call myself a beauty, but one should not be bored with my features. I love children and look forward to being a mother one day if the Good Lord blesses.

Sincerely,
Tilda Green

The ground rumbled beneath his feet as heavy wheels braked on the steel rails amid clouds of steam and the shrill warning of the train's whistle. He tucked the letter back in his right coat pocket and stepped forward. *Dear Lord, I hope I haven't made a mistake.*

◆ ◆ ◆

Tilda grabbed her carpetbag as the train came to a stop. Steam released into the air with a great gasp as the big iron horse finally stood still. Her body continued to vibrate. She'd been riding on the train for a day and a half. Jeffery Oliver had spared no expense with her ticket, reserving a spot on a Pullman Palace Car. She'd never traveled in such luxury. She'd had her own bedchamber, and he'd paid for all her meals. She'd probably gained five pounds.

Inside her one small trunk, she'd packed a few mementos, a couple of dresses, undergarments, and a picture of her parents. Her letter to Mr. Oliver had been sent on a whim—or was it desperation? Never in a million years would she have guessed she'd be moving to the South to marry a man she'd never met before.

Pushing a stray hair behind her ear, she slipped into the private bath chamber, glanced into the mirror, and pinned her chestnut brown hair back in place. She checked the pins in her hat, then straightened her dress. She'd heard that Savannah was a beautiful and historic city. Tilda loved exploring, and Savannah sounded perfect. She couldn't wait to become familiar with this new place.

The train jerked as she stepped into the passageway. She grabbed the doorframe so she didn't land on her backside. Out the window, people milled about, waiting for the passengers to exit. She scanned their faces. One of them was her husband, though she'd been given no description of Mr. Jeffery Oliver.

Her heart thudded in her chest.

The others in the car stepped forward as the smiling porter—proud in his uniform and white gloves—opened the door and wished each passenger well.

Tilda noticed folks were slipping him a coin as they departed. She'd learned that a quarter was the proper tip to give the porter for any and every service he performed. She reached into her drawstring bag and pulled out a coin.

"Pleasure to have you on board, Miss Green."

"Pleasure was mine." She handed him the coin as she shook his hand. A smile inched across her face realizing how practiced he was in accepting the gratuity.

"Your fiancé is a blessed man."

"Thank you." Tilda hoped he would be a good husband. He had to be better than the man she'd left behind in New York. Reginald Murphy had pledged to her father he would oversee her assets. Instead, he attempted to trick her into marrying him in order to gain possession of her inheritance. Mr. Oliver didn't know about her inheritance. If he proved to be an honorable man, she would tell him. Until then, she would keep that part of her life a secret.

Marrying a man she didn't know seemed a whole lot better than marrying the man who only wanted her money. Reginald was twenty years her senior. . . Mr. Oliver's advertisement didn't state his age. *Dear Lord*—she closed her eyes and prayed—*I hope I followed your lead.*

◆　◆　◆

Jeffery watched as an unescorted woman descended the stairs. His bride. She had a regal set to her shoulders. Her brown hair was tied in a loose braid slipped up under her hat. It was a conservative hat, not given to a lot of adornment. *She may think she's plain,* he thought, noting her delicate nose and soft chin, *but she is beautiful.* He stepped forward. "Miss Green?"

She turned in his direction, smiled, and assessed him as carefully as he had been scrutinizing her. "Mr. Oliver?"

He nodded with the removal of his hat. "At your service. I trust your accommodations were sufficient."

"Superb, thank you. I've never ridden in a Pullman Palace before. It was quite comfortable."

Jeffery smiled. "I had heard, although I have not had the pleasure. My carriage is over there," he said, indicating the location with an outstretched arm. "Are your trunks labeled with my address?" He took her carpetbag in his left hand and offered the elbow of his right. As she placed her hand in its crook, he moved to place his hand on top of hers. . . but held back, chastising himself for such a foolishly intimate impulse, especially while carrying her carpetbag.

"Yes, as you instructed."

"Wonderful." He lifted his grandfather's watch from his waistcoat pocket and flicked it open. "If we hurry, we'll get to the courthouse in time to get married."

She halted. "We're not going to have a church wedding?"

"I'm sorry. I assumed—since you didn't know anyone—a courthouse wedding seemed appropriate."

Her chest heaved, and she nodded. "I understand. A courthouse wedding is fine."

"Excellent." He led her to a stately, highly polished landau carriage. "I know the judge; he's a deacon in the church. I'm certain he wouldn't mind saying a prayer of blessing over the vows."

"I would feel better knowing the Lord is a part of our marriage."

"I'll make the arrangements. This is my carriage," he said, handing her bag to his driver. He then opened the door for her to step inside its plush black-and-red interior.

Being the gentleman his parents raised, he held out his hand to assist her. Its soft warmth sent a wave of calm over him. Jeffery shook off the surprising reaction to their contact and walked around the carriage as James secured the carpetbag in the carriage boot. He climbed in, latching the door behind him, and settled beside his bride.

The carriage roof provided modest shade for Miss Green. Normally, he would travel with the top down. But Savannah heat could be quite challenging for the uninitiated. So he gambled on the side of caution, figuring the northern climes of New York City were bound to be much cooler. In fact, in anticipation of his marriage, he'd purchased the home where they would begin their married lives precisely because of its location under a grove of oaks. In addition to the ample shade they provided, the house was positioned so as to capture the cool breezes off the Savannah River. Prior to that, he'd made his home with his parents in the same house he'd been born in nearly thirty years prior. That family home sat proudly on one of the famous city squares designed by Oglethorpe back in the sixteen hundreds.

"Courthouse, James." He'd hired the young man who had worked for his father in the stables to drive the carriage this day.

"Yes, sir." James flicked the reins, and the horse plodded forward. The harness jangled with each step.

Jeffery turned to his bride. She really was quite handsome to look at. "Are you familiar with driving a buggy?"

She nodded. "Yes. I didn't have many opportunities, nor was there much need in the city, but on Sundays our family would rent a carriage and ride through and around Central Park. Mother would make a basket of food, and we would stop for a picnic."

Her eyes glistened. He recalled she had mentioned in her second letter that she no longer had any living relatives. "If you don't mind me asking, what happened to your parents?"

She glanced down at her lap and fiddled with the drawstrings of her purse. "They died about a year ago." She swallowed. "They were traveling to the Cape, and the train derailed."

"My condolences." He turned and faced the front. "If it is of any comfort, my parents are still alive."

Out of the corner of his eye he saw her give a brief nod, then turn her attention to the various houses as they rode down West Broad Street toward Broughton and the Courthouse. "If you look down there"—he pointed to the right—"you'll see Liberty Square. General James Oglethorpe designed the city with numerous squares. Each community has a place to gather, sit in the shade of the trees, and enjoy their neighbors. It's a marvelous plan." He was rambling, he knew.

He pointed up ahead. "That's the back of the white marble courthouse. A bit farther up ahead is Bay Street and the Savannah River."

Her eyes widened—with excitement, he hoped. "It is clearly a city," she commented, "but much smaller than New York."

Jeffery's back stiffened. Did she regret her decision to come to Savannah?

Chapter Two

Tilda's mind couldn't stay on one subject. The new sights, sounds, and smells all piqued her curiosity. Then the reality of her situation slammed back to the forefront. The courthouse. She was about to marry a man she didn't know. They hadn't said more than a couple of words to each other. Didn't he want to get to know her better? Or was this going to be a marriage one of her friends had warned her about, a marriage where the wife was a second-class citizen. Where the man made all the decisions, and the wife cooked, cleaned, and raised children. Her heart pulsed in her chest. She sucked in a deep pull of air. It was hot, humid, and stuck to her teeth. "It's a beautiful city."

His shoulders relaxed. "I love it." He smiled.

"You should see New York sometime. The height of the buildings, the—"

He stiffened.

She narrowed her gaze. "Are you one of those southerners who hate the North?"

"What?" He turned to her.

"You stiffen up every time I mention New York. Why would you seek a wife from the North if—"

"Forgive me. I was merely concerned that Savannah might not be to your taste, coming from such an affluent city."

"Oh." Tilda relaxed. "I love history and architecture. I can see that I will be fascinated by the delightful buildings of your city."

His smile returned. A very pleasant smile, she decided, that sent a wave of peace down her spine. Perhaps she hadn't made the wrong decision, after all.

"There is a lot of history here in Savannah," he offered. "In fact, there is a historical society you might wish to explore."

The carriage slowed as James pulled it toward the stone curb. Jeffery Oliver jumped out of the carriage and rounded it to open her door. He was a gentleman. He hadn't waited for his servant to open the door for both of them. "Here we are, my dear," Mr. Oliver said with a slight bow.

She placed her hand in his and stepped down off the carriage. It was a nice carriage, not overly ornate but representative of modest income. Her father often rented a landau. She scanned the area and could see a bit of the Savannah River between the buildings that crowded the shoreline. The mastheads of tall ships poked up over their roofs.

Jeffery led her up the stairs, through the great doors into the hall, and down the hallway to Judge Burrow's office. A young man seated behind a polished wooden desk stood as they entered the office. "Evening, Mr. Oliver. The judge will be right with you. Excuse me while I notify him."

"He knows you?" she asked. Her knees were beginning to shake.

"Only because I came in earlier and made arrangements for our wedding ceremony," he whispered.

"Oh." Jeffery Oliver was a planner.

"His Honor says to come right in," the young man said as he exited the judge's chambers.

"Thank you." Jeffery led her in.

"Good afternoon, Mr. Oliver." Judge Burrow extended his hand as he stood up from behind his desk. "And who might this beautiful lady be?"

Jeffery placed a hand upon hers. "This is Tilda Green from New York City. She's done me the honor of consenting to be my wife."

The judge, a broad man with a round belly and equally round face, smiled. "Ah, a man who findeth a wife. . ."

Jeffery Oliver's eyebrows shot up. "Yes, my grandfather often quoted that verse."

"Joseph was a good man, God rest his soul. I still miss him." The judge turned to her. "A pleasure to meet you, Miss Green."

"The pleasure is mine, Your Honor." He smiled, though Tilda didn't know if it was because she said the right thing or that she'd used the wrong title. She hadn't had any encounters with judges or magistrates until the death of her parents. Then she'd seen more than she'd hoped to see in her lifetime.

He clapped his hands. "Shall we get down to business? Did you file the papers with the clerk, Mr. Oliver?"

"Yes, Your Honor." He pulled the folded document from inside his dress coat pocket. Tilda examined the cut of Jeffery's clothes. He wore a well-tailored suitcoat without tails, but the cut was below his backside. The lapels were double-breasted and broad, though not as broad as some. The bow tie was made of a rich blue silk, bringing out the blue in his eyes. The vest was of a shade of ivory, a bit darker than his shirt, which seemed to be a lighter ivory color. The jacket sported a pattern of dark gray stripes offset by a seemingly single strand of lighter gray thread. Tilda knew fabric well enough to recognize the delicate line was composed of more than a single strand. The cuffs of the jacket were also light gray and had the same accent of blue silk covering the buttons on the cuffs as his tie.

Tilda examined the buttons more closely. They were cufflinks. . .button-shaped cufflinks that could be changed to fit the attire. *Interesting,* she reflected. *Jeffery Oliver is clearly a man who takes great care with his appearance.* She wondered what that might mean for his personal life overall.

"Wonderful." The judge's words brought her back from her musings. "Let us begin."

"One moment, please," Jeffery spoke up. "My wife-to-be would like it if you could add a prayer for the Lord to bless our marriage."

The judge smiled. "I'd be honored." He opened a small black book and began. "Let us pray."

Tilda's heartbeat pounded in her ears.

Three minutes later they were signing a piece of paper and the judge was pumping her husband's hand. *Husband.* It was hard to believe. It didn't seem possible.

"Thank you, Your Honor," Jeffery Oliver said as he picked up the marriage license.

"Pleasure was all mine, Mr. Oliver. Congratulations. Best wishes, Mrs. Oliver. I trust you'll find Savannah pleasing to your sensibilities. It is a fine city."

"I'm certain I will, Your Honor, thank you." Tilda nodded. Judging from how quickly they were married, no doubt they'd soon be consummating their marital arrangement. Tilda looked upon the face of her new husband as they turned to leave. Fear washed over her. She didn't even know this man.

Jeffery took her elbow and led her out of the judge's chambers, past the attendant's desk, through the hall, and back to the awaiting carriage where James stood at attention.

Jeffery opened the door, helped Tilda in, then stepped back. "James will take you home. I have work I need to finish. I should be home at six." Jeffery tapped the top of the carriage. "I'll see you later, Mrs. Oliver."

The carriage jolted forward, and Tilda leaned back. *What just happened?*

◆　◆　◆

Jeffery watched as the carriage drove off and headed down Bay Street. He'd seen the fear in her eyes after they signed the marriage certificate. He'd give her a bit of time to adjust to their married status. He turned and walked to his office.

As he entered the building he was greeted by his assistant, Max, who had pulled-up sleeves, messed-up hair, and drooped shoulders. "I thought you weren't coming back," Max said in startled surprise, then narrowed his gaze. "Isn't your bride arriving?" His eyebrows rose. "Oh no, she didn't arrive?"

"She has arrived, and we are married."

Max leaned back on his heels, shook his head in wonder, and said, "Well, I'm glad you're here."

"What seems to be the problem?" Jeffery took off his jacket and rolled up his sleeves.

"Everything that could go wrong has," Max began.

Jeffery leaned over the small table and looked through the scattered papers, plans and hand notes covering a surface normally reserved for reviewing proposals with clients. His practiced eye quickly discovered the contract associated with the plans Max was all up in arms about. He fixed his gaze on them, took in a deep breath, and waited for Max to begin.

"Here, look at these numbers. The delivery charges are high, but that doesn't bother me as much as. . ."

Jeffery's concern for Tilda shifted to the mountains of work in front of him. One thing he didn't care for from a business standpoint was construction. There always seemed to be too many hidden costs and delays. And Max was right: these new expenditures and delays were quite disconcerting. Investing in diverse industries—that's where lucrative profits were made. Dealing with these attempts by contractors to fudge the numbers, however. . . "I'll take care of it, Max. Turn your attention to the Forester and Whitaker accounts today."

Max gathered the appropriate paperwork and took it back to his office. Jeffery worked on his papers for two hours, then gathered his notebooks to confront the contractor. Price gouging was going to stop, and it was going to stop today—tonight, he realized, looking at the clock—or he'd cancel the contract and work with another. Jeffery stood, rolled his shoulders to calm himself, and headed out the door. The walk would be beneficial. The sun was setting in the west. He preferred not to speak to a man in his home, but he was upset enough that this couldn't wait.

He walked up the many steps to the first-floor entrance to the palatial home, which for more modest homes would lead to the second floor. The staircase was broad, capable of supporting many ladies in ball gowns, escorted by gentlemen in evening dress, as they made their way up to the veranda. Raymond Price was a man of notable worth. Jeffery had trouble believing he would knowingly produce such poor records. Not only had Max found that the charges were high, but he had also found two invoices for the same work. Jeffery had found four more.

He knocked on the door. The doorman answered.

"I would like to speak with Mr. Price. Let him know that Jeffery Oliver is here."

"Yes, sir." The doorman bowed. His hands were gloved in white. His ebony skin and dark, tightly knit hair spoke of his heritage. He was dressed in a heavy woolen jacket and slacks, neatly pressed for proper appearance. Jeffery closed his mind to the thoughts of the past and slavery. "Please step inside. I'll get Mr. Price."

Jeffery stepped into the grand southern mansion. The entryway opened into a large foyer. He'd been here more than once for various balls and gatherings.

The doorman walked off. Jeffery scanned the surroundings. A few minutes later, Mr. Price came into the foyer. "Mr. Oliver, what a pleasure to see you. How may I be of service?"

"Forgive me for coming to your home, but I needed to speak with you on matters of business and, well, I felt it might be best to converse in private."

Concern etched Raymond Price's face. "Certainly." He stepped back and waved his arm to the right. "Come into my den."

Jeffery walked toward the man's office, Mr. Price's footfalls echoing behind him. Once inside the walnut-paneled room, he heard the oversized door click shut. Mr. Price went to the chair behind his desk and sat. He offered a seat opposite the desk to Jeffery with a polite gesture of his hand. "What seems to be the problem?"

Jeffery showed him the double billing, the excessive shipping fees, and everything else he'd found.

"I don't know what to say. I'm sorry. I will look into the matter first thing in the morning. You have my apologies, sir. This is not how I run my business. But I do have a new foreman. Perhaps he'd forgotten and resubmitted. I honestly don't know, but the matter will be straightened out as soon as possible. This was repair work done on your personal house, correct?"

"Yes, sir. I purchased it for my bride."

Mr. Price smiled. "Wonderful! Let me make a cedar-lined cabinet in the master suite for your bride as a gift, and as an apology for your troubles."

"That isn't necessary. A reimbursement—"

Mr. Price waved him off. "Of course you will be reimbursed. I'm truly horrified by this. I shall look into the matter at once. I pray you are the only one of my customers who has been affected in such a way."

Jeffery stood. "I thank you for your time."

"Pleasure, and my apologies. And I shall be making that cabinet for your bride."

"Thank you, sir."

Mr. Price escorted him out to the front door. Within seconds Jeffery was working his way down the stairs and toward his house. He pulled out his grandfather's pocket watch beneath a streetlight. It was nearly eight o'clock, and he'd told Tilda he'd be home at six.

As he entered his home, he marveled at the thought that this was now his home. He had a wife and one day would have children of his own. Amazing how life could change one day to the next.

◆　◆　◆

Tilda paced. She didn't know where her husband was. She certainly wasn't going to endure a marriage where she was treated as a second-class citizen. She'd heard about how slaves had been treated in the South. Apparently, Mr. Oliver felt that way toward his wife. She looked at the now dry, cold food on the dinner table. She'd lost her appetite by seven. The food had lost its appeal not too long after that. She'd cleared the table and brought their meals into the kitchen, where she covered his dish and dumped her own, too upset to eat. It was hard enough considering a marriage bed with a man she didn't know, but now. . . It was unthinkable. Going to the parlor, Tilda went to a chair and tried to pray to calm herself down for the hundredth time. It was no use.

The back door opened and closed. Footsteps echoed off the hardwood floors.

She folded her arms across her waist.

He stepped into the parlor. "Hellooo. . ." His word drifted off.

She met his gaze; his sparkling eyes lost their cheer. "Your supper is on the table in the kitchen."

"Thank you," he muttered, and left her.

She marched into the kitchen. "I'm sorry it's dry and cold. You said you would be home at six."

He sat down at the table and spread the cloth napkin across his lap. He bowed his head for a moment, then picked up his fork and knife. He sawed his knife back and forth across the overcooked pork chop.

"I am a good cook," she said in defense.

He chomped on the tough, dried-out meat, struggled through a second piece then moved to the potatoes. The grease had congealed. "Would you like me to heat that up?"

"No, thank you." He wiped his mouth with the napkin and sipped his beverage. His face contorted. "What is this?"

"Iced tea—without the ice, obviously."

"This is not iced tea." He plopped his glass down on the table and stood. "You said you could cook in your correspondence."

"I can. You said you'd be home at six. It is nearly nine."

"Fine. I'll expect a better dinner tomorrow. I think before I say anything regrettable, I shall say good night." He stepped away from the table, away from her, and left the room. His footsteps fell like exclamation points on the stairs.

Lord, what have I done. Tilda sobbed as she picked up her husband's plate and tossed the uneaten food into the trash. She washed the dishes and hung up her apron until morning.

Rolling her shoulders, Tilda took in a deep breath. It was now or never. She left the kitchen, turning down the lamps as she made her way through the house, and headed toward the stairs. After Mercy, the woman he'd hired to help her settle in, had left for the afternoon and said she would return later in the evening, she had explored her new home, prepared a delicious meal, and waited for her husband. Now, her hand on the bannister, the house felt so empty.

At the top of the stairs, she turned down the hall to her room. She placed her hand on the marble doorknob, tried to settle her breathing and the knot in her stomach, and gave a gentle twist. The door opened quietly to reveal soft, moonlit curtains of lace lifted on a summer breeze toward the bed.

Jeffery Oliver was not there.

She stepped back. Had she entered the wrong room? She looked down the hallway. No, this was definitely the room the servant had said was hers. Tilda stepped inside. Her carpetbag was right where she had left it. Puzzled, she poked her head out into the hall again just as Mercy appeared in the passageway between her room and who knew where. "May I help you, miss?" she asked in polite, hushed tones.

"Yes, thank you." Tilda didn't wear corsets often but today she had, and having someone help her untie the contraption would be helpful.

"The tub is warm, if you wish. I tried to anticipate your needs. Tomorrow we shall get to know one another, and you can give me your list. . ." The servant prattled on.

Tilda stepped out of her dress. Mercy was perhaps twenty years her senior. "Thank you for your help, Miss Mercy."

"'Tis my job, Miss. Mr. Oliver, he hired me to help you for today as your chambermaid."

"Thank you."

So, her chambermaid was not a permanent servant. Which was fine. She'd taken care of herself most of her life. But if wearing fancy ball gowns was expected for attendance at important social events, well then she would need the assistance of a chambermaid. Tilda turned and Mercy undid the lacing. "Most women wear these tighter."

"I am aware. But I was traveling and didn't want to be uncomfortable."

"I have no use for those contraptions myself. Thank the good Lord, I don't have to attend social events that require them."

Tilda giggled. She liked Mercy. "Mercy, I am going to depend on you to help me learn this new city."

"It will be my pleasure, Miss. Now, shoo, and git into that bath. It is your wedding night!"

Two hours later she fell asleep in her bed, alone. She had waited, prayed, and read before finally falling asleep. It was becoming clear that Jeffery Oliver was not interested in having a "real" wife, just someone who could fulfill a role. But what kind of role?

The next morning, she woke feeling worthless. She grabbed her Bible and reread what she'd read the previous night. "Whoso findeth a wife findeth a good *thing*, and obtaineth favour of the Lord" (Proverbs 18:22).

"What about the wife, Lord?" Tilda prayed. "What's the 'good' for her? Was there favor for the wife to find a husband? How is a wife supposed to behave when the husband doesn't want or respect her?"

Tilda threw off the bedcovers and dressed for the day. Tonight she would cook a supper that—no matter what time of day or night he should come home—would be fine. Fried chicken was good hot, cold or even room temperature, she reasoned. However, coming from the North and cooking a southern dish. . . Tilda hoped it would be good enough for her husband.

That night, however, he came home even later and went straight to his room. Not their room but his. This pattern repeated night after night. At the end of a week, Tilda packed her bags and ordered a ticket to return home.

Jeffery came home earlier than normal, surprised to find James with the carriage waiting to take her back to the train station. "What's going on here?" he demanded.

Chapter Three

Jeffery had left work early to speak with his wife. He didn't know what to do. He knew she wasn't pleased with him coming home late and not sitting down to dinner with her. And admittedly the fried chicken had looked and smelled quite good. But he'd eaten a large meal with the Frederick & Miller associates while going over their investments. The next night he'd come home so late she hadn't even been up. Since then, he'd come home to no plate of food on the table or wife in the parlor waiting for him. Instead, she holed up in her bedroom with the door locked. So much for marriage.

She stood ramrod straight on the back steps, dressed for travel, as he approached. James was loading her trunk on a hand dolly.

"I'm leaving," she said as she stared him down. "I'll have my attorney draw up an annulment." Tilda secured her bonnet with a neat bow.

"Leave," he repeated, stopping in his tracks as if the word were an invisible barrier. "You can't leave," he ordered. "You're my wife."

She stepped to the edge of the porch and lowered her voice. He felt frozen to the driveway beneath her icy stare. "I am not your wife. I don't know why you even want a wife. You certainly don't want me to cook for you. You have servants to clean for you. You don't need a wife."

"Of course I need a wife."

"No, Mr. Oliver, you do not. A man who has a wife wants to come home to her. He wants to spend time with her. I don't know anything about you except what you wrote in your letter. And as I've reflected on that letter for the past week I've realized you didn't reveal all that much about yourself."

Jeffery paused. "I came home to speak with you."

"Well then, speak!"

Color inflamed her soft cheeks. Tilda made a pretty picture when she was riled up. He grinned.

"What?" she demanded.

"You are a beautiful woman, Tilda Oliver."

"That's Tilda Green. We may have said our vows in front of a judge, but we have certainly not become married."

James fidgeted nervously, the trunk still unloaded. Jeffery pulled two dollars out of his wallet. "Forgive us. We won't be needing your services today."

Tilda placed her hands on her hips. "Yes, we will. You can't dismiss—"

Jeffery took the steps up the porch and stood as close as humanly possible without touching her. "Tilda," he whispered. "Give me the afternoon and evening to discuss the matter. If you feel the same, then I will not prevent you from returning to your home."

She closed her eyes. A small tear rolled down her cheek.

He lifted his hand and brushed the tear away. "Forgive me, please. Give me a chance."

Her rigid shoulders sagged. She nodded, her eyes squeezed shut, her lips tight and flushed. He leaned in until a wisp of her hair brushed his face. "Thank you," he whispered into her ear. "Forgive me. I am new to marriage. My parents told me so this very morn, and I invited them to dinner to meet you."

"Today?" Her eyes popped open.

"Yes," he nodded, taking half a step back. "I can send a messenger and let them know you are a bit under the weather."

Her rich green eyes moistened and pulled at his heart.

He'd never meant to hurt her. "I know we—I mean, I—haven't been a good husband. I want to try and be a better man but. . ." He glanced around. "Let's retreat into the house and discuss this in private, please?"

She gave him a curt nod and turned back into the house. He gathered her carpetbag and carried it in. He'd come back later for the trunk. He found her in the parlor, a figure of feminine beauty and strength, with her back turned to him. *If only she knew how to cook!* Cooking lessons he could provide, he'd decided earlier. For now, he had a bigger problem on his hands than inedible meals.

"Why did you want a wife?" Tilda whispered.

Jeffery cleared his throat. "I wanted a companion to grow old with and have children with. However, my business takes up most of my time. As you could tell by the late hours I've kept this past week."

She turned and faced him. "Were you honestly at work? I've known men who would go out all hours of the night and return to their wives under the influence of spirits."

"I do not drink, other than an occasional glass of wine with a client over a meal. But I'll hardly drink more than a sip or two."

"What is your business?"

"Investments. I help my clients manage their investments, as well as invest in some opportunities myself."

"I know a little about investing in real estate and such. Business closes down by four or five in the afternoon. You've come home as late as nine and ten o'clock and without so much as a word that you would be late."

Frustration and fear washed over him. Should he be honest about his fears? "It's been a difficult week." He sat down on the sofa. "The night we married, my employee, Max, discovered that I'd been double billed by a contractor I had hired to get this house ready. . ." He glanced at his soiled boots. He wanted to wipe the smudges off but knew he would appear to be indifferent about their conversation. "To get this house ready for my bride," he finished, not looking up. "After I went through all the receipts, I went to the contractor's home and addressed him about the matter. He claimed to be unaware and said he would take care of it. But he took three days before getting back with me and then claimed some of the charges were not overcharges but simply bad bookwork from his filing clerk. Since that time I've learned of other cases in which this contractor has other—shall we say—unsatisfied customers." Jeffery jumped to his feet and paced. "It's the principal of the matter. I will not be cheated, nor do I wish to pay more for a service than is proper, but—"

"I'm sorry. What can you do?"

"I will have to take the man to court if I am to see my money returned. But I also learned that he's been caring for some ill family members. It doesn't excuse the man from cheating others, but—"

"You're certain he was aware of this?"

"I don't know. He seemed genuinely horrified at the prospect when I first brought it to his attention."

She came up beside him and placed a loving hand on his arm. He could smell her perfume, a delicate blend of some unknown flowers. He squared his shoulders against the unexpected reaction her close presence ignited. Determined not to show any impropriety toward his wife, he placed his hand upon hers and tapped. "I'll figure it out. I wouldn't want to worry your pretty little head over such business matters."

She pulled her hand away and stepped back.

◆　◆　◆

Tilda closed her eyes and counted to ten. "Women can, and do, understand business."

His forehead bunched together in the center, as if she'd grown two heads. "I'm sorry," he said, "but—"

"Don't, or I certainly will be gone in the morning." She walked back to the window and looked over the garden. She'd spent her days weeding out the neglected soil, getting it ready for plants. What little she'd gathered from others was that the planting season here differed considerably from up north. She nibbled her lower lip, then turned around. "I know some men do not consider women to have as much intelligence as a man. But I was an only child, and my father saw fit to educate me in various fields of study. I am proficient in French. I have a good hand for painting and a flair for poetry. I also have a mind for business and accept that a woman's opinion is not highly regarded in business matters. As your wife, however, I'd like to think you would be interested in my opinion. I will understand if you disagree with me, but at least show me the courtesy of speaking to me as an adult and not a child."

Jeffery leaned back on his heels. The shock on his face at being so caught off guard presented an almost boyish innocence. He was incredibly handsome, she realized, with his square chin, chiseled cheekbones, and blue eyes so vibrant a woman could get lost in them. "Your issues with this contractor were not the only reasons you have not come home early this week, are they?"

He rubbed the back of his neck. "If we are being truly honest with one another, then no. He provided a convenient excuse the first night. In truth, I was not certain you were ready to be. . .um. . .well. . .a married woman. And I believed it would be best if we got to know one another better before. . ." He nodded his head toward the upstairs.

"But why not discuss the matter? I—I—" How could she tell him she had bathed and prepared herself in anticipation of their wedding night without sounding foolish? "When I agreed to come, I accepted that as part of our marriage arrangement."

He folded and unfolded his hands three times before he spoke. "Tilda, you are a beautiful woman, and it is my sincere desire to consummate our marriage. However, I believe it would be best to wait until we get to know one another."

"How? You're never home."

"Touché. I will try to come home earlier."

Tilda rolled her upper lip under her teeth for a moment. "For dinner? I really can cook. You just come home so late."

Jeffery smiled and came beside her at the window. "I am no good at personal relationships. I never have been. I understand business. I excel at closing deals and maximizing profits. I get along with my clients just fine as long as I stick to business. Put me in a social setting and I'm a puddle of confusion. Tilda, I want our marriage to work. Can you give me some more time?"

"I will try."

"That's all I ask." His smile lit up his countenance and warmed her right to the center of her heart. She might just be falling in love with her husband. "Let me have your trunk put back in your room. What would you like to make for my parents tonight? I can run to the butcher and get some fresh seafood for dinner."

Her eyes widened. "Your parents?" He had mentioned them coming over—even suggested canceling with them.

"Would you like me to postpone to another night? I can send a messenger."

"No," she replied. Her mind drifted to what she had in the cabinets. "Do you like pasta?"

"Sure. What are you thinking?"

"I could make a white sauce for the fish and serve it over a bed of fresh pasta. We have flour and eggs, so I can make some."

"What else do you need?"

"Lemon, for the fish. And what about a vegetable or salad? I don't know what is in season down here right now."

"I'll find some summer squashes."

"Wonderful. I'll go change and start making the pasta. You go ahead and get the fish and vegetables."

Jeffery smiled. He gently touched her shoulder, turning her, placed a hand on each of her arms and faced her. "Thank you. And I'm sorry. I shall try to do better."

Tilda swallowed the tears that threatened to fall. *Perhaps we have a chance.*

Once he had gone, she ran up the stairs and opened her carpetbag, pulled out a work dress and changed. She had decided not to wear her corset for travel. It had left too many bruises on her ribs after days on the train. Jeffery had opened up—not all that much, but enough to give her some hope for the future. *Father, God, please make it so.*

Changed, she headed into the kitchen, poured a couple cups of flour into a mound on the counter, made a well in the center and cracked an egg to put in the well. Grabbing a fork, she whipped the egg, slowly gathering in the flour, then sprinkled in some salt and added a touch of olive oil. Once the dough was holding together, she put a large pan of water on the stove to boil. Then she went back to the pasta and began to knead until it was smooth and pliable. She let it rest for a moment, cleared the counter, and put a new sprinkling of flour down. Then she began to roll a quarter of the dough into a very thin circle. The thinner the pasta, the better it tasted, in her humble opinion anyway. She knew some who liked it thick, real thick. She paused. What did Jeffery like? Fear of failure washed over her again.

She shook off the thought. She'd make it to her taste, and if he liked it thicker he could just let her know.

◆　◆　◆

Jeffery stopped at the fishmonger first and picked up four fillets of fresh bass and a lemon. Thankfully, George Mueller had both a lemon and a lime tree in his yard. Next, he headed over to the market and gathered an assortment of summer and zucchini squash. He spied a bushel basket of fresh tomatoes—one of his favorite vegetables— sitting in a bin next to the zucchini. He picked up a dozen. *Perhaps Tilda knows how to can.* He replaced the dozen tomatoes and grabbed the entire bushel basket. Marsha Maciel, the owner's wife, raised her gray eyebrows. "I've never known your mother to can before, Mr. Oliver."

Jeffery shrugged. "These are for my wife."

"Your wife! Congratulations. When did this happen?" she asked, weighing the produce.

"Last week. Her name is Tilda. Would you put her on my account to charge whatever she might need?"

"Certainly. And your account is to be separate from your parents?"

"Yes, ma'am."

"That'll be two dollars and twenty today. On your account?"

Jeffery reached into his front pocket and pulled out enough change. "No, thank you. I have the funds today."

"Very well. And congratulations again, Mr. Oliver, I can't wait to meet your wife."

"Thank you." At that moment, he realized how much he truly would like to meet his wife and really get to know her. She was articulate and smart. He hadn't fooled her with his late nights at the office, though unfortunately she'd gotten the wrong impression. He grabbed the bushel of tomatoes. "I'll bring the basket back in the morning."

"That will be fine, Mr. Oliver. Good day."

Jeffery put the bushel basket, along with his other purchases, in the buggy and headed home. He hadn't expected to see Tilda packed and ready to leave, but his mother's words—"*You've been awfully busy with work for a man who just got married*"—had run around and around in his head all morning. *Thank You, Lord. I don't have a clue how to be a good husband. Help me become a man Tilda can trust and respect so we can take our relationship further.*

Childhood memories of his parents, who always seemed so. . .*together*, so. . .*at one* with each other, brought a smile to his face. His dad had such a gift for gab. Then again, so did his mom. And when they both got going, even in social settings, it often turned to playful banter. Something he'd never learned and, more importantly, had never wanted to. Now? Now it seemed like a foreign language. How could he open up and speak about things he wasn't even certain about himself? he wondered.

As he arrived home, he found Tilda in the kitchen, cutting very thin strips out of some kind of dough. "What are you doing?"

She jerked to attention. "I'm making pasta."

"How'd you learn to do that?"

Tilda shrugged. "I had some Italian friends. They taught me. What I wouldn't give to have one of their pasta machines. With those you can roll the dough very thin and can cut the pasta as well."

Pasta machine. Jeffery stored that for future reference.

"What did you purchase?" she asked, pointing with the knife at his bushel basket.

"Tomatoes. I love fresh tomatoes. I thought you might be able to can some."

"Sure." She shrugged. "I can make catsup also. However, that will take most of the tomatoes you have there. But there's nothing like catsup on hash browns."

"Yum, that sounds good. Do you know how to cook bass?"

"Sea or freshwater?"

"Fresh."

"Yes. But I'm more skilled with the sea bass." She dried off her hands. "Let me see what you purchased."

He handed her the paper-wrapped fillets. She placed the package on the counter, opened it, and smelled the meat. "They're fresh."

"George Mueller has never sold me a bad piece of fish. I've opened an account for you at the Muellers' place as well as at Maciel's Fresh Foods. I'll show you where they are later."

She paused and looked up, her gaze locked on to his. "Thank you. I appreciate that."

Jeffery nodded. "You're welcome. I apologize for not thinking about such things earlier."

She smiled. "We both have a lot to learn."

"Tell me, how I can help?"

"Do you know how to set a table?"

Jeffery chuckled. "I know the basics, not much more. However, I'd be happy to set the table, and you can come in and rearrange anything I put out of order."

"Thank you." She pushed a strand of her brown hair behind her ear. "I need to finish this. I'm going to make a white sauce for the fish; then I'll broil the fillets in the pan instead of frying them."

"I picked up some summer squash as well as some zucchini." He pointed to the brown paper bag on the counter.

"I can work with those, too. What time are you expecting your parents?"

"Five."

She glanced up at the clock and paled. "I don't have time to bake a dessert."

Jeffery came to her side and placed a hand on her shoulder. "I should have stopped at the bakery. I'm sorry."

"I'll see what I can do."

"Don't worry about it. We did not have dessert after dinner every night when I was growing up. Not to mention they are last-minute guests."

She bit her lower lip and nodded.

He brushed the errant strand of hair that had slipped back out from behind her ear. "Tilda, trust me, my mother will not find fault in you for not having a dessert ready on short notice."

Tilda gave a weak smile. *How can I trust you?*

Chapter Four

Tilda finished cutting and cooking the fresh pasta, then went on to prepare the vegetables, cream sauce, and bass. Minutes later, she pulled the sizzling fillets, white and fluffy, from the flame. "Perfect," she said, carefully removing them from the frying pan. She knew southerners liked their fried food, which she enjoyed as well on occasion. Hopefully she would not offend the Olivers by cooking the bass in the lighter fashion she preferred.

A glance up at the clock told her she still had a few spare minutes. She should go upstairs and freshen up. But her searching eyes caught sight of some fresh bananas in a fruit bowl. There were plenty of milk and eggs. . .and a half-dozen vanilla cookies she'd made a couple days ago remained untouched in the cookie jar.

She put a pan on the stove, dropped in a pad of butter, then mixed together some sugar and eggs. After crushing up the cookies, she returned to the egg and butter mixture and added some flour, then some milk, whisked it well, and combined it with the melted butter in the pan. She took a pie tin down and spread it with butter, lined it with the cookie crumbs, and placed the two fresh bananas —thinly sliced—on top of the cookie crumbs. She stirred the sweet pudding in the pan and added some vanilla. Once it thickened, she removed it from the stove and beat up the egg whites into a meringue. She layered the pudding over the bananas and topped it with the meringue, slid it into the oven, and ran upstairs. She changed quickly out of her housedress and into a casual but nice dress to meet Jeffery's parents.

She glanced in the mirror, poured some cool water into the basin and washed her face. Freshened up her lilac perfume with a tiny dab behind each ear and went down the stairs.

At the bottom of the stairs, a woman waited for her, looking to be about fifty or more years old, her eyes beaming. Just behind her stood Jeffery and a silver-haired gentleman Tilda took to be the senior Mr. Oliver engaged in conversation. "You must be Tilda," the woman said, seeming genuinely pleased.

"Yes," she choked out.

"I'm so happy to meet you."

As she reached the last step, Jeffery came up beside her and offered his hand. She slipped her fingers into its warm and gentle embrace, and a calm flowed through her. He winked and led her to the parlor and his parents followed. "Dinner is ready," Tilda offered. "Would you like me to serve?"

"Nonsense." Mrs. Oliver, a trim woman with impeccable taste in clothing and movement, sat down on the sofa and tapped the cushion. "Let us get to know one another first."

Fear washed over Tilda. She had worked hard to prepare a perfect dinner. This delay would mean the food would be cold and not up to Jeffery's standards. "But. . ." her voice trailed off. How do you tell your mother-in-law no?

As if sensing her concerns, Jeffery spoke up. "Mother, Tilda has worked hard putting together our dinner with little notice. If she feels it is best to eat our meal now, we should. There will be plenty of time to visit during and after."

Mrs. Oliver, who shared the same blue eyes with her son, let her assessing gaze linger for a moment on her new daughter-in-law. "Of course, dear. Shall we go to the dining room?"

Tilda smiled. "It's a simple fare. One I hope you will enjoy." Tilda glanced at Jeffery, looking for affirmation in her decision and mouthed *thank you*. He nodded while offering his elbow to his mother.

"Excuse me." Tilda hustled into the kitchen and placed the pasta in the water already heated on the stove, warming up the white sauce as she placed the pasta and fish on each plate. Then she placed the vegetables in a serving dish and brought it into the dining room. Without saying a word, she went back to the kitchen, poured the hot white sauce over the fish and pasta, and carried two plates at a time out to the table, serving her in-laws first.

"This looks wonderful," Mrs. Oliver purred.

Mr. Oliver placed his napkin in his lap. "Smells delicious."

Tilda caught the hint of an approving smile from Jeffery, who sat at the head of the table. "I'll be right back with the rest of our dinners."

Back in the kitchen, she turned the oven off and opened the door a little to let the hot air vent. She returned with the last two plates, placed one before Jeffery, and sat opposite him at the other end of the table.

"Father, will you offer the blessing tonight?" Jeffery asked.

Mr. Oliver cleared his throat. "I'd be honored." He went into a lengthy prayer, one she sensed was genuine, if not a little stiff.

"Amen," everyone said after he finished.

"So, tell me about yourself, Tilda. Where is your family?" Mrs. Oliver asked.

Tears threatened to build, but Tilda held them back. "My parents died nearly a year ago in a train wreck. I am an only child."

"I'm so sorry. I didn't mean. . . ." Mrs. Oliver took a forkful of the main course. "This is delicious."

"Thank you. And you couldn't have known. Jeffery and I don't have a traditional relationship. There is much we don't know about each other."

"Traditional, no. But I'm glad he found someone," Mr. Oliver said. "My father wasn't too sure he ever would."

She smiled. "My father probably felt very similar toward me, as well."

Jeffery spoke up. "This is very good, Tilda. Thank you."

"You're welcome." *See, I told you I could cook*, she wanted to say, but she held her tongue. *There's no sense airing our laundry in front of his parents*, she told herself and wondered just how much or how little they knew about their relationship.

The evening progressed with simple questions followed by simple answers, and Tilda decided she liked the Olivers, though it seemed they were not as deep or as open as her parents had been with her. *Is that why Jeffery had trouble getting to know people socially?*

They finished the evening in the parlor over cups of coffee. "Well, it was wonderful getting to meet you, Tilda," Mrs. Oliver said as she stood up from the sofa. "And I ate too much. I loved that banana pudding you made. I look forward to seeing you at church on Sunday."

"Yes, ma'am."

Mrs. Oliver grinned at Tilda's use of the southern sign of respect.

Mr. Oliver extended his hand. "Thank you again, Tilda. I look forward to getting to know you better."

"Oh, and don't forget to start working on those grandbabies." Mrs. Oliver winked.

"Mother!" Jeffery chastised.

Tilda could feel the heat on her cheeks as her in-laws slipped out the front door without a hug. The most contact she had received was a handshake from Mr. Oliver—another reason, she guessed, as to why Jeffery hadn't done more than extend his hand and his elbow to her all evening. If she was going to stay in this marriage, there was a lot of work to do.

◆   ◆   ◆

Jeffery turned and faced his wife. "You're amazing. That dinner was fantastic—and dessert. . . . You actually made dessert! How?"

"I told you I could cook," she responded with an impish grin.

"Consider me reprimanded. Can I help you with the clean up?"

"I won't say no. The kitchen is a disaster," Tilda warned, heading that way.

"I'll clear the table."

"Thank you." She retreated to the kitchen, and Jeffery entered the dining area. He picked up a plate and scraped it onto another until all the plates were cleared and stacked. These he carried to the kitchen counter by the sink. A pot of hot water was already heating on the stove as Tilda scrubbed down the counter where she'd made the pasta earlier. "That was delicious pasta. I didn't know it could taste so good, being fresh like that."

"Oh, there is so much I could do with it. Have you ever had lobster ravioli?"

"No, I don't believe I have. It sounds delicious." He headed back toward the dining room, stopped, and turned back. "You mentioned a pasta machine?"

"Yes, it's an Italian tool. It helps to knead and thin the pasta."

"Can you make the ravioli without a pasta machine?"

Tilda laughed, a warm, lilting sound he decided he liked.

"Yes, I can. All we need is the lobster meat to fill them."

Jeffery smiled. "I'll speak with George Mueller about Maine lobsters. I presume you would want to use them over southern lobsters."

"What is the difference?" she asked as she continued to clean.

"The southern variety don't have claws, and the meat is not quite as sweet."

She nibbled her lower lip. "I will try southern lobster because I have not had them before. However, if they are not as tasty as Maine lobsters. . ."

"I understand, and I agree. My preference is the Maine lobster." He turned back to the dining room and finished clearing the table as fast as possible. To be in the same room with his wife, to get to know this fascinating person now sharing his home, became an overwhelming desire.

Back in the kitchen, he found her at the sink, scrubbing away at the dishes as soap-suds worked their way up her arms. For a brief moment, he wanted to be those suds. Jeffery squared his shoulders. He would be a gentleman; he would not be presumptuous with his wife. On the other hand, he didn't want to end their time together. "I'll admit I've never washed a dish—or dried one, for that matter—but I'm willing to give it a try."

Tilda's smile edged up to her eyes. "It's not that difficult, and I'm glad for the help." She looked away and mumbled, "and the company."

Jeffery relaxed and walked up to her. "Tilda, I appreciate your willingness to stay in our marriage."

"I want our marriage to work," she said as she placed another dish in the rack draining into the sink.

"Thank you." He wanted to sweep her into his arms and hug her. But that would not be appropriate. He'd never seen his father carry on with his mother like that. *"Men need to respect their wives and not treat them like a woman of ill repute."* His father's words resounded in his head. But then images of friends with their wives, holding hands, hugging. . . Honestly, he didn't know what was proper.

She banged his side with her hip. "What are you thinking?"

He could feel the heat rise on his neck. "I—I'm not certain whether or not it is proper to speak of such things with a woman."

Her eyebrows raised, then pinched together in the center of her forehead.

"Forgive me. I was raised to treat a wife with the greatest respect and to protect her from the harshness of life."

She said nothing at first as she continued to wash and put items in the rack for him to dry. But he could see the wheels turning. Jeffery finished drying a dish, set it down, and grabbed another, waiting. "Jeffery," she nearly whispered his name, "from what little I saw of your parents tonight, I can tell we've been raised very differently. Did you ever receive hugs and kisses from your parents?"

Jeffery leaned back on his heels. "When I was a boy, yes."

"Ah, I thought that might be the case because your parents didn't hug me or kiss me. The most contact I had with them was a handshake from your father. In my home, my parents would hug and kiss me all the time. And Mother would welcome just about everyone she met with a hug. Father would slap a man on the back as he shook hands with an old friend and even give an occasional hug. I say all of that because you mentioned feeling socially inadequate. I'm willing to bet that you never had any really deep, personal conversations with your parents—possibly never with anyone."

Jeffery felt his temper start to flare and fought to keep it under control.

She pulled her hands from the soapy water, dried them off as she turned to face him, and wrapped her arms around him.

The anger dissipated. He wrapped her in his arms and pulled her close, praying he wasn't being disrespectful to his wife. She rested her face against him, and he wanted to kiss the top of her head but held back.

"I need this," she mumbled into his chest. "I haven't had a hug in so long."

Jeffery held her tighter. He could do this. She wanted and needed this physical contact. Yes, he could do this, and it felt too good to not want to hug her for the rest of his life.

She stepped out of his arms. "Promise me to be honest with me always, and we'll make it."

"I promise. I'll admit it won't be easy. I've been raised to hold my thoughts."

"I understand." She grabbed his hands, stepped back, and searched his eyes. "Why are we in separate bedrooms?"

Jeffery paled. His eyes widened as round as saucers. "You don't mean that your parents slept in the same room. Did they?"

Tilda giggled, in part to hide her shock that his parents didn't but in part to lighten the tension she sensed in him. "Yes, they did, and they shared one bed."

"Ah, well, ah. . . I think I better get ready for bed." His neck reddened. "I mean." He closed his eyes. "Tilda." He opened his eyes and focused on her again. "I want us to get to know one another more before. . ."

"I know. And I do not want to shock you, but I can see that our upbringings will shock one another for a while. I look forward to getting to know you, Jeffery."

He relaxed. "As do I, my sweet."

"Sweet, huh?" She reached up and touched his cheek now thoroughly red with embarrassment. "I like that."

He took her fingers from his face and kissed them. "Then I bid you adieu. I shall try to be home by five tomorrow. Good night, and Tilda, I look forward to getting to know you."

He stepped away and exited the kitchen as if the hounds of hell were nipping at his heels.

"Jeffery," she called out to him. "Read the Song of Solomon. My mother said it was a great book of poetry and explained married love very well."

He nodded and headed out of the room. She could hear his footfalls on the steps. She turned back to the sink and plunged her hands back into the warm soapy water. She thought back on her day. On her anger this morning and packing her bags, to the conversation she had with Jeffery before his parents came to dinner, the dinner, and most importantly, the moments they shared with each other in the kitchen. She was exhausted. Her emotions had run the full spectrum. Yet she was excited about the future. They seemed to connect with one another. Could this marriage really work?

The possibility played on her mind as she finished her chores, washed, and dressed for bed. A smile curled up her cheek remembering the horror on Jeffery's face when he learned that her parents actually shared a room and bed together. Then the smile slipped. Would he ever be able to open up and be free with her, or would his upbringing prevent them from having a future?

The next morning she found a note on the table informing her that he had hired Mercy to help around the house and any other tasks that Tilda needed help with. He signed it "affectionately, your husband." Tilda smiled.

"Good morning, Miss Oliver. How can I help you this morning?" Mercy said as she dropped a tray of fresh-cut flowers on the table.

"Good morning, Mercy. Please, call me Tilda."

"No, ma'am, it ain't right. I calls you *miss* as a form of affection rather than *Mrs.*, but

I can't use your first name."

Tilda puckered her lips. "All right, I understand. *Miss* it is then."

Mercy's brown eyes sparkled. "Thank you, miss."

"The first thing we need to do is stock this kitchen. Let's make a list, and I'll speak with my husband about the budget to fill the cupboards."

"I'd be happy to. Every good kitchen needs its herbs."

"Amen to that," Tilda said. She pulled out a pad of paper and a pencil. "Let's get started."

They worked until noon going over all the details of the kitchen, taking stock of what Jeffery had purchased and what he hadn't. Amazingly, the cookware and dishes were fairly well planned and stocked.

"Mercy, I need a dozen eggs and some cake flour. Where is the best place to get them? Oh, wait. Mr. Oliver said he opened an account at—what was the name?" Tilda nibbled her upper lip up under her teeth.

"Maciel's?" Mercy asked.

"Yes, that's it. Maciel's Fresh Foods."

"They'll have the eggs, but the cake flour you will find at Barnes Grain Market. They have all the grains you want to cook with. You can have them milled there, as well. Of course, you might ask at the bakery where they get their cake flour."

Tilda nodded. "Shall we go shopping at Maciel's?"

"What about your laundry? I really should get started on that."

"Oh. You're right. Tell me how to get to Maciel's."

Mercy did, and Tilda ventured out toward the business section of the city. From the way Jeffery had eaten the banana pudding last night, she knew he had a sweet tooth. *Personally, I would love a good angel food cake.* But that required eleven egg whites. . . *And I could use most of the yolks to make more puddings for Jeffery!*

Tilda spent the next couple of hours going in and out of shops. Fortunately, Maciel's provided a delivery service, saving her the trouble of carrying around the purchased items. She stepped into a small shop near the river's edge where a fine variety of trinkets and other items were available for sale. Tilda fingered the quilts, her thoughts focused more on the various skills she could put to work. A middle-aged woman with graying hair and an unusually wide hip span came up beside her. "How may I help you?" she asked.

"I'm just browsing. I'm new to Savannah."

"Oh! What brought you to our fine city?" she asked in her rich southern accent.

How does one answer that? I'm a mail-order bride? "I recently married, and this is my husband's hometown."

"Congratulations! Who is your husband? Perhaps I know him."

"Jeffery Oliver."

"I know of the family, but I've never met the son." The woman smiled. "In either case, it is a pleasure to have you in Savannah. I trust you will find it suitable."

"I love history, and there is so much here to explore."

"My name is Mrs. James," she offered, her hand extended, "and there is plenty of history here. From the American Revolution, and before there were pirates who made their homes here. The Savannah River has helped make our city prosperous. Not to mention Sherman didn't burn our city down, thanks to some creative thinking by our townsfolk at the time. The War of Aggression was a bad time, but we're recovering. Did you know the first steam-powered boat to cross the Atlantic left from Savannah?"

"I didn't know that." She smiled, appreciative of the woman's friendliness. "My name is Tilda Gr—I mean Oliver."

"Does take some getting used to, doesn't it?" Tilda nodded as Mrs. James continued on. "The S.S. *Savannah* left here in 1818. She was both sail and steam ship. She sank in 1821 off the coast of Long Island. But she was from here and made history from here."

Tilda looked to the wall clock. If she was going to get the angel food cake done in time for dessert, she would need to get started. "It's a pleasure to meet you, Mrs. James."

"Ya'll come back and see me sometime. I also love history and can tell you a tale or two." Mrs. James winked.

"Thank you. I might just do that." Tilda hurried back to the house, all in a sweat as she rushed through the humid air. She made a mental note: Plan more time and a slower pace for errands, or else plan time to bathe after each trip.

Chapter Five

Jeffery glanced at the clock. It was already past five. He penned a note. "Max, would you hire someone to run this over to my wife?"

Max took the proffered paper. "I'd be happy to. Do you mind if I do it? I have some guests coming to the house this evening and, well. . ."

Jeffery waved him off. "Fine."

Max grinned. "Thank you. I'll drop this off for your wife before I go home."

Jeffery turned back to the paperwork in front of him. He'd been working all afternoon on his analysis of the figures and reports concerning California Assets. Everyone in the market seemed to be jumping on board with this company's expansions, and several of his clients wanted to support the business. But Jeffery had reservations. Huge reservations—the kind that sent knots in your intestines—but he couldn't put his finger on any particular problem. The facts and figures seemed to indicate the company was poised for rapid growth. Investors could expect to double or triple their money in six months. *But.* . . Jeffery pushed his chair back and started to pace. "Why don't I have peace about it?" he mumbled.

The company wanted to expand out their California holdings. It even made sense. *Still.* . .

Again, he felt the check in his spirit.

Jeffery groaned. Then his stomach groaned in protest. He hadn't eaten lunch. He hadn't really eaten breakfast. His mind drifted to the meal Tilda had prepared for him. He put the papers together and slipped them in his case. He could work on this at home with a full belly rather than remain here producing nothing.

Ten minutes later he was walking up his street toward his house. Jeffery smiled. He'd purchased the house with all its contents from the widow Hoffman. She had moved in with her daughter and family because she was unable to stay by herself, not to mention she could no longer handle the stairs.

The first couple of weeks following the sale, Mrs. Hoffman and her daughter had come by daily, removing family mementos. A few items still remained in the attic and carriage house, but the house furnishings were all his now. *The gardens need work,* he thought. *I wonder if Tilda likes gardening or if I should hire a gardener?*

Even as his thoughts shifted to the amazing creature who just so happened to be his wife, she appeared on the back steps, carrying a hot pan. "Hello, Mrs. Oliver," he called out.

Tilda jumped.

"Jeffery, what are you doing here? I received your note." Her cheeks turned a brilliant shade of crimson.

"I was frustrated with this current project and thought I might as well be frustrated at home with a full belly than at the office with an empty one."

Tilda giggled. "Ah, so your tummy has a stronger will than your mind."

Jeffery grinned and shrugged. "Possibly. If whatever you're making tonight is as good as last night, I'd say my 'tummy,' as you put it, has an astute mind of its own."

Tilda nearly doubled over in laughter. "Come on in, Husband. I have a surprise for you. It is for dessert, however. I have not started our dinner." She wiped her hands on a towel. "Actually, that isn't quite true. I have made a potato salad to go with corn on the cob and beef patties called podovies."

"I don't believe I've had podovies before. Are they similar to lamb or veal patties?"

"Yes. Just different spices." Tilda went to the counter. It was cleaner than last night after making pasta, but he could tell she'd been baking.

"What did you set outside to cool?"

"A raspberry sauce." She turned and winked at him. "For dessert. So tell me, what wasn't going well at work?"

He clenched his jaw. A part of him wanted to open up and tell his wife about his day but... "Several clients want to invest in a company poised for expansion, and well, I don't believe it is a wise investment at this time." He lifted his case and tapped it. "On paper it appears to have the right balance of assets and liabilities planned out, but..."

"It doesn't sit well with you?" she asked.

"Yeah, but I can't tell my clients that. I have to have a logical reason for my concern, and I can't find one, at least not yet. And I'll admit, the idea of enjoying a meal with you after eating hardly anything all day sounded a lot better than sitting at the office accomplishing nothing."

Tilda smiled. "Then I shall have your dinner ready in fifteen, twenty minutes at the most. Go ahead into the study and lay out your paperwork. I'll bring you some southern sweet tea."

"Thank you."

"You're welcome. And Jeffery, I'm glad you're home."

"It is good to be home." He squelched the desire to give her a hug and headed to his office. He could hear her working in the kitchen and fought the desire to turn around and watch her work as he had last night. There was something in the way she moved that captivated his attention. She was a marvel to him. His mother had never worked in the kitchen, content to organize social engagements and fundraisers to occupy her time, while the servants did all the cooking and cleaning. His father had always worked for banks, so running figures seemed to be a trait he'd inherited from his father and grandfather. Each man had done well for his family. Jeffery was the first to branch out and own his own company. His parents and grandparents were proud of him and his accomplishments. Truth be told, however, he knew his grandfather wanted him to enjoy life more.

Jeffery laid the paperwork out on the desk.

Tilda came in with a tall glass of iced tea.

"Thank you." He took the glass from her and sipped the sweet drink. *Perfect, just the way I like it,* he thought, realizing the surprise showed on his face. "How'd you know?"

"Your mother mentioned it in passing last night, so I asked Mercy how to make it."

"It's perfect." He smiled. *Like you,* he wanted to add but refrained. It wouldn't be proper.

"How long have you lived here?" she asked.

"Not long, why do you ask?"

Tilda shrugged. "Curious, is all." She turned to head back to the kitchen then faced him again. "Actually, it is more than curious. Who set up the kitchen? It has nearly every tool and pan a woman would want. There are a few minor things but—"

He held up his hand. "I purchased the house from Widow Hoffman. She could no longer handle the stairs. The attic still has some of their family items, as well as the carriage house, but everything left in the house is ours."

Tilda smiled. "I would like to have known Mrs. Hoffman. She and I seem to share a lot of the same tastes."

Jeffery relaxed. "So you like the house?"

"Yes. I would like to make one change." She blushed.

Did he dare ask? "What?"

"When we are. . .fully married, I would like for us to share one room."

Jeffery could feel his eyes widen. He had read the Song of Solomon last night. He couldn't understand how he'd never understood the imagery in its poetry before, but now he couldn't help but see it. "I shall consider it."

"Thank you." Tilda scurried off to the kitchen. Jeffery's feet felt as if they'd been nailed to the floor. He liked his wife—more than liked her, he was beginning to realize—but could he get used to her ideas of married life?

◆　◆　◆

Tilda knew she was pushing her husband into uncomfortable territory. But if they were ever going to have a true marriage, one she'd be happy to stay in, both would need to make some changes.

She finished preparing dinner and served it in the dining room. As the night before, Jeffery came and sat at the head of the table. Tilda set her plate, silverware, and glass to the right of her husband—his mother's place at dinner—and sat down. This was their first time to sit down and eat with one another alone.

She fiddled with the linen napkin in her lap.

"Shall we pray?"

Tilda nodded.

"What's the matter?"

"I. . ." She cleared her throat. "I don't want to be a pest about how I was raised and how you were raised, but in my house we held hands when we asked the blessing over our dinner."

"Isn't that disrespectful?" Jeffery straightened his shoulders. "I mean, praying is an act of being holy and righteous."

"I understand." Tilda swallowed a sudden rush of tears, angry with herself at being so sentimental. She knew many families who didn't hold hands when they prayed. "I'm sorry."

Jeffery reached over and took her hand. "Tilda." He waited until she glanced up at him. He continued. "I know you're missing your father and mother, and I am willing to pray holding your hand on occasion. Perhaps in time I will grow more comfortable with such intimacy during an act of holiness. But for now I shall hold your hand because you would like me to."

"Thank you. And I know there are things I will need to change from how they were done in my childhood home. And I, too, am willing."

"Good. Then let us proceed." Jeffery bowed his head. "Father, thank You for this meal, and lead us not into temptation, but help us create a marriage that honors You. In the name of the Father, Son, and Holy Ghost."

"Amen," Tilda said. He released her hand, and the relative cool of the evening swept across her fingers. She liked his touch. The realization struck how far different it felt from her mother's or father's, even though it calmed and comforted her in a similar fashion.

He picked up his fork and cut into his beef patty. "This smells wonderful. It was difficult concentrating on the figures smelling these delightful aromas coming from the kitchen."

"I hope you like it. I do love cooking."

"I can tell. I'm sorry I waited so long to figure that out. And I apologize again for not coming home on time last week." He bit down on his first forkful of the beef patty. Tilda held her breath in anticipation. A gentle smile spread across his face. "Yum. This is excellent."

"You're welcome. We need to discuss what you like and don't like with regard to food. I would prefer to plan meals I know you would like."

"Truthfully, I haven't met a dish I haven't liked." He paused. "I take that back. I do not like dried fish. The taste is just too fishy for me. Otherwise, I believe I like all other foods." He took a forkful of the potato salad.

"Then what are your favorites?"

"Hmm, this is also good. What is in there? Something a bit different. . ."

"Bits of apple. Very small pieces really, so you should only pick up on the sweetness of the apple, not the apple itself."

He munched another forkful and nodded. "I'm going to gain twenty pounds."

"You could afford it." The words were out before she realized. "I mean, you're handsome and all." She could feel the heat on her cheeks. "I mean, you're just a little thin, is all."

Jeffery laughed. "I am. I don't eat a lot. With the dishes I've tasted the past two days, however, that just might change."

"What about breakfast? I see you leave early in the morning. I'd be happy to make your breakfast before you go into the office."

"I arrive at the office before dawn. I wouldn't want to impose upon you."

"Why so early?" Tilda relaxed, seeing his enjoyment over the food, and started to eat her dinner.

"My grandfather used to say I was obsessive. Perhaps he is correct. However, I am not quite thirty years old and own my own business. I purchased my own home and still have money in the bank. I make a profit for my clients and have established a respectable name in business. I believe my attention to detail, arriving to work early and staying late, has helped me in this endeavor."

Tilda mulled over what to say next. "That is impressive. Is that why you sought for a mail-order bride? Because you couldn't take time to court a woman?"

Jeffery wiped his mouth and pushed back from the table. "If I didn't know any better, I'd say you were talking with my grandfather. To answer your question, I'd say yes. I sought a mail-order bride because I didn't have time in my schedule to court a woman as customs tend to dictate. I do wonder, though, why would you answer such an offer?"

Tilda felt the tables turn on her. "As I mentioned before, my parents died. There was a man who sought my affections, but his interest lay in my property, not me."

"Your parents' home?"

She nodded in the affirmative. The family property included more than the house, but she wasn't ready to tell him that. She didn't know how the laws in Georgia worked, but she knew that some states required the husband to hold legal control over the wife's property. Frankly, she didn't want Jeffery or anyone else in control of her parents' affairs at this time. "Reginald was only after the estate. He had no interest in me."

"Well, as you can tell, I have no need for your parents' estate." He scooted back to the table and continued to eat his meal. "If we are to stay married, you will eventually need to sell your parent's property."

"I know but—"

"I understand. You want to wait and see—"

"If our marriage grows," she finished for him.

"Yes," he agreed. "So tell me about your childhood."

"Not much to tell, I guess. I grew up in New York City. It's an exciting place with the theaters, museums, and such, and we would travel to Cape Cod for summers. That is where my parents were headed when the accident happened."

"Why would they go there in the wintertime?"

"Father wanted to open the cottage early. They were considering an early retirement and living on the Cape year round."

"What did your father do? I mean, I understood from your letters he was a professor. Professors don't make that much, do they?"

"He was a professor, and you are correct, he didn't have an extravagant salary." She nibbled her lower lip then looked up at him. "Father and Mother had other income sources."

"Obviously you don't trust me enough yet to tell me everything, and I shall not push you to reveal more than you wish. Just answer me one question, if you would. These other revenue streams—nothing. . .illegal?"

Tilda giggled. "No, nothing illegal. And yes, I do need to trust you more before I reveal everything to you."

"Fine."

She knew she was hurting him by not revealing the complete truth about her parents. But she'd already experienced enough in her life to see how friendships could change once people learned who her parents were.

◆　◆　◆

Jeffery decided not to push the matter. She would tell him when the time was right, he hoped. He prayed. For now, he needed to pursue a friendship. Something he'd really never had with anyone. He could investigate and discover on his own who her parents were and what properties or other assets they held. *Of course, I own half a dozen of my own.*

He sighed. *Best to drop this puzzle and wait on Tilda.*

After dinner, he went back to the frustrating paperwork in his study. Tilda came in about thirty minutes later. "Do you mind if I read?"

"Of course not. I know little of the books on these shelves. Mrs. Hoffman had most of these shelves filled. They took several volumes with them, mostly first editions I believe, but left all of these." Jeffery stood and scanned the books. "Honestly, I haven't sat down to enjoy a novel since I was in school." He clasped his hands behind his back and walked over to the shelves. "Perhaps I should take up reading as a pastime."

Tilda perused the volumes for a bit, then looked down at his desk. "What seems to be the problem?" she asked, picking up a paper.

"As I mentioned earlier, I don't feel this company represents a good investment. Even so, I can't find any indication from the figures. . ."

She put the first paper down and picked up another, scanning each page carefully but quickly, then moved on to a third.

He held back from voicing his concern over her attempt to make sense of such complex financial documents. *What would it hurt to let her look?* he mused.

"Where is the budget for the projected expenses for this project?"

Jeffery rifled through the pages. "Here."

She scanned the columned pages and went back to the other papers. Fifteen minutes later, she spoke. "I see your concern and agree. Several steps are missing in their projections."

"Several? I found one. What did you see?"

"My father invested in a venture out in California three years ago. He lost money not because it was a bad investment per se but because the business suffered an earthquake before they reached a profit. They hadn't raised enough capital to absorb the loss they incurred. This company you are reviewing is seeking substantial investment, offering low payout, and showing rather high expenses. The salaries alone are nearly double those reflected on the profit-and-loss sheets of the similar company my father invested in two years ago."

"Ah, I didn't know that about the salaries in California. I thought they were high but. . ." He turned to his wife. "Thank you. Notice that the ratio of money going back into the company is very low for the first year. In most cases, the greater share goes back into the company in the early years rather than into the owner's pockets." He pointed to the figures on the page.

She nodded. "Yes. I see your point, although I wouldn't have picked that up. I have not had formal business training, just what my father has shown me over the years."

"Well, you are quite astute. I may just bring home more of my work when I find myself stuck."

Tilda's green eyes sparkled as she smiled.

"I know I said I would not push you for the source of your parents' income. Obviously he made investments. But if you should need my advice…"

She cut him off. "Thank you. Yes, he had investments. Most were profitable; occasionally, some were not. I appreciate your offer to help." She paused and looked into his eyes. He felt the heat of her gaze piercing his heart. "Jeffery, I want to trust you."

He opened his arms and stepped toward her. He'd been missing her closeness all day. She might be the one feeling the need for a hug, but he now found them equally comforting.

She stepped into his arms and wrapped hers around him. A warmth spread through his entire body, a peace that calmed him, a love that engulfed him. She leaned in, her head up.

He brushed stray hair from her face and focused on her delicate pink lips. "May I?" he whispered.

"Yes," she whispered back.

He brought his lips on to hers. A wave of passion, fire, and calmness converged as he lost himself in her arms.

"'Let him kiss me with the kisses of his mouth: for thy love *is* better than wine.'" Tilda whispered.

He'd read that passage last night from the Song of Solomon. "Tilda. . ." His voice cracked. He hadn't done that since he was thirteen.

Her eyes flooded open, then flickered with fear.

"Shh," he whispered. "It is fine. But we have promised to get to know one another first."

She stepped out of his embrace. "Forgive me."

He reached for her hand. "There is nothing to forgive. We are married."

The gentle pink rose on her cheeks.

"I am surprised by my own desires. I promise I will not dishonor you."

She tilted her head to the left.

"Now it is I who needs to ask your forgiveness. I am attracted to you, Tilda. But I want my—I mean our—love to be genuine, not sparked by a momentary pleasure."

"I think I understand."

He prayed she really did. He was still trying to figure it out for himself as well. His reading of the Song of Solomon showed there was more to marriage and love than he'd ever thought possible. This was not his parents' love. And though he knew his parents truly loved one another, they were not demonstrative in their affections. Yet here standing before him was a woman who thrived on affection, offered affection, and Jeffery decided he liked it. "I want our union to be special. I can't explain it. I just know that if I were to press for our union now it might not be for the right reasons. What little I know of you intrigues me—in fact, I am in awe of you. I believe I could easily fall in love with you. But I feel you need to be certain that I love you. Does that make sense?"

"Yes. And I will be patient." She stepped away and picked a book off the shelf. "If you'll excuse me, it is getting late. I have some chores I'd like to start early tomorrow morning."

"Good night, Tilda."

"Good night, Jeffery."

She left, her footsteps barely audible on the stairs.

◆　◆　◆

Each day throughout the following week it seemed to Jeffery that they drew closer and closer. Each night he tried to read through the Song of Solomon. The second verse of the tenth chapter kept repeating over and over in his mind: "Rise up, my love, my fair one, and come away." The verse had been permanently branded upon his heart. *"Come away,"* it said, and he contemplated a trip out to California. *We could enjoy a bit of a honeymoon,* he thought, his excitement rising, *and I could look into some of my clients' investments while we're there.*

But events early the following week caused him to pause. He came home to find a stranger in the house, a Mr. Reginald Murphy, the solicitor for Tilda's father.

"How may I help you, Mr. Murphy?" Jeffery said as he walked toward the man and ushered him to a seat in the parlor, then sat as well.

"I'm here for Tilda. Her father and I had an agreement. She is to be my wife."

"I'm afraid she cannot be your wife, since she has married me," Jeffery declared, coming to his feet.

"Mr. Oliver, I'm certain I can persuade you to change your mind. Would a thousand dollars do?"

Jeffery leaned back on his heels. "No."

He heard the back door slam shut and Tilda call out to Mercy.

"Tilda, would you come to the parlor?" Jeffery ordered more than requested.

She came in, and her smile faded as she realized who was sitting on the sofa. "Reginald?"

"So you do know this man?"

"Well, yes. He was Father's solicitor. I mentioned him to you when I first arrived."

Jeffery searched his memory. *Was this the same man. . .? Yes, of course.* "He claims that he had an arrangement with your father."

"He did not. He has taken liberties with the agreement. He was to help me with Father's estate in the event that something were to happen to him and Mother. Reginald presumed that meant he was to become my husband, which he is not, and he has been told in no uncertain terms on more than one occasion that I am not interested."

"Tilda, I love you," Reginald protested. "I came all this way to prove my motives are pure."

"Then you won't mind if I transfer all of my assets to the oversight of my husband, Jeffery Oliver."

Reginald paled.

"How much have you spent?" Tilda asked.

Jeffery put his arm around his wife and examined the man.

"Of Father's money," she added.

"I purchased a house for us in New Rochelle. I spent it for us," he defended.

"Without my consent and in spite of my repeated refusals to marry you, which means you had no authority to spend those funds. I should have you arrested."

"Mr. Murphy," Jeffery spoke up. "I believe my wife has made the matter quite clear. You will be hearing from my attorneys in the morning. We will be transferring oversight of my wife's assets to my firm as soon as you return to New York. You will have ninety days to return the funds you spent without my wife's or her parents' consent. If you have not returned all the funds by that time, I will have an arrest warrant secured by the New York authorities. Do you understand?"

Reginald Murphy nodded.

Jeffery motioned for him to leave.

"Are you certain, Tilda?" Reginald pleaded one more time.

"I do not love you, Reginald, and I am married."

He nodded and slipped out the front door.

"Just how large is your estate?" Jeffery asked.

Chapter Six

Tilda couldn't believe the change in Jeffery since he'd learned the true value of her inheritance. She'd presumed it would create some difficulty, but to find him so defensive at her insistence that he earn her trust—that she didn't expect. Prior to Reginald's visit, they'd been learning to quietly exist together in the same house. She found herself dreaming of the possibility they might celebrate their marriage as a true husband and wife. There were even conversations about having children, possibly several, as they opened up with each other about growing up as an only child.

At least, that's where she had thought things were headed. Now, she didn't know. Jeffery had become distant, coming home late from the office again, always with the excuse that he was too busy with work. And she wanted to believe him....

Tonight was no different.

"Tilda, where's my supper?" Jeffery demanded.

She came into the kitchen and watched him remove his coat and hat. "I thought we might go out tonight."

"If I wanted to go out, I would have told you. I never realized you were so spoiled."

"Fine." She stomped out of the room. "I'll pack my bags and file to have our marriage annulled."

"Fine."

She turned before she left the kitchen and addressed him on his accusation. "How can you say such a thing to me? I've been nothing but thoughtful and considerate to you and your horrible hours. I've never once asked you for a thing. Have I gone to the finery and ordered a dozen dresses? Have I gone to the store and ordered all new furnishings? When, pray tell, have I done anything to indicate I desire a life of pampered indulgence? Even though it's obvious now I don't need your money to do any of those things. And I certainly don't need to put up with your childish jealousy over the fact that I happen to hold more assets than you."

"I never said anything about you having more assets than me," Jeffery barked back at her.

"No, of course not. You communicate your feelings just fine without dropping a single word! Do you think for a moment I don't see through that 'gentleman' facade? There's a reason I didn't tell you right away, Jeffery Oliver. I wanted to. But I didn't dare until you and I were committed to one another unconditionally. Well, that obviously isn't going to happen."

"You never told me how your parents earned that kind of money. I'm no fool. I know professors don't earn that kind of wealth."

"As I told you before, you are correct, they don't. Father was a writer as well as a professor. He taught abroad and lectured during the summer months on his books. And as I've also mentioned before, I speak fluent French. We spent a couple of summers in France as Father and Mother toured. Mother was an accomplished painter. Politicians, university officials, and other well-known people paid quite well to have their portraits done by her.

"We never lived as if we were wealthy. In fact, I didn't know myself until after they died. And now you know—not that it concerns you." Tilda turned and headed back toward the stairs. "I'm leaving, Mr. Oliver. I'll be leaving on the five o'clock train this evening."

"Don't go, Tilda," she thought she heard him say, but it was too little too late. She couldn't continue to live like this. She thought she could be patient and wait for her husband to warm up to the idea of having a wife. What man would not want to fulfill his conjugal rights? They'd been married for a month. They had been growing closer, little by little—or so she thought. They had kissed more than once, the heat of passion certainly overcoming her more than once. Apparently, not so with Jeffery.

"I can't stay where I'm not loved, Lord," she sniffed and pulled out her carpetbag.

◆　◆　◆

Jeffery slammed his fist against the counter. Tilda couldn't leave. He'd been working late to allow himself a month away from his business. Most of his investors understood his need for some time away, but he'd lost another just this evening.

An insistent knock rattled the back door. "Jeffery," his father called as he knocked. "Jeffery, open up, we need to talk. Richard Thompson came by and said he was leaving your firm."

Jeffery rolled his eyes and opened the back door. "Yes," he said and led the way back into the kitchen. "Apparently, he doesn't believe I am allowed to take a trip with my wife."

"A trip?"

Jeffery blew out a pent-up breath. "Father, I've made a mess of my marriage, of everything. There won't be a trip now anyway."

"What's the matter, Son?"

"Tilda's leaving and will be seeking an annulment."

"Annulment? Not a divorce?"

"Yes, an annulment. I wanted us to get to know one another before we. . . You always said to treat my wife as if she were fine china."

"Son, you haven't?"

"No, we haven't. When I met Tilda, I was overwhelmed by how attracted to her I was. I felt it best not to let my passion get the better of me, so after the ceremony with the judge I left her off at the house and I went to the office. I came home late. In fact, I made excuses to come home late that entire first week. She was about to leave the night you and Mother came to dinner, but we managed to work out a truce and decided to get to know one another. All was well until her father's solicitor came from New York, saying her father had arranged for him to marry Tilda. Tilda made it clear she wasn't interested in him. In fact, she believed he was only interested in her money. And now, knowing the true extent of her wealth, I believe she was correct. Her estate is far more substantial than

I imagined." Jeffery gripped the counter, his knuckles white. "I didn't handle the knowledge well. I was hurt that she hadn't confided in me. But I hadn't confided in her, either."

His father placed his hands behind his back and stepped back. "I don't know what to say."

Jeffery chuckled and looked away. "Tilda has pointed out some shortcomings in my upbringing. Do you know that her parents shared the same bedroom—the same bed—and that most married people do? That was not the case in our home. Mother had her room, you had yours, and I had mine."

"But that doesn't mean we were not affectionate, not intimate with each other. Your mother can't sleep with my snoring. So we spent time together every evening before I retired for the night in my room."

Jeffery looked up in shock.

"Son, perhaps our family is not as. . .tactile. . .as some, but I love your mother very much, and I know she feels the same about me. The question is, do you love Tilda? Do you want her to be your wife?"

Did he love her? "I have great affection for her. . .and yes, I do want her to be my wife."

"Son, if you love her, let her know. Saying I love you—and meaning it—defuses a lot of anger. At least, that's my experience with your mother." His father tapped him on the shoulder. "Admit you're wrong when you are. Listen to the words she's *not* saying. Now go! Fix this."

Jeffery closed his eyes. *How do I listen to the words she's not saying?* He didn't have a clue. *I should have never buckled to my family's wishes. I'm no good with relationships, and now I've hurt a beautiful woman who has had more than her share of heartache. Father God, help me. I don't know what to do.*

After a few moments to collect his thoughts and get a handle on his emotions, Jeffery went upstairs and faced the closed door to her room.

"Tilda," Jeffery knocked on the door. "The train does not leave until Thursday for New York."

He heard her sniffles. His heart cinched in his chest. "Forgive me," he whispered.

"I'll stay out of your way until I can leave," she said.

He fought the desire to bust open the door and take her into his arms. "I'll fetch us some dinner," he said instead. She needed him, and he'd failed her, again. "I'm sorry," he mumbled and ran away from her door, away from his commitment and his desires to love her the way she wanted. The way he wanted, he had to admit. She'd made it clear she wanted to become his wife, so why couldn't he allow that to happen? What was holding him back?

Truth be told, he knew his parents spent time alone before his father left his mother's bedroom each night. He'd never really thought about it. And all his growing-up years his father's snoring could be heard down the hall. So it made sense his mother would want to get some sleep at night. But it was also true that his parents had never been openly demonstrative in their affections toward one another. He'd never once seen them hug or kiss in his presence. If he were to open up to Tilda the way she wanted—a smile emerged at the thought—he'd have her in his arms constantly. He'd kiss her every chance he got. Her kisses meant more than baiting passion; they were a seal of affection, a warm promise of their love. Jeffery closed his eyes. He did love her. More than anything else in this world, he loved her. He loved his wife, and now it was too late. She was leaving, and he couldn't prevent it.

He collapsed on a chair in the parlor, covered his face with his hands, and wept.

◆　◆　◆

The next morning, Tilda waited until after Jeffery left for the office before opening her door and leaving her room. He never had returned with food, not that she could have eaten anything. She'd spent the night pacing, crying, and praying.

She headed down the stairs into the kitchen.

"Good morning, Miss Oliver," Mercy called over her shoulder. Then she turned. "How can I—what's the matter, child?"

Tilda collapsed in Mercy's outstretched arms. "My marriage is over," she bawled, surprised she had any more tears to shed. "I'm returning home on Thursday's train to New York."

"Gracious, child! You sit right there and let Mercy fix you a batch of Grandma's tea. It will lift you right up." Mercy ushered her to a chair at the kitchen table and hustled back to the stove, where she removed the teakettle, filled it with water, and returned it to the stove.

Tilda closed her eyes. She could get through this. *God never gives more than we can handle,* she reminded herself, as she had all night.

Mercy blanketed Tilda's hands with her own. She felt the warmth and compassion from her new, old friend. "Now, why don't you tell me what's troubling you? It has something to do with that awful man from the North, doesn't it?"

Tilda gave a weak chuckle. "You could say that. Reginald had it all worked out that I should marry him so he could have access to my parents' funds."

Mercy nodded in understanding. The laws were the same in the North and the South. A woman owning property was a rare thing, and while she could own property, her husband possessed legal oversight of all assets. He couldn't sell the property without her say-so, but he could use up all the funds, leaving the woman with nothing, forced to sell her home as a last resort if she couldn't find a way to make those assets work for her. Tilda had heard several stories along those lines over the years.

Oddly enough, Jeffery had made no attempt to gain access to her funds following Reginald's visit.

"I hadn't informed Mr. Oliver of my inheritance," she explained to Mercy, "or rather, how substantial it is, prior to Reginald's inappropriate visit."

Mercy held her tongue. The kettle whistled. She tapped Tilda's hands and stood up, somehow not scraping the floor with her chair—a curious mystery to Tilda since day one—then went to the stove and poured the hot water into the awaiting teapot. She dunked the silver tea ball into the pot and let it steep, then joined her back at the table after setting it for tea. "What can I do to help?" she asked.

"Nothing. Mr. Oliver does not want me as his wife, and I will not stay in a marriage where I am not wanted."

"I think, if I may say so, Mr. Oliver does want you. He looked horrible when I passed him on the street this morning."

Tilda made no comment. She wanted to hope but couldn't. There was nothing left. She'd put everything into trying to make this courting marriage work. Jeffery simply wasn't interested in having a genuine wife, only someone to bear the title. He didn't want to open his heart and let someone in.

Mercy sat in silence and poured them cups of tea.

Tilda's fingers wrapped around the fine bone china and savored the warmth the heated cup offered. She took a sip. The refreshing liquid touched her lips and awakened her hunger.

"How's 'bout I fetch you a biscuit to go with the tea?" Mercy asked.

Tilda nodded. She ate the biscuit, still warm from the oven and lathered in melted butter, but it brought no joy. Life had lost its flavor. "Thank you for the tea and biscuit, Mercy. I'll be upstairs packing."

Tilda spent the rest of the day and the evening in her room. The next morning, her trunk already packed, she put the last few items in her bag, having decided to leave her corset off. The trip south had bruised her ribs, and she didn't need any more pain in her life. Last night, Jeffery had made one more attempt to speak with her, but she had refused to answer. She had reached her limit. The five o'clock train could not come fast enough. The cab came at noon. She wasn't going to risk having Jeffery come home and stop her from leaving again. She'd tried. She really had. Fresh tears welled in her eyes.

The taxi took her on a slow route around the city. She saw the sights she never had enough time to see. It wasn't much of a trip, a few mentions of various places. Where Sherman made his headquarters, the various houses that hosted many of the social balls. Oddly enough, history and historic homes often piqued her interest. Today she could do little more than quickly scan them. She had no desire to know the ins and outs, to feel the polished stonework, the rough stones. She wanted to go home. She wanted her parents back. She wanted her life back.

She arrived at the station. The cab driver dropped off her trunk. She handed him a dollar, then headed toward the ticket office.

The man behind the counter looked at her for a moment then asked, "Y'all wouldn't happen to be a Mrs. Oliver, would ya?"

"Yes." Fear gripped her heart. Had Jeffery told them not to sell her a ticket?

He smiled and handed her a boarding pass. "Here's your ticket, ma'am. The train will be leaving in thirty minutes."

"My ticket? I haven't paid for it yet," she protested.

"Ah, but your husband did." He smiled. "Next."

A porter came up. "Is this your trunk, ma'am?"

"Yes."

"You leaving on this train?"

She nodded.

"I'll take care of it, ma'am."

She nodded again as he lifted the trunk and headed for the train. She looked at the sleeve for the ticket: Pullman 526. She followed the porter to the caboose, where he carried her trunk through the door at the back into the car. He reappeared shortly after and exited the train. "Have a pleasant journey, ma'am," the porter said with a tip of his hat.

She felt numb, her feet momentarily glued to the platform. How could her life change so dramatically in such a short period of time? She looked back toward the beautiful, bustling city of Savannah. It would have been nice to get to know the town.

With a sigh, Tilda took the few steps up into the car and glanced once more at her ticket. To her left was the necessary room, to her right, storage. She walked down the hall, checking room numbers on the doors. The first was not hers, the second—*No, not this one*—and stopped in front of the third. *Yes.* She opened the door and stepped inside.

"Jeffery? What are you doing here?"

Chapter Seven

Jeffery greeted her, standing at attention, with flowers in his hands. "Tilda, I've come to apologize."

She glanced around the room. He'd rented the master bedroom suite.

"The entire car is ours," he explained. "We have the car to ourselves all the way to California for our honeymoon, if you agree."

"You made it clear—"

He cut her off. "I'm not saying this right. I didn't know what else to do. Tilda, I'm sorry. I love you. I want you to be my wife."

Tears glistened in her wonderful green eyes. She shook her head. "I can't."

He came up beside her and wrapped her in his arms. She stiffened but did not pull away. "I've been out late every night," he whispered against her ear, "because I was planning our wedding trip. The night I came home and snapped at you I had just lost another client—one of several. It seems that letting them know I was taking this trip shook their confidence in my ability to manage their investments. I was angry—not at you, but them. Please, Tilda. Please forgive me. I want us to become man and wife."

She sniffled. He kissed the top of her head.

"I've rented this entire car for our trip out to California, or any place you would like to go. I will change the tickets. I don't care. I only want to be with you. You've shaken up my life, Tilda, and I'm a better man for it. Please say you'll be my wife and travel this country with me."

She pulled away enough to wipe her eyes with a dainty white handkerchief.

He stepped back a bit as well to better read the expression on her face. "Please tell me I'm not too late." He searched the green pools of her eyes for any sign of interest.

She looked down at her ticket. "California?"

"Yes. I'm guessing you have not been there. I know I haven't. And, well, you brought up some interesting points about California investments, and I thought—"

"You're going to be working?"

"Well, yes. . . No, not really."

She marched to the window and held her sides.

He came up beside her and reached out for her. "Tilda, my sweet."

She lowered her shoulder and slipped out of his embrace. "You're working. I don't understand. Just a moment ago you tell me you want to take a marriage trip, but in the very next breath you tell me this is another excuse to build your business. It's always work for you, isn't it?"

She didn't give him a chance to reply. "You have no idea how to do anything but work, do you?" He felt himself wilt inside as she started to pace, her eyes riveted on his.

"A woman wants more. I understand the place for hard work, for a man to provide for his household. I understand we are all under Adam's curse from the Garden of Eden, that the man would have to toil and labor for his survival. But this preoccupation, this—"

She was all together beautiful when she was riled, and suddenly he knew why. She was not an angry woman, a tinderbox ignited by the slightest spark of irritation. Tilda was passionate—passionate about life, about right and wrong, about what was good and just and fair.

She turned and faced him.

"What?"

The whistle blew. The train started to move.

"Great, now I can't get off!" She found an overstuffed armchair and sat down.

"Tilda, let me convince you."

She held up her hand to him and shook her head.

Jeffery sucked in a breath and held it. He could feel the pulse of his heartbeat against his vest. He took off his suit coat and hung it on the specially designed rack. He removed his cufflinks and plopped them on top of the dresser, then rolled up his sleeves.

He turned and was startled by a look of fear written all over her face. She glanced at the bed then back to him. "After all these days of unconsummated marriage, you want to. . ." She gestured toward the bed.

"I would like to, of course. But I would never force myself upon you, Tilda. I am an honorable man. Perhaps ignorant in the ways of love, but I am honorable."

She relaxed.

"I rented the entire car for privacy. We are alone. No one will disturb us. The porters will come with our meals when we order them, or we can join others in the dining car. It is up to you. If you wish, I shall stay in one of the other staterooms. I will not pressure you. If nothing else remains between us, you should at least know that about me."

She nodded.

"Good. Now with regard to my business in California, I thought we could take a look at some of the companies my clients might wish to invest in. Also, I received the final papers on your father's estate. He still has holdings in California, albeit not of much value, according to his records. But wouldn't it be nice to check out this business of your father's that has shown such poor returns on his investment?"

"You have all my parents' paperwork?"

"Your father's, yes. It appears your mother's earnings from some of her paintings have not come in yet. I thought we could finish our trip in New York and take care of all your family assets. I'm also hoping that your mother's work is not all gone. I would very much like to see some of her artwork."

Tilda smiled.

"I also thought we could use our many free days on this trip to discuss our hopes and plans for the future. We had begun discussing the matter of children before Mr. Murphy so crudely came to my—correction, to our door."

Tilda shook her head no. "I'm not certain I can open my heart again."

Jeffery's heart stopped. Tears pooled in his eyes, and he turned away. "I understand," he said, his voice low and polite, and exited to the hallway to leave her alone in their room. His body shuddered, wave upon wave, as a lifetime of self-control cracked and gave way. The restrained tears now streamed down his face. He'd ruined it. He'd hurt her so badly she could not recover.

He pulled out his handkerchief, wiped his eyes, and headed to the private living and dining areas at the front of the car. He plopped down on the plush sofa. Only Tilda could make him do something so foolish as to put off his customers for a month and spend a ton of money on private accommodations. He shook his head and rubbed his hands over his face and through his hair. *Dear God, please help me. I don't think I can recover from this.*

◆　◆　◆

Tilda wanted to jump up and run after Jeffery. But she found herself unable to move, stunned by the fact that he'd rented the entire car, stunned that he'd planned a long wedding trip without consulting her. That, perhaps, was a little less unbelievable since he'd done the same with regard to purchasing the house before her arrival. The first thing she had noticed about Jeffery Oliver was his talent as a planner. It was a part of who he was. If—and she did mean if—she agreed to continue in their marriage, he would need to change. She needed to be a part of the decision-making for the household.

She looked around the lavish bedroom. Pullman spared no expense in his private cars, of which this was one. From the mahogany woodwork to the stuffed, silk-covered chairs and fine lace curtains—all testified to the highest standards of quality a society could produce and those with means could afford. Yet it wasn't gaudy. The large, ornately crafted bed filled much of the room, but still allowed plenty of room for a private toilet, a couple of chairs, and comfortable space to walk around two sides of the bed.

The bed. Tilda sighed. She'd been wanting Jeffery to join her in their marriage bed, but he'd wanted to wait. Now he was ready, and she wasn't. She shook her head. *Father God, help me understand what is going on.*

There was a knock at the door. "Tilda, the porter is here with our dinner."

"I'll join you in a minute."

The gentle rock of the train as it rolled down the rails lulled her to a place of calmness. She took in a deep breath, stood up, and exited the master suite. She turned to her left and walked toward the front of the train.

The next room took her breath away. She entered a private living area decked out with a sofa, a couple of chairs, and a reading lamp on a small, decorative table. The walls were lined with books, knickknacks—all the comforts of home.

Jeffery leaned against the doorway. "Impressive, isn't it?"

"Yes, quite."

He stood tall. "Come, sit with me in the dining room."

He reached out his hand. She didn't take it. She wanted to, but she had to protect her heart. His hand swung down to his side. With his left hand outstretched, he ushered her to the dining area. Again, the room was decorated with the best of modern furnishings. The tables, as well as the chairs, were made of polished cherry.

Jeffery pulled out a chair for her.

She tucked the back of her dress toward her legs and sat down. "Thank you."

"You're welcome, my sweet."

A smile curled on her lips. Perhaps her heart was already giving into this man once again. He sat down and held out his hand. "Shall we pray?"

She placed her hand in his. He wrapped his fingers around hers, his touch so gentle and warm. "Father," he prayed, "we ask for Your guidance and thank You for Your provisions. Be with us as we begin this journey. In the name of the Father, the Son, and the Holy Ghost, amen."

"Amen," Tilda said and gently pulled her hand away. She grabbed the silver fork and knife expertly set beside her plate filled with roast beef, gravy, mashed potatoes, and green beans. "It smells good."

"I have it on good authority that this railroad serves quality meals." Jeffery dug into his dinner. "It is good," he said a moment later, "but your gravy is better."

She smiled. "Thank you."

He nodded and continued with his meal. When he had polished off half of his plate he glanced up at her. "Tilda, I know I've made a mess of our marriage. Is there anything I can do to fix it? Anything at all?"

She put down her fork. "Before I answer that, tell me: did your father make all the decisions in your house?"

Jeffery shrugged. "I don't know. I never thought about it." He leaned back in his chair. "Oh no, I did it again, didn't I?"

She nodded, unable to speak due to a lump in her throat that had nothing to do with the dinner.

"I'm sorry, Tilda. I meant this trip as a surprise, and if I hadn't gotten so upset with my clients I would have told you about my plans." He paused. "Well, maybe not. I was planning this as a surprise. A man isn't supposed to tell his spouse about a surprise, is he?"

"I suppose not. But since I was heading home to New York, don't you think you should have talked with me before I arrived on the train?"

He knitted his eyebrows together. "How? You wouldn't speak with me. I tried every night, but you refused to talk. When do you think I should have told you?"

Tilda clamped down on her jaw. "Perhaps you have a point there." She placed her silverware down and folded her hands in her lap. "You hurt me. I want to love you Jeffery, I really do but—"

"It will take a week before we're out to California. We have time." He reached over and took her hand. "Tilda, I love you. Give me the week to prove it. We have all day to spend with one another. I won't be running off to the office. I won't even wire my office until I'm in California, and then simply to let Max know that we've arrived. Is that fair?"

Her words caught in her throat again, and she nodded.

He leaned back in his chair, relieved. "So, why don't you tell me about Paris? I have never been. In fact, today is the first time I ever left Savannah."

Tilda sat back. "You've never left Savannah?"

"Never. Another sign that I love you. I never had a reason to leave the city. It was home, all I ever knew or cared to know. You, my sweet, have changed me in so many ways. Now I am curious about the places you have been, the places I once read about in books. My grandfather was right about me. To be fair, you should know I was ordered by my grandfather— before my thirtieth birthday —to marry. If I did not, my inheritance would go to charity. Even back then Grandpa felt I was too focused on work rather than life. He also knew I would have a hard time giving up my inheritance, even if I didn't need it."

Tilda laughed.

"What's so funny?"

"I didn't tell you about my inheritance because I wanted a man to marry me for love, not for money."

Jeffery laughed. "I see your point. It is true, I did marry you for that purpose. However, the reason I did not come home with you the night we married was because I was afraid of you. You were so beautiful, so. . .alive! Marriage had been a task to accomplish until then, a goal to achieve. Meeting you that very first time changed all of that. You changed me. I knew I needed to respect you, not simply make you my wife and move on to other tasks. I hope that makes sense to you, because I don't believe I can explain it better than that. I have no education on how to speak with a woman, much less on how to speak to my bride. But if you're willing to allow me to make mistakes and forgive me, I will work with everything I have to get it right. I wish my words would never hurt you, Tilda. But I'd be a fool to believe otherwise. I promise you this, however: I will never hurt you intentionally."

Tilda picked up the water glass and twirled it between her fingers for a moment. "After years of marriage, my parents still managed to hurt and offend one another from time to time. I believe that is a part of love and marriage."

"You are probably right, though I wish it were not so."

◆　◆　◆

They talked for hours before settling down for the night. He kissed her at the doorway to the master suite before heading to a guest bedroom, and though he had not planned on it, she kissed him in return. A flicker of hope ignited in the pit of his stomach, and he prayed the flame would not go out.

The next morning, he rose in time for breakfast. He went to the dining area and found her in her morning clothes. "You look fetching this morning, my sweet. May I kiss you?"

"Hmm," she teased. "I suppose a little kiss would be acceptable."

He swooped her into his arms and kissed her with the passion he'd been wanting to show her for weeks, if he had only been honest with himself.

"My, my, Mr. Oliver! Where did that come from?"

"From you, from the hope that we might possibly become one."

She laced her fingers through his. "I'd like that."

He leaned in and gave her a light kiss on the lips. "I would like that, too, Mrs. Oliver," he said with a playful wink.

Her smile seemed to brighten the room. More than that, it unlocked another chamber in his heart. "Has anyone ever told you how beautiful you are, Mrs. Oliver?"

"My parents."

"No one else?"

"Well there was this one young man in Paris. . ." She smiled.

He groaned. "I don't know that I want to hear this."

"Perhaps not, but it was very serious. I was six and he was seven."

Jeffery doubled over in laughter. "Oh my, life with you is going to be interesting, Mrs. Oliver."

"You have no idea."

"No, I don't, but I'm looking forward to it." He lifted the cover off his breakfast plate. "Where's my bacon?"

"Sorry, I ate it," she confessed.

"That will never do, Mrs. Oliver. A man needs his bacon."

Tilda's giggle tickled his ears. So much had changed since the day he'd waited for her at the railway station. "I love you, Tilda."

"I love you, too, Jeffery. And I will stay married with you, if you still want me."

"Goodness, Tilda, there is no question. I'd be a fool to not want the most enchanting, challenging woman on this planet. I love you."

Tilda's smile evoked the same from him.

"Will you sleep in the same room as me?" she asked. "I don't think I could handle separate bedrooms."

Jeffery leaned back. "Ah." He wiped his mouth with the linen napkin. "I spoke to my father about that. It seems my mother could not abide his snoring. Which, to be truthful, I found difficult to tolerate at times, and my room was down the hall from his. To this day they spend time alone with one another each night until he is ready for sleep. Then he goes to his own room."

Tilda smiled. "Do you snore, Mr. Oliver?"

"I don't believe so, Mrs. Oliver."

"Good."

"How would you like to spend our day?" he asked.

A delicate pink rose on her cheeks. "With you."

He jumped up, swooped her in his arms, and twirled her around. "I have great affection for the railroad." He carried her toward the master suite.

"Pardon?"

"The railroad brought me the love of my life, and we recognized our love for one another while riding the rails. For that, I will be eternally grateful."

"Ah, love on the rails. I like that."

He kissed her lips. "Grandpa was right, you know."

"What do you mean?" she asked.

"'Whoso findeth a wife,'" he quoted from Proverbs, "'findeth a good thing, and obtaineth favour of the Lord.'" He pulled the pocket watch out and flipped it open for her to see. "This is what he was trying to teach me. Now I understand. I love you, Tilda."

"I love you, too."

Lynn A. Coleman is an award-winning and best-selling author of *Key West* and other books. She began her writing and speaking career with how to utilize the Internet. Since October 1998, when her first fiction novel sold, she's sold thirty-eight books and novellas. Lynn is also the founder of American Christian Fiction Writers, Inc. and served as the group's first president for two years and two years on the Advisory Board. One of her primary reasons for starting ACFW was to help writers develop their writing skills and encourage others to go deeper in their relationship with God. "God has given me a gift, but it is my responsibility to develop that gift."

Some of her other interests are photography, camping, cooking, and boating. Having grown up on Martha's Vineyard, she finds water to be very exciting and soothing. She can sit and watch the waves for hours. If time permitted, she would like to travel.

She makes her home in Keystone Heights, Florida, where her husband of forty-two years serves as pastor of Friendship Bible Church. Together they are blessed with three children, two living and one in glory, and eight grandchildren.

The Honeymoon
Express

by Susanne Dietze

Dedication

To Hannah and Matthew, two of the most amazing people on the planet. I love your jokes, your desire to please Jesus, and your willingness to brainstorm plots with me (I just couldn't work in a hamster or epic battle this time—sorry, guys). I'm blessed and proud to be your mom.

God sets the lonely in families,
he leads out the prisoners with singing.
PSALM 68:6 NIV

Chapter One

Jersey City, New Jersey
Evening of August 27, 1876

Ellen Blanchard cringed. She had no business standing in the ticket queue at the Pennsylvania Railroad Station. At least, no business standing under a banner which read BON VOYAGE, HONEYMOON EXPRESS.

She—a woman most definitely lacking a husband—did not belong on a transcontinental train occupied by celebrating newlyweds. The awkwardness of it all set her body afire, dampening her with perspiration. Heat suffused her face. And when she blushed, she splotched like a half-ripe tomato.

With fumbling fingers, she tugged her fan from her reticule and flicked it open with a snap, flapping blessedly cooler air over her hot cheeks. Thankfully, an observer might attribute her flush to the summer evening heat trapped inside the stuffy depot and the crush of bodies—canoodling couples, reporters, photographers, and a brass band performing a polka—pressed into the platform.

No one would likely suspect the true reason for her presence. Which was going on a wedding trip. By herself.

Enough foolish embarrassment. Ellen may not belong on this train, but it was open to the public if not enough newlyweds purchased tickets, so she had every right to ride it. She squared her shoulders and fixed her gaze smack between the buckskin-clad shoulder blades of the man in queue ahead of her, right where his too-long hair fell in gold-streaked brown curls.

This was not a wedding trip. It was an adventure. The start of a new life.

As long as she could procure a ticket. She peeked at the station clock—a quarter to seven. The train might leave without her.

Dash dot dash dot. Dot. Dot dot dot.

Jesus, please. Her fingers tapped out a prayer in Morse code against her thigh while she waited an interminable time, unmoving in the queue.

The haircut-shy man ahead of her was broad-shouldered enough that she had to bend at the waist to peek around him at the ticket agent. What took so long? The bespectacled agent adjusted his glasses and then took bills from the gray-haired, smartly dressed gentleman at the front of the line. A towheaded boy clung to the gentleman's coat. "Welcome to the Express," the agent hollered over the brass band's *oom-pahs*, his expression not the least bit welcoming.

His grimace didn't dampen Ellen's burgeoning excitement. If a father and son—no more newlyweds than she—could purchase a berth on the Express, then tickets were still available. She bounced on her toes.

Moving forward in the queue, her fingers tapped against her thigh, repeating her prayer. *Dash dot dash dot. Dot.* On the second *S* in *Jesus*, the buckskin-clad man ahead of her took his ticket and stepped aside, leaving her first in the queue. My, that was faster this time.

Stuffing her fan into her reticule, she leaned over the counter, the better to not be overheard. "One for the Express, please."

He cupped his ear. "Speak up, ma'am. Can't hear nothin' over them flugelhorns."

So much for trying to be discreet. "The Honeymoon train. I was told if any berths went unsold, they would be available for purchase by, er, nonhoneymooners. I'd like one ticket."

"No single tickets, this being a promotion for newly-hitched couples. Tickets-for-two are all we sell."

Double the expense, but she had no choice. "Then I'd like a ticket-for-two."

"If'n there was any more left, but I just sold the last one. You got somewhere to go, ma'am, I can get you a spot on another train tomorrow morning."

Ellen's head shook so hard her hat slipped toward her ear. No other train would do. Only the Express, this only-once-before attempted coast-to-coast mastery of engineering and cooperation, would get her to California in time to claim employment.

She shoved her hat aright. "I must reach Sacramento by September first. Any other train will take days longer than that."

He sighed. "Sorry, ma'am."

"If the berths are sold, I'll take a seat in the passenger car." Although she'd miss the privacy of one at nighttime.

"No seats were ever for sale. Just berths in the Pullman. The final coach on the train ain't a passenger car, either. It's repurposed with a galley, dining area, and gentleman's lounge." From his weary tone, it sounded as if he'd had this conversation already and resented repeating himself. "These advertising stunts cause nothin' but headaches. Sorry, but if you don't want a ticket for a different train, move aside."

"Forgive me." She stepped to the side, uncertain what to do next.

She couldn't go home—she didn't have one anymore. Once Father died, she'd been granted a few weeks to vacate their rooms above the telegraph office. She'd applied for Father's job, of course, but the company preferred a man. As had every other place she applied.

Rawlings Mining and Transport Company in the pleasant-sounding town of Poppy, California, hadn't minded her being a woman, however, so long as she started work September 1. Five days from now—something that wouldn't have been a problem had Ambrose not misplaced the telegram offering her the job.

Misplaced, her eye.

At least she'd discovered what he'd done. She'd telegraphed Rawlings, accepting the job, tidied Father's grave a final time, and packed her necessities in the valise and two trunks now waiting for her on the platform. There was no going back.

Squaring her shoulders, Ellen returned to the end of the ticket queue. She'd telegraph Rawlings Company regarding her tardiness and pray they'd take her nevertheless.

Her fingers tapped against her leg. *God, help me.*

"Ma'am?"

"I'm sorry, sir, were you here first?" The words were hardly out before she recognized the man who'd stood ahead of her in line. Not that she'd seen his face, just his broad back, but who else stood out in a crowd like this? The fellow's gold-streaked hair curled to the shoulders of his buckskin jacket. His trousers and shoes appeared sewn of similar-looking leather, as did the thong threading a necklace of white beads around his neck. Beneath the jacket, however, he wore an orthodox blue-striped shirt that matched the hue of his eyes.

His unconventional dress could mean but one thing. He was a man of the West, some sort of outdoorsman or mountain man. Ellen's hand pressed her chest. She'd read about fellows like him in novels, but those were grizzled fellows with beards to their ribcages who reeked like skunks. This one, however, was shaven, clean, and indisputably handsome.

"I'm not in line." He was polite, too. "I purchased the last berth on the Express, but I couldn't help overhearing your exchange with the ticket agent. I can tell it's mighty important for you to be in California. I have a proposition for you."

"You'll sell me your berth?" This mountain man was a gem of a gentleman. Even if he raised the price to make a little money for his trouble. "How much?"

"Oh, no." He smiled. "I thought we could share the ticket-for-two."

Ellen blinked. Then it all made sense. She might be a fool about many things, but she was not stupid.

"Mister. . . ?" She'd behave like the lady she was, rather than screech at him. For now.

"Nash."

"Mr. Nash—"

"Just Nash."

"Step away before I summon assistance."

His eyes went wide. Then one of his fringe-laden sleeves reached for her.

She lifted her knee. Not enough so anyone would notice it beneath the bustled bell of her amethyst silk skirt. But it was ready should she need to kick him to make her point understood.

◆ ◆ ◆

"Not like that." Nash yanked back his hand. What was he thinking, almost touching a strange woman, much less phrasing his offer as if he had foul intentions? *Try to remember how to be around females, at least until you get home. Then you can go back to being normal.*

Which was what, lonely? Nash shoved away the thought. Alone didn't necessarily mean lonely. Things were fine as they were.

Meanwhile the blond in the dress the color of grape jelly glared up at him with rich brown eyes. She was a pretty thing, despite the glower.

His hands raised in a gesture of peace. "I thought we could split the ticket, all businesslike. That's it. I want to go home, you need to get west, no more than that."

Her scowl didn't soften. "There is but one berth per ticket."

"True." At least that was how Pullman cars worked, as far as he knew. Beds formed out of two seats or folded down from the ceiling. Despite a curtain, there was scant privacy for anyone on this ridiculous honeymoon trip, but it didn't concern Nash. "I won't be using the berth, whether you come or not."

She crossed her arms. The fingers of one hand tapped against the purple fabric of her opposite sleeve. A sign of her anxiety? "How can I be assured of this?"

When was the last time he'd had to defend his honor? Then again, when was the last time he'd made such an idiot of himself? He couldn't fight the smile that tugged his lips. "Truth is, I don't like being closed up. Most nights I sleep outdoors so I can watch the stars—in warm weather, anyway. So I'll sleep in the train lounge where I'll have a good view of the sky. If you don't take the berth, it'll go empty."

She chewed her lip. Debating—it wasn't hard to figure that out. Then she sighed. "At least I shall be well chaperoned with so many others on the train."

So would the newlyweds. He grinned and passed her the ticket.

"Thank you, Mr. Nash. I insist on paying you."

"Just Nash. Miss—?"

She hesitated half a second. "Blanchard."

She directed a porter to her trunks just as the band's song ended on a flourish.

"Honeymooners!"

The yell made her jump. Set Nash's nerves on edge, too. Give him the quiet of his mountain home any day.

A thickset fellow waved from atop a bunting-draped platform several feet off the ground. His hand rested in a protective gesture on a camera. "Time for a commemorative photograph," he hollered. "Stand in front of the engine, please."

Couples murmured and hurried over to find places before the black steam engine, but Miss Blanchard shook her head. "We're not honeymooners."

"Nope." Nash pulled his satchel strap over his shoulder. Truth was, he didn't cotton to spending four days on a honeymoon train. Not that he wasn't happy for the lovebirds clustering together, twittering while the photographer issued instructions. These folks had their whole lives ahead of them. At least, he prayed so.

But happy honeymoons didn't always lead to happily ever afters.

Miss Blanchard stepped back, colliding with the little boy who'd preceded Nash in the ticket queue. She wobbled, and Nash caught her arm. She smelled nice. Like almonds.

Her cheeks blotched pink. "Thank you."

Nash released her arm as if it were quilled like a porcupine's hide, then stepped back to a more proper distance. Nodded, because saying *you're welcome* seemed idiotic when he should apologize for—what, liking how she smelled? Holding on a second too long?

"Gabe." The boy's father gripped the boy's shoulder. "Apologize to these folks. Almost knocked them over."

Miss Blanchard's smile was as pretty as she was. "Not at all. He's excited, and who can blame him, riding such a fine train?"

Gabe grinned. As ever when Nash encountered little boys, it was impossible not to think of his own. Would they have loved trains—the noise and smoke and excitement?

The photographer clambered down from his perch to herd the gathered folks with his arms, and Gabe's gaze riveted to him. "Sorry, ma'am. Come on, Papa, the photograph's waiting."

"Not for us." He drew Gabe to his side. "Honeymooners only."

The photographer beckoned them. "Every Express passenger, please, honeymooner or child and parent."

"No, thank you," the man said. His boy's face crumpled.

"Sir. In the buckskins." The photographer pointed. "Stand here."

Nash hadn't posed for a camera since he wore the uniform of the Army of the Potomac. Didn't want to start now, but the photographer took his arm and pulled. "Step closer to the group with your wife so we can finish and you can begin your bridal tour."

His wife. Nash should've expected folks to make that assumption, this being a honeymoon trip and all. But he hadn't thought it through. Just tried to help somebody in need.

The photographer had Miss Blanchard by the arm, too, ushering them to the right flank of the group and pushing them together so her shoulder touched his bicep. "What a fine-looking couple you make, if I do say so myself."

Chapter Two

O h, we aren't married. Just traveling together."

That sounded horrible. Ellen's face scorched. "That is, we are strangers sharing the convenience of a ticket-for-two."

The photographer didn't appear to be listening. "Hold still, folks." He scurried back up the ladder to his camera and hid under the black-cloth hood.

She looked to Mr. Nash for help, but he just stood with a straight face. Traitor. Why hadn't he spoken up? She spun, pressing into his shoulder since they were pressed cheek by jowl. "Mr. Nash, say something—"

"Mrs. Buckskins." She spun back. The photographer had thrust aside the hood to scowl down at her. "Please refrain from speaking to your husband."

"It'll be over in a minute." The way the words came out, it was clear her "husband" spoke without moving his lips—in obedience to the photographer. She couldn't turn her head to prove it, though.

Instead she answered him in kind, through clenched teeth. "We're not married."

"He doesn't care."

Well, Ellen did. Mrs. Buckskins, indeed. And to think she'd responded to it! Heat pricked her cheeks, just in time to look blotchy for the photograph.

With a burst of light and puff of smoke from the flash lamp, it was over. The pressure of Mr. Nash's arm disappeared from her shoulder.

"All aboard!" The dark-coated conductor held up his arm. The crowd of honeymooners moved as one to board the Express.

"My portion of the ticket." Ellen opened her handbag, but Mr. Nash held up a hand.

"Later. We don't want to hold up the departure."

Not with its urgent itinerary, with every other train traveling the same lines waiting on side tracks while this one passed. And not with water, coal, and crews standing ready to replenish the train on its brief stops along the way.

A porter gripped Ellen's elbow and hoisted her onto the gleaming-red passenger car—oh, the hotel car. The plush upholstered sofas were far more luxurious than the wooden benches she'd occupied on other trains. So were the shining silver accents, the carved woodwork, and carpet underfoot.

"Take a seat, enjoy the complimentary newspaper you'll find there provided by our sponsor, the *New York Daily*, and congratulations on your nuptials." The conductor waved her through.

"But—"

"Thank you, sir." Mr. Nash spoke over her.

"Mr. Nash, really." Negotiating her skirt around a gleaming brass spittoon in the aisle, she found the closest empty seat, scooped the newspaper and a guidebook from it, sat down, and plunked the publications on her lap. Headlines blared about the Express and those bank robbers terrorizing New York; she'd read the articles later.

"It's not worth correcting everybody about our status. Twenty-four passengers and staff? Can't get to all of them." To her surprise, Mr. Nash took the seat beside her. A glance assured her there weren't other options available. Half a dozen rows of sofas flanked the aisle, with two sofas facing each other so four people could speak easily. It appeared all the seats in the car were taken, except the one beside her. Ellen sighed. Of course. Everyone on this train traveled in pairs.

Would she and Mr. Nash sit together the entire journey? A strange current of excitement traversed her bones. Something she hadn't felt since Ambrose leaned over her shoulder that first time to decipher an incoming telegraph.

Ridiculous. But it would behoove her to take advantage of Mr. Nash's proximity to ask him questions about California.

That notion proved fruitless the moment the train whistle blew. Cries of "Godspeed" and "Bon voyage" carried through the open windows. The engine pulled from the station, and the couples cheered. Ellen joined in, catching a mouthful of sooty smoke that must've come in through the open window. And coughed.

"Here, ma'am." A silver cup was thrust under her nose.

"How kind," she choked, glancing up at the porter holding out the beverage. She took a gulp, washing the soot from her throat. And coughed anew at the sickly-sweet cherry flavor. It wasn't the water she'd expected.

"Celebratory punch." He offered cups to the others. At once, chatter broke out across the aisle, and cups clanked with cheers.

Small talk was not Ellen's strong suit. *Just ask Ambrose.*

"How do?" The dashing young man in the seat facing her leaned forward. "I'm Lincoln Dewey, and this is my bride, Primrose."

Primrose, a pretty blond, blushed a becoming shade of rose. It was difficult not to envy Primrose's coloring. Or the enormous emerald brooch at her throat. Ellen was not a connoisseur of gems, but its value was obvious.

The groom across the aisle from the Deweys thrust out his hand for shaking. "Clifford and Stella Howell."

The men shook hands while Ellen nodded at Stella. Dark haired and thin boned, she appeared not much older than Ellen's twenty-seven years. *See, Ambrose? I'm not too old for matrimony. One need not be eighteen, like your bride—*

"You're from New York?" Stella leaned forward toward the Deweys. "What do you do?"

"Banking." He looked it, with his tailored suit. "You, Mr. Howell?"

"City management." Clifford's eyes narrowed. "Say, you're a banker? Have any problems with those two robbers at your branch? The ones everyone in town's talking about?"

"None. More punch?" Lincoln hailed the porter.

Ellen smiled to herself. No one asked what she did. Or Mr. Nash, either.

"We're from New York, too, Papa." Gabe, the lad who'd almost bowled her over on the train platform, hopped from his seat across from Stella. "We're goin' to San Francisco.

Not on our honeymoon. But it's just us, leavin' on an a–venture."

Everyone laughed but his father, who introduced himself as Jerome Prewett. "That's enough, Son. Don't want to disturb these nice people."

"Nonsense," Ellen burst out, but Jerome Prewett bent to murmur to his pouting son. Lincoln whispered something to Primrose that made her giggle, and Clifford spoke softly to Stella—but they frowned.

Unsure what to do, Ellen sipped her punch.

"You a New Yorker, too?" Lincoln gestured at Mr. Nash's fringed sleeves.

Mr. Nash brushed a lock of hair from his brow. "I'm from Maine."

Ellen swallowed her sip too fast, stinging her throat again. "I thought you were a Californian."

"I am now." My, his eyes were the loveliest shade of blue.

Lincoln hooted. "And I thought Primrose and I didn't know each other well enough when we swapped vows. You two must not do much talking."

His brows wiggled suggestively. The others laughed. And Ellen flushed hotter (and no doubt redder) than a brick oven.

"We're sharing the ticket-for-two, just like the Prewetts," Mr. Nash said before Ellen could speak. "We didn't know one another before today."

So much for not declaring their status to the other passengers. Maybe he was horrified by the suggestion of being married to her. Just like Ambrose. His face didn't show disgust, however. But he was occupied with getting his ticket punched by the conductor. She handed hers over, too.

"Look at all you fine honeymooners on this train." He punched and then grinned at Gabe. "And folks wanting to get somewhere fast."

"Or get *away* from somewhere fast." Stella held out her ticket. "This would be ideal, wouldn't it? Hypothetically?"

Lincoln's laugh was loud. "Now that's an idea."

Primrose pulled him close to whisper. Clifford did the same to Stella, leaving Ellen and Mr. Nash awkward with their punch. After a minute, he drained his up. "I think I'll stretch my legs. Look at the other coach."

Understanding dawned. Soon the porters would convert these sofas to berths. And he'd sleep in the so-called gentleman's lounge, just as he'd promised.

His thoughtfulness touched her. "Enjoy the view."

"Seems unfair, the gentlemen getting their own car." Primrose rolled her eyes.

Maybe, but without it, Mr. Nash would have nowhere else to sleep.

"You go, too." Stella shooed her husband to stand. If Ellen ever married, she'd not want to part from her groom so soon, would she?

Lincoln rose, too. "I'll join you fellows."

So did several other men, including grooms who introduced themselves as Mr. Ridley and Mr. Fisher, whose wives jabbered with enthusiasm.

Little Gabe hopped up, but his father shook his head. "You need to stay here."

"Aw. I'm a gentleman." Gabe's chin jutted forward.

"Would you like to sit with me?" Ellen patted Nash's vacated seat. She'd far prefer chatting with a child than her peers. Stella crossed the aisle to sit by Primrose, and soon they'd start discussing hats or husbands, and Ellen would sit there ignored as the spittoon in the aisle.

Gabe hopped on the seat beside her, pointing at the guidebook left on their seats, *The Honeymoon Express: Sponsored by the "New York Daily."* "What's it say?"

"Let's see." She was curious, too, and thumbed open the booklet, holding it at an angle to catch the last rays of sun before dusk fell. "Many things, like when to look for buffalo."

"Papa says we may go sixty miles an hour, like the Jarrett-Palmer Express," Gabe added.

"This book says we won't go as fast as they did, because we have more cars."

It was still a short train. The engine-tender first, then the baggage car/staff commissary, and then the hotel car, where they rode, which included the saloons, or necessaries. Last in the train was the converted car containing the dining area and gentlemen's lounge. Still, they might make top speeds.

Traveling that fast sounded thrilling. Then the car lurched around a curve. Ellen wavered into Gabe. Stella swayed toward Primrose, or rather, the open valise at Primrose's feet. "My, what a pretty bag."

Did her fingers sweep inside it? Or did the motion of the train pull her down?

"It's new." Primrose helped Stella upright. "I didn't imagine we'd be jostled about like this, but it's worth it to make the speed record."

Ellen didn't care about the record. Just getting to California. Then Gabe shoved the guidebook in Ellen's face. "Read, please? Like my mama does?"

Tears spilled over his baby-round cheeks. Oh dear. "What's wrong?"

"I miss Mama. But Papa says don't talk about her."

Ellen's lips compressed. He'd just spoken of his mother in present tense, but perhaps she'd recently died. Maybe the train trip west was a distraction for the Prewetts, poor things. "Let's read, then."

She did until Gabe patted her neck.

"Mama's in New York, but don't tell Papa I told. This trip is our secret."

Ellen's heart thumped out of time. "Secret?"

"Gabe." At Mr. Prewett's voice, Ellen startled. Before she could blink, Mr. Prewett lifted Gabe from beside her. "Not bothering the nice lady, are you?"

"Of course not." Her voice croaked. "We were just—"

"Dusk is falling. Time to make up the berths. Let's visit the saloon."

Ellen should prepare for bed, too, but her legs had begun to shake, and it had naught to do with the jerky car. The Prewetts' trip was none of her business, and Gabe was such a young fellow he may have misunderstood the situation. Nevertheless, her stomach clenched with unease. She tapped a prayer in Morse code on her left leg. *What am I to do, Lord?*

The face that popped into her mind was that of Mr. Nash.

◆　◆　◆

In the morning, Nash ambled from the lounge into the dining area for breakfast, shaking his head. "That's enough, Ridley."

The large fellow at his heels thumped Nash's shoulder as a comrade would, almost knocking him into a table occupied by the breakfasting Howells, Clifford and Stella.

"Sure looked like you were sleeping in the lounge. Got booted from your berth by your bride on your honeymoon? Must've been some sort of disagreement." Ridley plunged his elbow toward Nash's ribcage. It might have hurt, if the train's swaying motions hadn't prevented Ridley from making contact.

"It's not like that." Folks and their assumptions.

"All women are naggers. Maybe Mrs. Nash wants you to wear real shoes, eh?"

Nash was accustomed to folks teasing him about his moccasins. And his hair, and the cabin he slept in during winter. But he wouldn't stand someone casting aspersions about another, "Mrs. Nash" or not. "She's a fine lady, Ridley, and I'll thank you to remember it."

From the disapproving looks on the Howells' faces, it was clear they'd overheard. Clifford's head tipped to the side. "Mr. Ridley, where's your bride? And what were you doing in the lounge this early morn?"

Ridley's jowls trembled in time with the train's *chug-a-chug*s. "All that noise switching to the Pittsburgh, Fort Wayne, and Chicago line woke me. Not that I slept well to begin with. Got cinders on my face from the open windows."

Clifford exchanged meaningful looks with Nash. "So it wasn't an argument with your bride that drew you to the gentlemen's lounge, either."

Ridley snorted, then pushed past to exit the car.

Nash extended his hand to Clifford. "Thanks."

Clifford's handshake was firm. "Think nothing of it, Mr. Nash."

"Nash." He hardly knew the fellow, but he liked him already.

"Join us, please," Stella offered.

Nash was about to sit when Ellen Blanchard wobbled into the dining area. Wherever they were in Ohio right now, they traveled so fast the train seemed ready to fly off the rails, making everyone and everything on it struggle to hold its place. The pale bun at her nape was askew, just like her steps. But her eyes sparkled, and her smile was brighter than the early morning light that streamed through the windows. Made him almost forget the ache in his bones from resting on the hard bench in the lounge.

He made his way to Miss Blanchard's side, hand extended to help her. "You all right?"

She nodded. "How can you walk without stumbling?"

"Moccasins. And years walking on uneven ground, I s'pose." But then the train lurched, and he did, too. They both laughed.

"Did you sleep well?" Her whisper was conspiratorial.

"Fair enough." He whispered back, grinning.

"Me, too. Oh, good morning." She greeted the Howells and took the seat Nash pulled out for her, landing hard on her bustle as the train braked. "We'll all be black and blue before we reach California."

She laughed again, testifying to her good humor, and Nash's appreciation of her rose a notch. She wasn't concerned with appearances, unlike Primrose Dewey, who almost fell out of her chair at the train's pitch and then snapped angrily at their porter for not holding the chair in the right spot.

A second porter arrived at Nash's elbow with a pot of coffee, biscuits, and boiled ham. All cold. But after Nash offered grace, their table of four ate, holding their cups in place with one hand while they forked food from skidding plates with the other. The dining area filled with the other passengers.

"Eight years," Stella answered Miss Blanchard's query of how long the Howells had been wed.

Clifford held up a hand. "That is, we've known one another eight years. The wedding was a fortnight ago."

"Congratulations." Nash remembered when he'd been married a fortnight. He'd kissed Leora goodbye and marched south with the Twentieth Maine. The recollection filled his mouth with a sourness that couldn't be washed away with tepid coffee.

"Pretty bad, isn't it?" Clifford held up his coffee.

"I've had worse." Like in the war. It'd been over ten years, but he could still taste stale hard tack dunked in muddy camp coffee.

"I'm certain it's difficult to cook, the way we're all heaving to and fro," Miss Blanchard suggested.

"Hear, hear." Stella eyed her husband in that way wives had, communicating something only he would understand. At once, Clifford rose and assisted Stella up.

"See you in the hotel coach," Clifford said. And they were gone, leaving Nash and Miss Blanchard with their near-finished ham. Miss Blanchard smiled, but her finger tapped the side of her coffee cup in an odd rhythm.

He recognized it. "Is that Morse code?"

Her cheeks flushed—no, that was too gentle a word for it. They enflamed. "I'm a telegrapher Mr. Nash." Her tone sounded both proud and defensive. As if she'd received no end of judgment over her profession.

She'd get none from him. "An admirable skill. And I'm just Nash. Please."

"Nash." Her cheeks muted to roses.

Not a nosy sort, he usually let folks be. But he didn't want to leave the table just yet. Didn't want to stop talking to her. "What made you decide to head west?"

"My father—he's the one who taught me how to be a telegrapher—passed away. There was nothing to hold me in New Jersey, so I answered an advertisement for a job."

"I'm sorry for your loss."

"You've had loss, too, I think." Her tone was matter-of-fact, sympathetic but not melodramatic the way some people were, so he decided to tell her.

"I lost my wife and twin boys during the war. So I came to California." Suddenly, he became all too aware of the clattering of silver and china around him, murmuring couples, and Primrose Dewey's grumbles. "I needed a new start. Guess you feel that way, too, to leave family and friends."

"Father was my only family. Friends? In truth, I'm most comfortable with a telegraph machine. It is straightforward, to the point, and one knows where one stands with it."

There was no artifice about her, something he admired. But a fine lady like her should never feel friendless. Nash frowned, praying for words.

"And you?" She spoke before he could. "What do you do?"

His index finger traced the brim of his cup. "This and that."

Her mouth twisted, as if she'd hoped for more of an answer. But it was true. He did a lot of different things these days.

"Did you ever mine for gold?"

He chuckled. "Sure did, although it's been a while. Here." He dug the quartz from the small pouch that hung from his belt and held it out to her. It was thick as two of her fingers and just as long, white and pink, sparkling in the morning sunlight.

"It's lovely." She fingered the streak of gold bisecting the quartz.

"It's the first gold I found after I came west eleven years ago. After I lost my family. I keep it to remind me where I came from. That God provided for me."

And that his heart could heal, but it did so with a long, ugly scar. Losing people he loved hurt too much to risk opening his heart again.

"Perhaps God will give me something to hold onto when I arrive in California, too. In the meantime I have my mother's cameo to remind me where I come from." She sipped her coffee. Then frowned. "Nash?"

He liked that she'd used his name without the Mister attached. But something in her tone aroused his concern. "Yes?"

Her gaze flickered to the Prewetts. "May I count on your discretion?"

Surprise skittered up his bones, but so did an odd sense of pleasure. Her confiding in him—and him helping her—felt right. "Of course."

She cleared her throat. "We were given copies of the *New York Daily* last night when we boarded the train, remember? I read our copy after Gabe went to sleep."

"Front page story about the Honeymoon Express, I'd bet. And probably something about that bank-robbing couple." Big news in New York, both of them. The robbers were especially notorious because, even though they wore handkerchiefs over their noses and mouths, one of them was female. And she didn't just take cash and coin, but she also nabbed the jewelry off the customers.

"Their carriage driver was caught two days back and admitted the duo planned to escape town yesterday on a train." She shuddered. "But there was something else, an article about an heiress, Magdalena Pierce, whose husband, Jerome, and son are missing. She's offering five hundred dollars for information leading to her son's return. The boy is six, towheaded, and goes by the name of Gabriel." She glanced at the Prewetts again, and Nash's stomach churned.

"You're saying Jerome Prewett could be Jerome Pierce?" He leaned in to whisper.

She leaned forward, too. Their foreheads were a hairsbreadth apart. "Last night Gabe told me his mother was alone and his trip was a secret. He cried for missing her."

Lord, have mercy. He'd heard of this before. Read the legal debt disclaimers placed in newspapers by parents seeking the return of children their spouses took away. "A father taking a child from its mother isn't necessarily illegal. I'm not saying it's right, but I don't know if there's anything to be done."

"That poor mother should know where her son is, if the Prewetts are in fact the Pierces. At first opportunity I'll send a telegram to a friend of my father's in New York. I'll ask for more details before I inform the conductor of a possible problem."

Her intent to seek more information and not to jump to conclusions was noble. But tricky. "They won't let you off the train since they're trying to set a speed record."

"We're taking on supplies in Chicago. Maybe then."

Helping her—and Gabriel, if he was a Pierce and not a Prewett—was the right thing to do. "I'll make sure you get on and off somewhere. In the meantime I'll keep my ears open. Thanks for trusting me, Miss Blanchard."

"Thank you. And…if I'm to call you Nash, I suppose you may call me Ellen."

A name as pretty as her eyes—

Something thumped his shoulder. "Ho, lovebirds."

Nash and Ellen flung apart. Ridley stood above them, waggling his bushy eyebrows. "Honeymoon back on, eh? No sleeping in the lounge tonight."

Ellen's cheeks enflamed, red as blisters. "Excuse me." She hopped from the table and fled from the car.

"Or maybe you will." Ridley guffawed and walked off.

Nash ran a hand through his hair. That Ridley—but maybe Nash should be grateful. He could be friends with Ellen, sure. But thinking her pretty?

He washed the thought down with a gulp of tepid coffee.

Chapter Three

Ellen couldn't hide in the saloon forever, so she splashed water on her face for the third time, patted dry her flush-hot cheeks, and held her head high when she made her way back to the hotel car.

Ridley and his teasing. To think, the entire train thought her "husband" Nash slept in the lounge because they quarreled. They must think her a shrew.

It doesn't matter. A few more days and she'd never see any of them again. Not even Nash. Although the thought that she might come across him someday in California brightened her spirits.

Bracing herself with a hand against the compartment wall, she made her way to the hotel car. The berths had been transformed back into sofas. Only one other person occupied the car, Stella Howell. The long-nosed woman crouched at the front of the car, rifling through a brocade valise that had accompanied a strawberry-haired bride aboard the train.

"Ma'am?" Ellen blurted. "Is that Mrs. Fisher's bag?"

Stella unbent. "My, you gave me a fright. She said I could borrow a spool of green thread for my sampler, but I can't find it anywhere. I'll just wait until she finishes breakfast."

Ah. "I couldn't sew a straight stitch, as fast as we're going." The train wobbled on the rails, as if to illustrate her point. "Truth be told, I can't sew a straight stitch, anyway."

Stella's laugh sounded forced. Well, Ellen wasn't known for her humor.

Primrose flounced past to her seat. "What an odd honeymoon. I thought it would be exciting, but I fear boredom looms ahead."

"Hmm." Ellen's murmur expressed agreement about the oddness of this honeymoon, not the boring part. Not if Gabe had indeed been taken from his mother. She was blessed to have Nash to help her. What a gallant man. Like a knight in stories of old, except he wore buckskin and moccasins. Perhaps they'd share luncheon together, or supper. No, she'd not be bored—

"Time for some fun." The conductor strode up the aisle. Behind him, the others followed from the dining area, including Nash. "Settle down, folks, and take your seats."

"What's happening?" Ellen sat up.

"Something to break the boredom." Primrose clapped.

Nash sat by Ellen, his brows lifted in a question.

"Time to play a game." The conductor beckoned porters, who passed out paper and pencils. "Which newlywed couple knows each other the best? Winners get supper at the Palace Hotel in San Francisco."

Stella patted Clifford's knee and gave him a resolute nod.

264

"Can we win, Papa?" Gabe climbed to his knees.

Nash bent toward Ellen. "Here's to paying for our own suppers."

She giggled like she hadn't done since Ambrose—well, enough of Ambrose. Forever. "I shall do my best, anyway."

"I reckon that's your motto 'bout everything."

How kind that he thought so. Then she gasped. "Quick. What's your middle name?"

"Jethro. Yours?"

"Marcheline."

"Marsha-what?"

"Leen." They were both grinning.

Before she could ask his favorite color, the conductor called for silence. Then she realized she should have asked for Nash's first name, not his middle name. He was Something Jethro Nash. But what? Why didn't he use it?

"One of every pair, switch seats so you can't cheat."

Nash saluted goodbye and ambled to the opposite end of the car. Then she caught Gabe's tearing gaze. "Come here."

"I can't write yet." He scrambled beside her.

"Then tell me what you want me to write, and I'll jot it down."

"Exactly?"

"I'm a telegrapher. Part of my job is sending messages precisely as given to me."

Across the aisle, Primrose flexed her pencil-holding hand, sending the many bracelets at her wrist jangling. "Ready."

The conductor looked at each of them in turn. "I'll ask a question. Answer first for yourself, then your spouse—or, er, traveling partner, since we've got a father and son with us."

"That's me." Gabe stood on the seat.

"And me." But the conductor didn't hear and it didn't matter for the game, so she pulled Gabe back down to the seat.

"Number one." The conductor grinned, as if this was the most fun he'd had all week. "What is your partner's favorite color?"

"I like red. Papa, you like red, too?" Gabe shouted. "Put red."

She dutifully wrote *red* twice, and then her favorite but—Nash's? She might as well toss the pencil into the spittoon. Everything he wore was brown, except for his shirt. Yesterday's was blue, but today's shirt was white, and in desperate need of ironing.

Except—what did she know of Nash? He slept under the stars. He wore clothing that was neither white nor native, from her albeit limited knowledge, but some sort of combination of the two. She scrawled a guess.

She chewed her lip as the game progressed, using her gut to guide her answers for Nash once she finished with Gabe's answers. A few minutes later, everyone returned to their original seats and the porter collected pencils.

Nash chuckled. "I'm sure we'll come in last, but it passed some time, didn't it?"

"And it was fun."

"It was." Nash looked like he meant it.

"Number one." The porter raised his voice over the train's rumbling. "Your partner's favorite color. Share your answers and raise your hands if you both get it right."

"I guessed green for you," Ellen blurted.

"You're right." Nash smiled. "How'd you figure?"

"I pictured you in a meadow. It just seemed right." She was babbling, a telltale indicator of excitement or nervousness. Either way, she was embarrassed now. She swiveled to look out the window at the passing blur of scenery. "Look at that farm."

"I guessed purple. For your favorite." Nash's voice pulled her back around.

"Why?"

"Your dress yesterday." His finger drew lazy circles on his paper. Was he embarrassed, too?

"It's my favorite. Dress. And color." She turned her paper to show him.

In tandem, they smiled and raised their hands for the conductor's scorekeeping.

Primrose howled at Lincoln when it became evident she did not know what he did when he was worried, but Ellen's guess that Nash took long walks and prayed was right.

"You tap Morse code with your fingers," he said.

No one had ever noticed that before. Not Father. Not Ambrose.

They raised their hands again for another point.

Ellen and Nash did not know one another's first pet's name, favorite nursery rhyme, or best Christmas memory. But they'd guessed correctly about one another's prized possessions: his quartz and her mother's cameo. And they laughed over their failed guesses.

"Hangtown Fry?" Nash's bemused expression started her giggling when they swapped answers for favorite foods. "I'm shocked you know what that is."

The legend of the Gold Rush prospector ordering the most expensive meal in town—eggs fried with bacon and oysters—made its way east over the decades. "I made it my business to learn what foods are popular in my new state."

Lincoln bent and flicked the string of beads around Nash's throat. "You dress like a native. I bet your favorite supper is acorn stew. With chunks of squirrel. Am I right?"

Ellen's face heated. How many times had others spoken to her like that, pretending to joke, but with cutting words? Her hands clenched on her lap as remembered voices filled her ears.

No dance lessons at that fancy college, eh?

We'd invite you, but everybody knows you're not one for social evenings.

I've never seen someone have such a hard time with a simple stitch. Good thing you're unwed and don't need to smock baby clothes.

Men who asked everyone else to dance. Conversations carried on around her. Labels of *loner* and *spinster* cloaking her like a shawl. Until Ambrose. And then—

Nash's voice drew her gaze. Something about his beads being a gift. His smile hadn't faltered at all. "But no, the Miwoks don't dress like this, and as for acorns?" He smacked his lips in an exaggerated display. "More mush than stew. Tasty, too."

He ended it with a wink for Ellen.

How did he do that—make light of others' rude comments? In some ways, he embodied on the outside what she felt on the inside. His appearance made him stand out; her awkwardness kept her isolated. But Nash didn't seem to mind Lincoln's derision. He smiled as if Lincoln's attitude didn't bother him a lick.

How did he have that sort of confidence?

Lincoln snorted and returned to Primrose.

Nash turned to Ellen. "Seriously, now." His face was not the least bit serious, with that smile. "My favorite food is peach pie. What's yours?"

If he could ignore Lincoln, maybe she could try to squelch the voices in her head, too. "Squirrel." The tease blurted out.

He burst into laughter. "I said you liked cake."

"It's mashed potatoes. No point for us." She leaned closer, so Lincoln wouldn't overhear. "Do Californians really eat squirrel?"

"People eat squirrel everywhere. We eat gold-dusted lizards."

A giggle escaped her throat. And multiplied until she laughed so loud she covered her mouth with her hand. Really, this game wasn't that funny. Neither was joking about lizards and squirrel, or the baffled looks they received from Lincoln and Primrose. But she couldn't help it, and apparently neither could Nash, because he laughed, too.

It was hard not to stare at Nash when he laughed. He was handsome, but there was so much more to him. He was kind. Didn't dismiss her when she told him about Gabe. He didn't rise to the bait of those who found humor at others' expense, like Lincoln.

Thanks for sending me a good partner for the trip, Lord. Her fingers tapped code against her lap.

"Are you two finished?" Stella leaned around Clifford, grinning.

Had Ellen and Nash held up the game by giggling? "Sorry."

Nash snickered, which made her snigger again.

Five minutes later, the Howells won a dinner at the San Francisco Palace Hotel. Ellen's jaw dropped at the announcement she and Nash had not come in last place, however. They'd scored somewhere in the middle. He gazed at her with his lips parted, surprise in his eyes.

"We didn't lose." His arm went around her shoulders for a brief, brotherly hug.

The nerves along her arm caught fire. *Say something humorous—*

"Huzzah!" Oh, she could kick herself.

"My word." Primrose's brows were high. "I've never before seen anyone so happy to *lose* a game."

"Um-hmm." Lincoln waggled his brows.

"That was fun." Nash rose. "Think I'll visit the lounge. Stretch my legs."

She nodded, disappointment and relief warring for supremacy in her stomach. It was probably for the best he left so she could chide herself for responding to his platonic gesture like a lovesick girl. And *huzzah?* She shuddered.

She mustn't forget, she had work to do. For today, it was investigating the Prewetts. A few days from now, work entailed starting life anew at Rawlings Mining and Transport. And Nash, a man who slept outdoors and ate acorn mush and squirrel, would never fit into that sort of structured life. Even if she'd liked his arm around her.

"Before you go, here's yesterday's paper." She withdrew it from her valise and tapped her finger over the article about the heiress and her stolen boy, Gabriel. With a grim set to his lips, Nash glanced at the Prewetts.

God had given her Nash to help her on the trip—a trip to a job and a new life. She was beyond blessed for that mercy. She shouldn't yearn for more than that.

◆ ◆ ◆

A few hours later, Nash peered out at the passing scenery, but his attention remained fixed on Gabe. When Nash came upon him a minute ago, the boy was standing on the sofa, his upper half hanging out the open window, waving at the folks gathered along the tracks. At once, Nash came up behind him and wrapped an arm around the boy's midsection to keep him from falling out onto the tracks.

Nash couldn't blame Gabe. Boys got antsy cooped up like this. But an accident could've happened, so Nash stayed put, waiting until Mr. Prewett—or Pierce, if Ellen was right—returned to his son.

"You're good to wave at those folks." Nash patted Gabe's white-blond head.

"There must be thousands of 'em watchin' us go by," Gabe said with gravity, as if it was his job to provide the viewers, a few hundred, not thousands, acknowledgement.

Was this as many as the number who mobbed the tracks when the Jarrett-Palmer Express made this trip in June? Word was schools let out, businesses closed, and funerals paused so folks could get a gander at the first express train.

It seemed the Honeymoon Express was cause for celebration, too. Here on the outskirts of Chicago, people waved and shouted, just as they had all along the way today.

Nash craned his head. Ellen sat with her arms crossed, tapping dots and dashes on her lap. That, more than the set of her jaw, told him she fretted. The train had stopped four times today to switch engines, take on coal and water, and switch personnel. Who'd have guessed an engine could be changed in just thirty seconds? There'd been no time for anyone to peek at the depot, much less to send a telegram.

Ellen wanted to send that query to her father's friend about the possibility of Gabe Prewett being Gabe Pierce. Needed to send it. Her fingers probably itched to send the telegram herself.

The conductor traversed the aisle. "May I have your attention, please? It's four aught one p.m., and we are coming up on Chicago five minutes ahead of schedule."

The passengers cheered.

"We'll stop for ten minutes to pick up a new engineer." The conductor held up his pocket watch. "You may detrain, but you must reboard when the whistle sounds. We'd like to cross the Mississippi River during daylight."

The train slowed beneath Nash's feet. As he swayed forward with the momentum, he locked gazes with Ellen. This might be her best opportunity.

She hopped up. "Are you coming?"

He couldn't, not when Mr. Prewett hadn't come to collect Gabe. "I'd best stay here."

She gave a curt nod. The moment the train lurched to a stop she was out the door.

Most of the passengers followed in her wake. Mr. Prewett collected Gabe, leaving Nash in the hotel car with the Howells.

"After you." Clifford gestured to Nash.

It would feel good to stand on solid ground. Nash nodded and bounded down the steps.

The number of enthusiasts gathered at the depot brought Nash to a halt. Scores, to Nash's quick count. Some lifted painted signs offering felicitations while others waved their arms, but all were held back from the train by more than a dozen policemen. Not that the use of force was necessary. Faces in the crowd grinned, attesting to their enjoyment of the spectacle of the Express. Wasn't much to see, though, except porters tossing bundles of the *New York Daily* off the train while others loaded crates aboard.

Was there sufficient time for Ellen to send the telegram? He appreciated her determination to find proof before she accused Jerome Prewett of taking his child from his mother. Nash had exchanged few words with Prewett today; the man was private, something Nash could relate to, but it was clear Prewett wasn't a particularly attentive parent. Nevertheless, he appeared to care for his son, and Gabe was not afraid of him.

The whistle hadn't blown, but Nash mounted the steps to the hotel car. *Lord, help Ellen send that telegram fast—*

A movement at the opposite end of the coach drew his eye. Stella in someone else's seat, her hands deep in another's bag.

Stealing? Snooping? While Nash didn't like to judge, something wasn't right. The whistle blew, making her jump. Then she looked up at Nash.

They stared at each other a half second before stomping sounded behind him. Clifford pushed past Nash to take his wife's shoulder.

"Stella." His voice was low, but Nash could detect frustration. So the fellow knew his wife had a tendency to snoop, or steal, or whatever she did. Hopefully she wouldn't do it again.

Unless—

Nash mulled the thought, stepping back so the reboarding honeymooners could find their seats. He'd share his suspicions with Ellen when she returned. His gaze fixed on the door. Gabe burst through, chomping a fragrant peppermint stick, but Ellen didn't reappear. The conductor sidestepped down the aisle. "Tickets!"

Alarm clogged his throat. "Ellen isn't back yet."

"Sir, we are on the tightest of schedules."

"She'll be right here." He prayed so. He should've gone with her. If she'd come to harm by some brigands in the depot. . .

His stomach clenched. So did his fists.

"This is not a sightseeing trip." The conductor's mouth pinched. "We are attempting to set a speed record, sir. Perhaps you should detrain with your wife."

It wasn't worth correcting him. But there was no question what he should do. "Fine."

The conductor stood aside. "We'll drop your luggage in Fulton, sir."

Clifford stood, holding Nash back. "Surely the train can wait another minute."

"Aw, get off the train, Mr. Nash. You and the missus are ruining the schedule." Ridley pulled out his pocket watch.

Primrose and Lincoln argued amongst themselves. Which of them wanted to leave Ellen behind?

"What will your sponsor, the *New York Daily*, say about leaving a lady behind?" Nash's arms crossed.

Mouth softening, the conductor nodded. "I'll speak to the engineer. Five minutes."

Nash exhaled in relief even as he pushed his way to the door to watch for Ellen. Maybe he should hop off and find her—

The train lurched forward.

"Wait." Nash's yell was lost under the train's rumble, fruitless though it was to even ask. The train couldn't be stopped now, so he had no choice but to hop off so Ellen wouldn't be stuck alone in Chicago. He leaned out the door, ready to jump.

"Nash!" Ellen ran, skirts hiked, one hand pressing her bonnet to her head.

They weren't going fast yet. He gripped the door rail with one hand and held out the other. "Take my hand."

She reached. Then looked down and stumbled.

Another move like that and she wouldn't make it. "Look at me."

"Nash." Her fear came out in his name. But she kept running. And she looked him in the eye.

"I've got you."

But it was only the tips of her fingers that met his when the train bowled forward in a burst of speed.

Chapter Four

Ellen's wrist still ached from Nash's grip a full ten minutes after he yanked her onto the train. He'd had to stretch to haul her aboard, and she'd barreled into his arms. His limbs must hurt worse than her wrist, but perhaps not as much as her pride. Shame swamped her innards.

After Nash hauled her aboard the train, a few ladies swooned at his heroics, but others began sniping about her tardiness. She'd apologized to the conductor—twice—as well as the group, but Mr. Ridley still grumbled to whomever sat near him about how if they didn't get across the Mississippi River before sunset, they'd be stuck all night.

"That's not true, by the way." Nash's voice was soft as breath on her cheek. "It's slow going over the river, night or day. It's just easier to see before dusk. We'll make it."

"I know, but—" She peeked up. "Mrs. Ridley is glaring at me."

"Mrs. Ridley doesn't know you're trying to return a boy to his ma. Besides, who cares what she thinks?"

Ellen shouldn't care, but she did. She'd have preferred to send the telegram *and* return before the whistle, so the train could make its speed record and no one would be vexed with her. Those voices in her head started up again. Her fingers tapped against her thigh. Nash saw and frowned.

Her fingers stilled.

He nudged her shoulder with his, another fraternal gesture that sent her heart out of beat. "Did you send that telegram?"

"At last." Her tone revealed her irritation.

His mouth quirked. "Slow telegrapher?"

"Like molasses." Professional pride trumped her embarrassment, and her spine stiffened.

"I'm sure you could have sent the telegram faster yourself."

Thrice over, but it would be boastful to admit it. Instead she glanced at Gabe, whose mouth was shiny with candy residue. Her fingers twitched to take a hanky to it, but his father didn't seem to notice. "I asked Father's friend to send his reply to me in Omaha. According to our guidebook, we'll pause to switch engines and take on supplies. All I need to do is lean out the window and reach out my hand for it, and perhaps we shall have an answer."

She hadn't meant it as a joke, but Nash chortled. It *was* a funny image, so she smiled, too. "Did you get off the train?"

His face sobered. "Let's stretch our legs."

They'd stretched plenty when she sprinted like a jackrabbit to catch the train, but she followed anyway. He led her to the back of the car, shielding her from the other passengers with his broad shoulders.

"Notice anything odd about Stella Howell?"

Her head jerked back in surprise. Stella was perhaps the nicest woman on the train. "She's tense, perhaps, but she's a new bride and I imagine honeymooning like this would strain anyone. I like her."

"I caught her in somebody's valise while everyone was off the train."

Ellen's stomach clenched. "I found her searching Mrs. Fisher's bag, but she said she received permission to borrow thread."

"I don't think she had permission."

"She's snooping?"

"Remember yesterday's newspaper? The headlines were about the Express, the boy, and that bank-robbing couple." His voice was so low his breath warmed her ear.

"A man and woman. The paper said they told their accomplice they'd flee town on a train yesterday." Her mouth went dry. "Surely not the Howells."

"They stayed on the train when everyone else got off. He was upset with her when he saw what happened, but who's to say he wasn't more upset she was caught than by what she was doing. Maybe they were taking advantage of the empty train to take cash or jewels. And remember how she mentioned fleeing town when we first met? I can't help thinking something isn't right, and that might be it."

Her fingers fluttered over her lips. They felt cold despite the stifling heat in the car. "I would hate it if it were true."

His hand squeezed her arm. "Me, too. But it bears watching."

He'd watched the Prewetts—or Prices—for her. She'd do the same with the Howells. "I'm going to the lounge. See what I hear."

"I'll do the same." She nodded farewell.

Still, it wasn't easy to return Stella's smile when she returned to her seat.

◆ ◆ ◆

At the announcement of supper, Nash hopped to his feet. The feeble partition between the lounge and the dining area couldn't hold back the savory smell of meat roasting in the galley all afternoon. His stomach rumbled. His steps were sure.

Until he crossed the threshold of the dimly lit dining area.

In his thirty-two years, he'd survived war, negotiations with Native tribes, and cold and drought while living off the land. But he wasn't sure he could do—this.

A romantic dinner with a pretty lady.

Fool, Nash. You forgot what sort of train you're on.

Ellen sat at a table for two, her fingers tapping the white-clothed table squeezed between a dozen like it. The chair across from her remained empty. His chair. He couldn't leave. Couldn't humiliate her like that.

But he never thought he'd sit alone at a table with a pretty lady again. Why would he, since he had no plans to remarry? His head understood the plan.

Then why was his heart starting to forget?

That's why a romantic dinner with her scared him. Yes, scared. Because his traitorous heart enjoyed it too much.

Ridley bumped past, jarring Nash to the present. Coward. He plastered on a smile and marched to the table.

"This seat taken?"

She shook her head and smiled.

"How was your afternoon? Oh." The porter placed soup bowls before them. Consommé, thin and brown. "I'd like to offer grace, if you don't mind."

After he prayed, she dove into her soup with relish. "It's warm. I wasn't sure it would be, after our earlier meals."

"Train's going slower so it's easier for the staff to cook." He tilted his jaw toward the window. "We're about to cross the bridge. See?"

The sun sank low, dappling the Mississippi River with gold. As pretty a scene as Nash had ever seen, and at this slow speed, he had time to appreciate the lapping waves and thin-streaked clouds overhead.

Her eyes shone with appreciation for the view. And something else. "You said we'd make it by nightfall. You were right."

"Don't hear that too often," he joked. Her smile widened. She didn't know how pretty she was, which made her all the more fetching—

He immobilized, spoon aloft.

Stop it. You've got no business thinking about anyone like this.

Nash swallowed his thoughts down with his consommé. The porter exchanged their empty bowls for fragrant plates of roast beef. Around them, honeymooners twittered, except for the Howells. Clifford and Stella's gazes fixed everywhere but on one another.

Speaking about the Howells was far safer than mulling his emotions, so Nash took advantage of the freedom sitting like this offered him and Ellen to speak quietly. He leaned forward. "You learn anything this afternoon?"

Ellen peeked at Stella. "I didn't say a word about you catching her, but she wasn't interested in chatting with me."

He gulped a leathery cube of beef. He'd expected dinner to be more palatable, considering the tracks were smoother here. Maybe the chefs couldn't cook, no matter the speed or terrain. "Clifford asked more questions than he answered. Nothing new with Prewett, either. He played possum in the lounge."

"He should have spent that time with Gabe, but I enjoyed him." Ellen's brow quirked. "I taught him Morse code: His name. *Train. Mama.*"

Smart. "Did he react? Talk about his ma?"

"He teared up but wouldn't speak of her." Her lips pressed into a line.

The moment the porter cleared plates, the conductor appeared. "Would you folks care for another game before dessert?"

Ellen chuckled. "Perhaps we'll truly get last place this time."

They probably would. But he found himself looking forward to it all the same. Ellen was fun to be with—not that he'd dwell on it. No, sir.

"I want to win," Primrose encouraged Lincoln.

"C'mon, Papa!" Gabe was on his knees.

Stella and Clifford muttered and frowned.

Without explanation, the porter placed a pasteboard box on each table. Within, wood rattled on wood. "It's a puzzle."

Her eyes sparked. "Wonderful."

The conductor looked as excited as Ellen. "Dump the contents onto the table. Use the pieces to form a solid square, one foot by one foot. It's not as easy as it sounds. First couple to finish wins."

She set to work at once. "I have a tangram puzzle like this at home."

"Tangram?" He didn't know what he was doing, but he could sort out the wood pieces, which were all different-sized triangles and rectangles and such.

"It's Chinese. Geometric shapes fit together to form images. Rabbits, flowers." She shrugged. "A square won't be difficult."

Since she was experienced, he expected her to take over, but instead she pointed at the square in his hand. "Should we try putting it on an angle, like this?"

Once it was turned like a diamond, it made sense, and together they made progress. It proved somewhat challenging, however, requiring some trial and error.

A bump from the tracks jiggled the train, and others lost pieces to the floor. Primrose huffed. Gabe crawled past, picking up pieces. Stella looked out the window while Clifford fiddled with a block. Meanwhile, Ellen adjusted a shape. "What about this one, here?"

"Then this triangle won't work."

"How astute, Nash."

Her praise warmed him. They passed pieces back and forth. After a minute she pulled a frustrated face, and with exaggerated motions, pretended to shove an unwilling piece into place.

They laughed. And in another minute they'd created a square. Their hands shot in the air.

"Already?" The conductor bustled over and grinned. "This game took cooperation and communication, two components of every good marriage. The prize is same as the last game, supper at the Palace Hotel. Congratulations, Mr. and Mrs. Nash!"

Ellen's hand lifted, as if to correct the conductor. Then it fell, and she blushed.

Primrose stood by their table, eyes narrow. "Are you certain you two met yesterday?"

"Yup." Nash brushed back his hair.

Ellen handed the prize letter to Nash. "You take it."

"No, you." He pushed it back.

"I'm getting off the train at Sacramento."

"So am I." Hope rose in his chest. Maybe they could—

What? Unless he took an official interest in Ellen, he had no business thinking like this. "Guess we'll give it away, then."

Then he pictured her in the dining room of a fancy hotel, pretty and dining on exquisite fare, not this hide-tough stuff. For the first time in a long time, he wished things were different.

Like his heart.

The conductor invited everyone to stay in the dining area until bedtime, and by unspoken agreement everyone except the Prewetts stayed in their seats, sipping coffee in the light of the kerosene lamps. Nash and Ellen could have used the opportunity to compare notes on the Prewetts and Howells, but instead they talked about her father, his twin sons he met but once, and a dozen mindless things. While talking about her college days, Ellen waved her hands and accidentally knocked Clifford as he passed in the aisle.

"Pardon me—"

"My fault." Clifford gave her a hesitant half smile, as if he were embarrassed. Worry creased Stella's brow, too. They stood there, stiff and awkward, like they wanted to do something but didn't know how, or what.

They didn't act like confident bank robbers, but as much as Nash wanted to believe the couple innocent, he couldn't shake the feeling something was wrong with these two.

"We're off to bed," Stella said. "Near midnight, and all."

Ellen sat up straight. "I'd no idea it was so late."

Nash had. But he hadn't minded. "We should probably go, too." He offered her his arm, even though the track was smooth. They walked slowly.

Seeing they were alone in the saloon corridor, she paused. "We'll reach Omaha early. The conductor knows I'm expecting a telegram and asked to have it brought to the train."

"Good." He'd be awake to make sure, too. Hopefully it would be good news, and Gabe Prewett wasn't Gabe Pierce after all.

Ellen leaned to look up through the open window. "You're right. I'd wondered—" Even in the dim light, he could see her face mottle red.

"Wondered what?"

"You sleep under the stars. I wasn't sure how well you could see them from the train, but there they are. Like they're following us west."

"And they'll greet us there, too. Always with us."

The faintest trace of almond wafted from her hair. "What's your first name?"

A smile tugged at his lips. "I go by Nash."

"You can be most exasperating." Her light tone belied any frustration. "Goodnight, Nash."

"Goodnight." He almost tacked on *sweetheart*. Which would have been a disaster. Wouldn't it?

God, what's happening to me?

Chapter Five

Dot dot dot dot dot. Long dash. Dot. Ellen tapped a prayer of petition against the open doorjamb, waiting where the porter bid her stay. In the predawn light, she couldn't make out much on the Omaha platform beyond the loading of crates. But where was her telegram? It was supposed to be waiting here for her, no matter the time. She'd seen to it.

Someone moved to stand beside her. Nash, smiling his greeting.

She smiled back, at once regretting her hastily pinned hair and rumpled appearance.

"Nothing yet?" His voice was low, out of respect for the passengers snug in their berths—but there hadn't been a single snore or murmur of sleep-talk since they'd stopped earlier in Council Bluffs to fill the water tanks. Everyone was probably as wide awake as Ellen and Nash, just playing possum. Except Gabe. That child slept no matter how hot, loud, or bouncy the ride.

She shook her head. "The telegraph wasn't awaiting us, so the porter—oh, here he comes."

A uniformed employee bounded aboard, extending a paper. She pressed coins into his palm just as the whistle blew. "Thank you, sir."

She forgot to whisper. Her palm covered her mouth.

"Let's find some light." Nash tilted his head toward the dining area.

Instead, they paused under a sconce outside the saloons, an unoccupied space that proved well enough lit to read by. As the train rumbled to life, Ellen held out the telegram so Nash could read, too:

DESCRIPTIONS ACCURATE *Stop* PREWETT A FAMILY NAME OF JEROME
PRICE *Stop* AUTHORITIES WILL INTERCEPT IN SACRAMENTO TO
VERIFY *Stop* WELL DONE *Stop* WITH AFFECTION, HARRY

Ellen peered up at Nash. "It sounds like our Gabe is likely Gabriel Price."

"Poor lad." Stubble covered Nash's chin and cheeks, shining ginger in the lamplight. "Who's Harry?"

"Father's friend. He's like my uncle." She lowered the telegram. "I thought I'd feel vindicated having my suspicions validated, but all I feel is sad. The Price family. . ." Her throat thickened with emotion. What made one parent take a child from the other? Desperation, violence, fear, anger. . .with Gabe caught in the center.

"Because of you, Mrs. Price has hope she'll see her boy again."

True. But if Ellen talked about it further, she might cry. "I'm sorry this woke you."

"I wanted to be here. Besides, the lounge isn't the most comfortable place. I imagine the berths aren't, either."

They weren't, despite the luxury of the palace car. Her back hurt, her neck had a crick and—

Ooph. Something barreled into her backside, shoving her into Nash. He caught her fall, drawing her to his chest.

"You're up with the chickens, too!" Gabe's arms wrapped around her legs.

"Ah, to be excited to wake up early." Nash's voice rumbled under Ellen's cheek before he helped her stand. "You hurt?"

She shook her head, reaching down to pat the white-blond hairs on Gabe's crown. "Good morning, sir."

"Cock-a-doodle-do!" Gabe crowed.

"That's enough, Son." Jerome led Gabe into the men's saloon.

Nash's hand reached for hers, sending her heart to thumping. But oh, he pressed her fingers to fold the telegram, not to link hands. "Put this somewhere safe."

"I'll do that now."

But once she'd stuffed the telegram in her valise, she curled atop her berth, her breath hitching as if in silent sobs. Yet no tears flowed. What was wrong with her? Grief for Gabe and his feuding parents? Yes, but more. Fatigue? Loneliness? Fear of starting a new life?

All those things were true. She was tired, alone, and moving far from home. Who wouldn't feel peculiar?

But it was Nash's face at the forefront of her brain.

Before meeting him, she'd known she had value in God's eyes, but in her head, not her heart. She'd listened to everyone who called her awkward or who overlooked her. Nash was the first man she'd met who truly seemed to value God's opinions more than others'. That obedience gave him freedom to be the man God made him to be. She admired his liberty, and she'd take that lesson off the train with her.

It was harder to deny now, though, that she also wanted to take her relationship with Nash off the train, too. Even though his life was foreign, and she didn't know his first name or if he had a job, it didn't matter. When she was with him, she felt wonderful.

She felt like *Ellen.* Like one of those tangram puzzles, composed of pieces that, on their own, accomplished nothing. But set the right way, made a lovely design.

Nash. You scarcely know him. Oh, maybe she was exhausted after all.

Her fingers tapped a prayer against the blanket.

When daylight streamed through the window, she dug Mother's cameo out of her valise, pinned it at her throat, and stumbled to the saloon. The tracks across the plains might be pin-straight, but that only meant the engineer could push the train faster. Primrose perched before the looking glass, fastening an enormous brooch at her throat when the train swerved.

The brooch fell from her fingers. "A drawback to the speed."

Ellen retrieved the piece, filigree surrounding a pink garnet. "It's stunning."

"So's yours." With a dainty finger, Primrose tapped Ellen's cameo before taking the brooch from Ellen. "Those pearls?"

Small ones, but it wasn't the value that made the cameo sentimental. She nodded and turned to wash up. "My father gave it to my mother when they married."

She opened the tap. Out dripped brownish-yellow liquid.

Primrose laughed. "We took on muddy river water at Council Bluffs. With or without it, you still look fresh as a flower."

A lie if Ellen had ever heard one. She was caked in sweat and smelled like soot. "You're kind."

"It's the truth. No wonder Mr. Nash can't stop staring at you."

"What?" Ellen swayed, but not from the train's motion.

With a chuckle, Primrose left the saloon. Ellen spun back to the tap and scrubbed with a leaf of soap and the suspect water. Primrose, like many females Ellen had known, might have been laughing at Ellen's expense. Or perhaps she'd simply misinterpreted Ellen's friendship with Nash.

She really should assume the latter. It was far better to assume the best of people, not the worst, which she had a habit of doing. Expelling a large puff of breath, she tottered to the dining area.

Nash and the Howells sat at the same table they'd occupied yesterday. Nash rose to seat her. Neither Nash nor Clifford had taken a razor to their cheeks, but a glance assured her none of the men had—probably too dangerous at such high speed.

Stella offered a small smile. "What a pretty cameo."

"Thank you." An awkward silence fell.

Clifford's jaw set. My, how uncomfortable this was, sitting together after Nash caught Stella snooping and thought it possible the Howells could be criminals. They seemed tense for honeymooners, true, but they did seem to care for one another.

Ellen snapped open her napkin and set it on her lap. Nash had to be mistaken in this. Those bank robbers probably hopped another train out of New York.

She'd take Stella's cue and speak of something neutral. "Ah, coffee. A warm cup will be just the thing."

They all sipped. Nash smiled. "It was a nice thought."

Equally cold were chunks of leftover roast and the toughest biscuits Ellen had ever put a tooth to. Gabe tossed his onto the floor.

"Son," his father chided.

"Don't like it!" Gabe crawled under his chair.

Mrs. Ridley huffed. "A child on this train for married couples—"

"Shh, everyone can hear you." Mr. Ridley's whisper was plenty loud, too.

"You should talk. Sawin' logs all night, keeping everyone awake."

"Anyone want my biscuit?" Nash's grin made Ellen smile. She couldn't help but appreciate how he lightened things.

Meanwhile Gabe burst into tears.

"He's been cooped up too long. Poor boy." Stella's eyes moistened. Clifford handed her his pocket handkerchief. Something sad passed between them.

Perhaps Stella had lost a younger brother. Or she knew, even at this early stage in her marriage, she couldn't bear children. One never knew what another person suffered. A strange affection for Stella rose in Ellen's chest. Criminal or snoop, Stella was not without her own private griefs. . .or hopes of redemption.

"Come on." Nash helped Ellen rise. "Let's visit with Gabe."

Mr. Prewett—or Price—was all too happy for them to take Gabe, who quieted when Nash carried him to the hotel car. Out the windows, the plains stretched vast and golden under a bright blue sky, so different from anything Ellen had ever seen. Peaceful, too, the way the grasses waved in the wind. If she stared out the window all day, she couldn't imagine being bored.

Bright sunflowers clustered along the tracks, some taller than a man. But not as tall as something else lining the tracks.

"It does my heart good to see the telegraph poles." It was a half joke.

Nash returned her grin. "Looks like the woodpeckers like 'em, too."

Sure enough, red-crested black birds with telltale curved beaks clung to several poles. "Shoo, birds!" She waved her hands as if they could see and hear her from the train.

"Shoo!" Gabe echoed.

Behind them, a few men read or talked, while the ladies swapped lists of their wedding presents. Mrs. Ridley received an impressive-sounding necklace from her mother-in-law.

"Willow Island," the conductor announced as he made his way up the aisle. "Halfway across the continent now, folks."

"Huzzah." Nash winked at her.

"Cheeky fellow."

Further along, they took turns pointing out things to Gabe. Soddy homes. Farmers. The strange towered dome of Chimney Rock. They scanned the horizon for buffalo but only spotted antelope. Then a few dappled horses with buckskin-clad figures on their backs.

"Nash?" A trickle of fear skittered her spine. She'd never seen a native before.

"They're just curious."

"You sure?" Lincoln leaned between them.

"No reason to think otherwise."

"You should know, eh?" Mr. Ridley jutted in. "You're practically one yourself, the way you dress. Your missus going to sew you real trousers?"

Ellen gasped, but Nash just smiled. "Buckskin's mighty comfortable, Ridley. Wanna borrow a pair?"

"It wouldn't fit," Gabe observed. "He's bigger 'n you. He'd prob'ly rip your pants down the backside."

Mr. Ridley stomped off. Lincoln retreated to his seat. Ellen hid her smile behind her hand.

"I'm sorry," she said. "I'm not laughing at what he said. That was mean."

"Nothing compared to how the tribes have been treated." Nash's jaw set.

"Tell me what you—Nash?"

His gaze was fixed forward. On a plume of black smoke.

Her fingers started tapping. Even a young'un like Gabe could figure what the thickening gray cloud meant.

Primrose bolted to her feet and pointed out the window. "Prairie fire!"

◆ ◆ ◆

Nash held up his hand. "Not prairie." Best stop the panic before it took hold.

Ellen nodded, but Lincoln shook his head. "How do you know?"

"It's not always easy to read smoke, but this doesn't seem to be spreading fast. Yet." A home or barn may be aflame, but fire could spread quickly. His muscles tensed.

With a banshee's shriek, the train braked. Folks swayed forward. Primrose glared at Nash. "You said it wasn't a prairie fire."

"Scheduled stop." Nash forced a smile. "Right, Ellen?"

"Oh—yes." She thumbed through the itinerary. "North Platte."

"I bet we'll be stuck," Lincoln grumbled.

Unlike other stations they passed, this one boasted no waving bystanders. Was everyone else fighting the fire? The conductor hurried down the aisle.

"Switchin' engines, folks. I'm sure the fire's not near us a'tall." The instant the train paused, however, he leapt from the car.

Ellen's fingers tapped against the sofa. *Dash dot. A J for Jesus?*

"Fire will set us back hours." Primrose rubbed her temple.

Lincoln patted her hand. Stella and Clifford murmured quietly. Gabe clambered back onto the sofa beside Ellen, stumbled, and knocked her in the temple with his elbow. Her head snapped back, then smacked against the train wall with a crack.

Nash caught her to his chest. "Ellen?"

"Yes." She blinked, as if dazed.

He smoothed back the hair from her brow, then glanced at Stella. "Water, please?"

Ellen grunted. "Not that wretched yellow stuff."

"Mercy, woman, I didn't take you for a picky sort."

To his immense relief, she rolled her eyes. Then groaned. "That hurts."

Gabe started crying. Again. "Sorry!"

"It's not your fault, dear." Ellen patted his sleeve.

The conductor bounded aboard the train. "Looks like a barn caught fire. It's close enough to the tracks that it could cause a problem for us, so we're stuck for now. A few of our men'll go help to make things quicker."

Primrose groaned. So did a few other passengers, as if the speed record was more important than some family's livelihood. Nash settled Ellen on the seat as Stella brought a cup of the nasty water from the saloon. "Take care of her."

"Of course." A half-smile split Stella's usually stern countenance.

For a dazed woman, Ellen's grip on his arm felt firm. "Where are you going?"

She already knew, so he smiled. "The more hands, the faster it'll go."

"I'll go, too." Clifford removed his jacket.

Still, Ellen didn't let go of his shirtsleeve. "Nash—"

She didn't finish. Instead, her eyes watered. So he bent down and kissed a spot just east of her mouth. "I'll be back."

He and Clifford jumped from the train and followed a crowd of men toward the source of the smoke.

It was an hour, maybe more. Nash beat flames away from the farmhouse while others pumped buckets of water. When the barn was a smoldering heap, he and Clifford gathered the animals in the yard and fenced them behind the house with rope. It wouldn't hold well, but with the paddock fence burnt, it was better than nothing.

The rail crew headed back, so he and Clifford followed. Nash was stretching his aching shoulders when Clifford started to laugh.

"Something funny?" The moment Nash spoke, he knew what it was—the same thing he saw—a man covered head to toe in soot, his tooth-white smile the only clean thing about him. He joined Clifford's laughter.

"Here." Clifford yanked a handkerchief from his trouser pocket, handed it to Nash, and pointed at his own cheek. "Right there. Just shy of your mouth."

"Just there?" He'd need a horse trough to get clean.

"You'll want the spot fresh so Ellen can kiss you back."

Nash lost his footing for half a step. Expelled a long breath. Then thrust the handkerchief back, unused. "It wasn't like that."

"So were you kissing her to make it better, or counting on her being so addlepated from the goose egg on her head she won't remember what you did?" Clifford wiped his face with the handkerchief, smearing more soot than he removed. "You don't know women."

He knew better than to kiss one. "I wanted to set her at ease." And she looked so sweet. So concerned.

"Everyone can see you're sweet on each other."

Nash took a long draw of air. "It's complicated."

"Isn't it always? I love Stella, for better or worse. Doesn't mean things are perfect. There's no such thing. But even in the rough times, I'm glad we have each other." He rubbed his filthy chin as they rounded the corner to the depot. The whole train had emptied while they waited to move on, not that Nash could blame them. Folks stood in groups talking or nibbling fruit or candy from the nearby general store. Ellen was nowhere in sight, not even chasing Gabe, who ran in circles, pausing to dip his hands into the horse troughs and splash water in the air.

"Speaking of Stella—what you saw? It's not what you think."

"What is it then?"

Clifford shrugged. "Nothing. Just—oh, look. There's Stella now."

Nash covered his disappointment with a nod. For a minute, he'd thought Clifford would be honest.

Stella hurried forward, bearing bundles. "There's a pump out back. Here's a shawl to dry with, soap, and one of Clifford's shirts for you, Nash. Didn't want to dig into your bags."

Well, that was ironic. "Thanks, ma'am." Nash took a bundle and searched for the pump. He washed his face, hair, and arms before Clifford joined him. Clifford's spare shirt strained at the seams, but it was better than his filthy one. "Thanks for the loan. I'll get it back to you as soon as I don my own on the train."

Clifford, still scrubbing soot from his hair, nodded. Nash hurried back, anxious to find Ellen. Maybe she'd hurt her head worse than he thought and rested on the train.

She wasn't. She stood on the depot, waving at him and holding a paper-wrapped package. "My hero."

He snorted. "The fire was pretty much out when we got there."

"So humble."

Mercy if he didn't want to kiss her again.

The whistle sounded. While they boarded, Ellen passed him the package. "Trade. I'll rinse out your shirt while you enjoy this."

"What is it?"

"They were out of squirrel at the restaurant, so you'll have to make due with buttered bread and turkey."

He definitely wanted to kiss her now.

This was getting worse, not better. He'd have to think. And pray. But he was starting to wonder if his desire to kiss her would fade when they got off this train.

If it didn't, he'd be in a world of hurt.

Mrs. Ridley screamed.

"What's wrong?" Nash dropped his snack on the sofa.

Mrs. Ridley gripped her husband's arm. "Your mother's necklace, Irving, it's gone!"

"You dropped it?"

"Of course not. It's been in its case until this minute, so I could show Mrs. Fisher."

"Can we help?" Nash peered under the sofas, but his gut told him the necklace was already in someone else's possession.

Ridley grunted. "I bet a porter took it."

"Impossible, sir." The conductor stepped aside with Mr. Ridley. "I supervised the porters as they loaded supplies."

Nash ambled back to his seat. With all the commotion in the other end of the car, this might be the best time to apologize for taking liberties. "Ellen?"

"I know what you want to say—the necklace. But Stella left with me. Everyone did. No one wanted to stay on board when we could walk on terra firma." Her voice was low as she unwrapped his luncheon.

"Stella could have taken it before now, you know."

Her shoulders slumped. "I suppose you're right."

"I didn't want to talk about the necklace. I'm sorry I took liberties."

Her lips parted. Then she smiled, but her gaze fixed on his shoulder. "What are you talking about? Now, I'll rinse out this filthy shirt, and you eat that bread while it's warm. Extra butter. Like heaven after this morning's biscuit." She hopped to her feet and dashed toward the saloon in a blur of green plaid.

Nash prayed for his food. He was almost finished before he realized she hadn't accepted his apology. She'd dismissed the kiss, like it hadn't happened.

He wadded up the wrapping paper and rubbed his now-throbbing forehead. Pretending the kiss didn't happen was probably best. He'd been stupid to do it. Ellen wasn't the sort of gal you kissed without meaning. Not that he was that sort of fellow.

Which was worse: That he'd gone and kissed her once, or that he wanted to do it again?

Chapter Six

Ellen stood at the window staring at the Laramie Mountains. The altering landscape seemed a good reminder that change, like God's love, was one of life's only constants. She'd expected a change, moving west, but meeting Nash had shifted things around inside her. Her fingers fluttered to her lips.

Stella tapped her elbow. "Didn't you hear the supper call?"

She shook her head. "Woolgathering, I fear. Shall we go?"

Nash had remained in the lounge with the men the rest of the afternoon. Ellen had helped the womenfolk dig through cushions and inspect the spittoons for Mrs. Ridley's necklace until Gabe awoke from a nap, when she taught him more Morse code. Her mind, however, had fixed on Nash. Would they dine alone again tonight?

Oh, she hoped not. He'd apologized, so he regretted kissing her. Even if she didn't. Her chin and cheek still felt enflamed, as if he'd branded her. He'd surely read it on her face, and then he'd feel bad. She should skip supper—

Stella guided her through the threshold, directly into Nash's line of vision. "There they are."

No turning back now. At least they were sitting at tables of four tonight. *Act normal, silly.* If she simpered or refused to look at him, he'd know how much the kiss meant to her.

She met every gaze. "I'm famished."

"More cold ham." Clifford poked at his plate.

"And lima beans. That's new. At least they're soft." Nash took a hearty forkful and grinned—at Ellen.

If he grinned like that, then he couldn't be totally put off by her. She returned his smile and shoveled a scoop of lima beans. And almost spat them out.

"They're soft. But saltier than Lot's wife."

The Howells chuckled, but Nash leaned back in his chair. "Reminds me of when I first came west. My cooking was so bad, I was about to give up. Until I found this."

As he reached into the pouch at his belt, Ellen clutched her napkin. What was he doing, showing off his quartz? Not just showing—passing it around.

Clifford and Stella. The Fishers. Then Gabe, who smeared butter on it before his father took it. Did Nash want it stolen? She kicked him under the table.

Not hard. But enough that he glanced at her and mouthed *ow*.

"You oughtta liquidate that. Make a few cents," Ridley insisted. "What're interest rates now, Mr. Dewey?"

Lincoln started. "Oh, you know."

"Three percent? Four?"

"Yessir." Lincoln passed the quartz to Primrose.

When every eye had seen the gold and the dinner plates cleared, Nash stood. "I'm putting this back in my satchel, Ellen, but would you share some coffee with me when I return?"

She nodded, waiting while the Howells and almost everyone else left the dining area to prepare for bed. Darkness had long fallen, and though she strained, she saw nothing but her blurred reflection in the window.

Nash slipped back into his chair. "No game tonight."

"Oh, yes, there is. The who-will-steal-your-quartz game."

"I'll get it back. Don't fret."

"You keep telling me that." She pushed back her cold mug. "A hunk of gold is tempting bait, but it's risky. It's possible to pass off Mrs. Ridley's missing necklace as her being neglectful, but if something else goes missing, everyone will know there's a thief on the train."

"But we could catch them in the act." Nash sipped his coffee. "It's worth it to me."

"But it's your special quartz."

He shrugged. "What it represents is still with me, and that's more valuable than the gold inside it."

"You've lost a lot." She sighed. "I'd hate for you to lose more."

Nash leaned forward. "You lost plenty to make this trip."

Maybe it was the hush in the dining car—everyone else was gone. Maybe it was the way their images reflected off the windows, blurry against the darkness outside, like this was a dream. Maybe it was his kiss, and the knowledge they'd soon part ways. But Ellen wanted to tell him.

"I had a fiancé." She fiddled with her cup. "Ambrose, my father's protégé whilst I went to college. Once my father died, he broke it off. Telegraphy was not as interesting to him as politics, and he'd require a spouse more comfortable with society than I. He chose a girl I tutored in multiplication nine years ago when she was a third grader."

"So you're going to California because of Ambrose?"

"I almost stayed home because of Ambrose. He substituted at the telegraph office while I handled Father's funeral arrangements. He took the telegram offering me this job and said he placed it on my desk, but I found it in the dustbin a few days ago."

His jaw gaped. "What did you do?"

"Confronted him. He said he'd no idea what happened. Laziness or contempt, I don't know. But I put my foot down. It might have landed on his toes." It was hard not to giggle. Funny how the thought of Ambrose didn't hurt much tonight. "I'm glad now. He wasn't the man for me."

"No, he wasn't." Nash's strong fingers played with his cup.

A charged silence stretched between them. Then Nash stirred.

"I saw my sons once when I received a few weeks' leave." His Adam's apple jerked. "That autumn, Leora packed them in the back of the wagon and went to town. Storm came up. The wagon overturned."

How tragic, to lose his wife and babies at once. Her hand started to touch his, then fell. "I'm sure that ache never goes away."

"It doesn't. But it changes. I've changed. I'm not the same fellow who kissed Leora goodbye and marched off to war in '61."

Ellen understood why he shared this. He wanted her to know she'd heal, too.

So she went ahead and touched his hand. It was brazen, foolish, and unwise, considering the way it tingled to her bones.

But he took hold. And smiled. And Ellen held back, fixed in the moment. She'd pull out the memory, like Nash with his quartz, on the cold, quiet nights ahead when she was alone, and she'd remember the sweetness of this moment.

◆ ◆ ◆

The sun was bright the next morning when Nash rubbed his growling midsection. "I haven't had trout for breakfast in a good while."

"I haven't had it for breakfast ever." Ellen took a knife to the last bite of fish on her plate. A midnight stop at Green River, Wyoming, had provided fresh supplies, the trout, and the news of a storm to the west. Now the train rolled to a stop. Nash hadn't recalled a scheduled stop at this hour.

"Washout in Utah," the conductor announced. Primrose groaned.

"Can I help dig?" Nash sat up straighter.

The conductor shook his head. "Men working on it now. We'll wait here in Evanston until we hear it's clear. You can get off the train, folks, till you hear the whistle."

Ellen patted her lips with her napkin. "Are you trying to ruin every shirt you packed?"

Nash laughed and took Ellen's arm. It fit just right in his. "Walk? We won't go far."

"I imagine we'll keep the train in view."

"Yep." They hopped down and walked a short distance. "The Howells are still on the train."

"I know. I wish they weren't." She sighed.

Gabe barreled into them, his cheek bulging like a chipmunk's. "Pa got me a jaw-breaker at the general store."

"So I see." Nash puffed out his cheek.

"Can't catch me, Miss Ellen."

"No chasing with that in your mouth. You could choke."

Gabe gripped her purple skirt. "Chase me."

Nash wrapped an arm around the boy. "C'mon, let's go sit on the bench until you've swallowed that thing—"

Gabe twisted away, swatting Ellen's legs. Nash scooped Gabe in his arms. Enough was enough, and if the boy's pa wasn't going to do anything, Nash didn't have a choice. "Gabe, you can't go hitting folks."

Ellen hastened alongside as he marched to a bench by the depot. "He's tired, Nash, and misses his mother. This is taking a toll on him."

"True enough, but that's no excuse."

"Mama!" Gabe sobbed. The jawbreaker slid from his mouth to the dirt, setting off a new round of cries. Nash waved his arm at Jerome Prewett, who reluctantly shuffled over.

Mrs. Ridley's hand fisted on her hip. "A child shouldn't have been allowed on this train. It's ruining my honeymoon!"

"I would imagine the tough biscuits and bone-rattling speed might have accomplished the same," Ellen said. "Leave the boy be."

In all the commotion, Nash forgot to watch the train. The Howells strolled close, clearly off the train now. Was his quartz missing yet?

With Gabe ensconced on Ellen's lap, Nash pulled Jerome Prewett aside. "Your boy needs you. This trip is hard on him."

"He's fine with Miss Blanchard." Prewett made to step away.

"She's not his parent." Nash's arms folded. "Wherever Gabe's ma is, he misses her. He's tired and uncertain, and he needs more than candy from you."

"It's none of your business." Prewett stomped off, but at least he took Gabe from Ellen.

She ambled to Nash, shaking her head.

"You hurt?"

"No, just fearing for Gabe. Once he's returned to his mother, will he ever see his father again? Should he?"

Nash didn't have an answer. He squeezed Ellen's elbow. "I'll be right back."

Back aboard the train, all was quiet except for a porter cleaning the spittoons. "Excuse me, has anyone else reboarded the train?"

"I just started. No one here but me."

"Thanks." Nash reached under the sofa he and Ellen shared, unlaced his satchel, and reached in. No evidence of the stone's rough exterior touched his fingertips. His heart hammering, he raced off the train. Ellen rushed to his side, her brows lifted in query. At his nod, she sighed.

Clifford and Stella came over at his beckoning. Nash tipped his head. "Walk this way?"

"Sure." Clifford's shoulders tensed.

Stella's fingers twisted at her waist. "It does us all good to stretch our legs—"

"I noticed you two stayed on the train. Now my quartz is missing, just like Mrs. Ridley's necklace." Nash stopped walking, bringing them all to a halt. "You know anything about that?"

"Not at all." Stella was a lousy actress. Her gaze darted left, and her tone held a forced lightness.

"Sorry to hear it's missing, Nash, but maybe you shouldn't have flaunted it like that." Clifford's smile seemed strained.

"Enough." Nash's arms folded. "The bank robberies in New York? The newspapers said the duo would board a train three days' back. The Express is perfect for someone hurrying out of town. The female robber has a penchant for other folks' jewelry, and Ellen and I have both seen enough to make us more than suspicious. So should we handle this with local law enforcement, or should Ellen march back to the depot and telegraph New York?"

Stella teared up.

"If you do that, it'll ruin everything." Clifford stiffened, shifting to block Ellen.

If he dared touch her, he'd be in a world of hurt. Nash's arms tensed.

"It isn't what you think," Stella whispered.

"Stella." Clifford glared at his wife.

"What are we to think?" Ellen's brow furrowed. "You're in everyone's bags. Are you even newlyweds?"

Stella's chest heaved. "We're on official business for Pinkerton."

"Pinkerton agents?" Nash exchanged looks with Ellen.

"Not Stella. Just me." Clifford ran a hand through his hair. "And Stella, you can't tell everyone—"

"They aren't who you're looking for, Cliff. They just met. Nash's hair is too long."

Still, Clifford scowled. "Doesn't matter. This is my job, Stella."

Nash held up a hand. "So you're investigating what?"

"The bank robberies. We learned the criminals were getting on the Express, not just any train—we kept that detail from the papers. I had to act fast." Clifford sighed and pulled papers from his vest pocket. Nash and Ellen read together. Looked legitimate. Nash passed them back.

"He couldn't come on a honeymoon train without a wife." Stella's chin tilted a notch. "We're not newlyweds, but I wanted to come, though I've been more hindrance than help. It's not like it's my nature to search ladies' bags."

Clifford's expression softened. "You didn't have to do that. All you had to do was be here."

"I'm so weary of you being gone." Tears streaked her cheeks. She took Ellen's lacy handkerchief.

It all made sense now. The tension. The snooping. Even Stella's sadness over Gabe, if she'd had no children of her own.

None of them moved when the train whistle blasted.

"We'll keep quiet." Nash nudged Ellen with his shoulder.

Clifford nodded his thanks. "But we're no closer to discovering their identities. Tomorrow afternoon, we'll be in San Francisco."

Nash watched the folks reboarding the train. Which pair was responsible? If they didn't figure it out soon—well, God would see justice done. But Nash would like to have a hand in it.

"We'll do what we can with the time we have left." Ellen took Stella's free hand. "In the meantime, you can help us with another mystery. It's about Gabe."

Nash and Clifford followed the ladies as Ellen enlightened them to the probability Gabe was taken from his mother. Onboard, the men congregated in the lounge, but after crossing into Utah, with eight hundred miles to go before Sacramento, Nash returned to the hotel car.

Ellen tucked a coat over a sleeping Gabe, a soft smile on her face. "Ellen?"

She spun. "I didn't expect to see—I mean, you learned something?"

"No." He memorized her features. "I thought maybe we could sit together. Watch the scenery."

Not talk about the robbers. Or anything at all. Just look out at the red cliffs and stone spires.

She seemed to read it in his eyes. After a moment, she nodded. "I'd like that."

They sat together through the sagebrush of Utah, past a Shoshone village, into Nevada. They pointed out things to Gabe and read to him when he woke up from his nap. Chatted with Primrose and Stella and whoever came by. Watched for anyone poking into others' bags. Ate their lukewarm supper. But they didn't part company. They sat in the dining area until midnight when the resounding blast of cannon outside announced they'd crossed yet another state line.

Nash took her hand. "Welcome to California."

Ellen's delicate fingers curled around his. "We're almost to the end."

He let go of her hand. It felt like he was letting go forever. But what else could he do? She had a job waiting for her. So did he, and a life she didn't fit into. "Tomorrow's a big day. You should get some sleep."

She nodded. "You, too." But as she reached the threshold, she looked back over her shoulder. "Welcome home."

It was home. The place where he felt most himself. But he'd never imagined he'd feel so sad to have reached the end of the line.

Chapter Seven

Ellen gasped, stumbling in the aisle of the hotel car as the train took a curve too fast for her liking. It felt as if they'd flip onto their sides.

I won't miss this come morning. Though if she slept, it would be a miracle. They'd reach Sacramento before breakfast, where the law would speak to Mr. Prewett about him being Mr. Price.

And then there was Nash and never seeing him again. Even if her brain wasn't spinning, the way the train rattled and shook she'd probably roll all over her mattress—

Gabe spilled through the curtains of his berth into the aisle.

She had him in her arms before he fully woke. "It's all right, dear. Just a tumble."

"Mama?" Gabe's eyes blinked, and then filled with tears. "Mama!"

"Shh, now." Oh, the lad was heavy. Especially now that he was fighting her. "Mr. Prewett?"

Heads poked out from berth curtains. At last, Mr. Prewett's did, too. But Gabe was sobbing so hard for his mother, Ellen couldn't hear Mr. Prewett's mumblings.

"Wanna go home to Mama." Gabe clung to her neck. "Take me home."

Instead she carried Gabe to the dining car, away from the passengers who tried to sleep, stumbling as she went. "Follow me, Mr. Prewett."

Nash was still where she'd left him, staring out the window. At her entrance, he jumped to his feet and took the thrashing boy from her arms.

"Fell out of bed. Wants his mother."

"So I hear." Nash bounced the boy on his lap.

"Wanna go home," Gabe cried.

"Home is California, Son." Mr. Prewett touched Gabe's head. "Now quiet down and leave these folks in peace."

Ellen's foot thumped the floor. "Where is his mother, Mr. Prewett?"

He blinked like a fish. "I say."

"That's all?" Ellen's vision reddened. "You *say*? *Say* the truth, I implore you."

"New York." Gabe's voice was muffled against Nash's neck. Ellen reached for the boy again, overcome by the need to protect him.

Nash's eyes blazed into Mr. Prewett. "Time to come clean, Price. That's your name, isn't it?"

"Gabriel Ar–fur Price," Gabe answered instead. "We're pretending it's Prewett."

"What do you say now?" Ellen shifted Gabe on her hip.

Mr. Prewett—Price, rather—didn't speak. Instead he flopped onto a chair and burst into noisy sobs.

Nash shook his head. "Didn't turn out quite like you wanted, did it?"

"I wanted her to be the one with no control for a change. It's her money, her connections." He sniffed. "I wanted to hurt her."

"Gabe is the one who was hurt most of all." Ellen shifted again so she could pull her spare hankie from her sleeve. Nash took it from her fingers and pressed it into Mr. Price's hand.

"I know. I can't—I'm sorry. I regret it."

Nash leaned against a table. "Ellen figured it out and telegraphed east. There will be lawmen waiting for us in Sacramento who want to take the boy back to his mother. Maybe you should go back with him."

"Is that what you want?" Ellen stroked Gabe's hair. He didn't respond, and a peek assured her he was close to sleep.

Mr. Price wadded her hankie in his fist. "I was so angry, but I want to be a family again."

"I hope you'll set things right."

Mr. Price nodded, then stood and reached for his boy. "I'd like to take him back to bed now. My wife may not let me back in the house, so I'd best take advantage of tonight and hold him close."

"Wise course. See you in the morning, then." Nash's blue eyes, gray in the dim, fixed on her. "You, too, Ellen."

Oh. Was he angry she'd tipped their hand? "I hope he doesn't run tomorrow."

"Where can he go? Men will be waiting at the depot, and it's not like he can jump off the moving train before that."

"I jumped on." She smiled. "But you pulled me."

He smiled, too. "So I did."

She wanted to stay, but he didn't indicate that he wanted her to, so she nodded and trod off to bed. The hotel car was dark and quiet again.

It wasn't until Ellen was curled on her berth that she realized her curtain had been wide open.

◆ ◆ ◆

A pink-and-coral sunrise illumined the lounge car. Almost time. Nash stretched his legs and stood, but it was his arms that ached the most this morning. Not from holding Gabe last night, but for lack of something to hold.

He'd never thought he'd feel this way again, and the good Lord knew Nash never wanted to. Caring about someone—like this—brought pain and loss.

But it also brought warmth. Fun. Humor and light. Companionship and—

Nash shook his head, as if it would shake those thoughts out through his ears in the process. Ellen was starting a new life. He shouldn't interfere with it, even if he knew his own mind. *God help me, I don't know what to do.*

Sure he did. For starters, he had the Prices to deal with. And another matter. The puzzle of the bank robbers had played through his brain all night, while he'd stayed awake. It helped distract him from the realization that dawned with the sun, that Nash might want a roof over his head again. And other things. Like a family.

As if conjured by his thoughts, Ellen stood in the dining area. She wore her dress the color of grape jelly and a tentative smile. "Good morning."

"Morning."

By unspoken agreement, they stepped to a southeast-facing window. The pink clouds had dispersed, and the sky looked clear blue as turquoise. He'd miss this, just being with her. Talking. Not talking. Just being.

After a while, she sighed. "We're almost there."

"You nervous?" He stroked her upper arm.

"For Gabe? No. He'll be on his way home."

"About you. Starting a new job tomorrow."

"It's an adventure, isn't it?" Her face held anxious tension despite her smile. "I'm sorry we didn't recover your quartz, though. And I—I wasn't going to tell you, but my mother's cameo is gone."

His hand fell. "I'm sorry." Learning of her loss felt far worse than losing his quartz.

"Sacramento," the conductor called from the doorway. "Brief stop before breakfast."

"Let's go." Ellen squared her shoulders. "I expect most folks are still sleeping, but the Prices were up when I left the palace car."

Her prediction proved wrong. The passengers milled about the aisle. "Can't wait to get off this train." Lincoln mock-punched Nash's arm.

"Three hours to the ferry, and we'll be in San Francisco at last." Mrs. Ridley patted the arm of her strawberry-haired friend.

"Ocean breeze and a solid bed." Even Ridley looked jovial at the prospect of getting off the train.

"It'll be wonderful, won't it, darling?" Primrose reached to straighten Lincoln's tie, revealing a bracelet dangling under the lace at her cuff. The piece of jewelry appeared so large it seemed it might slip off her hand. Like it wasn't hers.

The only soul not jubilant was Jerome Price, who held Gabe close and nodded at Nash. "We're ready."

Two porters appeared. "Those gettin' off the train in Sacramento, your bags, please?"

Nash hoisted his satchel over his shoulder while the Prices' and Ellen's valises were collected. A few ladies kissed Ellen on the cheek. "Happy honeymoon, Mr. and Mrs. Nash," one called.

Ellen didn't contradict her. "Thank you. Same to you."

At the train's lurching stop, the Howells got off with their small party. A group of five men waited on the depot—three lawmen and two men in string ties who identified themselves as lawyers for Magdalena Price.

"I'm ready to return home with my son," Jerome Price said, hoisting Gabe into his arms. "It's time to go see Mama again, and we won't go away from her again. Neither of us."

One of the lawyers took out a folder. "There's the matter of the reward money offered by Mrs. Price. Miss Blanchard telegraphed, is that correct?"

"Gabe's happiness is reward enough." Ellen kissed the boy and wrote her name and address on a scrap of paper. "Let me know when you're home."

"I can't write yet, remember?"

"I'll help. I'm not leaving you or your mother again." Mr. Price turned to go with the lawyers.

Nash held up his hand to the lawmen. "Wait a moment, sirs. If you could board the train with us, it'd just take a minute. I think there's a matter you might be interested in."

Clifford's brows scrunched. "What is it, Nash?"

"Come on." Nash pulled a porter aside with a quick message for the engineer. The train couldn't move yet.

The hotel car was stifling after the fresher air of the depot, but this wouldn't take long. The passengers had abandoned the palace car for the dining area, allowing porters to take down the beds and return them to sofas. Nash pointed at a berth. "One of your men may want to search this one for money and jewels stolen in the New York bank heists, but I think we'll find what we're looking for this way."

Ellen was at his elbow. "What's going on?"

"I'm getting your cameo back."

In the dining car, Ridley looked up and groaned. "You're back?"

"Miss us already?" Lincoln hoisted his cup.

"We'll never make the speed record now." Primrose toyed with her cuff.

"I don't think it's the speed record you're concerned with." Nash stopped at her side.

"That and getting off this stuffy train." She laughed.

Clifford came alongside. "Nash? Are you sure?"

"Yep. She brought an awful lot of jewelry for such a short trip. Like she couldn't leave it behind. I expect there's more in her handbag as well as her luggage. And the money stolen from the banks in New York, too. Lincoln doesn't know about interest; he's no more a banker than I am. They're the two you're looking for, Clifford."

"How dare you." Lincoln tossed his napkin aside.

Primrose gripped her reticule and stood. "That's it, Lincoln. Let's get off the train here. I can't bear to listen to this presumptuous, pompous man a minute longer."

Ellen stood back to make way for her to pass, but failed to remove her foot from the aisle. Primrose stumbled over it. Nash caught her fall, but her reticule tipped, spilling coins, chains, a string of pearls, a cameo, and a chunk of quartz with a vein of gold in it.

Chapter Eight

With a puff of smoke and a long, loud whistle, the Honeymoon Express departed the station, leaving Stella, Nash, and Ellen on the depot while Clifford and the lawmen took the Deweys into custody. Ellen waved goodbye to the train.

"I cannot believe you tripped Primrose," Stella said, almost chiding.

"I didn't try, truly. I thought to block her a moment so I could think of a way to stop her." This was the first time—and probably the last—her clumsiness would be to her credit.

Clifford jogged to join them. "Everything's set. We'll take them back East to stand trial. Found a few thousand dollars in their luggage. If it weren't for the jewels, however, we couldn't prove it was from the bank robberies."

"Greed's an odd thing." Nash's hair glinted gold in the sun. Ellen had never liked longer hair, but she liked his. And she started to understand a thing or two about greed. Right now, a voracious yearning flooded her veins—for Nash's continued presence.

Was that greed? Or was it grief at never seeing him again? *Maybe he'll write, from his home beneath a tree.* Ellen smiled, but her fingers tapped a prayer against her arm.

"Breakfast?" Nash offered. Ellen and the Howells agreed, and the meal was pleasant, if not tinged with the sad awareness they'd part ways. But they all agreed a hot meal of eggs and flapjacks was a nice change.

"We'll be on a train again later today, though." Clifford drained his coffee.

"With the Deweys to New York?"

"San Francisco first." Clifford and Stella exchanged happy glances. "We won that meal at the Palace Hotel. We're almost there, after all. Go there today, come back tomorrow. Like a second honeymoon. Stella deserves a holiday."

Stella blushed. Ellen patted her friend's hand.

"May I write to you?" She pulled a pencil from her bag for Stella's address. Maybe Nash would take the hint.

He didn't. He chatted with Clifford about Pinkerton work. At last, Ellen couldn't pretend to linger over her coffee anymore. Or postpone the necessary. She stood. "I need to find a stagecoach east. Work tomorrow."

Stella and Clifford kissed her cheeks and left Ellen and Nash on the street in front of the restaurant.

Best do this clean and quick. Ellen thrust out her hand. "Goodbye—"

"Ellen?" He spoke at the same time.

"Yes?" *Please. Say you'll write.*

He looked at her collar. "The day of the barn fire? I'm sorry."

Ah. She waved her hand as if she'd forgotten about it, although she'd feel the effects of that kiss if she lived to a hundred. "You already said you regret kissing me."

His stern gaze lifted. "I regret not asking your permission, not the kiss."

His words sank to her bones. "You aren't sorry?"

"I'd like to do it again, actually."

Oh!

He led her around the corner, away from the street. "I was young when I married and went to war. Only a year or so older when my family died. After that, I kept everything at a distance, except the one thing I'd never lose, and that's the Lord. My work's fulfilling, and I care about my friends, but something's different now. This is the first time in a long while I've wanted something more than I feared I'd lose it."

"What do you want?" Her voice sounded croaky.

He twisted a tendril of her hair around his finger. "To not let you go."

His fingers didn't even touch her skin, but her cheeks burned anyway.

"I'd like to call on you." His fingers fell. "But if you don't feel the same, I'll be grateful to call you friend."

"No." She took a shaky breath. "Not friends. I'd like you to call. On me."

She'd never seen a smile brighter than the one stretching his handsome face. "I'd like to show you where I live."

She'd gladly eat squirrel and acorn mush with him, but she couldn't resist a tease. "Don't you live under a tree?"

"I'm thinking it's time I had a roof. My land's been cleared for a long while."

"You own land? I thought you were a bit of a wanderer."

"I'm a bit of everything. But yes, I own land. And a few businesses. My brothers in Maine invested, and every few years I go back to handle things. But enough of that. Where's your job, so I can take you to a supper where the coffee's hot and the biscuits are soft?"

She couldn't resist giggling. "I don't even know your first name."

"Nash."

The joker. Her eyes rolled.

"It's my last name you don't know, 'cause everyone calls me Nash. It's Rawlings."

"What a coincidence. I'm working for Rawlings Mining and Transport, in a town called Poppy." The change on his face made her stomach flip. "What's wrong?"

"You're my new telegrapher?"

My?

He was *Mr. Rawlings*. Her wealthy boss, not a mountain man. And his *business*, as he called it, involved several industries that employed everyone in Poppy.

"You didn't know it was me?" How much gold had he found, to be this rich? And shouldn't he look happier about her working for him?

"My secretary compiled a report of applicants' experience, without names. I picked the best of the lot. You." Nash puffed out a breath. "I don't want to be your boss."

"Because I'm a woman?"

"Because I think I love you, Ellen, and I'd never want you to fear for your job on my account."

His words tumbled in her brain. At last she picked out the ones she liked most. "You love me? Maybe?"

"No." He smiled. "I'm sure I do, even though I've not known you long. But don't worry about your job. The telegrapher's office is in town, not on site, so you don't report to me. You don't even have to see me if—"

"I think I love you, too."

He didn't blink. After a moment, his hand cupped her cheek—the one he'd kissed the day of the fire. "Even though it's crazy, after four days?"

"Even though."

"And we can get to know each other off the train?"

"I'd like that."

His gaze was on her mouth. "I want to kiss you, but it's not proper for the boss to kiss an employee."

"I don't report to you, remember?"

That was all he needed. His head lowered, and he covered her lips with his. She relished the warmth of his closeness, the strength of his arms about hers.

Too quick, he pulled away. "Sorry, Ellen."

"Again?"

"We're in public."

So they were. She flushed hot. Probably blotched. But didn't really mind.

Nash hoisted her valise onto his shoulder with his satchel. Then took her hand. "We made pretty good partners on the train. What do you say we share a stagecoach to Poppy?"

She met his smile. "There's no one else I'd rather travel with."

He held her hand the entire trip. And she hoped he'd never let go.

Epilogue

April, 1877

The town of Poppy lived up to its name, as golden poppies blanketed the surrounding hills alongside yellow mustard, purple lupine, and pale green grasses. The town of Poppy had also turned up, every last member, to the newly completed stone-and-timber Rawlings house for Nash and Ellen's wedding. Ellen flushed hot as the townsfolk clapped and cheered at their first kiss as husband and wife. She no doubt splotched like a tomato.

Who cared? Nash was her husband now. She popped to her tiptoes to kiss his cheek.

"That's enough, you two." Stella, her matron-of-honor gown straining over her round midsection, fisted a hand on her hip. "Cut the cake before your train leaves without you."

Best man Clifford slipped an arm around his pregnant wife's shoulders. "Can't believe you're honeymooning on a train, after the last time."

"Seems fitting, but it's not a long trip. Just to Oakland, then the ferry to San Francisco. We won that fancy dinner at the Palace Hotel, after all. Although you're right, we did everything backwards." Nash led the way to the cake table. "A honeymoon trip first, courtship second."

Ellen shook her head. "That wasn't a honeymoon. A crazy stunt with honeymooners, yes. But I doubt any of them found it romantic."

Nash's fingers tightened on hers. "I did."

"Me, too."

Stella smiled at her husband. Since they'd settled in San Francisco, they'd grown closer again. Ellen hugged her friend.

It seemed they'd scarcely had a taste of the fruity cake Stella crafted before Nash lifted her into a beribboned carriage, they said their farewells, and were off to the train depot. Ellen smoothed the flounces of her white dress, but since she'd spotted Nash in his wool suit—no buckskin in sight—she hadn't thought once of her appearance, just his.

Not that their clothes mattered. She curled her arm into his. "I love that you take me as I am, quirks and all."

"I love who you are. You're who God made you to be." He grinned down at her. To think, this compassionate, handsome man loved her.

In August, she'd boarded the Honeymoon Express to begin a new life. Little had she known the miracles God had planned for her. A purpose. Friends in the Howells and even in little Gabe, whose mother often wrote to Ellen on his behalf. And a beautiful home built by her new husband's own two hands.

"Something fretting you, sweetheart?" Nash kissed the top of her head.

"No, why?"

"Your fingers are tapping my arm. Thought you might be telegraphing something."

She was. She just hadn't realized it.

Dash. Dot dot dot dot. . .

Thank You, Lord.

Author's Note

Today, we use the international version of Morse code adopted in 1912, not the original developed in the 1840s by Samuel Morse (now called American Morse Code). For example, when Ellen prays *Please*, her *P* is comprised of five dots—not the *dot dash dash dot* in use today.

The Jarrett-Palmer Express, a promotional cross-country railroad trip, traveled from New Jersey to San Francisco in under eighty-four hours in June 1876.

Susanne Dietze began writing love stories in high school, casting her friends in the starring roles. Today she's blessed to be the author of over half-dozen historical romances. Married to a pastor and the mom of two, Susanne loves fancy-schmancy tea parties, genealogy, and curling up on the couch with a costume drama and a plate of nachos. She loves to hear from readers! Come say hi on her website, www.susannedietze.com.

Just for Lucy

by Kim Vogel Sawyer

Chapter One

Near Kingsley, Kansas
Spring 1891

"Miss Emmett?"

Amelia gave a start and sat upright, careful not to dislodge Lucy's tousled head from her lap. She fixed her bleary eyes on the gray-haired conductor. "Yes, sir?"

"It's almost eleven o'clock."

She looked out the window. Sunshine bathed the passing landscape. Nearly midday then, not nighttime. She shook her head, trying to bring herself to full wakefulness. The week of forcing herself to stay awake both day and night to keep watch over her charges had finally caught up with her. Tiredness weighted her like a millstone.

"We'll be pulling into the Kingsley station in roughly ten minutes. You and the little girl are the only ones departing the train in Kingsley, and no passengers are waiting to board, so the engineer says the stop'll be brief—just long enough to make use of the water tank."

The man spoke nonsense. Why did she need to know about passengers' comings and goings or the water-tank usage? Amelia blinked several times. "A—all right. . ."

"It's been a long journey, hasn't it?" An understanding smile crinkled his eyes. "But it's almost over now. As I said, only ten more minutes. I'll get your things gathered up. Why don't you wake the little girl and. . .er. . .ready her and yourself to depart."

Finally Amelia understood. After her days and nights of jostling along the rails, delivering children from the New York City orphanage to their new parents in various towns in Indiana, Illinois, Missouri, and Kansas, she must be a rumpled mess from head to toe. And the engineer required a hasty leave-taking so he could be on his way. She wouldn't inconvenience him. "Thank you very much. We'll be ready when the train reaches the station."

The kindly conductor hurried up the aisle, his gait matching the rocking motion of the train.

Amelia turned her attention to the child curled on the padded bench. From the moment little Lucy had arrived at the Good Shepherd Asylum a year ago, orphaned by the influenza that marched from apartment to apartment in her family's tenement building, she'd been Amelia's pint-sized companion. Saying goodbye to the child would be torture, but what other choice did she have? The matron of Good Shepherd, Miss Agnes, only allowed two-parent families to adopt, claiming it was in the best interest of the children. Amelia couldn't argue. God Himself created man and wife. She could only trust that Lucy's new mama and papa would grow to love her as much as Amelia already did.

She petted Lucy's silky brown ringlets, crooning softly, "Lucy, sweetheart, you need to wake up."

Lucy's thick eyelashes threw a shadow across her rosy cheeks, and her sweet lips released a little sigh of contentment. She nestled more thoroughly into the folds of Amelia's brown plaid skirt.

Tenderness filled Amelia. If only she could let Lucy sleep until she was ready to rouse. The days of being cooped up in such a small space had been so difficult for the little girl. But in less than ten minutes they would vacate the train. She would deliver Lucy into the care of Edwin and Ruby Early. Both she and Lucy would begin new lives.

Dear God, now that it's upon me, I'm not sure I'm ready to—

Pain stabbed, tears threatening. Ready or not, the arrangements were made. She couldn't change them now. Miss Agnes had already hired someone to take Amelia's place at the orphans' asylum. She'd emptied her small room that had been her home for the past eight years—all of her earthly goods traveled with her. After this last duty to Good Shepherd—delivering Lucy—she'd be free to pursue a different life than caring for other people's abandoned or orphaned children. But what would that life be?

With a sigh, she took hold of Lucy's narrow shoulders and gently lifted her. The child yawned, rubbed her eyes with her fists, and then looked around in confusion. Her gaze met Amelia's, and a precious smile broke across her features.

"Miss Meela." Lucy flopped forward into Amelia's arms.

Amelia choked back a sob. She set the child aside and rose. "Come along now. We'll visit the necessary room and freshen ourselves. Your mama and papa are waiting."

Lucy took Amelia's hand and followed obediently. Trustingly. More tears threatened.

As Amelia led Lucy to the little room in the corner of the car where a washstand and chamber pot awaited passengers' use, she set her lips in a firm line and sent up a silent petition. Or perhaps more accurately, a command. *God, let Lucy's new parents be good to her.*

They finished freshening as best they could with the bit of water remaining in the bowl and a cloth already sorely in need of laundering and exited the washroom. Back in their booth, Amelia pulled her trim-fitting jacket over her shirtwaist and settled her flower- and ribbon-bedecked straw hat, her going-away gift from Miss Agnes, over her hair. She smiled at Lucy. "Now then, we—"

The train's brakes began to screech, and the car jolted. Lucy flung herself into Amelia's arms. Amelia held tight to the little girl, whispering assurances. Thank goodness they'd reached their final destination. The poor child had reacted in fear with each raucous start and stop of the mighty locomotive. With a series of shrill shrieks and noisy blasts, the train came to a halt outside a small clapboard building.

Releasing a sigh of relief, Amelia took Lucy's hand and guided her to the back landing of the passenger car. As he'd promised, the conductor had retrieved Amelia's trunk and Lucy's bag from the storage car. Both items waited on the landing next to the man's feet.

He hopped to the dusty ground with more grace than she'd expect from someone of his seemingly advanced age and set out a little wooden stool for Amelia. She stepped down while he lifted Lucy, swooping her through the air and making her giggle as he did so. He set Lucy beside Amelia and then reached for her trunk.

"Let me carry these to the station porch so you can keep hold of the little one. Wouldn't want her dashing off and getting trampled by a passing wagon."

The streets were nearly empty, the town especially quiet compared to the boisterous bustle of New York. The likelihood of getting trampled seemed slim, but Amelia didn't argue. She'd rather hold Lucy's hand than lug her secondhand trunk. She smiled her thanks and trailed the man to the porch. He thumped the trunk on the edge, flopped Lucy's bag on top of it, and then turned as if he intended to speak to her. But the train whistle split the air. He tipped his hat, whirled, and leaped onto the passenger car's platform as the steel wheels began rolling forward.

Amelia pulled Lucy to her side, and they waved at folks behind the train windows. When the caboose rolled past, she searched the area, expecting Mr. and Mrs. Early to emerge from the station's waiting area. In their correspondence with the orphanage, they'd promised to meet the train. The blaring whistle had surely alerted the entire town to the locomotive's arrival. So where was the couple?

She guided Lucy to a bench pressed against the station's yellow-painted siding, and they sat. With her hand on the child's knee, she kept her alert gaze on the street. Wagons passed, the horses' hooves and rattling wheels stirring dust. People ambled in and out of the few businesses lining the street. A few folks glanced in Amelia's direction, some even smiled, but no one approached the station.

Lucy fidgeted as the wait lengthened. Although Amelia had hoped to keep the child's hair neat and her apron fresh until her new parents arrived, guilt bade her to allow Lucy the freedom to skip up and down the boardwalk and release some pent-up energy from the long days on the train. While Lucy cheerfully hopped from knothole to knothole on the wide planked porch floor, Amelia moved to the station ticket window and tapped lightly on the glass.

A slender man in a crisp blue uniform immediately stepped to the opposite side of the window and slid the pane upward. "Yes, miss?"

Amelia rested her fingertips on the ledge. "I wondered if Mr. or Mrs. Early left a message with you."

The man drew back. "Early, did you say?"

"Yes, sir." She patted her reticule, imagining the paperwork inside. "Edwin and Ruby Early."

"Edwin an'. . .an' Ruby?"

Did the man have a hearing problem? Amelia nodded.

"You're askin' if they left a message?"

"That's right."

He glanced back and forth as if seeking rescue. "What about?"

She wasn't in the habit of divulging private matters to strangers, but she needed answers. "About being delayed. I expected Mr. Early and his wife to meet me at the station, but—"

He slammed the window closed and hustled away from the glass. Such a peculiar reaction to a simple statement. Moments later, the man darted from the station and crossed the street. He disappeared inside the building on the corner of the next block—the one with a sign marked SHERIFF'S OFFICE hanging from a bracket above the door.

Amelia stared after him, trepidation making her pulse skip as erratically as little Lucy's clumsy game of knothole hopping. She wove her fingers together, pressing her joined hands to her ribs, and watched for the station worker's return. Within a few minutes the clerk and a man with a bold silver star on his chest strode in her direction. The depot worker headed back inside the station, but the lawman stopped directly in front of Amelia.

He pinned her in place with an unsmiling gaze. "Marv said you're hunting Ed and Ruby Early."

Amelia's knees began to quake, and she offered a jerky nod. "Yes, sir."

"For what reason?"

"My name is Amelia Emmett. I work—er, worked—for the Good Shepherd Asylum for Orphans and Half-Orphans in New York City. Mr. and Mrs. Early adopted a little girl"—she caught Lucy's shoulders and pulled the child tight against her leg, grateful for something to which to cling—"from Good Shepherd. I'm to deliver her to them today. Do you know where they are?" *Dear God, please don't let them be sitting in one of his jail cells.*

The sheriff's thick eyebrows descended. He stared at her long and hard for several tense seconds, and then he blew out a breath. "Yes, miss, I know where they are. And they won't be comin' here to collect this child." He glanced at Lucy. For a moment his stern gaze softened, something akin to sorrow shimmering in his steel blue eyes. "We put Mr. an' Mrs. Early to rest in the Kingsley cemetery only this mornin'."

Dead? Oh, so much worse than arrested. Lucy was orphaned yet again. Amelia's knees gave way. She dropped onto the bench.

Lucy touched Amelia's cheek, her sweet face puckered. "Miss Meela, what's a matter?"

"Shh, darling, everything's all right." Such a bold lie. Amelia cupped Lucy's head and guided it to her shoulder. The child's silky curls tickled her jaw, a welcome distraction. She gaped up at the sheriff. "How did they. . .?"

He grimaced. "Fire broke out in their farmhouse two nights ago while they were sleepin'. Neither one got out."

Amelia pressed her palm to her throat, closed her eyes, and forced herself to think rationally. Miss Agnes always had adoptive parents list next-of-kin for emergencies. If she remembered correctly, Mr. Early had a brother residing in Kingsley. She popped her eyes open and zinged her gaze to the sheriff. "Mr. Early's brother…"

"Abe," the sheriff said.

She recalled the name from her paperwork. "Yes, Abraham Early. Did he survive the fire?"

"Ed an' Abe worked the ground together, but they didn't live together. Abe has his own place a short piece from his brother's house. So he wasn't affected by the fire."

If the brothers lived side by side and tilled their farmland together, he was certainly affected. Sympathy wove its way through her. She planted a quick kiss on Lucy's curls and pushed to her feet, taking hold of the little girl's hand as she rose. "Will you direct me to his farm, please? I need to speak with him."

The sheriff shrugged. "I doubt he's at his farm yet seein' as how we buried his brother an' sister-to-law less than an hour ago. You'll likely find him at the cemetery."

She shuddered. Such a dismal place for a meeting. She pulled in a steadying breath and straightened her spine. "I need to put my trunk and Lucy's bag in a safe place. Then, sir, I ask that you take me to the cemetery."

Chapter Two

How long would he stay with his knees pressed in the fresh-turned soil? The noonday sun, hot already for late April, scorched his uncovered head. Underneath his good Sunday suit, perspiration dampened his shirt. Work waited at home. Lots of work. He should go.

Abe braced his palm on the thigh of his trousers, intending to push himself upright and move away from the moist mound of richly scented earth, but instead he settled his backside on the heel of his boot. Sorrow sat as heavy as a boulder in his chest. He wanted to pray—add his request for the peace and comfort the preacher asked God to give him during Ed and Ruby's service—but no words would form.

He rested his hand on the bar of Ed's simple wood cross and let his head hang low. He sighed. What would he do without Ed? Without his brother, his partner, his best friend? His chin started to quiver. He scrunched his eyes closed.

"Abe?"

The voice startled him so badly he almost yanked Ed's cross from the ground. He jolted to his feet and spun. Sheriff Bailey stood a few feet away. A timid-looking woman and a little girl, both strangers to Kingsley, were with the man. Heat filled his face. How long had they been gawking at him?

The woman's gaze traveled from his dirty knees to the top of his head. Her green eyes went wide, her mouth formed an *O*, and pink splashed her cheeks. He'd seen that reaction before. Not for the first time, he wished he could shrink himself to a normal height. Why'd he have to be such a flagpole of a man anyway?

He sniffed hard and slapped his hat on his head, trying to ignore the woman's startled expression. "Whatcha need, Sheriff?"

The lawman jabbed his thumb toward the woman. "This here is Miss Amelia Emmett. She came from New York, expected Ed an' Ruby to meet the train. But. . ."

Understanding washed through Abe. He dropped his attention to the little girl—the one his brother had claimed would call him Uncle Abe. Ed and Ruby made all the arrangements over the wires and through back-and-forth mailed exchanges with the orphanage in New York, accepting responsibility for a child sight unseen. When Abe questioned the wisdom of such a venture, Ed laughed and said, *Are you worried she won't be as pretty as my Ruby? Well, how could she be? But it don't matter. Me an' Ruby can love a homely child if need be. After all, we both love you, you big galoot!* The memory sat pleasantly in the back of Abe's mind.

Now, looking at the child from the orphanage in New York, he decided that neither Ed nor Ruby would've called this one homely. The little thing stared at him with big eyes as blue as the Kansas sky. Brown ringlets, sparkling with gold in the sunshine, framed her heart-shaped face. Her button nose and pink lips were as perfect as those he'd seen on a porcelain doll in a store window. She was probably as fragile as a doll, too.

He frowned at the sheriff. "Didn't you tell her about. . .?" He held his hand toward the pair of crosses.

"Sure I told her."

"So then why not put her back on the train?"

"'Cause she asked me to bring her to you. Figured you'd still be here."

Abe slipped his hands into his suit pockets. Sweat dribbled down his forehead and stung his eyes. "I won't be for long. I've finished my goodbyes." Pain stabbed his chest like somebody'd impaled him with an arrow. "Gotta get back an'—"

"Is everything all right?" Preacher Henry strode across the yard from the direction of the church and joined their circle. He shook hands with the sheriff and then fixed his attention on Abe.

Abe bobbed his head toward the woman and child. "Remember Ed an' Ruby saying they were gonna adopt an orphan? Well, that little girl is the orphan, and that lady is the one who brought her. Preacher Henry, I'd appreciate it if you'd—"

"Mr. Early." Miss Amelia Emmett moved toward him. Just two steps with her brown-and-tan skirt sweeping the tips of the scraggly grass blades poking up from the ground. The little girl held to the woman's skirts and came, too.

Instinctively, Abe eased backward the same distance and almost stepped on the preacher's toes.

The woman's fine brown eyebrows pinched together. "I wish to offer my condolences for your unexpected loss. I realize you are in mourning, and I don't intend to sound shrewish, but would you speak to me rather than speaking of me?"

More sweat dripped down Abe's forehead. She wasn't harsh. Actually, her voice was soft, gentle as a spring rain shower, and matched the soft turn of her jaw. But the words pricked him as hard as marble-sized hailstones. His ma had taught him better manners. He cleared his throat. "I'm sorry, miss. Didn't mean any disrespect." He shifted himself behind Ruby's cross and fingered its smooth, warm top. "I'm real sorry, too, that you came all this way for nothing. Seein' as how my brother an' his wife planned to adopt the little girl, I probably ought to pay for your tickets back to New York." He reached for his pocket where his money pouch held a few coins. Would he have enough to cover their fare? Paying for two carved maple caskets lined with fine linen—he couldn't bear to bury his brother and sister-in-law in plain pine boxes—had used up a good portion of his bank account.

The woman shook her head slowly. A strand of hair the color of ripe wheat fell from underneath the brim of the fanciest hat he'd ever seen in Kingsley and waved beside her smooth cheek. "Mr. Early, I don't think you understand. Your brother and his wife didn't *plan* to adopt Lucy. The adoption was finalized before I made the journey."

Abe gnawed the inside of his cheek. What did she expect him to do? "Well, I—"

"Miss Agnes Swenson, the matron of the Good Shepherd Asylum for Orphans and Half-Orphans, is always very thorough. She required Edwin and Ruby to choose a next-of-kin who would assume responsibility for Lucy should illness or accident befall them." Pink filled the woman's face again. "They chose you."

Abe raised his eyebrows and touched his chest. "Me?" He gulped. "For what?"

"To take care of Lucy in their stead."

He barked a laugh. "No, they didn't."

She patted a pouch hanging from a cord over her shoulder. "I assure you they did."

The woman was mistaken. Or flat-out lying. Weren't the big cities full of swindlers? This gal must be pulling a trick on him. Ed and Ruby wouldn't make Abe responsible for a child. They knew better than anyone how inept he was around delicate things. Hadn't Ruby always given him tin cups instead of china ones for his milk or coffee? And Ed always told him to stay out of the chicken coop until the chicks were full grown in case his big feet crushed one of the fuzzy little fowl.

Abe folded his arms over his chest. "I don't believe you."

She opened the bag, pulled out several sheets of paper folded together, and offered them to him. "See for yourself."

He kept his arms tight over his thudding heart. "Don't want to."

Sympathy pursed her face. "Are you illiterate, Mr. Early?"

He pondered the unusual word. Meaning struck, and his face grew hot. He jammed his hands into his pockets. "I can read just fine, miss. But I don't need to read it. Even if my name is on there somewhere, it don't mean anything."

Sympathy changed to stubbornness. "I assure you, Mr. Early, it means a great deal." She opened the pages and pointed to several lines. "This is a legally binding document naming you as Lucy's guardian in the event of Edwin and Ruby Early's demise."

For a small person, she sure had starch. He admired her stick-to-itiveness, but she wasn't going to push him into taking that child. Neither he nor that little one would come out of the deal unscathed. He shook his head. "Huh-uh."

Miss Emmett offered the pages to Preacher Henry. "Sir, would you please read this and confirm its contents for Mr. Early?"

The older man scratched his chin and chuckled. "I'm not much for legal reading, Miss Emmett. Maybe we ought to take these to Ben Cleaver. He's an attorney-at-law."

"I believe you'll discover the document is very straightforward."

Abe snorted. Wasn't she a pushy thing?

The preacher flicked an uncertain look at Abe. He took the pages and held them at arm's length. Sheriff Bailey ambled up behind, and they both scanned the lines on each page. Miss Emmett stood close, one hand on Lucy's curly hair and the other balled on her hip.

Abe kept his gaze angled off to the church steeple while they read. The sun nearly roasted his head through his hat. He twitched in his suit coat. The shoulders were too tight, and the collar scratched the back of his neck. Why hadn't he left the graveside earlier? By now he could be in his comfortable dungarees and chambray shirt, walking behind the plow, turning the soil, working off the sadness that made his stomach ache with a hunger food couldn't fill. Instead, he stood here waiting for the preacher to tell Miss Amelia Emmett from New York City her paperwork was all a farce and she should take her shenanigans back to the big city.

Preacher Henry shuffled the pages, scowled at the top paper, and let out a big sigh. He nudged Abe's elbow and pointed to a paragraph in the middle of the page. "Abe, this part talks about what will happen to the child if the adoptive parents die before she reaches the 'age of majority.' She's supposed to go to the guardian named by the adoptive parents." The man aimed a sheepish grimace at Abe. "Your name is right here. Ed and Ruby made you the guardian."

Abe grabbed the papers and stared at the block of print. Sweat slid along his temple and dripped onto the sheet. A couple of the letters smudged. But he could still read his name. He shook his head. "Ed wouldn't do this. Not without tellin' me."

Miss Emmett toyed with Lucy's curls and turned a pensive gaze on Abe. "Listing a guardian is required of all adoptive parents. Miss Agnes wouldn't have considered the application without it."

Abe closed his eyes. *Lord, let me be dreamin'*. He opened them. Nope. The lady was still there, her fingers in the child's hair. *Thanks a lot.*

"Are you his closest relative?"

Abe nodded.

"Then you would be his most likely choice."

"But—"

"I'm sure he had every intention of honoring his commitment to Lucy himself, but. . ."

But he died. Abe wadded the pages and shoved them into the woman's hand. "Well, it don't matter anyway. No matter what that paper says, I can't take care of a little girl." More sweat broke out over his body, and not from the sun's heat. The little one wouldn't last a week with him and his bumbling ways. "Take her back to New York."

"I can't."

"Yes, you can."

She glowered at him and held the rumpled papers under his nose. "Unless a judge severs this agreement, no, I cannot."

Abe could be stubborn, too. "Then I'll get the judge to sever it. Sheriff Bailey, when's the circuit judge comin' to Kingsley?"

"You know his schedule as well as I do, Abe. He'll be here sometime durin' the first week of June."

Abe stifled a groan. Still six weeks away.

Miss Emmett slipped the adoption papers into her bag. "Mr. Early, did you come to town in a wagon or on horseback?"

Now what was she up to? "In a wagon."

"Good. Would you kindly meet Lucy and me at the train station?"

His pulse gave a hopeful leap. "You want me to buy you some tickets?" He'd do it even if it cost him every penny in his pocket.

She frowned. "I left Lucy's bag at the station. Although it isn't terribly heavy, I'd rather not carry it here to the cemetery. I would appreciate you fetching it." She took hold of the little girl's shoulders and aimed her toward Abe. For a moment her chin quivered, and tears winked in her eyes. But then she blinked, set her lips in a grim line, and raised her chin. "Go to your uncle Abe now, Lucy."

Panic flooded Abe. Holding up both palms, he shuffled in reverse. "Wait!"

She frowned. "Why?"

"You ain't sendin' her home with me."

A mighty sigh left her throat. "What else am I to do with her, Mr. Early? Even the sheriff conceded she is your responsibility until the circuit judge changes the edict—if he changes it."

Abe unbuttoned his jacket and shrugged it off with jerky, impatient yanks. Threads popped, but he didn't care. He would suffocate if he had to stay in this suit one more minute. He wadded it and held it in front of him like a shield. "She can't come with me. I have to ready my ground for planting."

Preacher Henry cleared his throat. "Now, Abe, to be honest, I don't know that you have a choice in this. Ed and Ruby adopted that child. Ed made you guardian. She's yours whether you like it or not."

He hadn't slept more than an hour at a time or eaten more than a bite or two since Ed's house burned down with Ed and Ruby in it. Planning a burial, keeping up with the chores, wondering how in the name of all that was sensible he was going to survive had taxed him beyond anything, including losing his parents when he wasn't yet old enough to shave. Because for the first time he had to do it all on his own with no big brother lending encouragement or chiding him or delivering a good-natured kick on his back pockets.

He blew a breath skyward and let the frustration pour out. "I've got a farm to run—got a crop to put in the field. All day long, sunup to sundown, I work. Now with Ruby gone I'm gonna have to see to my own meals an' laundry an' housecleaning as well as carin' for the livestock. How can I do all that if I've got some little kid needin' my attention, too?"

Miss Emmett pulled the child against her skirts and cupped her head, her thumb gently stroking the little girl's temple. The gesture was sweet. Protective. Reassuring. All the things Abe didn't know how to be. The woman's green eyes met his. "Mr. Early, I'm sure all new parents feel the same way you do. But in time you'll find the means to—"

"Time won't make one bit of difference, Miss Emmett. The only way I could take that child with me is if I had a wife to see to her, an' there ain't no likely prospects in Kingsley." He coughed out a laugh. "Unless you'd like to hitch up with me."

Chapter Three

Every girl anticipated her marriage proposal. Amelia's daydream included a dapper beau bent on one knee offering a bouquet of fragrant flowers and a poetic promise of undying love and commitment. Her fantasy shattered with Mr. Early's outburst, even though she knew he'd spouted the suggestion in jest. Would she ever have the joy of a real proposal? She was twenty-six years old already—beyond the age of desirability. The realization stung. To ease her deep pain, she chose to pretend this one was real.

She met his surly gaze. "To be frank, Mr. Early, it's too soon for us to consider matrimony even for Lucy's sake. But I would be willing to stay in Kingsley for a time, help you ease into caretaking for Lucy, and become better acquainted."

All three men gaped at her, but she kept her gaze pinned on Mr. Early's eyes. Such an unusual color—gray irises rimmed with dark blue, the colors of a stormy sky. She shivered. Staying made more sense by the minute. She'd be able to assure herself that Lucy settled in well—that the child would be treated lovingly by this standoffish, unsmiling storm of a man.

With slow, steady steps, the way she might approach a wary street urchin, she advanced across the grass until she stood only inches in front of him. She gulped. The brim of her hat didn't even reach his chin, and she wore shoes with two-inch heels. He was an extraordinarily tall man. Her hand quivering, she touched the sleeve of his shirt with her fingertips. The taut muscles hiding beneath the cambric fabric gave her a start, but she remained in place. "You feel alone right now, Mr. Early, and for good reason, given your recent loss."

His gaze flicked to the crosses and then settled on her again. He swallowed, his Adam's apple bobbing against his tight collar.

"Now isn't the time to make brash decisions about sending Lucy away or. . ." She couldn't bring herself to say "taking a wife," knowing he hadn't truly meant what he'd said. The words would be a mockery and would scald her heart. She cleared her throat. "Or anything else. You need to give yourself time to heal from this wound."

"I'm not fit for seein' to youngsters."

He growled the statement, and Amelia couldn't decide if his tone held regret or a warning. Then an image of the man as she'd seen him when the sheriff guided her through the cemetery gate—bent before the crosses, his head low and shoulders slumped—flashed in her mind's eyes. His humble, sorrowful pose had stirred her sympathy, but she'd sensed tenderness and the ability to love deeply in him. Suddenly his eyes seemed less stormy than uncertain. The embers of sympathy flared to life.

She offered an encouraging smile and pressed her fingers more firmly on his forearm.

"You might surprise yourself, Mr. Early. I suspect that when your pain isn't so fresh you'll be able to see Lucy as the last gift your brother gave you rather than as a burden."

She glanced over her shoulder at Lucy, who crouched in the grass and played with a few new green stems. Fondness swelled upward and filled her chest. Lucy had won her heart. In time, the child would win Mr. Early's, too. Amelia faced the man again. "I'm willing to help you if you're willing to try."

He stepped away from her. His long shadow flowed across the grass and reached Lucy. The little girl looked up, her blue eyes wide. The muscles in his jaw formed a knot as he stared hard at the child. He crunched his jacket in his fists, his entire body tensing, and then he seemed to collapse. He aimed a weary look at Amelia.

"I don't reckon I've got much choice until the circuit judge comes. If you'll take care of her until then, I'd be obliged."

"Of course, Mr. Early." Her heart gave a happy skip. A few more weeks with Lucy was a blessing beyond compare. And a few weeks in Kingsley would give her time to plan where to go next. Certainly a bigger city where jobs were plentiful. But until then, she'd lavish her affection on Lucy. She would call these weeks her bridge from her former life to her future one.

The minister, a kindly looking older man with thick gray hair slicked back with oil, sent a frown at Mr. Early. "Where do you intend for Miss Emmett and the little girl to stay, Abe?"

The sheriff said, "Hotel'll be awful expensive for that many days. You could check at Miz Tooney's boarding house."

Amelia released a little huff of disbelief. How would Lucy and her new guardian become acquainted if they weren't together? She swung a firm look across the trio of male faces. "Mr. Early's home is now Lucy's home. She'll stay there."

"Huh-uh. Not unless somebody's there besides me to take of her. Not if you want her in one piece when the circuit judge gets here."

Mr. Early's statement sent apprehension dancing up Amelia's spine. She wouldn't abandon Lucy to the man until she was assured the child would be safe. "Then I suppose we both need to stay at your farm instead of in town."

The sheriff coughed—loudly—into his hand. He gave the preacher a bump with his elbow and whispered gratingly, "Didja hear that, Preacher Henry? City gals."

The preacher frowned first at the sheriff and then at Amelia. "You staying at Abe's farm wouldn't be seemly, Miss Emmett. A little thing like her"—he angled a glance at Lucy—"isn't what folks around here would consider a good chaperone. Tongues would wag nonstop if he put you up in his house without a clergy speaking words over you."

"Ain't that the truth!" Sheriff Bailey folded his arms over his chest and glowered at her. "No such immoral doings are gonna take place in my town."

Heat flooded Amelia's face. Did they really think so little of her? She'd be there as a caretaker for Lucy, nothing more. She started to say so.

Preacher Henry pinched his chin. "You're going to need a place to stay. Miz Tooney likely has a room available that would accommodate both Miss Emmett and the child."

The sheriff nodded, leaning close to the preacher. "She charges three dollars a week for one boarder. Seein' as how the little girl isn't hardly the size of a lamb, I doubt Miz Tooney'd ask for extra for her."

"So assuming Miz Tooney has a room, and she'd rent it for her standard rate, the cost of lodging for six weeks comes to. . ." Preacher Henry rolled his eyes skyward. "Nearly twenty dollars total."

Amelia gasped. Twenty dollars? Such a sum! And how had the town's minister and the sheriff gotten involved in her affairs? Why couldn't she and Mr. Early work things out together for Lucy's sake? She looked at the tall man, expecting him to intervene, but he stood off to the side with his black jacket all crumpled in a ball in his large hands, his mouth closed tight and his gaze fixed on the other two men. Apparently mourning had rendered him incapable of thinking for himself. She could be understanding. But she would also be very clear on her expectations.

"Sheriff? Reverend?"

The pair of men jerked their faces in her direction.

"As much as I appreciate your, er"—she pushed aside the word *interference* and searched for one less condescending—"concern, you seem to have lost sight of the most important issue at hand."

"An' what's that, Miss Emmett?" the sheriff said.

She curled her hands over Lucy's shoulders and set the child in front of the men. "Lucy."

Both of them gazed down at the little girl, but she noted Mr. Early turned sideways and stared across the cemetery rather than looking at the child.

Amelia sighed. "Lucy came to Kingsley to meet her parents and to settle in her new home. I certainly don't intend to sound indifferent to Mr. Early's tremendous loss, but Lucy has lost something, too. She's just a little girl, helpless and alone. Shouldn't we do what is best for her right now?"

Preacher Henry turned a serious look on Amelia. "What do you think is best, Miss Emmett?"

Finally they were listening. She smiled. "Since Mr. Early is Lucy's guardian as specified by the adoption papers, I think it best for them to become well acquainted. Thus, the child needs to stay at the farm where her legal guardian lives and works."

The preacher's eyebrows rose high.

The sheriff's jaw dropped open.

Amelia held up her hand. "I am not suggesting that I stay nights at the farm. You're correct, Preacher Henry, that my doing so would be unseemly. And I can assure you, Sheriff, despite my having grown up in the city, I do possess morals."

The two exchanged a sheepish look.

"But as Mr. Early has indicated, he'll require assistance so he can see to the responsibilities on his farm. What if I take a room at the boardinghouse by myself? Each morning I can travel to the farm to care for Lucy during Mr. Early's working hours and return to my lodgings in the evening after she is tucked in bed. Mr. Early wouldn't be inconvenienced, and Lucy would have a home."

Mr. Early whirled to face the group. "You'd be there all day? I wouldn't have to do anything for her?" He seemed more panicked than petulant.

She'd met nervous first-time parents in her years of delivering orphans to families across the Midwest, but Mr. Early won the prize for anxiety. She offered what she hoped would be received as an encouraging smile. "All day, Mr. Early." Until the circuit judge affirmed the adoption papers and she would be free to move on. But it was best not to mention the short-term arrangement when he was so clearly tense.

"Who's gonna pay for the boardinghouse?"

Amelia choked back a laugh. "I presume you will."

"Why me?"

"My responsibility toward Lucy is complete"—her heart panged—"with her delivery to her lawful guardian. I'm only staying to accommodate you. Does it not make sense then that you would provide for my lodging?"

"It does make sense, Abe," the sheriff said.

Mr. Early gave the lawman a sour look.

The sheriff ducked his head.

Preacher Henry cleared his throat. "I'm going to guess Abe's apprehension has more to do with finances than his sense of obligation. Am I correct, Abe?"

The tall man set his lips in a grim line and nodded.

The preacher pinched his chin for several seconds, his brow furrowing. Then he snapped his fingers and smiled. "I have a solution. Miss Emmett, our youngsters have all grown up and moved on, so my wife and I have a room you could use."

Amelia swallowed a laugh. No doubt the preacher and his wife would also monitor her comings and goings to be sure nothing of a questionable nature took place between her and Mr. Early. She didn't mind being held accountable—she had nothing to hide. "Are you sure I wouldn't be an intrusion?"

"Oh, now, my Lizzie has been lonesome for company since our youngest, Helen Marie, got married last fall and moved to Satanta. She'll welcome having a young woman under our roof again." He chuckled. "Only one word of warning. My Lizzie is a mother hen. She'll try to cluck over you the same way she does any young person who crosses our threshold. I hope you won't hold that against her."

Amelia hadn't been mothered by anyone since she was too young to remember. She smiled. "I promise." She held up one finger. "But I will see to my own needs—laundry, meals, and housekeeping. I won't be a burden on you."

"I'll let you fight that battle with Lizzie." The minister turned to Mr. Early. "Now you won't need to worry about providing lodging for Miss Emmett. Is there anything else we can do to help you, Abe? I'm sure you weren't expecting to become a papa the same day you laid your dear brother and sister-in-law to rest."

Tears briefly winked in the tall man's eyes, and Amelia's heart rolled over in compassion. He had been dealt a mighty blow. She would do her best to assist him in his new role as father to Lucy even though it meant giving the little girl a permanent farewell.

"I'm wonderin' how she'll get from town to my farm every day. Will you tote her, Preacher?"

"I keep my horse and buggy close at hand in case there's an emergency." Preacher Henry tilted his head and frowned at Abe. "But Ed and Ruby's barn didn't burn. Why not let Miss Emmett make use of their horse and wagon? We can put the horse in the lean-to with ours every night, and she can take herself to your place each morning. Then she'll have a wagon available for errands and such, too."

The sheriff clapped the preacher on the shoulder. "You've got a good thinker, Preacher Henry. An' since you've got things all solved, I'm headin' back to my office. Good to meet you, miss." He tipped his hat to Amelia and strode off.

Mr. Early's eyebrows pinched together so tightly they formed a knot between his eyes. "Do you know how to drive a rig?"

Amelia swallowed. She'd ridden in carriages, on streetcars, and across the country on trains hundreds of times. But she'd never been responsible for guiding any kind of conveyance. She grimaced. "I'm afraid not." Would the plan dissolve before it had a chance to take shape?

He sighed, his chest expanding and falling. He shook out his jacket, jammed his arms into the sleeves, and sighed again. Amelia held her breath, waiting for his response. At last he gestured toward a horse and wagon waiting on the street outside the cemetery fence. "I reckon I'll have to teach you then. Come on."

Chapter Four

For a city girl, she caught on quick. Abe sat beside Miss Emmett on the wooden seat and gripped his knees, sometimes offering low-voiced instruction, but mostly just letting her get the feel for driving. His trustworthy horse, Pet, held to a slow, steady *clop-clop*. Miss Emmett looped the traces between her gloved fingers instead of clutching them in her fists. If he hadn't known better, he would have suspected she grew up on a Kansas farm instead of the middle of a big city. Yep, she was doing fine. Even better than fine.

But no matter what Preacher Henry said or how she proved herself capable, he wouldn't hand over Ed's wagon or one of Ed's horses to this city gal. He'd let her stick with *his* wagon and *his* horse. Partly because out of the four horses owned by the Early boys, Pet was the gentlest and most cooperative. Partly because he couldn't stand the thought of anybody but Ed or Ruby using their wagon and team. Could his steadfast brother and his bubbly, always-laughing wife really be gone?

The little girl stood in the wagon bed and held onto the back of the seat, looking this way and that. Every now and then she murmured, "Ohhh," or pointed at something—a circling hawk, a rolling tumbleweed, a farmer trailing his horse with his hands on the plow—with wonder in her eyes. But mostly she just looked. The rolling farmland with houses and barns sitting in the middle of open ground probably made her think she'd landed on foreign soil.

Pressure built in Abe's chest. A deep ache that made drawing a breath pure torture. Ruby would've enjoyed teaching the child how to put seeds in the good Kansas ground and coax them to life. Ed would've relished holding her on his knee and letting her pretend to drive the team. His brother and sister-in-law were so natural with the town children, so eager to parent one of their own. They would have been the best pa and ma ever for Lucy.

Why'd You have to take them away, God? They were my whole family. They were supposed to be this little girl's whole family. I don't understand.

The wagon approached the turn in the road leading to the adjoining Early farms. Ed had always teased it wasn't fair that Abe got home quicker from town, his house being the first one on their property. He'd always felt a little guilty about it, seeing how Ed planned to be a family man and would have reasons to get home faster, but now he was happy he'd claimed the closer plot to town. He didn't have to pass the pile of charred timbers that was once Ed and Ruby's house every time he made the trek back and forth to Kingsley.

He cleared his throat and pointed to the bend. "Gonna turn in there on the left. Pet already knows that's home, an' she'll take us that way without you tellin' her, but it's good for you to know what to do. So when we're close, you'll wanna say"—he lowered his voice to a whisper—"G-E-E."

From behind them, Lucy echoed, "G-E-E."

"Hush, you," he told the child. He frowned at the woman. "You'll say the word, not spell it. But if you say it too soon, Pet'll get confused. So wait just a bit. I'll tell you when."

She nodded and set her face at a pert angle, gaze ahead.

Abe watched until they reached the second stone fence post from the corner. "Now."

"Gee," Miss Emmett called. Pet obediently pulled the wagon onto the lane. Miss Emmet smiled at Abe. "I did it."

Abe shrugged. "Well, Pet did it."

She nodded. "She listened to me."

Abe decided not to argue. "When we get to the yard, the barn'll be to the right of the house. When you want Pet to go right, you say H-A-W."

Another quick nod that made her hat bounce. This time Abe stayed silent and let her judge when to give the direction. Pet had already begun angling the wagon toward the barn when Miss Emmett announced firmly, "Haw," but she was right on target. Without thinking, he said, "Good job."

She beamed at him. When the horse neared the sliding barn door, she pulled back on the reins and called, "Whoa, Pet." The horse stopped. The moment the wagon's creaking fell silent, Miss Emmett thrust the reins into his hands, slumped back in the seat, and blew out a dainty breath. "I'm so glad that's done. It's quite disconcerting to be in control of such a muscular animal with only those slim lines of leather. I don't believe I truly breathed the entire drive."

Abe swallowed a reminder that she'd be taking herself back to town in the evening. "You did fine, miss. An' ol' Pet is a trustworthy beast who likes to take things slow. She's a good match for somebody just learnin' to handle a wagon an' team."

She smiled a thank-you that made Abe's heart do an odd little flip in his chest.

He cleared his throat and hopped down from the seat. "Climb on down from there an' I'll show you the house." This city girl would probably shrink away in shock when she got a good look at his simple dwelling. But maybe it'd be enough of a shock for her to take the little girl away even before the circuit judge came. He reached into the bed for the child's bag, and the little one scampered over to the open back and held her arms to him.

"Hewp me out?" she said, her angelic face expectant.

Sweat broke out over Abe's body. He looked at his hands—his big, calloused hands with their knobby knuckles and nails rimmed with dirt that he could never completely remove no matter how much he scrubbed. He shouldn't touch her. He'd soil her. Maybe even break her.

She bobbed her arms. "Please?"

Miss Emmett rounded the wagon. "Come here to me, Lucy. I'll help you."

Abe stepped aside, relieved he'd left the wagon's hatch door in the barn when he'd set out that morning. Miss Emmett wouldn't have been able to lift the child over the high side, but the floor of the bed was only a little over three feet from the ground. She had no trouble helping Lucy from that reasonable distance.

With the child riding her hip, she turned to Abe. "Please bring Lucy's bag and show me where she is to sleep. I'll put her things away for you."

She'd gone a little frosty in the last few minutes, probably because she was peeved at him, and guilt pricked. He'd never liked displeasing anyone. But he wouldn't risk hurting the little one. He headed for the house. "C'mon in." He felt obliged to add, "It's not much."

She trailed him across his dirt yard and onto the porch—just planked boards with a slanted roof held up by two plain posts. Nothing like the spindled, painted porch Ed built for Ruby. For the first time he wished he'd at least slapped some paint on the boards, but what difference did it make? These two weren't staying permanently.

He opened the front door and gestured the woman over the threshold into his small sitting room. Not that he did much sitting. Her gaze was flitting around the room, but he couldn't tell by her expression what she might be thinking. He said, "Follow me," and headed for the little room next to the kitchen. Only a storage room, but he didn't have much to store, so it would make a suitable bedroom for the child. Small as she was, she wouldn't take up much space.

He opened the door and entered the dark room. Shutters covered the windows, one looking north at the fields and one looking east where Ed and Ruby's house used to be, but once he flopped them open sunlight spilled into the space, revealing a jumble of crates and burlap bags stacked in the corner. And a whole lot of stringy cobwebs.

Abe slid his finger over the windowsill and grimaced at the pathway left in the dust. "Reckon it's gonna need some cleaning before she can sleep in here."

"I should say so." Miss Emmett spoke so staunchly it made Abe want to chortle. She turned a slow circle, still carrying the little one, her face pursed in distaste. "Where is the bed? And a chest of drawers? This is hardly a suitable arrangement for a child."

Her tart comment chased away his humor. "I'm sorry I don't have a guest room all ready. I didn't know I'd need one."

Immediately her expression turned repentant. "I apologize, Mr. Early. Of course you couldn't have known."

She set Lucy on the floor. The little one stayed close to the woman's skirts, but she pinned her gaze on Abe. As did the woman. He squirmed beneath their attentiveness. After several tense, silent seconds, Miss Emmett cleared her throat.

"Mr. Early, neither Lucy nor I have had our lunch. Might I fix her a little something while you clear these items out of the room?"

Abe shrugged. He didn't mind feeding them. Town ladies had brought out all kinds of food over the past two days the way folks always did when somebody lost a family member. His appetite had gotten buried with Ed, so he had plenty to share. But what did Miss Emmett expect him to do with these things he'd kept in his storeroom?

"Thank you."

He blinked, surprised. Why was she thanking him? He hadn't agreed to anything.

"After we eat," she went on, a cheery smile lighting her face, "I'll borrow your broom, mop, and cleaning cloths, and this room will be sparkling in no time. If you have some extra blankets, I can make a pallet on the floor for Lucy, and her belongings can simply remain in her bag until you're able to locate furnishings."

Miss Emmett swung the little one's hand, her smile never dimming. "Well! Since that's all settled, let's go have lunch, shall we, Lucy?" She scurried out of the room, her skirts raising a little cloud of dust.

Abe gawked after her.

She paused on the other side of the doorjamb and peeked over her shoulder at him. "Of course, Mr. Early, you are more than welcome to join Lucy and me at the table when you've finished moving those boxes." Then she disappeared around the corner.

Chapter Five

Amelia prepared a simple lunch of sliced ham, bread, and boiled eggs. She set three plates and cups of milk at the table, but she and Lucy ate alone. Mr. Early stomped in and out of the small room where Lucy would be sleeping, transporting items to a lean-to tacked on the back of the house. By the stern look on his face, she knew she'd irritated him by asking him to empty the room, but what else did he expect? Lucy needed a clean, furnished room if she was to stay in this small but cozy house.

While she ate, she examined her surroundings. Such a simple dwelling—unplastered walls empty of paint, raw beams overhead, not even a throw rug warming the unstained planked floor. Yet something about the structure appealed to her. It seemed a blank slate waiting for the touches that would make it a home, and deep inside she experienced an itch to perform the transformation. But Mr. Early would not appreciate her making changes in his house. Regardless of how he felt, she would change the room where Lucy would sleep. For the child's sake. And Mr. Early would have to understand.

Mr. Early plopped a burlap sack on the stack in the lean-to and crossed to the table. He settled his unsmiling gaze on the plate and cup in front of the empty chair.

Amelia offered a hopeful smile. "One nice thing about a cold lunch—it's ready whenever you are." Would he sit? She wanted a chance to get to know him a bit before she left Lucy with him for the evening. She was a fairly good judge of character, and she wouldn't brand him as unkind, but his standoffishness concerned her. Was the air of indifference a pretense to hide his mourning? Men were such odd creatures when it came to expressing their true feelings.

"I'm not hungry. Got work waitin' in the field."

She bit the corner of her lower lip, stung by his sharp tone.

He curled his hands over the back of the chair and kept his head low. "But thanks." The words emerged gravelly, as if his throat was dry, but with no harshness. He flicked a glance at her, the hint of an apology glimmering in his unusual eyes. Then he turned and strode out the door. His long legs carried him quickly.

The moment the door closed behind him, Amelia released her breath in a whoosh, unaware she'd even been holding it. "My, that is a taciturn man."

"A tackerter man," Lucy echoed, emulating Amelia's tone perfectly.

She turned to the child, who wore a circle of crumbs around her mouth. As always, the child's innocence melted her. She used her napkin to clean the little girl's face. "Now that we're done eating, we have work to do, yes?"

Lucy bobbed her head, making her ringlets bounce. "Work to do, yes."

"Then let's get busy."

If Lucy hadn't helped, Amelia could have cleaned the room in less than an hour. But Lucy whacked the straw broom like a club against the floor, sending dust over the surfaces Amelia scrubbed. The child was so eager to help, so cheerful in her labors, Amelia couldn't complain. However, she traded tasks long enough to thoroughly sweep the floor, then allowed Lucy to slap the broom against the now dust-free floorboards while she once again scrubbed windowsills, windows, and shutters.

When the room sparkled beneath its cleaning, Amelia put her hands on her hips and frowned at the empty space. "Hmm. . ."

Lucy imitated her stance. "Hummm. . ."

Amelia laughed and scooped the child into a hug. "Silly girl, we need to find you a bed. Where do you think we should look?"

Lucy giggled and slipped free of Amelia's grasp. She darted into the slanted paths of sunshine streaming through the open windows and spun joyous circles, her arms outstretched and her face lifted. Giggles spilled from her throat.

Watching the little girl, Amelia experienced a stab of pain. How would she bear to leave Lucy behind when she departed from Kingsley? If only the adoption wasn't final. If only she had a husband who loved Lucy as much as she did. If only—

She stomped her foot against the floor, sending the *if-only*s away. What good would these thoughts accomplish? None whatsoever. Lucy belonged to Mr. Early now. Unless a judge overturned the adoption—in her experience, adoptions were only voided when the child was grossly mistreated, something she didn't expect from the tall, solemn farmer—she would have to tell Lucy goodbye.

"But I have today," she whispered. Today was a gift she shouldn't squander.

Lucy ceased her spinning and gazed up at Amelia, her little face puckered. "We find a bed, Miss Meela?"

Amelia jolted. Evening would be upon them soon enough. She needed to finish readying Lucy's room. But how? She didn't want to rifle through Mr. Early's cupboards and closets like a common snoop. Her gaze shifted to the open window, and in idea formed quickly.

She held out her hand, and Lucy caught hold. "Come, Lucy, I have an idea for your bed."

◆ ◆ ◆

Abe tugged the reins that stretched from the plow to Jerry's broad back and brought the horse to a halt. He frowned across the landscape. Miss Emmett, the little one skipping along beside her, was heading for the barn. Was she leaving? And was she taking the child with her?

His heart pounding in half hope, half trepidation, he watched her and the little one disappear into the barn. He stared at the open doorway, frowning and counting off the seconds until they emerged. But not in the wagon. Still on foot. And they both carried armloads of straw. Puzzlement filled him. He and Jerry remained rooted in place while the woman and child made two more trips, each time carting more hay into his house.

When they stayed inside, he clicked his tongue on his teeth and set Jerry in motion again. But while he guided the plow, folding back the rich Kansas soil to receive seeds, he couldn't resist sending glances toward the house. What was she doing with that straw?

Besides making a mess, that is. Maybe he shouldn't have left the two of them in there alone.

Curiosity and nervousness drove him to end his day early. Besides, his empty stomach growled. For the first time since Ed's house burned down, he thought he might be able to eat something. The hours of hard work had done their duty in restoring his appetite. Maybe the woman was in there using that straw to build a fire in the cookstove. A city gal likely wouldn't know to look for a woodbox. Even if she was burning up his straw, he wouldn't complain about having a hot meal on the table. It'd almost be like having Ruby back.

He released Jerry into the stall, saw to the horse's needs, and then hurried to the house. Wisps of hay formed a trail to the back door, but not a single bit littered the floor inside. Soft voices carried from the spare room, and the cookstove was cold. Disappointment momentarily struck, but the lunch Miss Emmett had set out earlier waited on the corner of the dry sink with a checkered cloth covering the plate. He lifted the edge, snagged a piece of ham, and crossed slowly to the open doorway leading to the spare room, drawn by the cheerful sound of the mingled chatter and laughter.

Abe stopped in the doorway and peered in. The woman knelt, smoothing a blanket over a mound in the corner of the room, while the child paced back and forth, seeming to supervise. He swallowed the ham and then cleared his throat.

They both turned, the child shrinking against the woman's frame. Miss Emmett curled her arm around the little one's waist and smiled. "Mr. Early, I hope you don't mind me helping myself to some of your sweet-smelling straw. I often slept on a straw mattress when I was a child, and I thought some straw and one of the blankets I found in the lean-to would make a fine bed for Lucy."

He cringed. "That blanket's wool. Plenty scratchy."

The woman rose and brushed her hands against her skirt. "I presume you have some extra sheets somewhere, but I didn't want to"—her cheeks blushed pink—"snoop."

Except through the lean-to. She'd prowled plenty in there to find that blanket and a pair of crates which were now stacked one on top of the other against the wall and holding the child's clothes. Sadness clawed at his midsection. Ruby wouldn't let the little one sleep on a mound of straw on the floor or store her clothes in old crates.

He backed up a step. "Got some extra sheets in the bottom drawer of the chifforobe in my room." Now why'd he tell her that? Did he want her going after it herself? "Wait here. I'll fetch them." He held the stack away from his sweaty, dust-smeared shirt as he carried them to the spare room and handed them to the woman.

She took them with a smile and knelt again to prepare the little one's bed. While he watched the woman show the child how to smooth the sheets flat and tuck them under, a worry struck. Come Saturday, he'd need to switch out the sheets on his bed, and this was his only extra set. Who would wash his sheets and hang them to dry? He glanced down at his shirt and britches. Who would launder his work clothes? He'd come to depend on Ruby for so many things.

As his mother had taught him, his worries formed into a prayer. *Lord, don'tcha think I'll have enough trouble just takin' care of myself? You can't mean for this little one to stay here with me. Find her a good home with a ma an' a pa who'll love her the way Ed an' Ruby would've done. An' please show me how I'm gonna get along without Ruby doin' for me all the things a wife would do. I can't take care o' things on my own.*

The woman had the straw bed looking neat and tidy. She rose, swishing her palms together. "Well, now, that should do nicely." She aimed her perky gaze at Abe. "Now that Lucy's bed is ready, I'll put a hot supper on the table for the two of you. Would fried potatoes and ham suffice, Mr. Early?"

His stomach growled. He nodded wordlessly.

A soft smile curved her lips and turned her cheeks into rosy apples. "I promise not to dally." She scurried past him and out the door, little Lucy scampering after her the way the barn cats chased a mouse. On the other side of the threshold, she paused and looked over her shoulder at him, her eyebrows high. "There will be sufficient time for you to freshen up. I put water in your washbowl, so please make use of it."

Heat filled his face. Not even Ruby had ever come right out and told him he needed to wash.

"And Mr. Early, while I was readying Lucy's room, I made a decision."

He drew a sharp breath, half afraid of what she'd say next. For a small woman, she had a big measure of spunk.

"Until the circuit judge comes, I will serve as your housekeeper as well as Lucy's caretaker. This way you can plant your crop without worry, and you should have ample time to locate a woman to see to your household tasks when it's time for me to move on." For a moment, tears brightened her eyes. But she blinked several times, clearing the moisture. "Supper will be ready soon. Go wash up now." She cupped her hand behind the child's head and ushered her to the stove.

Abe angled a wry gaze toward the ceiling. *You sure got a funny way of answerin' a man's prayers, God.* Shaking his head, he made his way to the washstand to do as the woman had requested.

Chapter Six

Within two weeks in Kingsley, Amelia felt completely at home. She didn't puzzle over the sense of belonging, either, even though living in the little Kansas town was quite different from living in New York. She credited the Reverend and Mrs. Voth, who treated her like family and, by their very acceptance, encouraged everyone else in Kingsley to do the same.

Wherever she went, folks greeted her with smiles and cheerful nods. She received a half-dozen invitations to supper, all of which she politely declined since she stayed at Mr. Early's farm through the supper hour and tucked Lucy into bed shortly after washing his dishes and putting them away. No one took offense at her refusals, and Mrs. Voth assured her they would ask again "once that young'un is settled an' don't have need of you anymore." Although it pained her to think of the day that little Lucy wouldn't need her, she began to imagine staying in Kingsley permanently with these friendly folks. Then, at least, she could watch Lucy grow up.

On her second Saturday morning in Kansas while the predawn shadows lay heavily across the land, she stood by with a bundle of laundry in her arms and watched Preacher Henry hitch Pet to Mr. Early's wagon for her drive to the farm. The man whistled as he worked, and she swallowed a chortle when she recognized the tune—"Buffalo Gals." Such a strange song for a minister.

He must have caught her amused grin, because he abruptly ceased whistling and shrugged, his expression sheepish. "I'll count on you not to tell Lizzie I was lettin' loose with such a heathen melody. It's just one of those tunes that gets stuck in a fellow's head, and you have to get it out somehow."

"Don't worry. I won't tell." She tossed the bundle into the back of the wagon.

Preacher Henry raised his eyebrows. "What's that you've got there? You running away from home?"

She laughed. "No, sir. It's my laundry. I'm going to do Mr. Early's and Lucy's wash today, so I'll do mine at the same time."

The man chuckled as he helped Amelia up onto the wagon seat. "I reckon that'll keep Lizzie from doing them up for you again."

Amelia nodded. "Exactly." She adored the good-natured, open-hearted woman, and she didn't intend to burden her with additional chores. The couple provided her with a place to sleep and sweet companionship. That was more than enough. She took the reins and smiled down at the preacher. "Have a good day. I'll see you this evening."

"Or maybe earlier if the rain Doc Freely predicted swoops in." Preacher Henry scratched Pet's ear and frowned. "We get some sudden gully-washers around here, and the road between town and the Early farms can become impassable. So you keep watch. The clouds get to building, you skedaddle back to town even if you haven't tucked that little girl in bed yet. Abe can see to the child if need be. Reckon he ought to start practicing anyway."

Despite their many days of eating breakfasts, lunches, and suppers together, Mr. Early seemed no more comfortable around Lucy than he had during the first few minutes of meeting. Rain or not, she wouldn't abandon Lucy to the man's caretaking unless she knew he wouldn't ignore the child.

Amelia forced a smile. "Well, I have a lot of clothes to hang on the line, and I would prefer they didn't receive a soaking. So you say a prayer that the rain holds off until tomorrow, hm?"

He laughed and stepped away from the horse. "I'll see what I can do. Have a good day, and tell Abe he's invited to our place for dinner tomorrow after church."

Would the man lose his taciturn ways in the presence of the affable Voths? She would like to witness such a change. She flicked the reins, and Pet obediently lunged forward. She glanced skyward. Still gray, cloudless, with pink blooming in the east. The doctor's prediction of rain seemed unlikely, but storms would brew inside the house if she wasn't there when Lucy awakened.

She called, "Hurry now, Pet."

◆　◆　◆

Something tapped Abe's shoulder. He snuffled and brushed at his arm. The *tap-tap* came again, more insistent this time. With a low growl of annoyance, Abe forced his bleary eyes open. Then he sat up so abruptly his sheet slipped off the edge of the bed. He scrambled to retrieve it. "You?"

The little girl stood close, big blue eyes unblinking. In the dim light sneaking through the window, her hair stood out like the snarled strings of a mop. She puckered her lips. Was she going to cry?

"What you want?"

She danced in place.

"Then go on out."

She shook her head, making her tangled hair bounce. "I scared."

Abe glanced at the window. Dawn was breaking, but things were a mite gray out there. If he was no bigger than a nubbin, he'd be scared, too. He groaned. "All right, all right." He swung his legs out of bed and stood.

The child angled her head back to peer up at him. He expected her to recoil in fear at the up close look at his taller-than-any-other-man-in-town frame. But instead she lifted her arms.

Abe grimaced. "Just come on, you." He put his fingers on the back of her head and turned her toward the door. He scuffed across the floor on his bare feet with the child scampering ahead of him. The morning air, moist and cool, greeted him when he opened the back door. He started to step outside, but the child froze on the doorjamb, once more holding her arms to him.

"Me up, please?"

Abe chewed his lower lip. The little girl was barefooted, like him. He didn't mind trooping across the dewy grass with no shoes on, but her feet were more tender than his. What if she found a cocklebur? Those blasted weeds popped up no matter how hard he fought against them. He started for her room. "We'll get your shoes on."

Panic widened her eyes. She wriggled, her arms quivering.

Apparently she couldn't wait. Quick, before he could change his mind, Abe hooked his hands under her arms and lifted. Holding her in front of him the way someone might carry a skunk-sprayed critter, he hustled her across the yard to the outhouse. He set her inside and stepped back. "There. Do what. . .needs doin'."

To his great relief, she took care of herself without asking for help. By the time she emerged, the sun had peeked his head over the horizon, and the entire sky was robin's-egg blue, a shade lighter than the child's eyes. She smiled at him, and something warm bloomed inside Abe's chest. This time when she lifted her arms to him, he settled her on his hip the way he'd seen Miss Emmett do. Surprisingly, she fit well there, and his lips twitched into a small smile.

The rattle of wagon wheels on gravel intruded.

"Miss Meela!" the child crowed.

Abe whirled to look. Sure enough, Miss Emmett was bringing his wagon to a stop on the patch of ground between the house and barn. And there Abe stood in the morning sunlight, wearing nothing but his union suit. He took off at a gallop for the house with the little girl squealing in his ears. He plopped the child on her straw mattress then darted into his bedroom and slammed the door. Faster than he'd ever dressed before, he scrambled into a shirt, britches, socks, and boots.

The light patter of footsteps crossed the porch and knuckles rapped the front door. He smacked a comb through his hair then tossed it onto his bureau top before racing through the living room to the door. He swung it open and forced a raspy greeting. "Mornin', Miss Emmett."

The red flush on her cheeks let him know she'd seen his mad dash across the yard.

His face went hot. He shuffled aside so she could enter and muttered, "I gotta shave." He closed himself in his room again. He decided to shave slow, give him—and her—time to recover from the awkward start to the day.

Familiar sounds—the woman stoking the stove, cracking eggs in a bowl, talking soft to the child—crept under the door while he carved away the prickly whiskers shadowing his jaw. He gave himself extra swipes, hoping to remove all traces of embarrassment along with the stubble. But the razor blade did nothing to remove the pink stain from his face. He finished, then paced the floor, considering sneaking out the window. But he'd have to face her sometime. So he sent up a silent prayer that God would erase her memory of him standing in the yard in his underwear and stepped into the main room.

She turned from placing tin plates on the table. Her gaze met his. Fresh red flooded her already pink cheeks. "Mr. Early. . .This morning, when I arrived. . ."

He gulped. Fire blazed in his face. Didn't the Lord listen to anything he said? She remembered, and she was still mortified. Who could blame her? He should've gone out the window. "Yeah?"

Tears glistened in her eyes. "You were holding Lucy."

He frowned, confused. "Y–yeah."

"It was a beautiful sight."

She remembered all right, but not his union suit. He couldn't decide if he was happy or sad about what her memory held. Then he thought about the comfortable weight of the child in his arms, and something inside of him melted. He took an uncertain forward step. "You. . .you think so?"

A shy smile curved her lips. "Yes, Mr. Early. I do."

"She needed the outhouse." He shrugged. "Needed it bad. So I took her." Would that satisfy her curiosity about why he hadn't been dressed?

The woman nodded, and slowly her face faded to its normal color. "I'm sorry I didn't arrive in time to take her. She woke earlier today than usual."

Abe grimaced. He toed the floor. "That's probably my fault. I gave her an extra cup of milk after you put her to bed last night."

Her eyebrows shot up. "You did?"

"Yeah. She couldn't sleep, said she was thirsty. So. . .I gave her a drink. So she'd hush an' drift off to sleep." Why was he blathering this way? They both had work to do. He hurried to the stove and reached for the coffee pot. "I won't do it again."

The woman's smile changed to a frown.

He angled a glance at her. Her shoulders sagged, her head drooping low. He scowled. "Somethin' wrong?"

She looked at him. The disappointment in her expression made his stomach roll over in a funny way. "Mr. Early, I hope you didn't mean that."

He drew back. "Mean what?"

"That you won't give Lucy a drink the next time she asks for one."

"Well, I—"

"Because an important part of parenting is meeting a child's need as it arises. If she was thirsty, then giving her a drink was the appropriate thing to do. I sincerely hope you won't ignore future requests."

Only at bedtime, since that extra liquid made her wake up earlier than usual and let him get caught standing outside in his under drawers for Miss Emmett to see. But then again, neither the woman nor the child would be around forever. They were two weeks closer to the circuit judge coming and reversing the adoption. How likely was it that he'd have to take the little girl to the outhouse at the break of dawn again? Maybe he'd sleep in his britches until the circuit judge came, just in case.

"You got breakfast ready, miss? I need to get into the fields."

His answer must have disappointed her, because her frown deepened, and much as he hated to admit it, her disappointment stung. But no matter how it'd felt to carry the little girl on his hip that morning, no matter how warmed up his insides got when the little girl smiled at him, it was only desperation that bade him to offer help. He wasn't fit for parenting.

God, let Miss Emmett see the truth.

He sure hoped God was listening to that prayer.

Chapter Seven

A be had enjoyed Sunday dinners with the Voths more times than he could count, and he'd never been uncomfortable around Preacher Henry or his always-smiling, always-friendly wife. But on this Sunday, he was as uneasy as a raccoon treed by a pack of hounds. The tender pot roast stuck in his throat. The gravy turned into sawdust in his mouth. Even the cold, frothy milk tried to choke him. What was the matter with him, anyway?

Foolish question. He knew the answer. It bothered him to be at odds with the woman. He wouldn't call her a friend. He couldn't even call her his housekeeper since her time on his farm would be so temporary. There was no relationship between them at all. So it shouldn't matter a bit if she was unhappy with him. Yet it did matter. It mattered a lot.

"Mr. Early, how is your planting comin'?" Mrs. Voth spooned more peas onto Abe's plate. "I reckon it's very different, workin' alone. Will you plant both yours and your brother's fields this year?"

Abe put down his fork, the remainder of his appetite fleeing. He sensed Miss Emmett sending him a sympathetic look from across the table, but he kept his gaze on the preacher's wife instead. He didn't want to see pity in anybody's eyes. "I want to get both fields planted." He hated looking at that empty stretch of ground, proof that Ed wasn't with him anymore. "But it's takin' a lot longer'n I expected. I guess I never realized how much work Ed put in."

"I don't rightly see how you'll manage without help." Mrs. Voth shook her head, her eyes sad. "If only you were married already. Then you'd have a helpmate, the same way Ed did."

Abe's flippant comment about the city woman marrying up with him haunted him. Did she ever think about it, too? He glanced at her. Her face filled with pink, and she looked down at her plate. Yep. She was thinking about it now.

"But I s'pose," Mrs. Voth went on, "that's somethin' best left to the good Lord's doin'."

"Indeed," Preacher Henry said firmly. He rested his elbows on the edge of the table.

"Maybe you should hire a farmhand. After all, havin' Miss Emmett doin' the housework has surely eased a burden for you. Wouldn't an extra pair of hands in the fields make things easier?"

Abe forced a chuckle. "Well, it ain't exactly the same thing, Preacher. Miss Emmett isn't costin' me anything except the food she eats." The woman ate like a bird—she hardly put a dent in his food stores. "But I'd have to pay a hired hand outright, an' my bank account is pretty limited until my crop comes in."

"Will you sell Ed's land then?"

How could he sell his brother's land? How could he watch somebody else till the soil, plant the seeds, harvest the grain? Whoever bought it would have to traipse across his acres to reach Ed's place. He didn't like the idea of somebody other than his brother using his land as a thoroughfare. Besides all that, if Lucy was Ed's child in the eyes of the law, that land rightly belonged to her now. He couldn't do anything until the judge reversed the adoption. Abe swallowed the lump in his throat. "Not unless I have to."

The minister sat back in his chair, pinning Abe with a serious look. "The church has a fair amount in its benevolent fund. If you'll recall, I offered some to you to help with Ed and Ruby's burial. You refused it, but maybe you'd take some to pay a hired hand."

Mrs. Voth chimed in again. "'Specially now that you've got a young'un, you can't be out in the field every wakin' hour of the day. That little girl needs attention, too, an'—"

Abe stood and dropped his napkin on the table. "I appreciate the good dinner, ma'am, an' your offer of help, Preacher, but I'm doin' all right on my own." He eased backward toward the hall tree where his church hat waited, still talking. "Soon as the child gets settled in someplace else an' Miss Emmett is free to move on, I'll be able to put more hours into my farm an' everything'll be just fine. Yes, sir, things'll return to the way it was before."

Preacher Henry rose. "It'll never be like it was before, Abe. 'Cause Ed an' Ruby'll never be with you again."

Abe's limbs turned to stone. He stood still as a statue beside the door, his chest hurting worse than the toothache he got when he was ten and ate a whole bag of taffy.

"You can't get back the family you lost." Preacher Henry spoke low, soft, kind as kind could be. Funny how even such kindly stated words stung. "But you can make yourself a new family by keeping Ed and Ruby's little girl."

Abe found the ability to move. "'Bye, Preacher." He stormed out the door.

◆　◆　◆

Amelia sighed. "I told you it wasn't any use."

Preacher Henry and Mrs. Voth exchanged sorrowful looks.

Amelia used her napkin to clean the gravy from Lucy's chin then lifted the little girl from the chair. "Let me tuck her into my bed for a nap. Then we can talk."

Lucy lay down without a fuss, and Amelia returned to the dining room, where the Voths remained in their chairs at either end of the long table, sipping coffee in companionable silence. She slid into her seat and picked up the conversation as if there'd been no interruption. "I admit I was hopeful when I saw him carrying her across the yard yesterday morning, but then he spent the rest of the day ignoring her. Just like he did here at your dinner table. I think it's hopeless. I'm probably wasting my time waiting for an edict from the circuit judge. That man is not interested in becoming Lucy's papa."

Mrs. Voth tilted her head and pursed her lips. "Not to be contrary, but I think you're wrong, Amelia. It isn't a lack of interest that holds him aloof from little Lucy."

Amelia arched her brows in silent disagreement.

The woman laughed. "Don't give me that sour look. I happened to notice the way he watched Lucy during the service this mornin' when she got wiggly and began whisperin' at you. Some folks frowned, but he was fightin' a grin. Even here at my table, every time he looked at you wipin' her mouth or holdin' her cup for her, his eyes took on a warm glow. I could almost hear him wishin' he was the one helpin' that way."

Amelia huffed and threw her hands wide. "Then why does he tiptoe around her as if he feared she carried the plague?" He did the same to her, which also stung. He was very polite, thanking her for preparing his meals, washing his clothes, or straightening his house. But he did so from a distance. Always stiff and formal. "The man has erected barriers around himself, and I doubt anyone will be able to penetrate them."

Preacher Henry cleared his throat and set his coffee cup aside. "Miss Emmett, I've known Abe Early since he was a boy of fifteen. Even back then, he was taller than most grown men. You've heard of boys goin' through a gangly stage during the years between boyhood and manhood? Abe Early was gangly an' then some. Probably 'cause he shot up so fast. He had a hard time findin' his footing, so to speak."

Amelia tried to imagine Mr. Early as a smooth-faced youth, clumsy and awkward. Images of his chiseled features, broad shoulders, and determined stride intruded.

The preacher continued. "If someone was gonna knock over a cup of milk at a church potluck, it would be Abe. If someone was gonna send a basket of fruit sailing over the edge of a counter, it would be Abe. If someone was gonna step on a cat's tail and send it yowlin'—"

The two Voths chorused, "It would be Abe."

The preacher chuckled. "Poor fella just couldn't seem to help it—his limbs flew out farther than he expected them to, I reckon."

Mrs. Voth shook her head. "He took a fair amount of ribbin' from the local youths because of his long shadow an' the way he stumbled over his own feet. I can't tell you how many times I heard his brother tease that if Abe ever married he better find himself a buxom girl who could hold up to bumps an' bruises 'cause she'd probably get knocked down every time he went to hug her."

"His own brother said such things?" Indignation stirred through Amelia's chest. "Why was everyone so unkind to him?"

"Oh, now, honey." The preacher's wife squeezed Amelia's hand. "I don't think any of it was done in meanness. Folks tend to josh other folks. But I suppose, over time, some of the teasin' started to feel like truth to Abe. An' now he's fearful of gettin' close to somebody. Most especially a little somebody like Lucy. Or you."

Heat attacked Amelia's face. She clapped her palms to her cheeks. "Me?"

"Why, of course you." A knowing grin climbed the woman's cheek. "I've lived long enough to recognize when someone's smitten. And you, Miss Amelia Emmett, are smitten with our Abe Early."

How had she been so transparent? She'd tried mightily to hide her fascination with the tall farmer, a fascination that bloomed the moment she saw him kneeling at his brother's graveside. And how could she reverse her feelings? Obviously they weren't reciprocated, and she was only setting herself up for heartache if she couldn't squelch her growing affection.

"Lizzie, you're embarrassing Miss Emmett." The preacher patted Amelia's shoulder. "Never mind Lizzie's speculations. She fancies herself a matchmaker and just can't seem to help herself."

Amelia sighed. "Unfortunately, Preacher Henry, her speculation about me is correct.

I am smitten with Mr. Early."

"I knew it!" Mrs. Voth clapped her palms together and beamed.

"But it's pointless. He isn't interested in caring for Lucy, and he isn't interested in me." Tears pricked her eyes. "If I had any sense at all, I would send a telegram to Miss Agnes and inform her that Lucy's placement failed and return to New York as quickly as possible."

Preacher Henry frowned. "But you said you'd cut your ties with the orphan's home."

How could she have forgotten? The orphanage was crowded enough with hapless children. Miss Agnes wouldn't be able to take in an adult even if she had nowhere else to go. Amelia groaned and buried her face in her hands.

The preacher's warm hand curled over her shoulder. "Now, don't despair, Miss Emmett. You're welcome to stay here for as long as you need to. An' there's still a month until the circuit judge comes. A whole lot can change in a whole month."

"That's right." Mrs. Voth caught Amelia's wrists and pulled her hands away from her face. "We all know Abe Early is a good man who'd provide a lovin' home for that little girl. He might be runnin' scared now, but that doesn't mean he can't change his mind. All it'll take is a little coaxin' an' a little teachin' an' a lot of prayers."

Amelia managed a weak smile. "Well, if you folks are willing to provide the prayers, I'll do my part to coax them together and teach him how to take care of Lucy."

"An' in case it don't work out," Preacher Henry said, "I'll start spreadin' the word about a little girl needin' a home. That way you don't need to worry any about Lucy, Miss Emmett. She'll be cared for."

Amelia nodded, but inwardly she cringed. Of course someone would welcome a sweet, adorable little girl into their home. But Amelia needed a home, too. Who from this little Kansas town would want to woo an old-maid, big-city woman?

Chapter Eight

After their conversation around the dinner table, Amelia and Mrs. Voth began a new habit of praying together before Amelia set out for the Early farm. She treasured those prayers, and she reflected on them in the moments when Mr. Early behaved particularly standoffish. Knowing Mrs. Voth was praying helped her hold to hope that the man's defensive walls would crumble and he would soften toward Lucy. But she didn't allow herself to hope he would soften toward her. She wouldn't risk her heart.

Lucy, although very young and without an ounce of guile, did her part to win the tall man's affection, too. Whenever she and Amelia stepped into the yard to hang laundry, dip water from the well, or feed the chickens, Lucy would race to the edge of the field, jump up and down, and call, "Uncoo Abe! Uncoo Abe!" until he finally waved back. When the man entered the house, Lucy pranced close and beamed up at him, raising her arms to be held. Amelia never witnessed him holding the child, but she wondered if he did so when the two of them were alone. Otherwise, why would Lucy continue to expect it?

Every evening for the next two weeks, when Amelia returned to the Voths she spent a few minutes in their small parlor sharing any changes in Abe's behavior toward Lucy. On one day she reported him waving at the child from the field; on another she shared how he helped Lucy with her napkin during lunch. She didn't tell them how he'd caught her watching him and went all pink in the face.

On another day she told them that he hadn't shooed the child to the other side of the room while he soaped up at the washbowl the way he had on previous days. The second Friday in May she could hardly wait to divulge how he invited her and Lucy to the barn to peek in on a new litter of kittens. He'd even put his hands on the child's waist to help her keep her balance on the stall wall. And when Amelia went up on tiptoe to look, too, he'd given her a rare, genuine smile and offered his hand to help her step onto the bottom railing. Now, hours later, her palm still tingled from the touch of his strong, callused fingers.

"An' tomorrow's Saturday, the last day of the week." Mrs. Voth tapped her chin with one finger and scowled. "Every Saturday you've brought Lucy here to stay through 'til Monday mornin', but..." She whirled to face her husband. "Henry, what would you think about leavin' the young'un out at the farm this time? Let Abe get the child up on Sunday mornin' and bring her in for service on his own? Do you think he's ready for it?"

The preacher sucked in his lips and rocked in his creaky old rocking chair, his forehead puckering. "That'd be a mighty big change from what he's used to. As I recall, there's only been the one day Lucy woke up before Amelia reached the farm, an' even then he didn't get her dressed or anything. He only took her to the outhouse."

Amelia ducked her head so they wouldn't see the blush she knew was stealing across her cheeks. She couldn't hang his clothes on the line without remembering how he'd looked standing in the yard with Lucy perched on his arm and the pink rays of dawn illuminating the long underwear that covered his tall frame.

"You might be right." Mrs. Voth blew out a breath. "Reckon he'd need to practice it a time or two before bein' expected to ready that child for Sunday service. Say!" Her expression brightened. "How 'bout you hold off on gettin' over there tomorrow mornin', Amelia? Give him the chance to take care of Lucy before you arrive. If you come late— say, eight or so—an' the little one's still in her nightgown an' he's ignorin' her, then you'll know he's not ready for time alone. But if he gets her in a little dress, maybe sets her at the table with a cold biscuit, that'll tell you he can do the same for Sunday mornin'. An' more important, it'll tell *him* he can do it."

Part of Amelia resisted the plan. She loved her early morning hours with Lucy. There was something special about the smell of the sleepy child. She cherished the trusting way the little girl leaned against her while Amelia ran a comb through her hair. Was she ready to give up those sweet moments?

"I don't reckon there's any harm in givin' him a chance. How much damage could he do in one hour on a Saturday mornin'?" Preacher Henry brought the rocker to a stop and beamed at his wife. "It's a good plan, Lizzie."

She sent a smug smile across the room. "I think so, too. 'Course..." She gazed intently at Amelia. "It's up to you, dearie. It'll take a heap of trust. Are you ready?"

◆　◆　◆

Where was she? Abe chewed his lip and sent another look out the window. No horse and wagon approaching. Not even a cloud of dust to show one might be coming soon. The sun had been up for over an hour already. He'd already dressed, milked the cow, and fed and watered the stock. He needed to put some breakfast in his stomach then head to the field. If she didn't hurry, the little girl would wake, and then—

A small hand tugged his pant leg. "Uncoo Abe?"

Abe swallowed a groan. Too late. He gazed down. The child's sleep-heavy eyes and tousled hair stirred protectiveness to life within him. She was so small. So helpless. Panic chased the flow of protectiveness away. He needed the woman's help. "Need the outhouse?"

The little girl nodded.

"Let's go then." Maybe by the time they were done in there, Miss Emmett would arrive. Lucy finished her morning business, and Abe carried her back to the house, but still no wagon rolled up the lane. So now what?

Lucy touched his cheek, then jerked her hand back and squealed. "Owie! Sharp!"

Abe put her on the floor, scowling. "Only one night's whiskers. Can't be that bad." He rubbed his jaw. More prickly than he'd expected. "Well, all right then, but you don't have to fuss at me. I'll shave 'em." Funny how good it felt to talk to somebody first thing in the morning.

The child stayed close, her fingertips resting on the edge of the washstand while Abe cleared his face of the dark shadow. When he was done, Lucy quirked her fingers at him. Confused, he bent low. She smoothed her fingers along his cheek then grinned. "Soft."

Abe straightened abruptly. He'd never been called soft before. He harrumphed. "Least I'm not sharp anymore. C'mon, you." He herded her to the table. "Sit yourself up there an' I'll see if I can find somethin' for you to eat." He didn't mind hardtack or even leftover beans for his own breakfast, but he wasn't sure how Miss Emmett would feel about the little girl eating such manly food.

He scrounged through the cupboards and located a half loaf of bread. He sawed off a good sized chunk, dropped it in a bowl, then poured milk over it. His ma had fixed him milk toast when he was a boy, usually when he had an upset stomach. Lucy didn't seem to be ailing, but the breakfast wouldn't do her any harm.

He plopped the bowl and a spoon in front of her. "There you go. Eat up."

The child folded her hands and closed her eyes.

Abe automatically did the same.

"Fank You fo' my food. Amen."

He looked at her.

She smiled.

His insides went all quivery. Maybe he needed a bowl of milk toast, too.

He returned to the dry sink to cut another piece of bread, and the clock on the fireplace mantle sent out its chime for half past the hour. Seven thirty already. Abe dropped the knife and moved to the window. He searched the sunlit horizon, but it was as peaceful as midnight out there. Had something happened to the woman? With spring came snakes. Had one spooked ol' Pet into bolting? His hunger departed, and he paced the room, checking the clock every other minute.

Lucy finished her bread and then drank every drop of milk from the bowl. She plunked the empty bowl on the table and shot a smile at Abe. "I aw done." She wriggled out of the chair and trotted to her doorway. "Put dress on, Uncoo Abe?"

He sent another hopeful look out the window. No sign of the woman. The fields were waiting for his attention, but he couldn't think about a crop until he knew Miss Emmett was safe. He'd hitch Ed's horse and wagon and go look for her. He'd had to take Lucy with him, and she needed to wear something besides her nightgown. "All right. Let's go."

◆　◆　◆

Amelia's heart beat double time, and her palms were slick from sweat. The entire drive from town she'd repeatedly prayed that Mr. Early and Lucy's morning had gone smoothly, but worry still tangled her in knots. Had she trusted him too soon?

She pulled up next to the barn, like always, and sent a glance around. The yard was empty, the surroundings quiet save the chickens' soft clucking from their pen. A bit of the worry eased. She set the brake and turned to climb down from the wagon's seat. As she placed her foot on the wagon wheel, which made a handy ladder, a series of thuds sounded inside the house followed by piercing screams. Lucy!

She leaped, landed hard enough to jar the soles of her feet, and took off at a stumbling run. For the first time since her daily treks to the farm, she didn't bother knocking on the door but simply burst in and darted for the little room where Lucy slept, guided by the child's continued wails.

Mr. Early sat on the floor holding his head. The pair of crates with Lucy's belongings lay on their side next to him, their contents scattered. Lucy—half-dressed, red faced, and screeching—crouched in the opposite corner.

Amelia went straight to Lucy and scooped her up. The child continued to wail, and Amelia spoke over the noise. "What happened? How did she get hurt?"

The man slowly lifted his head and squinted at Amelia. "She ain't hurt. Not sure why she's bellowin' except maybe I scared her when I fell. Lord knows I scared myself."

Now that she understood, Amelia gave the child a little shake. "Lucy, hush that. You're fine. No more crying." With a few hiccups, Lucy quieted. Amelia plopped her onto the straw bed. "Stay there. I need to see to Mr. Early."

Mr. Early slowly pushed to his feet. "No need for that. I've taken harder lumps than this one." He fingered a spot between his right eyebrow and hairline.

Amelia wrung her hands and stared at the purple knot forming on his forehead. "How did you fall?"

He grimaced. "I was tryin' to get her wrestled into a dress. She kept prancin' out of reach. I moved to catch her, she whirled and came back, and I tried to keep from steppin' on her. Went down so fast I hardly knew I was fallin'. Knocked the crates to kingdom come, but at least I didn't land on the child." He wobbled a bit.

Guilt smote Amelia. She grabbed his elbow and guided him to a chair at the table. "Oh, Mr. Early, I'm so sorry. Lucy likes playing little cat-and-mouse games in the morning. I—I should have been here."

He scowled. "Where were you anyway? Did Pet throw a shoe, or did a wheel come loose?"

"No, no, nothing like that. I. . ." She didn't want to tell him why she'd dallied. He might not take it well, considering.

"I'm glad you're all right."

The sincere relief in his muttered statement made tears sting Amelia's eyes. "Let me get a cold rag to put on that bump."

He rose, shaking his head. "Now that you're here, I need to get busy. Morning's gettin' away from me. I wanna be puttin' seeds in the ground come Monday, and my land needs one more goin' over with the tiller."

She gaped at him. "But you're hurt. You aren't even steady on your feet."

He planted his feet wide and stopped the slight swaying. "I'm fine."

He wasn't, but she knew he'd never admit it.

He headed for the back door. "Finish gettin' her dressed, then gather up her things. Take her to town with you. It just ain't gonna work for her to stay out here with me." His face contorted with pain Amelia sensed went deeper than physical discomfort, and his voice turned harsh. "I could've squashed her flat, even broken her bones. She ain't safe with me. Take her, Miss Emmett. Please. . .take her away."

Chapter Nine

By bedtime on Saturday, Abe regretted his hasty decision to send the little girl away. During his long evening alone, with no woman puttering at the dry sink or child jabbering, he experienced a deep loneliness. As deep as the early days of Ed's marriage to Ruby, when the two of them spent every spare minute alone and left him to himself. As he lay on his bed in the quiet house, he told himself he'd adjust. He'd used the woman and child to replace Ed and Ruby in his mind. He only needed to get used to being alone. It would take time, but he could do it.

Sure he could.

His convictions faltered the moment he spotted Miss Emmett and little Lucy in church Sunday morning. He hoped no one asked him about the sermon after the service, because he couldn't pull his attention from the woman and child. Miss Emmett wore her familiar flat-brimmed straw hat with roses shaped out of filmy fabric. Lucy, who sat in the woman's lap, kept reaching up to touch the flowers. Each time Miss Emmett caught the child's hand and lowered it to her lap, never once smiling or shifting her attention from Preacher Henry. Such a persistent imp, and such a patient woman. Abe tamped down chortles at their battle of wills.

Lucy finally gave up and tipped her head against Miss Emmett's shoulder. Miss Emmett rewarded the child with a warm smile and a kiss on the top of her tousled head. Abe had to bite the tip of his tongue to hold back a *hurrah* at the woman's victory. And all achieved without anger or threats or a smack on the hand the way lots of parents would have done. Miss Emmett was a natural mother. The image of the two of them settled in his heart and lingered.

Without any warning, his mind began tripping through other pictures of the woman—cooking at his stove, smiling shyly across the dinner table, washing dishes at his dry sink, tossing sheets over the line, scattering apple peels to the chickens, pointing him to the fresh bowl of water when he returned from the fields. . . She'd settled into wifely duties in his house as if she'd always lived on a farm.

He examined her wheat-colored hair smoothed into a roll that held the hat at a pert angle on her head, the sweet curve of her jaw, and the slight upturn of her rosy lips. Such a pretty woman. And capable beyond his expectations, given her slight figure and big-city background. The regret that stabbed his chest last night returned with a mighty thrust. What had he been thinking? In one big swoop, the reason he sent them away washed over him. He'd almost stepped on Lucy. He could've hurt her. Hurt her badly. Sweat broke out over his flesh, considering what might have happened.

"But it didn't."

Preacher Henry's staunch statement nearly sent Abe from his bench. Had the man been reading his thoughts? He jerked his attention forward and realized the preacher wasn't even looking in his direction. So the words were part of his sermon. Yet Abe's pulse continued to pound as he forced himself to listen.

"Nope, not a one of David's sins—and there were many!—prevented God from callin' him a man of His heart." Preacher Henry's warm smile drifted across the gathered worshippers, drifted over and then past Abe. "That's 'cause David was repentant. He asked God for forgiveness an' then made an effort to not make the same mistakes again. And God in His lovin' mercy answered David's prayer and equipped him with the strength to overcome temptation. That very same God loves us as much as He loved David. God'll do the same for each of us when we come to Him with repentant, open hearts."

Preacher Henry invited everyone to rise for a final hymn, and the congregation broke into "Leaning on the Everlasting Arms," one of the most rousing hymns from their new songbooks. Abe added his voice to the throng, but when they reached the third verse, his throat tightened and he could only listen.

"What have I to dread, what have I to fear, leaning on the everlasting arms. . ."

◆　◆　◆

Now that the service had ended, would Mr. Early come over and talk to her? Amelia had been aware of his gaze fixed on her the entire morning. It had taken every ounce of self-control she possessed to keep from looking back at him. Had it not been for Lucy's repeated attempts to play with the flowers on her hat, which gave her something else on which to focus, she wouldn't have been able to resist.

The little girl had fallen asleep with her head nestled in the curve of Amelia's neck. With effort, Amelia rose while holding the sleeping child and turned to make her way to the center aisle in the hopes of exchanging a few words with the tall farmer. But folks gathered in little clusters to chat, and Amelia found herself trapped by groups on either side of her.

He'd made his way to the center aisle, and his height let him look over the heads of the women and meet her gaze. A sheepish grin lifted the corners of his mouth. But what did it mean? Was he sorry he'd banished Lucy from his house or only sorry about the way he'd done it—in anger? She wanted to ask him. The group blocking her pathway moved, and she started in Mr. Early's direction.

"Miss Emmett?" Preacher Henry and a couple she hadn't yet met stepped into her pathway. "I'd like you to meet Bent and Millie Wilcox. They have a farm west of town."

Amelia nodded at the pair. The man stood with squared shoulders and a raised chin in a strong, proud pose, but his weathered face held a scowl that seemed etched in place. Amelia resisted a shiver and shifted her attention to the woman. Wearing a faded gray dress and bonnet, she appeared as weatherworn as her husband. She clasped her chapped hands against her ribs and hunched forward slightly as if she carried a weight on her back. Sympathy stirred for the woman.

"The Wilcoxes heard about Lucy." Preacher Henry touched Lucy's hair. The child snuffled and burrowed. "They wanted to take a gander at her, talk to you about adoptin' her since. . ." He flicked a glance toward Abe, who hadn't moved from his spot in the aisle.

"I'll let you all get acquainted." He hurried off.

Mrs. Wilcox gave Amelia a hopeful look. "Could'ja wake her? Lemme see her face?"

Amelia jostled her shoulder a bit, and Lucy stirred. Yawning, she raised her head and blinked at the circle of faces.

The woman released a little gasp. "Oh, so comely. Ain't she a pretty little thing, Bent?"

The man's scowl didn't fade. "Pretty don't matter. How old is she, lady?"

Instinctively Amelia tightened her hold on Lucy. Something in the man's demeanor unsettled her. "Three. She turned three two months ago."

The man snorted. "A three-year-old ain't gonna be much help. An' look how spindly she is. Probably couldn't even carry a bucket o' water from the well."

"But she'll grow, Bent, an' the bigger she gets, the more help she'll be."

Amelia bristled. Did they want a child or a farmhand?

Mr. Wilcox jammed his hands into the pockets of his baggy pants. "Me an' the missus've visited orphanages twice before, took home youngsters both times. Bigger ones. But they run off first chance they got. Ungrateful brats. . ." He crunched his lips to the side and stared hard at Lucy. "S'pose takin' in one this young might be good. She's too small to get far if she tried to run off, an' probably easier to train, too."

Trepidation gripped her. Why hadn't Preacher Henry stayed? She needed him. She glanced toward the aisle, intending to beseech Mr. Early with her eyes, but he was gone, too. Her breakfast curdled in her stomach.

The wife lifted a hopeful look to her husband. "So we can have her?"

"Reckon so." The man reached for Lucy.

Amelia took a backward step, shaking her head. "You can't just take her."

Mr. Wilcox's eyes glittered with fury. "Don't you be tellin' me what I can or can't do, lady. Preacher said the child needs a home. We're offerin' one. Now give her over."

"But I can't!" Panic turned Amelia's voice shrill. "There's protocol to follow. Lucy has already been adopted."

The farmer snorted. "Those folks're dead. They ain't gonna care what happens to her."

Perhaps Mr. Early didn't care, either. If he cared, he wouldn't have left her to face this vile man alone. Amelia swallowed bile. "That may be true, but the agreement between Edwin and Ruby Early and the Good Shepherd Asylum must be severed by the circuit judge. Then a new application has to be made to the director of the orphanage in New York before I can grant your request to adopt Lucy. I—I don't have the authority to—"

Mr. Wilcox grabbed his wife by the elbow and jerked her toward the aisle. "C'mon, Millie. Circuit judge'll be through next week. He'll do right by us." He pushed his wife out of the church.

◆　◆　◆

It was too late. He'd told Miss Emmett to take the child away, and she'd done it. Now someone else would take in the little girl. Abe gripped the reins so tight they cut into his bare palms. If only it was some other couple besides Bent and Millie Wilcox.

Abe couldn't find any fault with Millie. Meek, kindly, never complaining—everyone in town said she was a good woman. But she stayed with Bent, and no one had a good word for that man. Nobody could prove it, but folks suspected he abused his wife. Probably the youngsters they'd taken in, too, which is why they never stayed. And now Miss

Emmett was going to let the Wilcoxes take Lucy. A sick feeling flooded his gut. He couldn't let it happen. But how to stop it?

He knew how. By keeping her himself. It was what Ed and Ruby wanted. Truth was, he wanted it, too.

Abe lowered his head and contemplated the bit of the sermon he'd heard. He hadn't exactly sinned by sending Miss Emmett and the child away, but he'd hurt them. He'd seen it in their eyes. Could they forgive him? Hope flickered within him. But then he remembered how his clumsiness had almost hurt little Lucy!

But it didn't.

He sucked in a breath. He hadn't hurt her. He'd avoided stepping on her, avoided falling on her. He touched the tender spot on his head. He'd hurt himself, but he hadn't hurt Lucy. Except for her feelings when he'd barked at her to get back. Was he being too hard on himself, thinking he was irredeemable when really all he needed was to try harder?

It was time for him to stop fearing what might happen and let God guide him to a family of his own. He opened his mouth and bellowed out the refrain of their closing hymn. "Leanin' on the everlastin' arms!"

Chapter Ten

The first Wednesday in June, Amelia awakened early and filled the washtub with warm water. She bathed Lucy, using her best lilac-scented soap, and let the little girl splash and play with the bubbles until the water turned tepid. Then she dressed Lucy in her finest dress—the one of cream linen with ruffled lace sleeves—and combed her silky hair into perfect, sausage-shaped curls. She battled tears the entire time. Because today she would say goodbye to her precious Lucy. And then she would say goodbye to the little Kansas town and its residents. Including Mr. Abraham Early.

Yesterday evening after tucking Lucy into bed, she and the Voths had talked about her future. Given her experience with caretaking, she could easily find a job as governess in a large city. As soon as the hearing was over, she would purchase a ticket and make her way to Kansas City or maybe Lincoln, Nebraska. Mrs. Voth hinted that she should stay in Kingsley, at least for a while. But her heart would wither and die if she was in this town but couldn't claim Lucy and Mr. Early for herself. She had to leave.

As she adjusted the bow on the back of Lucy's frock, part of the prayer Preacher Henry offered right before Amelia went to bed drifted through her memory. *"Work Your perfect will concernin' little Lucy, our Amelia, and Abe. Your plans are best, dear Lord, an' we trust You to use the judge to bring 'em to pass."* Amelia closed her eyes and echoed the prayer in her heart. She would trust God to guide the judge into making the right decisions today.

The Voths accompanied Amelia and Lucy to the church, where the circuit judge set up court during his visits to town. As they walked side by side up the boardwalk, Mrs. Voth took Amelia's hand. "Now, no worryin', Amelia, you hear me? I have faith Abe'll come to his senses and show up to do his duty toward Lucy. He loved his brother somethin' fierce, an' he won't do anything that would make Ed roll over in his grave."

Amelia's heart pattered in hopeful beats, but when they reached the churchyard, Abe's wagon was nowhere in sight. The hope flickered and died. He wouldn't come. Not for Ed, not for her, and not for Lucy.

Other townsfolk needing to talk to the judge waited in the chapel though, including the Wilcoxes who sat in the back corner away from everyone else. Amelia kept her gaze forward. It hurt too much to envision the surly man and timorous woman with her vibrant, sweet-natured little Lucy.

The sheriff called names one by one. Folks stated their cases, and Amelia listened carefully to the judge's edicts. He seemed knowledgeable and fair, and her hope that he would make the right decision for Lucy increased with every announced decision.

As the morning stretched toward noon, the room grew stuffy, and the sheriff and

Preacher Henry circled the room, opening the windows. Street sounds and children's voices from the schoolyard nearby filtered in.

Mrs. Voth leaned close to Amelia. "There's still a lot of folks waitin' to see Judge Parker. Hard to say when they'll call your name. Lucy's gettin' fidgety. Want me to take her outside, let her get some wiggles out? I'll be able to hear when you get called if we stay close to the windows."

Amelia didn't want Lucy to muss her dress or hair, but it wasn't fair to make the child sit so still for hours. She nodded. "Yes. That's fine. Thank you."

Mrs. Voth reached for Lucy, but the sheriff announced, "Mr. and Mrs. Bent Wilcox in the matter of the adoption of Lucy Early."

Amelia's heart fired into her throat. She searched the room. Mr. Early hadn't come.

◆　◆　◆

Of Abe and Ed's four horses, only one was saddle broke—Jerry. And of all the mornings for Jerry to throw a shoe, he had to choose this one. They'd only made it halfway to town when the horse's back left shoe dropped off. Abe came close to riding in anyway, but he couldn't risk crippling the horse. So he'd walked the long distance to his land, put Jerry in a stall, then hitched Pet to the wagon and taken off again.

Now the sun beat directly overhead. Sweat poured down Abe's face and into his eyes. He blinked against the sting and prayed he'd make it in time. He drove directly to the church, ignoring folks' smiles and waves. The churchyard was crowded with wagons. So the judge was still doing business. He parked at the edge of the yard and set the brake. A voice escaped the open windows—Bent Wilcox, scornful and brash.

"You ain't in New York no more, city lady, an' your fancy ways don't mean nothin' around here. The folks who adopted that girl are dead an' buried, an' that means the adoption's buried, too. So you just step aside an' let the judge finish writin' papers that make me an' my missus the legal guardians now."

Abe's heart sank. He was too late. He started to flick the reins, instruct Pet to take him home again, but deep within him a longing rose up and propelled him from the seat. He might be too late to claim the child, but at the very least he would have his say to Bent Wilcox. The man would listen, too, when looking up into Abe's face.

Miss Emmett, holding Lucy, was at the edge of a scarred table carried in to serve as the judge's bench. The Wilcoxes stood opposite her, Mrs. Wilcox chewing her fingernails and Mr. Wilcox scowling at little Lucy. The judge appeared to be examining a document. Abe strode up the center aisle and stopped at the edge of the dais. He cleared his throat.

All five people on the dais turned toward him at the same time. Wilcox's lip curled into a snarl. Mrs. Wilcox's eyes went wide. The judge's eyebrows dipped as if annoyed by the intrusion. Miss Emmett seemed to wilt, and little Lucy reached for him and crowed, "Uncoo Abe!"

Abe stepped forward and plucked Lucy from Miss Emmett's arms. "Judge Parker, have you rendered your decision yet?"

The judge leaned back in his chair. "I was just about to sign my name to these transfer of guardianship papers. But if you've got something to add, I—"

"He's just tryin' to cause trouble." Wilcox flung his arm toward Abe. "If he wanted the girl, he would've been here first thing."

Abe wished he could push his fist through Wilcox's lumpy nose. "My horse threw a shoe. Slowed me up, or I would've been here earlier. I'm here now, though. An' I'd like to have my say."

The judge shrugged. "I'm listening."

Wilcox muttered, but the judge's frown silenced him.

With Miss Emmett's gaze fixed on him and Lucy playing with his ear, Abe gathered his courage and spoke his heart. "You've been given some papers that show my brother an' his wife adopted this child as their own. In those same papers, there's a part that says if somethin' happens to Ed and Ruby, I'm to take care of the child. I confess, I was pretty scared about it at first. That's why I told Miss Emmett we'd meet with you, Judge Parker, an' have the agreement severed. But that was six weeks ago, and I've changed my mind."

Miss Emmett gasped.

Abe shifted to address her. "I wanna be Lucy's uncle. I wanna raise her, the way my brother would've if he hadn't died. I don't want the adoption severed."

Judge Parker pushed the papers and pen aside. "Well, if there's no opposition to the original documents, then I don't need to change a thing. Mr. and Mrs. Wilcox, your petition to take guardianship of the child is denied."

Mr. Wilcox erupted with angry oaths. Mrs. Wilcox began to cry. He grabbed his wife by the arm and charged down the aisle and out the church doors.

Miss Emmett darted close, her tear-filled eyes pinned to his face. "Do you mean it? You intend to keep Lucy?"

A smile pulled on Abe's lips. "I mean it. 'Course, I still have a problem. Don't see how I'll do all my farmin' an' take care of her at the same time. I'll need. . .help." His mouth went dry, and he swallowed twice before adding, "Would. . .would'ja help me?"

◆　◆　◆

Her heart ached. She loved the child. She loved the man. Staying would let her spend her days with both of them. But being his housekeeper and Lucy's governess would never satisfy her now. She wanted more. She hung her head.

He cupped her chin and lifted her face. "Amelia?"

Oh, what joy to hear her name on his tongue. Slowly, so slowly she might have imagined it, he set Lucy on the edge of the table and then went down on one knee in front of her. Titters and muffled gasps rose from those waiting their turn to see the judge, but he didn't even blink. He kept his gaze locked on her.

"Amelia," he said again in his deep, throaty, gentle tone. "Would you marry up with me?"

She glanced at Lucy's sweet, innocent face. She dared a glance into the congregation and caught Preacher Henry and Mrs. Voth leaning forward, eagerness lighting their faces. She turned to Abe, who knelt before her with one hand extended and hope glowing in his unusual gray eyes. She gulped. "Why? Just for Lucy, or. . .?" She held her breath, unwilling to risk her heart until she knew. What if this was all a farce, like the first time he'd asked?

He shook his head, the movement slow and deliberate, his eyes never wavering from hers. "I'm askin' 'cause I love you, Amelia Emmett. The three of us"—he gestured to include Lucy—"belong together." He caught her hand and brushed a kiss on her knuckles, the touch igniting a fire in her chest that spread to her limbs and sent her heart soaring. "Marry me."

Tears filled her eyes, blurring his dear face. She nodded. "Yes."

"Today."

She gaped. "Today?"

"Now."

She clasped her throat, holding back a laugh. "Now?"

"Why not? We got the judge here, the preacher, and a flower girl." He rose and scooped Lucy onto his hip. He shrugged. "It's a fine day for a wedding, don't you think?"

His grin was so boyish, she let her laughter escape. "Yes. Yes, Abe." What glory in speaking his name—her soon-to-be-husband's name. "There's no finer day or no finer moment."

With a broad smile, Abe turned to the judge. "You heard the lady, Judge Parker. And while we're at it, how about changin' those adoption papers after all."

Amelia tipped her head, puzzled.

"I'd rather be Papa than Uncle Abe."

Which meant she'd be Mama instead of Aunt Amelia. She'd prayed that Lucy's new mama and papa would love her, but she'd never expected God to allow her to be part of the prayer's answer. Fresh tears flooded her eyes and spilled down her cheeks.

He folded his arm around her and jostled her a bit. "You all right?"

She smiled up at him through her tears. "I'm more than all right. I'm blessed beyond all expectation." She curled her arm around Lucy's waist and pressed her cheek to Abe's solid chest. The steady thrum of his heartbeat in her ear was the prettiest wedding march ever. From her nestling spot, she grinned at the judge. "Well? Do you have a wedding certificate in your portfolio or not?"

The man winked. "That I do. Preacher Henry?"

The minister charged onto the dais and spread his arms wide. "Dearly beloved, what God hath brought together, let no man pull asunder."

Kim Vogel Sawyer, a Kansas resident, is a wife, mother, grandmother, teacher, writer, speaker, and lover of cats and chocolate. From the time she was a very little girl, she knew she wanted to be a writer, and seeing her words in print is the culmination of a lifelong dream. Kim relishes her time with family and friends, and stays active in her church by teaching adult Sunday school, singing in the choir, and being a "ding-a-ling" (playing in the bell choir). In her spare time, she enjoys drama, quilting, and calligraphy.

My Soul Waits

by Connie Stevens

*My soul, wait thou only upon God; for my expectation is
from him. He only is my rock and my salvation:
he is my defence; I shall not be moved.*
PSALM 62:5–6

Soli Deo Gloria

Chapter One

Ten miles north of Laramie, Wyoming, 1875

Pa, you can't be serious." Rosemary Denton's mouth dropped open as she stared at her father. "Philadelphia? Why would you want to send me halfway across the country to spend time with relatives I can barely remember?"

Daniel Denton folded his arms across his chest. "Don't pull that innocent act with me, young lady. I ain't blind. I've seen the way you and Wade Renfroe flirt with each other when you think nobody's watchin'."

Heat rushed up her neck. "Pa—"

He narrowed his eyes. "Renfroe is one of my top hands, and I can't do without him right now. But if it weren't for spring roundup and brandin', I'd send Renfroe packin'." Pa huffed—that noise he always made when he grabbed a problem by the horns.

Rosemary's stomach tightened. "So you want to send *me* packin' instead? Pa, how could you? We—we haven't done anything wrong." Was it wrong to let Wade steal a kiss? A whirlwind of panic spiraled through her, and she tried to force her thoughts into a logical, practical reason to make Pa change his mind. But her brain froze and stumbled.

Pa waved his thick finger at her. "If I thought anything wrong had already happened I'd knock Renfroe's jaw back so far he could scratch the back of his neck with his front teeth." He planted his hands on his hips. "I ain't gonna let a roughneck cowboy come sniffin' around here after you. As long as I'm your pa, Renfroe ain't got no more chance of wooin' you than a stump-tailed bull at fly time."

Her face flamed, and she had to pull her gaze away from Pa, lest he read her thoughts. She had to admit Wade's roguish grin charmed her, but his reckless manners and wild ways did frighten her a little. Perhaps that was part of the thrill. Wasn't love supposed to be thrilling?

"But, Pa, Philadelphia? I haven't seen Aunt Florence and Uncle Quentin since I was six years old. I have nothin' in common with my cousins. Every year, all they talk about in their Christmas letter is their fancy ball gowns and attendin' debutante cotillions and how some society matron is hostin' a tea party. What do I know or care about ball gowns and tea parties? I've grown up on this ranch. I can ride and shoot and do ranch chores alongside my brothers, but I'd have no more idea how to act at a parlor social than a steer knows how to—"

Pa's dark glare halted her words. "Now you see? That's just what I mean. I won't abide watchin' my daughter grow up without a lick o' ladylike polish. Your ma, God rest her soul, woulda known what to do with you. The good Lord knows I don't. But your aunt Florence will. And your cousins—what's their names?—will help you learn all those things ladies are supposed to know."

Rosemary suppressed a shudder. "Gloria and Penelope. In the letter we received from them last year, Penelope went on and on about her 'comin' out,' whatever that is, and about the plays and concerts they attended, and Philadelphia's social register." She wrapped her arms around herself. "Pa, I'd sooner track mavericks through a briar patch on foot than sit at a fancy table with my snooty cousins tryin' to figure out which fork to use."

"You'll learn." Pa rubbed his hand over his stubbled chin.

"And what about those balls? I can keep up with the best square dance caller in Wyoming, and I can reel and two-step, but I'd be a laughingstock at one of those high-falutin' cotillions where the women get all gussied up in silks and satin." She hated the way her voice took on a high-pitched whine of desperation, but the sinking feeling in her gut told her she was losing this argument.

One look at Pa's hard-set jaw confirmed her fear. "I'm ridin' into town tomorrow to wire your uncle and purchase your train ticket. You'd best start packin'." Pa snatched his hat from the cattle horns mounted on the wall and jammed it on his head. He stopped in the doorway and stood like an impassable mountain. "And if I catch you anywhere near Wade Renfroe between now and when you leave, I'll hogtie you like a calf at brandin' time and you won't see the outside o' your room till it's time to take you to the train station." He harrumphed and stomped out the door.

Rosemary sank down on the nearest chair and buried her face in her hands. For the first time in years, she wished she knew how to pray.

Chicago, Illinois
May 1875

Jeremy Reide Forbes leaned back in the leather chair and sipped his coffee. He'd hoped to have at least a few weeks of relaxation upon receipt of his diploma from Yale University, but Father apparently had other plans.

His father, John Murray Forbes, ran his hand over the gilded edge of the framed diploma waiting to be hung on the wall. "A degree in humanities and sciences is a fine thing, son, but it's hands-on experience that will hone you into the man who will one day step into my shoes. The Burlington and Missouri River Railroad is my legacy to you, and I want you to be well prepared for the challenge."

Jeremy set his cup on its saucer and leaned forward. "What do you have in mind, sir?"

Father beckoned Jeremy to the desk, where he pushed a piece of paper toward his son. "Look over this schedule. Between now and next spring, you will work in various positions—virtually every job on the railroad. Everything from porter to conductor to ticket agent, flagman, switchman, brakeman, and fireman. I want you to learn how freight is managed and how the trains are dispatched. Knowing the details of each of these jobs will enable you to guide the Burlington and Missouri into the next decade. When I'm ready to retire, that is. Which I'm not. . .yet." A tiny smirk twitched Father's thick mustache as he took a sip of coffee.

"Sounds like quite a challenge, certainly different from my activities of the past four years." Jeremy studied the schedule. "I like the idea of working with the people who perform those duties that keep the railroad running. But how will I handle the obvious name recognition? As soon as they learn my name is Jeremy Reide Forbes, they'll all know I'm your son. Won't that make things a bit awkward?"

Father lowered himself to the finely upholstered armchair beside the blazing fireplace. "I've already thought of that. It won't be awkward because you aren't going to tell them your name is Forbes."

A frown pulled at Jeremy's brow. "Oh?"

Father extracted a cigar from his inside coat pocket. "You'll go by your middle name: Jeremy Reide. You must be anonymous in order to make this plan successful. Otherwise, every employee you encounter will walk on eggshells and you won't get a realistic picture of the operation. The whole point of this work schedule is to give you a taste of every job on the Burlington and Missouri. Do you think you can handle it?"

Jeremy drained his coffee cup. "I find the idea intriguing. Not only will the experience prove personally valuable, I'll be able to empathize with the challenges faced by every employee." But Father's suggestion that he be duplicitous with those people with whom he'd be working lay unsettled in his chest.

Broaching his misgivings with Father required tact. "Eventually, these people with whom I'm working shoulder to shoulder are going to learn my real name. How will they feel when they find out I was deceptive? A Christian is commanded in scripture to be honest."

Father snorted. "Now, don't let your Bible-pounding get in the way of your common sense. You can be as religious as you want as long as it doesn't interfere with railroad business."

"But Father." Jeremy held out his open palms. "Being a Christian isn't something I put on and take off like a coat. It's part of who I am."

Father pointed at Jeremy with the end of his cigar. "I'll tell you who you are. You are Jeremy Reide Forbes, my son and heir to the Burlington and Missouri River Railroad. And for the next several months, you will go by Jeremy Reide."

◆　◆　◆

Sweetwater, Nebraska

Jeremy paid strict attention to Otto Gustafson, the ticket agent and depot manager. The man's belly hung over his belt, and his thick black eyebrows merged in the middle. Looking over his shoulder while he explained the different eastbound and westbound schedules was an odoriferous experience. Judging by the smell and sweat stains on Otto's shirt, the ticket agent wasn't well acquainted with the benefits of soap and water.

"This here's the list o' fares between here and each stop." The grime under Otto's fingernails created ragged black bows crowning each dirty finger as he pointed out the different columns for first class, second class, and third class passengers, livestock, and freight. "We don't take no checks nor bank drafts. Cash on the barrel. Iffen there's a connection"—Otto peered at Jeremy over his bent spectacles—"that means they gotta get offa the train and wait for another one on a different line." He pointed to the space on the ticket reserved for such information. "You write it here, and stamp beside it."

Jeremy turned his head momentarily and grabbed a breath of fresh air while Otto ran down the list of livestock regulations.

Otto frowned from his seat on the wobbly stool. "Ain't you got no questions? You gotta learn this job by the end of the week on account o' I'm goin' fishin' with my brother-in-law and you'll be here by yourself. You gettin' all this?"

"I've got it, Mr. Gustafson." Jeremy took a step back. He glanced around at the cramped cubicle with its tiny window. Thin wood peelings littered the floor, no doubt from Otto's whittling pastime. Peanut shells, dried muddy boot prints, and other unidentified soil decorated the floor. The customer area of the depot appeared as much a stranger to the business end of a mop as the cubicle. "Um, is there a broom somewhere?"

Otto grunted. "What for you need a broom?"

"Thought I'd clean up the place a bit."

Otto shrugged. "Old Man Forbes gripes about the depot needin' to be cleaner ever' time he comes through Sweetwater." He picked up his pocketknife and the stick he'd been carving on when Jeremy arrived. The blade sliced off another thin peeling of wood that dropped to the floor.

"What is that you're whittling, Otto?"

"Ain't nothin'. Jus' relaxin' to put knife to wood." Another sliver hit the floor. "Druther set an' whittle than sweep the floor. 'Sides, it's jes' gonna get dirty again. What's the point?"

Jeremy gestured toward the waiting area where two rickety chairs leaned against the wall. "There doesn't seem to be much in the way of comfortable seating for paying customers, either."

Something akin to a cackle left Otto's lips. "Ain't my job to make folks comfortable. It's my job to sell 'em a ticket."

Months of grime coated the windows. Jeremy scratched his fingernail across the glass, leaving a tiny carved canyon. "When was the last time the windows were cleaned?"

A yawn garbled Otto's reply. "The last time Old Man Forbes came through."

His first day on the job of his first assignment and Jeremy was sorely tempted to tell Otto that "Old Man Forbes" was his father. He explored and discovered a narrow door behind the office cubicle. The swelled wood screeched a protest as Jeremy forced the door open. Inside he discovered a small storage closet. He batted away cobwebs and shoved a few things around until he found a broom, and then he set to work on the littered floor. A half hour later, the place wasn't what Jeremy would call clean, but it was an improvement. More wood peelings encircled Otto's tipped-back chair while the ticket agent snored, the butchered stick he'd been whittling reduced to barely a toothpick resting on the man's filthy shirt.

Chapter Two

Laramie, Wyoming
May, 1875

Late spring rain dripped from the edge of Rosemary's bonnet, as if the sky were shedding the tears she wanted to release. The platform of the train depot in Laramie bustled with passengers and freight handlers while she stood under the cover of an overhang, her feet nailed in place by her great reluctance. She clutched her valise and reticule while Pa directed the porter to care for her trunks. All her arguments, pleading, and cajoling had fallen on deaf ears. Pa had cut off her every angle of debate, and here she was, moments from being carried hundreds of miles from the only home she'd ever known.

Pa returned to where she stood out of the rain and held out an envelope along with her ticket. "Here's enough cash for any travelin' expenses. I'll wire money to your uncle to put into a trust for you. Do you have everything? Did you pack enough sandwiches? You never know how long it will be between stops and whether or not there will be a decent place to eat close by the train station."

His apparent concern over making sure she had something to eat did nothing to ease her resentment. She stared at the raindrop-dotted ticket. It was now or never. "I won't go, Pa. I refuse to get on the train. You can't force me." She braced for his reaction to her blatant defiance. But instead of wrath, moisture filled his eyes.

Pa dipped his head for the space of several heartbeats. His chest swelled and then released a huge sigh. "Rosemary, I've failed your mother. It grieves me to admit it, but I broke my promise to her. Right before she died, she begged me to make sure you were raised to be a lady." When he raised his gaze to meet hers, tears welled in his eyes. Rosemary couldn't ever remember seeing Pa cry. Her heart hiccupped.

Pa cleared his throat, swallowed hard, and looked past her, as if staring at the gray, rain-bloated clouds eased his words. "You weren't but three years old. Seein' you turn out like a lady seemed so far away at the time, so I gave your mother my promise." He returned his gaze to her face, and his jaw muscle twitched beneath his salt-and-pepper beard. "I don't know where the years have gone. But here you are, all grown up, with cowboys comin' 'round like flies to buttermilk, and it's about time I keep my promise the only way I know how."

His Adam's apple jiggled again. "I know you don't want to go. But a father's gotta do what he thinks is best for his little girl." He blinked and narrowed his eyes. "So you're gettin' on that train if I have to pick you up and carry you."

She'd heard that tone before—right before he promised her a trip to the woodshed when she was eight. Pa wasn't in the habit of saying things he didn't mean. Besides, how was she supposed to stand up to him now? He'd never told her that story before, about his making that promise to her mother. Resignation drooped her shoulders.

"All aboard!" The conductor's bellow prompted the few people exchanging lingering good-byes to cut them short.

Rosemary took the envelope and tucked it into her reticule along with her ticket. Unwilling to even look at Pa, she kept her eyes downcast and tightened her grip on her valise. Pa cupped her elbow as she made her way to the mounting step. Once she ascended to the train car entrance, she paused. "Good-bye, Pa." She stiffened her spine and stepped into the railcar without looking back.

She chose a seat on the opposite side of the train so she wouldn't have to see Pa standing on the platform. Steam belched from the locomotive four cars ahead, and the train lurched. The depot and the town of Laramie began slowly rolling past the grit-darkened window, slipping beyond her reach. For a panic-filled moment, she considered running to the door and flinging herself off the train, but her next heartbeat brought sense and reason. No, she couldn't do such a foolhardy thing.

In the distance, a man sat aboard his horse on a hilltop, slicker hanging over the saddle and hat pulled low. Rosemary squinted through the raindrops. Was the man wearing a blue bandana? The blue bandana was how she always picked Wade out from the others, even at a distance. While the rest of the ranch hands used faded red bandanas, or even scraps of muslin, Wade's blue neckerchief—the same color as his eyes—caused her breath to hitch.

The foggy mist hung in wraithlike wisps around the hillside, preventing a clear look at the lone cowboy and whether or not he sported a blue bandana. But Rosemary wanted to believe it was Wade. As the train picked up speed, the man and his horse disappeared from sight, along with everything else comfortable and familiar.

Mountains shrank as the train chugged southeast, farther into the prairie. Every bone-jarring joggle took her where she didn't want to go. Her eyes burned with gathering tears, but she blinked them into obedience.

The conductor came through and checked her ticket. "Miss Denton? My name is Henry. Your pa said I was to keep an eye on you, make sure you don't get yourself into no trouble. If there's anything you need, you just ask." He tugged on the brim of his cap and moved on to the next passenger.

Her pa said? How much had Pa paid the man to act as her overseer? She gritted her teeth. Did he think she was a child? And how unfair of Pa to resort to tears and a heart-tugging story about her mother—a story he'd never mentioned before in sixteen years—in order to get the upper hand. An arrow of guilt skewered through her. All right, maybe the story was true, but why wait until now to tell her? Anger smoldered within her breast, but she squashed it. She'd need a clear, level head to come up with a plan.

She leaned her head back against the seat and closed her eyes to the landscape sliding past her window. Was this how a rabbit felt when it got caught in a snare?

"Can I get you a blanket, Miss Denton?"

Rosemary opened her eyes to find Henry peering down at her. Her lips quivered with the retort she wanted to fire back, but she swallowed the words. "No, thank you."

"Anything you need, miss, you just call on ol' Henry." He patted her shoulder.

Indeed. What she needed was for this train to turn around and take her home. Could he do that? Perhaps if she feigned sleep, her keeper would leave her alone.

She had to think.

Henry's solicitous attention only confirmed what she already knew: Pa didn't believe she was grown up enough to make her own decisions or take care of herself. She simply had to prove him wrong.

◆　◆　◆

Rosemary opened her eyes and groaned when she tried to stretch. Travel-weary, the rocking motion of the train had lulled her to sleep, but her cramped position left her muscles stiff.

"Swwweeeetwater, Nebraska." Henry's singsong voice echoed through the car. "Thirty minute stop here, folks. The train will blow the whistle five minutes before we get underway again. There's a café across the way, mercantile and emporium both just down the street. Post office around the corner. Sweetwater, Nebraska. Thirty minute stop." He kept up his spiel from one car into the next.

After two days of occupying an uncomfortable train seat, Rosemary didn't care for a café, mercantile, or post office. What she truly wanted was a place to freshen herself and don clean garments. She felt as grimy as the cinder-coated windows. She smoothed her dress and tidied her hair the best she could.

The forward motion of the train slowed, and the brakes began to squeal as the town of Sweetwater came into sight. She curbed her impatience to disembark until the train lurched to a full stop. Ducking her head to peek out the window afforded her a better view of the depot. Half the size of the Laramie station, the limestone building reflected the morning sun, giving it a nearly alabaster appearance. She squinted against the glare.

The passengers elbowed past Rosemary as they scrambled for the exits. She stuffed her reticule into the bottom of her valise, and then plopped the bag on her seat to indicate it was occupied before scurrying after the others.

Her legs wobbled when she set foot on the unmoving ground, and Henry reached out to steady her. "Careful there, missy." And he patted her shoulder again. She refrained from rolling her eyes.

While most of the passengers headed across the street to the café or the mercantile, Rosemary just wished for solitude. She'd decided the worst part of traveling was the lack of privacy. The billowing prairie grass and sprinkling of colorful wildflowers behind the depot beckoned. The wind teased tendrils of her hair from their pins, and the sun on her face lifted her spirits. The fragrance of the grass reminded her of the grazing range back home, and the ache in her chest grew.

As she walked, the fresh air blew the cobwebs from her mind. She bent and picked a few daisies and buttercups, twirling them between her fingers. She needed to think. She needed a plan.

"There's bound to be some kind of social event once I arrive in Philadelphia. I'll ask Uncle Quentin for some money for a new dress and whatever else my cousins think I need. Aunt Florence will get him to agree. But instead of buyin' a dress, I'll use the money to purchase a ticket home."

The plan might be deceitful, but she brushed aside pangs of conscience as she climbed up a gentle slope. She'd do whatever it took to go home. Wade had said he loved her when he coaxed her for a kiss. Was it love she felt for him in return, or was she simply caught up in the flattery? How was she to know how love felt? She'd never been in love before. But if her plan worked, she'd be back home soon, and love could have a chance to grow.

Stopping at the top of the rise, she closed her eyes and let the wind blow her hair, not caring if her tresses became tangled. There was nobody here to impress.

Pink wild roses in the distance caught her eye, and she hiked toward them through the rippling green waves of prairie vegetation. She plucked the blushing blooms and lifted them to her nose. Their sweet fragrance pulled her lips into a smile before she nestled them into her bouquet. Long strands of grass bound the stems together.

A train whistle sounded from afar off. Another train coming through the valley approaching the Sweetwater station?

She glanced back in the direction she'd come and nearly dropped her flowers. The prairie grass all but swallowed the town of Sweetwater, and the depot looked so tiny it could have been a toy. How could she have walked so far? Had thirty minutes passed already?

Rosemary began running, but the long grasses and thorny vines snaked out and snagged her skirt and entangled her ankles. She stumbled and fell. The thorns bit into her flesh, and she winced but frantically tried to free herself from the entrapping vine. Her efforts were mocked by the distinctive sound of ripping fabric.

"Nooo." Her heart pounded double time as she glanced up toward the train from her seat on the sun-warmed ground. It still sat in front of the depot, but was building up steam. Surely Henry would notice she wasn't on board and make the train wait until she got there. With resolute tugging, she finally freed her skirt. She pushed away from the ground and scrambled to her feet, her hem hoisted to her knees. And she ran. The long grass slapped at her, as if laughing at her impaired progress.

Black smoke billowed from the locomotive. A few hundred yards still stretched between her and the depot when the train began to roll forward. Its shrieking whistle drowned out her shout.

"Wait! I'm coming! Wait for me!"

Chapter Three

J eremy stowed the mail bag from the train in the compartment under the counter where Otto had instructed. The postmaster would come for it later in the afternoon. So far, he'd not run into any issues he couldn't handle in the agent's absence, and putting one more incident-free train layover under his belt boosted his confidence.

"Wait! Come back!"

Jeremy jerked his head up. What was the shouting about? He stepped to the door. A young woman in a dark blue dress ran alongside the tracks in the direction of the departed train, waving her hand.

The smoke from the train trailing in thick black puffs far down the tracks indicated it was picking up speed. The woman stopped and bent at the waist.

Jeremy strode to the edge of the platform, leaped off, and ran toward the woman. "Ma'am? What's wrong? Are you all right?"

The lace on her bodice heaved in and out along with her labored breathing, and her red face evidenced how hard she'd run.

But her eyes. . .

Jeremy's pulse staggered. He'd never seen eyes such a deep shade of violet. "M–ma'am, perhaps you should come and sit down. Can I get you some water?"

She gulped and nodded, but her mute expression screamed distress. Jeremy took her arm and gently steered her to the depot. Her quaking hand sent arrows of misgiving through him.

"Are you all right? Should I summon a doctor?"

They reached the shadow of the overhanging depot roof, and she gave a weak shake of her head. "No, I–I'm f–fine."

Jeremy wasn't convinced. He ushered her inside to one of the chairs, praying the flimsy thing wouldn't collapse. "Sit here while I get you a drink of water."

He rushed out the back door and yanked the pump handle up and down until cool water gushed forth. He caught the liquid in a dipper and returned, carefully balancing the vessel so as not to spill its contents. "Here. Sip this."

She did so and then drew trembling fingers across her brow. Tangles of askew chestnut hair fell from loosened pins.

"Thank you, Mr.—"

Forbes almost slipped out. "Reide. Jeremy Reide. Are you quite certain you don't need a doctor?"

Her shoulders slumped. She looked away from him, and her head dipped. "Miss

Rosemary Denton, and no, I don't need a doctor. I just missed my train is all."

Jeremy glanced out the filthy window, but the only evidence of the train was a dissipating puff of smoke far in the distance. "You were supposed to be on that train? I don't recall you purchasing a ticket."

Miss Denton tossed a sideways glare at him. "My ticket was purchased in Laramie. I got off the train while it was stopped to go for a walk, but I'm afraid I wandered too far."

Jeremy straightened. Otto hadn't included this kind of predicament in his instructions, but it shouldn't be too difficult to figure out. "I see. Well, I can get you on the next train. Let me see your ticket and I'll change it for you."

She pushed unruly locks of hair behind her ear. "I can't. My ticket is in my reticule, which is on the train along with my valise and trunks." She held up her empty hands.

"Oh." He bit the inside of his lip and sorted through possibilities. "Perhaps you could send a wire to someone, a family member or—"

She cocked her head. "You weren't listenin'. Everything I had with me is on the train, includin' my reticule. I have no luggage, no ticket, and no money to send a wire."

Staring into her eyes robbed him of reasonable thought, so he plunked his hands on his hips and studied the tips of his shoes. He certainly had money to help her; that wasn't an issue. He reached into his pocket and withdrew a few coins.

"The telegraph office is right next door." He held out the coins.

"No, no." She intertwined her fingers together at her waist. "I can't take your money."

Jeremy raised his eyebrows and smiled. "What other choice do you have?" He helped her to her feet. "Come on. I'll introduce you to Arne. He'll send your wire for you."

He walked her to the telegraph office and then set out down the street. Having only been in Sweetwater for less than two weeks, he knew few people. But the two folks who came to mind were the pastor of the local church and his sweet wife. The moment they'd seen his unfamiliar face in church last Sunday, they wasted no time inviting him to dinner and making him feel at home.

He hurried to their cottage and knocked. The pastor's wife opened the door, and her gray eyes twinkled. "Well, hello, Jeremy." She wiped her hands on her apron. "Now how did you know I was baking cookies today? Come on in and have some."

Jeremy grinned. The aroma of baking confections taunted him to take her up on the invitation, but he had to get back to the depot. "Thanks, Mrs. Collins, not today. But I do have a favor to ask." He glanced back toward the direction of the depot. "A young woman is stranded here in Sweetwater. She got off the train when it stopped for fuel and then missed reboarding when it left again. Everything she owns is on board, and she's alone. I wondered if—"

Mrs. Collins held up her hand. "Don't say another word. You bring her here and Reverend Collins and I will take good care of her until she can be on her way again."

Was it improper to hug a lady nearly old enough to be his grandmother? He grasped her hand instead. "Thank you, Mrs. Collins. She's sending a wire right now, but I'll bring her by when she's finished."

The lines around the woman's eyes deepened along with her smile. "I'll get the extra bedroom ready."

By the time Jeremy returned to the depot, Miss Denton sat on one of the chairs.

Telltale splashes on her dress indicated she had apparently found the pump out back and had put herself back together the best she could. Her face, no longer flushed, was framed by chestnut tendrils.

"Did you get your wire sent?"

"Yes." The word came out more like a sigh than a reply. "My father's ranch is about ten miles outside of Laramie, so it'll take a while for someone to carry the telegram all the way out there." She shaded her eyes against the midday sun.

Jeremy could almost read her thoughts. "Look, it might be tomorrow before you get a response to your wire." He shoved his hands in his pockets. "There is a railroad boardinghouse, but I don't recommend it for a lady."

She stood and twisted her fingers. "I don't have money for a boardinghouse or a hotel. Could I stay h–here inside the depot? I mean. . .th–the depot closes overnight, doesn't it?" Her face reddened, and she dropped her gaze.

Jeremy waved off her stammering entreaty. "The wife of the local pastor said they'd be delighted for you to stay with them. Reverend and Mrs. Collins are wonderful people, and you'll be safe there."

An odd combination of relief and discomfort filled Miss Denton's expression. "That's very nice of them, but I hate to be a bother. Besides, I can't pay them."

Jeremy suppressed a smile. So she had a proud streak, did she? "Reverend and Mrs. Collins will be happy for your company, but if you were to offer to help out with a few chores I'm sure it would be appreciated."

Miss Denton hesitated before she nodded. "All right, as long as I can work for my keep."

Jeremy extended his arm. "Right this way, Miss Denton."

◆　◆　◆

Rosemary opened her eyes and for a moment couldn't remember where she was. No rocking motion or clacking of wheels against the rails disturbed the quiet. Had the train stopped?

She sat up, groping her hand along the edge of the soft quilt. She remembered now. Reverend and Mrs. Collins had treated her like a long-lost relative yesterday. The still-dark bedroom was tiny but comfortable. She swung her legs over the edge of the cot. Pale streaks painted the sky through the east-facing window.

Rosemary donned her dress and made her way to the kitchen. She lit the lamp and found the wood bin. By the time Mrs. Collins came out of the other bedroom, Rosemary had the fire going in the stove, a pot of coffee boiling, and flapjacks on the griddle.

"Good morning, dear." The pastor's wife gave Rosemary's shoulders a squeeze, sending a twinge of regret skittering through Rosemary. She couldn't remember her mother's hugs.

Mrs. Collins reached for coffee mugs. "Why, look at this. I can't remember the last time someone cooked breakfast for me."

Reverend Collins emerged from the bedroom. "Good morning, ladies. Something smells mighty good out here." He poured himself a cup of coffee and leaned to peck his wife on the cheek.

The three sat down for their meal, and the pastor lifted his voice to heaven, giving God thanks for His provision and praise for His faithfulness. Rosemary listened, intrigued as the man spoke to God like He was right there at the table with them. Emotions she couldn't identify tangled in her middle. What might it be like to talk to God in such a way?

"What are your plans today, Rosemary?" Mrs. Collins's question jolted her out of her reverie.

She picked up her fork. "I'll go to the telegraph office this mornin' to see if there's any reply from my father." She drew in a deep breath, dreading what he'd say when he learned of her foolishness. "Thank you both, for bein' so kind and givin' me a place to stay."

"Oh, my dear." Mrs. Collins reached for Rosemary's hand. "It was our pleasure. I rather hope you can stay a few more days, but I know you're anxious to continue your trip."

Rosemary dropped her gaze to the flapjacks on her plate and bit her lip. Truth be told, she wasn't anxious at all. She insisted on doing the dishes and cleaning the kitchen, lingering to put off the inevitable. When she finished, she thanked her hosts again and relished the warm hug from Mrs. Collins. Reluctance weighted her feet as she trudged to the telegraph office.

Arne Rheinholdt, the telegrapher she'd met yesterday, looked up as she entered. Tufts of gray hair stuck out from around his visor, and black garters held up the sleeves of his faded shirt.

"Mornin', miss." Arne scratched his head. "Afraid I don't have very good news for you. That there wire you sent yesterday didn't go through. Seems the lines are down somewhere between here and Laramie."

She didn't know whether to frown or smile. "So my father still doesn't know I'm here?"

"Reckon not. Sure am sorry, but there ain't nothin' I can do from this end 'cept wait till I get word the lines are back up and workin'." Arne rubbed his gnarly hand over several days' growth of whiskers. "Sometimes it's a couple o' weeks before they get it repaired."

She mumbled a thank-you and stepped back out into the brilliant sunlight. Now what?

"Miss Denton?" Mr. Reide from the train depot walked toward her. "Did you get a reply?"

She shook her head and repeated Arne's grim report. "It looks like I'll be stayin' in Sweetwater longer than I thought. Do you know where I can find a temporary job?"

Mr. Reide pinched his chin between his thumb and forefinger. "As a matter of fact, I do. You can work right here in the depot. I've tried to clean the place, but I'm afraid I'm not very good at it."

Rosemary glanced around the train station. It surely needed a good scouring. She shuddered to think how many layers of grime coated the floor, and the view out the windows was barely discernible. But hard work didn't scare her. She nodded. "I can do that."

He stepped behind the counter and opened the cash box. "The job pays two dollars a week, and I'll advance you two weeks' wages so you can buy what you need." He held out four silver dollars.

She pulled her hand back in hesitation, but Mr. Reide grinned. "Look around. You'll earn it."

He spoke the truth. She took the four dollars. "Where will I find a mop and bucket?"

Chapter Four

Jeremy led Miss Denton to the tiny supply closet tucked into a niche behind the office. She'd declared the rags and mop she found there would have to be washed out first before they'd be of any use, and she'd gotten right to work. He had to admire her spunk—she certainly wasn't feeling sorry for herself.

He pulled out his watch and flipped it open. Just over an hour before the 11:15 a.m. eastbound arrived. Plenty of time. He jogged down the street to the Collins' house. He found Mrs. Collins on her knees in the garden.

When he called to her, she looked up and adjusted her bonnet. "Well, land sakes, Jeremy, what brings you around here again so soon?" Her smile faded. "Is Rosemary all right?"

Jeremy helped Mrs. Collins to her feet. "Yes, ma'am, she's fine. But she is why I'm here."

Mrs. Collins shaded her eyes. "Go on."

Jeremy explained about the telegraph lines being down and the length of time it could take before Rosemary's wire could be sent. "So she is going to need a place to stay for an indefinite length of time."

Mrs. Collins flapped her hand. "Pshaw, that's not a problem. I told her this morning I wished she could stay longer."

"Well. . ." Jeremy rubbed his chin. "The problem is she'll likely refuse any offer she sees as charity. I gave her a job cleaning the depot, so may I suggest you come to an agreement on a small amount of rent and let her do some chores?"

Exasperation spread across the woman's face. "If you say so, I'll let her pay her way, much as I dislike it. It's our pleasure having her stay. You go tell her she has a home here for as long as she needs it."

"Thank you, Mrs. Collins. You're an angel." He headed back to the depot with a lightness in his step. The prospect of having Rosemary Denton around for a couple of weeks made him giddier than it ought. His father would berate him for not keeping his mind on his work, but after all, didn't scripture direct him to minister to those in need?

Who was he fooling? Certainly not God. Were he honest, he'd have to admit her presence rendered more than an opportunity to minister. The moment he'd laid eyes on her, his tongue tied and he had to remind himself to breathe. Last night's dream of wide, violet eyes and tendrils of chestnut hair bore witness of his ulterior motive.

As he leaped over the rails and bounded up the steps, a thought struck him. Nobody knew he was the son of John Murray Forbes. Everyone knew him as Jeremy Reide. How would he justify giving Miss Denton a job without anyone's permission? And what would Otto say when he returned to work?

◆ ◆ ◆

Jeremy meticulously recorded the purchase of the three tickets from Sweetwater to Chicago in the daily ledger, noting the transfer in Omaha. He glanced at the older couple with the little girl—obviously a grandchild—sitting on the two flimsy chairs as they waited for the arrival of the eastbound train. The grandmother's attempts to control the restless, fretful youngster were fruitless. No doubt it would be a long trip for the trio.

To the right of the grandparents, Miss Denton polished the last of the front windows. From time to time she sent a smile to the tyke. Jeremy watched as she sorted through her pile of clean rags until she found one she liked. Then she sat on the floor and beckoned to the little girl.

"Come and look what I can do." She bent her head over the piece of cloth and carefully tore a wide strip off one end. The child stopped and fixed her mischievous eyes on Miss Denton's activity.

Miss Denton held up the pieces of cloth and scrunched the smaller one into a wad, tucking it into the center of the large square piece.

Jeremy propped his elbow on the counter with his chin in his palm and watched, as fascinated as the child. The little girl took a few tentative steps toward the depot cleaning woman.

"Whatcha doin'?"

A tiny smile tipped the corners of Miss Denton's lips. "I was a little lonely, so I thought I would make a new friend. Do you want to see?"

The tyke's gold curls tumbled as she nodded and stepped closer. Miss Denton pulled a few threads from the frayed edge of the cloth, which she used to tie around the wadded up ball in the middle. "What's your name?"

"M'inda."

Miss Denton looked over at the frazzled grandmother. The older woman managed a half smile. "Her name is Melinda."

With a barely perceptible nod, Miss Denton returned her attention to Melinda, who edged a bit closer.

"What is it?"

Miss Denton's smile deepened. "You'll see. Watch." She smoothed out one edge of the material to the corner, twisted it and tied a knot, and then repeated the process on the opposite side. Melinda stood transfixed.

Jeremy couldn't stop the smile that grew on his face. After a few tucks, tugs, and adjustments, Miss Denton held up her creation for the child's assessment.

"Doll!" The little girl clapped her hands to accompany the delight in her voice.

The amazing young woman who he'd hired to scrub floors pointed to Jeremy. "Why don't you go over and ask Mr. Reide if you can borrow his pencil."

Melinda observed Jeremy with shyness but made her way to the counter. "Pencil?"

Jeremy withdrew the pencil from behind his ear and handed it over. Melinda reached out a hesitant hand and took the pencil, murmured something that sounded a little like thank you, and scampered back to Miss Denton.

"Whatcha do wi' the pencil?"

Miss Denton patted the floor beside her. Melinda plopped down and leaned close while Miss Denton used the pencil to create two dots for eyes and curving smile on the face of the rag doll.

Melinda looked up at Miss Denton and grinned. "C'n I hold her?"

Miss Denton held the doll up to her ear, as if the doll whispered a secret. "She tells me she's been hopin' a little girl named Melinda would come along. She says she wants to stay with you, because she thinks you're beautiful."

A knot formed in Jeremy's throat. The young woman sitting before him on the floor was beautiful.

Little Melinda's eyes widened, and her mouth fell open. "She's mine?"

Miss Denton nodded. "She can be yours, on one condition. You must listen to your grandparents and obey them. Because you don't want to teach your new doll bad habits."

The little imp glanced at her grandparents, and a slow smile stretched her lips. "C'n I name her Ruth? That was my mama's name."

Jeremy could tell by Miss Denton's reaction that she understood the ramifications of the child's statement. She pressed her lips together and closed her eyes for a moment, as if in empathy with the tiny soul beside her. "I think that's the perfect name." She laid the rag doll in the child's hands like it was a priceless thing.

Melinda stared at the doll for a moment and then scrambled to her feet. She threw her arms around the neck of the stranger in the train station who had become a friend for a lonely child. Then she dashed back to her grandparents to show them her new treasure.

Jeremy ducked his head and rubbed his palm over his eyes while he struggled to swallow the lump in his throat. Whether she knew it or not, Miss Denton had just demonstrated Christ's command to comfort the brokenhearted.

"Here's your pencil." A soft voice tugged his attention, and deep violet eyes greeted him when he looked up.

Jeremy cleared his throat. "That was a very nice thing you did."

She shrugged. "That little girl reminded me of myself at that age. She just needed somethin' to love."

Her words touched him deeply, and he wished he could wrap her in his protective embrace. Instead, he took his pencil and sent his focus to the child, now sitting on her grandmother's lap, cuddling her doll.

"Well, she looks happy now, thanks to you."

The whistle of the approaching train sounded in the distance, and the little family gathered their belongings. The grandmother nodded her thanks as they exited the depot, and Melinda turned. "G'bye, lady."

Miss Denton waved. "Good-bye, Melinda. Remember what I said." She glanced at Jeremy. "Well, I'd best get back to work before I get fired."

Jeremy studied her retreating form. *Not much chance of that happening, Miss Denton.* With all the challenges of learning the ins and outs of managing a depot, the brightest part of his job was seeing Rosemary Denton every day.

◆ ◆ ◆

Rosemary smoothed her hands down the lavender calico dress Mrs. Collins had given her. When she'd tried to refuse the gift, the dear lady had clucked her tongue and declared she couldn't fit into it anymore and Rosemary might as well put it to good use. A slightly faded green gingham dress also hung from a peg in her room along with one of Mrs. Collins's old aprons.

She'd risen early to help Mrs. Collins with the washing, assuring her new friend she'd retrieve the dry laundry off the clothesline when she came home at lunchtime.

Home. The word gave her pause. Home was on the Double D Ranch in Wyoming. Her intention was to return there as soon as she could. But thinking of this place as a temporary home wasn't in the least distasteful.

Her first stop was the post office to mail the letter she'd written to her father. She'd struggled over the missive for hours, explaining how she felt and why she disagreed with him. But how would he react to the request she'd scribbled in at the end? She'd find out soon enough. At least he'd know where she was and that she had a safe place to stay. Reverend Collins added a note, assuring her father they'd take good care of his daughter.

Since Arne had assured her the lines eastward were operating, she stopped at the telegraph office and sent a short wire to Philadelphia informing her aunt and uncle she'd not be arriving as scheduled and promised a letter to follow.

The clean windows of the depot winked at her in the morning sun as she made her way down the boardwalk. A thread of pride twined through her. It had taken three full days, but the Sweetwater depot fairly sparkled.

Mr. Reide greeted her when she stepped through the door. "Good morning. New dress?"

Now why did it please her that he'd noticed? "Mrs. Collins made over a couple of her old dresses she can't wear anymore."

"The color becomes you." Mr. Reide's appreciative expression made her face heat.

She mumbled a thank-you and headed for the storage closet. Her broom offered no compliment, but the depot agent's words sang in her ears.

Rosemary set her mind on her duties, sweeping and mopping between passengers and freighters coming and going. During a lull, she paused at the counter. "Might I get into the office to clean?"

"Sure." He stepped aside to allow her access to the cubicle.

She took stock of the wood shavings littering the corners, disorganized papers in haphazard stacks, and stains on the desk that defied description. First, she attacked the floor with her broom.

Mr. Reide leaned against the doorframe. "So, you're from Wyoming."

She nodded. "I grew up on a ranch not far from Laramie." She angled the broom to capture every bit of debris.

"Brothers and sisters?"

"Three brothers. No sisters." She maneuvered the dirt toward her dustpan.

Mr. Reide scooted out of the broom's path. "Why were you going east?"

Rosemary straightened and raised her eyes to meet his. Should she tell him her father was sending her away because one of the ranch hands had flirted with her? "To visit relatives. Why?"

Red stole into Mr. Reide's face. "Sorry. That's really none of my business. It's just that you struck me as. . .not very anxious to get where you were going."

She sighed and leaned on the broom handle. "I wasn't. This interruption in my travel plans isn't really an inconvenience. I've barely been here a week, but I like Sweetwater. I love Reverend and Mrs. Collins, and I've met some interestin' people workin' here."

Mr. Reide grinned. "Does that include me?" The redness in his face deepened. "I guess that was a bit forward."

Rosemary cocked her head. It especially included him, but propriety dictated she respond with discretion. "People comin' and goin'. Makes me wonder where they're headed and if they're happy to go home."

There was that word again. How could a word that drew such deep longing a week ago stir up such confusion now?

Chapter Five

The tapping of a hammer pulled Jeremy's attention from the ledger in which he was recording a stack of freight bills of lading. He laid aside his pencil and leaned around the corner of the office.

Miss Denton knelt on the floor beside an overturned chair, her head bent in concentration. Her small tack hammer rat-a-tatted on the stretcher bracing the two back legs.

He edged closer and peered over her shoulder. "What are you doing?"

She glanced up. "I'm fixin' these chairs so nobody gets hurt. Both of them are ready to fall apart." She directed a dab of glue into the mortise slot and tapped in the tenon, finishing it off by driving a nail through the joint. "My father would have a conniption if he saw me usin' a nail on a mortise and tenon, but since it already came apart once, the nail'll make it more secure."

Jeremy pinched his chin. Neither his privileged background nor his Yale education ever afforded him the opportunity to become acquainted with tools or their use. Still, shouldn't a gentleman take the hammer and perform the repair for her? He was half-afraid to offer for fear she'd take him up on it. "Need some help?"

She arched her brows. "I know how to handle a hammer."

He didn't know whether to be rebuffed or relieved. "I can see that. I just thought I ought to ask."

The corners of her lips twitched. "By the time I was ten years old, I could hammer barbed wire onto fence posts as well as my brothers." She turned the chair right-side up. "Care to try it out?"

Jeremy drew in a breath. If he refused, he'd offend her. If he sat on the chair and her repairs weren't sound, he could end up on the floor looking foolish. He lifted his shoulders and held out his hand toward the chair. "Ladies first."

She folded her arms and huffed. "You don't trust me."

He made a gallant bow. "Just being a gentleman."

A girlish giggle escaped her lips, and mischief twinkled in her eyes. "Well, it might be a good idea to let the glue dry first."

Jeremy threw his head back and laughed. "Miss Denton, remind me to never allow you to serve as a switchman." He shook his head. "I'll wager you can hold your own, whether on a cattle ranch with your brothers or back east fending off the dandies."

A rosy blush stole into her cheeks, causing her eyes to take on a deeper hue of violet. "You'd be right about that."

His heart stuttered. Unable to pull his gaze away from her, he allowed himself to be captured by her charm. He'd known many young women in his social circles, but he'd never met one quite like Rosemary Denton. He ran his hand through his hair. "Would you mind terribly—that is, would you find it offensive if I asked you to call me Jeremy?"

Her smile deepened two beguiling indentations on either side of her lips, and she lowered her lashes. "I wouldn't be offended at all, as long as you call me Rosemary."

◆　◆　◆

Rosemary glanced up from the windowsill she was dusting to see Jeremy emerge from the telegraph office next door. Apprehension poked her. Her father had certainly received her letter by now.

Pa would be annoyed that she'd been so careless as to miss her train. He might even believe she'd done it on purpose out of spite. But the stirring in her heart was about more than Wade's flirtation or Pa's insistence that she go east to become a lady. Over the past two weeks, her reluctance had taken on a different sentiment. She'd discovered she liked Sweetwater and working at the train depot. Despite having to sweep floors and clean windows to support herself, she found the job offered her something she'd never had before: independence. The feeling of accomplishment when she finished a day's work bolstered her confidence.

She checked the mail daily to see if she'd received a reply to her letter. Maybe Pa would wait until the telegraph lines were working again, or he might even jump on the next train and come for her himself. Every time an eastbound train pulled into the station, she held her breath, expecting to see her father or one of her brothers disembark. A knot tightened in her stomach. She only hoped Pa would take her entreaty to heart and see that she was no longer a little girl but a resourceful and industrious grown woman, capable of making her own choices. It took more than tea parties and fancy dresses to make a lady. She hoped he would look past her imprudent mistake and think her resourceful and levelheaded in the face of her dilemma.

She moved to run her dustcloth over the chairs. Every time she imagined Pa's insistence on her going to Philadelphia, she gritted her teeth. If he refused her request and still made her go, she just wouldn't stay, that's all. He couldn't force her to stay.

Jeremy entered the depot. "Arne says word is the lines should be up later today. He suggested you check with him in the morning."

Rosemary pushed out a sigh. "Thanks. I will."

Jeremy straddled one of the newly repaired—and now sturdy—chairs. "You don't sound terribly enthusiastic."

Unsure if sharing her tangled feelings with Jeremy was a good idea, she shrugged. Pastor Collins's Sunday sermon lingered in her mind, and she'd started a half-dozen times to tell Mrs. Collins what weighed on her heart but doubted the woman would approve of her intention to defy her father. In all likelihood, Jeremy would agree with the pastor's wife.

He ran his fingers over the worn edge of the chair back. "I remember you said you were going to visit relatives. Where do they live?"

"In a village just outside of Philadelphia called Ardmore."

"Ardmore." Jeremy blinked, and his eyebrows arched before dipping into a frown. "It's on the main line. I know the area."

Rosemary focused her attention on polishing the brass hardware at the entrance. A sliver of panic needled her. What if Jeremy knew her aunt and uncle? Should she tell him she'd never been east of Cheyenne until two and a half weeks ago? "I've never been there. My cousins wrote about the parties and balls they attend. Suppose I'll be joinin' them."

"No doubt." Jeremy rose from the chair. "Well, I should get back to those shipping invoices. Otto is due back today, and I want to make sure everything is caught up."

Otto? She frowned. Who was Otto?

"Oh, I remember. You said Otto is the regular depot agent." Her stomach tightened. Did this mean Otto was the boss? What if he didn't think the depot needed a cleaning woman and fired her?

"Does Otto know you hired me?"

A smile eased the furrow in Jeremy's brow. "No, but I'll introduce you when he gets here. Don't worry."

Don't worry? He'd read her mind.

◆　◆　◆

Jeremy settled in behind the tidy desk and opened the ledger. Each entry reflected the care he'd taken to record every transaction with accuracy. But Rosemary's words echoed in his mind and distracted him from the columns of figures.

She had family living in Ardmore—one of the rural areas where Philadelphia's wealthiest families built summer houses to escape the heat of the low-lying parts of center city. His own parents had spent a couple of summers there when he was in college.

He propped his elbows on the desk and held his head in his hands. What had he done? A young woman from the upper crust of society, probably on her way east to become a debutante, and he offered her a job mopping floors and washing windows. She hadn't given the impression she was insulted, but perhaps she was just being kind. Or she may have realized she had no choice. She was, after all, in a rather desperate situation, having been stranded without any money and no way to reach her father. He could only imagine what went through her mind.

It seemed odd, though, that she wasn't more anxious to be on her way. If she had wealthy relatives waiting for her arrival, she could have wired them of her predicament and asked them to send her funds for a new ticket, even if she couldn't reach her father in Wyoming. Yes, she could handle a hammer and perhaps even string barbed wire fencing. But why in heaven's name was she here cleaning the depot and living in a modest little cottage when she could be living in a mansion in Ardmore being waited on and pampered? No doubt about it, Rosemary Denton was a mystery.

He recorded the last invoice and filed it. Otto wouldn't recognize the place when he returned. The office was spotless and the desk clear of all clutter, every piece of paper filed properly and the ledgers all up to date. He checked the clock. Westbound wasn't due for another hour.

He pulled his Bible from his satchel. The envelope from his father's latest letter marked the place where he wanted to pick up reading. He noted with an element of chagrin that his father had omitted his name from the return address—no doubt to maintain Jeremy's anonymity. Guilt pinched him again. He understood his father's reasons for not wanting anyone to know Jeremy was his son during this time. The best way to learn the railroad industry, starting with the lowliest jobs, was to step into the experience as an equal. People like Otto needed to view him as nothing more than an apprentice, and that wouldn't happen if they knew his true identity. But he didn't like being less than honest. Especially with Rosemary.

He tucked the envelope into the back flap and began soaking in God's Word.

"What are you reading?"

Jeremy jerked his head up. Rosemary stood in front of the counter, peering at his open Bible.

"Psalm 62." He pointed to the page and began to read aloud. "My soul, wait thou only upon God; for my expectation is from him. He only is my rock and my salvation; he is my defence; I shall not be moved." He looked up at her, and his breath caught.

Moisture brimmed in her eyes. "I wish I knew what to expect from God."

Jeremy reached across the counter and touched her fingers. "Do you pray?"

She shook her head. "I listen when Reverend Collins prays. Sometimes I feel like I'm eavesdroppin' on a personal conversation. I never knew you could talk to God like that. I found my mother's Bible a few years ago and read parts of it, but it confused me. I wish I knew what my mother believed. Maybe if she'd lived, she might've taught me to pray."

Compassion flooded Jeremy's soul, and his heart quickened. "I'm sure no expert, but I read God's Word, and He speaks to me through it. Praying is like talking to my best friend, only better, because I'm talking to the One who created me and loves me."

An expression of wonderment fell across Rosemary's face. "I never heard anyone ever talk about God like that, except maybe Pastor Collins. I wish I knew if my mother talked to Him like you're sayin'."

The wistfulness in her voice tugged at him. "Do you still have her Bible? Maybe she made some notations in it."

Rosemary lifted her shoulders. "I suppose it's back home—at the ranch, I mean."

Jeremy turned the Bible around so Rosemary could read it, and he pointed to the verse. "This is what you can expect from God: His strength, His salvation, His defense, and more. He will give you peace, comfort, mercy, and best of all, His love. When you trust God, He will never leave you alone."

She stared at the page for a full minute. "Truly?"

"Truly. God will never promise something and then betray you."

She blinked and swallowed. He wished he could read her thoughts. Turmoil was evident in her eyes. Had someone broken a promise to her? Or worse, betrayed her? Jeremy kept his tone gentle. "The Bible is full of God's promises. I'd like the chance to show them to you."

A tremulous smile wobbled over her face. "I'd like that."

"Well, ain't that nice." Otto's voice growled from the doorway. "Thought I'd come back to find you workin', not holdin' a Sunday school class."

Chapter Six

Queasiness unsettled Rosemary for the remainder of the day. Every time she looked up, Otto's eyes were fixed on her, following her around the depot. His scowl sent a shudder through her.

From the window, she caught sight of Jeremy out on the platform, talking with a man about a load of freight. He pointed and scribbled notations on his clipboard as sturdy crates of various sizes disappeared into the gaping jaws of the boxcars.

She let his words linger in her memory. *"When you trust God, He will never leave you alone."* His voice had rung with assurance, as if he knew by experience what he said was true. The idea of God always being close by when she was frightened or lonely or confused appealed to her. It was that first part—the trusting part—that she couldn't quite grasp. Did it mean she was supposed to trust God the way she trusted her father? He'd forced her into something she didn't want to do. Wouldn't it require a very special kind of person to trust in a God she couldn't see? Her questions certainly weren't leaving her alone.

The activity out on the platform stepped up with the blowing of the train's whistle. When the final container was stowed and the door of the boxcar closed and secure, Jeremy glanced toward the depot windows and their gazes connected. A smile tipped his lips, and he lifted his fingers in acknowledgement.

They'd not had an opportunity to speak since Otto's arrival. The regular agent settled himself in the cubicle, and she went about her tasks with his scrutiny boring a hole in the back of her head. The two men had conversed, and though she couldn't hear their exchange, judging by Otto's sharp glances in her direction she suspected she was the topic of debate. When Jeremy calmly retrieved the clipboard, he'd sent her a reassuring smile as he headed out the door. But even now, as she paused by the window to watch Jeremy perform his duties, she sorely wished she knew what they'd discussed.

"All aboard." The conductor's bellow drew her attention. Jeremy tossed the mail bag to the conductor and waved. The train engine's growl began to build from a rumble to a roar.

The westbound 5:15 pulled out of the station, hissing steam and chugging great black clouds in its wake. As soon as the train departed and the smoke cleared, Rosemary retrieved her bucket and rags and scurried outside to remove the grime left on the windows by the steam and cinders.

"You cleaned the windows this morning."

Rosemary glanced up to find Jeremy leaning against the door frame. She shrugged.

"I know. But when I come to work in the mornin', I like for them to shine in the sunlight." She halted the motion of her rag against the glass. "Am I comin' to work in the mornin'?"

Jeremy's brow dipped slightly. "Yes, of course you are. But I'm not."

Rosemary dropped her rag, and her hand clutched her stomach. "What? Did Otto fire you? Was he angry because you hired me?"

Amusement pulled Jeremy's face into a cockeyed half smile. "No. Otto isn't my boss, and your job with the Burlington and Missouri is safe." He hesitated, and the smile faded. "My training requires that I work many different jobs. My time here as a depot agent is over, and the next job is learning to manage freight." He appeared to study the window she'd just finished wiping. "Tomorrow I head up the line to the Grand Island station."

A cloak of heaviness fell over her. "Will you. . ." She pressed her lips together. Asking about his intentions wasn't ladylike, but the desire to throw propriety to the winds was nearly her undoing.

"Will I. . .what? Are you asking if I'll be coming through Sweetwater?" A hint of teasing threaded his voice.

He'd read her thoughts again. Could he also hear her heart plummet upon hearing the news he'd no longer be working out of the Sweetwater station? Her cheeks burned, and she stooped to pick up her rag. Maybe her father was right and she needed to learn to become a lady after all. "Guess I've just gotten used to seein' you every day."

He reached and caught her fingers, pulling her gently upright. "Me, too." After a brief squeeze, he released her hand, but his touch made an indelible imprint on her heart if not her skin.

"I'll be based in Grand Island, but the line I'm working on will run between there and North Platte, so I'll come through Sweetwater regularly. I hope to be here on Sundays for church."

Her heart, slumped only moments ago, lifted. She tried to school her features but couldn't stop the smile that grew on her face. "I'll look forward to seein' you."

He cocked his head toward the depot door and winked. "You always have Otto to talk to."

◆ ◆ ◆

That night, Jeremy sat up in bed with his Bible on his lap, but the picture of Rosemary's face in his mind distracted him. He flipped the pages back to the book of Psalms and reread the same verses he'd read to her that morning.

"My soul, wait thou only upon God; for my expectation is from him. He only is my rock and my salvation: he is my defence; I shall not be moved."

The impact on Rosemary's heart had evidenced itself in her tear-filled eyes and the way she'd wrapped her arms around herself. Her faraway expression spoke of conflict within her spirit. If only Otto hadn't chosen that moment to walk in, he might have been able to get her to open up and talk about what was troubling her.

He longed to share with her how the passage also spoke to him, but couldn't do so without breaking his father's trust. Working incognito side by side with the very people who would one day work *for* him pricked his conscience. They knew him as Jeremy Reide, just a common, hardworking fellow who carried a Bible. They'd think him a hypocrite when they learned the truth. He grimaced. How would Rosemary feel when she learned he'd been less than forthcoming about himself? "Lord, please show me what to do."

God alone was his refuge. He prayed Rosemary would find the same sanctuary and solace in the Lord. He whispered, "Amen," and God gave him an idea—to purchase a Bible for Rosemary before he left for Grand Island. "I can't always be with her, but You can, Lord. Thank You."

At least he'd ensured her job was safe. The funds he'd left with Otto would pay her wages for the next several weeks, if she stayed in Sweetwater that long.

◆　◆　◆

Rosemary folded her father's letter and tucked it into her apron pocket. The telegraph lines had been restored for a week, but he'd chosen instead to reply by letter. Pa had never been a man who wasted words, but his missive was short even by his standards.

Was it possible? She read it over three times just to be sure she didn't misunderstand.

> *Your uncle wired me the same day you left, saying your aunt had fallen and broken her ankle. In addition, your cousin Penelope has the mumps. But your train had already left the station when I got the wire. So it seems you've won, at least for now. I've decided to allow you to stay with the Collinses for the summer. But when your aunt and cousin are recuperated, you will go to Philadelphia.*

Despite a twinge of sympathy for Penelope and Aunt Florence, Rosemary couldn't hold back her smile. At the beginning of the whole ordeal, she thought she wanted to stay at the ranch. She was attracted to Wade and thought he was attracted to her. Was it love? Would she even recognize love? She wasn't so sure.

The swirl of confused thoughts dogged her as she went through her morning duties. At least she knew what to do with dirt-tracked floors and dusty windowsills.

The warm afternoon sun pulled sweat to her brow as she tackled a filth-encrusted bench outside at the end of the platform.

"What's that thing?" Otto's bark behind her yanked Rosemary's attention from the task.

She sat back on her heels and shook dirty water from her scrub brush. "It's an old bench."

"I can see that. I ain't a ninny, y'know." Otto tramped to stand beside her and pointed to her latest project. "What're you doin' with it?"

She set the scrub brush aside and emptied the dirty water from her bucket into the alley beside the depot. "I'm cleanin' it up so people can sit on it. There aren't but two chairs in the waitin' area, and until a couple of weeks ago they weren't much better than kindling." She gestured to the bench. "The blacksmith down the street, Mr. Gilstrap, said I could have this bench since he wasn't usin' it. It just needs a good scrubbin'."

Otto snorted. "What for? This place was just fine the way it was." He jerked his thumb toward the waiting room inside. "All that cleanin' and sweepin'. I never seen so much lye soap in all my days. This here is a train depot, not a ladies' tea room. What's next? Flowerpots and doilies? Y'know, the sunlight glare hurts my eyes since you keep cleanin' them windows. All that soap makes the place smell funny."

He stomped back to the door where he stopped to fire a parting shot. "And it makes me feel all itchy." He entered and slammed the door behind him, but not before she caught sight of his whiskers twitching.

After several days of working with Otto without Jeremy's presence, she'd finally begun to realize the grizzled man was all bark and no bite. Even when he groused about her telling him to wipe his feet or move his chair so she could sweep, she got the distinct impression he was amused by her. Of course, it didn't hurt that she brought him cookies and cinnamon rolls from Ada Collins's kitchen. She carried her bucket to the pump out back to refill it with clean water. One more scrub and she could set the bench in the sun to dry.

As she worked the pump handle up and down, her thoughts drifted to Jeremy. He'd said he hoped to be in Sweetwater for Sunday, but thus far she'd only seen him once since he moved on to his new job. The westbound train on which he came in only stopped long enough to unload a few crates and drop off the mail. They barely had time to say hello, and a hollowness took up residence in her chest when the train pulled out again.

That evening she sat with Ada Collins, the two of them working together to stitch a cushion for the bench to hide some of the stains she couldn't scrub out. Rosemary found more than friendship in Ada—the dear woman was a counselor, a confidante, and a patient answerer of questions.

"You know that scripture Pastor Collins read after supper this evening?"

Ada replied with an *mm-hmm* without looking up from her sewing.

Rosemary plied her needle to the cushion. "I don't understand how those men who followed Jesus and acted like they were His best friends could suddenly turn their backs on Him. One betrayed Him to the soldiers and another denied even knowing Him. How could they do that after He'd been so good to them?"

Ada's needle halted midstitch, and the wrinkles around her eyes deepened with her smile. "Pastor Collins will be pleased you were listening. But in answer to your question, the disciples' behavior didn't take Christ by surprise. He knew all along that would happen. Do you remember what He said as He hung on the cross? Forgive them. When those closest to Jesus turned away from Him, it not only demonstrated His own sinlessness, but also His ability to forgive sin."

Rosemary chewed on Ada's words for a moment. "I don't think I'd respond that way if someone betrayed me."

Before she could poke her needle into the cloth again, her own words convicted her. Hadn't she plotted to betray her father? Perhaps not in the same way, but she'd planned to circumvent his will.

She lowered her sewing to her lap and stared into the flame of the kerosene lamp. A startling realization grew in her conscious thought. Her being stranded in Sweetwater was no accident. God had planned it all along. Encountering people like Reverend and Mrs. Collins and Jeremy had introduced her to God in a way she never recognized before. With that new revelation came an understanding of how wrong her plans were. A sudden ache in her middle made her wish she could share the epiphany with Jeremy.

Chapter Seven

Jeremy chafed at the message that came across the wire Saturday afternoon. The urge to kick the nearest object into the next county tempted him, but instead he leaned forward and planted his hands on the desk.

"When did this happen?"

Jonesy, the telegrapher at Grand Island, glanced up at Jeremy's tone. "Look, it ain't my fault a band o' knucklehead outlaws decided to dynamite the track and hold up the train. I'm waitin' on two replies out of the Chicago office before we know when the tracks'll be repaired. Right now, I got a stack o' telegrams to send between here and Omaha and Chicago, 'cause Mr. Forbes is fit to be tied about this. So you're gonna hafta wait."

Caution poked Jeremy with the reminder that he was just a new employee learning the ropes, and he sent Jonesy an apologetic smile.

"Sorry. Didn't mean to bite your head off. It's just that I have. . .an appointment."

The gap between Jonesy's front teeth peeked out underneath his scraggly mustache. "Had a date, did ya?" He guffawed. "Well, the last time somethin' like this happened, it took two days to replace the section of track that got damaged. Don't look like you're gonna keep your date today. Where was you headed?"

"Sweetwater."

Jonesy snorted. "Sweetwater? Ain't nothin' much happenin' in a little town like that."

Jeremy opened his mouth to reply but thought better of it. With Jonesy tapping out messages to and from the different railroad offices, it might be hours before he could send a wire to notify Rosemary of the reason for his absence. He pulled loose one end of his tie and headed back to his room at the boardinghouse. There might not be much happening in Sweetwater, but he'd asked Rosemary if he could escort her to church.

His jaw muscle tightened, and he sucked in a deep breath intended to calm his nerves. No doubt his father was angry and frustrated by the robbery and damage done to his railroad. A sliver of guilt stabbed. After Jonesy assured him nobody had been hurt during the holdup, Jeremy hadn't given much thought to the business ramifications. As the company's future vice president, he should contact his father to inquire if there was anything he could do. But the thoughts taking center stage in his mind now were of Rosemary and whether she'd think he'd broken his word.

He unlocked the door to his room and plopped down into the lumpy chair next to the window. The view from the second-floor window pulled a halfhearted smile onto his face. Between the dust and smears, the vista across the street and down the railroad tracks was partially obscured. Rosemary would never tolerate such dirty windows in *her* depot.

While still stationed in Sweetwater, he couldn't deny his attraction to Rosemary.

Since his departure, the separation left a gaping hole in his heart. He longed to be near her, to share the scriptures together, to learn everything there was to know about her. He'd memorized every curve and plane of her face, the depth of her eyes, and the sound of her voice. He dreamed of touching the tendrils of her hair to see if they felt as silky as they looked. But it was the hidden places of her heart he most wanted to explore—to discover what made her happy and the reason for her tears.

Growing realization startled him. Was this what he thought it was? He stared out the dirt-streaked window. "Lord, am I in love with her?"

And what if he was? Not only had she told him her father insisted she continue her trip to Philadelphia by summer's end, his own father had mapped out an intricate plan Jeremy was expected to follow. What could come of a romance with a thousand miles between them? The thought made his stomach ache.

◆ ◆ ◆

Staring out the window trying to catch a glimpse of someone who didn't show up was a depressing way to spend a Sunday afternoon. After a restless night, Monday morning wasn't a welcome sight. Rosemary donned her lavender calico dress—the one Jeremy liked—and hurried off to the depot. Ada had fussed at her for not eating any of her special doughnuts, but Rosemary had claimed a queasy stomach. It wasn't a lie. Wondering why Jeremy hadn't come unsettled her more than she wanted to admit.

She stepped in the front door of the depot, her gaze scanning the area for those chores she needed to address first. Otto was grumbling and slamming things about in the cubicle office.

"Good mornin', Otto."

The agent growled back. "Ain't nothin' good about it."

Rosemary peeked across the counter at him. "Should I have brought you some of Ada Collins's fresh doughnuts?"

Otto looked up, his thick black eyebrows knitted together like a fat caterpillar. "Wouldn't hurt." He returned his attention to the mess on his desk. "Whadja do with the Lincoln schedule?"

Rosemary pointed. "It's there beside the blotter, where it always is."

He muttered something unintelligible and then added, "How am I s'posed to find anything if you keep puttin' it where it belongs?"

Otto's grouchiness wasn't new. He greeted her most mornings with a grumpy demeanor. But an urgency Otto normally didn't employ accompanied this morning's tirade. Deciding to give him a wide berth, Rosemary turned toward the storage closet.

"Ever' time a band o' road agents holds up a train, the schedules get more scrambled than Aunt Sally's eggs."

Rosemary's feet halted. "Hold up a train?" She returned to the cubicle door. "What are you talkin' about?"

He thrust his fist holding the schedule toward the east. "Some yayhoos dynamited the track Saturday afternoon an' held up the westbound. Ain't no trains comin' from Grand Island till at least t'marra. The express from Omaha even has to be rerouted."

Fear rose up and strangled her. Was that the train Jeremy. . .? Her heart hammered against her rib cage. "Was anyone hurt?"

Otto tossed the schedule on the desk. "No. S'pose we can be thankful for that. It just makes ever'thing a lot more complicated. Now they'll throw some confounded new regulation at us, and the folks wantin' to ship goods or buy a ticket are gonna blame me."

Rosemary found the breath she'd been holding and released it in a *whoosh*. "Thank God."

"Huh? These here schedules are more tangled than a wad o' barbed wire an' my job jus' got harder, an' you're gonna hold a revival meetin' over that? An' here I thought you was a nice little lady."

Rosemary laughed and threw her arms around Otto. She squeezed his neck and gave him a peck on his whiskery cheek.

"Here now, cut that out." Otto flapped his hand and wiped the spot where she'd kissed.

"Thanks, Otto." She dashed to the closet and grabbed her bucket, fairly skipping out the back door to the pump. Jeremy hadn't put her off or forgotten about his promise to escort her to church. The trains weren't running because of the damage to the rails. Relief flooded her that no one had been hurt, but comfort snuggled around her heart to think Jeremy's absence wasn't due to uncaring.

The morning flew by, and Rosemary hummed while she worked, despite Otto's grousing about "workin' with a confounded canary-bird." The scripture Jeremy had read to her, the one about waiting upon God, kept returning to her mind. The words reminded her she wasn't in control of her life's events. God's very fingerprint was visible on her life, and the thought both frightened and thrilled her. The concept that God cared enough about her to direct her path filled her with awe, but what if God desired something for her that she didn't desire for herself? The weight of the "what if" pressed down on her. Such ruminations were too deep for casual consideration. These questions required the wisdom of someone like Ada.

The large railroad clock read 12:15 p.m. when Otto grabbed a box of therapeutic papers and headed for the door.

Rosemary glanced out the window to the empty tracks. "Otto, didn't you say the express out of Omaha is due at twelve-thirty?"

"Ain't none of the trains keepin' to a schedule today. I'll be back in a while."

Rosemary kept pushing her mop back and forth. Perhaps tonight she'd write a letter to Jeremy assuring him she understood why he hadn't come. Tentative wording ran through her mind as she bent over the bucket and wrung out the mop. Would it be lady-like to express how disappointed she'd been or how much she missed him?

The echo of a distant train whistle met her ear. She glanced at the clock. Otto had been gone almost twenty minutes, and he'd implied the train wouldn't be on time. She dropped her mop, and it hit the floor with a loud *thunk* as she hurried to the open door.

The rumble on the tracks grew like the approach of thunderstorm. The train slowed, preparing to stop, but Otto was nowhere in sight. She glanced to and fro but saw no passengers waiting to board. What if someone wanted to unload freight or needed to purchase a connecting ticket? Her palms grew sweaty.

The train's huge wheels spewed steam as they screeched to a halt. A lone conductor jumped down and strode to the next-to-the-last car—a rather ornate vehicle. He pulled out a mounting step and opened the door. A distinguished-looking gentleman in a finely tailored gray suit stepped out and descended the step to the platform.

Rosemary backed up, seeking the confines of the depot as her hiding place. The man brushed his sleeve with his fingertips and pulled a handkerchief from his inside coat pocket to dab his forehead before walking to the depot. As he approached the door, Rosemary begged God to let Otto come back *now*.

The gentleman stepped inside and removed his hat, moving his gaze slowly from one end of the depot to the other. He seemed vaguely familiar, though Rosemary felt certain she'd never met him before. His brow furrowed, and he stepped to the ticket window. Rosemary swallowed hard and took a deep breath.

"Good afternoon, sir."

He turned in her direction and studied her for a moment. "Good afternoon, miss. I'm looking for Otto Gustafson. He is supposed to be on duty."

"Yes, sir, he is. . . That is, he was. . . I mean. . ." Her throat tightened.

"What exactly do you mean, young lady?" He tucked the fingers of his free hand into his vest.

"He—that is, Otto. . .uh, Mr. Gustafson. . .went out to—"

"He went out?" The gentleman's frown deepened. "Do you know where?"

Rosemary forced her head to nod. "To the. . .n–necessary." Heat galloped up her neck and flooded her face.

"Ah." As if aware of the embarrassment his inquiry had caused, he turned his head away from her and walked a few more steps into the depot. He tossed his hat on one of the chairs and scrutinized the new bench over which Rosemary had labored before returning his gaze to her. "And what exactly is your position here, miss, if I may ask?"

Confident the man could find no fault in the way she performed her duties, she swallowed back her intimidation. "I'm the cleaning woman."

"Cleaning woman?" His gruff tone made Rosemary cringe. "I was not aware we had hired women to clean the depots. That's supposed to be Gustafson's job."

He walked around the waiting area with measured steps, running his finger over the windowsills, sweeping his focus across the floors, and eventually staring at the windows. Her stomach knotted when the man turned to fix his eyes on her. "Now this is what every depot up and down the line should look like. What is your name, young lady, and who hired you?"

"R–Rosemary Denton, sir. The agent that was here a few weeks ago hired me. Jeremy Reide."

A light flickered across the man's eyes. "I see."

The back door flung open, and Otto came barreling in. "I heard the train whis—" He came to a stumbling halt. "Mr. Forbes. I weren't expectin' you, sir."

The gentleman in the fine gray suit, Mr. Forbes, narrowed his eyes. "Obviously."

Chapter Eight

The North Platte Hotel wasn't exactly the Palmer House in Chicago, but it was nicer than the boardinghouse where Jeremy had been staying in Grand Island. After a very long day and a mediocre supper, he'd begged a couple of pieces of paper and pot of ink from the desk clerk. Bone weary, his body longed for sleep. But before he'd give in to the temptation to collapse on the lumpy mattress, he wanted to write to Rosemary.

> *Dear Rosemary,*
>
> *I was glad to finally see you last Tuesday. The other freight man didn't mind me taking his place on the Sweetwater run at all. But I do regret not being able to escort you to church last Sunday. Thank you for understanding and forgiving me for not being able to contact you.*

Disappointed. That was the word she'd used. Some might say he should feel flattered that she'd been disappointed by his absence. But instead, grief skewered him to think he'd failed her—albeit unintentionally. He knew in that moment he never wanted to let her down again.

The future dangled before him. Their paths were destined to go separate directions in another month. An emotion deeper than disappointment made his chest ache. He heaved a sigh and returned pen to paper.

> *You surprised me, in a good way, with your new faith. I had a hard time stopping joyous tears when you shared with me the way God has been speaking to you. Selfishly, I wish I'd been the one to witness that moment when you understood and accepted God's love and forgiveness, but I'm thankful Reverend and Mrs. Collins prayed with you. Likewise, I'm grateful for being used of God to plant the seeds of faith. What an exquisite joy! I look forward to spending time with you over God's Word, hopefully next Sunday if outlaws and thugs don't do any more damage to the rails.*

Jeremy paused with the nib of his pen poised over the inkwell. Even now, days later, a smile spread across his face when he recalled Rosemary's eyes lighting up when she told him of her search through her new Bible. He prayed she wouldn't lose the hunger for God's Word.

It appears my time learning freight management in Grand Island is growing short. By the first of August, I will move on to the next step in my training, which I believe will be learning the mechanics of the locomotives, including fuel and steam production. At this time, I am uncertain to which routes I will be assigned. I will request the Sweetwater route, although I've been told the Omaha to Chicago route will provide the most experience.

When Rosemary had asked why he moved from one job to another, he'd merely told her he was going through a training program to become a well-rounded employee with knowledge in multiple areas of the railroad industry. She'd given him a quizzical look but appeared to accept what he'd told her. It wasn't a lie. The description of his father's plan was basically the explanation he'd given Rosemary. He'd just left out a few important details.

His gaze landed on the latest missive from his father lying on the desk to his right. Learning his father had made an unexpected visit to the Sweetwater depot caused momentary misgiving, but the elder Forbes had only commended him on hiring "the cleaning woman," and went on to reiterate the importance of Jeremy's anonymity.

Jeremy leaned back in his chair and sighed. His father put great importance on putting oneself in a position to lead the corporation into the next decade through sharp business astuteness, ambition, and cunning efficiency. How he wished his father valued integrity as highly as he revered ambition.

He couldn't see how telling Rosemary the truth about who he was would hinder the agenda's purpose, but he was honor bound to obey his father's mandate.

Honor. Wasn't it a contradiction to honor his father by being deceitful about his identity?

He returned his focus to the incomplete letter to Rosemary. One day he'd be able to tell her he was Jeremy Reide Forbes, son of John Murray Forbes, the president of the Burlington and Missouri Railroad. For now, all he could do was pray she wouldn't hate him when she learned the truth.

I look forward to seeing you again soon.

Should he tell her how special she was to him? Or would that imply something he couldn't promise? He dipped his pen tip into the inkwell, hesitating. Then he added *Affectionately, Jeremy.*

Night had fallen and he had to be up before dawn. He sealed and addressed the envelope, setting it beside his Bible where he wouldn't forget it in the morning.

◆　◆　◆

Rosemary sat in the Collins's kitchen and read over the first page of the latest letter she'd written to her father. Hopefully he'd be pleased to hear how she was working hard, learning to stand on her own two feet and be responsible for herself. He'd always seemed to think it important for his sons to be independent and industrious. Surely he'd be proud to know his only daughter possessed the same work ethic.

Would he be able to discern the delight she took in her job? She described Otto and how the grumpy depot agent was really soft hearted underneath the gruffness. The story of the group of greenhorn cowboys trying to load a cantankerous prize bull into one of the boxcars ought to make him chuckle. She told him about the little girl with her grandparents and how she'd made a rag doll like the ones Pa used to make out of his handkerchiefs. Would he smile to know she remembered him doing that when she was a little girl?

But nothing she'd written thus far reflected his reason for sending her away in the first place. She tapped her fingers on the tabletop. "He said he wanted me to become a lady."

Ada stood at the stove removing two loaves of fresh bread. "What was that, dear?"

Rosemary pulled her attention away from the paper in front of her, not realizing she'd spoken aloud. "Nothing. Just wondering what else to write to my father."

The aroma of the bread teased Rosemary's senses as Ada wiped her hands on her apron. "Honey, I know you told me you disagreed with your father for sending you east." She sat down and covered Rosemary's hand with hers.

The warmth of Ada's fingers lent comfort and acceptance, giving her the encouragement she needed to speak freely. "I still do, but my reasons for disagreein' with him are changin'. I wanted to be independent, make my own choices, control my own life. And I resented Pa for takin' that away from me. But then God brought me here, and you and Reverend Collins and Jeremy showed me how I could know Him." Moisture burned behind her eyes, and she curled her fingers around Ada's. "I found real freedom when I surrendered my selfish wants and let God have control of my life." She tightened her grip.

Ada returned the squeeze. "I'm so very glad you've found that peace and contentment in the Lord. He promises to never leave you, no matter what you face along the way. Your difficulties and struggles may not change, but at least you won't have to struggle alone."

Rosemary swallowed the lump in her throat. "I know that now. I believe God stranded me in Sweetwater for the purpose of comin' to know Him. I just wish I knew what else God has in mind for me."

"Are you talking about Jeremy?" A tiny smile tipped the corners of Ada's mouth.

Rosemary wasn't surprised that Ada suspected she had growing feelings for Jeremy, but heat crept into her face anyway, and she nodded.

Ada patted her hand. "Well, give it time and see what God has in store. As for what to write to your Pa—I expect he just wants to know you love him."

Ada rose and returned to the stove, humming as she went. Rosemary followed her with her eyes. Everything Ada did, she did with love and grace. A candle of understanding flared to life. Pa had sent her east so she'd become a lady. God brought her to the very place and the right person to do just that. Because being a lady wasn't about attending fancy balls or dining at a formal table. It wasn't going to tea parties or wearing the latest fashion or having her name listed on a social register. Being a true lady—the kind of lady she wanted to believe her mother was—meant demonstrating compassion and gentleness, generosity and kindness. Love and inner joy defined a lady who sought to minister to another whose heart was confused and fearful, because a true lady was a woman of God. Ada Collins was a lady, and Rosemary wanted to be like her.

She knew now what to write to Pa.

Pa, I hope you can meet Reverend and Mrs. Collins someday. I know you would like them. With their help, I've discovered the kind of faith that can carry me through hardship and uncertain times. Ada Collins has taught me so much just by watching her. I've never met anyone with such a heart of grace. God has used her to demonstrate what a real lady is. She's been the example to me that I believe Mama would have been, and for that, I will always be grateful for becoming stranded here in Sweetwater and meeting these wonderful folks.

When she'd started the letter, she planned to beg her father to allow her to return to the ranch at the end of summer instead of making her go on to Philadelphia. But now she wasn't sure she wanted to go back. Yes, she missed the ranch and her family, but the draw to go home was no longer as strong as it had been over two months ago. Truth be told, she wasn't sure what she wanted. Going back to the ranch meant leaving Jeremy, and the very thought grieved her. Not seeing him for days at a time left a void in her life. She didn't think she could bear never seeing him again.

She signed the letter and tucked it away to mail in the morning. Ada was busy making yeast dough for cinnamon rolls, and Rosemary joined her. If the day was soon approaching when she'd have to tell Ada and her husband good-bye, she wanted to take advantage of every moment with them.

◆ ◆ ◆

Thick gray clouds blotted out the rising sun as Rosemary detoured by the post office on her way to the depot. As she'd lain in bed last night, she'd struggled to know how to pray, and she'd wrestled most of the night wondering about the direction of her future. The depth of her feelings toward Jeremy startled her. When had her heart grown so in tune with him that being without him left her desolate? The murky dawn didn't bring with it any answers other than to just keep asking God to guide her, and that is exactly what she suspected Jeremy would advise her to do. Maybe he'd be working on one of the trains coming through today.

She entered the post office and purchased a stamp for Pa's letter. She handed the letter across the counter and turned to leave.

"Oh, Miss Denton, you have a letter." The postmaster pulled an envelope from one of the cubbyholes behind the counter. "Here you are." He slid the missive to her. The envelope bore Jeremy's handwriting, and her heart soared.

Otto might be grouchier than usual if she was late, but she couldn't wait to read Jeremy's letter. She tore open the envelope and hungrily took in every line, the enduring sound of Jeremy's voice whispering in her heart as she read.

Chapter Nine

Rosemary dipped her scrub brush into the soapy water bucket. Ada had said more than once that time spent on one's knees was never wasted. She didn't think the Lord would mind if she talked to Him while she scrubbed the depot floor, seeing as how she was already on her knees.

Otto was happy with the muffins she'd brought him this morning, so he'd only grumbled a little bit about her making him move his feet so she could sweep up the wood chips from his whittling knife. He didn't even complain about her humming while she worked. In fact, she thought she heard him humming along with her a time or two.

Still unsure how to pray regarding her future, she'd taken Ada's wise advice. *"Give it to the Lord,"* she'd admonished. So with a thread of apprehension, Rosemary told God she didn't know where He'd have her go and asked Him to choose for her. Even now, as she pushed her scrub brush across the floor, chagrin poked her. She'd already engaged in a tug-o'-war with God over the matter, and wondered if people like Ada and Pastor Collins and Jeremy ever struggled to surrender their own will to the Lord. She'd gone back and forth just like her scrub brush. She straightened and sat on her heels. God must surely be mighty patient with her.

She didn't want to think about suffering through any length of time with her snooty cousins and their high society lifestyle. Pa hadn't yet responded to her letter in which she'd related the influence Ada Collins had been to her. Oh how she hoped he'd see that she didn't need to become a Philadelphia debutante in order to be a lady.

She scooted back and continued scouring the floor, the *swish swish* sound of her brush creating a rhythm to cloak her whispered prayers into privacy between her and God. What if He steered her path home to the life she'd left behind?

"So many things've changed since I left Wyoming. My life isn't the same as it was. I expect things there have changed as well." She dipped her brush into the bucket again and continued. "I wonder if Wade misses me."

She'd not received a single letter from him, but it didn't really surprise her. Pa wouldn't have shared her whereabouts with Wade. His purpose had been to separate them, after all. She'd written him a brief letter on the train and mailed it when the train stopped in North Platte to take on fuel and water. Did he know she'd spent the past three months in Sweetwater, Nebraska? Unlikely.

She paused the motion of her brush. "God, I don't know how to feel about Wade now. I thought I loved him back in May. What if he's forgotten about me?"

Leaning forward on her hands and knees, a thought—so clear it could have only been prompted by God—startled her. Why hadn't she written Wade another letter from

Sweetwater telling him where she was? A second question, more eye opening than the first, intruded.

Do you miss Wade?

How long had it been since she'd entertained thoughts of him and his blue neckerchief the same shade as his eyes? She couldn't remember. Those first few days on the train, every time she'd dozed off, images of his roguish smile and flirting eyes filled her dreams.

Miss him? This was the first time in weeks she'd thought about him. Truth be told, the only dreams she could remember in the past couple of months had been of Jeremy.

Was this God's answer?

"Lord, am I that fickle? Wasn't Wade the reason I fought Pa so hard?"

She didn't know the answer. Was Wade really the reason she'd dug her heels in, or was it her own hardheaded petulance over wanting to do as she pleased?

"Miss Rosemary, you all right?" Otto's gravelly voice interrupted her communion with God, and she realized she was still planted on her hands and knees.

She raised her head and forced a smile. "I'm just taking a break from scrubbing." She clambered to her feet and grabbed the rope handle of her bucket. The dirty water sloshed against her skirt as she hastened to the back door.

The hot breeze did little to cool her when she stepped outside. She tossed out the contents of her bucket and plodded to the pump. The pump's handle chafed at her hands when she worked it up and down, just as her unsettled spirit rubbed an abrasive sore on her heart. Clear water spilled into the bucket. She cupped her hands beneath the flow and let the water refresh her. But it did nothing to wash away her confusion.

"God, please make these feelin's clear to me. In the beginnin', I begged You to let me go home instead of Philadelphia. But if I go home, Wade will be there, and Jeremy won't. What should I do, Lord?"

She waited and listened for a word of direction from God in the wind sighing through the cottonwood trees.

◆　◆　◆

Jeremy heaved another shovelful of coal from the tender into the firebox and then checked the steam gauge and water level in the boiler. He mopped his face and neck with his bandana before refilling his shovel. The giant roaring locomotive depended on how well he'd learned the job of fireman in order to chug its way down the track and stay on schedule.

"Back off a little on the coal, Reide." Roscoe, the engineer, peered at the safety valve and then leveled a scrutinizing look at Jeremy, as if trying to read his mind. "This head o' steam you're buildin' up is gonna get us into Sweetwater pert near twenty minutes early."

Jeremy gave a nod and uncorked his canteen. He gulped down a few swallows and then poured the tepid water over his bandana and tied the wet rag around his neck. They couldn't pull into Sweetwater too early as far as he was concerned. He couldn't wait to see Rosemary.

After spending nearly the entire night in prayer, he'd written a note to his father, explaining why he must break his word and tell Rosemary the truth about who he was. Included in the note was a request for a meeting at which he planned to propose a compromise—tell the people with whom he worked that his name was Jeremy and at the end of each individual training period inform them of his true identity. He prayed his father would react with acceptance, but if not, Jeremy was still determined to be honest with Rosemary and ask her to forgive him. He prayed she'd listen.

Sweat and coal dust blended on his skin, running in blackened rivulets down his arms. He'd never been this dirty in his entire life. Despite the grime, however, he vowed to seek out Rosemary straightaway upon arriving in Sweetwater before seeing to his own comfort.

Roscoe reached up and pulled the cord, sounding the whistle. Jeremy leaned out the window, using his hand to deflect the flying cinders from his eyes. Yes, that was Sweetwater in the distance. His pulse stepped up. Rosemary was just another minute or two away.

The locomotive began to slow, preparing to pull into the station. Impatience gnawed at him. He could get there faster if he jumped out and ran. Instead, he scanned the area to see if he could catch a glimpse of her.

Steam hissed, the brakes squealed metal against metal, and the great iron beast screeched to a halt. Jeremy leapt down to the platform. The depot windows gleamed like they always did—evidence that Rosemary was nearby. He strode to the door and paused, allowing his eyes to adjust.

There she was, across the spacious waiting area, on her knees scrubbing the floor. He only advanced a few steps when she looked up. But instead of a welcoming smile, she frowned and pointed to his feet.

"Stop right there, mister. The floor is still wet, and you're tracking dirt. . ."

Her gaze traveled upward, apparently taking in his dirty work clothes. Maybe he should have taken time to clean up first.

Her eyes widened with disconcertment and her mouth formed an *O*. "Wade? How did you find—"

Jeremy halted. The air left his lungs like he'd been punched in the stomach. Wade? Who was Wade? Ice ran through his veins.

He pulled the blue bandana off his neck and wiped the sweat and soot from his face. Rosemary's eyes riveted on him, and her expression shifted from shock to despair. She pushed away from the floor and rose, shaking her head, as if trying to make sense of his presence. Whoever she'd been expecting, it wasn't him.

"Oh, J–Jeremy. . . I–I. . ."

He backed up and mumbled an apology for dirtying her clean floor.

She stepped toward him, nearly upsetting her water bucket. "No. Jeremy, I–I'm. . ."

He turned and exited, lengthening his stride and putting space between him and the woman he loved. With each step, the conflict in his chest thickened. All the while he'd fought with a guilty conscience over his deception, Rosemary apparently had held back a few important details of her own. In all the time they'd spent together, he couldn't remember her mentioning anyone named Wade. His chest burned, and his stomach hardened. Perhaps weariness from working so hard after a sleepless night caused him to jump to conclusions, but he couldn't talk to her right now. Was there anything more hurtful than hearing the woman who meant more than life itself call you by another man's name?

The train whistle blew, and he turned and jogged back to the depot, climbing aboard without looking to see if Rosemary was anywhere in sight. He focused on his job, heaving shovelful after shovelful of coal into the firebox to fire up the boiler. As much as he couldn't wait to get here less than a half hour ago, now he couldn't wait to leave.

◆　◆　◆

If Jeremy thought the exhausting work of a train fireman would keep his mind occupied and off Rosemary, he was wrong. He fumed by day and fought with the bedcovers at night, allowing his imagination to fuel his claim that he had every right to feel betrayed. But after four days speculating and guessing, praying and agonizing, he couldn't stand it any longer.

In the predawn hours, God reminded him of his own prayer the night before he saw Rosemary—how he'd prayed that she would listen to him and forgive him. How could he do any less for her?

"All right, Lord. I'll do whatever You say."

He fell into a bone-weary sleep for a few hours. His dreams were filled with Rosemary's face and the expression of anguish in her eyes. She cried out his name, and he jolted awake. He had to go to her. Dawn was barely a streak of pink and gold on the eastern horizon. He rose and dressed in a gray suit, crisp white shirt, and black tie.

The sun was barely up when he walked to the Lincoln depot and sought out Roscoe. The engineer gave a low whistle in assessment of Jeremy's attire. But the man's eyebrows arched up to his hairline when Jeremy told him he was taking the day to attend to a private matter.

Roscoe scratched his head. "Reckon I can get Barton to take your place. But you'd best be ready to return the favor when you get back."

Jeremy hopped aboard a westbound out of Lincoln and fidgeted for three and a half hours until the conductor called out, "Sweetwater. Sweetwater, folks."

The train hadn't yet come to a complete stop when Jeremy leapt to the platform and strode inside. He glanced left and right, but the place was strangely quiet.

"You're too late."

Jeremy spun to find Otto standing in the doorway of the office, arms akimbo. Otto's scowl carved deep lines across his forehead.

"She ain't here."

"She—" Dread plummeted into the pit of his stomach. "What do you mean, too late?"

"She up and left," Otto growled. "Back to Wyoming. And she was cryin'."

Chapter Ten

His father had blustered and bellowed, but in the end, Jeremy stood firm. He refused to perpetuate the deception any longer and told his father of his plans to travel to Laramie. Finally, John Murray Forbes had lifted his glass toward his son. "She must be quite a young lady."

The memory of the confrontation lingered as Jeremy peered through the train window. "She is, Father. She is." Once again he prayed Otto's assessment of being *"too late"* wasn't accurate as he watched the Laramie depot come into view.

But the sting of Otto's declaration—*"she was cryin'"*—hadn't lessened one bit. He drew in a deep breath and prayed for favor.

Cowboys, cattle brokers, and other travelers milled about the platform, impeding Jeremy's progress to inquire where he might rent a rig. Obtaining a hotel room could wait. The desire to see Rosemary drove him toward a crude sign announcing the location of a livery.

The livery man took his sweet time harnessing the horse, so Jeremy helped fasten a few of the straps.

"Do you happen to know how to get to the Denton place?"

The man straightened. "The Double D? Sure, everyone around here knows where Daniel Denton's ranch is." He pointed northwest. "Take Sentinel Street out of town till you come to the Laramie River. Follow the river road about six miles till it branches off. Take the left fork for another three or four miles. You'll see the Double D on the rise to the west."

Jeremy tossed his valise into the buggy and climbed into the seat. "Thanks."

"Daniel Denton don't take kindly to strangers."

"I'll keep that in mind." He slapped the reins on the horse's rump and moved out in the direction of Sentinel Street. Praying all the way, he followed the stableman's directions until a large gate bearing an overhead DOUBLE D loomed ahead. A half mile past the gate, a sprawling log home sat between towering fir trees, with expansive fenced enclosures and grazing land as far as he could see.

He tied the horse to the hitching rail and strode to the wide front porch. Before he reached the door, it opened and a mountain of a man with an intimidating scowl filled the doorway.

"Help ya?"

"Yes, sir. My name is Jeremy Reide For—"

Before he could get his whole name out, the huge man grabbed his hand and pumped it. "I sure am glad to make your acquaintance. I'm Daniel Denton. When my daughter wired that she was comin' home, an' I went into town to git her, she was a bawlin' like an orphan calf. Now I can handle a calf but never could figger out what to do with teary-eyed woman. I felt about as useless as a twenty-two cartridge in an eight-gauge shotgun. She ain't stopped cryin' since she got home. Keeps sayin' if only she could explain to Jeremy. So I reckon I'm glad you're here."

Denton led the way through the house and stopped short of a pair of doors that stood open to a covered back porch. He pointed. "She's out there. Sure hope you can do somethin' to stop them waterworks."

Jeremy took a step, but Denton put one meaty hand in the middle of Jeremy's chest and narrowed his eyes. "But if you hurt her worse, me an' my shotgun are close by."

Jeremy swallowed hard. "I don't plan to hurt her, sir. God willing, I hope to help dry her tears."

Denton nodded and stepped aside.

◆　◆　◆

Rosemary blotted her tears with the corner of her apron, so heartsore she could barely raise her eyes at the sound of footsteps. Her mind played cruel tricks on her. After pining for Jeremy for days, his image now formed a mirage before her.

He positioned a chair in front of hers and sat, fidgeting with his hat. "Rosemary."

Mirages didn't speak.

"Jeremy, it's really you." The words barely slipped out on a raspy breath.

"It's me." He reached for her hands. "I couldn't stay away. I had to tell you how sorry I am for walking away without giving you a chance to say what you wanted to say. You must admit, though, hearing you call me by another man's name wasn't exactly flattering."

She shook her head, loosening tendrils of hair, but she didn't care. "Wade is, or was, one of Pa's cowhands. He'd been flirtin' and tryin' to charm me, and said he loved me."

She went on to explain Pa's reasons for sending her away and shared how she'd begged God to help her sort out her feelings. "I realized I didn't love Wade. The day you came in all covered in soot, I'd been talkin' with God about him, knowin' he'd be here when I came home. It was the blue bandana. That's why I thought for a moment you were Wade. He always wore one."

Jeremy glanced out toward the cattle enclosures. "So he's one of your father's hands?"

"Not anymore." A tiny smile tipped her lips. "Pa tells me he took up with a saloon girl in Laramie and ran off just a week after I left. I'm glad he's gone."

His gaze appeared to lock on their clasped hands. "I have something I need to tell you as well. I've been less than honest with you—with a lot of people."

She stared wide eyed as he told her about his father's plan to indoctrinate him in the workings of the business from the lowliest job to the boardroom. Hearing him speak his full name gave her pause.

She rolled the revelation over in her mind. So many things made sense now. "I wish you would've told me, wish you'd felt you could've trusted me. But I think I understand. We were both strugglin' to honor our fathers."

Jeremy dipped his head. "Please forgive me."

She tugged his hands. "Jeremy, your name doesn't change who you are. You're still a gentle, compassionate, hardworkin' Christian man. . . ."

Jeremy lifted his shoulders and finished her sentence. "Whose father just happens to be the president of the Burlington and Missouri River Railroad."

Heat climbed into her face. "I've already told Pa."

Jeremy jerked his head up. "Told him what?"

The burning in her cheeks intensified, and her heart drummed. "That I've fallen in love with a man who works on the railroad."

A smile stretched across his face. His gaze slid to her lips, and he leaned toward her, pausing barely an inch away. "I think I fell in love with you the day you missed your train."

His lips brushed hers ever so gently, and she murmured, "Promise me somethin'?"

He arched one eyebrow. "What's that?"

She pulled back just far enough to lose herself in the depth of his eyes. "Promise you'll never wear a blue bandana again."

Connie Stevens lives with her husband of forty-plus years in north Georgia, within sight of her beloved mountains. She and her husband are both active in a variety of ministries at their church. A lifelong reader, Connie began creating stories by the time she was ten. Her office manager and writing muse is a cat, but she's never more than a phone call or email away from her critique partners. She enjoys gardening and quilting, but one of her favorite pastimes is browsing antique shops where story ideas often take root in her imagination. Connie has been a member of American Christian Fiction Writers since 2000.

World's Greatest Love

by Liz Tolsma

Chapter One

Monday, May 18, 1896
Peoria, Illinois

From her vantage point in the doorway of the wardrobe tent as she mended the bareback rider's torn skirt, Ellen Meyer glanced at the sky blackening in the west. None of the flimsy tents scattered about the circus grounds offered any true protection from a fierce summer storm. And right now, hundreds and maybe thousands of men, women, and children packed the main show tent, thrilled by snarling lions and dazzled by trapeze artists.

Geraldine Warner tapped her slippered foot on the dusty ground. "Can't you hurry up? I'm in the next act. Harriet wouldn't have let this happen. She made sure the wardrobe was always in tip-top shape."

No sense telling Geraldine that Harriet was the one who sewed this costume. The former wardrobe designer was well beloved and much missed. Ellen didn't hold a candle to her. "Stand still. I'll be finished in just a minute." A rolling peal of thunder punctuated her words.

The band under the big top played louder. Geraldine rubbed her arms. "Look at how green the sky's gotten. Like an ugly bruise. I don't care for the sight of it much."

"I've never seen anything to compare. Does this happen much in the Midwest?" Ellen finished another stitch.

"All the time. Where are you from?"

"Boston."

"And they don't have storms like this?"

Ellen shook her head.

"Maybe I should move there. But then I'd miss all of this." Geraldine gestured wide. The horse trainer clung to the leather lead of a pair of nervous white steeds. At the railroad siding, roustabouts loaded cages containing pacing tigers. One let out a mighty roar, and goosebumps pricked Ellen's skin. Even Bertha, the fat lady, lumbered with haste over the trampled grass toward the train.

If possible, the sky darkened more. The wind picked up, beating the flap of the wardrobe tent into a fury. The metal support poles rattled, the grommets clanging against them.

"Ellen, can you help me?" Constance Hefner stood frowning in the tent's doorway.

"As soon as I finish Geraldine's skirt." She forced the needle through the gauzy material.

"But the storm is coming. I want to pack the costumes so they don't get ruined." The wind whipped the golden ringlets escaping from Constance's Gibson-girl hairstyle.

Ellen resisted the urge to huff. "Get started. I'll be right there." She, too, wanted to move her work to keep the storm from damaging it. In her haste, her needle struck her thimble. She blew her bangs from her eyes and tried to concentrate.

"Ellen, please." Constance's whine matched that of the wind.

Ellen whipped the last stitch into place and tied off the thread. "There, Geraldine. Good as new."

The performer examined Ellen's work. "I guess that will do for now. I only hope it holds."

Ellen shared that sentiment. She rose from her stool. "Now, Constance, let's put away what we can." Another bolt of lightning streaked across the sky. Thunder rumbled under her feet.

She grabbed her repair kit and hurried into the tent. Earlier in the morning, as she'd set up, Ellen organized the costumes she had responsibility for. Each of them hung on a hanger on a metal pole. To keep from having to press them, she refrained from jamming them together.

In Constance's area, costumes that required many hours of work to create lay scattered across the benches where the performers dressed. One of the purple velvet gowns used in the spectacular hung into the dirt.

Ellen scooped it up. "You have to be more careful with the clothes. The dust is bad enough, but when it rains, this will get wet."

"Yes, Mother." Constance cackled. "Don't you think I know how to do my job after five years? You're nothing but an upstart."

Ellen brushed off the skirt and folded the gown, each move calculated to keep the finery from wrinkling. "It's common sense, that's all." A gust of wind shook the tent, the canvas sides heaving inward under the strain.

Constance grabbed the dress from her hands. "I'll do it. I'm capable."

Ellen shrugged and moved to store her costumes before the full wrath of the storm unleashed. The roll of thunder didn't stop. The tent poles leaned under the force of the gale. Her heart beat a little faster. Her hands shook. "Lucy, come help me." She motioned for one of the seamstresses.

Speaking was impossible over the cry of the wind. Together, she and Lucy loaded the trunks and shut the lids. Constance lagged. Ellen crossed the tent to help her.

The roar of the gale filled her ears.

Pressure built in her chest. She couldn't draw a deep breath. What was going on?

Shrieks rose from the big top. She pressed her lips together to stifle her own scream.

The wardrobe tent's canvas tore away.

One pole sailed through the air. Her knees trembled.

She tried to run, tried to get away. Her skirts tripped her.

She fell.

Blinding pain seared her head.

Her world went black.

◆　　◆　　◆

"Get that wagon loaded." Will Jorgensen yelled for the roustabouts to hear him above the storm. The men rushed to secure the tiger cage on the flat car. The wind drowned out their communication with each other. He wiped his sweaty hands on his pants. This was when accidents happened.

And despite the storm, Mr. Ringling would expect them in the next town tomorrow morning, ready for the day's shows.

Will was responsible for making it happen.

One of the men guiding the carved, gilded wagon slipped.

"Watch out." Will rushed forward. As first-year trainmaster, the well-being of all the workers fell to his care.

The man popped up.

"Are you hurt?" Will examined him up and down.

He shook his head. "Naw, ain't nothing. Been hurt worse than this just getting out of bed in the morning."

Will relaxed. Until he scanned the skies. Black clouds rolled across the heavens, their underbellies dark green. Lightning burst across the scene every few seconds. After living his entire life traveling with the circus, he'd seen plenty of summer squalls come and go. But none like this.

"Looks like a nasty storm's brewing." Art Pavlovic, the wagon master, slapped Will's shoulder, his hand as big as a bear's.

"It's been a long time since I've seen such a bad one. Let's get those wagons on as soon as possible. I'll light a fire under the tent crews. We need to get as much tied down as we can before it hits."

"Go on. I'll keep an eye out here."

"Thanks." Will yanked down his cap to keep it from flying away and scurried across the hard-packed dirt toward the menagerie tent. Once the rain fell, this place would be a quagmire.

The storm raced in their direction, the clouds each vying for first place. He picked up his pace. Damage to the equipment or injuries to the staff or patrons would be devastating. They had another show tomorrow in Geneseo. Mr. Ringling wouldn't be pleased if they had to cancel. Not at all.

And it would be Will he would fire.

The roustabouts struggled to pull the pegs from the menagerie tent. They needed to hurry. The scent of rain filled the air. Not long until the deluge hit. "Need some help?"

The short muscular man leading the crew nodded. "Get that one out there. Wind's making it mighty hard to get the job done."

Will pulled a pair of leather gloves from his pocket and slipped them on. He tugged on the stake. This area of the country must have been pretty dry this spring. The peg didn't want to budge.

Another lightning bolt flashed almost at the same time as the thunder cracked. Will's heart leapt like a bareback rider onto her horse. The wind intensified, swirling clouds of dust. An elephant trumpeted.

He wiggled the stake, and only after he worked himself into a sweat did it release. "Let's fold it and load it, boys. There's no time to waste. Going to be some blow down."

Like the tremors from a locomotive, the ground under Will's feet rumbled. The wind buffeted him, snatching his cap from his head. He chased his hat as it skittered across the staging grounds. Before he reached it, the gale picked up his cap and carried it away. No sense in following it. The storm bore down. He had to get back to the train and oversee the loading. They needed to finish as soon as possible.

Crack. Bang. More lightning.

His ears popped. His stomach froze, even as sweat dripped down his face.

Horses whinnied.

Women's screams erupted from the big top.

The band hit a sour note.

The canvas ripped from the wardrobe tent.

He watched, unable to move, as a pole flew through the air, striking the new wardrobe mistress.

No, no. He had to get to her.

The rain came then, in sheets. Before he took three steps in her direction, the dirt transformed into mud. He slipped and slid. His muscles strained forward in his desperation to get to the injured woman.

Soaking wet and slimy with mud, he reached her at last. He dropped to his knees in the muck.

Blood gushed from her head.

No, Lord. Not her, too.

Chapter Two

Will touched the wardrobe mistress's bloodied head, his mouth as dry as if he'd swallowed a handful of sawdust. Broken bits of memories exploded in his mind. He was little, so little. His own mother lay in a pool of blood. The other trapeze artists clustered around her, as if they could restore her life.

Screams slashed through his thoughts and brought him back to the moment. The assistant, Constance, stood beside him, yelling.

"Stop it. That's not going to help." He watched the wardrobe mistress take a breath. *Thank You, Lord.* "Help me get her out of the water." Rain gushed into the middle of where the tent once stood.

Constance didn't budge.

Without help, Will picked up the wardrobe manager with as much gentleness as he could muster. By now, the rain soaked him to the skin. He shivered.

"What's her name?"

"Ellen Meyer." Constance spit out the words.

Miss Meyer stirred in his arms, her dark eyelashes fluttering. She moaned.

"Don't move too much. I'll get you somewhere dry." The thick mud sucked his shoes, threatening to tear them right from his feet.

She opened her eyes. The green of them shocked him. He'd never seen eyes the color of prairie grass.

"What happened?"

When she spoke, he wilted. "You got a mighty nasty bump on the head." This time had a different ending. He'd seen so much worse.

She struggled against him. "The costumes. We have to get them loaded before the rain hits."

"It's already pouring."

"Then we have to hurry. Put me down. I'm fine."

"You're not."

"I insist."

"Are you sure?"

"Thousands of dollars' worth of dresses and shoes and hats will be ruined if I don't get them on the train."

Still supporting her around her waist, he set her on the ground.

She wobbled for a moment. "Oh my."

"You need to see a doctor."

"Nonsense. As soon as the world stops spinning, I'll be fine." She bit her lip for a moment before smiling, even as rivulets of water trickled down her face. "See, right as rain."

He couldn't control the laughter that burst out of him. "I suppose you are. Let me help you." He whistled for one of the roustabouts from the flat car. "We need the wardrobe trunks on next."

"Oh no. No, this can't be happening." Still in his embrace, Miss Meyer trembled.

He followed her gaze. The depression where the wardrobe tent used to stand had filled with water. Turned into a pond. He couldn't guess as to how many inches now covered it. But it was enough for the trunks to float.

He put out another call to his men. "Let's go, on the double. No time to waste. We still may be able to save the contents."

Holding Miss Meyer's hand, he sloshed toward the trunks. The petite blond assistant, Constance, occupied the same spot he'd left her. Instead of screaming, she now bawled like a black bear cub. Miss Meyer broke away, pulling a trunk onto dry ground.

He turned his attention to Constance. "There's nothing to be frightened of. We're safe."

She blubbered. "But my costumes. Look at them." What creations the gale hadn't torn from the rack now hung sodden on the rod.

He didn't know much about clothes but doubted saving them was possible. "Ruined. Let's concentrate on what we can rescue."

No sooner did he turn his back than her shrieking resumed. "No. That's all my hard work. We have to save them."

Three of his crew members arrived with a wagon. "Help Miss Meyer. I'll take care of this mess."

Figuring it would be faster to load up the few remaining dresses than arguing with the woman, Will got to work. He really needed to supervise the loading of the train, especially considering the weather. Everything must move with precision if he wanted to retain his new position. He only stayed to keep a watch on Miss Meyer. Once or twice, he caught a glimpse of a grimace on her face, but otherwise, she worked alongside them, showing no ill effects.

She could be dead right now, just like. . .

Shaking off the thought, he commandeered a water-logged trunk and stuffed the once-showy costumes inside before hoisting it onto the waiting wagon with the others. "Get them to their car, boys."

Miss Meyer, her wet hair hanging in curls down her back, watched the roustabouts take away the trunks. He stood beside her. "I hope you can salvage them."

She closed her eyes, then opened them. Were those tears or raindrops? "I don't think so. The trunks aren't waterproof. There must have been two feet of water in that depression."

He touched her damp cheek. "I'm sorry."

The assistant's strident voice startled him. "At least she had hers packed. She helped herself before she gave me a hand, so hers would be saved and mine ruined."

"That's not true." Miss Meyer leaned forward. "You told me you could do it yourself."

"I told you I could fold the dress myself, not get everything put away in time. You're selfish. Your underlings should be your first priority. I have never been treated like this before." The assistant spun, almost slipping in the mud, and splashed away.

Will's skin prickled. "Watch out for that one."

◆ ◆ ◆

Ellen's head pounded in a most awful way, the beat of it matching the clacking train wheels. She sat on her lower berth, the one she shared with Lucy Hanson, and tried to focus on the tiny stitches in the ringmaster's coat. All to no avail. The hem blurred before her eyes.

Compounding the headache caused by her bump on the head was the knowledge that she and her seamstresses would be busy in the coming days repairing or, in most cases, remaking many of the costumes. Only a few of the floating trunks remained dry. Most were waterlogged.

"You look worn out, Ellen."

She glanced at Lucy, who also sat stitching. "I am. And I hate to think of all the work left in front of us. Hopefully in Geneseo tomorrow, I'll be able to get some of the material we need. I don't know if they'll have all of our specialty fabrics. I might have to telegram to procure some of the tulle and spangles."

"And the milliners in town. They might be able to help."

"That's a good idea. I hadn't thought of them."

Constance picked that moment to flounce down the aisle dressed in a light-weight yellow gown with the poofiest sleeves Ellen had ever seen. She dared to glance at Lucy, who clenched her lips together. Laughter simmered inside of Ellen. She bit her cheeks to keep it from spilling out. While the gown might be appropriate for a stroll in Central Park, it had no place on a train in the middle of a very muddy Illinois prairie.

Lucy leaned over to whisper to Ellen. "Those sleeves take up almost as much room as Constance herself."

"Stop it. That's so naughty." But Ellen couldn't keep the lilt from her voice.

Constance spun around. She pointed at Ellen's heart, her finger almost daggerlike. "It's all your fault. If you had helped me pack, those costumes wouldn't be ruined."

"Packed or not packed, it didn't matter. Do you forget that most of mine floated away, too? Yours actually fared better still hanging on the rods."

Constance fluttered like a butterfly as she collapsed onto her berth. "All that hard work, nothing but a soggy mess. And I only have you to blame."

"Me? You blame me for what happened, as if I control the rain?"

"Why not? You favor Lucy and the other girls. I don't know why you have it out for me."

"I don't dislike any of you. Lucy and I sleep next to each other, that's all. And she's helpful to me." Her headache ratcheted up several notches.

"And she's helpful to me." Constance spoke in a singsong manner.

Lucy stood. "That's enough. Ellen's not done anything to you. Leave her be. If you'd get to work, you could finish a few repairs before we get to Geneseo."

"I'm worn out. All that work I did on my own exhausted me. I need to take it easy. Maybe go to the pie car to unwind."

Ellen crushed the delicate velvet in her fist. She forced herself to relax her fingers. "We're all going to have to work extra-long hours and help each other in order to get this done. That includes you, Constance."

"Me? How about you? The way you order everyone about, like you've worked here forever instead of a few weeks."

"Ladies." The sharp male voice startled Ellen. In an instant, the Alvena, the women's sleeping car, fell silent.

She looked up to find the trainmaster in the doorway, a steaming cup of something in his hand.

"I knocked several times, but I suppose you didn't hear me with all the shouting. What's the matter?"

Ellen came to her feet, a wave of dizziness swirling around her. As the train lurched, she reached for the berth to balance herself.

Within seconds, Will was at her side. "What's wrong?" He steadied her, the warmth of his hand seeping through her cotton shirtwaist's sleeve.

"I'm fine." The car came back into focus. "Just a tiny dizzy spell."

"You need to be careful. That was a nasty bump on the head."

She stared into his hazel eyes and couldn't think of a thing to say.

"She's fine." Constance's high-pitched voice grated in Ellen's ears. "It's just like her to play up a little injury to her own advantage."

"I brought you some tea. Chamomile. My mother swore by it." Will handed her the cup.

"Thank you. That's very kind."

"What, no tea for the rest of us? Is it only Ellen who's special?" Constance's voice grated on Ellen's nerves.

"If you want to knock yourself unconscious, I'll be happy to make you some."

How could he be so gracious? All Ellen wanted to do was to light into Constance like she'd seen her brother do to the schoolyard bully.

She rubbed her temple. "I do have a headache."

Will turned his back to Constance. "I'm sorry we weren't able to get the trunks loaded on time. That storm came up fast."

"It's not your fault. You had no idea—none of us did—that the dressing tent would turn into a lake."

"Did you lose much?"

"Quite a bit, I'm afraid. I hope Geneseo is a large enough town that I'll be able to buy a good deal of what I need there."

"From what I remember, it is."

"You've been there before?"

He nodded.

"How long have you been with the circus?"

"Born and bred."

"Impressive. It's quite the life."

"I don't know anything else." He nodded at her, a bit of a frown marring his handsome, angular face. "Well, it will be an early morning yet again, so I'll leave you to get some sleep. Good night."

He strode away, needing just three long steps to reach the end of the car.

"What was that all about?" Lucy returned to her position next to Ellen.

"I have no idea. Why would the trainmaster check up on the humble wardrobe mistress?"

"Exactly my question." Constance glared at Ellen. "Watch that you don't get too big for your britches. Oh, but you already are."

Chapter Three

H urry up, Lucy. We're already running late." The wind whipped Ellen's skirts around her ankles as she exited the Alvena. Good thing she'd pinned her hat well.

Lucy answered from inside. "Shouldn't we wait for Constance?"

"She only just got up. With our late arrival, we don't have much time to shop before we have to be back. She can meet us in town." Ellen didn't know what time she heard Constance return to the Alvena last night. Late, for sure. For someone who complained about being exhausted, she didn't get to bed at a reasonable hour.

Ellen descended the stairs and waited for Lucy beside the tracks. She watched as Will ordered the train's unloading. The process moved with precision and a great deal of order. First, the cookhouse wagon came off. The thought of breakfast tickled her stomach, but they didn't have time to wait for the dining tent to be set up and the meal prepared. Will hooked the horses to pull off the menagerie wagons next, the lions and tigers roaring in their cages, the bears pacing, the hippos yawning.

At last, still pinning her red velvet hat in place, Lucy hustled to join Ellen. "Leaving Constance behind won't make her happy."

A headache niggled at Ellen's temples. "That can't be helped. If she wouldn't have stayed so late in the pie car, she would be ready to come with us. As it is, I don't know how we'll get everything done before the first show. Or if the costumes hung on the lines this morning will dry in time for the afternoon performance."

"At least this lot looks high and water-free."

"I suppose we should be thankful for small blessings."

A short but breathless walk brought them into view of the town. Brick buildings lined the wide main street. At the very end of it, a church's steeple rose into the blue sky. "Good. Will was right. This town is big enough for us to find much of what we need. Do you have your list?"

Lucy held up the piece of paper she and Ellen had labored over the night before. "And here's the milliner."

Through the clean window, Ellen spied a wide array of hats, many adorned with enough feathers to cover a bird. She pressed against the glass. "Perfect. I see chiffon and velvet. And look, this one even has a few spangles. We might clean the woman out of her inventory, but we'll be able to check a good number of items off that list. Meet me in the telegraph office when you're finished."

The bell above the shop's door tinkled as Lucy entered. A walk of another block brought Ellen to the general store. This shop's window boasted boots and shoes, several pieces of crockery, and three ready-made dresses.

She visited several mercantiles that sold similar items, managing to purchase a number of gowns in royal blue, dark purple, and cream with red trim that would do well for the grand triumphal pageant at the beginning of the show. Much to her surprise, she managed to procure a few bolts of silk and velvet. Her last stop would be the telegraph office to place an order with her supplier for the items they couldn't find. She had to meet up with Lucy to see if she had any success.

Though the proprietors offered to deliver the goods, she didn't want to take any chance with the premade dresses getting crushed, so she had them wrapped. By the time she left the last store, she couldn't see over the top of the boxes. She peered around the side of the stack to navigate the couple of steps. The townspeople and the excursionists from the outlying areas jammed the edge of the street, waiting for the parade to begin.

She had to hurry, but in addition to not being able to see, she couldn't remember which way she came. Her head pounded worse than ever as tears formed in the corners of her eyes. Did she turn left or right? She didn't even know if she'd remember the shop if she stumbled on it.

Boston was much bigger than this, but she'd never felt so lost in all of her life.

She couldn't very well stand in front of the shop the rest of the day. Choosing to turn right, she struck out. *Please, Lord, let this be the correct way.*

Whoomp. She ran straight into something solid.

She peered around the boxes. Correction. Someone solid.

◆　◆　◆

"Pardon me, ma'am. I'm so sorry." Will reached around the stack of boxes to steady the woman he ran into, then peered over the edge. "Miss Meyer. What a surprise."

"Oh, Mr. Jorgensen. It's all my fault. I thought I could carry these boxes and see and find my way to the train, but I can't." Her frenetic words spilled over each other.

He relieved her of the entire lot. "I should have been watching where I was going. My apologies. Where are you headed?"

"To find Miss Hanson at the telegraph office."

"Allow me to escort you there."

"Really, there isn't any need. If you could point me in the right direction, that would be helpful."

"I insist."

She flashed him a dimpled smile he hadn't noticed before. Today, her hair was pinned under her hat. He liked it better yesterday, when her curls dropped over her shoulders.

"What are you doing in town, Mr. Jorgensen? You must be very busy."

"Everything's in place, so I have a break before we have to start loading." He didn't dare tell her he hoped he'd run into her. "Looks like we'll have a good crowd."

"Which is why I need to hurry. Already I've missed getting the performers ready for the parade."

"You have capable assistants. Harriet Riley was proud of her staff."

"Even of Miss Hefner?" Her face flushed. "I'm sorry. That wasn't kind."

How did he explain Constance to Miss Meyer? Could he tell her she'd targeted almost every male star and officer with the show in the five years since she'd joined the staff? "She's a bit of a handful."

"And I'm younger than her. I'm sure Mrs. Riley kept her under better control."

"You're doing fine. Be firm but kind. And put your foot down when you need to. You must be a talented seamstress to be wardrobe mistress already."

More red suffused her face. "I worked hard to get out of Boston to escape my family's poverty and make a better life for myself. And them."

"I think Constance is envious. This is her fifth season."

"That makes sense. She thought the position should be hers. Maybe it should be. I don't have much experience with this kind of life."

"I've heard no complaints about you. Well, withstanding the one."

She bit her lip. "I can't lose this position. My family depends on the money I send them to survive. What would I do if the Ringling brothers fired me?"

"Don't worry. Keep doing your job, and you'll be fine." He told himself the same thing every day.

She nodded, the feather on her hat bobbing in time. "Thank you."

"How are you feeling?"

"I still have a rather bad headache. And I didn't sleep much. Every time I rolled over, I bumped my bump." She giggled, the sound reminding him of his mother's laugh.

He didn't want her to stop. "You should take the day off and rest. I'm sure your staff can manage without you."

"Because the rain ruined so much, there's a pile of work. I'll be fine. Don't worry."

They met up with Miss Hanson at the telegraph office, and the women placed their order. They wriggled out of town as the parade stepped off, led by the large band chariot, covered in carvings of lions and gargoyles and hauled by eight white horses.

More than once, Will slowed his pace so the women didn't fall behind. Still, they huffed and puffed by the time the train and lot came into sight. Multitudes of colorful flags waved on top of the numerous tents scattered about the grounds. How could he grow tired of the sight? "To the ladies' dressing room, I assume?"

Miss Meyer reached for the top box. "We can take it from here. Thank you."

He turned to leave when Constance called to him. "Will, oh Will, there you are." She flounced over to him and pulled him into a tight embrace. "The most terrible, awful thing has happened."

Chapter Four

Constance grasped Will around the waist almost tight enough to squeeze his breakfast out of him. "The most terrible thing has happened."

He stared down at her chalky face. "What is it?"

"I've been robbed."

Beside him, Lucy muffled a cry, and Ellen gasped.

He cleared his throat. "What happened?"

"While I searched the grounds for Ellen, who went off without me, someone spilled my trunk, took my satchel with all my money, and even found the secret drawer and stole my grandmother's cameo." Constance wiped away a lone tear. "She gave it to me because I was her most special grandchild. There's no way to replace it."

Ellen shook her head. "Was anything else taken?"

Constance let go of him and turned to her. "No, not a thing. Just my belongings. My dresses, stockings, and unmentionables are strewn about the car." She touched her flaming cheek. "But I shouldn't be talking about such things in a man's presence."

"Let's take a look." Not that he wanted to be involved, but Constance needed help.

"Shouldn't we go to the police?" She leaned against him. "I'm so afraid. Someone has it out for me, I know it. I want them arrested and jailed for a long time."

Will pushed her from him and led the way to the Alvena. "How do you know they targeted you? It might have been a random act."

"It had to be one of the girls from my car. Someone who watched me take out my grandmother's cameo. Who else would have known about the secret compartment?"

"The robber might have gotten lucky. Could be a smart fellow who figured it out. Everyone knows most trunks have a hidden drawer." The entire affair left a bitter taste in his mouth.

Mr. Ringling wouldn't appreciate this brouhaha.

The women confirmed everyone in the compartment was decent before he stepped in. The girls had made their living quarters bright and cheery, covering the walls with rose-flecked wallpaper and hanging pink curtains.

Constance's description of the scene proved accurate. The worn trunk gaped open. Dresses and shoes littered the floor. The drawer he presumed to be the hidden one lay on the bunk Ellen had sat on last night.

"Who was in here when you left? Did you see anyone entering?"

"I—I don't know. I'm too upset to think. This is the most terrible thing ever to happen to me. What am I going to do? I have no money. And no mementos from my grandmother. This is the worst day of my life." She sniffled.

Will wiped his damp forehead with his handkerchief. "I suppose we'll have to get law enforcement involved."

Ellen bent down. "Let me help you fold these things and put them away."

Will reached out to stop her. "No."

She startled at the abruptness of his voice.

"I'm sorry. You're only trying to be helpful, but the police will want to view the scene the way we found it. That might help them in their investigation."

Ellen stood. "Oh, I never thought about that. You're right, of course."

"In the meantime, keep everyone out. I'll be back as soon as possible. With the crowds in town and the parade going on, it may take a bit of time to find the sheriff." What a chore stretched in front of him.

Ellen nodded. "We have a show to get ready for. We're behind schedule."

"You're sure you're up to this? You look a little peaked."

"Nothing that's going to prevent me from doing my work." She rubbed her temple.

"Will, please don't leave me. I'm too afraid to be alone." Constance's hand trembled as she touched his forearm.

He backed away. "You won't be alone. The ladies' dressing room will be loaded with women."

"One of whom stole my most precious possession. I can't trust them."

"If you want this resolved, I have to find the sheriff."

He made his escape and hurried back in the direction he'd come. A robbery among the close-knit circus family didn't happen often. He should feel unsettled, and he did. But why did he break out in goose bumps every time he thought about Constance?

◆　◆　◆

Ellen, the seamstresses, and the wardrobe assistants busied themselves preparing for the show. As many women as Ellen could do without sat at their sewing machines, the needles whipping up and down. For today's shows, they would have to make do with what they'd salvaged. At least they'd purchased a few ready-made gowns.

But the hum in the tent didn't come from women busy at work. Gossip swirled under the canvas.

"Who could have done it?"

"What a terrible thing."

"I hope they catch the culprit soon."

As Ellen dressed Polly, the fat lady, Lucy worked beside her, mending a tear in the midget's tiny costume. "This whole business turns my stomach. I don't understand how someone could do such a thing."

Ellen's own stomach churned. "I don't want to believe it was anyone from this department. We get along so well."

Lucy nodded in Constance's direction. She stood in the corner, wringing her hands.

Ellen grimaced. "Do you think it's possible someone did this to get back at her?"

"Don't you?"

Ellen didn't know. She trembled a little as she tugged the voluminous gown over Polly. "Maybe you're right. I hate to think that's the case."

The women finished their work and sent the two sideshow performers to their jobs.

Ellen rummaged through the trunk holding some of the accessories for the main show acts. "Did the acrobats' leotards dry?"

"Here they are."

Ellen almost fell backward at the sound of Lucy's voice behind her.

"You're jumpy."

"I can't put my finger on it." Ellen glanced at each woman in the tent. "I'm not scared, but I guess I'm uneasy."

"We all are."

The wardrobe staff muddled their way through the afternoon show. Some days, Ellen managed to get a bit of rest between performances, but not today. She and her crew stayed busy during intermission, repairing and creating costumes in preparation for the evening.

"Is it safe to come in?"

Ellen recognized Will's voice. "It's fine." She wiped her sweaty hands on her apron.

He lifted the flap and entered, but he wasn't alone. The man with him sported blue trousers and a blue jacket with polished brass buttons. A tall, rounded helmet sat atop his head. He shook Ellen's hand. "How do you do?"

"I'm fine." Her midsection tightened. What could the police want with her? What if she gave him the wrong answer?

"I'm interviewing everyone who sleeps in the Alvena and has knowledge of where the victim kept her valuables."

His deep voice and forceful tone did nothing to still her quivering knees. "I don't know much, but I'll help you any way I can."

"Very good."

Will moved to her side. She appreciated his nearness. As the officer interrogated her, she took a deep breath.

"Where were you at ten o'clock this morning?"

She allowed her breath to escape. Her alibi stood beside her. "In town, purchasing items to replace the costumes damaged in the rain yesterday. Mr. Jorgensen was with me part of the time. So was my assistant."

She glanced at Will. His face didn't register any emotion. Why not? What was going on?

The policeman cleared his throat. "Were you alone at any time?"

"Yes, in the shops. The store owners can corroborate my story."

"That will help. Give me the shop names, and I'll speak with the clerks. But you were alone at no time?"

"No. Even when I moved between stores, people crowded the streets. Someone must have seen me."

"A witness reports spotting you on the circus grounds in the area of the sleeping car around noon. What do you say to that?"

The room warmed. A trickle of sweat stood at the edge of her jaw. "The witness must be mistaken. I left for town about an hour before then and didn't arrive back until Constance reported the robbery. Mr. Jorgensen was with me."

Beside her, Will stiffened. "I'm afraid it was closer to one o'clock when we ran into each other."

She struggled for breath. "I got turned around searching for one store. There was a time gap between my departing one shop and arriving at another. But I never left town. Mr. Jorgensen, you saw my boxes. If I returned here, wouldn't I have left them behind? Please, you have to believe me."

Will grabbed her stool. "Sit down. Don't get the vapors."

"I'm fine. But I didn't commit this crime. Ask around. You'll find that's the case."

The police officer reached into his jacket pocket. He slid out something and opened his hand.

Ellen gasped. "Constance's cameo."

Will knelt beside her. "He found it in the top of your trunk."

Chapter Five

Ellen stared at the delicate cameo in the officer's large, calloused hand. "I didn't take it." Her chest tightened. "You have to believe me."

"Then how did it get there?"

"I don't have any idea. Someone put it there. Someone is framing me." She didn't want to think it, but no other theory explained the jewelry's mysterious appearance in her belongings.

Constance zipped over from the other side of the tent. "My cameo. You found it." She clapped, then swiped it from the officer's hand. A few tears, crocodile ones in Ellen's estimation, slipped down her cheeks. "I never thought I'd see it again."

The officer cleared his throat. "This is the missing item, then?"

Constance nodded. "And you found it in Ellen's trunk?"

"That's correct, miss."

Constance turned to Ellen, her skirts swirling. "How could you? This means everything to me. You waltz in here, take my job, and now you steal my grandmother's cameo. I hope they lock you in jail."

Ellen stood, knocking over the stool. "But I didn't do it." She clenched her fists, her heart racing faster than the chariot around the hippodrome. "Officer, I'm innocent. Check with the stores. They'll tell you I shopped in their establishments. There is no way I had time to do this."

"You can be sure I'll do just that."

Will touched her shoulder and smiled, his mustache rising. "This will all work out." He directed his attention to the policeman. "The train leaves within a couple of hours of the show's end. This matter needs to be cleared up before we depart."

The man nodded. "I'll do the best I can. In the meantime, Miss Meyer will have to stay in her train compartment."

"But the show. There's so much to do. I have to finish these costumes."

Constance fluffed her hair. "I'm the senior member of this staff. I'm more than capable of overseeing the job. Besides, we don't want this kind of influence around innocent young women."

The officer shook his head. "I'm sorry, Miss Meyer, but that's the way it has to be. Is there a responsible person who can guard her?"

Will nodded. "I don't have any duties at this point. I'll sit outside the car. Can she work while we await the results of your investigation?"

"I don't have any problem with that. I'll do my best to speed things along. I can't guarantee I'll be done by the time you leave, but I hope to wrap this up soon."

"Just make sure to keep a careful watch on her." Constance glared at Ellen. "Who knows what she's capable of."

With gentle pressure on the small of her back, Will led Ellen to the tent's entrance. He glanced behind. "Make sure all of the performer's costumes are in good repair and ready to go when they're needed. The show comes first."

Will clasped Ellen's hand as they wound their way through the crowd gathering on the circus grounds. Already, the sideshow hawkers beckoned the curiosity seekers to peek inside their tents. They sidestepped the wagons, painted in an array of garish hues, returning from town. An elephant trumpeted. The smell of peanuts wafted on the afternoon air.

Ellen didn't enjoy a bit of it. "I'm sorry. I'm sure you have work to do."

"I believe you. Perhaps the real thief panicked when they heard I went to town to involve the authorities. Whoever did it might have stashed it in the nearest trunk."

"Is it really such a simple explanation?"

"Sometimes, yes."

"Thanks for believing me. You might be the only one."

"Are you having a difficult time adjusting to this life?"

"The girls have been nice enough, but they don't welcome me with open arms."

"The circus is like a family. Many of these people were born into families of performers. This Gypsy-style existence is all they know. And the former wardrobe mistress worked for the Ringling brothers since the beginning. Give them time. They'll warm up."

She stopped as they reached the train's steps, doubt filling her. "But you've been with the show your entire life. Why are you being nice to me?"

A handsome deep pink infused his smooth cheeks. Did he get too much sun? Or had she embarrassed him?

How?

◆ ◆ ◆

Will toed a rock stuck in the dirt. How did he answer Ellen's question? He couldn't tell her he noticed her yesterday in the rainstorm. That compassion rose in his chest at the sight of her bloody head. Or that some mysterious part of her reminded him of his sweet, departed mother. "It's the Christian thing to do."

"Oh." She skipped up the stairs and disappeared into the Alvena.

"I'll be out here if you need anything." He sat on the warm metallic step. The first woman who sparked any kind of emotion in him, and he made a mess of things. Most of the girls on this train were more like sisters to him. He grew up with many of them. And those he met during the winter harbored no desire to spend their lives on a stuffy train crisscrossing the country.

Anyway, he worked from first thing in the morning until late in the night. He remembered the long, lonely hours he'd spent as a child wandering the grounds, looking for anyone to pay him a bit of attention. This was no life for anyone who wanted to settle down. That's what his mother told his father.

Before the circus took her life.

Still, he loved the excitement and pageantry of it all.

"Mr. Jorgensen?"

He straightened, her soft voice piercing him. "Please, call me Will."

"Would you mind talking to me? Just to keep me company."

"Not at all."

"I'm frightened. What if the store owners don't remember me? I don't stand out in a crowd. In fact, I'm rather forgettable. And if they can't tell the police I was there, they'll throw me in jail."

"You have nothing to worry about." Dimpled cheeks. Light brown curly hair. She was anything but forgettable.

"How can you be so sure?"

"You're innocent, right?"

"Yes. The only thing I ever stole was a cookie from Miriam Taylor in school. And I only did that because I was hungry."

"You have nothing to worry about."

"What if the investigation takes too long? What will I do if the train moves on without me? Will I lose my job?" Her voice tightened until it almost squeaked.

"My mother would tell me not to borrow trouble."

"I'm not borrowing it. It's found me."

"Havoc follows Constance in her wake. One disaster or another befalls her on a regular basis. You had the misfortune of standing too close to her. Keep your distance, and you'll be fine."

"That's wise advice. I wish you would've told me that twenty-four hours ago."

"And don't worry about the train leaving. You happen to be talking to the right person."

She giggled. "True. But I can't allow you to hold up the entire production for me. You have a schedule to keep. A show to put on tomorrow."

"It's a short run. Rock Island is only twenty-five miles away. We can wait." He'd risk Mr. Ringling's ire, if need be.

"Thank you."

"For what?"

"You calmed me down. Now, if I could only get this skirt to the wardrobe tent. One of the Nelson sisters needs it for the contortionist act."

He scanned the grounds. The call of the ringmaster heralded from the main tent. The afternoon performance was well underway. For now, the grounds were quiet. He stood and peeked into the Alvena. "Give it to me. I'll run it over. You stay put." He winked.

"I'll be right here."

He scampered across the field and made it to the ladies' dressing room within a few minutes. "I have a delivery from Miss Meyer."

Of course, Constance met him at the entrance. "Mr. Jorgensen, what are you doing here? You're supposed to be guarding the prisoner."

"She isn't a prisoner. No one has convicted her of a crime."

She blinked several times, until he thought she must have sand in her eyes. "I'm sure the little vixen worked her magic on you and has you running at her beck and call. She's hoodwinked you like she has everyone else, made you believe she's perfect and innocent when she's nothing of the sort."

"I'm just delivering this skirt for one of the Nelson sisters."

"I'll walk back with you to make sure she hasn't escaped. What a perfect time it would be. With the entire town inside the big top, she could slip away unnoticed and be halfway to Chicago before anyone realized she disappeared."

"Let's go. I'll prove she's trustworthy."

When he spun around to return to the train, he spotted the police officer climbing the steps.

He'd returned with his verdict.

Chapter Six

Ellen paced the railcar up and down between the berths. What if no one corroborated her story? What if no one remembered her? How would she survive jail? Her family. They depended on her. With Mama's health declining, she couldn't lose her job. If she did, Mama wouldn't be able to afford her tuberculosis treatments.

And Ellen couldn't bear to think of the consequences.

When she heard men's voices outside of the compartment, she broke into a cold sweat. She recognized the police officer's tenor timbre and Will's much deeper one.

He'd been so kind. Would he continue to believe her even if she was found guilty?

"Miss Meyer, you may come out. The officer is back, and he has some news." Will's soft, steady words gave her a glimmer of hope. Her hands didn't shake quite as much as she made her way down the steps and over to the men.

At least, not until she saw Constance. What was she doing here? How did she know the officer had returned?

"You're going to get your comeuppance, Ellen. You can't steal from me and get away with it. I'll make sure you receive justice."

Will shook his head. "Let's hear what the officer has to say. Don't rush to judgment."

The officer nodded to Ellen. "Especially since the young lady here told the truth. The shop owners verified her story. At the time of the robbery, they were doing business with her in town. At no point was she gone long enough to return here, steal the cameo, and get back to the next store."

Ellen's knees buckled. Will grabbed her around the waist and steadied her. Out of impulse, she hugged him. "Thank you for believing in me."

"You're free to go, Miss Meyer. I'll question the rest of your staff before you pull out tonight."

"But, she stole my cameo. You're letting this thief get away." Constance stood on her tiptoes, almost shouting. "Who knows what she'll steal from me next."

Ellen's bubble of patience popped. "Didn't you hear the officer? I'm innocent. Whoever thought they saw me here at the time of the theft was mistaken. I was in town shopping for wardrobe items." She clenched her fists. "Let's put this behind us and move on. There's too much work to be done for us to stand here bickering."

Ellen couldn't hold back a smile as Constance stood moving her mouth, no words coming out. With a swish of her skirt, Ellen headed in the direction of the wardrobe tent.

A few moments later, Constance caught up to her, her voice as smooth as ice. "Just so you know, Mr. Jorgensen and I have an understanding."

Ellen stopped in her tracks, Constance flying a few steps ahead of her. "What do you mean?" Why did the urge to claw at Constance strike her?

"You know. Don't play dumb. In fact, we're planning to be married at the end of the season. Maybe even before."

"I'm very happy for the two of you. Congratulations. If you need help sewing your wedding gown, let me know."

"I believe I can make that just fine on my own."

The pain behind Ellen's eyes ramped up. She told herself the disappointment that ate away at her chest was the result of nothing more than a trying day.

Too bad she couldn't make herself believe it.

◆ ◆ ◆

Friday, May 22, 1896

Ellen clutched her satchel in one hand and her parasol in the other as she and Lucy made their way to the Des Moines post office. "I hope there's a letter waiting for me. With Mama's delicate health, I'm concerned about the cold Poppa said she contracted."

Lucy patted her hand. "Don't worry. I'm sure you'll hear that she's much improved."

"That's the hardest part of the job. Being away from your loved ones when they need you."

"You do what you have to at times."

"You're right. With much better pay than I received at the Boston shop, I couldn't pass up this opportunity. At least with the nonsense about Constance's cameo over, I don't have to fear losing my job. Mama can get medical care."

"I'm glad Constance is behaving herself. She's been almost nice to me and civil to you."

"She told me that she and Mr. Jorgensen plan to be married at the end of the season."

Lucy covered her mouth and laughed. "Over the years, she's fancied herself engaged to almost every man associated with the circus. I wouldn't put too much stock in it."

"You never know."

They made their way into the bustling city. Lithograph posters plastered the sides of many of the buildings. Their bright colors livened the brown brick landscape. "I've never seen so much advertising in one place."

Lucy pointed to one on the side of the drugstore. "I love that one. I almost believe the tigers are going to jump off the page."

"Wait, that's not for Ringling Brothers. It's for Forepaugh."

Lucy held on to her hat as she spun in a circle. "None of them are for Ringling."

"What's going on? Didn't the advertising car get here on time?"

"No, the Forepaugh advance men are opposing us, plastering over our posters."

Ellen jumped at the sound of Will's deep voice in her ear. Her heart cartwheeled in a way any acrobat would envy. "Mr. Jorgensen. I didn't know you were in town."

A moment too late, she spied Constance hanging on to him. "We're having a lovely day. I begged him to show me around, and he was only too happy to indulge me."

Will tightened his lips into a straight line. "You said you were afraid of the commotion in the big city."

Constance's giggle couldn't have been any more fake than the gorilla boy's fur.

"I trust you're feeling better, Miss Meyer."

"I am, thank you. I haven't had a headache in a few days." She didn't miss the ruddiness that highlighted his cheeks, enhancing his handsomeness.

"Where are you ladies headed?"

"To the post office. I'm hoping for a letter from my father."

"We'll walk with you."

Constance tugged on Will's arm. "I really do need to get to the five and dime. You promised to show me the way."

"We can head over there after Miss Meyer checks for her letter. Who knows? Maybe one of us will have mail, too."

"I'm not sure I can wait. Besides, there won't be anything in the post for me. My family disowned me after I joined the circus. It's simply too painful for me to watch others at mail call."

"The five and dime is on the next block on the left. We'll meet you there."

Constance flashed a most unbecoming pout. "That is quite ungentlemanly to leave a single lady alone in a strange city."

"We won't be long. With the crowds here for the performances, you'll be fine."

Constance stomped off in a cloud of dust.

Not that Ellen was sad about it. "Are you sure you should let her go like that? Maybe you should follow her."

"No, I don't think so."

"If she's your fiancée, that's the right thing to do."

Will coughed until Ellen thought he might pass out. "My fiancée?"

"She told me you're planning to get married at the end of the season."

"So, I'm to be her latest victim." He shrugged.

Lucy elbowed her in the ribs. "I told you."

Ellen glanced between Will and her friend. "I need an explanation."

Will took off his bowler hat, wiped his forehead with his handkerchief, and returned his hat to its rightful place. "Let me explain. Every year, Constance chooses a man to set her cap on. Problem is, the young man never knows anything of the plan until it's almost too late."

Lucy swung her satchel back and forth. "Last year, it was poor Mr. Quincy, the ticket taker. She almost had him to the altar before his head stopped spinning."

"Oh dear. I do feel sorry for you."

"No sorrier than I feel for myself."

They entered the cool, dark post office. Much to her delight, the clerk handed Ellen a letter with her address inscribed in Poppa's strong hand.

She slit the envelope open with a hairpin and withdrew the piece of Mama's lavender-scented stationery. She'd saved her pennies and given it to Mama right before she left for Baraboo.

But when she read the words on the page, the letter fluttered from her hand.

Chapter Seven

Ellen held the letter in her trembling hand. Her face turned as white as the sheet. The paper floated to the ground.

Will picked up the page. Did it contain terrible news? "What's wrong? What did it say?"

Ellen stared straight ahead, not blinking.

Though he didn't want to violate her privacy, he did want to help her. Something he couldn't do unless he knew the problem. He scanned the letter until he found the reason for Ellen's shock.

> *Mama is not responding to the medication. The doctor recommends a sanatorium, though how we will pay for it is a mystery only God knows the answer to. Thank you for what you send to us each month. We could not get along without your help. You are a blessing to us. Perhaps we'll be able to save some of your contribution and send her there in time. Please continue to pray for her. She is very weak.*

Will shivered, a memory of the cold chills that had racked him when he'd looked at his mother's lifeless body. "I had no idea your mother was ill." Will drew Ellen into an embrace, her muscles taut.

She whispered into his shoulder. "Take me to the train."

He released her. "Sure. Lucy, can you please meet Constance at the five and dime and tell her what happened?"

"Of course." Lucy nodded, the flower on her hat bouncing. "Everything will be fine. Trust and believe that."

"Thank you." Ellen's soft voice held no trace of emotion.

They wove their way through the throngs of circus goers, the festive party out of place with the news she'd received.

"How can I help?"

"Unless you have the money for the sanatorium, there isn't much to be done. My immigrant parents have small resources and five mouths to feed beside their own. Poppa works hard, but because of Mama's illness my siblings are his responsibility. What am I going to do? How can I pay for what she needs? I have little enough."

He stopped. "Look at me."

She gazed into his eyes. Without words, she pled with him for a solution.

He didn't have one. "I'll pray for you. And her."

"What if He takes her away?"

"It'll be hard. God says to trust Him." But had Will trusted the Lord since his mother's death?

"Easier said than done."

"That's true. I lost my own mother when I was ten. In a circus accident. She fell from the trapeze."

"Oh, Will, how awful. I'm so sorry."

"So you see, I understand your struggle. I know what it's like to lose a parent." They resumed their walk.

"I can tell myself to trust God when the trunks float away or when I can't find a costume. When it comes to my mother's life, that's harder. When God doesn't act, I have to." Her staccato words matched the rhythm of her feet.

They returned to the Alvena. "Why don't you lie down? A bit of rest will do you good. You've been fiendish in repairing and replacing the costumes."

"I have to sew. When difficulties come, I block them out by stitching."

"Stay on the train. The peace and quiet will do you good."

She nodded and slipped off her gloves before climbing the steps. "Thank you again. You're a dear friend."

His heart tripped over itself. She considered him a friend. "I'm glad I could help. That's what friends do." But this fluttering, somersaulting, diving sensation in the pit of his stomach had to be more than friendship.

She disappeared into the compartment, then appeared at the window, waving. He sauntered across the grounds, the fragrance of the cook staff's stew mingling with that of elephant dung and popped corn. The unique smell of the circus.

His hunger pains evaporated when he thought of Ellen. He ached for her. He knew what it was to lose a mother. He would have done anything to save his.

How could he help her? As trainmaster, he earned a decent wage. To pay for a sanatorium, though, was beyond his means. Did they take charity cases? Could he help them find a good low-cost facility?

Yes, of course. And he would. Des Moines had a large enough population to support several doctors. One of them had to know the answer.

He turned toward town. If he hurried, he could ask and be back in time to load the train. Little sleep for him tonight, but when he thought of Ellen's sad, green eyes, it spurred him on.

Until a hyena-like scream erupted from the wardrobe tent.

◆　◆　◆

"Ellen, hurry. Come to the wardrobe tent." Lucy's breathless voice broke Ellen's concentration as she stitched spangles onto the elephant's headdress.

"What's wrong? Can't it wait until I'm finished?" The heaviness in her heart weighed down her entire body. Even lifting a needle took enormous effort.

Lucy dragged her to her feet. "There's an emergency. With Constance."

Lord, give me strength. "What now? No, don't tell me. I don't want to know."

She followed Lucy across the grassy lot. After a moment to adjust to the tent's dim interior, she discovered the reason for the pandemonium.

Contortionist, acrobat, and equestrian outfits lay strewn about the dirt floor. She bent down. Cut. Slashed. Ruined. The lot of them.

"And all of them my creations." Constance stood over her, her legs akimbo, a scowl marring her flawless features.

Sweat covered Ellen's palms. "You don't think—"

"I certainly do. You came back ahead of the rest of us." A glint shimmered in Constance's eye, almost triumphant.

"Ida." Ellen nodded in the direction of one of her assistants. "Were you here the entire time?" The girl did a very good job, but she sewed slower than anyone. She often worked while the rest of them went to town.

"No, ma'am. I had coffee with Renee in the dining tent."

Constance tilted her chin and stared at Ellen. "You had the time to come in here and destroy all of my work. Do you know how many hours I labored over them? Gone. You're jealous of my relationship with Will. You want me fired so you can have him." Her neck muscles tightened. "Well, it won't work. We all know who did it, don't we?"

Constance scanned the crowd of seamstresses and performers gathered near the tent flap.

They all stared at Ellen. Their glares drove her down like a tent peg into the soft sand. "You can't believe I had anything to do with this. Where's Mr. Jorgensen? He can attest to my whereabouts."

He popped through the crowd as if she'd produced him by magic. "What on earth happened?"

"Someone destroyed Constance's costumes." She held up one of the aerialist's leotards.

"Who would do this?"

Constance nestled against Will. "I'm glad you're here. She's the only one who could have ruined my work. The other girls were in town or the dining tent. You left her alone, and this is what happened."

"She didn't have time. I left her only ten minutes before you screamed."

"Plenty of opportunity." Constance crowed and harrumphed.

A murmur rippled through the spectators.

"Why would I wreck my assistant's work? Her claims on Mr. Jorgensen are in her imagination, so I heard. This makes more work for all of us. The real culprit needs to be stopped."

The crowd cheered. Were they turning against her? She fought for breath. She couldn't lose her job. Not now. Not ever.

One of the men Ellen recognized from the big top crew stepped forward and apprehended her. "We know who's behind this mischief. I'll sit on her meself, so's to stop it."

Her chest squeezed.

A sideshow man wrested her away. "You're talking crazy. We know Miss Constance. She set her sights on me two years ago. Looks like she's aiming higher now. Let the mistress go. I'd bet my last dollar she didn't do it."

Will stepped in front of her, forcing the man to release his hold. She rubbed her painful wrists.

"No one is apprehending anyone. Miss Meyer is innocent. I'll attest to it myself."

"How can you side with her?" A perfect tear clung to Constance's blond lashes. "Why can't you see her for what she is?"

The tent walls closed in. The room spun.

In her haze, Ellen spotted a man in the crowd. His thick mustache gave him away. Al Ringling.

Chapter Eight

"W hat is going on?"

Ellen gasped for breath as the imposing Al Ringling entered the wardrobe tent. Such a commotion had attracted the attention of the circus's founder. And chief.

Will tightened his grip on her waist. "Sir, the situation is under control. A mysterious suspect ruined several of Miss Hefner's costumes, but I will get to the bottom of the matter and ensure nothing like this happens again."

Mr. Ringling nodded. "I trust you, Mr. Jorgensen. You haven't let me down. See to it the miscreant is dealt with." The man strode off.

Beside her, Will straightened. "You heard him. I'll make sure the person who did this will be held responsible. We won't tolerate this kind of behavior."

The crowd dispersed.

Constance clutched her ruined items. "Why are you hesitating? You're standing next to the culprit." She stepped between Will and Ellen. "I demand justice."

Ellen held her breath. What if he wanted to placate Constance? And Mr. Ringling? He didn't have to investigate. He could blame her and be done with it.

"You'll have it. As soon as I get to the bottom of it. Not a minute before."

"I see." Constance glanced over her shoulder at Ellen. "Mark my words. You'll be sorry." She flounced off. "Mr. Ringling. Wait, Mr. Ringling. I must speak with you."

Ellen sunk back onto the stool. She smoothed her black skirt with shaky hands. "She's going to the boss. He won't suffer this. I'll be dismissed by the end of the day. Then what will my family do?" She fought back bitter tears.

Will circled her. "You won't be fired. I'll make sure of that. Don't worry about your mother. She'll be fine."

Ellen didn't understand his words. How did he know all would be well? Only God knew.

Some of the performers arrived to prepare for the show. She stood and rubbed the back of her neck. "Well, for now I have a job. The show waits for no one."

Somehow, she and her assistants dressed the ladies. The matinee went off without a hitch. Constance didn't put in an appearance. What might that mean? Had Mr. Ringling refused to listen to her? That would be the best possible outcome. Were they still discussing? Maybe he was promoting her to wardrobe mistress this moment.

Much to her surprise, she had an appetite for dinner, so in the lull between shows she wandered to the dining tent. A few of the tent crews and the roustabouts gave her sideways looks as she worked her way through the line. Even her own crew whispered.

She took her plate and found a seat at the end of one of the long tables, away from the other behind-the-scenes workers. The performers had their own tent. The circus officers ate in the dining car.

She buttered her bread. The yeasty odor reminded her of home. Mama loved to bake. Her hearty, dark loaves had filled Ellen's belly many nights. Sometimes it was all they had, but Mama made them delicious.

The bench creaked as someone sat across from her. "Is this spot taken?"

Will's voice might as well have been the honey on the bread. "What are you doing? People might get the wrong idea."

"Tell them I questioned you."

"Questioned me?"

He leaned across the table. "I know you're innocent. The best way for me to prove that is to figure out who really stole that cameo and cut up the clothes. But I need your help."

"What can I do?"

"A good deal. Who has a reason to get you into trouble? Who wants to be rid of you?"

"I don't know. So far, I get along well with all the girls." She glanced at the younger seamstresses staring at her. "Until today. Only Constance gave me problems. I'm not much help."

"No, that's not much to go on." He rubbed his hazel eyes.

"I wish I could do more."

He twitched his mustache. "I know a way you can."

◆ ◆ ◆

Searching the Alvena posed danger. If one of the women caught them, Will and Ellen might both lose their jobs. His mouth turned as dry as coal dust. But he'd told Mr. Ringling and Ellen he'd find the perpetrator.

He meant to do just that.

When he stared into her eyes, he believed her to be innocent. Now, he had to convince everyone else.

She bit her lower lip.

"We have to get in your car and hunt for anything useful. Now. Soon you'll have to prepare for the evening show, and I'll have to load the train. If we don't seize this opportunity, it will be a while before we can get in there. Are you with me?"

She rubbed her hands together. "It's risky. What if one of the seamstresses comes in and catches us? I'm not sure about this."

He couldn't solve the mystery without her help. "If you do nothing, you take the chance you'll get fired."

A small smile played on her lips. "You're right. But if we get caught, I'll tell them you dreamed up the idea."

"Fair enough." His body warmed at her playful side. "Success or failure, I'll take the blame."

But he intended to prove to Mr. Ringling he had been right to hire such a young trainmaster.

They walked together toward the quiet sleeper. The roustabouts, who would soon start their shift, meandered in the direction of the dining tent, the tantalizing smell of roasted chicken beckoning.

Will and Ellen reached the car. She climbed the steps, her black skirt brushing her black boots as she went. "Stay here. Make sure no one spies you. I'll see if the coast is clear." She disappeared inside.

One of his crew passed him. He whistled and attempted to appear as nonchalant as possible.

"Will we get out of here early tonight, Mr. Jorgensen?"

"It's a short haul from the lot to the rail yard, and the weather's good, so we should. Enjoy your dinner." He tipped his bowler hat.

As soon as the man left, Ellen gave a loud whisper. "Hurry in."

He glanced around to be sure no one watched, then bounded up the steps. His heart beat double time. At least daylight lingered long this time of year. No need to turn on the gas lamps.

Her curly hair escaped the knot on top of her head. "What should I look for?"

"Anything suspicious that might be a clue as to who is after Constance."

"That could be anyone."

"Move fast. We don't know how much time we have." He took a deep breath, then lifted the creaky lid of a woman's trunk. A hint of lace greeted him. He slammed the top shut. "Maybe you should look through the personal belongings. I'll search the girls' papers."

Her cheeks pinked like a Dakota sunset. "Good idea."

She bent over a painted steamer trunk, while he moved to unlatch the brass straps of a lap desk. He searched every drawer. Nothing. There might be secret compartments, but he couldn't find any.

Time ticked. He rummaged through every scrap of paper, every receipt, every letter from a loved one. Nothing. "What have you found?"

"Not much."

The sound of female laughter floated through an open window. The lilt of several soft voices carried on the air.

"That's Lucy and Martha. You have to hide."

"Where?" He spun in a circle, his mind whirring.

"Under the berth."

He examined his neat trousers.

"I have to get my thimble. I don't know why I took it from the tent or why I left it here after my rest."

"That's Lucy." Ellen hissed. "Hurry."

In one motion, he rolled under the narrow bed, sharing the space with numerous dust bunnies.

But what he spied made the dive worth it.

Chapter Nine

Ellen's hands turned icy as Lucy and Martha entered the train compartment. Was that Will's breathing she heard? Would the girls notice they'd rummaged through their belongings?

"Ellen, what are you doing here? I thought you'd be getting ready for tonight's show." Lucy moved past her to her trunk.

"I, uh, I—"

"That's strange." Lucy knelt in front of her valise. "I always keep Mother's picture on the top so it doesn't get damaged. Why is it on the bottom?"

Ellen wanted to smack her forehead. She'd searched Lucy's possessions. How could she have forgotten to put the photograph back?

"Who knows? So many strange things are happening." She wished Lucy would hurry. The sooner Will left, the better. They shouldn't have come in here.

"And my thimble. I can't find it."

Ellen knew where it was. She'd found it in the pocket of the skirt Lucy wore earlier. "Have you checked all your pockets?"

"Here it is." Lucy stood and brushed the dirt from her gown. "It's almost like you knew it was there. Are you ready to get back to work? You can walk with us."

"I'll be there in just a minute. I need some headache powders."

The two women left. Ellen slumped against a berth.

"I'm glad I rolled under there." Will emerged from his hiding spot holding a piece of paper.

"What's that?"

"Something tells me it's the clue we're looking for."

He unfolded it. "'Dearest Mama.'" He scanned the page. "Ah, here. 'Constance is a continuous thorn in my side.'"

She flew at Will, diving for the scrap in his hand.

He snatched it out of her reach and spun with his back to her. "'I wish some calamity would befall her so she would be forced to leave the circus. Nothing grand, but some misfortune. Then, I could work in peace. Without her, the wardrobe would run with greater efficiency. My job would be easier.'"

She reached around him and snatched the letter from his hand. "I meant to throw that in the stove."

He turned to face her, his hazel eyes empty. "I'm sure you did. You never hid the fact you disliked her. But I believed you wouldn't do such a terrible thing."

A drip of sweat rolled down her back. "I didn't. I wrote that when I was upset. As soon as I put the words to paper, I regretted them. That's why I wanted it destroyed. You have to believe me. I have an alibi."

"I don't know how or when you did it, but you fooled everyone." His words held no hint of warmth. "I'm sorry I trusted you."

He headed for the exit.

"Will, don't go. I'm telling the truth." She swallowed around the lump in her throat.

He didn't look back.

Ellen sat on her berth and hugged herself. She had come to care for him. Why had she opened her heart? Now, she would run into him and Constance every day. For the rest of the season.

If she stayed that long. He might be in Mr. Ringling's car right now. Would they give her train fare home after they fired her?

What about the toll on her family? She'd failed to help them when they needed it most. That note sealed Mama's death sentence.

How many times had Poppa warned her to watch her tongue? That applied to the pen, too. She'd brought this on herself.

Digging her fingernails into her palms to keep the tears at bay, she shuffled toward the dressing tent. By this time tomorrow, she expected to be on an eastbound train. In the meantime, she'd oversee one last show.

◆　◆　◆

Wednesday, June 17, 1896

"Mr. Jorgensen, wake up. The devil's on the train. We need your help. Fast."

Will rolled over in bed as the train clacked its way through Iowa. What a strange dream. He covered his head with his pillow.

"Mr. Jorgensen."

He was sleeping, wasn't he?

"Sir, the devil's visiting us."

He opened his eyes and sat up. Frank Brown, the brakeman, stood at the foot of the bed holding a lantern, his eyes wide, his hair wild.

"What's going on?"

"There's an awful racket on top of the cars. I went investigating like the conductor told me to, and I met the devil. Large horns and a long beard, just like in all the drawings I seen of him."

Will rolled out of bed and yanked on a pair of pants. "I don't know what it was, but you didn't see the devil. Let me have a look."

"Thanks so much, sir. But you be careful, now. Don't go falling off. And don't sell him your soul."

Will followed Frank through the cars until they came to a flatbed piled with tent canvases and poles.

"I seen him on top of that there car." Frank handed Will the lantern.

The train raced across the dark farmland while Will shimmied up a tent pole and onto the top of the car. Like a newborn foal, he used great caution as he stood. Laughter welled inside of him and burst from his lips when he saw what Frank called the devil. The Nepalese mountain goat used in the menagerie stared back at him. "How on earth did you get up here?"

The goat lowered his head.

The lights of a little town whipped past. His fingers tingled, and his foot slid on the dewy metal. He lowered himself to all fours and, as fast as possible, crawled back the way he'd come, down the pole.

"Did you see him? Wasn't I right?"

The goat followed Will, and in one flying leap, landed on a roll of canvas. Frank bellowed, stumbling backward.

The animal jumped on the car's floor and back into his cage.

"Secure that door. If it was open enough for him to get in, it must have been open enough for him to get out." Will leaned forward to catch his breath.

Frank locked the latch. "When he lunged at me, I thought I was done for."

"Just a rogue out for a midnight stroll." He and Frank returned through the men's sleeping car.

Mr. Ringling stood in the middle of the compartment, wrapped in his dressing robe. "What's going on?"

Not what Will needed. Especially since he never went to Mr. Ringling about his suspicions regarding Ellen. Something held him back. Stopped him from sharing his worst fear. "Nothing, sir. A little incident with the Nepalese goat, but that's been handled."

"My porter woke me claiming the brakeman saw the devil."

"My apologies. I handled the incident. Let me walk you back to your car."

"The devil, of all things. That man better not have been drinking."

The prohibition on alcohol set the Ringling circus apart. "Not at all. Shadows in the middle of the night played tricks on his mind."

They crossed into the dining car. "Now that this matter is cleared up, tell me about your investigation into the happenings in the wardrobe department."

The costume cutting happened a week ago. Will thought of the desperation in Ellen's voice, the pleading in her eyes. He wanted to believe her. But that slip of paper taunted him. "I have a suspect."

Mr. Ringling smoothed down his mustache. "And who might that be?"

Should he say? Keep quiet, hoping to find evidence that pointed away from Ellen? He rubbed the back of his neck. "I want to complete the investigation first."

They entered another car and stopped in front of Will's compartment. "This is my operation, my train, my employees. I have a duty to take care of them. Share with me what you've found. I'll determine what happens."

Like one of the caged lions, Will was trapped. "A few days ago, I found a letter written by—"

Will's porter rushed breathless into the car. "Sorry to disturb you." The man tipped his hat.

"What is it, Harry?"

"You'd better come. Some ruckus in the Alvena."

Will clung to the brass rail along the wall as the train swung a wide turn. Something involving Ellen? He should have gone to Mr. Ringling earlier. "I'll be right there."

Mr. Ringling poked Will's arm. "This better not be about those two wardrobe women. I'll hold you personally responsible if it is."

"I hope not, sir."

More than anything.

Chapter Ten

Will hustled from his car, following his porter. Trouble in the Alvena. His entire body tingled.

He pushed by Mr. Ringling and raced toward the sleeping car. He didn't care that he bumped into the berths where his roustabouts and the canvas men slept. All he cared about was keeping his job.

He refused to go down in history as the shortest-lived trainmaster.

And, if he had to be honest with himself, he cared about Ellen.

He heard women's cries and shouts before he arrived. He entered and leaned against the wall to catch his breath. One voice rang above them.

"Let me go. I'm innocent."

Ellen. Tears laced her words.

He pushed through the crowd, which fell silent. Mr. Ringling must have entered. Will worked his way to the inner circle of women.

Constance stood behind Ellen, pinning her arms behind her back. Tears streamed down Ellen's cheeks.

Constance narrowed her eyes. "She tried to suffocate me."

The train lurched. Will stumbled, then regained his balance. "She what?"

"You're lying."

"I caught her standing over me."

"She grabbed me as I walked past." Ellen sucked in her breath as Constance tightened her grip.

"They should have locked you up in Geneseo. Will might have saved you then. Not this time. Not if I have anything to say about it."

Mr. Ringling stepped into the center of the action, legs akimbo, arms crossed.

Will cleared his throat and forced his voice to remain steady. "Let go of her."

"What?" Constance dragged Ellen in Will's direction. "You want me to free a murderer?"

"You're alive."

"Only because I'm stronger. If I wasn't, I'd be dead."

"I said let her go. She won't get away. Not with this mob."

Constance released her grip. Ellen rubbed her wrists. She swiped away a few tears. "Thank you."

"I didn't exonerate you. Far from it. We're going to get to the bottom of this. No one goes to sleep until I hear the story. And the truth."

"She—"

Will signaled for Constance to be quiet. "I know your version. I want to hear Miss Meyer's."

"I got up to . . ."

"To what? Tell the truth. All of it."

Red flooded her face, rivaling the scarlet of the ringmaster's coat. "To use the chamber pot." She studied her bare feet.

He wanted to fold her into his embrace. To make this all go away. Why did he want to do that when he believed she'd perpetrated the earlier crimes? What brought out this protective streak? "Go on."

"I was walking back when Constance grabbed me and screamed. That's all. It's my word against hers."

Will sighed. They had no proof either way.

"Who else would it have been? She's the one I fought off and grabbed. I can't be mistaken." Constance crowed like a proud rooster.

Mr. Ringling rubbed his lower back. "The evidence isn't in your favor, Miss Meyer."

Ellen's voice regained a measure of strength. "It's not in hers, either. There's no proof I did this. She's making it up. Look. She doesn't have a single mark on her."

Will examined Constance. Her hair hung down her back in a neat braid. If she'd struggled with Ellen, it would be mussed. Instead, not a hair was out of place.

He studied Ellen, her arms bare midway up. Constance said she fought her attacker. Yet Ellen's arms showed no fresh bruises or scratches. Her hair hung in wild curls.

What should he do? He had to please Mr. Ringling. But the helpless, frightened look in Ellen's wide green eyes ate at him.

He drew in a deep breath, prepared to answer.

◆ ◆ ◆

Ellen couldn't control the shaking that racked her.

Murder.

Constance accused her of attempted murder.

Falsely.

Would anyone believe her?

She wanted to crumple to the ground in a puddle of tears. She'd failed her family. Failed Mama. The woman who gave her everything.

Mama would die. Her younger brothers and sisters would grow up without her love.

Mr. Ringling's voice penetrated her fear-laced haze. "Never have I encountered such trouble. It's not becoming to a family like ours. If the public learns about these problems, our sales will be affected, our reputation sullied. I refuse to have that. Ringling Brothers is a family-friendly show, and I aim to keep it that way."

Ellen went numb. Did Marie Antoinette feel this way as the henchmen led her to the guillotine?

"Miss Meyer, we will let you off at the next station. As soon as we arrive, you are to disembark and leave the circus. Since there is no evidence against you, I won't involve the authorities. But these disruptions happened after I employed you. I have to maintain peace and order in my show."

Constance stood on her tiptoes and almost jumped up and down, like an eager schoolchild ready to give the answer. "Who will replace her?"

"You're the longest serving wardrobe staff member?"

"That's correct." Constance out-beamed the gas lights.

"Then you're the new wardrobe mistress. I trust there will be no further incidents once Miss Meyer is gone."

"There won't be. I'll do my utmost to make my department a model of efficiency."

If Ellen's mouth hadn't gone dry, she might have laughed. Or shouted at Mr. Ringling and everyone else. How could they believe Constance over her?

Will was right. The circus was a family. One she didn't belong to. She wasn't part of them. Never would be. Maybe Miss Anna would give her back her old dress shop job. The low pay wouldn't be enough to send Mama to the sanatorium, but it would help the rest of her family.

"Do you understand, Miss Meyer?"

She nodded. "Yes, sir."

The crowd dissipated. She returned to her berth and lay beside Lucy.

"I'm so sorry, Ellen. For what it's worth, I don't believe Constance. She's vengeful and spiteful. She wanted your job. It looks like she did whatever it took to get it."

"Thanks." She swallowed a sob.

The train's wheels clacked out the miles until arriving in Independence, Iowa. Since she'd lain awake for hours, Ellen decided not to waste time. She dressed and packed her belongings. The job didn't take long.

The other women filed off the train, heading for the dining tent. Lucy lagged behind, enveloping Ellen in a long hug.

Ellen's throat stung. "I'll miss you. Thank you for believing in me. You're the only one."

"There are more, I'm sure. What about Will? He stared at you last night."

"Only pity. Everyone stared at me."

"Don't say that. I know you're worried about your mother."

"I can't talk about her. She's going to die because I failed."

Lucy pressed a piece of paper into Ellen's hand. "Here. I read this last night. It's been on my mind. The words might comfort you."

Ellen unfolded the lilac page.

> *Trust in the LORD, and do good; so shalt thou dwell in the land, and verily thou shalt be fed. Delight thyself also in the LORD: and he shall give thee the desires of thine heart. Commit thy way unto the LORD; trust also in him; and he shall bring it to pass. And he shall bring forth thy righteousness as the light, and thy judgment as the noonday.*
> *Psalm 37:3–6*

Trust in the Lord. Over the years, she had heard that admonition a thousand times. But how difficult to trust when your mother's life lay in your hands. When your family relied on you to make enough money to get her the treatment she needed to live.

"He shall give thee the desires of thine heart."

She wanted to believe. Right now, the desires of her heart lay in tatters at her feet. "Thank you, Lucy. I'll miss you most of all." Ellen picked up her valise. Once they unloaded, she'd have one of the roustabouts bring her trunk inside the station.

The Alvena's porter, Mr. Hickley, knocked and entered when she answered. "I'm sorry to see you go, miss. Constance don't hold a candle to you. Anyways, the station master gave me this telegram for you."

Ellen tried to take the message from Mr. Hickley, but she couldn't hold it in her trembling hands. "Read it to me, Lucy."

She feared the news to be the worst kind about Mama.

Chapter Eleven

Ellen sat on the edge of her berth and covered her eyes. She wanted to cover her ears and not hear what Lucy was about to read. She already knew. The lump in her throat clogged her airway.

Lucy sat beside her. In a soft voice meant only for Ellen's ears, she dealt the news.

MOTHER ILL. *Stop.* MEDICINE RUNNING LOW. *Stop.* SEND MONEY. *Stop.*

Her pent-up tears burst through the dam. Ellen doubled over and sobbed. Lucy rubbed her back.

Today, she would travel home, a disgrace. Poppa had pinned his hopes on her. And she'd let him down. How could she face him? What would she say to Mama?

At last, she composed herself.

Lucy leaned close. "God will provide. He has so far. Trust Him."

"I did. I trusted Him to give me a job."

"And He provided one."

"Only to rip it away a few weeks later." Ellen wiped her face with an embroidered handkerchief. "I won't make this kind of money elsewhere. I'll give them everything from my last paycheck, but that will be all."

Lucy squeezed her. "I'll pray for you. You'll never be far from my thoughts. I hope we meet again."

"You've been a true friend. Thank you."

Lucy left the car with one final wave.

Ellen picked up her valise and made her way to the door. The Alvena had become her home. She would miss it. All of it.

She stepped from the train for the last time and made her way toward the station. The ticket home would sap her money. What she'd saved in her trunk's secret compartment to send Mama to the sanatorium. Perhaps she could find work in Independence. But she wanted to see Mama. To hold her hand and kiss her cheek. What should she do? Where should she go?

Gravel crunched under her feet, each step taking her farther from the life she'd come to love. The band's music. Bright flags flapping. Children's laughter. Pomp and daring and opulence.

Her new life would never measure up.

"Ellen."

She jumped at the sound of Will's voice, but checked herself from racing away from him. "I thought you were my friend." *Maybe even more.*

"I was. I am."

"You don't believe me. Because of one scrap of paper, you tossed away everything I proved to you and believed a woman who'd do anything for my job." Her heart pumped in rhythm with her legs.

He grabbed her by the arm and stopped her. "Last night taught me something."

"What? That you were wrong to trust me? You already told me that." The lump in her throat grew until she thought she might suffocate. In vain, she tried to wrest herself from him.

"I was wrong to not believe you."

She ceased struggling. Was this an apology? "What?"

"I panicked. Mr. Ringling is after me to stop whatever is going on in the wardrobe department. I don't want to lose my job. The circus has been my life. I was born into it. It's all I know."

"So, to please him, you intended to sacrifice me."

He finger-combed his brown, slicked-back hair. "Nothing like that."

"Then tell me what it was like."

"People have duped me. Last season, I brought on an assistant who told me he'd been with Barnum and Bailey for several years. What he didn't tell me was that he was here to discover where we planned to go and how we ran our operation so they would be bigger, better, and faster. I almost lost my position. Now, Mr. Ringling entrusted me with the trainmaster's job, at my age. I can't make another mistake."

"You broke my trust. How can I depend on you?"

"Because I'm about to go in to Mr. Ringling's office to tell him you're innocent."

"Telling him that won't change his belief I tried to murder Constance."

"That's not what he thinks."

"I'm the one who lost my job. A job I needed to save my mother." She clenched her fists.

"Lucy told me your mother needs medicine."

"She shouldn't have."

"I'm going to fight for you, because I believe you. Constance is making up everything. The stolen cameo. The shredded costumes. The attempted suffocation."

Ellen took a deep breath. Like a train coming to a station, her heart slowed. "That's your theory?"

He nodded, smiling. "She had motive."

"My job. And you."

"Opportunity."

"She doesn't have an alibi for any of the times the events took place."

"And I studied the two of you last night. She didn't look like she struggled. You didn't bear any marks, either."

Her ears rang. He really believed her. "Is it possible? You can clear me?"

"Am I forgiven for my stupidity?"

Should she? Could she trust a man who didn't trust her?

"We all make mistakes. I don't want my big one to ruin what's happening between us."

"I looked guilty. If Constance was behind this, she did a good job of setting me up."

"I don't want you to leave. You're important to me." He caressed her cheek, then cupped her chin.

"I would have missed you." More than she wanted to admit.

"Then let's meet with Mr. Ringling. Show him our proof. I'll convince him to give you your job back. You can take care of your mother."

Maybe the Lord did provide. Perhaps she should have trusted Him more. "Lucy gave me a verse. Something about committing your ways to the Lord, and He will bring forth your righteousness as the light."

Will rubbed the dirt with his shoe. "I need to depend on Him more. Less on myself."

"I'm scared. What if He lets me down?"

He gazed at her. "I'll disappoint you. He never will."

"Will you pray with me?"

And so they stood in the rail yard, heads bowed, and beseeched the Lord to sustain them. When they finished, peace flooded her. The worry lines on Will's brow relaxed.

She followed him to Mr. Ringling's private car. Through the window, she spotted rich mahogany and brass fittings. Sumptuous luxury. Not her two-to-a-berth accommodations.

She stopped Will at the bottom step. "Are you sure I should go in? He might throw me out on my ear. He told me he wanted me off the train as soon as we arrived at the station. It's late."

"You need to show him your arms. The ones that aren't scratched and don't bear nail marks. You can do this. For your mother."

He'd touched a nerve. For Mama, she would do almost anything. She steeled her back and climbed the steps.

When given the go-ahead, Will entered the red velvet–draped car. Mr. Ringling sat behind a large, polished desk, his long legs outstretched. "Mr. Jorgensen. Mr. Piel said you had an urgent matter. I didn't realize Miss Meyer would join us. I made it clear last night she was to disembark as soon as we reached Independence."

Her stomach turned to a block of ice. Coming to Mr. Ringling's office was the wrong move. She tugged on Will's dark jacket.

He ignored her. "What I tell you will change your opinion."

The middle-aged circus founder puffed on his pipe. "Make it fast. You should be unloading."

"Miss Meyer is innocent of all charges. She had nothing to do with any of this, other than being wardrobe mistress and spending time with me."

Ellen clasped her hands together, concentrating on remaining upright.

"Miss Hefner orchestrated this entire charade. When Harriet Wilson left, Constance believed she'd get the job. She never thought you'd hire a young seamstress not associated with the circus. If she got rid of Miss Meyer, she'd have another chance."

"And she was right." Mr. Ringling nodded. "But this is nothing more than a theory."

"Did you notice her last night? She claimed Miss Meyer tried to suffocate her, yet her hair was neat. And she said she fought back, yet Miss Meyer's arms aren't scratched. Isn't that strange?"

Al Ringling sat forward. "Let me see."

She hung back, not wanting to bare her arms in front of two men.

Will gave her a small shove.

"It's not too immodest?"

Mr. Ringling chuckled. "If you wish to exonerate yourself, I need to see them."

She loosened the buttons of her white shirtwaist's cuffs and pushed up the sleeves. Then she stepped toward Mr. Ringling.

He studied her for a moment. "Thank you." He turned his attention to Will. "You're correct about Miss Meyer. I don't see evidence of the struggle Miss Hefner described. Your theory is solid. But not proof."

Ellen rolled down her sleeves. They didn't know for sure Constance invented these crimes. For the good of the circus, one of them had to go. She knew it would be her. "Thank you for your time, Mr. Ringling. I'm glad you believe me. I appreciated my opportunity here." She turned to leave, determined not to weep.

"Stop." Will blocked her path. "We can show Mr. Ringling Constance was behind this. I have a plan."

Chapter Twelve

The song of hammers against tent pegs rang out around Will as Ellen and Mr. Ringling stared at him.

He'd put a hard-won job on the line for this woman. But she was worth it.

Ellen stood on her tiptoes. "If you have a plan that will save my job, I want to hear it."

Will swallowed. Why had he said he had a plan? "It's not completely formulated."

"Let's hear what you have." Mr. Ringling's booming voice echoed through his mahogany-paneled private car.

"We have to catch Miss Hefner in the act."

Ellen licked her lips. "How?"

"Set a trap. Give her a noose so she can hang herself."

"I hope you meant that figuratively." Ellen cracked the day's first smile.

He wanted to keep her smiling. "First of all, Mr. Ringling, you have to rehire Ellen."

The man nodded. "You are hereby reinstated as wardrobe mistresses."

Ellen's gorgeous grin widened. An urge to kiss her almost overwhelmed him. He held himself back. "That will make Constance furious. She won't wait long to react. I'll tail her, watching her every move."

Mr. Ringling tented his fingers. "So, your plan is to wait for her to act?"

Will gulped. Trust the Lord. "Yes, it is."

"That's not much."

"I know, but it's all we have. Like I said, she'll dream up another way to get rid of Ellen soon. I'm sure of it."

"Fine. But I need proof. I won't tolerate any more mischief. If you can't provide it, Miss Meyer will be terminated."

"But sir—"

"That's all." Mr. Ringling stood.

Will led Ellen from the lavish car into the bright light. "I'm sorry I didn't have a better plan. That should teach me to think before I speak. But I want to help." He'd already gone to town this morning to set an idea into motion to make up for not believing her. "I'd do anything for you."

She tugged on his jacket sleeve, and he turned to face her. "That means so much. But why?"

Did he dare say the words that fought to leap from his mouth? Blood pounded in his ears. "I care about you."

"Oh, Will."

"I should have believed you."

"You've been good to me. I know it's been hard. I looked guilty. Even with your doubts, you searched for a way to help. That counts in your favor. You're special to me."

He wanted to whoop. Instead, he brushed a strand of curly hair from her cheek. "I think I love you."

She stood on her tiptoes and whispered in his ear. "I know I love you."

Little shivers traversed his spine. "Then let's see that Constance gets justice. I don't want to lose you."

"Let's do so. I don't want to go anywhere. Because of Mama. And because of you."

◆　◆　◆

Ellen sailed into the wardrobe tent with as much bravado as she could muster. Too bad she didn't feel it. Her mouth went dry. Her palms sweated.

Constance sat in the center of the tent, her back straight, her eyes narrow. "Lucy, haven't you finished that hem? Anna needs the costume for her high-wire act now. Sophia, patch Ella's dress. Make sure no one can tell her performing goat nibbled it."

She continued to demand compliance from her staff. *No, from my staff.* The assistants spotted Ellen and stood stock still.

Constance's face reddened. "Let's get to work. Costumes don't sew themselves."

"That's right. Why don't you work on Ella's dress yourself?"

Constance wobbled on her stool. "What? Why? You should be halfway to Boston. If you don't leave, I'm going to report you to Mr. Ringling."

"Go ahead. He'll tell you he reinstated me. You're no longer wardrobe mistress."

"He wouldn't give me the job and take it away again." She stood so fast she knocked over her seat. "Did you go to him with some sad story and pitiful lie?"

"I went to him with the truth. And with proof I didn't suffocate you."

"This is ridiculous. I'll speak with Mr. Ringling. Don't get too comfortable. You won't be here long." Constance marched from the tent.

Lucy and the other assistants swarmed Ellen. "It's good to have you back. I hope you stay. Constance is terrible. It's only been a few hours, and I'm ready to quit."

Ellen laughed, never expecting such a warm reception. Perhaps she had been part of the circus family. "While it would be good to see my mother, I'm glad I'm here." She breathed a sigh of relief. Though she couldn't afford the sanatorium, she could give her parents a few dollars for medication.

"He shall give thee the desires of thine heart."

He just might do so.

And the desires of her heart included a certain trainmaster.

In a way, she pitied Constance. Maybe she had family back home that relied on her income. To see a job that would afford them a better standard of living go to another must be difficult. Perhaps it wasn't necessary to trap her.

Maybe she just needed a listening ear.

After the other women left for dinner, Ellen remained in the tent, working on a new headdress for one of the elephants. He'd trampled his old one, apparently not fond of it.

"Knock, knock."

She peered up to see Will. "Come in. The coast is clear. The menagerie performers won't be here for another half hour."

"How is it?"

"Wonderful."

"I'm glad." He brushed a kiss across her cheek.

A thrill raced through her middle. "What was that for?"

"To show you how glad I am you didn't leave. How did Constance take the news?"

"Not well. She stormed out, on her way to Mr. Ringling's office. I haven't seen her since." She paused. How would Will feel about her wanting to reason with Constance?

"You're deep in thought."

"I was wondering something."

"Care to share?"

"What if she's in a similar situation? What if she needs the income the job provides? That would explain why she's so set on it, so angry I got it, and so determined to get rid of me."

He scooted one of the assistant's stools closer. "Do you always think the best of others?"

"No. It's a terrible fault of mine, in fact. But there has to be a reason behind her behavior."

"Jealousy."

"Why?"

"That's what I'd like to know. I'm going to stick close. Who knows what she'll try next. But if you want to talk to her, go ahead. It can't hurt. You know what?"

"Hmm?"

"I love you."

"You'd better leave before the others get back. I don't want them to find us unsupervised. Mr. Ringling doesn't need another reason to dismiss me."

"Fair enough. I'll be close. If you need me, holler." He turned to leave.

"Okay. And Will?"

He turned back.

"I love you, too."

A quick grin, and he left. She was so engrossed in her work, she didn't think about the time ticking away. The outside world faded. All that existed was her needle and the scarlet headdress. She sang the doxology, praising God from whom all blessings flowed. And she thought about what she would say to Constance.

Maybe they'd work out a solution to her problem. Maybe they'd become friends. Maybe she needed nothing more than someone who cared. She searched for it hard enough in a man. If she searched for it in God instead. . .

"Why are you still here?" Constance swept into the tent, her eyes sparkling, her jaw set.

God, give me the words to say. And open her heart to me.

Ellen drew in a deep breath and let it out little by little. "I'm glad you're here before the other girls. I'd like to talk to you."

Chapter Thirteen

Will crouched behind the wardrobe tent, listening to every noise inside. He'd seen the flash of Constance's blue gown as she blustered toward the area. Ellen might think she could reason with her.

He doubted it.

Constance's voice came through the canvas, loud and demanding. He couldn't pick out Ellen's words, but her tone was soft and gentle. Why hadn't he trusted her? Today proved her good heart. She believed the best about people.

"I don't want to talk to you. I have nothing to say."

A pause as Ellen answered. He wished he could hear her.

"Keep your pity for yourself. You know nothing about me. I deserved that job. Not you. You waltz in here, thinking you own the place. You steal the man I love from me."

Ellen's voice pitched higher, clearer. "You exaggerated the nature of your relationship with Will. At no time were you a couple. He's a nice man, and you took advantage, setting your sights on him. But he isn't interested."

"Don't tell me about my life. I can make yours miserable. I will. I have."

Will shifted positions. Was she admitting her guilt? Should he run in there?

As he debated with himself, Constance scurried from the tent toward the train. He stood and breathed a sigh of relief. The conversation hadn't gone the way Ellen hoped, but at least it didn't end in an altercation.

"Mr. Jorgensen?" Hiram, a tall, strong roustabout, came alongside him. "One of the boards on the tiger flatbed is broken. Can you come look at it before we have to load?"

He should follow Constance. Who knew what kind of mischief she might be getting into? But his job called. If they didn't fix this problem now, it would put them behind schedule. Nothing riled Mr. Ringling more than a late train.

He didn't need Mr. Ringling riled. Not now.

Torn, he plodded after Hiram. He was proud of Ellen. She didn't blow up when Constance went after her. She wanted to work things out. That was a sign of a good woman. A woman he'd be a fool to let get away.

"See how it snapped under the weight of the wagon? Rotten wood. Just crumbling. That's what you get for buying used railcars."

Will inspected the damage. He'd have to run into town to get a few boards to fix it. What a bother. He said he'd watch Constance, wait for her to make a move. This crisis forced him to break that promise.

At least Ellen remained busy in the wardrobe tent. The presence of the assistants might keep Constance on good behavior.

Because he didn't know what he'd do without Ellen in his life.

◆　◆　◆

Ellen's assistants trickled back to the tent to get ready for the evening show. Constance, however, didn't appear. Where was she? What was she up to?

Knowing Will kept a close watch on her brought Ellen comfort. And more worry. Constance must be insane. That was Ellen's only explanation for her behavior. If Will had to confront her, no telling what she might do.

Lucy sat beside her. "I saw you and Will talking earlier. He can't stop staring at you. I've seen that look before—on my father's face when he gazes at my mother. Will's in love with you."

"Hush. I don't want the other girls to know."

"Too late. They already do. The tiger is out of the cage, so to speak."

Ellen giggled. "I'm in love with him, too. He's the man for me. I just hope he catches Constance trying to sabotage me again."

"Do you think she will?"

"No telling what she is capable of. But I have to trust God, don't I?"

"'Commit thy way unto the Lord; trust also in him; and he shall bring it to pass.' That's His promise to us."

"So easy to say. So hard to do." Ellen bent over her work once more. A few more stitches and she would finish the hem on this band member's jacket. He wouldn't need it until tomorrow's parade, but it would be good to get the job accomplished.

The albino twins came in to dress for the menagerie. How difficult it must be for them to travel without their parents. Ellen missed her family, but she couldn't imagine being a child in the circus. Because she shared her name with one of the girls, they had a special place in her heart. "Ready for tonight's show?"

Little Ellen nodded, her white curls bouncing.

Ellen went to the rack to pull out their costumes. Though she searched twice, she couldn't find them. "Does anyone know where the McPherson children's clothes are?"

Lucy rummaged through a rack. "Constance had them when she stormed out of here this afternoon. She must still have them."

Great. Ellen surmised Constance planned some crime to pin on her. At least Will would be with her when she confronted her.

Ellen scurried from the tent and scanned the area for Will. He wasn't around. Neither was Constance. He must be following her. Maybe she went into town. But where did she put the costumes?

Perhaps she took them to the Alvena to work alone, away from Ellen. She trudged across the grounds. The tracks sat some distance from the lot. She hoped the items would be there and this wouldn't be a wasted trip.

The odor of smoke hung in the air. What was Mr. Haley cooking? Shouldn't he be about ready to pack up for the night?

As she approached the Alvena, she realized the smell of smoke didn't come from the cook wagon but from her own sleeping car.

She grasped her skirts and sprinted toward the train. As fast as possible, she bounded up the steps.

When she saw the sight, she stopped in her tracks.

Flames leapt from her trunk, licking at the blankets hanging from the berth beside it. And Constance stood transfixed, watching the fire consume all Ellen's worldly goods.

No! Not her money. Her chest tightened, her stomach tumbling in her middle.

She kept a roll of cash in a secret compartment. Every dime of what she'd saved to send Mama to the sanatorium.

Not much.

But all she had.

She rushed forward, her throat constricting.

Constance snapped to attention and blocked her way. "You're getting what you deserve."

Ellen tried to push her to the side. "Let me go. I have to get in there."

Constance dug in her heels. "Never. Not until all you own is ashes."

The fire traveled along the berth and up the wall. Smoke filled the compartment. Ellen coughed. She labored for each breath.

A handkerchief. She grabbed one from her skirt's pocket and covered her mouth. She pushed and shoved with all of her might. Constance pushed back. Ellen stumbled to the ground. With one booted foot on her chest, Constance stood over her.

What was she going to do? The money was gone. Gone. Though the chance of earning enough to help Mama was slim, there was one. Now, that small hope went up in smoke.

Ellen's eyes watered. "Get off of me."

Constance pressed harder on Ellen's chest. What little air she managed to get in her lungs came filtered through the handkerchief.

Blackness edged her vision. If she passed out, she might never emerge alive. She fought to remain conscious.

Oh God, I'm trusting You to get me out of here. Only by His saving grace might she survive. *Help me. Please, help me.*

The blackness closed in. The crackling of the fire faded into the background.

Chapter Fourteen

Smoke drifted from the Alvena's window, catching Will's attention as he returned to the circus grounds from town.

Constance. What was she doing?

He sprinted toward the sleeper car. Why had he left? Why had it taken so long to find a sawmill employee?

Beads of sweat formed under his shirt collar. He loosened it so he could breathe better.

God, help me! Though he pumped his arms and legs as fast as possible, the cars passed with maddening slowness. He reached the Alvena after what seemed like miles and miles of racing.

He took the steps in one flying leap.

When he opened the door, heat from the fire slapped his face.

Constance stood in the middle of the room, flames surrounding her, her foot on something.

Not something.

Someone.

Ellen.

Will rushed forward. With one giant shove, he pushed Constance to the side. He bent down and dragged Ellen across the floor, toward the exit. Her eyelids fluttered.

"Hang on, sweetheart. You'll be fine. I'll have you in clean air in a minute."

Constance barreled at him, knocking him off balance. "You're not going anywhere."

He staggered and bumped against a berth. A moment later, he regained his balance and picked up Ellen.

"Will?"

He wanted to brush the brown curl from her damp forehead. "Yes, I'm here. Don't worry. I have you."

"God sent you to me."

"Yes, He did."

Constance rushed him again. This time, he steeled himself. When she plowed into him, he grabbed her and tossed her to the side. A moment later, he and Ellen emerged into the daylight.

By this time, a crowd had formed, drawn by the smoke. He handed her off to Lucy and went inside to confront Constance.

"There's no more use in fighting. This is the end for you."

She narrowed her watery eyes. "Not until I get what I want."

"It's not yours to have." He stepped forward. She backed up. They repeated this dance until she stumbled into the flames. She screamed. In one motion, he scooped her up. She wriggled. Kicked. Scratched. He held firm. Sweat rolled down his face, his back, his chest. He coughed. So did she.

The door. So far away. He lurched forward. He couldn't breathe.

◆ ◆ ◆

Ellen sat on the hard-packed dirt, coughing, crying, waiting for Will to emerge from the burning train car. What was happening to him? *God, please save him. I've lost so much. I can't lose him.*

She remembered praying for help as the darkness consumed her. And God answered her. Will came. He pulled her out. He saved her.

He shall give you the desires of your heart.

There is one thing I desire, Lord. A life with Will. Please, make that possible.

"He'll be fine." Lucy sat next to her and rubbed her back.

"I pray you're right."

A crowd of roustabouts and kitchen staff gathered. Most of the crew continued with the show. Nothing must stop it.

How long had he been in there? She jiggled her foot. *Come on, let me see you. Just one glimpse.* "What's taking him so long?"

"He'll be out. You'll see." Lucy's words brought small comfort.

And then, the most beautiful sight. Will tumbled through the door, Constance in his arms. Several of the tent men not yet busy with teardown rushed forward. One took Constance. The other steadied Will.

Ellen jumped up. Still shaky herself, she ignored the dizziness and staggered forward. A wide grin spread across his face. He enveloped her in a hug.

"Oh, Will, I thought you were going to die. What would I do without you?"

He kissed her forehead, her cheeks, her lips. Though he tasted of smoke, she didn't care. Nothing had ever been sweeter to her.

He broke away. "You'll never have to find out. Ellen Meyer, I love you. I want you to be my wife. Will you marry me?"

Her body tingled. "Yes, yes, yes, of course I will. I love you, too."

A cheer went up from the circus family surrounding them.

"And I have one more surprise for you." He reached into his back pocket and drew out a piece of paper. A telegram.

No, not more bad news. Couldn't she be happy for a few moments?

"It's from a fine sanatorium in Boston. They have accepted your mother as a patient. Her care is paid for in full."

"You did this for me?"

"For you. For us. I can't be happy unless you are." With that, he kissed her again.

She returned the kiss, deepening it until she couldn't catch her breath.

The World's Greatest Show brought them together. And together they'd live out the world's greatest love.

Epilogue

Sunday, July 12, 1896
Baraboo, Wisconsin

Ellen sat in the upstairs bedroom of Will's father's home as Lucy fussed with her hair. "You're going to be the most beautiful bride ever."

Ellen peered at herself in the mirror. Did she glow from happiness? "I can't wait. It's fast, I know, but why put it off?"

"Not at all. If you're truly in love, there's no reason to."

"And it worked out that we're near the Ringling's home base, so Will's dad can be a part of our special day. Even if my parents can't."

"They'll meet him when you go east this winter. And they'll love him."

"Maybe Mama will be well enough by then to be home."

A knock sounded at the door. "Are you ready?"

Lucy pinned one last curl and admitted Mr. Ringling. "She is."

"Your groom awaits." He offered Ellen his elbow and escorted her downstairs.

Flowers adorned the small parlor, the scent of roses perfuming the air. Will stood between the long front windows waiting for her, straight and tall, his eyes bright. She'd never met anyone so handsome.

She smoothed down the light gray silk of the gown her assistants had created for her and descended the steps. Once in front of the minister, Mr. Ringling handed her off to Will.

"You're gorgeous," Will said. "I can't believe I get to spend the rest of my life with you."

Her cheeks warmed. "I'm the most blessed woman in the world to call you my husband."

The pastor cleared his throat and began the ceremony. Though she tried to listen to his admonition to them, the service passed in a blur. Before she knew it, the reverend declared them to be husband and wife.

She tingled from head to toe.

"You may kiss your bride."

Will bent over and pulled her close. "I love you, Mrs. Jorgensen."

"I love you, too."

They kissed, a long, deep kiss.

No circus would be as thrilling as this moment.

The world's greatest love, indeed.

Liz Tolsma is a popular speaker and an editor and the owner of the Write Direction Editing. An almost-native Wisconsinite, she resides in a quiet corner of the state with her husband and their two daughters. Her son proudly serves as a U.S. Marine. They adopted all of their children internationally, and one has special needs. When she gets a few spare minutes, she enjoys reading, relaxing on the front porch, walking, working in her large perennial garden, and camping with her family.

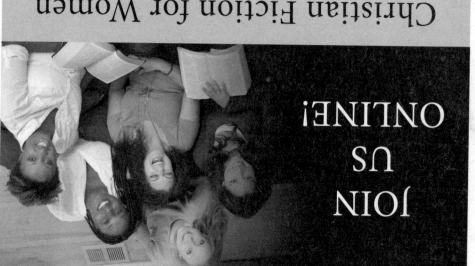

JOIN US ONLINE!

Christian Fiction for Women

Christian Fiction for Women is your online home for the latest in Christian fiction.

Check us out online for:

- Giveaways
- Recipes
- Info about Upcoming Releases
- Book Trailers
- News and More!

Find Christian Fiction for Women at Your Favorite Social Media Site:

 Search "Christian Fiction for Women"

 @fictionforwomen